A

TALE

OF

FOUR

PLANETS

A Tale of Four Planets

Book Three: Centers of the Universe

A Novel by David Taylor

Cover photo: New Course, St. Andrews, Scotland, courtesy of Eddie Taylor.

ISBN: 978-1-949756-53-1 (softcover)

ISBN: 978-1-949756-72-2 (hardcover)

ISBN: 978-1-949756-54-8 (ebook)

Library of Congress Number on file with publisher.

BOOK THREE:
Centers
Of the
Universe

a novel by David Taylor

"The whole difference between construction and creation is exactly this: that a thing constructed can only be loved after it is constructed; but a thing created is loved before it ever exists."

– Charles Dickens

dedicated to Maria

Contents

Philadelphia No-Zone, 2063

A phantasmal specter was the last thing Shelly Taylor expected to find when she returned to the Philadelphia "No-Zone." Shelly hoped to find Flamboyo Sanchez. If she succeeded, she would tell him she didn't care what he thought of her. And that it also made no difference, his seemingly fathomless depth of bitter cynicism. She still loved him.

"Ms. Shelly Taylor. Can't say I expected to see *you* around here, ever again. What, it's been months, hasn't it?" The guard waved off Shelly's identification card and certificate for re-entering the walled-off two-thirds of the city.

The Philly No-Zone entrance facilitated foot traffic only, thereby disempowering roving No-Zone gangs. They were forestalled the opportunity to seize any other means of transportation besides the gondolas and canoes already crowding No-Zone canals.

The entrance façade's bleakish gray structure loomed high above the electric barbed wire fences extending for miles to either side of it. Shelly found herself reminded of the entrance to a haunted castle ride at an amusement park. She well knew, however, the horrors contained beyond this access point were all too dangerously, despairingly real.

"Can't tell you the harsh winter weather kept me away," Captain Taylor's daughter responded to the guard at last. "Don't think the temp's been down below the upper thirties since December. No, the boss said time for follow-up on my previous No-Zone story."

"What I heard was: This is what we get. This is our new normal when we go a full year without a volcano really blowing its stack."

"Oh?" Like Shelly didn't know exactly what the guard was referring to.

"Better believe it, Ms. Taylor," Officer Calo nodded, oblivious to her humoring him. "Less volcanic activity means less of some particular chemical in the upper atmosphere, umm, sulfur dioxide? Which means less pushback against the prevailing trend. At least that's the explanation I've heard."

"Sounds about right."

"Yeah, so with less sulfur dioxide or whatever, less sunlight is refracted into space, more heat trapped in the atmosphere. Then Bingo! Warmer and warmer weather!"

Shelly nodded stiff-upper-lip grim acknowledgement. She could have made the causal connection herself. Climate change physics had been the small talk of choice for months. Didn't matter. The grimness many were feeling over the implications remained inexhaustibly fresh.

Shelly Taylor checked herself on adding something to the effect of: *Let's hope a human volcano doesn't blow its stack because of the No-Zones*. Such a remark might have spurred Officer Calo to insist on seeing Shelly's identification card and re-entry certificate, after all.

As matters stood, the priority dialogue transpiring between Taylor and the guard was nonverbal.

Even before Officer Calo opened his mouth to utter the name of the famous spaceship captain's daughter, he noticed the drone accompanying her high overhead. Its appearance reminded him of a spider he'd read about that rode webbing like a hang glider. Calo had also read about cow-sized spiders reported to be flourishing on Fafama. Fafama was the planet where Earth's civilization made first, formal contact with an extraterrestrial civilization.

Officer Calo knew that once Shelly got over to the quarantine side, her airborne robotic security wouldn't make itself so obvious. Rather, it would behave like any good spider stalking its prey, or in this case protecting its brood. It would zip from one sheltered rooftop to another while shadowing Ms. Shelly Taylor.

Officer Calo also noticed what looked to be two unusually large starlings in a bother over their quietly whirring mechanical company. They made their typical, arcing swoops here and there, round about the drone. Calo thought nothing more of them than that. His eyes darted from the drone to a nodding glance at Shelly. Shelly reciprocated with her own, confirming nod.

"Well, duty calls," Shelly sighed, like if it were up to her she would have taken a different course of action. She would have continued exchanging anti-controversial banalities with this guy who was trying not to be too obvious about checking out her figure. Sure.

The reality was that Shelly was anxious beyond anxious to have another go at searching for Flamboyo.

"No camcorder crew this time, huh?" said Officer Calo. He feigned nonchalance when he gestured one of his partners to punch in the No-Zone entrance access code.

"Yeah." Shelly shrugged her shoulders with her own semblance of nonchalance. "There's journalism, and then there's journalism."

"I hear that," Officer Calo chuckled. Shelly well knew if she pressed him, he would have confessed he hadn't a clue what she meant, let alone why it was worth laughing over. Her stuff about journalism was total nonsense meant to disarm any slightest suspicion.

When the security code unlocked the extra-reinforced metal door, it slid open with a hiss. Shelly was reminded of an old-fashioned tea kettle letting off steam. Where she was concerned, the metal door's hiss might as well have issued from growing rage simmering towards a full boil.

After Shelly Taylor finished this particular crossover to the No-Zone side of the wall, the entrance slid shut with a thud of finality. In reaction, Shelly twisted her head around. She found the edifice through which she left the Philly Yes-Zone to appear more looming, more starkly foreboding than ever before.

Where her editors were concerned, the real mission of Captain Helena Taylor's daughter was to update the outside world on life inside the No-Zone. The pretext, the excuse was that she wanted to see how Flamboyo was doing. One year earlier, she wove him into her televised account of social outreach in quarantined North Philadelphia. So what had happened with him since then? Whether or not Shelly Taylor found the answer, perhaps she would uncover pleasantly surprising grounds for a new feel-good report. Such a report would push back against Congressional inaction.

By a torturously slim margin, the United Americas Congress fell short on passing No-Zone redevelopment legislation. Besides the redevelopment itself, that legislation would have opened more opportunities for No-Zone residents. They could have visited Yes-Zone areas, at least on a short-term trial basis.

All well and good. But where Shelly Taylor was concerned, the pretext was the real mission. The update for the outer world to put more pressure on Congress was her cover story, while her search for Flamboyo was her everything.

Shelly's pause continued at the top of a stairwell leading down to ground level inside the No-Zone. She was taking in the most elevated, most encompassing view she could hope to gain of an urban region crowded with tenement buildings. Her admittedly slim hope was that she might chance to espy Señor Flamboyo Sanchez rounding a corner or some such. Perhaps she would catch him stepping into a gondola.

No luck. But a pervasive situation did make an especially strong impression on Shelly amidst the grime and gloom under yet another overcast day. In several places, the canal water lapping at sidewalk edges was actually spilling onto those cracking and crumbling-apart cement surfaces. Aggravated by recent heavy rains, the water level was the highest she'd ever seen.

To accommodate the steadily rising sea level from global warming, former roads through the tenement district were dug out to create a canal network. Thereby flooding was minimized where city streets were still maintained. In recent months however, one thing was becoming clear not only in Philadelphia, but in the rest of the world as well. A lot more needed to be done.

In strong second place for Shelly's attention was the extensiveness of rooftop terrace gardens. The rooftop garden project continued to gain momentum as a win-win-win. More greenery meant more greenhouse-gas absorption, and more food of a healthier character grown within the No-Zone. Not only that, but fewer airlifted supplies were required, with their attendant security risks.

However, funding for the so-called Green Roof Initiative had been eliminated. This was thanks in large part to some ugly agri-business lobbying on behalf of processed food packagers. Processed food packagers fretted over losing a not-inconsiderable share of their market. And so, the proliferation of rooftop farming was growing to depend far more on its proponents' imaginative resourcefulness. They achieved makeshift dredging of mud from the street canal bottoms to provide rooftop soil. And they stitched together large-item shrink-wrap sheets to undergird that soil for new rooftop gardening development. Unfortunately, though, such covering proved far less leak-proof than the exhausted supply of government-contributed tarps.

Shelly contemplated the inadequately tended greenery, inadequately tended thanks to other funding cuts. It was growing out of control. Vines were creeping down the sides of buildings, even as the ever-prevalent soot and grime lent them the same gray tint as everything else.

Herbs might have still been flourishing, insinuating themselves amidst the other wildly spreading flora. But Shelly caught only fleeting scents of oregano, parsley and mint amidst the overwhelming stench of sea brine littered with sewage.

Shelly feared an even worse state of affairs within many buildings. She suspected that leaks in the rooftop covering were allowing mold to fester to an ever-more-dangerous extent.

Shelly Taylor could easily imagine what was in store another fifty years from then if not sooner. As the sea level continued to rise, the greenery would continue to descend already crumbling walls. Sea and greenery would meet in a transformation of this area comparable to how Central American jungle reclaimed Mayan ruins.

With these many despairing thoughts, Shelly realized she better proceed pronto. She better force herself to make her descent straight away into this increasingly forbidden-feeling No-Zone. Otherwise she might just chicken out, turn around and leave. She might, as it were, abandon her search for what remained of the ruins of a relationship before it was even begun. She might leave that relationship for a jungle's worth of fear and hopelessness to reclaim alongside real jungle reclaiming the decaying city.

Helena Taylor's daughter hardly noticed the faint whoosh of the small sphere launched by a slingshot. That whoosh was nearly drowned out by the din of seawater lapping rhythmically against sidewalk curbs. Ditto for the pea-sized explosive launched in turn from the whooshing sphere.

The explosive sounded like a firecracker as it made impact with its target. The noise was plenty loud enough to draw Shelly's attention skyward. She looked up just in time to see what happened to the more obvious drone hovering like some giant mechanical airborne spider. Two of its three silently whirring helicopter blades were blown scattered apart. The rest came crashing down literally at Shelly's feet. Pieces of the drone made plopping sounds when they bounced off the cement sidewalk into the street canal.

"Allow us to introduce ourselves. We already know about you, Ms. Shelly Taylor. Oh, and fakin' jacks if you say you know or care a thing about us." The tall gang leader made a low bow towards Helena Taylor's daughter. Shelly could tell it was a mocking bow, black leather trench coat notwithstanding. She could also finally tell something about the two seeming starlings that sporadically darted from building to building overhead.

They were actually animatronic drones. With the demise of the more obvious drone, they continued to keep her security detail well apprised of her situation. The idea was that Shelly's protection could move in at any moment, if needed.

Trench Coat Guy and his two associates had still easily managed to surround Shelly hot on the heels of one of them downing the more obvious drone. Unnerved, her response left her lips before she could check herself, reflecting on its sheer stupidity. "'Sup?"

"''Sup'?! Hear that, boys?! ''Sup'!" The gang leader made a strutting jaunt in a circle around Shelly as he unbuttoned his pants and yanked them halfway down. "Ms. Taylor, would you like we should give you some 'yo-yo-yo,' then top that off with a couple of peace-outs?!?"

"I'm an idiot." Shelly stretched out her hands, palms open to the world. Her voice cracked tearfully on her utterance of "idiot." "Please go on with your introductions." As the gang leader pulled up his pants to re-zip them, Shelly feared for her life. She well knew her security couldn't be anywhere close to acting quickly enough. Quickly enough, that is, were Trench Coat Guy to decide she had earned a bullet through her skull. Pursuant to which bloodshed, she was also certain he and his associates would melt back into the prevailing gloom of decay. They would succeed as effortlessly as they had materialized out of the gloom in the first place, to present themselves before her as people not to be ignored.

"'Please go on with your introductions.' Yes, okay. We have nothing better to do. Unlike yourself who can count on safe deliverance out of here any time you wish. Name's T-Lamp, like you really give a f-." T-Lamp bowed his clean-shaven head to draw Shelly's attention to the colorful Tiffany Lamp design tattooed there. More precisely, it was a Tiffany Lamp design depicted explosively shattering apart.

"Ms. Taylor" refrained from comment. She knew better than to give this potentially unstable person another something to mock. There was the risk of propelling him uncontrollably into a reckless act against her. Still, she couldn't help being struck by something about T-Lamp's tattoo. Perhaps unwittingly, it seemed to express what his habitat had done to him, the damage wrought. If his body was a sacred dwelling place, the cathedral of his soul, didn't that make the design more stained glass window than Tiffany Lamp? And didn't the explosively shattering apart effect signify the violence of being walled away in the No-Zone, beyond redemption?

"More useless trivia for you..."

Shelly Taylor struggled not to shake her head in protest.

"This here's the Marksman. That's all he knows, all he needs to know."

The Marksman smiled broadly. He nodded his head proudly. And oddly enough, his eyes' vacant look emitted a certain warmth and kindness. Shelly guessed the Marksman was too mentally challenged to comprehend his leader didn't exactly pay him an unqualified compliment.

Helena's daughter noticed the Marksman fidgeting with the slingshot he held upside down to his side. Clearly, he anxiously awaited the next opportunity to demonstrate his prowess, especially for a pretty lady.

"We watch out for him," added T-Lamp. "Let's say someone doesn't quite appreciate the props he deserves. Farmer Deadbulb here, he plants that someone's severed head in rooftop soil to grow the necessary respect. Amazing how that works."

Farmer Deadbulb impressed Shelly as being the scariest of a scary lot. There was a wild, crazed look in his eyes when he bit off the top half of an oversized Oort Cloud candy bar. That proved unsettling enough. But he kept tossing skyward a long, two-bladed knife with his hand not busy holding the Oort Cloud to his mouth. His catching it safely, again and again, made no difference where Shelly's discomfort was concerned.

What little stability remained of the social compact within the No-Zones hung by a thread. From her research, Shelly well knew it depended on the clear thinking of gang leaders such as T-Lamp. Followers were crippled in so many ways by the lethal combination of wretched environment with a wretched, limited diet, including water of suspect quality.

Despite her sense of T-Lamp's mental well-being, Shelly Taylor worried how hard she could push her inquiry as to Flamboyo's whereabouts. That is, before she set off T-Lamp in fatally dangerous ways. She had to hope her sincerity would mollify his distrust.

Steeling herself, Shelly Taylor pretended to ignore Deadbulb's routine like he didn't faze her in the least. She addressed T-Lamp. "I'm sure Flamboyo Sanchez is the last person you want to talk about," she said. "And that you already knew I was intent on asking about him regardless."

"Oh....," T-Lamp nodded sarcastically towards Deadbulb and the Marksman. They nodded "Oh" right back, though not having the faintest clue what this was about. "'Nother words, you're 'fessing you don't give a f- about us; you're after the Mexican."

"Actually, he's of Puerto Rican descent."

The Marksman and Deadbulb reacted dramatically to Shelly correcting T-Lamp. They both leapt into a ready-to-pounce crouch. She might as well have issued their leader a threatening challenge.

T-Lamp anticipated this result with a hand held high. Thereby he cautioned both men to hold off on doing anything violent, at least until the lady finished having her say.

"However," Shelly went on, trying to still seem unfazed, "with what his, uh..." She checked herself on using the word, *crew.* "With what his associates have done, their indefensible savagery..." She shook her head with heartfelt disparagement. "If I were you having to listen to me inquire after him, uh, I wouldn't be happy."

"You wouldn't be, 'uh,' happy," T-Lamp reacted mockingly again.

Shelly could tell that T-Lamp's held-high hand was the merest subtle gesture away from unleashing his two "associates."

"I see," T-Lamp nodded. "So, would you be, 'uh,' surprised if your friend Flamboyo is gone? Like there are not enough things that can go way wrong in here, away from your Never-Neverland?"

Shelly strained not to let her relief show regarding her personal welfare. For sure, T-Lamp had continued to practically spit out every word. And he had made crystal clear his power over the Marksman and Farmer Deadbulb was the only thing standing between Captain Helena Taylor's daughter and a gruesome fate. But he avoided any direct comment on her attempt to empathize with his hatred of all things Flamboyo. There was no pride-maintaining way he could have acknowledged she understood even the most minimal of what he was feeling. Changing the subject was the best she could have hoped for, and plenty good enough. This, even though what T-Lamp changed the subject to was how easily life could be lost in the No-Zone.

"By 'gone,' do you mean killed?" asked Shelly, embracing the direction T-Lamp took the conversation.

Locked in eye contact with her, T-Lamp took a step towards Shelly. "I mean nature abhors a vacuum," he said.

Ms. Taylor stood her ground. She resisted her strong impulse to break off the stare-down and run. She also resisted pretending innocence, pretending not to understand T-Lamp's double-entendre insinuation he had reason to rape her. Rather, she braved saying, "So you're here to fill that vacuum, you and your associates?"

"Me and my associates. When it suits us. At our leisure." T-Lamp nodded the Marksman and Farmer Deadbulb's way, and they nodded back.

Sound ready to rampage, full vengeance, but choose to hold off. Shelly got it. She also got that all it would take to unleash horror upon her own self would be to make T-Lamp feel the least bit patronized.

"Something else about Flamboyo and company. Their ancestors - Mexican, Puerto Rican, Cuban, don't give a shit. They mostly chose to come to this country. Our ancestors were shipped here and sold."

"I don't think the Mexicans chose to have their land taken out from under them." Shelly regretted her remark the instant it left her lips. At least she stifled herself before she could have gone on about Puerto Rico and Cuba. But she worried that didn't matter. That she had already taken enough of T-Lamp's bait to get one of the Marksman's remote-controlled explosives slingshot into her forehead. Or Deadbulb's knife slicing across her throat.

"Three steps behind." T-Lamp shook his head matter-of-factly. Shelly's cringe in expectation of something barbarously else plainly delighted him. "There are people you are too f-n' naïve to think bad enough of. They were counting on, counting on gangs to keep tearing one another apart when they were isolated from the rest of the world. But that's not what's happening! Hell, I've even got a little action going myself with a chiquitita! That's the future, and that's why *your* f-n' associates have wasted their time erecting the quarantine zones! They're going to prove about as effective against us as the levees and canals against the rising sea level!

"But that's not what we have seized your attention for, famous lady. There is something we want you to see. Concluded by a commentary."

"Is your commentary something you want me to share with people on the outside? Any chance it would help resurrect efforts to open up the No-Zones?"

"Maybe, for all you know, I just want to give you a little something to ponder, a little food for thought while you're drawing your final breath.

"Get in the boat."

Shelly stole a glance skyward. She was checking the animatronic starling drones, assuring herself they weren't flitting about in too obvious a manner. Following which, she most obligingly stepped down into the motorized canal gondola she didn't even notice until T-Lamp mentioned it.

"You have the slightest idea what this is about, Ms. Taylor? I'm not necessarily going to buy your answer. Just curious what you're going to say." These were T-Lamp's only words on the canal ride.

"I have *no* idea what you are talking about, and you don't have to pay a cent for that answer. Free of charge." Shelly looked from side to side of the canal while she responded. What distressed her as much as anything else was how far the briny, dirty water sloshed onto the sidewalks from the gondola's passing. But she could feel, sense T-Lamp's genuine amusement over her brazen wit. And she also just as strongly intuited something more crucial.

T-Lamp was bluffing with his insinuation of murderous intent. Whatever came next, "concluded by a commentary," would not end with her summary execution. T-Lamp was going to release her.

Nothing would have stopped T-Lamp from just emailing a description of whatever was in store, plus his commentary, to the Yes-Zone authorities. He didn't really need Shelly for that. Or did he?

The conclusion seemed obvious. T-Lamp's bluster notwithstanding, he still did hold out hope that "famous lady" could produce a meaningful political breakthrough.

The importance of such a breakthrough could not be overstated. How much longer could the quarantined wretched of the Earth be contained? How much longer before they finally did erupt with waves of violence that overwhelmed, collapsed the walls sealing them off from the rest of the world?

NORTH HANCOCK

Shelly Taylor noticed this relic street sign when the motorized gondola made a right turn into the North Hancock canal. She was doubly glad she'd kept her attention focused away from her three captors, on the dreary scene set before her. Otherwise, there was no way T-Lamp wouldn't have been able to plainly see the color draining from her face.

They cruised very close to where Shelly's relatives on her father's side were spirited out of the neighborhood sixty years earlier. They were spirited out by the Smoke and Mirrors under her mother's leadership. That time travel experiment remained largely secret from all but a handful of people on the entire planet Earth.

Ms. Taylor helped dock the gondola, tying one of its ropes to a century-old fire hydrant. She kept her head bowed humbly low. She wanted to delay as long as possible T-Lamp glimpsing her countenance, because she sensed that the chill down her neck had turned it ghostly pale.

The problem was that Shelly Taylor found herself disembarked right in front of the residence of her father's granduncle and grandaunt. *What were their names? Something Perez?*

The Marksman and Farmer Deadbulb forced Shelly to precede them on the front stoop into the tenement building. T-Lamp brought up the rear.

Before Shelly entered, she stole one final glance heavenward to confirm the two starling drones kept pace. She also noticed a larger blackbird, a crow, showing special interest in the drones. That real creature could provide a most unwanted complication. What if it attacked, sending one of those pieces of animatronic machinery crashing onto the sidewalk or into the side of the building? Such an eventuality would allow the gang members close inspection of that machinery.

Stepping inside the building did not help at all, where Captain Taylor's daughter feeling spooked was concerned. The place was packed, and yet the silence reminded her of a church's interior during a moment for silent prayer.

The crowd hastened to make way for Shelly to wade through to the front, once they realized this was a T-Lamp operation.

Shelly counted no fewer than eight women lying on their backs. They were reclined on a large, pastel-green carpet section used as a throw rug for the otherwise empty living room. Stranger still, the women's arms and legs were stretched out in various odd positions. They could have been performing a yoga variation Shelly had never seen before. Another notable something was the abundance of fake jewelry, rings and toe rings alike, sporting equally fake oversized gems.

The arm and leg positions kept in constant yet slow motion, until one woman's set of limbs froze. There was a poof of what looked to be faint blue smoke over that woman's belly. The other women's limbs proceeded to freeze one by one as their bellies presented with their own faint blue poofs.

With the reclined women's arms and legs frozen still, more faint bluish smoke appeared to swirl together, forming a whirlpool set amidst them. That whirlpool resolved into a phantasmal human figure floating several inches above the carpet section. What none of the people gathered there could have known, including Shelly Taylor, was that figure's identity. Namely, Doña Galleta, Cookie Lady, from back in 2004...while channeling herself through Samantha Santiago trillions of miles away on the starship, Eisenhower. The Eisenhower was presently headed for the planet Oomb.

Shelly found herself straining along with everyone else to hear whether any sound issued from the ghostly presence...until she realized something also along with everyone else. This proved true even for those who had experienced this phenomenon on several earlier occasions. They couldn't help finding their senses misdirected again. There was a faint sound long since disregarded, discounted as nothing more than the din from outside, of canal water lapping at sidewalk curbs. But that sound was resolving, becoming enveloped in a soft voice perfectly synced with the apparition's moving lips. "She is wondering," the apparition said. "What could be so important about the object entrusted to her, that it must be personally delivered to her son across several light-years?

"I try to reassure her of something, as I strain to reassure you. A cycle nears its full circuit connection, to summon the intervention for the Great Healing. I would serve you my cookies in the meantime, while you wait, but there is a constraint. It is a constraint I find ridiculously arbitrary. Especially given this seemingly boundless feat I am able to perform, that you have become parts of. There is only one other comfort with which I can provide you, to try to secure your patience for just a little while longer. To quote a popular phrase from the planet Fafama: The sunset storm line cannot arrive before the sunset storm line arrives."

Shelly Taylor thought the apparition went on. She thought this even though the apparition's voice withered and became too garbled for continued understanding of what she was saying. But then Shelly realized she was focused once more on the ebb and flow of canal water lapping at the sidewalk outdoors. And that Doña Galleta's image had dissolved into a mix of shadows and light.

The assembled locals mumbled about what happened. Participation in that discussion included the eight women who summoned Galleta's apparition by moving about their limbs as though they were antique television antennae.

While the impromptu debriefing was transpiring, Shelly allowed herself to be yanked back outside by Deadbulb. He was careful not to look at her. He well knew how little he would subsequently have been able to control himself, keep from raping her, gleeful into the bargain.

"Cookie in the sky instead of pie in the sky, Famous Lady!" sputtered T-Lamp, self-consciously rubbing his bald head.

The Marksman and Farmer Deadbulb nodded agreement. As usual, they did not even begin to comprehend what their leader was referencing.

"Be sure to tell this to anyone and everyone chosen *not* to live damned: Sooner or later, we'll figure out how to breach their f-n' No-Zone walls!" T-Lamp blustered. "Make sure they understand most of us no longer take the drug bait to keep us in a don't-give-a-f- daze! We will not be distracted! The waters of our righteous rage will not be calmed by some hi-tech false promise of a second coming!"

"And *you* be sure to understand I know nothing about that ghost!" insisted Shelly. "Don't think I'm not going to be pestering the authorities about this, the first chance I get! What?" With her sudden realization, Shelly nearly stepped off the sidewalk and fell into the canal. She had been discounting something as dust unaccountably stirred up off the crumbling, cracking cement, despite the cement's dampness and the absence of any breeze. But that something resolved into another slow whirlwind of seeming faint blue smoke, from where the apparition was re-emerging.

As a faint breeze did finally kick up, T-Lamp, Deadbulb and the Marksman all three scanned the perimeter. T-

Lamp was intent on determining the apparition's artificial origins, while his two followers were watching not to be ambushed. They feared that the haunting re-visitation outside where they'd been used to seeing it was meant to divert attention away from a trap.

"That crow! Damn!" T-Lamp shouted. He pointed at the real bird swooping after the animatronic starling drones. "That has to be the holographic projector for this spooky shit! Marksman?! You're on!"

The Marksman let fly a spherical object from his slingshot. The object wasn't three feet slung into the sky before producing an exhaust like firecracker sparklers, for accelerating its ascent. The Marksman made expert practiced motion of his slingshot, employing its joystick capability. He remote-controlled the spherical object into the crow's chest, mid-flight, where it burst apart.

The two drones descended to rooftop perches while the dead crow fell in pieces at T-Lamp's feet.

"At least it can't poop on us! One less of those!" said Farmer Deadbulb with a wild-eyed grin. He resumed the juggling act with his two-edged mini-sword.

By then, the whisper of faint breeze had evolved into a gentle voice issuing from the persisting apparition. "This is not over. Ultimately, this is not how it happens," said Doña Galleta. She pointed towards the blood-soaked mess of feathers and charred crow's flesh. Her attention from wherever she actually presided was drawn across the light-years to this tragic happening on a sidewalk in the Philadelphia No-Zone of 2063. "None of this," she went on, looking up and around. "That is what the Great Healing is about."

Doña Galleta's further whispers rapidly blurred to no more than additional hints of wind. Her physical projection faded back into an illusory play of light and shadow on tenement building window panes.

By that time, T-Lamp and his crew had long since fled the area.

Chapter 1

The flying saucer spacecraft christened Dek-Fook-Tek's Fifth Celestial Breath was following the course set by decelerated photon sparkles too small for the naked eye to see. Those sparkles left a bread crumb trail all the way from the planet Tictoctic into the Alpha Centauri C system. The trail stretched for trillions and trillions of miles, of light favoring the material aspect of its character over its wavelength aspect. Saucer propulsion engineer Kwit-Nik discovered this curious phenomenon soon after being appointed commander of the Tictoctic defensive invasion force by Tictoctic's Supreme Authority, Dek-Fook-Tek.

The photon sparkle trail was the first lead anyone had picked up concerning the fate of a Tictoctickian reconnaissance saucer. That is, ever since its disappearance from the Second Celestial Breath a year and a half earlier. The reconnaissance saucer was presumed to have been hijacked by a pair of traitors. Perhaps they were bent on warning other civilizations of Dek-Fook-Tek's plans to defend the Tictoctickian Empire.

Of course, the Supreme Authority Dek-Fook-Tek wanted to be credited with discovery of the photon sparkle bread-crumb trail. But Commander Kwit-Nik had to perform logic-bending mental contortions in order to make that case. And he needed to do it in a way the Supreme Authority found plausible, sincerely adulatory, not condescending. This proved doubly hard given how diminished had become Kwit-Nik's respect for his mentally unstable leader. So diminished, in fact, he was plotting something of a rebellion...

"Captain Gekalek, a message from Dek-Fook-Tek..."

"'A message from Dek-Fook-Tek,' Officer Wek-bek?!" Captain Gekalek's nostrils became so agitated from his rage, they might just as easily have been freaking over sniffs at a gourmet dish featuring the finest cut of Chonoran meat. "'A message from Dek-Fook-Tek'?!" the captain of the Fifth Celestial Breath repeated. "Why not say, then: A turd from one of the last surviving Chonorans?!"

"That was not what I meant at all, Captain Gekalek!" Officer Wek-bek reared back onto his two hind legs to swell out his uniformed chest. Unprompted, he was making himself available for possibly fatal impalement on the captain's antlers. He knew his chances were better of avoiding such punishment if he literally rose for the occasion rather than trying to avoid it. Officer Wek-bek had garnered this lesson from fellow deer creatures' most unfortunate experiences. "After my reckless language," he went on to humbly bray, "suppose you were to order me transformed into the next meal. Served up sliced, diced and fried in the feeding trough would still be a far better fate than I have so deservedly earned."

Captain Gekalek was down on all fours, impatiently pawing at the thick, corrugated plastic floor of the saucer's navigation bridge. He itched, indeed, for an impaling charge at his officer's chest. His moist breath produced tiny bursts of visible steam from his still-twitching nostrils on their every rage-filled snort.

What Wek-bek could not have known was that the captain's anger had more than one origin. It erupted not simply over Wek-bek's plain announcement of an incoming communication from the Supreme Authority of the Tictoctic Empire. Far more important were the captain's conflicted feelings. The orders given by Commander Kwit-Nik smelled to Captain Gekalek close to treason. They carried that sweet carrion scent of betrayal. But maybe treason and betrayal were what Dek-Fook-Tek deserved, if certain indications of his unhinged mental state were not entirely misrepresentative.

Originally, Captain Gekalek had been operating under a certain impression regarding the Tictoctickian battle saucers' mission. They were to neutralize the offense capabilities of three inhabited planets in three separate solar systems. The species responsible for those capabilities was destined to become an additional food resource, lasting for centuries. To that end, the Tictoctickians would wisely bring to bear lessons learned from the overkill of Chonorans.

The planet named Chonora was pulse-beamed into submission as a defensive response to Chonoran aggression. But during this military action, certain Chonorans unwittingly bombed themselves to the brink of extinction with their thermonuclear weapons. In the wake of that terrible mess, too little thought was given over to breeding, where the few Chonoran survivors were concerned. Before very long, the only usable Chonoran flesh remaining was already stored away in meat caskets. Nobody could count on certain rumors having any factual foundation.

This time, there were to be no extinction events. Immediately pursuant to the defensive onslaught, breeding pens were to be established. The young and the elderly would even find themselves allowed to roam free, in what was to be hailed as the bountiful mercy of Dek-Fook-Tek.

Again, this *had* been Captain Gekalek's impression of the mission. However, there was a secret meeting of Celestial Breath captains aboard Kwit-Nik's command control saucer, christened Nostril-Dek-Fook-Tus as the name would have translated into English. During this meeting, Commander Kwit-Nik took a different tack. The commander argued most persuasively his fellow Tictoctickians should bargain rather than battle with the target civilizations. As he explained it, the revised goal should include obtaining herds of the other-worlders' beasts of burden for Tictoctickian breeding and consumption. The goal should also include the securement of other-world seedlings for reviving Tictoctic's failing eco-system. The Tictoctickians would hold back military measures as a final resort. They would only implement such measures should reasoned discourse prove the other-world civilizations to be more on a par with Tictoctic's hill-building insect colonies than with its apex intelligent species. And of course, that apex species consisted of the deer creature Tictoctickians, themselves.

In preparation for the defensive conquest, Supreme Authority Dek-Fook-Tek expected Captain Gekalek of the Fifth Celestial Breath to perform one simple task. Or at least he assumed it should be simple. Gekalek was to confirm the fate of the renegade couple who made off with a scout saucer from the Second Celestial Breath.

What Dek-Fook-Tek did not know was that Commander Kwit-Nik had entrusted Captain Gekalek with an additional task, as well. Gekalek was to exude a diplomatic scent to the inhabitants of the first planet on the defensive conquest itinerary.

But suppose that planet did end up being the renegade couple's destination, maybe even their final resting place? And suppose they went there with a traitorous thought towards warning the inhabitants of an impending invasion? In such an eventuality, Captain Gekalek's diplomatic scent would need to fill the air with special assurance. To wit, nothing smelling of an invasion was actually in the works.

Complications abounded across the bigger picture, however. As though Captain Gekalek's conflicted feelings were not complication enough.

Doubtless, many crew members would agree to a saner course in defiance of Dek-Fook-Tek's manic-driven orders. But Captain Gekalek well knew many other crew members were still blindly worshipping Dek-Fook-Tek. Moreover, they had made common bond with kindred worshippers down on Tictoctic's surface. Whether planet-bound or aboard the battle saucer, those worshippers habitually bought certain lotto tickets. The winners enjoyed the privilege of eating the Supreme Authority's excrement prepared by some of the finest Tictoctickian gourmet chefs. This scheme for fattening the royal treasury was entitled: Nibble-down Economics.

Relatives of some of the Supreme Authority's devoted fanatics were victims of Chonoran atrocities. Understandably, those relatives did not want to take a chance on any other extraterrestrial civilization having the opportunity to perform an atrocity encore. Where Dek-Fook-Tek loyalists posted aboard the Fifth Celestial Breath were concerned, no mercy should be shown to other-worlders. The least kindness afforded other-worlders was in the same league with anything less than untempered adulation for the Supreme Authority. It could be sufficient grounds for mutiny.

Captain Gekalek and fellow captains did commiserate in private before the Fifth Celestial Breath's departure. They shared mixed feelings over what Commander Kwit-Nik was about. They were uncertain they wouldn't ultimately come back around to total obeisance for Dek-Fook-Tek, and expose the commander as a traitor.

"What I meant to say, Captain Gekalek," continued Officer Wek-bek with his contrition, "what there was no good excuse for me not saying in the first place, is that we are about to be blessed with, baa... It is imminent! The only worse offense would be for my worthless groveling to delay even the smallest portion of a mini-pektel longer the Supreme Authority's most blessed counsel. So here..."

Wek-bek stepped aside from the navigation deck view-screen, and he made a presenting sweep towards it with a fearfully trembling foreleg.

On the view-screen, transmission snow resolved into a still-grainy picture of Supreme Authority Dek-Fook-Tek. Crossing trillions of lek-leks of space severely degraded the transmission quality. Consequently, even the best eyes would have had an impossible time discerning the nylon-thin filaments. Those filaments were holding stable Dek-Fook-Tek's mighty antlers so they wouldn't tip over and possibly break his neck.

Every deer creature on the navigation deck of Dek-Fook-Tek's Fifth Celestial Breath rose up onto his hind legs in a noisily clumsy commotion, antlers bumping antlers. They every last one faced the view-screen with chests swelled out. Pursuant to which, Captain Gekalek led them in his latest adulatory litany.

"What might have proven a nibble-less day," he began.

"What might have proven a nibble-less day," the rest repeated.

"can now be regurgitated,"

"can now be regurgitated,"

"full of joyful celebration, nibble-less or not!"

"full of joyful celebration, nibble-less or not!"

"For you have honored us, so undeservingly,"

"For you have honored us, so undeservingly,"

"with your inspiring presence,"

"with your inspiring presence,"

"oh great, wise, all-powerful Dek-Fook-Tek,"

"oh great, wise, all-powerful Dek-Fook-Tek,"

"whose respiration now marks entire other solar systems as his own,"

"whose respiration now marks entire other solar systems as his own,"

"even as the oskynt marks its territory with its urine."

"even as the oskynt marks its territory with its urine."

Captain and crew bleated relief. They had galloped through the adulatory litany without a hitch. And down to the last one, they strongly suspected Dek-Fook-Tek would approve. There was merely the matter of having to wait out the considerable transmission time. Space-debris-disguised patrol markers were relaying their ritualized greeting, to be followed by the return relay of the Supreme Authority's reaction. Again, though, their confidence was high. Didn't matter whether they had grown to revile Dek-Fook-Tek, or still felt sincere, if often fearful, adulation.

On Captain Gekalek's sheep-like "Baa!" the Tictoctickians' celebratory dance began in tight unison. There were two steps forward followed by a kick of their right hind limbs, then two steps backward followed by a kick of their left hind limbs. Observers from Earth might have thought they were performing a Texas line dance.

At last the grainy image went into motion, of the Supreme Authority on the view-screen. That's when the dance came to clomp-clomping halt with a militaristic march step, left-right, of the deer creatures' hind hooves.

Supreme Authority Dek-Fook-Tek was heard to tongue-click, albeit with lots of accompanying static, "Captain Gekalek, your new salutation I find not altogether demeaning. Regardless, matters of the highest priority occupy me on Tictoctic..." He paused. The way his head moved ever so slightly with a definite rhythm, Captain Gekalek suffered a fleeting intuition... *No, it can't be. In the Supreme Authority's foreground, out of camera range, he couldn't, he wouldn't be conjoining with one of his harem while he was addressing us, would he?* "...so this is a reminder not requiring a response," Dek-Fook-Tek finally continued. "And incidentally, my modesty dictates no commemorative statues to honor this historic occasion. At least for now! Anyway, my reminder is this: Once you have verified the fate of the scout saucer hijackers, notify Commander Kwit-Nik immediately! The commander knows that upon receipt of such verification, the multi-planet defense of Tictoctic must begin! For the primitive, barbaric other-world civilizations, their experience of that defense is to be as a hurl of vomit would be for a niki-nik colony on Tictoctic!

"One last thing: I could predict what you will discover regarding the traitorous hijackers, wherever they finally spit out their venom. But as our saying goes, a child should not be expected to gore an oskynt on the word of his parents, before seeing the oskynt gore his sister. This is the Tictoctic Empire." Dek-Fook-Tek punctuated that concluding remark with a most pronounced nod. He was ably assisted by his antler handlers in the ceiling directly above him. Those handlers could have been puppeteers manipulating marionettes, rather than guiding the Supreme Authority's prolific head growths.

The view-screen aboard the Fifth Celestial Breath went blank. It remained that way but for a moment before filling with starry firmament. The largest star was Alpha Centauri C. The second largest star was the fourth planet of the Alpha Centauri C system. That planet was known by its inhabitants, when they were still alive, as Fafama.

"For how his guidance sustains us," said Captain Gekalek, "we could fast for ten days, and still feel gorged."

Gekalek had gone on with more ritual praise for Dek-Fook-Tek, despite Dek-Fook-Tek having brought their encounter to a close. Officer Wek-bek well understood why. One never knew when Dek-Fook-Tek might be surreptitiously continuing to listen in after he presumably had moved on to other matters. Nevertheless, Wek-bek couldn't help exclaiming, soon as the captain was done, "New information, Captain Gekalek!" He realized his outburst was over-the-top the instant he finished.

Earlier on, Wek-bek could not have been more distracted from the adulatory litany and the celebratory dance. Both might as well have never happened where he was concerned. But he couldn't help it. Ever since the giant flying saucer dropped out of light-speed excess in the Alpha Centauri C system, the navigation panel readouts were indicating something amazingly ominous. Nevertheless, Officer Wek-bek figured presently that he better make up for his rudeness. "No one can doubt Dek-Fook-Tek would have detailed far more than I am able to," he said, despite how full of doubt he actually felt in this regard. "But there are untold urgencies against which he must head-charge his massive antlers back on Tictoctic." Captain Gekalek remained quietly shocked by Wek-bek's behavior, affording Wek-bek the opportunity to proceed without interruption. "Our sensors, adapted as per Commander Kwit-Nik's Dek-Fook-Tek-inspired directives," Wek-bek was careful to add, "have detected two additional dissipated photon-stream signatures. Each signature is much larger than the photon decay signature from the hijacked scout saucer vessel. And both signatures take paths parallel to the scout saucer signature. In addition, it is clear that all three photon decay signatures converged on this solar system's fourth planet."

"Officer Pekkyspek, place the targeted magnetic pulse-beam on standby," crisply tongue-clicked Captain Gekalek. Then he trotted over behind Navigation Officer Wek-bek. He wanted to find out what Wek-bek was making such a big fuss about. With knowing nods at the navigation console data screens, he pretended to understand. "Officer Wek-bek," he said finally, "I will scan here to assure you are not missing any significant detail. Meanwhile, I insist you perform a task for the edification of the rest of the navigation crew. Relate to them what else you and I already know we can apprise from this data."

Ah, yes, Officer Wek-bek thought to himself. *Superiors in the command chain can never admit requiring assistance with this co-opted technology. Captain Gekalek will surely attend closely to my "edification for the rest of the crew."* "Something bears repeating, Captain Gekalek," Wek-bek deferentially brayed rather than tongue-clicked, putting himself in his place in the hierarchy. "You are as a full moon, lighting up the night with the reflected wisdom of Dek-Fook-Tek."

"Always the full moon when Dek-Fook-Tek is our sun," ritually baaed the other officers.

"We can discern nothing of a currently active spacecraft signature," Wek-bek went on, following the captain's orders. "This is the reality whether we scan near or afar in respect to the solar system's fourth planet."

The captain pretended to be too consumed by panel screen data to be sniffing at Wek-bek with any least attention.

"However," Wek-bek tongue-clicked with a sharpness meant to impress upon his audience the significance of what he was about to report, "we *are* picking up something in orbit around the target planet. It is too large to be a satellite."

Captain Gekalek couldn't help his ears twitching anxiously. So much for having insinuated there was nothing Wek-bek could relate from the data screens that would catch him unawares!

"It is most likely a space station in high orbit around the target planet," added Wek-bek.

Captain Gekalek nodded as though he'd just calmly completed taking in every last bit of screen data, no anxious ear-twitching about it. He raised his antlered head to tongue-click in rapid staccato tones, "Officer Wek-bek, you have alerted the crew to the likelihood of a space station orbiting the target planet?" Gekalek spoke as if nobody else were present overhearing his every remark and Wek-bek's as well.

"I have. But only because your very demeanor reminded me this detail was of the utmost importance, Captain Gekalek."

The captain nodded approvingly. Well did he know that Navigation Officer Wek-bek was feeding him verbal excrement. Yet he appreciated Wek-bek doing far better at ritual obeisance than he did earlier, when he said, *A message from Dek-Fook-Tek.* "Officer Wek-bek," Captain Gekalek proceeded, "transmit the pictograph to the fourth planet other-worlders. I am referring to the pictograph which details our most noble intent, thanks be to Dek-Fook-Tek."

"Thanks be to Dek-Fook-Tek," everyone else ritually repeated.

"Captain Gekalek, I can confirm pictograph transmission," tongue-clicked Officer Wek-bek after some button-pushing on the navigation control console.

"We should expect a response sooner rather than later, issuing directly from the other-worlders' space station," Captain Gekalek declared. He thought to himself on how Officer Wek-bek might require a ritual chest wounding, also sooner rather than later. Yes, Wek-bek was doing better where ritual adulation was concerned. But in the captain's estimation, he was also getting too full of himself as one of the few on board who totally understood control console output.

Several more minutes elapsed with still no answer from the space station orbiting Fafama. Captain Gekalek spent that time clip-clopping back and forth. He had long since grown weary of nibbling off the pektels with some antler-sharpening, courtesy of his captain's-issue bahvek. Anyway, when he finally paused from his impatient pacing, he tersely tongue-clicked, "What bray you, Officer Wek-bek? Should we fire a magnetic pulse-beam at the target planet, set on harmless tremor? Give its inhabitants a firm reminder that somewhere, shadows are lengthening?"

Let's see: How do I parry my boss's unreasonable expectation in the form of a compliment? "Magnificent Captain Gekalek," Officer Wek-bek made a self-effacing point of baaing rather than tongue-clicking. "Our superior intelligence is inspired to its maximum by the ever-flowing example of our Supreme Authority, Dek-Fook-Tek. He has accustomed us to far more rapid reaction times to communication initiatives than are likely found among other-world intelligences. Those intelligences must rely on their instincts. Evidence bears this out from our exploration of the planet whose strange natives call it 'Koombt.' It often felt like we waited forever on their responses to the most basic inquiries." This was a lie, but Officer Wek-bek confidently assumed Captain Gekalek would accept it at face value.

"None of us needs reminding of something else," Wek-bek went on. "The other-worlders might be dealing with compatibility issues concerning the frequency level on which we made our transmission. It is probably not the frequency level they are instinctively used to. We can still hope they won't prove as dumb as our pet kokatoks back on Tictoctic. I regret to this day how kokatok sacrifice became so tragically required in order to stave off our fellow creatures' mass starvation. In any event, I expect the other-worlders' response will consist of more than a quizzical head tilt and a tail-wagged body!"

Fellow officers on the bridge baaed their amusement over Wek-bek's remark about the kokatoks, but Captain Gekalek would have none of it. "You believe the other-worlders on that space station keep us waiting for reasons other than preparing a surprise attack on us?!?! We cannot assume that, Officer Wek-bek!!!" Gekalek brayed at the top of his lungs. He stamped a cloven hind-hoof thumping hard against the floor on his every word. "Remember: three decelerated photon stream signatures have been tracked towards that planet!! Three!!"

Of course, Captain Gekalek had no way of knowing that one of the signatures was from Dek-Fook-Tek's Third Celestial Breath, after Earthlings seized it by ingenuous means. And that those same Earthlings sealed its doom. By remote control, they sent the giant battle saucer into the laser mesh shield protectively enveloping Fafama. They sent it there, intentionally not programmed with the protective passcode required in order to forestall a disintegrating barrage of laser cannon fire.

"Two things I order you to do, Officer Wek-bek!" went on Captain Gekalek presently. "First, send an additional pictograph demanding immediate acknowledgement of receipt of the previous pictograph series! The other-worlders can take however long they need for their full response. However, they must be made to understand that in the meantime, failure to quickly acknowledge will be taken as a show of hostility. And a show of hostility will oblige us to respond with the most severe consequences! Possibly including the cripplement if not total destruction of their space station!!

"And...now for your second order: Upon transmission of the additional pictograph sequence, you will place the Fifth Celestial Breath on a new course setting. That setting will hide our movement behind the most conveniently located asteroid available! From there we can launch a surprise attack if such dramatic projection of the full might of Dek-Fook-Tek becomes necessary!"

"In process, Captain," Wek-bek baaed in response. He was already applying himself furiously fast to the demanded pictograph. He might have tried to frame his effort in the usual, self-effacing terms with which an officer was expected to communicate to his superior. For example, Wek-bek could have humbly baaed there was no doubt Dek-Fook-Tek would have assembled the required pictograph communication in record time. Dek-Fook-Tek would have had the pictograph done and on its way well before someone finished re-sharpening an already needle-sharp antler prong with a bahvek. However, lesser mortals required more pektels, many more pektels, to achieve such a feat. Again, Wek-bek's self-effacement would have gone something like that. But as matters already stood, he sensed a chest scarring in his future; he didn't want it to turn into an all-out fatal goring. This was certainly possible, he feared, if the time he took for self-effacement ironically delayed completion of the task beyond what the captain could endure.

⁂

"Officer Pekkyspek, I am leaving you in charge of the Fifth Celestial Breath while Officer Wek-bek and I fly a scout saucer out from behind the asteroid. If we are met with hostile fire, execute magnetic pulse-beam retaliation. Target the other-world space station, maximum setting to assure its total obliteration. Thereafter, I will also expect three demonstration blasts directed at assorted high-population targets across the planet's surface."

"Would that Dek-Fook-Tek was here in my stead," somberly nodded Pekkyspek. "In such an eventuality as you have described, I can only aspire to approach remotely what he would have accomplished."

"We can only aspire to approach remotely what he would have accomplished," ritually repeated the rest of the crew on the navigation bridge.

Pekkyspek thought on how easily he could exploit this opportunity to seize command from Captain Gekalek. With the flick of a few switches, he could blast apart the captain's scout saucer once it flew a safe distance away from the Fifth Celestial Breath. But Officer Wek-bek was ordered to accompany Gekalek. And Wek-bek was the only other Tictoctickian aboard the Fifth Celestial Breath, apart from Pekkyspek himself, who possessed any operational understanding of the co-opted space-flight technology.

⁂

"Captain Gekalek, I am noticing something," timidly baaed Officer Wek-bek, seated beside the captain aboard the scout saucer. "I am sorry it has taken me so long to realize this. Now I understand why you have remained steadfastly measured in your displeasure with the persisting lack of response to our communication overtures."

"It is about time, Officer Wek-bek. Please detail what you are noticing, so I can confirm you are not mistaken." The captain grew anxious to learn what his chief navigation officer was talking about. He had no idea, himself.

Officer Wek-bek finished maneuvering the scout saucer into full sunlight, out from behind the shadows of a two-mile-wide asteroid.

The Fifth Celestial Breath kept concealed on the asteroid's dark side.

"Captain, I am noticing the other-world space station's orbit on a decay course. That course is certain to send it burning up through the planet's atmosphere in only a matter of days. Maybe it has been abandoned?"

"That is the station, yes?" Captain Gekalek pointed a cloven hoof-hand towards the scout saucer view-screen. More specifically, he pointed towards a large, bright object revealed there. It reminded the captain of colorfully bejeweled scabbards on exhibit in Tictoctic museums.

"Baa! Yes! Of course! You are correct!" Officer Wek-bek pretended to have required Captain Gekalek's assistance to locate the space station. In reality, his eyes had latched onto it several mini-pektels before his superior. "Without your Dek-Fook-Tek-inspired directing of my attention..." Wek-bek trailed off with feigned humility.

Captain Gekalek snorted disgust. He was picking up the foul scent farted by Officer Wek-bek pretending far greater stupidity than actually felt.

"Those beautifully colored objects as of various gems, embedded in the space station's hull," Wek-bek went on as though he didn't notice Gekalek's disgust. "We can suppose they are tinted windows. They convey a festive atmosphere. But I still have the stomach-regurgitating feeling there is nobody aboard. Could the strangely shaped vessel be abandoned?"

"Officer Wek-bek, your perceptiveness is nearly enough for you to have earned a deep chest-scar from the antlers of Dek-Fook-Tek himself! But he is nowhere near, except of course as he projects his supreme presence across trillions of lek-leks via the Fifth Celestial Breath. Therefore, at the first convenient opportunity it will be for me to try my best, inflicting that most deserved honor upon you. I will assume this task, well aware of my antlers' limited effectiveness. They are as the deflated sex organ of an impotent oskynt by comparison to Dek-Fook-Tek's antlers."

"Captain Gekalek, is it safe for the Fifth Celestial Breath to reveal itself from behind the asteroid?" Officer Pekkyspek's shrill brays suddenly filled the scout saucer from its intercom.

"Not just yet," answered Captain Gekalek. He held up a cautioning hoof-hand even though Pekkyspek wouldn't be seeing it back aboard the Celestial Breath. "Officer Wek-bek," he then proceeded to tongue-click, "can you confirm with our scout saucer's sensors what my visuals are suggesting about this solar system's fourth planet?"

The planet Fafama provided a distant backdrop to the abandoned-looking, scabbard-shaped space station. Fafama presented as an ominously dark orb, save for its thin crescent of light. That crescent was rapidly expanding as the scout saucer spun like a top towards the planet's day side. Erratic lightning flashes, plus equally erratic flashes of bright orange from explosive volcanic activity, disrupted the darkness on Fafama's night side.

"Captain Gekalek, sensors are not picking up flying vehicles in the planet's atmosphere. Nor are there any other obvious signs of an intelligence that has attained a significant level of technology.

"On the other hoof, spectrographic readings do confirm the presence of substances conducive to thriving life as we know it. Nevertheless, we must consider the elevated concentrations of radioactivity and poisonous gases in various locations. Taken together with volatile weather and tectonic activity, we have a strong suggestion of especially hostile conditions. Baa!" Officer Wek-bek suddenly baaed in horrified awe.

The light of day made Fafama's ruination more starkly evident. Cloud cover ranging from brown-tinged smoky gray to coal black enshrouded much of the planet. Only a few gaps in the clouds were large enough to accommodate peering all the way down to the surface. One such gap allowed glimpses of a large body of water, the Grand Basin as Fafamans used to call it. The Grand Basin no longer looked like an emerald blanket studded with sparkles whenever bathed in sunshine. Rather, it glistened oily black. With an ear-twitching shiver, Captain Gekalek imagined some impossibly monstrous creature lurking there, just beneath the waves. In reality, the life-choking birth of an undersea super-volcano led to the Grand Basin's discoloration.

Another gap in the cloud cover afforded dramatic peeks at a fully exposed, dry land super-volcano.

Voluminous ejections from its persistent eruption kept feeding the overcast with billowing black ash plumes.

Except for the super-volcano, Captain Gekalek was most reminded of the fate that befell Chonora. Chonora was the planet that shared Tictoctic's identical orbital path and velocity, to always keep it the opposite side of the Cygnitaurus sun from Tictoctic. Anyway, Chonora's devastation proved equally dramatic, simply from the Chonorans bombing themselves close to extinction. This became the case inadvertently, when Chonoran missiles launched against the Tictoctickians ran out of steam before they could free themselves from the planet's gravitational pull. Instead, they fell back to Chonoran earth with horrific results. But Chonoran devastation also became the case intentionally via homegrown terrorism. Supreme justice meted out for what the Chonorans tried to do to Tictoctic. Gekalek had long since conceded this point, despite his agreeing with Commander Kwit-Nik as to the complexities of present circumstances.

What Captain Gekalek and Officer Wek-bek had already borne witness to was plenty enthralling, in a most horrible way. Something additional, though, caused the captain to lean forward in his seat. His nostrils got extra-agitated in an impossible yet uncontrollably instinctive effort to detect the slightest relevant scent. That something additional was what he and Officer Wek-bek espied through a third gap in the cloud cover, the biggest gap. First glimpse suggested very mountainous terrain of a most peculiar character. If Officer Wek-bek didn't know better, he would have guessed a god from ancient Tictoctickian mythology somehow lifted up this planet's tallest peak. Then that god hurled it against the ground, shattering it into irregular chunks.

But Wek-bek, and Captain Gekalek too for that matter, *did* know better. Still, they noticed something even weirder than the peculiar terrain. Silvery-glinted straight edges lay scattered about the epic geological mess, too silvery and way too straight to have occurred naturally.

"If I didn't see it for myself, Officer Wek-bek, I would only have believed this scene existed had Dek-Fook-Tek lowered himself to describe it for us. Apparently, an entire mountain was thrown against an intelligently produced edifice of epic proportions!" tongue-clicked Captain Gekalek. "Officer Pekkyspek! You may proceed to emerge the Fifth Celestial Breath from behind the asteroid! You plus two other officers are going to trade places with us! The three of you will investigate something alarmingly odd down on the surface of this planet!"

Captain Gekalek figured if the away team were to meet their doom, at least he would still have Officer Wek-bek. Wek-bek's presence assured a safe return to their home solar system. *His well-earned chest-slashing might need to be postponed.*

⋅⧓⋅⧓⋅⧓⋅

Officer Pekkyspek piloted the scout saucer towards where Captain Gekalek and Officer Wek-bek espied mysterious terrain. Pekkyspek, Nik-Nak and Pattywak experienced only minor turbulence on the saucer's descent through the brownish-gray overcast. Still, Pekkyspek maneuvered to a low-altitude cruising level as quickly as possible. For the remaining approach to the region he was assigned to investigate, the scout saucer spun like a top not more than two thousand feet above the surface of Fafama. From that height, Pekkyspek took no time at all spotting something of unusual significance.

"Captain Gekalek, I would not have dared contact you again so soon. However, Dek-Fook-Tek's vision seems to have crossed the multi-trillion lek-leks to subsume mine. As a result, I have been made aware of another ground feature commanding most urgent interest."

"Proceed quickly, Officer Pekkyspek!" Captain Gekalek's severely staccato tongue-clicks burst from the scout saucer's intercom, albeit drowning in static from atmospheric disturbance. "Confirm most hastily that you have not made a mockery of our Supreme Authority!"

"Captain Gekalek, I am patching in our view-screen to the Fifth Celestial Breath's view-screen as I circle us back around to show you."

"Allow the patch-through, Officer Wek-bek," the captain gestured to his navigation officer back aboard the Fifth Celestial Breath. That giant flying saucer was hovering in geosynchronous orbit some twenty thousand miles above the surface of Fafama.

"There! There it is!" Pekkyspek pointed excitedly, his mouth drooling at both corners. "Do you see the wreckage embedded at an odd angle in this planet's soil?? Would that be our lost Celestial Breath?? Would that be the battle ship some other-worlders tricked an entire crew into abandoning??"

Captain Gekalek realized what he was seeing on the view-screen not only fit Officer Pekkyspek's description. Engraved on it were the unmistakable markings of the Tictoctickian language. They consisted of sets of carefully rendered striations. Their precedents were pawed into clay ground thousands of years earlier, by the first deer creatures to conceive written communication.

Captain Gekalek became so angry that he unbuckled his seat belt, stood up and turned to face his captain's chair. He held on tight to the chair's arms so his rage-exhausting kicking would not send him cartwheeling across the navigation bridge in the near-zero gravity. Then he cut loose with a shrill, deep-throated bray. *So! So! Commander Kwit-Nik might well be correct about Dek-Fook-Tek's mental state, but I hope he fully understands what we are dealing with!* This thought raged feverishly through Gekalek's head, until he finally calmed down enough to crisply tongue-click, "An excellent find, Officer Pekkyspek! It can only be that for precious pektels, Dek-Fook-Tek's vision was indeed informing your own!"

"His vision is welcomed through the thickest walls, even as his member is welcomed into the deepest womb," ritually spoke the crew aboard the Fifth Celestial Breath and the scout saucer alike.

"We are landing at the base of the target region!" proceeded to report Officer Pekkyspek. "Our close-in analysis suggests generally breathable air. However, there are also indications of randomly dispersed toxics. They could make for a potential hazard if reasonable precautions are not taken. I have ordered Officers Nik-Nak and Pattywak to join me in donning oxygenated suits for our venture outside. Air igniters will be kept at the ready, let me assure you!"

"That is exactly what I was about to command, Officer Pekkyspek! Continue your frequent updates, starting one pektel after disembarkation from the scout saucer!"

"Duly masticated, Captain!"

Captain Gekalek's order was easier said than done, however, once Pekkyspek and his away team descended off the landed scout saucer. It was one thing to spot silvery straight-edges from outer space, scattered randomly amidst jagged chunks of a seemingly collapsed-apart mountain. It was another matter altogether, though, to stand right beside them. The immensity of the bizarre geological tableau in which those shiny straight-edges played but a small, unnatural part literally took Officer Pekkyspek's breath away.

After a calming-down "Baa," Pekkyspek finally and firmly tongue-clicked his update into the transmission device embedded on his spacesuit. "We would appear to be standing beside the collapsed ruins of an intelligently produced structure," he reported. "It is nothing to compare with architecture Dek-Fook-Tek has inspired on Tictoctic. Perhaps, in fact, it is only short evolutionary steps removed from the quality of a niki-nik hill. Whatever the case might be, one receives the strong impression it was crushed to pieces by immense stone conglomerates. Dek-Fook-Tek inspires me to guess those conglomerates descended from space as either discreet meteorites, or parts of a rapidly disintegrating comet. We will attempt an ascent of one of the conglomerates to collect some samples. Oh, and scattered about our hooves, in amidst the rubble..." Officer Pekkyspek came down on all fours to paw at the ground with one space-suit-covered cloven hoof-hand. "...there are charred bones, bits of charred flesh, and... Baa, this would appear to be charred exoskeleton from the claw of a monstrously large insect. It is a shame we were not here sooner to gather up the flesh, when perhaps it was still palatable. Maybe we could have prepared beast jerky of the other-world variety."

"Dek-Fook-Tek cannot clone himself to be everywhere at once, which would have ensured our highest efficiency. This reality remains one of life's great regrets." By the time Captain Gekalek reached the end of this particular ritual litany, he was not alone. Everyone aboard the Fifth Celestial Breath and with the away team down on Fafama had joined in. Non-ritually, the captain added, "Careful, Officer Pekkyspek. Do not become the meal of choice for some surviving member of that monster insect species down there, the one whose claw you mentioned!"

"Your care for our safety extends like the hoof-hands of Dek-Fook-Tek's mercy, Captain Gekalek," humbly bleated Pekkyspek. He tugged on a hiking rope to assure it was successfully hammered securely deep into the rocky material of the conglomerate.

For several pektels Officer Pekkyspek climbed the rope, joining fellow officers Nik-Nak and Pattywak in that task. He wished to more closely inspect what appeared from ground level to be a giant, perfectly cylindrical hole bored into the side of bare stone.

All three Tictoctickian deer creatures did manage to ascend far enough to reach the giant hole. That's when Officer Pekkyspek tongue-clicked, "Officer Pattywak, you will enter this circular aperture with your flashlight and air igniter at the ready, while we stand guard outside."

None of the away team noticed before-hoof that translucent threads stretched haphazardly across the perfectly cylindrical hole. Consequently, Officer Pattywak soon found himself stuck helplessly. "No!" he bleated in a panic. "This must be the web of some fearsome insect monster! Like the one for which we found a short segment of exoskeleton below!"

Well before the Tictoctickian officer completed this terror-filled assessment, his cohorts succeeded in freeing him from the web filaments. The concentrated power of their air igniters did the trick. Then all three deer creatures aimed their fire-producing weapons towards the interior of the mysterious orifice. They were not to be disappointed in their anxious expectations.

The sky abruptly darkened, and a random lightning bolt unleashed concussive thunder. The deer creature officers from Tictoctic trembled even more anxiously than before. That is when an ahtpah, one of Fafama's cow-sized arthropods, appeared to emerge from a most hidden recess of the cylindrical hole.

The officers focused their air igniters on the monster spider, but to no good effect. The three blowtorch-like flames seemed to pass harmlessly through its shiny-black, bulbous body.

The ahtpah scurried closer and closer, panicking Nik-Nak into falling backwards off the precarious ledge. Sharp rock edges below sealed his doom.

Officers Pekkyspek and Pattywak shut their eyes. Any pektel, they expected to feel steely mandibles crushing their bodies. Yet they stood their ground; they did not desire their partner's cowardly, Dek-Fook-Tek-dishonoring form of death.

No body-crushing came. Both officers opened their eyes just in time for seeing the ahtpah's rear end fade into nothingness around and through them. They might as well have mistaken a bit of fog for a monster. Unexpectedly, though, they suddenly felt searing waves of heat. This furnace blast issued from the cylindrical hole where they unleashed their air igniters, trying to stop what turned out to be a phantom.

On a hunch, Officer Pekkyspek undid the helmet of his spacesuit to take a deep breath. His curiosity temporarily overwhelmed his judgment. But he detected exactly what he expected: the unmistakable fumes from rocket engine propellant.

Blessed Dek-Fook-Tek, the away team has uncovered the high-tech scent of an extremely barbaric other-world tribe! This was Captain Gekalek's conclusion once Officer

Pekkyspek completed his latest update. *Sending our Third Celestial Breath crashing into this planet's surface did not prove horrific enough for satisfying their destructive lust! No! They had to follow up by sending no less than an enormous celestial object, a comet, on essentially the same collision course! And clearly, they accomplished this awful deed by boring rocket engines into the chosen comet for propelling it downward! What monsters are these??!! And in that regard, when Commander Kwit-Nik learns of our discovery, where will that place his plans for usurping the authority of Dek-Fook-Tek? Indeed, hasn't our Supreme Authority's judgment now been vindicated? That we must approach foreign solar systems with overwhelming force? And wait to negotiate until after we have reined in whomever we are dealing with? Hmmm, I shall need to ponder this over a leg from Officer Nik-Nak, most tastefully prepared by Chef Glut-Gut in fitting tribute to his ultimate sacrifice!*

Chapter 2

"Stop aiming that thing at me!"

"I'm not aiming this thing at you!! I'm aiming it at the virtual reality quarry, a rather large quarry at that! Anyhow, I could be firing into the side of your head, point blank, and you wouldn't feel a thing!"

"You *are* aiming it at me! At my chest! And I don't care whether I would feel a thing or not! I don't like it!"

"Dearest Priscilla, Prissy dear..." Michel DeFarge lowered his game device replica of a vintage Remington rifle, and he lifted his virtual-reality goggled helmet off his head. That's when he gave his wife a lustful regard; anything less primal would have allowed his thoughts to wander places. And there were particular places he did not want those mind-reading tree dufusses from Oomb, as he regarded them, to access. "Prissy dear," he said, "you must not distract me from my distraction! I cannot control where the quarry chooses to bound about! If it happens to frolic in front of you, and that is where I can get off my best shot, then that is what I intend to do! Mais oui!"

"The pity of it... Oh, bother! Go! On with your hunt! I will endeavor to hit the floor softly when I pass out from terror over your firing that thing at me! I certainly wouldn't want to cause any further distraction from your distraction!" Priscilla DeFarge waved off Michel DeFarge's amorous advance as he tried encircling her shoulders with his free arm. She was going to say how ironically unfortunate his antics could prove. He might obstruct her observation of something significant happening with the Smoke and Mirrors. But she well knew such a remark ran the risk of opening the floodgates for thoughts her husband needed to avoid. The idea was to prevent those damnable tree people, as Priscilla and Michel both saw them, from mind-reading his plans. And so, rather than say anything, she turned away from the compact starship's panoramic view-screen. Her focus remained on the same cosmic vista, but as it was revealed on a far smaller scale by the control console. Priscilla also continued knitting socks for her husband, Michel. At least, she assured herself, his virtual bear hunt would not bring him between her and the console.

There was a time Michel DeFarge vented regularly to his wife. But presently, his aforementioned compact spaceship, the Elusive, had gotten to within mind-reading range of the Smoke and Mirrors. Anyway, in the days tree creatures were not picking his brain, he would rage early and often, "Damn, damn and more damn! It is not natural, it is damnably *unnatural* having to avoid detection by those who should be fellow hunters of a common quarry! And it is exponentially more unnaturally damnable that we should have to fear deer, any kind of deer! They could be from Earth, another planet, or an alternate universe for all I care. What could be worse than deer hunting *us*, hunting anyone or any*thing* beyond a truffle to be rooted from the ground?!"

Presently, Michel DeFarge would have liked to have been fussing over his trophy room housed by a log cabin in West Virginia. Even better, he would have liked to have been giving notables such as President Carey another guided tour of that room. But he would have settled with reliving his glorious boarding of the interstellar battleship, Barack Obama.

The thrill of the simulated bear hunt kept DeFarge's thoughts far, far afield from wistful contemplation of anything else. Such avoidances had become necessary thanks to that other damnably unnatural circumstance, as he saw it. Again, it was the business with mobile, mind-reading trees. DeFarge made the same point for anyone who would listen to him. He insisted the Oombian tree creatures must have gotten themselves infected by some ancient counter-culture freak, a hippie. Yes! Of course! A hippie from the 1960s somehow astral-projected himself all the way out to the planet Oomb! Yes! He accomplished that feat care of whatever hallucinogenic drugs hippies were using, every last one of them! Michel DeFarge swore this must be true!

"I have to say, Commander DeFarge, you took us completely by surprise how you crept up on us!" Dr. Magdalena "Maggie" Wang had effused back when Michel boarded the Obama. She clapped her hands together in pure delight as Michel clomp-clomp-clomp magnet-booted his way onto the navigation bridge of the battle-ready starship.

The Obama was "parked" on the outskirts of the Callaway X Centra System. That location placed it well out of range of anything stronger than the vague-est, blurred extrasensory eavesdropping even by Oomb's best mind-readers.

"I am impressed!" Dr. Wang added.

"You can take what Maggie said, Michel, and quadruple it for the rest of us!" boomed Secretary of Defense Michael Spinner. On a first-name basis with DeFarge, Secretary Spinner had enjoyed more than one admiring tour of Michel DeFarge's trophy room. "Oops! Hope I'm not going to get myself in trouble, speaking on behalf of these two extraordinary ladies here!" Spinner chortled. He waved towards the Chair of the Joint Chiefs of Staff, Sandy Warlor, and provisional Barak Obama captain, Louisa Entroper. They were standing beside him. "Don't want to put myself on the hit list of some ultra-feminist who might want to mount my head on a wall! Oops again! Can I say that? None of you heard me, did you?" Spinner gave the navigation bridge a wide-sweeping scan received with general laughter.

"It's no problem for me, you fat-assed bastard!" Michel DeFarge good-naturedly cussed as he swept greasy, sweaty, stringy, stray hair strands from his eyes. Over several years, DeFarge's legend had grown for being a fast study on state-of-the-art space flight technology. This was in addition to his warrior reputation. He unabashedly led whatever slaughter his superiors deemed necessary to enforce the more difficult portions of the quarantine zones, such as in Somalia. DeFarge accomplished the latter bloodthirsty feat without the least evident twinge of regret. Otherwise he could potentially have compromised the morale of fellow troops.

As a result of DeFarge's near-mythical status, he was allowed casual disregard of certain protocols without anyone questioning his loyalty, or otherwise calling him out. Most other male military personnel were required to keep their hair crew-cut neat, and their faces clean-shaven. But DeFarge's hair was shoulder-length, washed about once a month. And his sideburns burgeoned out of control, i.e. they had become full-blown mutton chops. Moreover, if he left his pants a bit unzipped, and his shirt partially unbuttoned...Then there was his wife who got to tag along on every assignment.

"So, explain what you did," Dr. Wang asked with her head shaking in delighted wonderment.

"It's like this, Ma'am." Michel DeFarge gave the weapons specialist a respectful bow. He even tugged self-consciously on his belt, the zipper close to two inches undone. "When you're hunting deer, the type back on Earth what can't fly saucers and fire air igniters, you want to make yourself invisible. A few shed skin cells, the oily sheen from your sweaty face, a shadow between leaves... Any one of those things, taken alone, will often be the only thing needed to scare your game leaping away before you get off a good shot. Far as I can tell, these particular deer, flyin' through space like they own the cosmos, they are really no different. Again, it's damnably unnatural, damn, damn, damnably unnatural we should have to be dealing with them! But it's the same difference."

"The same difference, exactly!" Secretary Spinner couldn't help interjecting, couldn't help effusing with a jab of his forefinger at DeFarge.

"Out here in space, okay, there aren't going to be any skin cells and such," Michel DeFarge conceded. "But you've got glints of light off the starships. The extraterrestrial deer might detect them glints, even if we're successfully radar-cloaked, or sitting stationary the dark side of some fat-assed ass-teroid! At least it's a simpler issue than having to worry about being in mind-reading range of tree critters. And let me say one more thing about mind-reading tree critters, while we're on the subject. If they knew what was good for them, they would be screaming in the ET deers' heads so those antlered demons wouldn't be able to think straight!"

"Two of those 'tree critters' demonstrated they could do exactly that!" said Secretary Spinner in support of DeFarge's thesis. "Back on Oomb during the brief Tictoctickian occupation, they gave our furry-assed enemy a collective migraine! But get this: They were reprimanded by their fellow up-rooters! Reprimanded!" repeated Spinner with another forefinger jab.

"I'll repeat this until I'm blue in the face: damnably unnatural! So anyway..."

Sandy Warlor and Entroper made urging nods as in, *Yes, on with it, DeFarge! Please!*

"...I conjured up something special, something additional for concealing my pint-sized interstellar battle cruiser, Elusive, from the bad guys. Then I had my personal metallurgist work out the details. Let me tell you about it in case you don't already know. Flat, non-reflective black is fused into the hull. It's also fused into the entry and exit cones for the tulip-array light-wave entrance, and the rose-array, light-particle exit. What inspired those cones, of course, was the special collar that people place round a dog's neck to keep him from scratching himself when he has a flea itch or some such. Where the light is funneled in, there's nothing left to see, no sign of the Elusive's presence. Out the ship's butt end, the photon stream does extend past the rear cone's outer limit. But it sprays every which way. You just have to make sure you fly with a fairly hefty star field in your backdrop. That way, the photon exhaust becomes camouflaged. How else do you think I snuck up so close to here with your being none the wiser?"

"If there's a word more emphatic, the next step beyond 'impressive,' that's the word I'm looking for," enthused Spinner. To keep out of earshot of the crew, he went on softly, "We need to show you something, give you the full sense of what this is about, just what we're up against."

"Must be damnably serious if you don't want the peanut gallery to overhear," commented DeFarge as he was hurriedly ushered into a conference room adjacent to the navigation bridge.

"I don't know how much pillow talk you are used to having with the little lady... Her name is Priscilla, right?"

"So I'm not going to have to shoot you after all, Mr. Secretary, for getting my wife's name incorrect." Michel leaned into Spinner for whispering. Nevertheless, his voice projected plenty loudly enough for Wang, Entroper and Warlor to easily overhear. "But regarding your concern I might blab to my wife," he went on, "well let's just say that when there's a pillow nearby, there's no time for talk! If you get my drift, har, har!" Michel DeFarge gave the Secretary of Defense a couple of elbow jabs.

The three women present shook their heads in a disgust tempered by their admiration for DeFarge and Spinner alike.

"We never talk about my business whether it's top secret, public knowledge, or after I've just left the potty if that's the business you mean!" Michel DeFarge proceeded to bellow for the whole world to know. "Prissy this minute is knitting me another pair of socks to poke my toes through. Or, she is indulging an additional hobby of hers. Wherever we fly, she's always reconciling the observable firmament with the star chart she brought from waaaayyyyy back home. All she knows about this mission is that sooner or later, she'll be cooking us up some extraterrestrial venison!"

Weapons specialist Wang nodded grimly. "That would appear to be the fate they deserve," she admitted. Pursuant to which, she wanted the Chair of the Joint Chiefs of Staff, Sandy Warlor, to continue from where Secretary Spinner left off. However, Warlor nodded for Wang to do those honors. "Okay, Commander DeFarge," Maggie Wang spoke in a blunt tone, "can we assume you followed the news coverage about Fafama?"

"Of course you can assume that! But things have been damnably quiet there in recent months. What gives?"

"This is from the Smoke and Mirrors, fifty-nine days ago."

The conference room view-screen filled with the apocalyptic aftermath of an ice comet crash-landing into the base of Fafama's great pyramid. It was the same ice comet corralled by the Smoke and Mirrors into orbit around Fafama, for shedding a new water supply into that planet's atmosphere. Studded by flashes of lightning, black smoke billowed everywhere. Ash and pumice spewed from a super-volcano.

"God damn!" DeFarge exclaimed when he could finally lift his jaw off the floor. He turned to Warlor and said, "You mean those antlered sons of furry, bleating bitches did *this*?!?!"

"What you see has been a consequence of the hostiles' threat." Warlor strained not to squirm when she noticed Dr. Wang hanging on her every word.

"The details are a little complicated," Louisa Entroper thusly entered the conversation to take some pressure off Warlor. "What we do know is this: A flying saucer from Tictoctic was brought into play, and the Tictoctickians have developed a magnetic pulse-beam of extraordinarily destructive power. Uhh..."

"We thought, um, at first we were led to believe," Dr. Wang continued, by way of picking up Entroper's slack, "that one of our own, the famous Buddy Leung, had hijacked the saucer, tricked the ETs off their own vessel. But now, we're not sure..."

"To hell with the details!!" bellowed DeFarge anew, this time with a stomp of his magnet boot for added emphasis. "And to double hell with being sure!! It's the God-damned fog of war! You've got to always remember this: No matter what exactly happened, the bad guys are counting on us to become mired in the minutiae, the damnably damned minutiae! Meanwhile, they march forward on their evil rampage!!"

The three women plus Spinner nodded encouragingly for this unapologetic warrior to proceed with his rant. They were all four of them desperate for whatever more heartening help they could get. That is, help to avoid thinking too carefully about the specifics of how events had actually transpired on Fafama. They feared where that journey would have taken them, what that journey would have forced them to face, to admit.

"I can see the bother in your eyes," Commander DeFarge obliged his associates by going on. "It's the bother of decent, civilized people! You have to keep reminding yourselves: Those flea-bitten demons in their planet-wrecking saucers aren't suffering the least self-doubt! No Hamlet for them! No 'to destroy or not to destroy'! That's obvious!" He waved a hand at the video documentation of Fafama's ruination. "I've always known what the good guys' sense of common decency does to them! It's like in that poem by who-the-God-damned-hell was it?? Yeats?? He wrote something to the effect of: 'the worst are full of passionate intensity while the best lack all conviction!' That's why we just gotta buck up!"

"Commander DeFarge," gushed provisional Captain Louisa Entroper, "you are the bright beacon we need, to cut through that fog of war and unwarranted uncertainty you have so eloquently described."

Wang and Warlor nodded their strong agreement, with exhalations of relief.

"So, here's one of many things I want to know," Michel proceeded. He tried to pretend the adulation wasn't going to his head even while his ears reddened. "Where is Captain Taylor on this? Will she ride the Smoke and Mirrors into battle, and you want me to provide sniper and drone support until Battleship... What is it, the Eisenhower?"

"The Eisenhower."

"Damn straight! So tell me if I've got this right. While I help the Smoke and Mirrors soften up the demon stag's war machine, you guys hang out near Oomb? Maybe you save those peacenik trees from themselves until the Eisenhower rides them light beams to town? Then we'll have all the firepower we need, hopefully, to stick those planet-wrecking antlered monsters on a permanent hunting reservation? That is, those we don't roast for the victory celebration feast?"

"How you put it, Commander, certainly makes a world of sense to me, based on our present info," Sandy Warlor nodded.

"But," said Secretary Spinner, "you know there's got to be a 'but'!"

"A big, hairy, stinky 'but,' Mr. Secretary!" growled DeFarge. "I can smell it a light-year away!"

"Permission to explain, General Warlor?" leapt in Dr. Wang.

"You should be the one, Maggie," nodded Sandy Warlor agreeably. Warlor hoped that Dr. Maggie Wang giving the explanation would lend more credibility to the righteousness of their cause.

Warlor, Spinner, and Entroper wanted to continue evading any focus on the details of what actually happened to Fafama. They wanted to maintain a deliberately self-numbing blur. They should have known better, but they feared the truth, every last one of them.

"Thank you, Sandy," said Dr. Wang ready to rumble. "Commander DeFarge, I am as peace-loving, as anti-violence, as anyone you are likely to meet. Still, I really do respect the need for game hunters like you back on

Earth, to keep the deer from overpopulating. I couldn't do it myself." Maggie shook her head definitively. Then she added, even more definitively, "That's why I went into this weapons business. Yes! You build a bomb, I build a bigger bomb, a bomb so big you are not going to want to mess with me! This is what has kept the peace. This is what has prevented all-out nuclear war on our planet! And I truly believe my business is also what is going to prevent all-out interstellar war!"

"That's how it works, Ma'am," DeFarge said with an approving frown. "Just let me assure you: I may not be quite your honey-and-cream sort. But the respect you expressed for me is a two-way street. You can always build a bigger bomb. But lots of luck building a bigger admiration for me than what I'm feeling for you over what animates your fine work! Double-straight!"

"Thank you, Commander," Dr. Wang smiled. "Here's the hard part, though. Here's that 'but' from where, unfortunately, we caught a bad whiff: Captain Helena Taylor and her idiot savant first officer have come too much under the sway of those 'peacenik trees.' They've taken two of them on board the Smoke and Mirrors, trimmed and pruned so they'd fit. And now they're off on a surveillance mission to learn more about Tictoctic. No harm in that; we actually thought they might glean some crucial information for overcoming the extraterrestrial military threat." Dr. Wang looked Spinner, Warlor and Entroper's way, seeking confirmation she had this part correct. They obliged with acknowledging nods. "But here we have it!" Wang proceeded. "Those 'peacenik trees' are calling the tune. And they are basing their input entirely, we can be sure, on limited, anomalously atypical events during their society's own most peculiar history.

They have convinced the captain and crew to go about their surveillance completely, recklessly unarmed!"

"What the- No shit! What about- I thought the Smoke and Mirrors was retrofitted with a laser cannon or some such!"

"The Smoke and Mirrors received that particular retrofit and more," confirmed provisional Captain Entroper. "But apparently Officer Leung, the 'idiot savant,' designed the whole shebang so that with a flick of a few switches, he could jettison it. More's the worse, once he set it adrift in deep space, every last piece of weaponry was remote-control detonated."

"They..." DeFarge's jaw dropped. He turned clomp-clomp-clomping the full way around. Like a dog chasing its tail, Warlor had the impression.

"Despite our weightless circumstances presently, Commander, you might want to station your hands in between your head and the floor. There's the off chance your jaw will drop even lower," warned Secretary Spinner. "They asked us... Captain Taylor and her deciduous amigos want us to keep holding off on any military action for at least a couple more weeks. They've given every indication they're beyond deluded, the next step past delusion. They seem to actually believe there is some peace-and-love miracle end-run they can make around antlered monsters who are wielding, as you put it, planet-wrecking pulse-beams."

"Wait." DeFarge held a pudgy hand towards his four associates as though he were fending off their assault. "Is this to say that my assistance...They will find *my* assistance persona non grata? So my hiding tactics will need be as much to keep them unawares of my presence as to sneak up on those damned infernal Tictoctickians??"

Sandy Warlor nodded grimly. "Your mission will be to stir up the Tictoctic hornets' nest with a drone or sniper attack. We want to accelerate, to rush, their conquest timetable before they are ready. Maybe even, suppose you are somehow able to tap into the time-travel capability Officer Leung uncovered with the light-speed technology. Possibly, you could go back to stir up that nest *long* before the Tictoctickians are ready."

"Of course," grumbled Secretary Spinner, "the Smoke and Mirrors is likely to come under attack as a consequence of your actions. Do your best to help the captain pull off a Houdini-style escape. But if things don't work out for them," Spinner shrugged his shoulders, "at least their tragic fate will drive home the important point for those naïve sociologist sons-a-bitches back on Earth. You know, the ones with their talk of bad guys self-destructing before they can project warfare outside their own solar system. They will end up with so much mud on their faces, lucky it's not alien weaponry *in* their faces! And *that* should rally the general population behind a no-bars-held effort to eradicate decisively this threat to our part of the galaxy. No soap-opera drag-out about it!" With his animation over this point, Spinner's jowls shook noticeably beneath his trademark Santa's beard.

"Yes! Yes!" eagerly nodded Louisa Entroper as though she had required convincing, and just been brought to revelatory understanding. "What, uh, has happened to Fafama cannot go unanswered!" Entroper checked herself on two counts. The first count was on saying, *what the Tictoctickians did to Fafama*. Enough honesty still seeped through her muddled brain to stay her from fouling the air she breathed with that level of untruth. The second check, however, was on what she really wanted to say. *Fafama's extinction-event devastation cannot have been for naught.* The voicing aloud of such a sentiment would have brought her too close to an unthinkably unbearable admission.

"Captain Entroper! Sorry to interrupt!" suddenly crackled from the intercom. "We have a UFO situation! You better take a look!"

The UFO situation provided an especially unsettling conclusion to the pep talk for Commander DeFarge's mission. A mysterious object showed remarkable similarities to what the Smoke and Mirrors detected during its first two missions. The UFO was travelling at speeds that put to shame the asparagus-stem-shaped starships from Earth as well as the saucer-shaped starships from Tictoctic. It did slow upon reaching within a half-billion miles of the Barack Obama, to a still-impressive ten times conventional light-speed. But then it made an impossible right-angle turn for accelerating back to some thousand-time-light-speed multiple. What also proved excessively weird was from how incredibly far away the object first became detectable. At a trillion mile distance, it should have had to have been no smaller than the moon for any teasing-out of its presence. And yet, as it came to within the billion-mile range, sensors clearly put it at no larger than a sports stadium.

"After we deal with Tictoctic," remarked Spinner, "we might need to reckon with them, whoever they are, next!"

"Yeah, about the light-speed thing," Commander DeFarge said in his most gravelly voice yet, so long had he gone since his last sip of water. "What I'm hearing, the latest thinking is that we don't actually, nobody actually beats the speed of light. Einstein still has it correct. It's just that something accelerates light, that the speed of light isn't a constant. In the case of our starships, the mirror array does the accelerating. In the case of that UFO, who knows?"

"You've got it," nodded Dr. Wang. "The first serious theoretical work on speed-of-light variability was done by the Portuguese physicist, João Magueijo, nearly eighty years ago."

"Triple damn!" DeFarge cussed anew. "Well, we already have plenty enough urgency about what we're on to already. But please allow me to bring up one last tidbit before I get my show back on the cosmic road."

"Of course," nodded Sandy Warlor.

"I was reading about this British legend what extends way, way back to the sixteenth century. It makes the Tictoctickian stuff really damned spooky. You see, there was this critter called the Huntsman. He was also known as Herme the Hunter, the collector of human souls. A stone sculpture of him was found in a stone cellar in Windsor. It was a gargoyle's head, basically a man with stag antlers. And in the 1800's, antlered man sightings were nearly as common on the royal hunting ground as ghost sightings in Windsor Castle.

"Well this situation has got me to wondering regarding that time travel element your dumb genius Leung stumbled across. What if those deer devils from Tictoctic managed to co-opt Leung's discovery from the now-defenseless Smoke and Mirrors? Meaning the stag-man legend is our historical memory from Tictoctic's first time-travel incursions to Earth, trying to turn the hunting tables on us? And then, what if it's only going to become a lot worse? What if one day we're going to wake up in some alternate universe run by the deer devils? Imagine them chasing us buck-naked through the woods with their air igniters transformed into human meat barbecuers!! Gentle ladies, gentle man, this possibility lends a certain urgency to my getting the show on the road, like an hour ago!"

"Double-damn straight! Don't let us stop you!" effused Secretary Spinner.

So there was Commander DeFarge short days later, Earth calendar time, back aboard his compact battle cruiser, the Elusive. He was tailing the Smoke and Mirrors by millions of miles. But that distance remained well within the mind-reading perimeter of the Oombian tree creatures on board the immense starship. No matter. DeFarge was successfully keeping every last thought of his mission suppressed, thanks to the immensely addicting distraction of a virtual reality bear hunt. Otherwise, he would have been intent on giving Earthlings and Oombians alike "what-ho," as he would have put it. He would have wanted, as he also would have put it, to have neatly filleted their argument for what they were doing. Then he would have tossed that fillet on a grill, and left it there until it was flame-broiled down to nothing but char. And then he would have hammered the char into dust, and blown it away with his own powerful breath in one giant exhale.

DeFarge also would have loved to have dwelt a little more on just what he had in mind for those bloodthirsty stags from Tictoctic. As he was wont to say to most anyone who would listen, he considered himself a humane sort. That's why he took pride, whenever whatever he got to hunt, in the one-shot instant kill. He made that kill with a particular Remington rifle, of the three handed down over four generations. It was the one with the barrel that accommodated the most appropriate cartridge size for the game involved. But with what he learned about those antlered monsters essentially wiping out a planet's entire ecosystem...

DeFarge wasn't sure how exactly he could arrange it. Nevertheless, one thought obsessed him, up until his compact battle cruiser named the Elusive flew to within mind-reading range of the Smoke and Mirrors. He fantasized a bow-and-arrow hunt for a specific Tictoctickian. It was to be the Tictoctickian behind the order to send some unimaginably destructive force slamming into Fafama. Better yet, DeFarge would round up "a whole herd of those critters" in Tictoctickian government and military leadership positions. He would set them loose on a game preserve in Pennsylvania, and declare open season until every last one was hunted down and slaughtered. Most preferably, the psychopaths among bow hunters would prevail. The particular "son a bitch" who gave the orders for Fafama's destruction would only be wounded in his hind leg. He would have no choice but to limp off awaiting a slow death from infection. Perhaps vultures and other raptors wouldn't wait for his life force to be extinguished completely. They would start picking and tearing away at his rotting, infected, gangrenous flesh while he could still feel the pain.

But again, DeFarge's every last bit of attention was presently most successfully diverted from dwelling on these bothers by the intrigue and drama of a simulated bear hunt. Presently, he was totally preoccupied over a certain human-scent-concealing honeysuckle fragrance. He worried whether he sprayed enough on himself so his big black quarry wouldn't be scared off. *Damnably amazing, how the olfactory part of this program works!* DeFarge could have used deer urine. The pee from young does worked the best. However, that would have reminded DeFarge about the mission. This was the same reason he was going after virtual reality bear rather than virtual reality stag.

Hot Damn!

DeFarge's obsession over the hunt got temporarily diminished by the distraction of his wife's complaint over where he aimed his virtual reality rifle. His obsession got so diminished, suppressed thoughts could have suddenly welled up from his memory banks. But then there was the quarry! There was the huge black bear! So huge, he would have had to have been a papa bear! If only he were more than mere data bits holographically projected inside DeFarge's virtual reality helmet... In so many other ways, the hunt was going much as DeFarge would have expected out in the actual wild. The digitally simulated, bee-devoid honeycombs piled into a digitally simulated bear bait barrel were proving an irresistible attractant. They might as well have comprised a boar, the female bear, moaning in heat. *Ha! Pooh Bear's Papa Pooh! Too bad those ignorant animal rights activists don't get it! They just don't understand how taking one of these big-bruising bruins out of play allows the cubs to grow into the next generation! That the adult males are known to eat their young with probably no more qualms than those stag-* Damn! *Back to where my mind was NOT supposed to stray!*

"Michel, you've got to see this!" Priscilla DeFarge shouted as her husband reprimanded himself for allowing his thoughts to course their way back around to the mission.

"What've you got there, Prissy?" Commander DeFarge croaked hoarsely. He had already pulled off his virtual reality helmet and resignedly tossed it aside.

"Prissy" gestured towards the panoramic view-screen with her sewing needle. "Something impossible," she said in her typically high-pitched voice. Her shaking head also shook the auburn locks of her Dutch boy haircut. "I still don't know what you've gotten yourself into, but…"

"Damn damn damn! I see it!"

"At first I thought, maybe it was a star field…"

"Enough, Prissy! I told you I see it!"

"Prissy" cowered with shoulders hunched. In the blink of an eye, however, she calmly resumed knitting. She deigned to say not another word, or to give either the panoramic view-screen or the control panel screen another look.

If her husband was going to be that way about it,…

The astounding phenomenon both screens revealed was following not more than twenty thousand miles behind sparkling photon exhaust from the Smoke and Mirrors. And sparkling photon exhaust was all Michel DeFarge could see of the enormous starship at that distance. Anyway, the phenomenon was a collection of orange-ish starry lights. They were configured in the shape of a classic, Chinese dragon.

DeFarge hoped his impressions were clearly mind-read by the Oombian tree creatures aboard the Smoke and Mirrors. The extraordinary light display, invoking a mythical beast, had to have been nearly the size of a planet. Especially for how it dwarfed the spacecraft it wasn't just following, but rather was fast approaching.

Chapter 3

The wedding aboard the Smoke and Mirrors could have been happening on the surface of a still-thriving Fafama. The whole idea was to create exactly that illusion for Yulala's sake. She was the last known living Fafaman of a conventionally physical nature, ever since two nuclear warhead missiles redirected a comet crashing into her planet.

Earthlings had already been going to great lengths to make Yulala feel at home aboard the starship. But since she would be pledging herself to Marine Corps Sergeant Guy Hanson in holy matrimony...

The choice for the wedding processional was a Puerto Rican folk tune entitled "Verde Luz" (Green Light). "Verde Luz" served a dual purpose. It invoked both the bioluminescence formerly widespread on Fafama, and the Puerto Rican heritage of Yulala's new good friend, Ciela.

Ciela accompanied Yulala down the aisle in a joint ceremony. Ciela was betrothing herself to Marine Corps Sergeant Fred Frankly.

The Oombian tree creature, Oodle-Noodle, strummed the wedding processional folk tune on four-dimensional strings. Oodle-Noodle provided herself with those strings by bouncing oof balls about the starship's main recreation hall prior to the event. She was basically plucking trails left by the balls in the space-time continuum. Her five-dimensional consciousness made this possible, of course.

The recreation hall was kept brightly lit before the ceremony. During the first strains of "Verde Luz," however, fluorescent illumination was faded to a faint, greenish cast. This allowed the nocturnally adapted Yulala to remove her anti-glare goggles before she started her entrance alongside Ciela. At the same time, a holographic program projected images of Fafama's fern-like trees to line both sides of the wedding aisle. Those images behaved like their real counterparts back on Fafama prior to the devastating impact of an ice comet. They uncoiled to reach towards the recreation room ceiling, one by one after Ciela and Yulala strode past them. This created the impression the holographic ferns were bowing down in advance of the brides' approach, and resuming growing upright in their wake. They could have comprised an Oombian tree creature honor guard were there such a thing, Officer Chris Olsen-Taylor mused. Back on Fafama, the actual fern-like trees used to uncoil at night. They did so in response to nocturnal resurfacing of the namalumina, nicknamed flounder mice by Earthlings.

Counselor Ali Magabu couldn't help thinking the on-board pair of Tictoctickians would have appreciated the shadowy forest ambience, albeit holographically simulated. But it was their choice not to attend the wedding even though they volunteered to join Mission Three of the Smoke and Mirrors. They could have remained behind on Oomb with fellow deer creatures in low-security, high-luxury imprisonment.

Ludi Perez sang the century-old Puerto Rican folk song by Antonio Caban Vale (El Topo) in beautiful, crystalline falsetto:

"Verde luz de monte y mar,
Isla virgen del coral,
Si me ausento de tus playas primorosas,
Si me alejo de tus palmas silenciosas,
Quiero volver, quiero volver.
"A sentir la tibia arena

Dormir en tus riberas,
Isla mía, flor cautiva,
Para ti quiero tener.
"Libre tu cielo, sola tu estralla isla doncella,
Quiero tener,
Verde luz de monte y mar."

Yulala and Ciela swayed rhythmically down the aisle to this tune while Wafoodle-boodle gently telepathed for those who didn't understand Spanish,

Green light of mountain and sea,
Virgin island of the coral,
If I stay away from your exquisite beaches,
If I move away from your silent palms,
I want to return, want to return
To feeling the lukewarm sand
To sleeping on your river banks,
My island, my captive flower,
For you I want to have.
Free your sky, alone your star island maiden,
I want to have green light of mountain and sea.

Pedro and Ludi Perez's young daughter Alexita kept just ahead of Yulala and Ciela's subdued dance forward. She was sprinkling crumbled-apart chocolate chip cookies from a basket full of them. The crumbs kept bursting into flaming flare-outs as they were torched by Effy the ephemeral dragon to benefit its own, mysterious chemistry.

Based on what anyone knew, Effy was the only other Fafaman creature left alive aside from Yulala. (Okay, there might have been a few teensy bugs and various bacterial entities still wandering the wrecked planet.) Anyhow, the faint green light occasionally combined with the cookie-crumble flare-outs just right. That's when members of the audience were able to catch glimpses of a bat-like wing here, and a reptilian-looking, extravagantly crested head there.

Professor Dauntilus Skepticus among the attendees could not watch without frequently checking his rear pants pockets. He needed to repeatedly assure himself there was nothing in them Effy would also want to set on fire.

Oodle-Noodle found herself somewhat distracted from the happy spectacle of Yulala and Ciela joining Guy and Fred at the makeshift wedding altar. She was mind-reading DeFarge's apprehension over a special conglomeration of glitters floating at incredible velocity through outer space. Those glitters were assuming the uncanny likeness to a planet-sized dragon, and they were following behind the Smoke and Mirrors. Whatever it was, it was gaining on the starship, more than matching the fifty-percent light-speed.

To officiate their wedding, Captain Helena Taylor welcomed both couples forward onto the altar. At the same time, she received the Oombian tree creature's telepath about what was worrying DeFarge. Helena endeavored not to let that pull her attention from the three Earthlings and one Fafaman standing before her. After all, they were anxiously anticipating her key role in the ceremony.

Over previous days, the Smoke and Mirrors crew had grown increasingly aware of the glitter conglomeration. It kept pacing the starship's journey headed into the Cygnitaurus solar system.

Early on, ship's counselor Ali Magabu voiced his opinion Yulala might be correct.

Yulala believed Fafama was more than simply a planet before the comet crashed into it. Rather, that it was a living thing whose spirit felt forced into exile, disembodied from its physical self by the comet calamity. Where Yulala was concerned, the planet spirit had taken to shadowing the Smoke and Mirrors.

In other words, the planet spirit was one and the same with the glitter conglomeration. It kept company with Captain Taylor and crew in the hope they would eventually be able to perform a miracle. Namely, they would resurrect the planet Fafama to all its odd, former glory.

There was other news from Oodle-Noodle that Captain Taylor considered relatively minor. A human being had flown a small space-faring vessel within mind-reading range of the Smoke and Mirrors. Whoever-he-was originally set his focus on a simulated bear hunt, but that focus switched over to the enigmatic glitter cluster. And there was a second person inside the small vessel. She divided her attention between knitting socks and maintaining surveillance of the Smoke and Mirrors.

Helena assumed the small spacecraft flown to within Oodle-Noodle's mindreading range was benefiting from detection-cloaking technology. Besides which, its photon exhaust would have been camouflaged by any number of star field background settings.

Anyway, Oodle-Noodle had been expecting someone or something to shadow the Smoke and Mirrors. She mind-read Secretary of Defense Spinner's planning for that happenstance from aboard the battle-ready starship, Barack Obama. Moreover, she didn't make a secret of it. So Captain Taylor considered the tree creature's vindication of her expectation no big deal. This made all the easier staying focused on wedding duties.

"We are gathered here to celebrate the joining of Ciela Sanchez with Frederick Frankly, and Yulala with Guy

Hanson, in holy matrimony," Captain Helena Taylor announced officiously.

Effy let out a snort, the first noise anyone had heard emitted by this curious creature. For a flashing instant, that snort made Effy's entire body visible. It crouched on all fours to Yulala's right side while Guy stood beside her, hand-in-hand, to her left.

Wow, Chris Olsen-Taylor wowed to himself. *Yulala has an ephemeral dragon for her guardian angel!*

Ciela and Fred repeated a set of traditional wedding vows read by Captain Taylor. Then Yulala and Guy recited the vows they opted to write for themselves.

"Guy Hahnsahn, I vowah thaht mah lahve fah youah, it is ahs thah pulpieahst, mahst cushahny trahlahlahfah. It fohevah sheltahs us frahm thah sthormlahns, howevah strahng, thaht regahlahly buffaht ouah existahnce," said Yulala. She still struggled with her pronunciation due to Fafaman language interference. Her insistence, nevertheless, on pledging to her betrothed in English endeared her that much more to Guy Hanson. "Youah ahmbrahce celahbrahtes owah lahve evahry day, ahntil thaht finahl stahs-out sends ahs unfurahlahng to sahch foah ouahsahlves ahnew, beyahnd thahs unahvahse ahof jahoy ahnd teahs!"

"Yulala, I vow that *my* love for *you* is also as the pulpiest, most cushiony tralalafa. It forever shelters us from the storm lines, however strong, that regularly buffet our existence. *Your* embrace celebrates our love every day, until the final stars-out sends us unfurling to search for ourselves anew, beyond this universe of joy and tears!"

During Guy and Yulala's collaboratively conceived vows, Helena marveled anew regarding the peculiar circumstances her crew had decided upon for the ceremony. Partly, she wanted to review everything yet again. Assure herself she hadn't overlooked some crucial detail, or made some critical error.

The top priority was selecting a time and location when and where Earthlings, Oombians, and Fafaman alike could be reasonably certain of no interruption.

It had to be a situation they could afford hazarding the Smoke and Mirrors essentially on autopilot. That way, every last being who wanted to could attend the ceremony.

The third mission of the starship Smoke and Mirrors was well underway. Totally unarmed, the starship had headed into the interstellar backyard of an advanced extraterrestrial intelligence already responsible for some pretty threatening behavior. Clearly, that intelligence was intent on collecting for consumption the inhabitants of planets from solar systems other than their own. And they were bent on accomplishing this gruesome task through invasion and conquest. The apocalyptic devastation of Fafama effectively took that particular planet off the extraterrestrials' table. It left them only one other major target, far as anyone knew: Earth.

The Oombian tree creatures had accumulated countless generations of experience in resolving conflicts peacefully. Captain Helena Taylor and crew hoped to tap into that experience, somehow develop a workable plan for neutralizing the menace from the planet Tictoctic. And not have to fire a shot in the process.

Captain Taylor managed to sell the mission to her superiors as simply information-gathering surveillance. She left out the pacifist part. Instead, she shamelessly allowed Secretary of Defense Michael Spinner to believe the real idea went a different direction. The Smoke and Mirrors would uncover weaknesses in the Tictoctic military. Hopefully, those weaknesses could be exploited with weaponry installed onto a small but growing fleet of interstellar battleships being stealthily constructed back in Earth orbit.

Soon as Captain Taylor received the go-ahead for the mission, she had First Officer Buddy Leung implement stage one. The Smoke and Mirrors jettisoned into space, and then harmlessly detonated, every last bit of retrofitted weaponry.

Secretary Spinner and his military complex associates found the implication most unpleasant. Captain Taylor had something very different in mind for surveillance from what they had in mind.

What Helena admitted up front did come close to giving away the real game. She asked that any military action be held off for as long as possible. The Chair of the Joint Chiefs of Military Staff, Sandy Warlor, might have explored this request more deeply, dug into what exactly was behind it. However, Captain Taylor predicted correctly. Warlor and the rest of her associates demurred from such probing. Taylor suspected they were shamed into letting go by how events transpired on Fafama. Those military officials could rationalize all they wanted, Helena Taylor supposed, but there was a grim reality. Whether they ever actually brought themselves to consciously face that reality, or not, didn't matter. The militarization of Fafama led to its total destruction without the deer creatures from Tictoctic having fired a shot.

Again, stage one of the third mission of the Smoke and Mirrors was the abandonment and harmless, deep-space destruction of its weapons retrofit.

Captain Taylor and company agreed stage two would involve scouting Tictoctic's binary twin planet. That planet took the precise, same orbit as Tictoctic, but always the opposite side of Cygnitaurus from Tictotic.

When Buddy Leung time-travelled to rescue Pedro Perez and several Marines from a Tictoctic saucer craft, he noticed something in the saucer's impressively large kitchen. Partial bodies of hitherto unknown creatures were mounted on a wall in plain view, for further dismemberment to facilitate future meals. More importantly, the head that was still intact on one of those bodies clearly had to have belonged to a highly intelligent species. Its mouth was surrounded by octopus-type, tiny tentacles, but so what? Its brain case was, if anything, larger than a typical human's. Also, the rest of the body was proportioned like a human body, though with suction cups up and down its arms and legs, like on octopus tentacles. Where its sex organs were likely to be located, there was a covering that looked to be a pair of boxer shorts. They were virtually indistinguishable from boxer shorts one might find worn by Earthlings.

The Smoke and Mirrors crew couldn't absolutely rule out the possibility two highly intelligent species had evolved on the same planet. However, they concluded that the far more likely possibility was humanoid creatures with octopus characteristics having evolved on another planet. And that Tictoctic's binary twin should be the prime suspect for where such evolution occurred.

There was more. Wafoodle-boodle and other Oombian tree beings mind-read most curious thoughts on the Tictoctickian deer creatures' part during their military occupation of the planet Oomb. Those thoughts were to the effect that few of the Tictoctickians actually understood the technology they were using. The most tantalizing cogitation was picked up from a creature named Kwit-Nik. Kwit-Nik wistfully pined away for a future when his kind "caught up" with the "co-opted" technology from the "sister planet." Only then, he determined, could they actually "make advancements" of their own.

Buddy Leung was the first to raise the question: Did the Tictoctickian deer creatures steal their technology from the creatures sporting tentacled mouths? Nobody had to even raise the second question, because it was purely rhetorical: What else could that "sister planet" be than Tictoctic's binary twin?

And so it was concluded the Earthlings would take the long way around into the Cygnitaurus solar system. Captain Taylor and company would see if they could safely check out Tictoctic's binary twin before, as Ali Magabu put it, "entering the belly of the beast, truly."

The Smoke and Mirrors "descended" onto the orbital plane following a mercifully uneventful circumnavigation of the Cygnitaurus-associated Oort Cloud. Ominously, though, neither Oodle-Noodle nor her significant other, Wafoodle-boodle, was able to pick up any significant mental activity from Tictoctic's sister planet. This didn't necessarily mean anything. For these two tree creatures, there could have been multiple poorly understood extrasensory interferences posed by assorted cosmic rays and dark matter. All that and more were likely to be found in the three hundred billion miles of outer space separating the Smoke and Mirrors from the sister planet.

What proved of more concern was a discovery not two million miles further into the Cygnitaurus system, cruising at one-tenth light-speed. There was a space-time rift indicative of some mass death disaster. Had there been a showdown in deep space between the civilizations from both planets? Who could tell? But agreement was quickly reached that, most ironically, hanging around the rift in question would prove the safest option, by far, for conducting the wedding.

The Smoke and Mirrors wasn't "anchored" there. Rather, it was accelerated into a one-half light-speed circular path around the space-time rift. Captain Taylor wanted to provide a modicum of gravity so that, among other things, Yulala and Ciela's wedding dresses wouldn't start randomly floating about with embarrassingly immodest results. Those dresses flowed spirally, as designed by Third Engineer Geena Murphy-Davis, Ludi Perez and the ever-versatile Buddy Leung. This lent the impression both brides were emerging from beige-colored, satiny-smooth tree trunks.

Again, the starship was kept close to the space-time rift. If any worst-case scenario developed, the starship could quickly dive into there, hideout mode. Officer Buddy Leung had already acquired plenty of experience time-travelling, so he could make the maneuver with assured safety. What's more, he specially programmed Captain Taylor's intercom device so she could command a rift dive remote-controlled from the wedding. Just the push of a button on her lapel was all it would take. Nobody would have to stay on the navigation bridge waiting on the emergency scenario, to receive the captain's order.

"Tomás? Jorge? The rings?" Helena returned her attention to the present to ask this question.

"Oh, yeah!" eight-year-old Tomás exclaimed from underneath a virtual reality tralalafa, to muted chuckles from the wedding congregation. He and Jorge popped up through that holographic simulation of a thick-trunked plant sporting one lone leaf the size of a bed comforter. They sauntered side-by-side up the aisle to the wedding altar. Their arms and shoulders were flouncy with their mischievous imitation of two Oonzy-Ootzies jiggling up the shore out of the surf on an Oombian coral sand beach.

At the altar Jorge said, "Here! Catch!" He and Tomás flipped two rings a-piece in the air like they were flipping pennies.

Guy and Fred were quick enough with their reflexes to snatch their respective rings from mid-flight.

Tomás and Jorge sauntered backwards down off the altar, on their return to hiding underneath the tralalafa simulation. Again it was as though they were two Oonzy-Ootzies. They could have been jiggle-waddling their re-submergence in the surf until it was up over their heads.

After the couples slid the rings onto each other's fingers, Captain Taylor said, "With the power vested in me by the American Union, I now pronounce you husband and wife, and husband and wife. Wives, you may kiss your husbands!"

"Is that *all* they get to do for now? Cripes!" complained Fred Frankly as Ciela laughingly, joyfully wound her arms round his neck.

The recessional originated from a suggestion by Chris Olsen-Taylor that enthused Guy and Yulala, especially. Legendary keyboard player Rick Wakeman's bold, majestic orchestral mellotron chords blended with Chris Squire's throbbing bass guitar to produce a most grandiose fanfare. Blasting from an amplet in lieu of the more traditional wedding march, it announced the final portion of "And You And I" from the British symphonic rock group, Yes. By the time the fanfare dissolved into piano ripples, the newly married couples had reached the end of the aisle, back where the brides entered originally.

Lead vocalist Jon Anderson sang joyfully in his special falsetto,

"And you and I climb crossing the shapes of the morning.

And you and I reach over the sun to the river.
And you and I climb clearer towards the movement.
And you and I called over valleys of endless seas."

Steve Howe's single, prolonged electric guitar modulation soared off like an eagle. It brought "And You And I" to its final, stirring conclusion.

The two newly married couples were set in silhouette, hand-in-hand, by the brightly-lit hallway past them.

Other couples in attendance included Deborah and Geena Davis-Murphy, Kevin and Yoon-hee Park-Smith, Ali and Tanya Magabu-Petrovsky, Oodle-Noodle and Wafoodle-boodle, and Ludi and Pedro Sanchez-Perez. They all felt moved to hold hands tightly, or branches in the case of the tree beings. Most were teary-eyed.

Chris was left to wonder what Helena would have done standing beside him. She needed to be at a far remove up on the altar, to officiate the wedding.

None of them knew how much closer the sparkle conglomerate had approached to the Smoke and Mirrors in the meantime. That is to say, the behemoth planetary dragon spirit Michel and Priscilla DeFarge were keeping an eye on from a million miles away.

⁕ ⁕⁖⁘⁙ ⁕⁖⁘⁙ ⁕⁖⁙

"Captain Kek-stek, I have received confirmation from Commander Kwit-Nik. The space vessel we have detected roaming the outer perimeter of Dek-Fook-Tek's solar system is not one of our own Celestial Breaths," crisply tongue-clicked Officer Rek-mek-a-nek. "The Third Celestial Breath is presumed hijacked by the other-world enemy in the solar system of the mobile trees. Apart from that, the other Celestial Breaths are accounted for, including the one on reconnaissance in a star system six light-years distant."

"Baa!" the captain of the battleship saucer, the Sixth Celestial Breath, sloppily bleated. He could have been some lower-class worker only a short trot removed from becoming converted into part of the emergency food source.

"Perhaps we have spotted a lone Chonoran vessel, the very last one to escape Dek-Fook-Tek's final vengeance!"

"Dek-Fook-Tek's justice bridges our food supply over to the interstellar abundance soon to be ours," Captain Kek-stek's crew ritually tongue-clicked in the wake of his speculating revelry.

"The last of the Chonorans!" the captain went on. "They must have decided it is finally safe for them to return from their long exile of cowardly retreat, and even more cowardly desertion of their fellow beasts! If this is true, then we feast extra well on our mission, even while contributing unexpected additional bodies to the bridge supply! Our regret, of course, is that we don't have Dek-Fook-Tek here to prepare our meal for us. Although were he present, with what other jobs would he be unfairly tasked? And how much more skillfully would he accomplish them than we could ever hope to accomplish for ourselves?"

"We suffice with other chefs' preparation of our daily nibbles. We can only dream of what culinary wonders Chef Dek-Fook-Tek might have produced, even as the lowly, legless, ground-clinging Kwirk can only dream of becoming a high flying kookek." All officers present on the navigation bridge of the Sixth Celestial Breath rose up onto their hind legs to tongue-click this ritual lament.

"Captain Kek-Stek," said Officer Rek-mek-a-nek. "Commander Kwit-Nik informs me he will not accept any least dismemberment of the other-world vessel for bridge supply foraging. He thinks it might not be of Chonoran origin. Rather, it might be a vessel from Akt. In fact, it might even be the same vessel detected earlier by one of our remote sensors. It was stationed in the solar system where that notorious deserter, Captain Mat-kek-tek, allowed the Third Celestial Breath to fall into other-worlder hooves! If Commander Kwit-Nik is correct, this particular vessel rid itself of every last piece of weaponry aboard! It jettisoned them into deep space where they were harmlessly destroyed! The other-world vessel's occupants left themselves defenseless on purpose!"

"We are well aware of Commander Kwit-Nik's new strategy, ever inspired by Dek-Fook-Tek," knowingly nodded Captain Kek-Stek. "He wants us to address our needs in more merciful ways when we pillage the larger universe. As a part of that strategy, we must investigate further the intent of this particular spacecraft's occupants! Whether they are from Chonora or Akt makes no difference! We use our magnetic pulse-beam on the diffuse setting. We deliver a crippling projection, only, of Dek-Fook-Tek's power, until we can learn more! But we still go about this with a skipping-stone-sudden ambush!"

How does Commander Kwik-Nik know the other-world beasts are not setting a trap for us, assuming they are indeed from Akt? How does he know that when they discarded their weapons, they were not still keeping on board other, much more powerful tools of aggression? And now WE are the ones who will be ambushed? Captain Kek-stek wanted to go on. Instead, he settled with, "Officer Rek-mek-a-nek, notify Commander Kwit-Nik we are executing his orders immediately forthwith. Then power up the skipping stone acceleration function for coming to within a thousand lek-leks of the other-world starship. And set our pulse-beam on diffuse, for automatic dispersal when we slow out of light-speed!"

While Officer Rek-mek-a-nek did as told, Captain Kek-stek thought further to himself, *I wonder when Commander Kwit-Nik will stop pretending worshipful allegiance to Dek-Fook-Tek. Exactly when will his bit-by-bit nibbling-away at the Supreme Authority's legitimacy become an all-out leading the charge for herding him off his throne? Depriving him of his antler handlers so his neck breaks under the weight of his out-of-control head growths?! I also wonder where my allegiance will finally settle...*

⸙⸙⸙⸙⸙

"What *is* that, Prissy?!?" a confounded Michel DeFarge exclaimed. He was contemplating the dragon-shaped conglomeration of sparkles the size of a planet, gaining rapidly on the Smoke and Mirrors. For once, he felt blithely uncaring of where his thoughts roamed while in mind-reading range of who he regarded as "those accursedly arrogant tree people." He was too intently focused on the exceedingly strange spectacle unfolding a mere couple hundred thousand miles away from his compact battle cruiser named the Elusive.

"I wouldn't know, dear."

"There's nothing on the sensors! Nothing! We might as well be dreaming or hallucinating! And yet that beastie looks almost large enough to engulf the moon whole, were it actually what it gives the appearance of being!"

"Indeed it is large enough, dear." One wouldn't know from Priscilla's disinterested-sounding remarks how absolutely riveted she was to the view-screen while she continued her knitting and stitching.

"In fact, Prissy, the way it is catching up to the Smoke and Mirrors, maybe it is all about gulping down that entire starship for an appetizer."

"Yes, dear." The only indication "Prissy" gave of her growing anxiety was the speed with which she knitted as the sparkles drifted ever closer to the cigar-shaped starship.

Commander Michel DeFarge hoped there might be some insight to be gained, were he to concentrate with just enough ferocious intensity on the unfolding spectacle. However, insight into another matter altogether was what Michel experienced when he rested his eyes for a moment from his determined squinting at the view-screen. He finally realized what his wife's blur of finger work with needles and thread recalled. Years ago back home, a garden spider wove an entombing cocoon round a hapless beetle, newly caught in its web.

⁕ ❦⁕❦⁕❦⁕

"This is just wonderful, Helena, just wonderful how well Yulala appears to be adjusting to life among the Earthlings!" enthused Cathy James-Leung to Captain Helena Taylor. Cathy and Helena stood apart from the center of wedding reception action, alongside Yoon-hee Park-Smith. "That was a popular tune on Fafama, am I correct?!"

"'Storm line in my feet,' by Faboompas Washed Ashore!" nodded Yoon-hee.

The women had to shout to get heard by one another above the fa-la-la crooning to a pulsing bass beat from the extraterrestrial music.

"It's fortunate that Chris enthuses over so many different kinds of music! He made a top priority out of streaming Fafaman tunes into the ship's data base on our first couple visits to Fafama!" noted Yoon-hee. She took every opportunity to make a point of reminding the captain what great contributions the captain's husband was making during the Smoke and Mirrors missions.

"How tragic, what little might be left of an entire planet's ecology! One adult female! A ghostly creature some scientists do not even agree is a living entity! And lastly, an encyclopedia set's worth of information stored onto a hard drive! That's it!" Buddy Leung's wife Cathy, one of the leading experts on exo-planet geology and weather, became teary-eyed with her reflection. Nevertheless, her big grin suddenly broke out. Yoon-hee would have likened it to the sun breaking through during a shower. This resulted from Cathy realizing what was happening on the dance floor during the final strains of "Storm line in my feet."

Making dance moves she had practiced since she was five years old, Yulala lifted her encircling arms high above her new husband, Guy Hanson. Guy crouched low, trying to perform his part. But as he did so, he lost balance and fell backwards onto the floor, albeit in slower motion than usual due to gravity at only forty percent.

"I would say Yulala has adjusted better to life aboard an alien spacecraft than our own husbands have adjusted to life at a wedding reception dance!" laughed Yoon-hee. "Look at them over there! They're pretending deep immersion in some important conversation from which they can't tear themselves away to come anywhere near us!!"

Kevin, Buddy, and Chris who managed the music on his amplet were nodding thoughtfully to a comment by Dr. Dauntilus Skepticus.

Dr. Timothy Aquinas offered a rebuttal which Skepticus met with a leaned-back head and eyes rolling back as well. This was so obvious as to be spotted easily across the dance floor.

"Shall we go over and ask them to dance?! And if they say no, we try to make them jealous by asking Aquinas and Skepticus?"

"Watch out, Yoon-hee!" laughed Cathy. "I think Skepticus heard you! Do you see how he's anxiously rubbing the seat of his pants?!"

"He's been rubbing the seat of his pants all evening! Haven't you noticed?!" said Helena while Yoon-hee modestly cupped her hands over her mouth to conceal her amusement. "He's making sure Tomás and Jorge haven't snuck in another chocolate chip cookie! And he's probably worried that whether they have or not, Effy might try to torch him again, simply on general principles!"

"We've done four already,

But now we're ready,

And everything's set…"

With that, "The Ocean" blasted from Chris's amplet with a bold, distinctive riff on drums and electric guitar. It was the original recording made nearly a century earlier by yet another British progressive rock band, Led Zeppelin.

Brief, shuffling percussion transitioned to the syncopated refrain on guitar and drums.

Tomás and Jorge, the two eight-year-old boys adopted by Ciela and Fred, looked to one another with mutually dawning delight. Not a word needed to transpire between them for their next actions to coordinate perfectly. On repeat of the opening riff, both boys took two steps backwards, side-by-side. Then, in exact lockstep with the shuffling percussion transition, they pulled down their pants and wiggled their bare butts. The repeat of the syncopated refrain gave them ample time to pull their pants back up, and step forward to where their back-stepping had begun. They made effortless back-steps for another bare-butt wiggle on the subsequent repetition of the opening riff.

"Tomás! Jorge!" Ciela shouted reprovingly. But Oodle-Noodle telepathed, *Please, Ciela, allow me to blossom in defense of your wonderful little boys' actions. They have managed to conceive a marvelous tribute to that time shrouded in Oomb's ancient past when love broke out instead of war. Their sheer genius roots itself in how they have blended our customary mid-day mooning with the ebb-and-flow dance, in and out of the surf, of our Oonzy-Ootzies.*

They help make us feel like we are back home, added Wafoodle-boodle. *We only wish we could somehow add comfortingly to Yulala's experience in similar fashion.*

Long before these telepaths concluded, Ciela and Fred tossed their hands in whimsical resignation to their adopted sons' behavior. They even joined them, though forgoing the pull-down-the-pants part prior to their own butt wiggles.

A final repetition of the instrumental opening preceded Robert Plant's distinctive vocals. By then, there was nobody on the makeshift dance floor who *wasn't* following the lead of Tomás and Jorge. Again, however, those two boys remained the only ones actually pulling down their pants. Although Pedro and Ludi's two-year-old daughter, Alexita, ran weaving in, out and around the small crowd, frequently clutching the edge of her dress to her chin.

"Singing in the sunshine,
Laughing in the rain..."

On the downbeat at the end of each line of verse, Tomás and Jorge merely stuck out their bare butts, no wiggle. But they kept the Oonzy-Ootzy ebb and flow going, back and forth. Kevin was reminded of line dancing in Texas. Where he was concerned, the two boys had concocted some crazy variation on what he saw in videos from a dance hall in Austin.

"-singing to the ocean,

Has the ocean lost its way..."

"The Ocean" returned to the instrumental anthem with which it opened, performed in a more elaborate manner. Elaborate or not, Jorge and Tomás were inspired to resume their butt wiggles.

However, Captain Helena Taylor's mind was already wandering to a more serious place. Carol James-Leung could tell. For Taylor's further contemplation of the dancers clearly enjoying themselves, she crooked her forefinger under her nose, and lodged her thumb under her chin. *It's wonderful to see Yulala having such fun,* Taylor thought to herself. *Can't imagine what I would feel, were I the lone human survivor of a planet-wide extinction event back on Earth. And it's just mind-boggling to see Pedro and Ludi laughing the simulated night away. They cannot have forgotten this was made possible by their being spirited out of an alternate universe where they might already have been hobbling around on walking canes. That is, if they hadn't yet succumbed to old age. Will this eventually become the deus ex machina of immortality? Will beings from the future continually reawaken beings from the past into fresh, alternative courses for their lives?*

What really has me concerned is the course I've chosen for these people in this existence, a course prompted by a voice inside my head. And it's dependent upon, relying upon the wisdom and guidance of tree creatures disposed to hitting golf balls with their rear ends! Speaking of which, look at them: Oodle-Noodle and Wafoodle-boodle, "Wafoodle-shake-your-caboodle" as Kevin would have it! They're having as much fun as anyone out there on the dance floor. Boogeying trees! Wafoodle really is shaking her caboodle! I wish I shared such blithe confidence in the future. I wish I could enthuse with something even remotely approaching their wild abandon. But, where does confidence leave off and arrogance begin? Where's the dividing line?

Yes, yes, yes, the blind faith of my superiors in the practical value of arming Fafama has led to destruction well beyond anything I could have imagined possible. However, one might argue it is no less extreme for us to be travelling without a single weapon, headlong into the midst of a heavily armed civilization intent on enslaving us for its food supply.

Did my revulsion in the face of what happened on Fafama overrule my reason? Was I left so emotionally vulnerable, I became a sucker for the oversimplified, wishful-thinking world view of the Oombians? And most unfortunately I was a powerful enough sucker, my seduction by Oombian naiveté has dictated the new mission for the Smoke and Mirrors? And my fellow crew members have gone along only because they were equally susceptible to the tree creatures' belief system? Thanks to their own emotional response to what happened on Fafama?

Or maybe it's a matter of my still struggling to shake off years of cultural conditioning, interrupted too infrequently by the occasional quote from Dr. Martin Luther King, Jr. Or by what gets framed as the fevered ranting of some drugged-out peace activist...

Captain, Oodle-Noodle suddenly telepathed, even while she continued wiggling her barked-over tree butt on the dance floor. *I think you and Yoon-hee are going to want to be making your way pronto fast for the navigation bridge.*

Helena's look Yoon-hee's way was met by her look right back.

Yoon-hee had been telepathed the same message.

Then the reception hall darkened, and scattered lights twinkled into being out of seemingly thin air.

※ ※ ※

"Michel, dear, do you see there in the southwest quadrant? A flying saucer has suddenly materialized! Would it have arrived from the clock planet?"

"I'll tell you one more time, Prissy! It's not 'the clock planet'! Its proper name, hell knows why, is Tictoctic! And the saucer didn't just suddenly materialize! That was an illusion created by deceleration below light-speed! If you really want to help me piece together what's going on, then determine what's happened to the Smoke and Mirrors! For all the damnably damned grizzlies in Alaska, looks to me like it's been engulfed by that sparkle dragon the size of Earth! Damn! If the saucer tosses an attack into the bargain, we might have our sufficient provocation for a formal war declaration much sooner than expected! I'll say this about those crazies flying their starship damnably defenseless into hostile territory! It would serve them right were they to get themselves blown apart, just one more falling star, before their mission's even properly begun!"

※ ※ ※

"Holographic disco lights, Chris?! Ha!" Buddy still had to shout to be heard above the party-hardy din.

"Nothing *I* did! Wo!" Chris exclaimed.

The ahtpah was Fafama's cow-sized, black-widow-spider lookalike, minus a red mark on the belly in the shape of an hourglass. And an ahtpah was what appeared to materialize at one end of the meeting room. It went scurrying directly for Tomás and Jorge. Panic-stricken, those two little boys fell backwards in their terrorized effort to simultaneously flee and pull their pants back up. Ciela screamed as husband Fred joined her mad rush in between their adopted sons and the rapidly approaching monster spider. The newlyweds cringed in full expectation of getting themselves sliced and diced by the ahtpah's steel-strong, knife-sharp mandibles. But it scurried right through and past them, followed by right through and past Tomás and Jorge.

The phantom ahtpah unwittingly supplemented the holographically simulated evocation of Fafama's fern-like trees and tralalafas. But it was far from the only mysteriously unexpected thing to suddenly most hauntingly infest the reception hall.

Fafaman plants similar to the tralalafa, animal-sheltering as well as carnivorous, came tumbling end over end. The sunset storm line could have been blowing them about like tumbleweed.

Groups of nocturnal-eyed Fafamans wandered aimlessly, confusion written all over their pale-green-glowing faces.

Private-jet-sized beetles called the blinding light prowlers joined the spectral circus procession. Said procession tumultuously made its way out of one wall of the large meeting area, and vanished through the opposite wall.

"This isn't funny, Chris!" shouted Dr. Deborah Murphy-Davis. She stormed over beside Officer Olsen-Taylor while nearly everyone else was gawking dumb-founded at the bizarre spectacle. "Turn it off! Right now!"

"I didn't turn it on! I don't know what's causing these phenomena!" But even as Chris made this protestation, he well understood how the ship's chief medical officer could have arrived at her assumption. He was the person responsible for the holographic simulation of Fafaman fern-like trees and tralalafas to enhance the wedding ceremony.

"It's thah plahnaht's spiraht, evahrywahn!" *It's the planet's spirit, everyone!* Yulala wasn't sure which way to turn when she tearfully offered this explanation. "It is fahllahwing us whahevah we go, to offah its prahtahcshahn!" *It is following us wherever we go, to offer its protection!*

Guy Hanson's new wife completed her remark just before there was a FWOOOOMPH! that only got louder and louder. On this odd noise's concluding reverberation, the reception hall shook. Then the floor tilted sharply as did, of course, the entire Smoke and Mirrors. If gravity had continued to mysteriously shed from the photon exhaust chamber, nobody would have known the difference. However, the impact from the diffuse magnetic pulse-beam temporarily compromised gravitational shedding. As a result, everyone in attendance spilled over to the side that the starship tilted.

Meanwhile, Yoon-hee and Helena were slammed against a wall on their rush to the navigation bridge.

"Yoon-hee?!" Captain Taylor shouted Officer Park-Smith's name in lieu of, *Are you okay?!* As for herself, through sheer determination she fought through pain in her right shoulder to get back on her feet.

"Captain!" was Yoon-hee's affirmation of being in good enough condition. She also fought through her own hurt, to pick herself up off the floor and resume the mad rush for the navigation bridge.

"I initiated the autopilot maneuver into the rift!" went on Captain Taylor. "But I suspect that jolt knocked it offline! We might have to make the maneuver manually! Hope there hasn't been any mirror array damage!"

Captain, Officer Park-Smith, I've mind-read the captain of a Tictoctickian saucer craft newly arrived to our vicinity. He has initiated a diffuse magnetic pulse-beam barrage, under orders to cripple the Smoke and Mirrors without destroying it. Hold the hallway railing; another jolt is coming.

FWOOOOMPH!!

⁎✧⊶⊷✧⊶⊷✧⊶⊷⁎

"That must be a diffuse magnetic pulse-beam, Prissy!"

"So return fire, dear." Priscilla tried to maintain at least a pretense of composure, even while she crawled across the floor of the Elusive's navigation deck. She sought to retrieve her knitting project jolted out of her hands by the second diffuse beam.

"Return fire is exactly what those animals would like! That way, they can learn where we are, knock out our propulsion, and then scoop us up like so many minnows netted from the ocean! We're going to sit still! Lay ourselves low!"

⁎✧⊶⊷✧⊶⊷✧⊶⊷⁎

KLUNK!

With his frustration, Captain Kek-stek of the Sixth Celestial Breath ran his antlers so hard against the nearest wall on the navigation deck, he made his neck stiff and sore. "Baa," he brayed half in pain, half in sheer aggravation. "Would that we could ground to bits the winged beast constellation! Would that it was pulverized into a fine dust beneath Dek-Fook-Tek's cloven hooves!

We can't make out one tiny kikitel of the marauding space vessel with that- that thing in the way!"

"Dek-Fook-Tek's hooves smooth jagged peaks down to smoothest sand, so we might trot gently after his passing through," ritually chanted the rest of the crew on the navigation deck.

"Agreed," Captain Kek-stek nodded with unconcealed impatience. "But we need a clear view of the enemy sooner rather than later, to more specifically set our sights. Otherwise, I must trust Commander Kwit-Nik will understand my subsequent decision! That he will not wish to gore me for launching targeted pulse-beams at various locations of the sparkle collective! Should we inadvertently blast apart the marauding vessel, we can always cast a net to retrieve flash-frozen other-world beast bodies! That is what we did when Dek-Fook-Tek led us to glorious victory over a Chonoran spacecraft in this same location!"

<hr />

FWOOOOOMPH!!!

"No!" exclaimed Helena Taylor, seated beside Yoon-hee at a control console on the navigation bridge.

The third jolt from the diffuse pulse-beam weapon lent ever more urgency to the haste by which Buddy, Kevin, Ali and Chris rushed to join Helena and Yoon-hee.

Meanwhile Dr. Deborah Davis-Murphy was working with Pedro, both Oombians, and her wife Geena. Under the doctor's direction, they were tending to the injuries and panic attacks of the adults and children still sprawled about the auditorium.

"The magnetic pulse-beam is ruining our trajectory!" complained Helena.

"I see that, Captain! Nay!" nodded Yoon-hee. She was furiously speeding her fingers across the control console keyboards. "I'm circling us around for another run at the space-time rift!"

"Oh, no! Just what we need!" Helena shouted. She wasn't complaining about Yoon-hee's efforts. Rather, she noticed strange mists suddenly filling the navigation bridge. The mists were resolving themselves into the shapes of strange, purplish-fleshed, uniformed creatures. Those creatures presented with a number of small tentacles about their mouths. And they were frozen into varied poses, with looks of horror in their eyes as they floated in and out of walls. "I hope the children aren't experiencing this!"

We've told them to keep their eyes shut, and focus on soothing delightful pictures we are painting in their heads, telepathed Wafoodle-boodle.

"I wish the fried fish that Wafoodle-lick-your-caboodle would paint some pretty pictures in *my* head! I'd like to get Mr. and Mrs. Calamari, all dressed up with no place to trick or treat, out of my mind!" complained Fred Frankly. He knelt beside Ciela to welcome Tomás cowering tremblingly into his chest.

⌁⧖⌁⧖⌁⧖

"Baa! Excellent!" crisply tongue-clicked Captain Kek-stek. "The winged beast has finally moved off! At last we are allowed a clear view of that oddly-shaped spacecraft! Officer Rek-mek-a-nek, target the magnetic pulse-beam on the enemy ship's rear end, from where the twinkly exhaust is issuing! Wait! What is the beast doing?! What *is* that?! Fire erupts like a volcano from its mouth?! Evasive maneuver! Evasive maneuver!!"

The Tictoctickian saucer broke off from launching a targeted attack on the Smoke and Mirrors. It made a sharp right-angle turn, the stuff of UFO legend, to dodge the planet-sized, dragon-shaped conglomeration of twinkles.

Blasts of fire blow-torched out for thousands of miles from what appeared to be the conglomeration's sharp-toothed maw.

⸱ℋⷨ°°ⷨⷨ°°ⷨⷨ°°ⷨ°⸱

Captain Taylor, Fafama's planet spirit has provided you plenty of time to execute the desired maneuver.

"Not a sentence one would ever expect to hear, let alone have infiltrate one's head, Oodle-Noodle," said Helena Taylor joining Yoon-hee to work the control console. "But we've got this...NOW!!"

When the Smoke and Mirrors traversed the space-time rift, everyone aboard endured a mild tingle. For those unfamiliar with such a sensation, Wafoodle-boodle quickly telepathed assurances it was okay.

Pedro, Ludi, Alexita and the two boys, Tomás and Jorge, experienced their first time travel beginning back in 2002. They journeyed to 2062 in post-quantum-wave suspended animation. This meant they essentially slept through it. Consequently, they needed the tree creature's gentle communication as much as anyone else.

⸱ℋⷨ°°ⷨⷨ°°ⷨⷨ°°ⷨ°⸱

"What happened to the Smoke and Mirrors, Prissy?! Where is it?!"

"You're asking me?! I thought it was still there when that dragon constellation thingie went after the enemy saucer."

"So maybe your 'dragon constellation thingie,' that damnably mysterious outer space critter, consumed our naïve peaceniks whole hog? Ah!" Michel DeFarge lifted a forefinger ceiling-ward. "I think I know, Prissy! But we're going to have to wait to confirm until the Tictoctic saucer makes a retreat. Maybe we will receive help from your 'thingie' for which there's no good animal trap comes to mind, just yet! Har! Maybe it will chase the saucer completely away from this corner of the solar system!"

Chapter 4

"Officer Rek-mek-a-nek?!?!?" shouted Captain Kek-stek. "Of course you have been inspired by the antler-hard resolve of our Supreme Authority Dek-Fook-Tek! As we all have been! Fueled by that inspiration, you must confirm for me what I forced myself not to flinch from seeing after the winged behemoth's assault proved impotent!"

This will be my most complicated grovel, yet, Rek-mek-a-nek literally ruminated on a preciously thin sliver of Chonoran jerky. *The winged, spectral space beast broke off from its illusory attack, only to be sucked down some invisible drain. And unquestionably the space beast's attack was illusory; its blow-torch exhalation did absolutely no harm at all to the Sixth Celestial Breath. It did indeed prove impotent. So I know exactly what Captain Kek-stek wants from me. He wants to know what happened to the marauding, inferiorly designed starship. That is what I "must confirm."*

Assume I actually had caught a glimpse of where that starship went. My regurgitation of something more ready for my intestinal tract than for my mouth still would have been tricky enough. I would have had to pretend to only thinking I saw so-and-so. And about hoping the captain could confirm I didn't hallucinate, given his that-much-more-reliable powers of observation. That probably would have salved the captain's ego, while still informing him of what his eyes had not managed to espy.

But the fact remains, I didn't procure even the briefest look at the marauding starship's fate. So what do I bray? If I had to guess, the starship was sucked down the same invisible drain as the chimeric beast. Do I gallop with that, and falsely claim I clearly saw what happened? Then hope the captain will never come into knowledge suggesting otherwise, thereby exposing my dishonesty?

Or do I tell him the truth, that I missed the whole thing? And add that if he, the great Captain Kek-stek, did not see what happened to the marauder, how did I have any chance? Especially given my inferior powers of observation? Will he accept such honesty, albeit marinated in self-deprecating brown-nosing? Or instead, will the captain succumb to his simmering paranoia, and accuse me of deliberately keeping information from him? Baa, I think I DO know how to handle this...

"Captain Kek-stek," Officer Rek-mek-a-nek made a point of baaing humbly, of emphasizing his own inferior status compared to Kek-stek's. He even bent his elbows to the rubbery hard floor of the navigation deck, tucking his fore-hooves under his chest in a bowing manner. "Captain Kek-stek, I am not even worthy of asking your forgiveness. I have taken way too long to recall the advice you expected me ever ready to apply in such a situation as this."

Captain Kek-stek nodded agreeably; he was straining not to reveal any least indication he didn't have the slightest idea what the officer was talking about. "Very well," he crisply tongue-clicked. "So are you prepared now to prove to me you *do* remember my advice?"

Officer Rek-mek-a-nek tried not to exhale too pronouncedly with his relief. Pursuant to which, he baaed, "Captain, you told us what to do in the event an enemy successfully distracts us from the manner of its withdrawal from our presence. You crisply tongue-clicked our next move must reinforce the home position. We cannot allow any sneak attacks there."

Captain Kek-stek surveyed the rest of the crew on the navigation bridge. He half-expected them to flutter their ears in puzzlement over what Officer Rek-mek-a-nek was baaing about. He didn't recall having said anything even remotely related to what Officer Rek-mek-a-nek claimed he had said. Although it did fit the present situation perfectly, if none of them saw exactly what happened to the marauding other-world vessel.

No fluttered-ear puzzlement was in evidence. Rather, Captain Kek-stek met nodding confirmation of Rek-mek-a-nek's claim from every direction he looked. The crew always backed up each other. They shared a common interest in not provoking the captain to any more chest scarrings than he was likely to perform regardless. Chest scarrings were how he kept reasserting his authority over them.

"I will never forget when you first presented us with this wise counsel, Captain. Dek-Fook-Tek himself could have been animating you," Officer Rek-mek-a-nek added.

The captain nodded approval. But he also pointedly tongue-clicked, "I *am* disappointed in your taking so long to chew these matters together into a well-ruminated mush of understanding. I will need to delay your next honorary chest-scarring as a result. Ditto for everyone else here present."

Officer Rek-mek-a-nek had to stifle an urge to celebrate this best of all possible outcomes. He really wanted to share an antler bump with every crew member.

"However," continued the captain, "take comfort from what Dek-Fook-Tek would say. And I quote, 'Better the rains come late to replenish the spring waters, than that they don't come at all.'"

"We make do with what we may sip from the gentle streams, as there is not enough of his most fragrant urine to go around." This is what Captain Kek-stek's crew scrambled up onto their hind hooves to ritually chant in response.

Captain Kek-stek strained to peer more discerningly into the star-studded void of space. He couldn't help thinking he missed something significant. He half-expected the saucer's sensors to detect telltale pieces of flotsam and jetsam. They would have constituted scattered wreckage from the twinkly space monster's destruction of the other-world vessel. But did that even happen? What went without saying was the twinkly, planet-sized space monster's having seemed sucked down an invisible drain. The other-world vessel's ultimate fate was far less certain, however.

Maybe the captain's sixth sense bothered him. After all, DeFarge's compact battle cruiser, the Elusive, sat waiting out there, camouflaged. Not to mention the firefly donut left behind as an anchor for the Smoke and Mirrors' safe return from its new travel through a space-time rift. The firefly donut was programmed to take a circuitous standby course, indistinguishable from asteroid fragments and other typical outer space debris. Maybe Captain Kek-stek's sixth sense bothered him about that.

Kek-stek did know for sure there had been a voice in his head. It entered there during the Celestial Breath's issuance of diffuse magnetic pulse-beams towards the other-world vessel. Most likely, it originated from someone aboard there, well prior to its indeterminate fate. And quite obviously, that voice was for him only. His officers would have shared their experience, no doubt, had they been receiving the voice in their heads, as well.

Captain Kek-stek gathered from the voice that Commander Kwit-Nik might be correct after all, about no need for interplanetary war. The voice prattled on gently about enough food for everyone, with nobody having to be slaughtered for meat. Sharing music and playing games could become the order of the day across several solar systems. Such oskynt pap must surely, in the captain's estimation, have originated from creatures of incredible naiveté. Negotiating their conquest without firing a shot should prove easy enough, he figured.

But suppose the telepath planted in his head resulted from Commander Kwit-Nik's collusion with the other-worlders? Eventually there could be great benefit, alerting Supreme Authority Dek-Fook-Tek to his commanding military officer's real plans. That Commander Kwit-Nik was trying to undermine his authority. Ironically, Kek-stek concluded he must share with Commander Kwit-Nik every last peace overture the voice telepathed him. He must further embolden Kwit-Nik to grow more reckless with his disloyalty.

"Officer Rek-mek-a-nek, set our course for the battleship rendezvous staging area near Tictoctic with all due speed. I will report directly to Commander Kwit-Nik before we resume our perimeter patrol!"

The Sixth Celestial Breath's outer hull resumed spinning like a top. It was impelled by an electromagnetically enhanced photon force. That force pushed against aluminum alloy slats rippling open and closed faster than the eye could see.

⊱⋅⋅⊰⋅⋅⊱⋅⋅⊰⋅⋅⊱⋅⋅⊰

Fifteen Earth years earlier, an electrical discharge suddenly materialized. This happened at the same location on the outer edge of the Cygnitaurus solar system from where the Sixth Celestial Breath had fast departed in the present. For Earthling observers, the discharge would have looked like cloud-to-cloud lightning, minus the clouds. It lasted far longer than a two-second flash, however. And it split open wide enough for the Smoke and Mirrors to emerge at incredibly high speed. The starship was already millions of miles along before the split-open slit could seal up, and the entire electrical discharge could dissipate. Down inside the Earth's stratosphere, concussive waves from superheated gas would have disintegrated the tallest buildings. And the noise would have carried for thousands of miles. In the depths of outer space, though, absolute silence prevailed.

The starship's panoramic view-screen revealed curious details as epic as they were disturbing. There was an intact saucer craft; an intact miniature saucer craft; a clutter of variously sized fragments from a blown-apart saucer craft; extraterrestrial bodies; and a net cast out by the miniature saucer for trawling those bodies. Spacecraft, spacecraft debris and bodies alike remained stuck in place at a particular past moment of their existence. The quantum wave of time's arrow had long since gone through. But the intrusion of the Smoke and Mirrors jostled them about. Chris drew on his memory of a baby jostling bathtub toys when gently lowered into warm, bubbly water.

"Yoon-hee, we can get a magnified view of those extraterrestrial bodies, I'm assuming?"

"Nay, Captain," nodded Yoon-hee, ever at work playing her fingers across her control console. "I'll display magnification on the left half of the split-screen. There!" she announced with a final, conclusive forefinger chicken-peck.

"Umm, that's *not* a deer creature from Tictoctic, Buddy, is it?" asked Captain Taylor. "Wait, is that..."

"It is, Captain," nodded Officer Buddy Leung. "The creature corpses displayed inside glass crypts mounted on a kitchen wall of the battle saucer I hijacked...These have to be the same species. The several small tentacles around their mouths..."

"So that's what they looked like. Deb, any chance-"

"No chance, Captain," Chief Medical Officer Davis-Murphy cut off Helena. She arrived on the bridge only a minute earlier, having just wrapped up emergency care at the disrupted wedding reception. She had needed to confirm everyone else was okay physically, and that Ali Magabu had the counseling aspect well in hand. "Let's assume we got here the shortest possible time after their saucer's destruction," Dr. Davis-Murphy went on. "They still would have been exposed to several seconds of near-absolute-zero temps, freezing them dead through and through. There was no prayer of resuscitation unless we retrieved them at the instant of magnetic pulse-beam impact."

"Of course," nodded Captain Taylor. "Pedro, um, Officer Perez, this is why we travelled back so many extra years to 'rapture' you. Rots of ruck, had we tried targeting the hours just before the Martian hurricane. But I digress. What we have here confirms your suspicion, Oodle-Noodle. The beings from Tictoctic were not the only ones in possession of flying saucer starships."

"Who wants to bet our antlered invaders *aren't* manning, stagging, whatever, that huge intact flying saucer out there? You know, the saucer we can safely assume disintegrated the other huge saucer via magnetic pulse-beam?" Kevin asked from beside Yoon-hee's control panel console.

"Well here's something else to consider!" blustered Sergeant Fred Frankly. He'd arrived on the navigation bridge not too many moments earlier from comforting his new wife and adopted kids. "Let's back it up again to the wedding crashers aboard the other flying saucer. I mean forward up to 2063. Begging your permission of course, Captain." He swept his hand Helena's direction.

"Proceed, Sergeant."

"Thank you kindly. I just want to know, with this whole peace-and-love mission you've undertaken, um... Look, I'm well aware I signed on again. I am not going to blame Sergeant Hanson for guilting me on board for round two. But suppose that Fafaman supersized ephemeral dragon beastie hadn't shown itself at just the right time to conceal us. And then given those damned Tictoctickians a good scare. Just how were we going to 'We shall overcome' our way out of that predicament without winding up on their dinner menu? Weren't we damned lucky?!"

May I, Captain?

After doing a double-take she couldn't conceal, Helena Taylor swept her hand the Oombian tree creature's way, similar to Fred Frankly's gesture. "Go for it, Oodle-Noodle."

Thank you, Captain. Sergeant Frankly, there was far more than damned luck involved. A carefully calculated risk is how I would characterize it. You see, I was in telepathic contact with the planet spirit of Fafama, your "supersized ephemeral dragon beastie." What I could mind-read made one thing perfectly clear where the planet spirit is concerned. It is set on doing everything in its power to protect the lone flesh-and-blood survivor of the extinction event precipitated by the crashing of an ice comet into Fafama. Of course I am referring to Yulala.

But okay, let us assume we were without its presence and help. Let's say the planet spirit of Fafama was not shadowing us. It never showed up, never sabotaged the Tictoctickians' efforts to target the Smoke and Mirrors with a magnetic pulse-beam. We did have a backup plan.

We were going to surrender fully to the Tictoctickians, albeit far earlier than originally conceived. Then we were going to proceed without the benefit of the additional information we hoped to gain from Tictoctic's binary twin.

Professor Dauntilus Skepticus popped from his seat where he so unobtrusively buckled himself down. He blurted out, "I am sorry, Captain. I cannot sit here taking in this foolish gibberish, unchallenged, any longer! Oodle-Noodle, what evidence do you provide us, evidence us non-mind-readers can replicate, that there really is anything to what you are claiming? That the noted phenomenon is not highly susceptible to conventional explanation? Which is to say, in lieu of some 'spirit of Fafama' acting as a planet-sized guide dog for Yulala?"

Professor Skepticus, of course you are well aware how I am able to telepath you, and read your thoughts.

"That has to do with your fourth dimensional acuity well superior to ours!! Nothing is happening with your telepathy, is claimed to be happening with your telepathy, beyond the bounds of normal physics! But when you allege some totally nonphysical existence..."

Imagine we better understood the world around us. In such a scenario, I am confident that spirits and other such aspects of reality would also be found to lie well within "the bounds of normal physics." For now, you are going to have to take me at my telepath. The enormous, dragon-shaped twinkle cluster that followed us, at least until we traversed the space-time rift, evidenced sentient characteristics.

It is true, I must admit to not presently being aware of how to provide you with physical proof, evidence to support my assertion. However, consider the ghostly apparitions from Fafama we experienced during the wedding reception. What better way to explain them than as reminiscences by the departed spirit of the planet?

On this telepathed question from Oodle-Noodle, Skepticus opened his mouth wide. He squinted at the Oombian tree creature as though what she communicated were blindingly shocking. "Pure speculation with absolutely nothing to support it!" he at last declared. "How do you know for sure you were mind-reading some absurdly conceived 'planet spirit'?! How do you know that a cosmic particle property of the twinkling anomaly didn't reflect your telepathy back to you, all distorted? That it is not unlike someone's image from a warped mirror in a fun house? That your desperation to invent some meaning out of the senseless obliteration of life on Fafama hasn't deluded you? Hasn't caused you to mistake such a distorted image for the cogitations of an impossible entity?

"And while we are at it, how do you know that's not of a piece with the whole matter of reading a dragon shape into the twinkle clusters? How do you know that's not the same as imagining various animals in cumulus cloud formations?

"Speaking of more plausible explanations, what about those 'ghostly apparitions' at the wedding reception? Couldn't people have been reading design into the random shadows of a room kept darkened to honor the lost world of the extraterrestrial bride? Couldn't that be of a piece with the fearful fantasies of children at bedtime, once their parents turn off the lights? That is, when children mistake their clothes tossed over the back of a chair for some bogeyman?

"Didn't the furor at the wedding reception start with one person screaming about what they misperceived? Then before you knew it, the power of suggestion had some of you hallucinating specters floating hither and yon outside the Smoke and Mirrors? Strange, unfortunate creatures with miniaturized tentacles about their mouths must have seemed like a nightmare, because that's all they were! Nothing more than a nightmare! And once we awake from nightmares, we realize they are not real! Hmmph!"

Professor Skepticus, aren't you simply substituting one set of speculations for another, rather than contributing anything qualitatively different? Besides, how did so many people, including my significant other, Wafoodle-boodle, know to make their nightmares include tentacles lining the mouths of the extraterrestrials? Officer Leung was the only person to previously see that, aboard a saucer from Tictoctic. Moreover, I think we have video of what we observed floating "hither and yon" outside the Smoke and Mirrors, after we traversed the space-time rift. That's proof of more than just nightmares.

"Mere coincidence!" Skepticus huffed and puffed at Oodle-Noodle's rebuttal.

Kevin mused to himself that had the professor been capable, he would have tried to blow down the tree person. He would have been like the big, bad wolf blowing down a little pig's house.

Instead, Skepticus said, "My point is simply this, Oodle-Noodle: Following your advice, our fates hinge on our luck holding out long enough! Long enough, I mean to say, for cruel reality not to come cutting through a thin tissue of fantasies, illusion and wishful thinking like the sharpest- OW!"

There was a brief, faint whoosh. To Helena's ears, a gas oven could have just been lit. That whoosh was accompanied by a flash of light from the seat of Professor Skepticus's pants.

"Careful there, Professor," said Buddy Leung. "I don't think Effy likes you insinuating he's nothing more than an illusion."

"Effy is *not* anything- OW!" With this new torching from seeming nowhere, Skepticus jumped forward and protectively held the seat of his pants by both hands.

"Better watch your words, there."

"Officer Leung!" Skepticus erupted admonishingly. "I am *not* going to watch my words in order to protect myself from- OW! There has to be an explanation for this! Whenever I speak, certain particulate matter in the air is profoundly disturbed by convection currents! Somehow, that particulate matter is rubbed together like pieces of flint! Only coincidentally is this happening in the vicinity of my rear- OW! Okay, not coincidentally! But not Effy either! OW! My pants must be shedding that particulate- OW! Maybe the flames are enhanced by certain autonomic flatulence I am not aware of producing, -OW! even though it originates- OW!"

"I would suggest you stop talking and go change your pants, Professor." Buddy Leung tried to keep a respectful tone, and not bust out laughing. The way Skepticus jumped about while still clutching at his concealed buttocks suggested he was being forced to do an Irish jig against his will.

"That is *exactly* what I intend to- OW!"

By this point, Skepticus had leapt out into the hall. Additional "ow"s could be heard from him as he sped off in erratic leaps towards his cabin.

After closing her eyes to shake her head, Captain Taylor turned to the Oombian and said, "Please tell me, Oodle-Noodle: Anything else you haven't gotten around to sharing with us? Perhaps some other predicament we don't know about yet, for which you have already foreseen the escape plan?"

Only this, Captain: When the Tictoctickians tried to force our surrender by firing the diffuse magnetic pulse-beam, I telepathed that we have come in peace. I asked why they attacked us even though we elected to enter their realm unprepared to attack them. And then I challenged their captain to dream how the future could be.

"So you gave away the game. Great." Sergeant Frankly rolled his eyes and crossed his arms. "I'd try sending a 'wish you were here' postcard to my AK-51, if I thought there was any chance it could respond!"

But here is a hopeful thing for us, Sergeant Frankly. The saucer captain to whom I telepathed, my sixth sense detected significant doubt along his mental horizon as to the wisest course of action. I also gathered that the commander to whom he answers is beholden to even deeper doubt than he is. Clearly we fuel this doubt with our deliberately pacifist approach while investigating the circumstances unique to their solar system.

"Hell, I'd bet that some of the most bloodthirsty mass murderers back home on Earth also entertained a doubt or two, also had their qualms. But did that matter? No! Not whether it was Mao Zedong ordering the slaughter of millions of fellow Chinese! Or Stalin having hordes of fellow Russians dig their own burial trenches for dropping straight down into, soon as they were shot! And of course there's always Adolf f-n' Hitler!

"You see, what I'm tryin' to spit out, Ms. Spaghetti Noodle, is this: What if we had ventured into the antlered demons' neck of the interstellar woods all weaponed up? Then, if your peace initiative became a big fail, we could at least have gone out with some damned heroics.

Maybe we could have bought our compadres and your fellow oof addicts enough time to fully prepare for interstellar war! But completely defenseless as we presently are, we could end up on their f-n' specialty menu, without a shot having been fired!"

Studying your civilization, Sergeant Frankly, here is one of the things I have noticed. Dying in the exercise of violence is nearly always regarded as heroic, worthy of numerous statues and tributes. But too rarely, in my estimation, is heroism attributed to those who in the name of peace would rather suffer, even die, than fight.

"We've got monuments to Dr. Martin Luther King..."

"Please, people..." Helena turned to Oodle-Noodle and footnoted, "I'm using that term loosely."

The Oombian tree creature scratched off a piece of bark lodged uncomfortably at the intersection of her trunk with one of her trimmed-down branches.

"But listen," the starship captain went on. "As much as I would enjoy hearing more of this conversation, we are on the clock. Right, Buddy?"

"Right, Captain. Before we know it the quantum wave will catch up, and everything will return to real time motion," Buddy confirmed. "We've probably got only a matter of seven, eight hours at most."

"So eight hours, max, to reconnoiter without worry of problematic encounters," Captain Taylor estimated. "And to decide what's next. I guess the first thing I want to know is the definitive answer to the chicken-egg question. That is, who 'laid' the saucer first? Was it the Tictoctickians, or the, um, octopus mouths?

"Sergeant Frankly, I'm not sure how familiar you are with Shakespeare, but you can think of me as the peace-and-love version of Lady MacBeth. Blame it on my visceral reaction to the consequences from our militarization of Fafama. Whatever the reason, I have committed very far into Oodle-Noodle's project. I have committed so far, it might prove at least as perilous for us to back out now as to continue the rest of the way.

"Yoon-hee, set a direct course for the binary planet, maximum light-speed from which we can successfully decelerate into geosynchronous orbit."

Don't you mean: Decelerate into sitting duck mode for the orbital shooting gallery, since we have no idea who the hell might be down there on the binary planet's surface? Fred stifled himself from saying.

"It's already calculated as a five-and-one-quarter-hour journey, Captain," Yoon-hee noted. "Rear laser lantern deployed, aft and fore blooms set to full, and advance guard firefly donuts providing us an open, uncluttered highway."

"Full bloom initiation, now, Yoon-hee!" Upon uttering, "now," Helena lowered her right forefinger pointed towards the panoramic view-screen.

The Smoke and Mirrors was flying well within solar powering range of the sun named Cygnitaurus by the Earthlings. However, Cygnitaurus's light shed could not be depended upon for more than one-quarter light-speed acceleration. The quantum wave passed through over a decade earlier. As a result, the photons were left in a dramatically decelerated state in the slice of space-time where the Smoke and Mirrors had emerged from the rift near the edge of the solar system. For any substantial speed-up, the starship depended heavily on the light emission source it brought along from 2063, namely a rear laser lantern. The first time he saw it, Chris was reminded of the bioluminescence that hung from the head of a certain deep sea fish to brighten its path forward. Only, that bioluminescence would have had to have hung from the fish's tail flukes.

Anyhow, the Smoke and Mirrors mirror array baffle system accelerated to a thirty times multiple the speed of all light that impacted with it. At least this was Officer Leung's latest thinking on the matter. But there was another possibility starting to haunt him. Maybe light wasn't actually being accelerated the least bit beyond a steady one hundred eighty-six thousand miles a second. Rather, maybe the mirror array propulsion was generating a river of space stretched out like a piece of soft taffy. One mile of space travelled near light speed within such a river was equal to thirty miles of space travelled outside the river. It was like walking up a moving escalator. You get from point A to point B faster than each escalator stair, even if you are walking slower than the escalator is moving.

Whatever was actually happening with the Smoke and Mirrors, to a well-placed observer the starship would have been seen to have vanished in the time it took to turn on a flashlight.

Only one indication remained of the Smoke and Mirrors' presence and departure. The saucers, saucer fragments and extraterrestrial corpses in post-quantum-wave suspended animation continued to look jostled about. Again as Chris would have imagined, they could have been bathtub toys after the baby has been lowered into or taken out of the water.

Some of the tentacle-mouthed creatures gathered into the net cast out by the smaller saucer were shaken free, to float in space. But soon enough they would be re-retrieved, re-netted, by the deer creatures from Tictoctic. That is, once the quantum wave retraced its steps for incorporating the Smoke and Mirrors into an altered space-time narrative.

Chapter 5

"Well," Secretary of Defense Michael Spinner shrugged his shoulders, "I suppose it was better for President Carey to get out ahead of the curve. And he did only admit to a sanitized version of the situation. We have to remember that lots more folks had to be brought into the loop for deploying a second battleship. Someone was bound to spring a leak sooner or later. Then people would have started wondering what else we were hiding, and journalists would have been poking around too much. Unfortunately, we can't throw every last snoopy reporter behind the quarantine walls, and keep them there until this entire matter gets resolved. We know how anal they are about giving up their precious investigations for even the shortest while. Same goes for all their conspiracy-seeking friends. Freedom to stick their nose in today is obviously two licks more important than the avoidance of us ending up on Tictoctic's dinner menu tomorrow!"

Secretary Spinner was referring to an address given by American Union President Carey, transmitted worldwide. In that speech, the president admitted concern over an extraterrestrial threat. Regarding Fafama, he said details were murky as to what exactly happened. They might take several more weeks to clarify. He added that the Callaway X Centra system was turned into a military staging area, seven long light-years away from Earth. Moreover, firefly donut monitors were dispersed at regular intervals between that solar system and Earth. Those monitors would assure early warning detection of any spacecraft issuing from even further out than Callaway X Centra, especially from the Cygnitaurus system. "But that is not all, fellow citizens of the world." A laser mesh shield was deployed, enveloping Earth. This shield would protect the planet from a potential if highly unlikely extraterrestrial invasion. Again, President Carey emphasized the whole idea was "we're containing any possible threat trillions of miles away."

The Eisenhower, Earth's second militarized starship, had raced to join the first militarized starship, the Barack Obama, in the Callaway X Centra solar system. Presently, both cigar-shaped vessels were maintaining solar orbit in amidst an asteroid belt. This belt was situated halfway between Oomb's solar orbit and the outermost planet's solar orbit within the Callaway X Centra system. The starships were programmed to mimic asteroids. That was how they would be passed off by any Tictoctickians who might perform remote sensor sweeps. Hopefully!

Once a navigation officer had locked in the Eisenhower's asteroid mimicry, strategy meetings ensued. Eisenhower Captain Kenny Robertson welcomed aboard Secretary Spinner, weapons specialist Dr. Magdalena Wang, General Sandy Warlor, and the Obama's provisional captain, Louisa Entroper.

Prior to receipt of President Carey's speech, Captain Robertson kicked off the high-level proceedings with a video. From inside Earth's Oort Cloud, the Eisenhower was shown demonstrating the full capability of its ball-lightning cannon. To get the party started, an oily-looking, amoebic, rainbow-colored blob of plasma shot from the battle-ready starship. That blob turned into a bright red flash of light, upon collision with an asteroid the size of New York City. The asteroid was disintegrated into chunks of rock conglomerate, none bigger than a compact car.

Dr. Wang clapped gleefully. "The application is not quite to magnetic pulse-beam capability, just yet," she cautioned, however effused she became over the test result. "Then again, we can already use these plasma condensations to set up deep-space mine fields where the enemy will not know what hit them!"

"Captain Robertson, we're receiving a high-security patch-through from the Barack Obama," suddenly interrupted Officer Emmeline Min over the Eisenhower's intercom presently.

"Let's have it, Officer. The intercom's fine; we've all got clearance. Just patch it through. And don't even dream of eavesdropping!"

"I *would* dream of eavesdropping, Captain. But I can assure you there will be scrambled gibberish on my end for the split second before the transfer mutes the communication."

"Your honesty is appreciated, Emme."

Next thing the assembled top officers were hearing, "Um, well, this is Michel DeFarge, Commander of the Elusive. I'll be damned, damnably damned, if I'll ever get used to these firefly donut bottles in the cosmic seas! I mean, it would be nice to hear some immediate response instead of having to wait for an hour! But I do appreciate the vast distance my communication has to travel. It's no small miracle we can expect your reckoning on my update sometime sooner than next decade. Burp! Sorry! Didn't mean for my indigestion to go interstellar as well."

"Commander DeFarge!" his wife exclaimed reprovingly. The chuckling audience aboard the Eisenhower was able to hear Priscilla clearly, despite her off-screen location.

"If time warn't the issue, there are certain things I'd already want to edit out of this piss-poor progress report. And I'm not just referring to my, errr, digestion-related indiscretion!" Michel tossed his right thumb back over his shoulder, Priscilla's way. "Anyway, there has been what you might call an incident here. In light of that incident, I want to know what your next marching orders are. Have an idea or two, myself, but I've been going it alone for long enough, as it is.

"So chew on this: Just an hour and a half ago, a big-assed flying saucer slowed to visibility out of its own ultra-light-speed. Its guns were ablaze with that magnetic pulse-beam doohickey."

Captain Robertson and Secretary Spinner's shoulders were heaving with their amusement.

Entroper, Warlor and Wang shook their heads in mild disapproval, however much they might still have admired DeFarge.

"But I don't think they were after the direct kill. Their pulse-beam sent us rocking and rolling. Probably spilled someone's bag of wacka-doodle-brocci-whatevers all over the Smoke and Mirrors. It was like we'd hit a rogue wave on the high seas. But no real harm. Maybe it was the demon stag's version of an underwater lake blast. You know, Secretary Spinner: the kind of explosion what sends all the sea critters floating unconscious-like to the surface for some good fishing, cheatin' style. Only, it didn't work. Got a ship-cam video for you to gnaw on like a sugar cane stick, see how much sweet you can take from it. I'll be providing the damned narration.

"So here, we're looking directly towards the Smoke and Mirrors, about a million miles from us," DeFarge went on as promised with his voice-over. The video revealed a planet-sized cluster of twinkles. Those twinkles were almost lost, camouflaged amidst a multitude of star and galaxy clusters far more distant. "Now correct me if I'm wrong, but damned if that assortment of nearby sparklers isn't assuming the shape of some damnably damned dragon! A few hours earlier, they weren't as proximate to the

Smoke and Mirrors as they are in this video. But during the intervening time, they kept getting closer. And with the saucer attack, I'll be triple-cursed if those sparklers didn't appear to scarf down our naïve friends. It was like it, they, who-the-hell-knows was trying to protect our folks!! That is, unless it was set on somehow actually eating them!

"Here's the real clincher: That magnetic pulse-beam whatchamacallit kept us a-rocking and a-rolling. Might as well have been ripples from the wake of some big-assed motor boat.

"Meanwhile, I'll be damned if that dragon constellation didn't suddenly go hauling after Mr. Flying Saucer. Look closely at *this* part of the show: Am I a monkey's furry butt, or was that flames spewing from the dragon monster's mouth? How else do you explain it?

"Well whatever it was, you can see that sparkle trail from the saucer high-tailing it outta there. But check out this film, courtesy of the magniview ship cam with sights still set on the Smoke and Mirrors. There's a thin, jagged line. Could have been cloud-to-cloud lightning what darted way off into deep space. The S and M seems to merge with the lightning, and the sparkle dragon looks sucked down a drain right after it. Not half an eye-blink later, that out-of-place lightning disappears in a flash.

"Now, I'm no damned fancy-pants physicist! But am guessing our peacenik friends jumped some space-time barrier, like you briefed me they've a habit of doing! And that their planet-sized seeing-eye dog what spewed flames at the enemy saucer broke that barrier as well! He wasn't going to be left behind!"

Secretary Spinner chuckled, "Well, well! Captain Taylor neglected to inform us their peace-and-love package included a planet-sized worth of char-broiling space monster!"

"So what are my marching orders now?" DeFarge continued on the video. "Should I go time-traveling after them? If I understand correctly, I'd have to prepare a firefly donut for my anchor near the rift. Bet you several thousand of what Prissy is knitting for me, that a close inspection of nearby space will reveal such an anchor for the Smoke and Mirrors. And bet several thousand more that it's programmed to wander round the rift like some freaking small cosmic particle what has nothing better to do. In any event, the instructions on time travel from Dr. Wang are plenty clear. A donkey with its head stuck up its damned ass could follow them. So if you want me to give immediate pursuit, well okay!

"Or, I would see two other options, hard to tell which of all three is the least damnable. Despite what I think went on, we don't really know what actually happened to the Smoke and Mirrors. Let's figure those damnably damned antlered bastards crippled or destroyed it. That would mean I should go ahead with the drone strike to stir the furry hornets' nest. Get the damned war started, assuming our second battleship will be on the scene in time.

"Second option is to just hang out by the space-time rift, and wait for the S and M's return. Hopefully they'll bring back enough valuable info to stick it to those damnably damned Tictoctickians. That is, before they can wipe out the entire hunting grounds of a whole other planet.

"Already mentioned plan three: We try giving pursuit across the space-time barrier.

"So there you have it. I await your good word. This is Commander Michel DeFarge, over!"

DeFarge's video message went blank.

The provisional captain of the Barack Obama, Louisa Entroper, shook her head and said, "I'd really like to have Professor Skepticus here to give us his take on the anomalies the commander filmed. I do understand the professor believed the greater priority was to continue his investigation of similar, perhaps related anomalies aboard the Smoke and Mirrors. He was up for that, despite Captain Taylor being embarked on a possibly fatal fool's errand. Still..."

Captain Robertson nodded agreeably. He added, "There was an article in one of the psychology journals I peruse for casual entertainment. It concerned our evolved face recognition ability, what that does to our perception in general. The author mentioned the kind of experience I've had which I'm guessing some of you have had as well."

"Nope. No such thing!" Spinner shook his head in deep mischief mode, with no idea what kind of experience Captain Robertson was going to reference. "You're the only crazy-assed person here! Proceed!"

"Thank you, Mr. Secretary," Robertson chuckled. "So what it is, you look at designs in floor tiles, for example."

"Do that all the time when I'm dumping a load. Sorry, ladies. The mike's not on, is it?" Secretary Spinner playfully checked under the conference table.

"You don't need to look at those tile designs for long," Robertson continued, taking Spinner's crude remark in stride. "It takes me only a few seconds before I start reading faces into them. So we really can't be sure-"

Knock! Knock!

With this unexpected knock on the door, puzzled looks circled around.

Entroper asked with mild reproof in her voice, "Captain Robertson, your communications officer did not alert you someone was on their way to interrupt us?"

"Oh," Kenny Robertson nodded as awareness dawned. "Think I know who." He bolted for the door while he noted, "Not the first time this has happened. I assure you she's perfectly harmless."

Secretary Spinner shrugged his shoulders in no-big-deal mode. But it was another matter for Dr. Wang, Captain Entroper and General Warlor. Warlor bowed her head and hunched her shoulders, feeling awkward; Dr. Wang studied her fingernails, unsure how she should feel or react; and Entroper closed her eyes. She thought to herself, *Well, this certainly isn't how I would ever handle whoever-it-is aboard MY ship!*

"Oh, I am so sorry, Captain Robertson. Looks like a very important meeting you're having."

"That's okay, Samantha. Allow me to introduce you to these good people." Turning back towards Entroper and company, the captain said, "This is Samantha Santiago-Olsen. She's the mother of Chris Olsen-Taylor, Captain Taylor's husband. I believe he's in charge of stress management aboard the Smoke and Mirrors. Samantha, I don't know whether you are already familiar with any of the gang here, but this is Secretary of Defense Michael Spinner..."

"Ahh," nodded Michael. "So you're the mother of the world-famous chocolate-chip cookie-maker!"

"Over to my right, this is Dr. Louisa Entroper, provisional captain of the Barack Obama..."

"I've seen good things about you in the news, Dr. Entroper," said Samantha. "You herded an asteroid into orbit around Fafama while my daughter-in-law was navigating their complex political situation down on the surface. Is that correct?"

"Yes, and I am in awe of your son, Samantha. Complete awe," Entroper reciprocated, disarmed by Samantha's compliment.

"And this is Chair of the Joint Chiefs of Staff, Sandy Warlor."

"It is an honor." Samantha bowed.

"It is an honor for me to meet a fellow Giants fan, all the way out here in the Callaway X Centra system."

"Oh." Samantha tugged on the brim of her Giants baseball hat self-consciously. She wore it nonstop as a security blanket, ever since the Eisenhower left Earth's solar system. Her team used to be the Baltimore Orioles, but ever since she moved for good to San Francisco... "I always have to be careful with news feeds, so I don't see any scores in advance of watching games on the two-day delay. I like to experience each loss as a fresh experience."

Surprise fueled the laughter at Samantha's sharp wit. How could that have emerged so soft-spokenly from such a meek-looking, wispy-slight figure of an elderly woman?

When the minor to-do subsided, Captain Robertson concluded, "And this is Dr. Magdalena Wang. She is one of our top applied physics advisors."

"Samantha, I must taste your son's secret weapon cookie, so I can learn how to prepare an even tastier one to defeat it! Although I hear that might be impossible, and we are doomed to forever craving it!"

"What brings you here, Sammy?" Captain Robertson asked with a nervous laugh. He had nowhere to go with Dr. Wang's bizarrely framed compliment.

"While I await my son's return from the latest mission of the Smoke and Mirrors, I should like to take a trip of my own, down to the surface of Oomb."

A Velcro-like material kept everyone securely seated whenever deceleration below light-speed reduced the gravity shedding to near zero. That material was making lots of static-type noises as the assembled officials shifted about uncomfortably. They were all thinking the same thing. Samantha should not be allowed to learn of the humans on Oomb. And that they were "raptured" out of their circumstances some sixty years earlier back on Earth. Some of them being her relatives didn't matter. Like everyone else aboard the Smoke and Mirrors, her son Chris had been sworn to secrecy about the humans on Oomb. Not even his own mother was supposed to find out, although of course his wife Helena already knew.

"Umm, this seems rather sudden," was the only thing Captain Robertson could think to say, for embarking on the path he initially thought must lead to "no."

Samantha Santiago-Olsen made a deep inhale followed by an even deeper exhale.

Louisa Entroper recalled an inhale and exhale made by someone else several months ago. Captain Helena Taylor. Helena breathed exactly that way just before explaining why she wanted to retrieve several people from the past, and resettle them on Oomb. The thought crossed Louisa's mind that Chris had married someone who reminded him of his mother.

"Captain Robertson, I don't know how much President Carey told you about why I sought passage aboard your vessel," Samantha went on finally.

"Well, I was informed you wanted to see Officer Olsen-Taylor after his current mission. That didn't seem like an unreasonable request, since you're his mother."

"President Carey said nothing about the pendant?"

"The president did mention a trinket he believed you might have received from Chris after his first journey to Fafama," answered Robertson. "He was under the impression you wanted to return it. Also, there was some suggestion of its being a souvenir from Fafama. With rumors flying of Fafama's apocalyptic fate, I'm guessing you've discovered it has real value."

Samantha looked up from her humbly bowed demeanor, right into Robertson's eyes. She gently shook her head. "A complete stranger handed me the 'trinket' sixty years ago. This happened while my parents were coping with the spooky disappearance of my Philadelphia relatives. The stranger's gentleness earned her my complete trust. She instructed me to give the 'trinket' to a loved one after he or she survived a most perilous adventure, sixty years later."

Dr. Wang gasped.

"I was taken by a most distinct impression," Samantha went on. "Fulfill the task assigned by the gentle stranger, and I would learn my relatives' fate, including why they vanished. What occurred to me in recent days was that somehow, those relatives must have ended up on Oomb. I'm also guessing a few of them might even be aboard the Smoke and Mirrors, wherever its mission. Therefore, I should like to visit with those of my relatives who remained behind on Oomb, see how they are doing at long last. Yes," she nodded, "their having been born before I was born will not matter. I will still find them far younger than me. I am well aware of that. But there is nothing to be done for it."

Latching onto the brim of her Giants' baseball cap for her security blanket proved beside the point. Samantha was able to proceed without interruption because she stunned her small audience speechless. Upon completion, she waited quietly patient for a response.

An awkward silence ensued.

It was Secretary Spinner, all shaking jowls and Santa's beard, who finally ventured, "Tell me honestly, Ms. Santiago-Olsen. Did your son confide your relatives' whereabouts?"

"Oh, no." Sammy could not have been any more matter-of-fact in her dismissal of Spinner's speculation. "I'm guessing he was not supposed to share that information with me, and likewise for his wife, Captain Taylor. I told you where my information came from, as incredible as it might seem."

"Did you relate your story to anyone else?" Provisional Captain Entroper couldn't avoid an accusatory tone creeping into her voice.

Samantha maintained her matter-of-fact composure, regardless, when she responded, "I did tell my late husband about the pendant. But I assumed that was odd enough, without bringing in the business about my vanished relatives."

"So, if there *was* anything to what you are saying – I'm not saying there is," Robertson qualified for the benefit of Warlor, Spinner and Entroper, whose heads seemed to him about to explode. "But if there was," he continued, "would you be sharing what you learned with anyone else after you concluded your family reunion? Again, we are assuming there is a family down there on Oomb for you to have a reunion with."

"Why would I want to do that? Especially since I gather you put a huge priority on keeping those family members' very existence a secret from the general public?"

Once Samantha left the presence of Captain Robertson and company, her interruption of their mini-conference prompted lots of discussion. How much more was the general public coming to learn of the potential interstellar crisis than President Carey had already admitted? And how much more might end up leaking out about everything else?

As for the way in which Samantha was responded to *before* she left, Chair of the Joint Chiefs of Staff Sandy Warlor did the honors. She became the point person following another awkward silence. That is, the awkward silence after Samantha asked why she would want to blab about her relatives on Oomb. "Well, Captain Robertson, of course the decision is yours," Sandy said. "But I don't see any harm obliging the request of the esteemed starship officer's most esteemed mother. Obviously there is no shortage of 'spooky action,' Einstein might have reiterated, attendant to our loosening the Earthly chains, as it were. But this particular eeriness would seem especially innocent and inconsequential in the larger schemata."

Permission granted for her excursion down to the surface of Oomb, Samantha exited the conference room immediately.

"The chocolate chip cookie; I still need to sample your son's chocolate chip cookie! Perhaps I will run a spectrographic analysis on it!" Dr. Wang called after her.

Samantha couldn't bring herself to admit that the whereabouts of her vanished relatives didn't simply just occur to her. That rather, the information was provided in a telepath from the Oombian tree creature named Moofoosoola.

Chapter 6

The Sixth Celestial Breath arrived home from its mission out the opposite side of the Cygnitaurus System. It came to hover in a saucer staging area near Tictoctic's lone moon, the same size as Earth's moon.

Captain and company found a flurry of activity. The Fourth Celestial Breath was firing targeted magnetic pulse-beams at mock cities scattered across the lunar surface. Scout saucers were emerging from the newly launched Eighth Celestial Breath, christened only two days earlier with an aged bottle full of Dek-Fook-Tek's urine. They would be deploying troops, as well as recovering other troops who had completed their ground exercises.

Ground exercises involved trot-marching from crater to crater. Along the way, troops used dart-firing replicas of their air igniters to take aim at tin-façade likenesses of other-world soldiers. As they sprang into view, those likenesses could have been metal oskynt in a Tictoctickian shooting gallery.

Commander Kwit-Nik didn't know how much longer he could keep Supreme Authority Dek-Fook-Tek satisfied with videos of these repeatedly performed military exercises. Sooner or later, the Supreme Authority would certainly insist he set an actual invasion in motion. But Kwit-Nik was stalling for time. He was holding out for information that might nudge the saucer captains placed under his command towards a significantly different course of action.

Commander Kwit-Nik was convinced his species could reap the additional food they needed without waging interstellar war. Moreover, he feared the consequences of such a war. It might not go as well as the interplanetary war the Tictoctickians had already successfully prosecuted against Chonora.

"I beg your pardon again, Commander Kwit-Nik, for my stubbornness requesting this expenditure of your valuable time. And insisting you have no more than one other officer present. I might as well be an oskynt pressing his sexual urges on a calf hardly yet able to stand, let alone mate." Captain Kek-stek rose onto his hind hooves to swell out his chest, offering it for goring if the commander was not satisfied.

Commander Kwit-Nik sat most comfortably in his armchair, complete with a perforation in the rear for his tail to poke through. He nodded serene acknowledgement of the captain's properly ritual obeisance that made reference to the oskynt.

There was something the commander dared not admit to anyone other than his very closest confidante, Chef Glork-tek. He actually preferred one-on-one audiences such as he was about to have with Captain Kek-stek. They usually transpired devoid of endless, fawning litanies in praise of Dek-Fook-Tek. And Kwit-Nik more and more considered Dek-Fook-Tek a dangerously imbalanced, mentally deranged individual.

Kwit-Nik wished history could be rewritten. That Dek-Fook-Tek had not successfully hijacked a Chonoran spacecraft. He never would have been able to take ultimate charge of the Tictoctickian Empire, otherwise.

Subsequent to Dek-Fook-Tek assuming the role of Supreme Authority, Commander Kwit-Nik found him an ever-growing threat to Tictoctic's future. What made matters exponentially worse was Dek-Fook-Tek's willingness to pretend, and delusionally believe what he pretended, about the origins of the Tictoctickian Empire's space-age technology. Such willingness only further cemented his hold on power, because it appealed to the vain ignorance of many Tictoctickians.

Commander Kwit-Nik hoped against hope that Captain Kek-stek brought the information he was holding out for, conducive to a dramatic change of plans. Why else would Kek-stek have practically insisted on a private audience?

So it was with good reason that Commander Kwit-Nik responded gently to Captain Kek-stek's self-effacing introduction. He said, "I hope you don't mind my first lieutenant, Lieutenant Ak-keek-teek, being that one other officer present."

"Mind? Commander, how could I mind the presence of Lieutenant Ak-keek-teek? Especially after the heroic role he played in the defensive subjugation of the Chonoran Kingdom? Far better I should ask whether he will mind *my* presence." Captain Kek-stek made a point of humbly bleating his response, rather than meeting Kwit-Nik's tongue-clicks with tongue-clicks of his own.

First Lieutenant Ak-keek-teek reacted to the captain's words with a dawning smile that slowly revealed two, oversized buck teeth. They were oddly complemented by the lieutenant's bulging eyes.

Kek-stek felt most uncomfortable. Just what exactly was going through Ak-kek-teek's head...and how much should Commander Kwit-Nik trust him? Although, of course, there was the additional issue of how much Commander Kwit-Nik ought to trust Kek-stek himself. Kek-stek worried over that young stag's naiveté where the larger universe was concerned. Regarding what one should expect on journeys to the stars, wasn't the experience with Chonora like the warning bellow from an oskynt about to charge?

"Stampede through with your report, Captain Kek-stek." Commander Kwit-Nik gestured with both articulated cloven hoof-hands. "Your transmission prior to your arrival noted an incident on the Chonoran side of the solar system."

"A most significant incident, Commander." Captain Kek-stek dropped down on all fours. Special magnetic hoof-socks kept him from floating ceiling-ward in the near-zero gravity. But they didn't keep him from pawing nervously at the floor. He knew Commander Kwit-Nik to be the fairest, most reasonable officer in the entire Tictoctickian Empire. It remained to be sniffed, though, how the commander would react to his most extraordinary account. "We ran across an other-world starship," Captain Kek-stek continued. "It might have been the same starship whose occupants reclaimed the plant people planet from our defensive occupation. Incidentally, didn't that happen in the solar system where Captain Mat-kek-tek totally disgraced himself? Where he got tricked off the Third Celestial Breath, leading to his traitorous desertion and dereliction of duty?"

"I was tricked off as well, don't forget," nodded Commander Kwit-Nik. "But go on, Captain Kek-stek. You ran across the other-world starship, and then?"

"The starship was spotted on a trajectory bound for Chonora. As per your orders, rather than attack with a targeted magnetic pulse-beam, we rippled out the diffuse beam. Plus, we transmitted universal pictographs calling for the other-worlders' peaceful surrender. Those pictographs included assurances none of them would be skinned and dressed for a culinary preparation."

"And that succeeded? You secured the other-worlders in captivity aboard the Sixth Celestial Breath?"

Kwit-nik leaned forward with intense interest. His ears fluttered accordingly.

"There was no surrender, Commander. But I think you are correct; they must have disarmed before they ever left the plant people's solar system. In response to our diffuse pulse-beam, they made no effort to fire back. But what did happen was another, most unusual matter I will detail, begging the continuation of your supremely inspired patience."

"Proceed with every last detail you deem necessary, Captain."

"Thank you, Commander. Since the other-worlders did not surrender, my contingency was to attempt a targeted magnetic pulse-beam. I focused on the other-world starship's rear propulsion unit. As you already know, this particular group of other-worlders has developed a cylindrically-shaped vehicle, rather than their own version of the flying saucer. But it still appears to rely on photon-induced acceleration."

"Of course. Please trot on." Kwit-Nik swayed his stubby antlers into an expression of his growing impatience. *Thank the gentle rains Kek-stek isn't drawing out his narrative even longer by ritual praise of Dek-Fook-Tek! For example, on how our Supreme Authority would have proven beyond persuasive for those other-worlders. On how they would have fought amongst themselves over who got to lie down in his plate first. Who got to lie down, that is, to await being carved up for dinner!*

"Whatever its means of propulsion, Commander Kwit-Nik, we couldn't get a lock on the other-world target due to bizarre interference. We are uncertain whether that interference was generated by the other-world starship, or constitutes an entirely unforeseen phenomenon."

First Lieutenant Ak-keek-teek came down on all fours to stamp a cloven hoof-hand on the floor with disapproval. "Commander Kwit-Nik will judge whether the phenomenon was entirely unforeseen! Assuming it was not a new weapon deployed by the hostiles!" he harshly brayed. Ak-keek-teek was about to go on with ritual "if only" praise for Dek-Fook-Tek. But he stifled himself.

"Here is the flash drive containing the video we filmed of the interference." Captain Kek-stek handed it over.

The three Tictoctickian deer creatures watched the video on the right half of the conference room panoramic view-screen. On the left half, Commander Kwit-Nik continued monitoring various military maneuvers round about Tictoctic's lone moon.

Captain Kek-stek narrated. "You can see the interference appearing to consume the other-world vessel. Now here's the part where the interference turns towards us, and spews what look like flames. We had no other safe recourse than to put more distance between ourselves and where we last spotted the other-world vessel. And then there! Look there! The interference appears caught in a whirlpool down some invisible drain!"

Commander Kwit-Nik intuited that his buck-tooth-grinning first lieutenant wanted him to make ritual noises about Dek-Fook-Tek. *Given half a chance, Dek-Fook-Tek would have tongue-clicked decisively what the interference was! His unexcelled, un-excellable powers of observation would also have resulted in quick determination of the other-world spacecraft's fate! If only he wasn't so preoccupied with more pressing matters!*

Kwit-Nik ignored what he felt Lieutenant Ak-keek-teek wanting him to say. Instead he tongue-clicked, albeit tentatively, "I assume both of you join me in being antler-impaled by the incredible likeness of the interference to a monster. Only, it's a monster of little more substance than sparkles that outline its form, and seeming flames that issue from its 'mouth'!"

"Most esteemed Commander Kwit-Nik," said Lieutenant Ak-keek-teek, rearing back up onto his hind hooves. "Couldn't that 'monster' be a special weapon deployed by the other-world marauders? Designed to terrorize more than to actually destroy?" The lieutenant thrust his chest vulnerably forward on his humble baaing of the "most esteemed" part, before he launched into his warning speculation.

"If I might interject, Commander," Captain Kek-stek ventured to crisply tongue-click. "There is a piece of information I have not shared with another person, until now. I believe it bears strongly on the question at cloven hoof, and is the main reason I requested this private audience with you. Honestly, I wasn't sure with whom else it ought to be trusted. Except the first lieutenant, of course," Kek-stek awkwardly bleated in afterthought; he noticed Lieutenant Ak-keek-teek's frown casting a shadow across his buck-tooth visage. Anyway, with Kwit-Nik's nodded assent, he continued, "The space monster, or whatever it was, seemed to enshroud the other-world vessel. Like I already said. This happened even as we continued with our diffuse magnetic pulse-beam ripples. We were still hoping to secure the other-world vessel's surrender. But we received nothing more than silence, where audible or visual transmissions were concerned. Not so in my particular case, however. A voice entered my head."

"A voice," First Lieutenant Ak-keek-teek repeated dubiously.

"Ba!" Commander Kwit-Nik baaed curtly for the lieutenant to keep quiet.

"The voice claimed to be telepathed by a tree-creature other-worlder. If truthful, she boarded the other-world vessel during its orbit around her planet," explained Kek-stek. "She proceeded with an additional claim. She said that she and her partner encouraged the successful disruption of our defensive occupation of their planet. Then she pleaded I acknowledge something from the more recent past. Namely, that the other-world space vessel did not retaliate or otherwise defend against our diffuse pulse-beam assault. She wanted me to reflect on this fact in the context of what she mind-read I already know from you, Commander. Please correct me if I'm wrong, Commander. Didn't you report that the other-world vessel discarded and then harmlessly detonated in deep space every weapon it was carrying?"

"I did," Commander Kwit-Nik admitted.

"Okay, well the next part seems to follow logically from the rest. The tree creature claims the other-worlders have come in peace. That they are here to investigate our circumstances and subsequently offer us alternatives for augmenting our food supplies. Purportedly, those alternatives would not involve the mass slaughter of other-world intelligent species."

"Commander Kwit-Nik!" Lieutenant Ak-keek-teek brayed intensely. The commander found Ak-keek-teek's tone insultingly suggestive that he was endeavoring to wake him from a trance state. But he didn't stop him from going on, "How do we know this isn't a clever trap? Do you recall the so-called 'peace initiative' from Chonora?"

"I recall the Chonoran emperor communicating that the Chonorans wanted to halt their offensive under certain preconditions," stiffly answered Kwit-Nik. "I do not recall, Lieutenant Ak-keek-teek, their demonstration of any unilateral disarmament whatsoever. That is in sharp contrast with what these other-worlders clearly executed prior to their own entrance of our solar system. And this flaming space beast, Captain Kek-stek: Let us assume the worst. Let us assume the other-worlders constructed it, rather than it being some unknown life form or natural phenomenon mimicking a life form. You suggested that on its approach towards the Sixth Celestial Breath, the whatever-it-is spewed flames like a volcano-sized blowtorch. But did even the slightest damage result?"

"Not that our maintenance crew has been able to detect, Commander. If I might finish, there was one other part to the intelligent tree creature's telepath. It is perhaps the most significant part of her entire communication."

"Oh?"

Both Commander Kwit-Nik and Lieutenant Ak-keek-teek's fur-lined ears shot straight up like attentive rabbit ears, rid of the slightest flutter.

"A portion of what the alleged tree creature telepathed, we already knew," said Captain Kek-stek. "Several of our Tictoctickian troopers were captured when the other-worlders from Akt intervened. That is, when those Akt beasts reclaimed the tree creatures' planet from us, on the tree creatures' behalf. What head-charges into my brain as especially significant, though, is what the telepather purported about two of our troopers. She purported they volunteered to board the cylindrically-designed starship of the other-world species from Akt. In other words, two of our own kind offered to aid and abet the other-worlders' proposed peace mission. The telepather further claimed that the offer by these Tictoctickians was accepted. Moreover, that they have been closely monitored to assure none of them, alone or as a group, attempts hijacking the Akt vessel like the other-worlders hijacked one of our saucers. But the telepather claimed they have been quite enjoying themselves. They have been playing the other-worlders' game called 'koof' on a virtual reality simulator. And they have been listening to music brought from the Akt planet, including dance instruction. Most astoundingly, I was also telepathically led to believe our two fellow deer creatures are eating food produced exclusively from plants!

"The telepather insisted our troopers will be released back to us, unconditionally. Again, if she is to be trusted, this will happen upon the Akt creatures' formal arrival at Tictoctic pursuant to their investigations, whatever that means."

Commander Kwit-Nik couldn't help flashing a happy face grin when Kek-stek mis-tongue-clicked 'oof' as 'koof' due to the pronunciation limitations. But it wasn't Kek-stek's mispronunciation that caused Kwit-Nik to let down his guard. Rather, it was the mere mention of that tantalizing game in the context of fellow deer creatures' enjoyment.

Commander Kwit-Nik's reaction was not lost on the first lieutenant. He noted it with a that-confirms-my-suspicions nod.

But the commander was quick to put his guard back up. With a show of clenched teeth, he sharply tongue-clicked, "You did say, Captain Kek-stek, the other-world starship was nowhere to be seen after the flame-spewing phenomenon seemed to consume it. And that the phenomenon appeared to be sucked down some invisible drain. Did you not?"

"That is what appeared to have happened, Commander."

"Well, then, I will make an educated conjecture."

You will make such a conjecture since our great Dek-Fook-Tek is not here to conjecture for us. Whose own conjecture, incidentally, I am certain would have shown up your conjecture for the idiocy it really is, Commander Kwit-Nik. By comparison, Dek-Fook-Tek's conjecture would have made your conjecture seem the mad ravings of a hunger-crazed idiot. I am thinking of a hunger-crazed idiot whose braincase spilled out when his antlers were uprooted in the course of a mating battle. During these bitter thoughts, First Lieutenant Ak-keek-teek kept his bulging-eye, buck-toothed grin plastered like a mask over his visage.

"Lieutenant, Captain," Commander Kwit-Nik continued, "you both recall, I am sure, what happened to the other-world specimens we secured from the planet of the telepathing trees. They abruptly vanished without a trace from the Third Celestial Breath's kitchen. A digital countdown device materialized in their place. Rumination upon these facts has brought me to the only possible conclusions. The other-worlders were set on rescuing their own kind from our dinner troughs. And they must have found a way to travel back through time in order to accomplish this deed. Either that or they must have developed a suspended animation machine. Whereby they froze us long enough to gallop in and retrieve their fellow creatures. Whichever, they left us totally unaware of what happened as it was happening."

"A suspended animation machine should be more properly brayed one of the most dangerous weapons of all!" The first lieutenant did not even deign to beg permission to tongue-click before he launched into his declaration. "If this is the reality, then the sooner we round up those other-worlders and place them within an electrified pen, the better! On the fast track for the slaughter house! That is what we must do before it is too late! Otherwise, they could use such a weapon to leave every last one of us waking up chained to a treadmill, and headed for our own slaughter!"

"Only, why didn't they already do that when they had the chance, Lieutenant Ak-keek-teek?" Commander Kwit-Nik made quick to rebut. "I am far from convinced they would have used a suspended animation device to imprison us, let alone prepare us for slaughter. Even if they somehow managed to drag such a device into existence, which is an 'if' the size, okay nearly the size of Dek-Fook-Tek's antlers." Commander Kwit-Nik was anxious to preclude Lieutenant Ak-keek-teek throwing a brown-nosing fit. The commander could imagine the lieutenant going on about how nothing, especially an "if," could be the size of Dek-Fook-Tek's antlers. Anyway, Kwit-Nik went on, "I believe time travel facilitated the other-worlders' nasty mischief aboard the Third Celestial Breath.

"Captain Kek-stek," Commander Kwit-Nik turned Kek-stek's way. "When the other-worlders' starship appeared to vanish, I am guessing they resorted to time travel anew. On this occasion, though, maybe they are taking a look into our past. Maybe they are curious to see how we got where we are presently, on the threshold of interstellar conquest.

"Based on this reasonable assumption, Captain, I order your immediate return to the scene of the other-world starship's disappearance. You will wait there for its reappearance. That is, until it becomes obvious they are never coming back, or your help is more urgently required elsewhere. Who knows? Maybe we will awaken to a memory of having already dealt decisively with the other-worlders, and further regurgitation will no longer be required."

"But when and if the other-worlder starship *does* reappear, Commander?"

"Captain Kekstek, you will communicate our interest in delivering them to our leadership for consideration of their supposed peace initiative. And you will accomplish that feat via a universal pictograph all ready to gallop!"

"And if they refuse, Commander?" interjected Ak-keek-teek.

"Then I would say that confirms your worst suspicions, Lieutenant. In such an eventuality, Captain Kek-stek, do not hesitate. Pulse-beam-disintegrate the other-world vessel in such manner as will produce the maximum possible number of flash-frozen bodies. If the other-worlders are up to no good, at least they will provide temporary additional replenishment of our food supply."

"Excellent, Commander," Lieutenant Ak-keek-teek nodded approvingly, for once. "But should you not share your ruminations on this situation with Dek-Fook-Tek? To nibble on what of supreme value he would most certainly add?" The lieutenant wished he could keep his nostrils from wrinkling so actively with his agitation while he tongue-clicked. Someone might as well have set before him a most fragrant bouquet clipped from one of the last remaining tek-tak-te-tum bushes on Tictoctic.

Captain Kek-stek looked anxiously from the lieutenant to Commander Kwit-Nik, wondering how the commander would respond. But he didn't have to wait for more than a small fraction of a mini-pektel.

"The Supreme Authority, Dek-Fook-Tek, selected *me* to become the commander of the interstellar defensive occupation forces!" brashly declared Kwit-Nik in brisk, staccato tongue-clicks. He had long since anticipated Lieutenant Ak-keek-teek's implicit challenge to his authority, and he was more than ready for it. "When Dek-

Fook-Tek made my selection to become commander, he gave me a specific order. I am to seek his advice only when I feel his wellspring of inspiration from previous advice has dried to a trickle. Lieutenant Ak-keek-teek, surely you above others must understand that Dek-Fook-Tek's wellspring of inspiration flows as if never-ending. And I am doubly certain you above *all* others would not want to suggest that his inspiration would ever, ever narrow to a trickle so quickly. You wouldn't have wanted to do that even in what would have amounted to a most demented jest, would you?"

"No, Commander, I most certainly would not." The lieutenant shook his head with his two buck teeth enhancing his shame-faced expression. But it was only another mask. He actually thought to himself, *Kwit-Nik has become an expert at giving ornately clever excuses for herding Dek-Fook-Tek away from awareness of his actions. It can only be a matter of time before he out-and-out leads an insurrection. On the verge of that insurrection is when I will alert our Supreme Authority, with enough damning evidence to get Kwit-Nik barbecued. And I should prefer that barbecue to happen slowly. I should prefer to see Kwit-Nik mounted still alive on a most sluggishly turning spit. Let him experience every last painfully burning sensation, every last moment of horror, on his journey to death. This, for his willfully refusing to understand that what we confront with the other-worlders is pure evil! Thankfully, I intercepted the transmission from Captain Gekalek detailing the planet-wide destruction those demonic other-worlders wrought in the Pek-tek-tek-mek solar system. How especially horrific, so much wasted meat charred to dust, plus the destruction of the Third Celestial Breath! Doubtless, Kwit-Nik would have concocted some ridiculous scenario to explain that* tragedy. Or he would have asked, "How can we be sure it was not some apocalyptic accident, intended by no-one?" NO!! Everyone needs to know the evil nature of the planet's destruction!

And what does- I cannot even bring myself to actually think of him with the word, "commander," attached to his name! I have seen him when he doubtless assumed no one was watching, pretending he was swinging a "koof" club! His body ought to be impaled on a "koof" club, for that slow turning over the barbecue spit!

But at least one thing I understand now. My memory of it has always been there, although it somehow feels newly implanted: During our triumphant defensive retaliation against Chonora, there was an inexplicable flash of a light-stream through space. It happened not more than a hundred lek-leks above the firmament of the Chonoran atmosphere. That had to have been from the other-world starship time-traveling in search of who-knows-what further atrocities they intended to perpetrate!

Chapter 7

"What do you think, Buddy? This isn't Fafama destroyed all over again, is it?"

"We will know more once we get closer, Captain. But at least from out here, I'm not seeing nearly the extent of black cloud cover as enshrouded Fafama."

"That's my impression as well, Captain," chimed in Officer Kevin Smith-Park. "There are sharply defined polar ice caps, so we also know this planet is revolving on a fixed axis. And, aren't those blue glimmers?"

"I'm seeing them," confirmed the chief navigation officer, Kevin's wife Yoon-hee Park-Smith.

"Wish it was my imagination, but aren't many of those glimmers tinged with gray?" said Captain Helena Taylor.

"Oh-oh, I'm seeing that too," said Yoon-hee.

These starship officers and others were variously standing and sitting on the navigation bridge of the Smoke and Mirrors. They pondered the panoramic view-screen while their spacecraft decelerated below one-tenth light-speed. Filling increasingly more of that screen was Tictoctic's twin planet, frozen like a holographic image several years into the past. The quantum wave of time's arrow would take a little while longer, yet, to backtrack to where the starship was intruding on "completed" space-time.

"Captain, I've just noticed something," First Officer Buddy Leung started with mild alarm in his voice. "Our reliance on our onboard laser for light acceleration hasn't helped quite as much as expected. We're closing in on the twin planet at a bit slower pace than originally calculated. That means we'll have an hour, tops, to assess the situation here before the quantum wave crashes our time travel party."

"Hopefully that will be long enough, Buddy. Kevin, let's try maximum magniview."

"Better than that, Captain; I rerouted our hull-monitoring firefly donut. It's already relaying from a one-thousand-mile altitude. Full screen...now!"

"Truly awful," ship's counselor Ali Magabu couldn't help remarking, although he tried to keep it under his breath. Only his wife, Tanya, seated beside him overheard.

Kevin, on the other hand, didn't care if someone walking down the hall outside the navigation bridge could overhear *him*. He just blurted out, "Too bad Sergeants Frankly and Hanson are busy with family, helping to keep the children entertained! I'd like their take on this! I'm guessing even Guy would have said we've just learned everything we need to know! For certain, he'd do a one-eighty on the pacifist approach! He'd recommend we get the hell outta here, ASAP, to re-arm, prepare for all-out war with Tictoctic! Sorry, Oodle-Noodle!"

Prompting these first reactions was the closer look at Tictoctic's twin planet facilitated by the repositioned firefly donut.

What the Earthlings plus two Oombian tree creatures beheld proved impossible to take in as a collective whole. They had to shift their gaze from part to part of the extraterrestrial vista. Yet everywhere they turned, grim variations on the theme of horrific devastation presented themselves.

There was the bluish, targeted magnetic pulse-beam, photographically frozen in its issuing from what had to be a Tictoctickian saucer. That beam ended in an explosive obliteration, also photographically frozen in a moment of "completed" space-time. The obliteration consumed three especially tall skyscrapers erected side by side.

On streets beside the buildings being destroyed, thousands of extraterrestrials were caught in still-life poses. Most curiously, they were hanging upside down from a complex of ropes comparable to an enormous spider web. The streets themselves could have been muddy throwbacks to unpaved roads of the eighteen hundreds, especially after a heavy rain. Such close-up details were revealed in a magnification of the magnification posted at one corner of the view-screen.

Again, citizenry fleeing the attack from outer space ornamented the rope complex. That was bizarre enough. But even more bizarre was the coliseum-sized net ensnaring said complex. One side of that net was attached to invisibly thin cables extending hundreds of miles back up out of the planet's atmosphere. Those cables led to a saucer about one-third the size of the mother saucer responsible for the pulse-beam attack on the trio of skyscrapers. Meanwhile, the other side of the net was pulled by small rockets. Those rockets had already dragged the net underneath the pedestrian rope complex, from one side of that complex to the other. Presently, they were frozen in a sharp ascent for returning to the saucer from where the net had been cast out in the first place. In other words, the rockets had made considerable progress towards dragging in the net. That is, considerable progress before the moment in completed space-time when the Smoke and Mirrors arrived.

Another terrible tableau was playing out at the boundary between upper atmosphere and space. That tableau displayed the awful fate awaiting the creatures ensnared closer to the planet's surface. Featured was a second cast-out net, already drawn halfway back. The second net originated from a different saucer than the first one. Clearly caught up in it were untold thousands of the planet's sentient beings. Strands of another pedestrian rope complex hung out from it like seaweed from a trawling net, as Buddy would have said.

Heaven help us all, Captain Taylor couldn't help thinking. *They are trawling people how we trawl seafood! And those people are becoming flash-frozen during the hauling-in process, thanks to the extreme cold of outer space!*

There was more. From several different locations, flames fed smoke into the upper atmosphere. That smoke joined together in places to conceal a good third of the planet in grayish cloud cover. Some of the flames were rising from enormous mushroom clouds, signatures of set-off thermonuclear devices.

"Captain, you noticed those contrails tipped by slender objects?" Buddy Leung broke the horror-induced silence to say. "Spectroscopic analysis confirms they are from intercontinental ballistic missile launches. In an act of desperation, presumably, those launches were reprogrammed heavenwards. The beings who were responsible must have hoped at least some of the missiles would strike the attacking saucers from Tictoctic."

"But the missiles are running out of fuel before they can get anywhere near..."

"As if those bloodthirsty stag monsters couldn't outmaneuver them, even if they *did* get anywhere near," Kevin vented.

"Yes, and- You see that one missile contrail in an arc? Am I correct?" the captain asked, hoping against all realistic hope she was not correct. "Some of the missiles didn't achieve full escape velocity? And now they are falling back into the atmosphere?"

"Those mushroom clouds," Buddy nodded grimly. "They must be self-inflicted wounds."

"So it is absolutely too dangerous down there," Helena shook her head and sighed. "We can't conduct our data-gathering on that planet at this time. We're going to have to travel further back."

"Further back, Captain?" Kevin couldn't help a pleading tone leaking into his voice as in, *Please, not that!*

"Shouldn't prove very difficult, Captain." Buddy strained to keep the excitement, the enthusiasm, out of his voice. He relished the prospect of ground-breaking time travel from an already time-travelled position. Time travel on top of time travel! But he knew he was unsuccessful in adequately stifling himself. He didn't require the additional evidence from Kevin rolling his eyes. Nevertheless, he went on, "I've developed a firefly donut anchor which would allow us to take up to a year on our return, um... Although of course I'm assuming we will require far less time than that."

It was becoming one of those rare instances for Kevin, when he wished Louisa Entroper was still aboard to provide backup for a protest. Or at least that Sergeant Frankly would come stomping in, enough already with entertaining the kiddies. Maybe even newlywed Hanson could have assisted. That is, had he gotten a good look at the epic vista full of unfathomable devastation frozen into the past-time diorama.

Kevin Smith-Park could definitely count on Dr. Deborah Davis-Murphy to chime in. But Deb was always chiming in when it came to second-guessing the captain's judgment. Her two cents were usually discounted on that basis. Moreover, Kevin knew it was only a matter of minutes, if that, before one or both Oombian tree creatures weighed in. All too soon, they would once again be filling their heads with that seductive peace-and-love opiate. And yet despite these inevitabilities, Kevin proceeded. "Captain," he said, caution in his voice. "I'm not sure how anyone else feels..." Kevin paused to send a look Yoon-hee's way. "But I know what I'm feeling from our widescreen snapshot, and it isn't good. Antlers or no antlers, the ETs from Tictoctic are a bunch of sick, heartless, deranged, psychopathic demons. That might be a redundant way of putting it, but the rot-gut shit we have freeze-framed them in the act of committing is also redundant. It's epic-scale atrocity!"

Kevin took heart from Yoon-hee, Ali, Tanya, and even Captain Taylor herself nodding agreeably. Add the expected buy-in from Dr. Deborah Davis-Murphy... "Captain," he went on, "I honestly, honestly don't understand what else of serious consequence to our mission you expect to learn. A trip down to the surface of that planet a year or two prior to now will accomplish what, exactly? Is the plan to alert the natives, help them thwart the coming invasion? Although I'm not convinced even heaven would know how. I would strongly, strongly advise we return to our present, pronto. We should make a beeline back for Oomb, eat all kinds of humble pie, then weapon-up to enjoin the battle!"

"Kevin, I'm not sure I don't agree with you. Seriously," Helena Taylor said in her most pleading tone.

"But...Sorry, Captain, after everything else..."

"Don't apologize." Helena waved off Kevin's self-admonishment. "You're correct; there is a 'but.' I am still troubled by that saucer we found blown apart by another saucer once we traversed the time rift. Those clothed corpses floating about there, with the little tentacles lining their mouths? We did comfortably conclude, didn't we, that the destroyed saucer was being flown by them? In other words, it was being flown by a different set of extraterrestrials, not the deer creatures of Tictoctic, yes? Well, we see corpses of the same species floating about here. I am assuming they issued from a blown-apart space station."

"Correct, Captain," added Buddy Leung at work on the navigation deck's info-gathering console. "We're picking up a clear time-rift signature in the vicinity of a debris field it makes most sense consists of space station remnants."

"Together with the bodies netted off the terrestrial surface, I think we have confirmation. The tentacle-mouthed ETs originate from this planet."

"Captain!" Buddy snapped his fingers. "Captain, I just realized something! Don't recall having thought enough of it at the time to include in my debriefing report. It's about the Tictoctic saucer we hijacked. When I first boarded it to rescue Pedro and the Marines, I noticed these ridges, concave surfaces and the like molded into the ceiling. They were everywhere! They didn't look to serve any conceivable, useful purpose, unless aesthetic. So, consider once more what we see covering an entire city block in the magniview of this planet's surface. There are crisscrossing lines, like antique clothes lines. The city residents are hanging from them, rather than traversing sidewalks underneath. And underneath looks like mud and dirt anyway, rather than stone and cement."

"Okay, Officer Leung," impatiently broke in Chief Medical Officer Dr. Davis-Murphy. "So that's additional proof, maybe, the extraterrestrials here were the original owners of the saucers. They hung upside down to fly them, perhaps. When the Tictoctickians stole them, the Tictoctickians retrofitted them for their own, right-side-up ends. In other words, the barbarians co-opted the technology to turn against their creators. Do we need to learn any more than that? Look at...God, there must be thousands of ETs caught up in that one net alone! Maybe what we should be doing is figuring out how to use our time travel to help these helpless beings. Maybe at the same time we can deprive the Tictoctickians of the saucers they are obviously set on using for their interplanetary conquest!"

Kevin piled on. "We start with those nukes that are falling back into the atmosphere! We seize their Styrofoam-light past-time existences. Then we Velcro them to the saucers conducting the trawl-net fishing operations and magnetic-pulse-beam skyscraper destruction! And we cut free those nets! Or maybe we can go back earlier than this! Maybe we'll be able to liberate the presently already-netted fishies before they are hauled up anywhere near becoming flash-frozen!"

Helena concluded her helpless-seeming, concessionary nod with, "I at least want to give Oodle-Noodle, or Wafoodle-boodle, a chance to respond."

Both tree creatures were nonverbally expressing profound sadness, despite their lack of mouths for exhibiting frowns. Deep sorrow showed clearly enough in their vertically set eyes.

Oodle-Noodle did the honors of sharing what both she and her mate Wafoodle-boodle were thinking, and thinking mournfully. They feared where the Earthlings' reasoning was headed. Oodle-Noodle telepathed, *I would agree the evidence argues most strongly for the creatures from Tictoctic having taken possession of these* other creatures' technology. However, we still don't know what led to this situation.

Dr. Deborah Davis-Murphy crossed her arms before she interjected. "In other words," she said, "you are seeking some way to excuse the large-scale violence the Tictoctic creatures have plainly committed. And which likely models what they have in mind for us, incidentally."

Chris could feel his fellow humans, his wife Helena included, finding Deb's appraisal especially compelling. Maybe it was as compelling as any diagnosis she might have given as the chief medical officer. But he found himself inhibited from fully accepting her logic. He could tell there was more than just a matter of his being enthralled by the Oombians' extrasensory vibes. Yet he also couldn't bring himself to fully *not* accept the good doctor's logic. He had to hope the continuation of the argument between her and the Oombian would somehow help at last to resolve matters for him.

No. Oodle-Noodle made her few leaves rustle when she twisted her trunk in protest to what Dr. Davis-Murphy said. *Determining why a group of creatures committed awful deeds is one thing. However, excusing those awful deeds because there is a reason why they were committed is an entirely different thing. What I am telepathing is this: We need a fuller understanding of how these two civilizations from two different planets arrived at this nightmare juncture. Otherwise, we could end up compounding the tragedy instead of turning it around. I do not wish to keep using the same example for a bludgeon, as that most violent saying goes. Nevertheless, the reality remains the reality. Your people armed the Fafaman Empire without a full appreciation for either its multiplicity of cultures or the root causes of its terrorism. This led directly to an extinction event perhaps even more* final in its consequences than the extinction event we perceive happening here. I repeat what your great spiritual leader, Dr. Martin Luther King, Jr., once said: "Darkness cannot drive out darkness; only light can do that. Hate cannot drive out hate; only love can do that."

With her lids closed, Captain Helena Taylor made a deep inhale and exhale. Images flashed through her head. There were children playing aboard the Smoke and Mirrors; Guy Hanson and Yulala in loving embrace at their wedding; daughter Shelly's holographic projection groaning over orders to clean her mess; and Chris looking forlorn. And there were flash-frozen extraterrestrial bodies floating through space... "Okay," she said when she reopened her eyes, having to squint for how long she kept them shut. "We're going back."

"Captain?" said Kevin hopefully.

"Sorry, Kevin. I meant further back, to a time on that planet before all hell broke loose. I'm assuming the best rift for our purposes will be where it would appear their space station blew apart. Buddy?"

"Loading in the course coordinates and none too soon, Captain. Look! The quantum wave is catching up!" Buddy pointed at the panoramic view-screen. "I'm going to send us on a slingshot course round the back side of their larger moon! An element of surprise should result when we re-emerge into the Tictoctickians' sight. That should stymie them for too long to get off a shot at us before we enter the rift!"

The one saucer had already shut off the magnetic pulse-beam directed at the three side-by-side skyscrapers. The saucer's Tictoctickian crew was focusing their attention on the Smoke and Mirrors. For them, the S and M was a most peculiar-looking spacecraft that seemed to have materialized out of nothing, from one instant to the next.

Captain Taylor, telepathed Oodle-Noodle. But she was sharing with everyone there assembled on the navigation bridge of the Smoke and Mirrors. *The planetary spirit that followed us through the other space-time rift should provide sufficient cover.*

"And if it hadn't followed us, and these antlered devils were able to get a clear shot at us?" grumbled Kevin, too angry to look Oodle-Noodle's way.

Then perhaps we would have been implementing our surrender plan far earlier than originally anticipated. We would have had less information to work from than we would have desired. All the same, though, Wafoodle-boodle and I would have exerted our mind-reading powers to the utmost, to fill in the gaps.

"Sure," Kevin nodded, still not deigning to look Oodle-Noodle's way. "And what if you two were wrong, about enough politically powerful Tictoctickians being accessible to reason? That would have been it! Our kiddies on board would have been transformed into the human version of veal cutlets! That is, unless those demon deer wanted to save them for breeding purposes! Oh, I know! I know! At least we would still have had a clean conscience while we were being sliced and diced!"

Yes, that, Oodle-Noodle actually nodded. *Too many within your civilization are willing to risk for war what they are unwilling to risk for peace. There were certain nuclear scientists of the nineteen forties on your timeline. They were placing bets on whether an above-ground nuclear test explosion would ignite the atmosphere.*

FWWWOOOM!!!!

"Okay, everyone, we need to focus!" shouted Captain Taylor. "We just got hit with a diffuse magnetic pulse-beam!"

"What the fried fish is happening up there?!" Sergeant Fred Frankly's crusty voice suddenly broke like so much static from the ship's intercom. "You're giving the pint-sized gals and guys a scare!"

"Strap them down, Sergeant! I should have addressed this earlier!"

FWWWOOOM!!!!

"Good news, Captain! The planet spirit, whatever it is, it is enrobing the Smoke and Mirrors! Between that and our speed, their saucer can't get off a good shot at us!" reported Yoon-hee in a panic-driven shout. "But the bad news is that their diffuse pulse-beam is keeping us all shook up!"

"Which is keeping us from the level of precision we require to make it through the rift!" shouted Helena in return. But she well knew she was belaboring the obvious.

FWWWOOOM!!!!

"Back behind the moon, Buddy!" Helena shouted anew. "We have to get out of their reach before they decide to take their chances with targeted magnetic pulse-beams! To try and hit the jackpot!"

"Done, Captain! We're on course!"

I have an idea, Kevin wanted to say. *With one of our laser cannons, we can zero in on where their pulse-beam is issuing from. That should take it out of commission long enough at least for us to successfully navigate the space-time rift. Oh, wait, I almost forgot. We jettisoned our laser cannon assemblies! We are totally disarmed! In psycho-reaction to the catastrophe on Fafama! And encouraged in that regard by our two absurdly naïve extraterrestrial guests from Oomb!*

"Captain, I have an idea!" Kevin's wife Yoon-hee mustered the courage to shout herself. But her idea was unlike Kevin's bitter concoction of regret over what a previous decision made impossible. Yoon-hee's idea was something they could actually attempt. From what Wafoodle-boodle mind-read, that made all the difference where speaking up was concerned.

"I've got nothing, Yoon-hee, except surrender!" Captain Taylor shouted anew. "So let's hear it!"

"Captain, why don't we keep circling the moon faster and faster, then unexpectedly break out on a course heading for the rift?! Maybe the Fafama dragon planet ghost will join the chase after us, and further confuse matters for the Tictoctickians! If so, we might be through the rift before anyone can stop us!"

"Oodle-Noodle, could you telepath the ghost dragon to keep circling the moon after we break lunar orbit?" said Buddy Leung, enthusiastically building on Yoon-hee's idea.

We have never before tried persuading a phantom! But also, of course, Wafoodle-boodle and I will both give it our very best effort! Oodle-Noodle telepathically responded, again for everyone present to mind-read.

"Go ahead, Yoon-hee!" said Helena Taylor, equal parts resigned to their fate, and hoping against hope.

"Captain, I've already loaded the program on a random trigger! Even I don't know when we will actually break orbit!"

One of the saucers trawling up sentient creatures off the planet's surface continued about its grisly work. But whoever was in charge was careful not to cast any nets where the ballistic missiles were falling back down into the atmosphere. Not unexpected, given that exploding nuclear weapons were likely to contaminate the potential food supply with radioactivity.

Meanwhile, the other saucer's captain took Yoon-hee's bait. He forsook additional net-casting to chase the Smoke and Mirrors around the moon, faster and faster. For the crew watching from aboard the saucer still on an epic fishing expedition, both spacecraft were transformed into a blur of motion. It was as if the alien planet's moon had suddenly acquired the rings of Saturn. Those rings were made that much more colorful by an orange swirl from the dragon spirit enjoining the chase. It was striving to keep up with the Smoke and Mirrors, to continue concealing that particular starship from hostile forces.

Everyone aboard the Smoke and Mirrors was already long since securely seat-belted. They anticipated extreme centripetal force when at last the starship did break into a run for the space-time rift of choice.

The plan worked. In fact, the plan worked too well where the planet spirit from Fafama was concerned. That dragon-shaped constellation of sparkles realized too late that its center of attention had broken from lunar orbit. It took almost as long as the crew of the pursuing Tictoctickian saucer. Subsequently, its own break-off from orbit couldn't quite catch up with the starship from Earth. It just missed getting sucked down the space-time-rift drain, as it had gotten itself sucked down before. The planet spirit was left stranded in the future, relative to the starship's new space-time location even further into the past.

Yulala was strapped to a seat beside her newly wedded husband, Guy, in the recreation center. From there, she didn't need the panoramic view-screen to notice the planet spirit's absence. It became evident to her right after head-to-toe tingles from passage through the wound in the space-time fabric. Mass deaths sliced open that wound, of course, when a targeted magnetic pulse-beam blew apart an extraterrestrial space station. Anyway, as a result of the planet spirit's absence, Yulala experienced sudden heart palpitations. They were succeeded by a bottomless, inexpressible yearning that caused her tears to flow freely.

Sergeant Guy Hanson encircled Yulala with his arms, but he still found himself helpless to provide effective consolation. He had no idea what suddenly brought on such extreme upset. At the same time, though, he admonished himself for not having every idea. Didn't his newlywed's sorrow over her home planet's apocalyptic devastation simply catch up with her again? What was so mysterious about that? Nevertheless, and despite how much lamer and more inadequate it made him feel, Guy couldn't help himself. He asked, "What's the matter, my dearest Yulala?"

There was only one thing Yulala could think to do, seemingly in response to her new husband's expressed concern. She unbuckled her seat belt, insisted on Guy unbuckling his as well, and wrapped one arm around his waist. Then she quietly guided him to their bedroom, intent on throwing caution to the wind.

≈ ⋈ ☙ ≈ ⋈ ☙ ≈ ⋈ ☙

"Goodness! All those lights! The night side looks much like the night side of Earth!" Yoon-hee enthused, clapping her hands together with delight. She had already set the Smoke and Mirrors into orbit ten thousand miles above the planet's surface.

Chonora remained photographically still in a past moment of space-time. All too soon, however, the quantum wave would catch up. Once more, time's arrow would deal with yet another detour taken by the Smoke and Mirrors from that arrow's forward advance.

"Approximately 1.0001 mass, it's virtually identical to our Earth's mass," observed Buddy, "more so even than Fafama and Oomb."

"The important thing is this," said Captain Helena Taylor. "We've time-travelled back to what appears to be a relatively tranquil period in this planet's history. But hopefully we've not travelled too far back. We need to learn what went wrong exactly in its civilization's association with Tictoctic civilization."

Kevin wondered whether what went wrong "exactly" really mattered. Who cared "exactly" how the antlered psychopaths stole technology from what did look to be the most Earth-like planet they had voyaged to, yet? Earth-like, that is, apart from their apex intelligent creatures, creatures who bore tentacles around their mouths. And oh, yeah, who went from place to place hanging upside down. Kevin wanted to vent anew, but he settled with observing, "Captain, it has just occurred to me: Back in the present, the present from where we travelled into the past, and now even further into the past..."

"Yes, of course," nodded Captain Taylor.

"It's regarding those Tictoctickians who first tried to disable the Smoke and Mirrors with their flying saucer's pulse-beam. Well, they now have in their memory, in their history, a far earlier encounter with us. Of course I'm talking about our crashing their party while they were treating this planet like their private fishing cove. For all we know, they were the very same Tictoctickians, aboard the very same saucer, who tried to zap us during the wedding reception. That would mean they are most certainly anticipating our return to the present. Sure, that planet spirit who-zy-what-zy might be patiently waiting for us in the time frame where we just left it, like a faithful puppy dog. After we finally reward that patience, it might do us another favor. Upon completion of the second leg of our return to the present, it might try once again to conceal the Smoke and Mirrors. But meanwhile, our interplanetary cattle rustlers might have concocted a scheme to target us, planet spirit be damned."

"Which is why, Officer Smith-Park," Helena Taylor said without hesitation, "should a saucer 'welcome' us back to year 2063, we will surrender immediately. That would be a trivial difference anyway, I would think, from our original surrender plan."

"Captain," interposed Dr. Davis-Murphy, "what if that additional information you are seeking here only confirms what we already suspect? What if the Tictoctic invasion was entirely without reasonable explanation, entirely unprovoked, entirely...evil? What if even our Oombian friends here would need to concede that? What then? Still surrender? Still surrender, but drop the pretext of this being anything other than a suicide mission as seen through rose-tinted lens?"

Captain Helena Taylor didn't want a disagreement, however huge, to devolve into something even worse given their already perilous circumstances. So she self-censored what her emotions would have otherwise driven her to spit out. *Dr., if this is what you have been thinking about our mission all along, can you run through for me again why you agreed to sign back aboard?* Instead of asking such a question, Helena took a few seconds to collect her thoughts. Then she responded, "Let's say we find the situation is as you suggest, Deb. In that case, I *will* want to explore sabotaging the attack we saw happening in this planet's more recent past. But we are not there yet."

"Captain, there's the space station, upper left quadrant," Buddy Leung pointed. "So at least we probably didn't travel too much further back in time, for our purposes."

"Truly fascinating architecture," nodded Ali Magabu.

"But I see no protective shell," observed Ali's wife, shuttle pod pilot Tanya Petrovsky. "They take their chances with random space debris degradations."

"What about that glint near their saucer in space dock?" Kevin pointed. "I'm pretty sure that's a protective 'soap bubble' like we use."

One observation shared by everyone had been experienced regularly on prior past-time excursions. It had been experienced so regularly as to no longer warrant comment. That observation was of a certain ripple effect providing a slight distortion to everything out the view-screen. Chris, Ali and Yoon-hee were struck by how especially appropriate such a ripple effect seemed, where the space station itself was concerned. The station in its entirety looked like something the Earthlings were more used to seeing underwater. The station's modules were interconnected and piled atop one another just so. They could have constituted an immense, free-floating coral formation. They were even molded in various pastel shades. For Chris, the saucer craft in dock might as well have been a monstrous, space-faring sea anemone.

"Okay," said Captain Helena Taylor, to finally break the awestruck silence and bring everyone back to task mode. "We have lots to put into place before the quantum wave catches us again. We need an away team headed up by you, Tanya, of course. And we also need to play hide and seek with the Smoke and Mirrors."

"Dark side of the moon, covered in crater dust?"

"Great minds think alike, Officer Leung."

"I will magniview scan for suitable landing locations on the planet, Captain."

"Another great mind, Tanya. Wafoodle-boodle, I'm supposing you've already read my mind to know I want you as part of the away team."

I will trim back my fronds immediately, Captain.

"Oh? Well, I suppose this confirms you really are striving to give us some measure of mental privacy. I was actually thinking, uh, I hope you don't mind the inconvenience of having to fold down your fronds around you aboard the shuttle pod. It would be better if you allowed your helicopter assembly to continue to grow out. On the off chance it might come in handy for getting the away team out of, um, a situation…"

Understood, Captain.

Through all the ensuing mission prep, Yoon-hee Park-Smith would have stuck a paper bag over her head. That is, if she weren't thereby going to draw even more attention to her than she feared her face and ears already did.

When she came to realize her good fortune, Yoon-hee couldn't believe it. Nobody was going to actually put her on the spot. Nobody was going to ask her to explain how she arrived at the idea for escaping the Tictoctic saucer's attentions in the past. That is, to exit through a space-time rift to even earlier in the past. Over her disbelief, Yoon-hee could feel her face and ears blushing as embarrassedly as though she had not been spared, after all.

What inspired Yoon-hee's solution was an old Bugs Bunny cartoon. In that cartoon, the gun-toting Yosemite Sam chased the "low-down varmint" round and round in a circle. The chase accelerated to such high speed, Bugs Bunny and Yosemite Sam both became a blur of motion. That's when Bugs cut out to watch Yosemite Sam keep running in a circle, virtually after nobody. Bugs also munched casually on a carrot.

Crew on the navigation deck dispersed to prepare for a targeted search of yet another new, unexplored planet. But Buddy Leung remained behind to sneak up behind Yoon-hee and whisper, "Ehhh, what's up, doc?"

Chapter 8

Samantha Santiago-Olsen received a detailed briefing. She was told exactly what to expect when a shuttle pod from the starship Eisenhower brought her down to the surface of Oomb. But her experience proved nonetheless overwhelming.

A flock of trees lifted off the island of Boombeeno all at once, on their helicopter-blade palm fronds. They escorted the shuttle pod's descent to a beach specially cleared for landings and liftoffs by Earthling spacecraft.

In reaction to the spectacle, Samantha's first thoughts concerned her long-deceased mother. *Would Mama have choked on a Life Saver or swallowed it whole, if she had gotten to see flying trees? Or would she have simply passed out, especially once she noticed those trees had eyes set in between their corrugations of bark?*

Samantha was recollecting the fateful trip her parents took to Philadelphia, to visit with relatives. Her brother's silly talk about a *Star Trek* comic book sent their mother ransacking her purse. She searched desperately for her Life Savers, rings of variously colored and flavored hard candy enclosed by a rainbow wrapper. However, the real freak-out had been finding the tenement residence of her Papa's sister mysteriously abandoned. Beans were left simmering fragrantly on a stove top.

This is beyond amazing, Samantha thought with a security-blanket tug on the brim of her Baltimore Orioles baseball cap. She had pointedly exhumed the cap from her storage chest for this part of her starship voyage. *So much of my life has been haunted by that one morning in Philadelphia. And now I might finally learn what happened to my relatives! There's still the matter of fulfilling the instructions from that little old lady who has been quite literally the ghost in my life. But I might have to wait a little while longer. Oh,* Samantha chuckled gently, *I am one to think of anybody else as "that little old lady"!*

Quite possibly, moments of truth were imminent that Samantha had been anticipating for decades. Despite this, she took most curious comfort from the eye-bearing trees helicoptering round the shuttle pod. Somehow, their accompaniment provided nearly the warm fuzzies as her Orioles cap. And that cap fit snuggly enough to have been an old shoe, Samantha mused. *Although I am not in the habit of wearing old shoes on my head,* she once again chuckled gently.

With your interest in baseball, you will want to see what your older relatives are doing, Oombian tree creature Mafoosoola telepathed Samantha, upon officiating her welcome to Oomb.

Incidentally, Samantha received an apology for the Oonzy-Ootzies' collective belch. It was putrid with fish they consumed just before their latest jiggly-bouncy waddle ashore. As always, those fifteen foot tall creatures' days were filled with perpetual emergence from and re-submergence back down into calm surf.

A baseball field was the first destination of Samantha's Oombian reception delegation, as hinted would be the case. They ushered her through a wood-constructed archway with the message carved into it, letters painted lime green,

BIENVENIDOS A OOMBINQUEN (WELCOME TO OOMBINQUEN)

Mafoosoola explained the origin of Oombinquen. Samantha's cousin, Pedro, blended "Oomb" with "Borinquen," what the Taino people called their island home before Spanish invaders renamed it Puerto Rico. Could there be a better honor for Puerto Ricans spirited to

Oomb from two entire city blocks in north Philadelphia, sixty years and many trillions of miles away?

Samantha took a seat on the front bleachers down the first base line. Her Oombian tree creature escorts situated themselves to the side of the bleacher assembly so they wouldn't block people's view. Like all tree creatures on the planet, mobile or otherwise, they favored standing. In fact, they were anatomically incapable of sitting. They worked their roots down comfortably into a specially prepared mud patch, but Samantha Santiago-Olsen didn't notice. Her eyes were drawn right away to her uncle, Don Placido. He was excitedly waggling his bat over the home plate, awaiting the next pitch. No more pale visage, how Samantha had last seen him before he vanished with the rest, sixty years ago. Instead, his sweaty sheen virtually glowed with a swarthy, healthy complexion from ample sun exposure. And he looked like he had lost weight. The overall effect was of his having grown far more youthful. Nevertheless, Sammy still found him instantly recognizable, if only for his big face. It somehow always reminded her of the cowardly lion in the movie, *The Wizard of Oz*.

Crack! Placido connected with the softball. He sent it flying over the second baseman's head...only to be caught by Ludi's grandma, Norma, way out in center field! At first, Norma blinked at the ball nestled snuggly in her glove, unable to believe what happened. But as reality sank in, she looked towards her husband Típico positioned in right field. He was already performing a one-man conga line to celebrate. His wide smile radiated pure joy. Norma's wandering eyes didn't come to rest there, however. On a sudden intuition, they strayed completely off field where they caught Samantha grinning at her, Samantha wearing her Orioles baseball cap. Norma gasped. She flung aside mitt and ball alike, to rush over where the unexpected visitor stood.

"Ay, Samantha, is you?!" Norma said as Placido also rushed over.

Rotonda threw off her umpire's protective gear to join in, and Típico came up behind Norma. He wended his way with merry-making salsa steps.

"Grand tía Norma, how can you possibly recognize me?" said Samantha. "I must look like someone excavated from a tomb!"

"Ay, no! Chica!" Norma shook her head laughing. "I can see you are still that little girl who wore her Baltimore Orioles cap everywhere!"

"I think my cap has aged more gracefully than I have!"

"Ay, no!"

"You noticed my cap?" Placido shoved Norma aside to focus Samantha's attention on the lettering and design woven into his head gear. "We are the Oombinquen Pirates!"

"And we are the Oonzy Ootzy Tostones, who caught his fly ball!" Norma shoved right back, to draw Samantha's attention to the lettering and design on her head gear.

A depiction of an Oombian tree creature sporting an eye patch was stitched into the Pirates cap. A skull and crossbones surmounted the creature's trunk, in place of helicopter fronds.

The Tostones cap featured an anthropomorphized flattened and fried slice of plantain banana emerging from the surf in a bikini. The scantily clad fried plantain slice was wielding a fish similar in appearance to a barracuda, as though that fish were a baseball bat.

"This is so wonderful!" Samantha shook her head in disbelief. "But after all these years…How do you manage, if anything, to look younger than you did six decades ago? What fountain of youth *is* this?!"

"We skipped those intervening years," Norma explained. "Your son and his wife came into our past on their spaceship. They transported us to this future where they provided many opportunities for a healthier, happier life!"

"I almost wish they would go back again, and bring my little girl self here so I could join one of your teams!" Tears welled in Samantha's eyes; the 'almost' part had to do with her late husband. She wouldn't have wanted her life to have passed him by. However, her desperate yearning led her to wonder something. Couldn't her husband's little boy self be brought there as well? Of course that would have meant their starting all over again. Their previous life together would have been forgotten save for perhaps an occasionally haunting déjà vu experience. Plus, there was the no small matter of their son, Chris…

On her ciliated root system, Mafoosoola approached Samantha from behind. She gently massaged Samantha's back with the lumps and bumps of one of her specially gnarled branches. And all that while, she telepathed, *The future is not pre-determined, set in stone…and neither is the past.*

Sammy was reminded of what that mysterious little old lady, little and old like her, mentioned to her those sixty years earlier. It was something about "the Great Healing."

"You *can* join one of our teams! Bendito!" Norma slapped Samantha's arm to protest her cheerless remark about wishing herself as a little girl had also been transported to the future. But she slapped her husband, Típico, on the arm admonishingly harder. And not because he added, "You can join our team!" Rather, because he succeeded his invite with lecherous eyebrow raises. "We will prepare you with several yoga exercises," Norma went on while Típico walked off, favoring his slapped arm and muttering, "Ay, caramba!"

I'm a big fan of downward-facing log, and tree pose, spoofed Mafoosoola.

Crack! Oondroomooda connected with the new softball pitch the same way many other of her fellow Oombian tree creatures hit their oof balls. She swung her trunk butt. She was playing for the Oombinquen Pirates, with her baseball cap pinned like a badge to her lower trunk.

"I guess anything *is* possible," Samantha laughed in wonderment as Oondroomooda helicoptered at ground level towards first base. "If a tree can successfully swing its butt at a baseball pitch...!" Another tear came to her eye. In addition to her late husband, she wished her late brother Eduardo could have been there, as well. She would have loved watching him complain about the impossibility of it all. There might have been a reprise of their argument sixty years earlier. That's when he said it was impossible for any batter to hit a warehouse window outside Camden Yards Stadium in Baltimore, Maryland. *Such an odd attitude, given his addiction to science fiction stories!*

"No!" protested Rotonda. She was racing for home plate with her umpire's gear. "You can't continue the game without me!"

Típico made salsa moves with a nonexistent dance partner. He was celebrating his return to the outfield just in time to catch the fly ball and get Oondroomooda out.

"Samantha?! Is you?!?!"

"Jerri?!" Samantha called out to the woman who called out to her. "You look terrific!"

Jerri, one of Samantha's cousins, took long strides Sammy's way. She was carrying a small guitar named a cuatro, and she sported a blouse-and-shorts outfit batiked in yellows and oranges. The outfit was woven from the unusually fibrous, cottony-smooth flower petals of the Oombian zoozooloola plant.

"But how did you recognize me?" asked Samantha. "I would have thought you more likely to mistake me for my great grandmother!"

"Nobody else I know, nadie," Jerri shook her head as she rushed over to Sammy and hugged her, "would think to wear a Baltimore Orioles cap trillions of miles away from Earth! But ay, chica, this isn't fair!" Jerri stepped back to take in her cousin's entirety with a most empathetic, pouty frown. "You were years younger than us," she said. The "us" included her sister Gloria, who was not present at that particular moment. "You look fantastic, but you should not also be looking older than Norma!"

"It is more than fair," Samantha patted Jerri gently on her arm. "Those years you skipped on time travel, for me they were full of rich experiences, and love. Now you, your family, and these marvelous tree creatures are providing me with more wonder, joy, and hilarity than I will ever be able to reciprocate. That is what is not fair!"

"What a lie! You have sixty years of 'rich experiences' to share! You can start with that bracelet!" Jerri pointed at the pendant on Samantha's left wrist. "We wondered what happened to that! How it ended up with you? Doña Galleta gave it to you after we were time travelled? Or is it another one that fell from the sky? But you missed your own ride into the future?"

"This pendant," Samantha latched onto and shook it, "this is the reason I came all the way out here. What do you know about it?! And who is Doña Galleta? Wait, she wasn't a little old lady with mousey gray hair, was she? I'm talking about someone who looked a bit like me, but wasn't wearing a baseball cap. Was that her?"

Jerri nodded emphatically. "That was her! So she gave you the pendant?"

"Yes! She was hiding in your old bedroom, waiting for anyone to enter. And I was the anyone who entered."

"In my old bedroom?!" Jerri exclaimed. "This happened after we were taken aboard the Smoke and Mirrors?"

"My parents drove up from Baltimore to spend the day with your family. None of you were home, but I remember beans left simmering on the stove. We must have arrived shortly after the spaceship took you on your time travel voyage. By the way, my son is Captain Taylor's husband."

"Ay, santo!" Jerri gasped. "That's right! Chris *is* your son!"

"He is my son."

"Ay!"

"So anyway," Samantha went on, "Doña Galleta did hand me this pendant. She said to hold onto it for sixty years, and be careful about sharing it with anyone else. In fact, I think she might have told me to NOT share it with anyone else."

"So you held this secret for sixty years?!"

"Sixty years, Jerri. And then I needed to hand it over to a loved one who suffered a bad adventure because, I will never forget her exact words, 'life and love are at stake.' So there I was, five months ago and a little over sixty years later, with still no indication of who exactly should receive the pendant. It felt like I wasted my life worrying over this thing. Especially since my husband who I loved so much had long since passed away! But that is when this Doña Galleta's voice came to me like a ghost. She told me the time had come, and that the loved one was my son, Chris. He needed to receive the pendant after the current mission of the Smoke and Mirrors. Within days, I asked President Carey for permission to hitch a ride out to Oomb, and he approved! So here I am, waiting on Chris's return! And what is even more incredible is this: Back in Philadelphia in your bedroom, Doña Galleta gave me the impression I would learn of your circumstances, Jerri! I would learn what happened to you, Gloria, and everyone else! Now that has finally happened!"

"Ay, so Doña Galleta still surprises over half a century later! Permit me to elaborate on the rest of the original events." Jerri related how Pedro claimed to have first come across the pendant bracelet. "He said it fell from cloud-to-cloud lightning. Then Doña Galleta went into these hypnotic trances, seeking the pendant's origin. We were not sure whether she was making up stuff, or was really channeling people from the future. One year later, we got the answer. We were all 'raptured,' literally waking into the future, along with close to two hundred other people in our neighborhood."

As for the "rapture" itself, different people experienced it differently. For some including Pedro, it seemed not to happen until after they got old and died. But for Jerri and the others it seemed to happen from one instant to the next, when it actually occurred. They blinked their eyes one moment, and when they opened them the next moment, they found themselves transported aboard the starship Smoke and Mirrors.

Jerri also mentioned to Samantha that long before the "rapture," Pedro grew to suspect the pendant was an extraterrestrial artifact. Wherefore its strange engraved lettering. They were hieroglyphics not unlike Egyptian hieroglyphics, but hieroglyphics that nobody on Earth had ever seen before.

I can examine the engraving? Mafoosoola telepathed. She had wanted to do this all along, after what she mind-read from Jerri and Samantha both. She figured, though, it was better to wait on asking until the conversation reached this particular juncture.

Samantha, Jerri, Placido and others gathered around. They waited anxiously for the Oombian tree creature to examine the lettering on the mysterious, greenish-gold pendant.

The resultant suspenseful moments produced a ripple effect. By the time Mafoosoola was ready to telepath what she determined, the softball game had already been put on hold at Rotonda's insistence.

An Oombian batter ceased attempting to take practice swings, with the handle of his baseball bat firmly inserted into his bark-concealed anal cavity. Three other Oombians helicoptering about for a fripe's perspective on the game slowly brought their palm-frond spinning to a halt. That way they were able to gently, quietly touch down on the outfield. Even Don Típico froze in mid-tango; his celebration over his and Norma's ball-catching exploits still had not quite finished running its course.

This artifact originates from the planet Fafama, Mafoosoola telepathed at last. *Our Fafaman guest, Yulala, has joined the others on their mission. But I am certain she will want to see this...when she returns.*

The Oombian's pause before completing her telepath was not lost on Samantha. *Was Mafoosoola* struggling with keeping a positive attitude to telepath "when" instead of "if"? Chris's mother couldn't help wondering despite her awareness the tree person would likely mind-read her concern. Her heart skipped a beat, for no telepath was forthcoming trying to disabuse her of her apprehension.

From my participation in a previous starship mission to Fafama, I have learned the Fafaman written language. So I understand the message that has been engraved. Dear Samantha, would you like me to share that message with you, with or without the presence of others?

This question, at least, Samantha found easy to navigate. "Dear Mafoosoola, my understanding is that the pendant is meant for my son. Therefore, I believe we best wait on his return. Allow him to decide who should learn what the pendant says."

That is a more than fair insistence, Mafoosoola's leaves rustled when she nodded her acceptance of the Earthling's response. At the same time, though, Mafoosoola was also carrying on a telepathic conversation with her significant other, Shmoodle-Coodle. That conversation was made available for mind-reading by the rest of the Oombian tree population. *What do you think?* telepathed Mafoosoola to Shmoodle-Coodle. *Will Samantha's fulfillment of the task suffice to at last persuade the Watchers to intervene?*

Samantha will be able to fulfill her task only if the Smoke and Mirrors mission concludes successfully. And that mission only has a chance of concluding successfully, a meager chance, if their strategy continues to be informed by pacifist perspectives. Therefore, I would think that fulfillment of the task should be ample to prompt the Watchers' intervention, responded Shmoodle-Coodle. At the same time, she was lining up a ten-foot putt on an oof course some two miles away from the baseball field.

Yes, there is no guarantee, is there? Even after all that. Mafoosoola struggled to not let a resinous, amber tear well very large in the bottom corner of her eye. She didn't want it streaming down the barky corrugated ridges of her cheek. The humans would notice.

Even after all that, Mafoosoola's mate nodded most somberly as her putter started her oof ball rolling towards the cup. *And without the Watchers' intervention, we must fear the doom of Earth, Tictoctic and the other world they are soon to be exploring. Such doom would certainly be on a scale to rival the extinction event on Fafama. Yet even with their intervention...*

Shmoodle-Coodle's oof ball started to fall into the cup. But its speed was a bit too fast for the putting line. It made a three-hundred-sixty degree circuit of the hole in the green before ultimately rimming out, failing to drop in completely.

Chapter 9

"Our canvasses are still practically spotless! We look like walking voids! If only I had known it was so dry out here! If only I had known the mud was turned to just so much non-clinging dust! I never would have allowed our outfits to be washed! At least then, our sweat stains would have provided some character, still made them presentable for display!"

"How many other ways can I say, 'I'm sorry,' Chwerp-chee?!"

Wrinkles multiplied below Chwerp-chee's eyes, well down across his bald, bulbous head. The numerous small tentacles surrounding his beaked mouth writhed chaotically. Both these reactions came courtesy of his sudden, disturbing self-recognition. Once again, he had lapsed into nagging mode with his same-sex love partner, Chig-cher. "Well one thing, at least," his new series of chirps and beak-clicks would have translated into English. "I am nearly ready to produce significant pee. That dried-out mud flat we are fast approaching should be the perfect place for us to unload. Our subsequent wallows ought to fill our canvases with a multiplicity of aesthetic intrigue! Wait. I do have to add something." Chwerp-chee affectionately reached out his finger tentacles to his partner's finger tentacles. This was a further effort to make up for his outburst borne of being such a control freak, he well knew. "Your pee ink, its vibrant purples upon your canvas are like no other purples out there!"

Chig-cher's body glowed. It lit up pastel blue. So did the body of his reconciliation-seeking lover. Indeed, their highly intelligent species never failed to glow one color or another whenever two or more of them were in physical contact. For Chig-cher, this stress-salving magic made especially excruciating what he knew he must tell his cherished partner. So excruciating, his own bald bulbous head wrinkled the same as had Chwerp-chee's. That is, when Chwerp-chee was reconsidering the harsh tenor of his remarks.

"Please, I'm sorry I'm sorry I'm sorry!" moaningly chirped Chig-cher. "I didn't drink more than a beetle-shell's-full before we left!"

Chwerp-chee tossed aside Chig-cher's tentacle fingers with uncontrollably reanimated disgust. He chirped and beak-clicked, "We have *talked* about this! Again and again! Whenever we go out, you should always drink at least one full tortoise shell of fluid beforehand! That is the only way to guarantee you will need to pee at least within the following two chirlas! Preferably, you choose chinga juice high in yellow-pigmenting vitamin B complex and carotene!"

"I *know!*" Chig-cher grievously slapped an arm against his forehead. The suction discs along that arm automatically sucked so hard there, they produced circular red marks certain to remain visible for days.

VROOOOM! BANG!!

"What on Chonora was *that?*" Chwerp-chee instinctively lifted his head from where it had been hanging upside down. He sought a better, if disorienting, downside up look skywards.

"I don't know for absolute certain!" said Chig-cher, his head also raised. "But I think some aerial object broke the sound barrier!"

The two Chonorans beheld an egg-shaped shuttle pod launched from the Smoke and Mirrors. It sailed through the air on its electrostatically clung-together, micron-layer wings. Those wings glowed translucent orange. Their bright outline, like neon lighting, etched them sharply against the deep blue firmament.

The shuttle pod's spiral descent brought it towards a sandy patch located underneath a diagonally tilted rock-layer outcropping. *Great for hiding purposes*, pilot Tanya Petrovsky decided.

Chwerp-chee dropped upside down again. He hung by only one tentacle leg from a vine strung along cactus-like trees. He and Chig-cher were availing themselves of this naturally occurring trail on their hike across the semi-arid region.

Chwerp-chee resumed his usual posture despite his curiosity. He still felt uncomfortable, dizzyingly disoriented, from the blood having rushed out of his head when he held it downside up. However, he still managed to chirp and click, "Tell me that isn't an unidentified flying object!"

"I can only lie like that when I am trying to flatter you, kelpy mouth!" Chig-cher responded. He joined Chwerp-chee to also resume hanging upside down, and for the same reason. He, too, was feeling uncomfortable from the blood having rushed out of his head. And "kelpy mouth" referred affectionately to Chwerp-chee's kisses. Far as Chig-cher was concerned, the tender commotion of several tiny tentacles encircling his love partner's mouth was like slimiest seaweed on the ebb and flow of ocean wavelets. In other words, it was a real turn-on. "I honestly have never seen such an aircraft before! Look!" Chig-cher pointed. "I think it has landed, or crashed, under that stone formation! In the spirit of adventure which brought us out here in the first place, shall we swing on over to investigate?"

"Okay, Chig-cher, three problems with that." Chwerp-chee strained not to sound condescending and lecturing. However, the way his lover's bulbous brain deflated and re-inflated, he realized he had already blown it. Again, he'd allowed his tone to incline too needlessly severe. Nevertheless, he eschewed any apology to go on instead, "One, I won't be able to wait to pee until we arrive over there. Two, I'm pretty sure the vine network leaves off at least a chingle before that rock formation. And three, we don't know who or what we should expect from the mysterious vehicle. For all we know, it's full of extraterrestrials from the sister planet, set on revenge for our demonstration bomb! But hey, if you want to swing on ahead while I remoisten this mud flat and at least give my canvas a barren landscape look...I mean, if their spacecraft engine hasn't finished cooling off yet, maybe you can burn something into your own canvas of sufficient interest for display."

"No, you're right, my briniest." Chig-cher shook his head in conceding despair. "You pee and design, and then we should return to our car as fast as possible. This entire hiking thing of mine was a bad idea."

"Nooo!" Chwerp-chee shook his head so vigorously in protest, his entire head wiggled like gelatin, most any Earthling would have thought. And the bright-purple, inky urine spurting from the side of his neck trailed off with his drawn-out chirp. "You really had no way of knowing. But you're right; let's leave here now. Our previous canvas soilings can remain posted for another couple of days, if need be. In any event, I'm not sure we're even going to have any guests before next full moon tide."

Please reconsider your plans. I am telepathing you from inside the space vehicle you saw land underneath a rock outcropping. No need for worry; we are not from your sister planet. But we are concerned about the interactions between that planet and yours.

Chwerp-chee and Chig-cher experienced such shock, they almost let go of the vine they were holding onto by only a few of their finger tentacles. Moreover, their mouth-framing mini-tentacles hung lifelessly limp.

I come from a planet that has renounced all war, all violence, going on for generations beyond count. I am accompanied here by creatures from a planet over eleven light-years away. Those creatures seek a peaceful settlement of the crisis aggravated by the highly intelligent beings of your sister planet. We ask for your assistance. With my mind-reading powers, we have ascertained you are two very nice, emotionally and mentally stable individuals. You are just the type to be of potentially immeasurable assistance to both us and yourselves, your planet's future. Not only that; we also sense you are the sort with whom we could become good friends, despite our many differences. As my Earthling friends would say, those differences ought to really spice things up!

Chig-cher glowed pastel violet with pride. He felt vindicated for what he had gotten his partner into for their weekend day trip. "Well then let me just say something, assuming you can mind-read whatever I voice aloud," he proceeded to chirp.

I can.

"Excellent." Chig-cher nodded Chwerp-chee's way. *You see?* was written all over Chig-cher's face. "I just wanted to say, um, to whom am I directing my brain waves?"

That is a more than reasonable question. My name is Wafoodle-boodle.

I come from the planet Oomb some five light-years away. My four associates are from the planet Earth, more than eleven light-years away as I previously telepathed.

They have made possible our presence in this particular time frame, for we have arrived here from the future. The Earthlings are the shuttle pod commander Tanya Petrovsky, her counselor and life mate Ali Magabu, stress relief manager Chris Olsen-Taylor, and military officer Sergeant Fred Frankly.

"Military officer?!" repeated Chwerp-chee in his chirped and beak-clicked language. He gave his partner a dubious *What's this?* look. Even so, though, he was not quite riled up enough to glow with his own bioluminescent chemistry.

Yes, military officer. But he, we, our flight vehicle and the larger starship from which it issued come completely unarmed, defenseless, no weapons. Sergeant Frankly is along as an observer. He wants to establish whether our nonviolent approach to onerous threats has even the smallest practical application.

"That is extremely fascinating, uh, was it Chafoodle-choodle?" As Chig-cher thus spoke, he nodded *You see?* his lover's direction again.

A life-time of uttering your language is certain to have placed certain constraints on how you speak particular words. Your pronunciation of my name is close enough. Incidentally, from my continued mind-reading I have gathered you are named Chig-cher, and your significant other is Chwerp-chee.

"Pronounced, errrr, telepathed absolutely correctly," Chig-cher nodded. His tone of voice was meant to convey to Chwerp-chee, *I told you so!*

One other thing before you at last proceed with what you wanted to say, Chig-cher: You are okay with my telepathically passing along, translating for my Earthling associates every utterance you and Chwerp-chee might make?

Chig-cher shrugged his suction-disk-covered legs when he responded, "I don't see why not. Chwerp-chee? Do you have any problem with that?"

"I suppose not." Chwerp-chee shook his head at his partner with a dazed, chagrined look.

I deeply appreciate, Chwerp-chee, your acceptance of an intensifying association with us treefolk from Oomb, and creatures not too unlike yourself from Earth. Trusting us other-worlders cannot be easy for you. There is a good argument to be made that your special one behaved too impulsively. That he should have sought more proof of our honorable intent before he proceeded this far. From your point of view, I can more than understand your wariness is well-warranted.

"Oh!" Chig-cher lifted his head and looked from side to side. He wanted to chirp, *Have I just been insulted by an other-worlder?* Courageously defiant where he was concerned, though, he chirped instead, "I just wanted to say, and the whole universe can listen in now for all I care- Oh, wait. Am I being too impulsive again?"

Chwerp-chee rolled his eyes.

"I just wanted to express my thankfulness for a certain someone's impulsiveness," Chig-cher went on. "I'm not going to say who that someone was, but he didn't think twice about us two Chonorans of the planet Chonora going on this hike. Otherwise, perhaps nobody would have showed up here to be of assistance to... I did understand your telepath accurately, didn't I, Chafoodle-choodle? You said we could provide valuable help for our planet's future, yes?"

Yes, Chig-cher, you did understand accurately. However, undoing the imminent damage will still take time, even after your help. Some other things have to happen first.

Chig-cher and Chwerp-chee exchanged looks of *Oh-oh*. But thereafter, Chwerp-chee tried to sound as nonchalant as possible when he chirped, "Okay, so what now? Are we to meet where we saw you land?" Under the circumstances, he wasn't about to ridicule his partner for thanking himself in the third person as "a certain someone."

Four of us will be waiting for you outside our vehicle. Tanya will need to remain inside, at the vehicle's controls. She is performing minor maintenance while she sustains verbal communications with our mother ship, the Smoke and Mirrors. Another Oombian mind-reading creature like myself is aboard the Smoke and Mirrors. She is keeping in constant telepathic touch from there.

Incidentally, you will find the three non-Oombian extraterrestrials to be wearing plain white, helmeted suits as part of their decontamination protocol. They will be wearing those suits until further notice. They need to establish with more certainty that lethal interactions are unlikely, of their Earth biochemistry with your planet's biochemistry. This is as much for your protection as it is for theirs. They have developed what they hope will prove a plausible enough cover story. That is for when you take them where they would like to go down here on your planet's surface.

As for myself, I will be the taller, unclothed creature. You might think me a "choop-choop" tree with its top lopped off, and crowned with "cherf-cherf" fronds radiating like the arms of an umbrella.

⚜ ⚜ ⚜ ⚜ ⚜

"I'm dizzy from splattering along wrong-side-up for so much distance with nothing to swing from, upside down!" complained Chig-cher. He paused from his steady trek across dusty, barren soil. He did that to pull at his bulbous forehead with lower arm suction cups not concealed by his shirt sleeves. This produced a massaging effect.

Chig-cher and Chwerp-chee were well on their way towards the rock outcropping where the shuttle pod landed. They had left far behind the cactus-type trees naturally interlaced with vines. To continue their steady progress forward, they clumsily wriggled their fluidly flexible legs across the ground, and lifted their heads high.

"At least if there had been a mud puddle for a luscious clothes staining!" Chig-cher continued complaining. "You're so lucky with your delightfully purplish pee markings! *I'm* going to have to explain to the other-worlders why my outfit looks like I just put it on, fresh from re-bleaching!"

"Chig-cher, I suspect that is not going to be a priority for beings from outer space, the unpreparedness of your clothes for wall mounting. Look, you were the one who insisted we rush to their assistance on blind faith!"

"Oh?? Is that how it is?" Chig-cher's bulbous head inflated and deflated with sudden, irrational fury. "Okay, let's quit! Let's go home! The other-worlders can search for two other 'very nice people' to help them save our world, plus maybe theirs as well! Let's just hope such other people even exist!"

Chwerp-chee's response was not immediately forthcoming. The minor spectacle ahead left him chirp-less.

Chwerp-chee had already come to terms with the shuttle pod parked in rock outcropping shade. But the other-worlders standing off to one side...! The unclothed other-worlder did appear an odd hybridization of choop-choop tree with oversized fronds from a cherf-cherf. And the remaining other-worlders' protective gear was plain white indeed, to an unaesthetically pristine extent. *They look so pathetic, so forlornly helpless!* But not only that! Standing there right-side up had to be an exceedingly uncomfortable experience for them, Chwerp-chee imagined. *All their blood must be rushing to their feet!* Chwerp-chee's two hearts couldn't help going out to them.

"I've turned around and am ready to sling back," resignedly chirped Chig-cher. He was oblivious to his mate's overwhelmed state.

"No, wait; I was wrong," said Chwerp-chee with his eyes remaining glued on the other-worlders. His right leg reached for a stray vine to swing him within touching range of them. "Of course we should help them! And if this be impulsive behavior, then call me impulsive too, and proud of it!"

"I can feel what little pee my body has managed to generate, despite woefully inadequate drinking habits! It's all going to my head!" happily exclaimed Chig-cher. He grabbed for the same vine Chwerp-chee had already used to propel himself forward, comfortably returned to hanging upside down.

⁕ ⁜⁚⁖⁚⁜⁚⁖⁚⁜⁕

"Octopus people suited up in cotton-white baggy slacks and dress shirts?! Save for a brownish purple stain on the one, I don't even want to know where *that* came from!" announced Sergeant Fred Frankly, his voice by turns warning and resigned. "Swingin' upside down on some f-n' bizarre vine, from cactus tree to cactus tree...They were like a couple of f-n' chimpanzees until they had to slinky-slink along a stretch of ground where the plants left off; f--- me! Are the Fafamans the only freakin' aliens we're going to ever meet who don't show off evolution run totally amok?!"

Ali was glad the communication mikes went from envirosuit to envirosuit only. He didn't want to see the approaching extraterrestrials inadvertently agitated into misapprehending hostile intent. The harsh sounds of Sergeant Frankly's first reaction to them had him especially worried. "Actually," Ali said, "marine biologists have found the typical Earth octopus highly intelligent. There are even documented cases where they have used empty shells and other sea bottom detritus as tools."

"Yeah? Well pigs are also supposedly 'highly intelligent,' or snortingly intelligent, whatever! Does that mean we're going to discover a real Miss Piggy out here, somewhere?"

"Sergeant Frankly," said Chris, "we wouldn't want you to meet a *real* Miss Piggy. Ciela might become jealous!"

"Yeah? Well I was thinkin' *Mister* Piggy might look pretty good to Captain Taylor after putting up with your happy horse manure for so long!"

"Gentlemen, truly!" intervened Ali.

Just so you are aware, added Wafoodle-boodle. *Your outside mikes might be turned off. Nevertheless, our alien hosts have noticed the friction between the two of you. One of them has said to the other, "I think he is nagging the other. Isn't that cute? Do you think we've not only made other-world contact, we've made other-world contact with fellow homosexuals?"*

"Oh, hell, no! How do I turn on this outer mike? I need to give them their first English lesson!" Sergeant Frankly tapped furiously on his envirosuit arm's built-in keyboard. "Have to teach them the meaning of the word, 'no'! Damn! Wish Hanson didn't need to stay aboard the S & M to take Yulala to the doctor. I could have remained aboard instead, away from this wackadoodle situation!"

For diplomacy's sake, Sergeant Frankly, said Wafoodle-boodle, *I'm not sure you want me to translate that for them.*

"Okay, so what are they chirpin' on about now, like two overgrown canaries?"

The shorter one to the left, named Chig-cher, he has just welcomed us to the planet Chonora. He also apologized for the lack of staining on his outfit despite their having been out here hiking for a while.

"Wait, he apologized for the lack of a mess on his outfit?! What the f--- is *that* all about?! Chigger or whatever the f...'s his name, he should have been on Oomb when those stag devils from Tictoctic attacked! Half the Earthling colony must have soiled themselves with fear! If what you're telepathing me is true, these octo-people probably would have made a whole freakin' art exhibition out of their undies!"

Introductions were completed with Fred finally managing to stifle his animated protests to the extreme absurdity, as he saw it.

Wafoodle-boodle continued to act as the translating intermediary. Wafoodle-boodle was also entrusted to explain the Earthlings' mission, and the important role the two Chonorans could play.

Without hesitation, Chwerp-chee and Chig-cher agreed to help. They led the three Earthlings to their car. Wafoodle-boodle lagged behind. And yet, she would still be playing a central role as translator and cross-cultural conflict mediator. Counselor Ali Magabu would assist her in this capacity, of course.

"Hey, Sergeant Frankly," said Chris. Both men were swerving about between twelve-foot-tall cacti while the two octo-humanoids kept just ahead of them, swinging along the naturally occurring vine network. "Do you want to try holding hands for a moment like Chig-cher and Chwerp-chee? See if we start to glow like them?"

"Stay away from me, you nut!"

"Oh, look back behind us, my inky pee-licious," chirped Chig-cher to Chwerp-chee. In aid of that suggestion, he paused from his swinging. "One is nagging the other again. I know we are supposed to believe their orientation is heterosexual, but I think they might be going through a little denial!"

Wafoodle-boodle spared Chris and Fred this translation.

Chapter 10

"Ahh, so there you are! This is perfect! Um, please have a seat." Dr. Deborah Davis-Murphy motioned Yulala and Sergeant Guy Hanson over towards padded chairs. They were securely fastened to the floor, the same as other furniture in the chief medical officer's consultation office, and no wonder. On more than a few occasions, gravity aboard the Smoke and Mirrors was less than optimal, if not totally non-existent.

The Smoke and Mirrors was parked buried in crater dust on the dark side of Chonora's larger moon, a dozen years into the past from year 2063. Whenceforth, the particular occasion of Yulala and Guy's visit featured a steady point two 'g,' one fifth Earth's gravity.

Dr. Davis-Murphy tried to behave warm and welcoming. She cleared aside assorted computerized medical analysis devices piled atop her desk that might have obstructed her view. Still, Guy Hanson could feel the chief medical officer radiating apprehension over the newlyweds' very presence. Furthermore, that she was set on postponing, delaying, putting off learning the reason for that presence as long as possible.

Well prior, Hanson sensed the good doctor's people skills were not always the best. She often appeared to struggle, strain to affect being sociable.

"I wanted to ask, Yulala, how things are going with the artificial tralalafa. Are you becoming more regular? Oh, sorry; should I enable the translator?" Dr. Davis-Murphy offered automatic translation assistance. She fervently hoped Yulala was reacting to her question about regularity with puzzlement more than shyness and embarrassment. How Yulala covered her mouth with one hand, though, came off like Officer Yoon-hee Park-Smith's usual reaction when *she* got embarrassed.

"That won't be necessary, Dr. Davis-Murphy," said Guy. "Yulala understands most English now. What she doesn't understand, she wants to try guessing through context clues. As a last resort, she will ask what a certain word here or there means. But I think she's a bit less constipated. Isn't that right, Angel Eyes?"

Yulala nodded in the affirmative though with her mouth still covered.

Deborah looked away.

If Yulala's husband didn't know better, he would have sworn the doctor wished to avoid learning what they came to see her about.

In regards to the artificial tralalafa, what the doctor referred to was a special contraption she designed with Buddy Leung's input. The goal was helping the nocturnal-eyed extraterrestrial woman with her bowel and urinary tract issues.

Back on Fafama before the ice comet ruined everything, tralalafas provided an important function for Yulala and her fellow intelligent creatures. Namely, tralalafas safely evacuated their bladders and intestines while they slept. Symbiotic relationships with these plants developed millions of Fafaman years earlier, and not just for nocturnal humanoids. Such an evolutionary response accrued for other creatures as well. It helped them survive the daily, planet-wide assault by a fierce set of thunder showers termed the sunset storm line.

Once the Earthlings spirited Yulala away from her devastated home planet, she tried really hard to adapt. She made every effort to sleep and take care of certain bodily functions unaided by a tralalafa. As a result, though, she soon developed constipation issues. A special, very limited diet provided a temporary fix. However, she needed something more dependable, safer for her health in the long term.

That's where the contraption invented by Dr. Davis-Murphy, again with First Officer Leung's help, came into play. Bed comforters were stitched together with a complex assembly of tubes and motors. Sump pump technology provided the inspiration. That same technology had already helped an increasing number of basements avoid flood damage back on Earth during growingly more frequent and powerful rain storms.

Sergeant Hanson's brainstorm contribution was a giant blow fan directed at the artificial tralalafa every morning in lieu of a storm line. This assured his wife waking up when she should.

Eventually, Dr. Davis-Murphy hoped to wean Yulala off such dependencies, get her toilet-trained and used to alarm clocks.

"I should thank you again, Dr. Davis-Murphy. You have put so much time and effort into helping Yulala with her, uhh, adjustments," said Guy Hanson presently. "But that's not-"

"Before you go on," Deborah held up a hand to halt the fellow Earthling mid-sentence, "I have good news to report. I know we could all use some good news. Plus, there is progress on what I am sure will be of critical interest."

Guy tossed a hand the doctor's direction. He affected a nonchalance he really wasn't feeling. "Okay," he said, "let's hear it."

"Yes." Dr. Davis-Murphy slapped her own hands together and gave them a good rub. This was *her* way of affecting a nonchalance she wasn't actually feeling, either. "I've completed my experimentation with long term exposure of your saliva samples to each other," she announced. "I can now say with confidence that, umm, your kissing mouth-to-mouth appears to be as safe as one can expect."

On Deborah's conclusion of this statement, Yulala cupped her hand over her mouth again, this time slapping it there. Then she leaned forward slightly and made an odd noise.

The chief medical officer wanted desperately to believe the female extraterrestrial was trying to stifle a giggle of embarrassment.

"Uhh, that's wonderful news." Guy could feel his ears turning beet red when he spoke. "So what's this progress…"

"Yes, that." Dr. Davis-Murphy nervously grabbed for her set-aside compu-pad. "The even more pressing matter, if you two want to start a family…"

Guy opened his mouth to interrupt, but Deborah wasn't going to allow that. She plowed on so the Marine Sergeant was left gaping silently. "I'm becoming more and more convinced you *might* be able to have children," she said. "Of course, fertilization will require carefully manipulated artificial insemination. And the obstacles still remain formidable. What is most helpful, Yulala, is what I've confirmed at the cell nucleus level. For Fafamans the same as for Earthlings, an xx chromosome pair marks females and the xy chromosome pair marks males. However, gene sequence mapping indicates the Fafaman DNA codes within Fafaman chromosome pairs are at considerable variance. Um, that is to say they are at considerable variance from DNA codes within the same chromosome pairs of Earthling men and women. And…" Once more, Deborah shut down Sergeant Hanson's effort to get a word in edgewise. Once more, he was left with his mouth hanging open, not the slightest peep emerging from it. "A far more imposing problem is your typical egg cell, Yulala. It contains twenty-four chromosome pairs versus the twenty-three chromosome pairs found in a typical human Earthling cell. The good news is that for the evolution of life on Earth, at least, there have been far more onerous obstacles overcome than this. For example, we have a large, pink starfish named *Luidia sarsii*. Like other starfish, the adult form has what we call radial symmetry. It can be cut up like an apple pie into five nearly identical slices, one slice for each of five arms. You see?" This time, Dr. Davis-Murphy stymied Guy's attempt to utter a sound by shoving a photo of the starfish into his face and Yulala's. She pulled up the photo on her paper-thin compu-pad. "But here's the amazing thing," she continued. "The starfish's larva form is bilaterally symmetrical. In other words, its larva is comparable to us. The larva's body has two sides, with an eye and an ear on each side. Our best evidence now is that even more ancient predecessors to this ancient-enough echinoderm somehow blended together their cell-building material. They were able to come from two places dramatically much farther apart than the two places you both are coming from. Genetically speaking, that is. So I feel comfortable emphasizing the hopeful aspect. However, I also feel obligated to warn you off the hazards possible from any physical contact beyond a fully clothed hug with mouth-to-mouth kissing."

That was as much as Yulala could bear. Without a word, she abruptly lurched from her chair, and ran for the nearest trash receptacle. There, she opened the special lid meant to keep its contents from floating loose when gravity was minimal or entirely absent. And then with the fiercest heaves, she vomited into it.

When she was through, Dr. Davis-Murphy's shock allowed Guy Hanson to finally get a word in edgewise.

"Um, I think Yulala is experiencing morning sickness."

Chapter 11

"Finally! Hot damn! Not exactly my AK-51, but it will do!" Sergeant Fred Frankly made close inspection, as close as he could confined by his envirosuit. He was examining a machine gun replica attached by rubber-encased wire to the front counter of a shooting gallery arcade game. "Fudge my brownies, wish I could shed this outfit! And tell the peanut gallery to quit their mocking-bird giggles so I can concentrate!"

The shooting gallery arcade game was part of a travelling circus on the planet Chonora. Tanya Petrovsky located the circus by studying aerial reconnaissance footage filmed during the shuttle pod's descent. Tanya and her husband Ali Magabu judged it the perfect venue for Magabu. There, accompanied by Chris and Fred, he could unobtrusively collect what he needed for computing an English-Chonoran linguistic algorithm.

Tanya remained behind while Chris, Fred, and her husband went to the circus. She guarded the shuttle pod where it sat concealed by a rock outcropping.

Anyway, the linguistic algorithm would facilitate Ali programming translators with yet another extraterrestrial language. The goal was near-effortless communication with the Chonorans of this particular region. A more specific near-term high priority objective would also be accommodated. The Earthlings could glean important news from local magazines and press.

At Wafoodle-boodle's telepathic request from Chonoran hosts Chwerp-chee and Chig-cher, local periodicals were secured in generous abundance. This happened on a most uncomfortable trip to the circus in the Chonoran couple's four-door sedan.

The circus itself was located off the main road, only a fifteen minute drive from where Chwerp-chee and Chig-cher parked for their wilderness hike. And the periodicals were bought at a small shop conveniently located along the same road only minutes from the circus.

The interior layout of the Chonorans' auto provided the main cause of discomfort for Earthlings. It accommodated the extraterrestrials' upside-down orientation, which meant it didn't accommodate Earthlings' rightside-up orientation. Seats were built into the ceiling, among other extreme peculiarities where the Earthlings were concerned.

Ali and company saw no other choice than to position themselves on the sedan's essentially barren floor. They sat in the back half of the vehicle where they weren't directly underneath Chwerp-chee and Chig-cher strapped onto the ceiling. And they held on for dear life to seat belts hanging over their heads.

What made the circus an especially appealing prospect was its location far distant from Chonoran population centers. The Earthlings hoped that out in the Chonoran boondocks, they could more easily get away with their cover story about why the envirosuits. Also, the circus's child-friendly aspect most likely meant numerous pictorial representations accompanied the texts found on various signs. It would be almost like walking through a picture dictionary. Moreover, circus barkers could be expected to add their clearly shouted renditions of those texts.

Ali was intent on surreptitiously filming everything.

Regarding envirosuits, the cover story received its do-or-die workout at the outset. That's when the three Earthlings and their Chonoran hosts sidled up to a ticket booth entrance.

Other Chonorans in attendance noticed something peculiar the moment Chris struggled to get out of Chwerp-chee and Chig-cher's car in the gravel parking lot. Chig-cher directed Chris to grab one of the thick ropes suspended overhead, forming part of an interlaced network. But Chris found moving along that network nearly impossible. He tried swinging from one rope to the next like a monkey, but he kept falling off. Frequently, he stumbled down onto his knees or landed on his bottom. But that was okay; his clumsiness fed into the cover story, and kept Chonoran onlookers very amused.

The far more athletic Fred Frankly swung himself along most facilely. He thereby staved off suspicion of something else, of something far more bizarre afoot where the Chonorans who didn't know them were concerned.

However, Fred couldn't stave off suspicion altogether. At least this was the case for a trio of police officers who decided they had better keep an eye on the entire curious bunch. Those officers were struck by how impressively well Fred was able to use his arms for moving along the rope line. That is, without showing the least inclination to swing by his legs. Such behavior didn't fit what those officers knew from their fellow Chonorans, including each other.

As for the rest of the sergeant's audience, his arms-only movement proved most entertaining. It was met with nearly the same amount of trilled laughter as met the ridiculous ineptness demonstrated by Chris and Ali.

"What exactly do you have there?" crisply chirped the ticket master. He extended a bare, suction-disc-covered arm out through a circular aperture in the ticket window. Then he pointed it wavingly, windshield-wiper style, at all three envirosuited Earthlings. His tone suggested to Chwerp-chee he wasn't sure whether to trill with laughter himself, or treat this situation as something more serious.

"These three fellows want an audition to become clowns." Chwerp-chee made a sweeping, mock-reverential bow their way. "Chig-cher and I are their agents. But here is the wonder of it; we are thrilled for you to see what value they add. We are so thrilled, we are happily willing to pay their way! Very quickly you will understand they enhance your customers' experience by their very presence!"

"They look awfully uncomfortable in those garishly clean, white suits! They could be from outer space or... Oh, I get it!" The ticket master made popping sounds by pressing together his fingers' suction discs, then rapidly pulling them apart. "That's supposed to be funny!"

Convolutions roiled Chwerp-chee's bare, bulbous head like a sudden breeze would have roiled an outdoor tablecloth. That's the comparison Chris would have made. "You see how your customers behind us are already clearly entertained?" Chwerp-chee boasted.

"Okay," the ticket master conceded with a nod. "But can you tell me how those two are able to stand that tall on their legs for so long without tipping over?" He pointed at Chris and Ali, who had both given up on swinging along the rope network.

A telepathed translation of the ticket master's question originated miles away, from Wafoodle-boodle keeping constant mindreading vigilance.

Anyway, the ticket master's concern worried the Earthlings. It prompted them to crouch down and try putting more weight on their hands than on their feet. Fred even committed to standing completely on his hands, upside down. An emboldened Chris tried the same, but he ended up falling to one side.

The most welcome result, for the Earthlings' clown pretensions, was another outburst of laughter from many nearby Chonorans, the children especially. Even one of the police officers swung back and forth with amusement, from his upside-down perch. But his two partners shook their heads in "What's next?" disgruntlement. They were still suspicious.

"It is a strain for them," chirped Chig-cher, responding finally to the ticket master's question. "Sometimes they make it look easy, but what that guy does, especially, his name is, err, Chisper." The Chonoran pointed towards Chris, who was struggling to reconstruct what he remembered about "downward facing dog" from yoga. "He has to train his muscles for long hours to fake clumsy swinging, and make standing on his legs appear so effortless."

⚬ɣֆ°⚬ɣֆ°⚬ɣֆ°

"What the f-n' hell is *this*?!" Sergeant Frankly complained presently.

The shooting gallery operator was handing over a large stuffed animal to Sergeant Frankly. It was his prize for having "shot" three metallic figures moving from side to side like proverbial ducks in a shooting gallery on Earth. Those figures had sported a horse's long legs, an elephant's trunk, a shark's dorsal fin, and a whale's tail flukes.

"This looks like Bigfoot saddled up!" Frankly went on to comment as he examined more closely the stuffed animal he won.

"Maybe, truly, you should win some more. When you give this one to Alexita or whoever, you don't want the others to feel left out," suggested Ali Magabu. Ali precipitated more laughter from Chonorans when he went up on his tippy toes to get a better look over Fred's shoulder at the extraterrestrial prize.

"What the f--- are you yappin' about, Mr. Magabu?! I might want to keep this for myself, for all those lonely nights when Ciela is too pissed at me to hop in the sack!"

"Um, I think you might have earned too much attention for yourself with that excellent aim." Chris tapped the Marine Sergeant urgently on his other shoulder from where Ali was peeking. "Every last one of the natives hangs upside down to take a shot, and none of them do even half as well. You win a few more saddled-up Sasquatch, and look out! The police might be swinging their way over here to demand a look inside our envirosuits. Between the hair on our heads and the lack of tentacles round our mouths,...Not to mention there aren't any suction discs running the length of our arms and fingers...we need to avoid this kind of attention."

"Officer Olsen-Taylor is correct," chimed in Ali.

Meanwhile, Wafoodle-boodle telepathed Chwerp-chee and Chig-cher what the Earthlings were discussing.

Wafoodle-boodle, still located miles away, was creeping closer bit by bit on her ciliated roots whenever there wasn't any traffic. She didn't want passengers or drivers wondering how a tree kept on the move, and such an odd-looking tree, at that.

"I think our best plan for the moment, truly, would be heading on over to the roller coaster ride," Ali went on. "Oh, and look! Even better, they have a minimum height requirement chart! That will provide me with additional valuable input for the linguistic algorithm!"

Embellishments made the roller coaster track appear to be the single tentacle of an impossibly large octopus.

The same as on Earth, a special ruler measured Chonoran heights to ascertain whether children especially were tall enough for the ride. Or in this case, it was designed to make sure they hung upside down far enough.

The Earthlings' cover story continued. They were simply other Chonorans auditioning for the role of full-time circus entertainers. So Chris especially had to find a way around his impossible time with the height measurement requirement that he literally hang by his toes. What he did was exaggerate his fumbling attempts, get the audience to chirp with more laughter. Chris pretended he was pretending to have trouble hanging upside down.

The Earthlings' charade went on for so long, the line behind them became seriously backed up from real Chonorans waiting to board the ride. That's when an official waved them through, too amused himself to make Chris and company prove they could actually dangle by their feet.

It was no joke however, when Chwerp-chee and Chig-cher had to help all three of the Earthlings strap themselves into a coaster car upside down.

"Well," started Ali as they sat there waiting. Blood was already going to his head. "At least the police seem to have lost interest. And there are a few loops in this thing where we will sit right-side up, if only for scattered instants."

"Are you almost done collecting what you need for your freakin' language algorithm?" Fred grumbled in response.

"So much so, Sergeant Frankly, I think we can have our kind hosts return us to our shuttle pod after this ride is over. That is, if they don't have to carry Chris out of here on a stretcher. Oh! Cough!" Taken by surprise, Ali nearly choked on his own saliva.

The roller coaster jerked suddenly when the chain for pulling the cars up the first steep incline latched onto the under-chassis.

"Here we go! Cough!"

By the first loop-de-loop, Chris already felt nauseous. By the second loop-de-loop, he was uncertain he could avoid vomiting until he ducked into a bathroom on the ride's completion. He met Ali's question, "Are you alright, Chris?" with a dry heave. And by the third loop-de-loop, actually a spiraling coil, he knew absolutely he would not be able to keep a lid on his nausea for even the shortest second longer. He threw up so forcefully, he completely covered the inside of his helmet with the putrid stuff. Long before the roller coaster finally slowed to a stop, he had already undone the upper portion of his envirosuit to avoid choking on his vomit, and finally catch a clean breath.

A child leapt out of his seat to swing on conveniently located ropes back down to the ground. He was the first to draw attention to Chris. Pointing with one leg, he chirped to his mother what would have translated as, "Mommy! That crazy guy has a nice stain dripping all over his clothes! I wish I could have that, too! But it really stinks! And he has hair on his head like a 'chungacho'! And his mouth and arms look really strange!"

"Mommy" screeched like a hawk Chris had heard in Muir Woods, California, several years ago. She swung her child up into her arms with one leg. Then with the other leg she swung them both far away from the Earthlings, fast as she could.

Ali, Fred, and Chris tumbled onto the ground when they hurriedly unlatched themselves from their coaster car.

"Oh, shit!" cursed Fred.

The hawkish screeches were spreading, and three policemen were swinging their way over where the Earthlings were getting back on their feet.

"Not that I ever expected to be saying this to anyone, were I to live a million years," went on the Marine Sergeant to Chris. "But this is the last time I ever take you on a roller coaster ride!"

Please get them out of there fast as possible, telepathed Wafoodle-boodle to Chwerp-chee and Chig-cher. The Oombian tree creature had finally inched her way parallel to where the circus was set up, though she was still standing the opposite side of the road. Pursuant to mindreading the Chonorans' response, she telepathed her Earthling friends, *Don't resist Chwerp-chee and Chig-cher; they will be carrying you on back of chungachos. Chungachos look like the stuffed animal you won, Sergeant Frankly.*

"Holy frijole!" exclaimed Fred. "I see people taking pony rides on those things! And I use the term, 'people,' pretty damned f-n' loosely! *And,* nobody needs to carry my sorry ass!" He leapt the four-foot fence for the chungacho rides. Then he leapt again, onto the back of what Chris would have sworn looked like the donkey-sized version of a Gigantopithecus. Chris had seen a wax museum rendition of that prehistoric creature inside a natural history museum back on Earth. But the chungacho's arms were longer, more muscular, serving as front legs. And it was saddled up just like the stuffed animal won by Fred Frankly at the shooting gallery.

Slapping at its flanks, Fred sent his disturbingly human-like steed galloping away on its exceptionally hairy hands and feet towards the rear of the circus layout. Easily, the chungacho leapt the height necessary to propel itself over the fence that was supposed to keep it caged for children's rides.

Meanwhile Chwerp-chee and Chig-cher successfully swung Ali and Chris, respectively, onto the saddles of two other chungachos. They seated the Earthlings in front so they could hold onto them securely with one suction-cup-bearing leg. With the other leg, they held the creatures' reins to urge them on, following Fred. Of course, even though both Chonorans rode atop their respective steeds, their posture remained upside down. They clutched at the chungacho's flanks by their elbow-less arms, every bit as flexible as octopus tentacles.

Within minutes the three police officers mounted three chungachos, and were in hot pursuit.

"Well how about that, space cowboy fans!" exclaimed Fred. He had left the circus grounds behind on his swiftly galloping chungacho, and was struggling not to let go of the stuffed animal version. "Somehow I expected we would be trying to outrun an old steam engine locomotive! But this approaching truck caravan will have to do!"

"I see it, Sergeant Frankly!" responded Ali Magabu.

The two Earthlings' back-and-forth communication still came crystal clear through the embedded speakers of their respective envirosuits. Chris, of course, shut off his transponder after vomiting.

"Wafoodle-boodle, you can telepath Chris and the Chonorans-"

Already done, Officer Ali Magabu-Petrovsky. I will be waiting on the other side of the road to helicopter you back to the shuttle pod!

Wafoodle-boodle wasn't about to bother telepathing the Earthlings, yet, about serious complications back out in space. *One thing at a time; first we have to concentrate on returning everyone safely to the shuttle pod,* she thought to herself. And she telepathed that to Oodle-Noodle aboard the Smoke and Mirrors, still covered in crater dust on the dark side of Chonora's larger moon.

⊱⋅ ☆ ⋅⊰ ⊱⋅ ☆ ⋅⊰ ⊱⋅ ☆ ⋅⊰

Preceding the onset of outer space complications was Yoon-hee's discovery of a significant situation overlooked originally. She happened upon it during the shuttle pod's descent to the surface of Chonora. The quantum wave had just finished backtracking to the new disruption of the space-time fabric. That is, the new disruption caused by the Smoke and Mirrors once more traversing one of the space-time fabric's multitudinous rifts. Anyway, Yoon-hee's routine sensor data review led to her discovery.

The location was not far from the space station. Yoon-hee noticed spectroscopic signatures for what had to be three additional saucers docked along a narrow rectangular edifice. Where she was concerned, they could have been three ships docked one after the other along a harbor pier. But somehow, saucers and rectangular edifice alike sat there hovering in space, entirely concealed.

"Wow," whistled Yoon-hee's husband, Kevin, in marvel at his wife's discovery. "Some sort of tarp must be cloaking that whole big enchilada. Maybe they're using the same sort of tarp Space Station 2 used to conceal construction of the Smoke and Mirrors. Only this is on a far larger scale!"

"Yes," nodded Captain Helena Taylor, arms crossed under her chest. "What doesn't make any sense is: Why the bother? One saucer is already parked in plain view at the space station. So it wasn't like they were hiding something new."

"Unless it wasn't fellow beings from whom they were trying to conceal expansion of their saucer fleet," said Buddy Leung. Buddy's remark earned him looks which read "Oh-oh" from Helena, Kevin and Yoon-hee. He wasn't able to help reciprocating with an "oh-oh" look of his own.

Aboard-ship apprehensions were vindicated the same time Fred Frankly was winning a stuffed animal at the Chonoran shooting gallery.

"Captain," reported Yoon-hee, "our patrol firefly donut is detecting a saucer-shaped object approaching Chonora. It's on a course heading roughly parallel to Chonora's orbit." (Oodle-Noodle was able to mind-read, and subsequently telepath to all the humans, what the extraterrestrials named their planet. She did this the instant the quantum wave caught up.)

"Parallel to Chonora's orbit," Captain Taylor repeated as she searched the panoramic video of outer space fed from the firefly donut. She wanted to discern as quickly as possible the approaching object. "That means it's probably coming from Tictoctic."

Captain Taylor, telepathed Oodle-Noodle, *I am mindreading cautious elation aboard the space station. They believe the approaching object is the saucer they lost contact with on its mission back to Tictoctic some sixty Chonoran days ago.*

"Back to Tictoctic?" This part of the Oombian's telepath, especially, really grabbed Helena Taylor's attention.

Yes, Captain. The missing saucer was actually on its third mission to Chonora's so-called sister planet, Tictoctic. I've pieced that information together reading four different minds.

"Okay, Captain, the saucer is coming into view on our firefly donut surveillance cam."

"I see it, Buddy."

The saucer is transmitting video to the space station. There is elated applause in the station's command center. No, the applause has abruptly died down. The message from the saucer captain isn't making any sense; it's from when the saucer was en route to Tictoctic. Oh-oh, in the command center they are realizing it's an old video, not live. Also, I am mindreading multiple creatures' intent to deceive from aboard the saucer. Whoever does occupy it, they are hoping the other Chonorans will taste as delicious as the ones they have already eaten...

"Captain!" Buddy pointed with alarm at what he was seeing in the view-screen feed from the firefly donut patrol. "They've hit both the space station and the docked saucer with a diffuse magnetic pulse-beam!"

Helena noticed right away, when the diffuse magnetic pulse-beam radiated out from along the rim of the newly arrived saucer. As neon blue ripples intersected with the saucer and the space station, those ripples rocked them about. This time, not just Chris was reminded of how bathtub toys were rocked about by a baby splashing water.

The diffuse beam has sent most systems offline aboard the space station and the docked saucer.

Before Oodle-Noodle was able to telepath any further, the attacking saucer sent out a targeted magnetic pulse-beam. But it was fired a different direction from the Chonoran space station.

The pulse-beam appeared to run up against an invisible wall, located precisely where the Smoke and Mirrors detected a cloaked collection of three flying saucers. But that wall didn't last for long. The pulse beam steadily cut it away and burned it apart until what little remained floated off. The three flying saucers parked along a narrow rectangular dock were revealed in all their enormous glory.

Oodle-Noodle was already telepathing to the Chonorans in charge of saucer fleet construction and maintenance. She was urging them to concoct a certain pictograph for immediate transmission. Oodle-Noodle wanted the pictograph to illustrate the Tictoctickian deer creatures making off with the three docked saucers. This is what she mind-read they were come to do. But she also wanted the Chonorans to depict the Chonoran construction workers and the maintenance dock itself left alone.

∗⋈°∘⋈°∘⋈°∘⋈°

Back down on Chonora, the Earthlings accompanied and assisted by Chwerp-chee and Chig-cher continued riding horseback on the chungachos. They were fleeing from the police in hot pursuit, also riding chungachos.

The Earthling-mounted chungachos came galloping up alongside the truck caravan well ahead of the police.

Chris couldn't help being struck by how similar the Chonoran trucks looked to huge three-wheelers back on Earth. However, at least one driver and his partner were hanging upside down from the ceiling of their cab. Chris caught a glimpse of them through the lead vehicle's windshield.

Meanwhile Sergeant Fred Frankly's chungacho steed easily outpaced the truck caravan. It galloped around front of the lead cab without getting run over.

"I must say," said Frankly, "it is right f-n' neighborly of these truck drivers to slow down so we can pass."

I might have telepathed them to please decelerate enough for friendly other-worlders to safely reach the other side. That is, away from the police and en route back to their spaceship. The truck drivers might have been spooked enough to most kindly oblige.

"Hold up, Sergeant Frankly!" Ali Magabu's voice suddenly erupted from inside Fred's envirosuit head gear. "Chwerp-chee and I have taken a spill behind you!"

Fred Frankly pulled on the reins of his chungacho, bringing it to a halt. He discovered that sure enough, there was a mess not twenty feet behind him. Ali, Chwerp-chee and their hairy primate steed were sprawled across the dusty, pebbly ground.

In no time, though, Counselor Magabu pushed himself back up on his unsteady feet.

Chwerp-chee reached with one leg for curling around a conveniently close overhanging branch. But that took longer than Magabu's recovery.

By then, Chig-cher holding onto Chris had brought his own steed to a halt beside the fallen chungacho.

Meanwhile, Fred Frankly had finished assessing the situation. He surmised that Chwerp-chee must have taken the turn round the truck caravan at too sharp an angle for his chungacho to maintain balance.

Chig-cher chirped and beak-clicked what would have translated as, "Oh, 'chachachal' poop! Both of you are displaying bloody rips and soily skid marks! You are looking ever so much more fashionable than I could ever hope to!"

"Yes," Chwerp-chee responded, wincing with pain. "It was a small price to pay, making a fashion statement that would humiliate you!"

"I don't know what you two are goin' on about, like a couple of cackling crows," said Fred Frankly. "But if we don't figure a way to vamoose quickly, the police will catch us!"

That was when Wafoodle-boodle descended amidst the disarray, courtesy of her spinning palm-frond helicopter struts. She telepathed, *Sergeant Frankly is correct; there is no time to lose! Chig-cher, please drape your companion about my branches here. The rest of you climb aboard and hold on tight.*

I think we can safely make it back to the shuttle pod in one load!

The Oombian tree creature achieved full liftoff just as the truck caravan finished clearing down the highway. As a result, the chungacho-mounted police could see where their quarry went. They looked up in stunned disbelief. Their mouth-framing tentacles went limp with their shock.

⋅ ⱶⲦⲅⓔ⋅ⱶⲦⲅⓔ⋅ⱶⲦⲅⓔ⋅

Some fifty thousand miles out in space, the Chonorans on the maintenance platform had herded themselves into one of the saucers docked there.

All three saucers were near completion of diagnostic review to assure space flight readiness.

The Chonorans rejected Oodle-Noodle's counsel, what for them was a spooky voice in their heads. They figured it was a trick of the hostile creatures from Tictoctic. Instead, having crowded one of the three new saucers, they were backing it out of dock. The Chonorans' plan was to bring it around with the intention of disabling the attacking saucer. But they weren't nearly far enough along getting a magnetic pulse-beam online. The saucer that crippled the space station was already firing away at them. Its magnetic pulse-beam targeted their saucer's upper mid-section, where most of them packed themselves in after they boarded.

Captain Taylor and her crew aboard the Smoke and Mirrors looked on helplessly at what the feed from their firefly donut revealed. The saucer launched by its Chonoran occupants from maintenance dock suddenly burst apart.

Within minutes, the attacking saucer spun over beside the two other newly constructed Chonoran spacecraft. Oodle-Noodle's mind-reading confirmed that Tictoctickian troops were pouring from the attack saucer to take control of them. Those troops included two engineers who were trained by an engineer aboard the attack saucer. They knew exactly how to successfully activate the two remaining saucers.

Captain Taylor and Buddy Leung couldn't help wondering how they might have been able to help. That is, if only they had come there with the Smoke and Mirrors fully armed.

Is this ultimately a fools' mission after all? Helena thought to herself. Although well did she know what Oodle-Noodle could have reminded her to consider. The Chonorans rejected the tree creature's counsel to seek a peaceful exit ramp. Oombian pacifist counsel had also been rejected by Earthlings back on Oomb and Fafama. With what results?

⸱⟊⊙⊙⸱⟊⊙⊙⸱⟊⊙⊙

Chris and Chig-cher gently lowered Chwerp-chee onto a mattress in the shuttle pod's small medical room. Meanwhile Ali Magabu was advising his wife, "We don't have much time, Tanya, truly. All too soon the Chonoran police will get past their shock from witnessing a flying tree, and resume their hunt."

Officer Tanya Petrovsky sighed in a manner her husband Ali knew well. It heightened his apprehension even more than he had already been experiencing. What did Tanya know that he didn't? Anyway, she succeeded her apprehension-promoting sigh with, "Um, in the time we do have, my Ali-papali, the question becomes what our injured extraterrestrial guest and his companion are going to want to do. Will they wish to leave our vessel after we bandage his scrapes? Or, um, I should think…"

Wafoodle-boodle telepathed Tanya's question to the two Chonorans.

Chig-cher chirped most animatedly in response. He assumed the tree person would understand him, which she did. Pursuant to which, Wafoodle-boodle telepathed the Earthlings, *This Chonoran named Chig-cher, he wants to know how homosexuals are treated in your culture.*

A wry smile dawned across Ali Magabu's face as Fred Frankly did a double-take. Frankly sputtered, "What the fried fish does *that* have to do with the price of eggs?"

Apparently, Sergeant Hanson, Chig-cher and his significant other here, Chwerp-chee, have had to always be careful. They have needed to exercise extreme caution with their relationship on Chonora, to avoid harsh persecution.

"Nothing like that on Earth, you can assure them, truly," said Ali, "excepting for a few, remote pockets of intolerance. But for that matter, if you search hard enough on our planet, you will also discover people still insisting the Earth is flat. Please add that our chief medical officer and third engineer are married, while both of the female persuasion."

"So they had to be *persuaded* to be female?? No wonder they're gay!" wisecracked Fred Frankly to Ali Magabu's wincing chagrin.

Wafoodle-boodle telepathed the counselor's response to Chig-cher and Chwerp-chee. She also apprised the Chonorans of her and Oodle-Noodle's own lesbian relationship.

What ensued was Chwerp-chee and Chig-cher intertwining their tentacle-fingered hands. They engaged in what the Earthlings clearly understood to be a decision-making discussion, despite the incomprehensible chirping. Their limbs and bare, bulbous heads glowed with an ebb and flow of various pastel colors.

Meanwhile, Ali wondered what conniptions Deborah was going to have. Once again, her decontamination protocol had been tossed to the wayside. Right from the get-go, Wafoodle-boodle had disembarked from the shuttle pod wearing no protective gear whatsoever. Ditto for how the two extraterrestrials from Chonora were welcomed aboard the shuttle pod. Moreover, the inky blue blood from Chwerp-chee's scrapes was allowed to drip all over the floor and medical room stretcher.

When at last the two Chonorans reached a decision, their head glows stabilized into a steady pastel orange. What Chwerp-chee chirped to Wafoodle-boodle, Wafoodle-boodle telepathed along to the Earthlings. *We would like to come aboard your mother ship for an extended visit, please.*

"Wow. Um, wow," Tanya repeated. "I guess I'm going to have to clear this with Captain Taylor. But, um, first there is something Chwerp-chee and Chig-cher need to understand. We are dealing with special circumstances, including time travel and, um, developing situation back up in space. We might have to delay our departure from planet's surface for as long as safely possible. Um, if the Chonoran couple accompanies us after that, it might not be for an extended visit. Or rather, their extended visit might need to be stretched out indefinitely, permanently even. And it will be fraught with danger, of course, once we arrive at, um, centerpiece of our mission."

"So what, we are going to turn the Smoke and Mirrors into some f-n' Noah's Ark?!" exclaimed Fred.

With a strained smile, Ali nervously asked his wife, "What 'developing situation' is that, Tanya?!"

"Um, well, a saucer under the control of Tictoctickians has arrived in general vicinity of Chonora. It's already destroyed one of three saucers that were undergoing deployment prep at a concealed maintenance pier. And now the Tictoctickians are taking possession of the other two saucers. Wait, there's more. The Tictoctickians have also seriously disabled the Chonoran space station along with the saucer docked there. In context of those events, Captain Taylor and crew are brainstorming what next. For starters, they are discussing a challenge we will face. How can we return safely to Smoke and Mirrors hidden on dark side of Chonora's larger moon, without drawing attention?"

"Hmm," hmmed Ali with forefinger contemplatively pressed against his face, just under his nose. "I suppose that would not be a problem if we could stay down here to wait out the Tictoctickians' rampage. But..."

"Captain Taylor knows, my Ali-papali." Tanya used her pet name for Officer Magabu again. "She knows from Wafoodle-boodle that police are on their way here to give us major headache. But she is also well aware that when and if we do lift off, we can only linger in atmosphere for so long before Chonoran air force comes after us. She assumes the Chonorans assume we are part of Tictoctickian strike force!"

Officer Petrovsky, telepathed Wafoodle-boodle, *I have finished apprising our Chonoran guests of the full ramifications. They understand what they will be getting themselves into if they remain on board the shuttle pod. But that doesn't seem to matter. They have assured me, in no uncertain terms, that if they were never to step a tentacle-toed foot upon their home planet's soil ever again, so be it.*

Something else for you, Officer Petrovsky, the Oombian tree creature went on telepathing. *I know how total your attention needs to be on your forthcoming tasks. Given that, I have gone ahead and taken the liberty of telepathing Captain Taylor about Chwerp-chee and Chig-cher's request for permission to join us. She has granted it.*

"Wo there cowgirl, cow-tree!" Fred Frankly waved a hand as in *Stop!* Wafoodle-boodle's way. "We already know these bird-calling fools have an upside-down orientation. What if there is something else about them even more extreme? Something what makes that imitation tralalafingy-dingy Dr. Davis-Murphy designed for Yulala's constipation crisis seem tame by comparison?! What if each time *they* take a poop, for example, they require an audience to give them a round of applause as each piece of you-know-what exits their rear ends?, like the crowds roar every time Lucas Feuillet drops a twenty foot putt at the Masters? Only, this will be for a foot-long deuce?!"

"If you're trying to say you want free season tickets to the Chonoran poop-fest," chuckled Chris, "I have an 'in' with the captain. I can make sure your presence is not only a given, but a requirement!"

"Yeah?! Then, how about if I make sure you're required to serve as their official butt-wipe?! I'll need front-row seating for that!

"WE'RE NOT GAY, OKAY?!?!" Fred suddenly turned around and shouted at Chwerp-chee and Chig-cher both. He could hear their crow-like cackles, and sensed they were pointing at him and Chris with unbridled amusement.

"Okay, everyone, enough!" Tanya said so firmly, so strictly, she earned total silence. "I've just received go-ahead from Captain Taylor for us to lift off. You better strap yourselves in promptly. It's going to be wild ride!"

Ali's heart skipped a beat on hearing the hint of delight in his wife's voice. With the maneuvers she had pulled off on previous missions, he dreaded even speculating to himself what she meant by "wild ride" this time.

On its departure, the shuttle pod kicked up dust clouds that billowed out from under the rock outcropping. But it left none too soon.

Not only had the police arrived on chungacho-back. Their reinforcements in patrol cars had also found their way there, bouncing across the desert terrain amidst the vine-draped cactus foliage. Already more than a dozen disembarked officers were slithering forward across the desert soil on their tentacle legs, firearms ready. Thankfully, though, not one of them bothered taking a shot at the hybrid flight vehicle, for having so quickly assessed the futility of that proposition.

214 | David Taylor

Officer Yoon-hee Park-Smith is sending a special live video feed to your shuttle pod, Officer Petrovsky, telepathed Oodle-Noodle. *Shortly after you exit Chonora's atmosphere, we expect you are going to receive a visual transmission from the Tictoctickian saucer. We are certain the Tictoctickians will demand you identify yourself. Instead of responding directly, forward that transmission to us. Simultaneously pass along our special video feed to the saucer. It will be as though you were our video feed's source, rather than acting as its intermediary after it was sent to you.*

"What about electronic compatibility issues, communicating with the saucer?"

No problem, Officer Petrovksy. We think the specs Officer Leung previously downloaded from his operation of a Tictoctickian-controlled saucer are good enough. Regardless, you might want to use a split-screen so you can see what the Tictoctickians receive from us. Don't forget to activate your translator, of course.

The shuttle pod sped out of Chonora's atmosphere well ahead of the interceptor jets deployed from the planet's surface. But Tanya still had to perform some wild maneuvers. Otherwise she wouldn't have been able to steer clear of fragments from the Chonoran saucer obliterated by a magnetic pulse-beam less than forty minutes earlier. Also mixed in amidst the wreckage, grotesquely, were Chonoran bodies. Expressions of horror were frozen on their faces, how they met their space vehicle's destruction.

"Wafoodle-boodle was correct, people. We are receiving transmission from the Tictoctickian saucer," reported Tanya Petrovsky. "Here it goes on our view-screen while we also forward it to Smoke and Mirrors."

The left half of the shuttle pod's view-screen filled with revelation of a flying saucer's navigation deck. Front and center loomed a deer creature from Tictoctic, seated upon a most regal armchair. His head featured antlers of such enormity that Chris was reminded of the antlers displayed by a full grown bull moose. On this extraterrestrial from Tictoctic, however, they appeared disproportionately large, oversized. It was like they should have been impossible for him to hold erect. Like they should have tipped his head so far over on one side, they broke his neck.

"I am Captain Dek-Fook-Tek of the People's Unified Resistance and Liberation Herd. Identify yourselves at once, in an understandable manner! Otherwise, for our defense we shall be forced to annihilate you with our targeted magnetic pulse-beam!"

Tanya Petrovsky followed Oodle-Noodle's directions on behalf of Captain Taylor. Tanya transmitted the live video feed from the Smoke and Mirrors to Dek-Fook-Tek's flying saucer. Hopefully the Tictoctickians would believe that feed was issuing directly from the shuttle rather than being passed along.

The video feed from the Smoke and Mirrors filled the right half of the shuttle pod's view-screen. Enjoined by those seated behind her, Tanya was surprised at what it revealed. There were two, fully-dressed deer creatures seated at a navigation panel. Their antlers were short and stubby compared to Dek-Fook-Tek's, but it was still obvious they were Tictoctickians. *Oh, of course,* Ali snapped his fingers as he remembered. *These are two of the deer creatures imprisoned on Oomb after we ended the Tictoctickian occupation. They are among those Tictoctickians who got hooked on oof and golf, and a vegetarian diet into the bargain. So hooked, Captain*

Taylor and our Oombian partners thought they could come in handy for our peace plan!

"Baa, Dek-Fook-Tek," humbly baaed one of the Tictoctickians with stunted antlers, although they were a wee bit longer than his partner's. "Your image on our video screen is as refreshing as the most gentle spring waters streaming down a rocky hillside! My name is Tlik-klok, and this is Fwok-bwahk. We are not even worthy of being two of the shortest prongs on your antlers.

"Please forgive our redundancy during the following exposition, Supreme Dek-Fook-Tek. There can be no doubt that you could provide far more details than we could ever hope to. But it all helps provide context. So here goes: An enemy vessel from this foul planet below us journeyed to Tictoctic. Upon arrival to your fair realm, it dropped a horror bomb on one of your defenseless cities. During the resultant confusion, enemy officers descended from their mother ship to the surface of your beloved planet. They landed on Tictoctic in a reconnaissance vessel like the one you see our having claimed from them for your own. Luckily, they captured us for interrogation purposes to which we did not succumb! I assure you! And I say luckily because of what our capture made possible! Inspired by your heroism, we were able to secure the enemy reconnaissance vessel from them, as I already just mentioned. If you are familiar with Kwit-Nik, he can vouch for us."

"Engineer Kwit-Nik, yes of course I am familiar with him. He is standing here by my side!"

Tlik-klok and Fwok-bwahk scrambled out of their seats, up onto their hind legs. They swelled their chests and brayed in unison, "Your bluntest antler prongs are still pine needle sharp! Impaled on them is far better than we deserve!"

"Of course it is," Dek-Fook-Tek tongue-clicked most dismissively. He added, "Needless to tongue-click, I am also well familiar with both of you. But because of uncounted pressing matters, I cannot be bothered keeping on the scent of your personal integrity, or lack thereof! That is why I now ask Engineer Kwit-Nik to vouch for you."

When Dek-Fook-Tek turned Kwit-Nik's way, Chris thought he spotted something. The thinnest of wires extended from one of the Tictoctickian leader's antler prongs, straight upwards. Presumably, it extended all the way into the ceiling of the cervine extraterrestrial's navigation deck. For the briefest instant that wire went lax, and DekFook-Tek's head started to tip over. But then it was drawn taut again, and his head resumed a perfectly raised balance.

"They are two officers of the finest gallop and unquestionable loyalty, most-free-range-roaming Commander Dek-Fook-Tek," Kwit-Nik made quick to offer by way of assurance.

Commander, captain… There were any number of roles the dictatorial deer creature had already succeeded in assuming for himself. They would soon be consolidated into a claim of absolute power by Dek-Fook-Tek's successful campaign for capturing other Chonoran saucer craft.

Incidentally, Officer Kwit-Nik gave his assurance despite his puzzlement. He could have sworn that Tlik-klok and Fwok-bwahk were stationed back aboard the space station in orbit around Tictoctic.

They were. Their slumbering bodies presently experienced a peculiar stasis near their home planet. Thanks to the Smoke and Mirrors having carried them back into the past, Officers Tlik-klik and Fwok-bwahk were in two different places, simultaneously. Wherefore the quantum wave forced their ever-restless spirits to make a choice. They could animate their bodies aboard the Smoke and Mirrors, or their bodies aboard the space station orbiting Tictoctic. The spirits of Tlik-klik and Fwok-bwahk could not be fully awake at both locations at the same time.

Tlik-klok and Fwok-bwahk could have been asleep and dreaming at both locations at the same time, though. That would have been comparable to an electron being everywhere at once in an electron shell. That is, until someone forced it to choose one specific location by trying to detect it. Buddy Leung might have invoked someone looking at a dinner menu. Before the waiter asked someone to make a selection, someone's choice for dinner could be anywhere on the menu. It could be anything from a veggie burger to meatballs with spaghetti. But then the waiter essentially detected the restaurant goer's choice, locating their meal in one specific location on the menu.

So yes, Tlik-klok and Fwok-bwahk were wide awake and putting on a show aboard the Smoke and Mirrors. However, they had no idea what was happening to them one hundred eighty million miles away, on the opposite side of the sun named Cygnitaurus by the Earthlings. They had no idea that their selves tossing and turning in bed aboard the Tictoctickian space station had suddenly dropped off beyond sleep.

Eventually, Officers Tlik-klik and Fwok-bwahk aboard the Smoke and Mirrors would return from whence they came, back to the future. That is when their past-time selves aboard the Tictoctickian space station would lapse into strange dreams. They would be dreams of enjoying a most oddly addictive game, only to get interrupted with a request for help by bizarre-looking other-worlders.

Lucky for Buddy and Helena's plan that Tlik-klok and Fwok-bwahk aboard the Tictoctickian space station had not been up and around, wide awake. Otherwise, their future counterparts aboard the Smoke and Mirrors would likely have fallen off most uselessly to sleep. Then what would the Earthlings' escape scheme have been?

"We were so inspired by your courageous example, Dek-Fook-Tek," Tlik-klok humbly baaed. "It is beyond amazing how you liberated your saucer from enemy control, on its treacherous return to Tictoctic for what could only have been further destruction. Without that heroic example, we would have lost our nerve. We never would have been able to keep from revealing anything other than made-up information during our interrogation. After which we never would have succeeded at escape from imprisonment on Chonora. Not to mention making off with one of the enemy's space patrol shuttles. All of this bears countless repeating, Supreme Dek-Fook-Tek.

"But there is something further. We dutifully ask your permission for performing yet another action in tribute to your endless glory. This action would take place before we docked with your mighty vessel made even mightier by your presence aboard it. We earnestly lick each other's anuses over our desire to be back in the company of so many good companions and fellow soldiers. Nevertheless, we ask that first you allow us to pursue a particular lead. We followed its scent along the way to our liberation of this small spacecraft.

"In a pine cone, we believe an enemy base is hidden away on the dark side of the enemy planet's larger moon. Once we are able to confirm this, we can perhaps assist you on your surprise attack thereof."

What Tlik-klok baaed for Dek-Fook-Tek so excited him, Dek-Fook-Tek rose from his throne and spontaneously licked at thin air.

Kwit-Nik couldn't help himself. He imagined the soon-to-be-anointed supreme ruler of Tictoctic in the thrall of one of his favorite concubine's tender private parts settled gently upon his snout.

But Dek-Fook-Tek wasn't finished expressing his excitement yet. He came down on all fours, and kicked out his rear limbs with such force that they splintered apart the back rest of his throne-like captain's chair.

Kwit-Nik knew that a stressful shame was in store for the chair's builders. They had put in hard work on the flying saucer spacecraft after its seizure from those heartless murderous Chonorans. Several days were required, just to remove all the Chonoran furniture built into the ceiling. Such strange beings were they, if delightfully tasty whether fried or grilled! Anyway, several more days were required for retrofitting new furniture built up from the floor, where really civilized beings expected to find it!

"I am missing anything of consequence pertaining to their proposal, Engineer Kwit-Nik?" Dek-Fook-Tek crisply, regally tongue-clicked once he finally settled down from his wild outburst.

"Anything you would miss, most masterful Dek-Fook-Tek, does not merit worry, as it surely does not exist. Only your supreme modesty herds you towards any such misapprehension." As Chief Engineering Physics Officer Kwit-Nik said this, a voice in his head was gently urging him, *Let them. Let them pursue their action on the dark side of the larger moon.* Moreover, Kwit-Nik noticed a suspicious absence in the fellow Tictoctickians' video monitor transmission. No Chonoran upside-down seating could be seen molded into the ceiling over Tlik-klok and Fwok-bwahk's stubbily antlered heads. If they really had absconded with a Chonoran spacecraft...but maybe the video monitor angle was so tight that it was removing them from view. Still... Kwit-Nik nevertheless decided to heed the telepathic calls from who he could not know was Oodle-Noodle. And he kept quiet about the seating. If Dek-Fook-Tek were to eventually notice that particular detail, no problem. Kwit-Nik would simply heap praise on him for seeing that to which his loyal subjects were so blind. For sure, none of the other crew on the navigation deck appeared to be ruminating on some undisclosed concern.

"I hereby command the both of you to conduct your dark-side-of-the-Chonoran-moon reconnaissance mission, immediately!" This is how Dek-Fook-Tek's official orders translated for Tanya and company. That is, as they looked on at the video feed from where they, not Tlik-klok and Fwok-bwahk, were situated on board the shuttle pod.

"Almighty crap!" Fred Frankly exclaimed in awe while Chwerp-chee and Chig-cher were still struggling. They couldn't find even a semi-comfortable way to remain buckled into their floor-based seats, not at all what they were normally used to. "We are actually getting away with this bluff, at least for now!" continued Frankly. "Okay, Officer Petrovsky, what's next?"

"You heard King Antler," Tanya murmured coolly. She worked her control panel the way Yoon-hee worked *her* control panel back aboard the Smoke and Mirrors. She was like a concert pianist tickling the ivory, so thought her always-adoring husband, Ali. "We are headed around to dark side of Chonora's larger moon. Smoke and Mirrors will be waiting for us there."

Back aboard the Smoke and Mirrors, of course, was where Tlik-klok and Fwok-bwahk were actually filmed. Those two Tictoctickian deer-like creatures were hearing a translation of Captain Taylor saying to them, "That was fantastic, both of you! Chris, where are they going to get to play on the golf virtual reality simulator after their acting debut?"

"Pebble Beach, Captain. They've already more than earned it!"

Dek-Fook-Tek saw the video transmission from the shuttle pod's exterior camera view while Tlik-klok narrated. Tlik-klok's narration was coached through a translator ear bud by Officer Buddy Leung. Where appropriate, Tlik-klok colored that narration with what he knew of Tictoctickian history, including the fawning ways in which Dek-Fook-Tek was accustomed to being addressed. "We are not sure how much a normal person would discern through this darkness so little relieved by available starlight," brayed Tlik-klok. "However, our faith is strong, great Dek-Fook-Tek. We do not doubt you must be seeing what we are seeing, as clearly as though during brightest mid-day. Meanwhile, our own merely functional eyes must squint and strain. And so, correct us if we are wrong. But there appears to be a large, cylindrical, intelligently produced artifact partially concealed by the moon dust of a large crater basin. For your benefit as well as for others who might be watching with you, but your benefit takes all priority..."

Dek-Fook-Tek was about to kick against his throne again, do further damage. However, Tlik-klok did quickly amend his remark suggestive there should be the least bother over the benefit of others. The soon-to-be-anointed Supreme Authority proved subsequently capable of constraint, limiting himself to a miffed snort.

"For your benefit alone, my Supreme Authority, we will descend closer to the cylindrical artifact," brayed on Tlik-klok. "One might easily conclude its immensity is dwarfed only by the immensity of your own achievement, Supreme Dek-Fook-Tek. After all, it is you who liberated a saucer craft from the Chonoran oppressors. It is you who freed that galloping edge of technology from brute animals who could not possibly have been the true inventors. Holding such technology within their grasp for even the briefest while must surely be one of the most unlikely accidents in the history of the universe!"

Tlik-klok artfully coupled his feigned adulation of Dek-Fook-Tek to an insult for the Chonorans.

It worked. Dek-Fook-Tek excitedly stepped down from his throne on the navigation bridge of what would be officially christened, upon his triumphant return to Tictoctic, the First Celestial Breath. He swaggered forward on his hind quarters, clip-clopping along. He thereby provided his antler handlers extra stress as they labored to prevent his overgrown cranial protrusions from pulling his neck muscles, or worse. Yet again, however, he remained too self-centered to care, or even be aware of the issue. Rather, he strutted up close to the navigation bridge's panoramic view-screen, and lapped at it. He slobbered his saliva all over the lower portion, most appreciatively.

"Baa, we've encountered an unexpected convenience, although we well know this is nothing you wouldn't have anticipated," continued Tlik-klok.

Meanwhile, Tanya Petrovsky flew the shuttle pod down ever closer to the lunar surface.

"One end of the enormous cylindrical artifact opens into a wide, empty chamber. There is plenty of room for us to actually land," further elaborated Tlik-klok concerning the "unexpected convenience."

"Unfortunately, however, we are kicking up a considerable lot of moon dust that is probably obscuring your view."

No sooner did Tlik-klok express his regret than brown haze filled Dek-Fook-Tek's view-screen, completely hiding the Smoke and Mirrors' photon exhaust chamber.

Dek-Fook-Tek stopped licking at the view-screen, as though he could have licked some of the haze. He returned to his throne, making himself comfortable as possible given he had kicked the backrest to splinters.

"Baa, we have discovered a convenience to perhaps countermand the inconvenience of such an obscured view. There are cable struts built into the roof of this empty chamber. We might be able to use them to drag the cylindrically shaped, other-world artifact out of the moon crater dust. Then we will see exactly what we've got. Although whatever it is, there are no signs of life. The artifact appears to have been abandoned. Or who knows? We will check deeper within. That way we can determine whether some Chonorans met an untimely if doubtless well-deserved fate. If we do find corpses inside, let us hope the heating system failed. That way they will have been flash-frozen for convenient addition to the general food supply. Those particular Chonorans' fate will have been well-preserved in addition to well-deserved! First, of course, we do need to drag the cylindrical artifact out of the moon crater dust."

There was something Dek-Fook-Tek could not have imagined, and none of his technical advisers been able to detect. That is, unless they knew exactly what to look for.

Tlik-klok submissively bleated away, describing the situation as directed telepathically by Oodle-Noodle. And he continued to embellish what he bleated with his local knowledge.

Meanwhile, Buddy Leung changed the video feed Dek-Fook-Tek's saucer was receiving. For the view from the shuttle pod he substituted a view from the forward end of the Smoke and Mirrors.

Nevertheless, Dek-Fook-Tek believed what Tlik-klok told him. Moon dust was clearing away from the shuttle pod as it dragged the "cylindrical artifact" out of hiding inside a Chonoran moon crater.

In reality, the "Supreme Authority" was seeing dust clear away from the artifact itself.

At long last, the shuttle pod pulled free the starship Smoke and Mirrors from the Chonoran moon's gravitational influence. Pursuant to which, Tanya unlatched the cable used for dragging it out of the dust layers. Next order of business was bringing the shuttle pod alongside the Smoke and Mirrors to dock within.

Shuttle pod and starship both remained concealed from Dek-Fook-Tek's direct view by moon shadow. Captain Taylor and company couldn't be more pleased. All the better for Tictoctickians not to learn of the cooperation transpiring between both space vehicles. And that the "intelligently designed cylindrical artifact" was clearly unfatally compromised.

Of course, it was important that Dek-Fook-Tek continue to believe he was receiving his video feed from the shuttle pod, operated by two of his fellow deer creatures.

"We have succeeded in retrieving the cylindrical artifact off the surface of the Chonoran moon," Tlik-klok went on with his coached narration. "You ought to see all that moon dust cleared from the cockpit window. Our liftoff from the lunar surface provides superior scouring out as from a most powerful air hose...or an exhalation of your most righteous, cleansing fury, Supreme Dek-Fook-Tek! It might as well be your celestial breath!"

Dek-Fook-Tek leaned forward to stamp a cloven hoof-hand against the navigation deck.

"Baa," baaed Tlik-klok, "Fwok-bwahk has been inspired by your example, Dek-Fook-Tek. He has been inspired to an achievement certainly dwarfed to near impertinence by even your humblest deeds. But it is an achievement nonetheless. He has hacked into the mainframe of this cylindrical artifact. And thereby he has determined something else of interest. Even though the cylindrical artifact is designed differently from the flying saucers, it is still a spacecraft of Chonoran origin! Let me qualify that: It is a spacecraft of fluke Chonoran origin more deservedly credited to your own genius, my Supreme Authority!"

On this news, Dek-Fook-Tek rose from his throne. Again to his antler handlers' stress-propelled chagrin, he came down on all fours. Even more to the handlers' chagrin, he proceeded to spin around and around in hoof-stamping celebration.

"For your glory, Dek-Fook-Tek, we are going to activate this starship! When she emerges from behind the dark side of the Chonoran moon, you will be able to see what she's got!" Tlik-klok baaed in feigned excitement. That is, once Oodle-Noodle telepathically advised him Dek-Fook-Tek had settled down from his triumphant hoof-stamping.

* * *

"Any issues stemming from the moon dust where the mirror arrays are concerned, Yoon-hee?" Captain Taylor asked her chief navigation officer. Taylor kept her eyes glued to the panoramic view of outer space. Part of

Chonora's larger, crater-covered moon lay in the foreground. This was the same view Dek-Fook-Tek mistakenly enjoyed as transmitting from the shuttle pod.

The shuttle pod was presently tucked away empty in the starship's shuttle bay.

"No, Captain, it looks like the arrays are pretty well cleansed. By the time we come into view for the Tictoctickians, we'll be close to forty percent bloom, EM fields fully charged. In addition, a slingshot effect will be ready. We should find ourselves launched on the perfect trajectory into the rift. We'll be going so fast, the Tictoctickians won't have any better look at the S and M than were it a falling star."

That was exactly what happened.

Dek-Fook-Tek experienced a most deceiving illusion, however. It had to do with the cylindrical starship's return through the rift opened by the Chonoran space station's future destruction. He mistook the Earthling space vessel's time travel departure for its catastrophic destruction.

"Fools!" Dek-Fook-Tek rose from his throne anew, this time to repeatedly stomp his two hind hooves against the floor in a raging fit. "Tlik-klok and Fwahk-bwok ought to have waited for further counsel from me, *and* from you, Engineer Kwit-Nik! They should have done that before attempting to power up a Chonoran space vessel of different design and operation specifications from ours! Now the cylindrical vessel is lost, and they're lost! We must assume the usable Chonoran meat of the perished crew is lost as well!"

"A senseless loss, indeed, precipitated by their momentary lapse of judgment, Supreme Dek-Fook-Tek. Clearly they forgot the peril of so hastily making things up as they go along, rather than taking the time to seek your wise counsel every step of the way." This is what Kwit-Nik at Dek-Fook-Tek's side tongue-clicked most soberly. "May the awful event we have just witnessed serve as a grim reminder to us all," he added. Even so, Kwit-Nik had to wonder. He had to wonder as one of only a few Tictoctickian engineers who deeply understood the technology they hijacked from the extraterrestrials of Tictoctic's sister planet. He had to wonder whether the cylindrically shaped other-world vessel was actually destroyed, and whether other things were actually as they seemed. There was no way Kwit-Nik could share what he was thinking with Dek-Fook-Tek. But if he didn't know better, he would have sworn the cylindrical vessel vanished rather than burst apart. The electrical discharge, the fireworks, perhaps they all pertained to a space portal or some sort of wormhole. Perhaps there was not really an explosion as such.

Kwit-Nik was also thinking about the other-world spacecraft itself. Such an unusual design, with the appearance of enormous bloomed flowers, one fore and one aft! Those "flowers" appeared to have caused light to stream in, and then exit out its rear in a beautiful spray of twinkles. Was the spacecraft even from Chonora? Wasn't it more likely to have arrived there from another planet, a different civilization altogether?

Incidentally, there was only one reason Kwit-Nik even knew to compare the cylindrical spacecraft's fore and aft to bloomed-open flowers. A long while back, he had seen old photos in Tictoctickian history texts of certain extravagant plants that had gone nearly extinct. The surviving exceptions were a few lone wild flowers. They managed to self-fertilize in two of the few "green zones" still remaining in the sub-arctic region of Tictoctic's north pole.

There was one other thing Kwit-Nik noticed. Dek-Fook-Tek or someone else would most certainly have commented on it had they also noticed. They all saw the large cylindrical spacecraft appear to self-destruct. But what happened to the smaller one? Where was the vessel Tlik-klok told them had towed the "cylindrical artifact" up off the surface of the Chonoran moon? It was nowhere in evidence. Dek-Fook-Tek assumed it was caught up in whatever consumed the larger craft. But shouldn't Fwok-bwahk have been able to unhook the smaller vessel from the larger one before the fireworks? What really happened to it...if it didn't dock inside the larger one?

There was something Kwit-Nik, the Tictoctickian space flight engineer, could not possibly have known while pondering these weighty matters. It was happening a few years later where the Smoke and Mirrors traversed an intermediary time period, en route to a cosmic rift for return to Earth year 2063. Having put on their elaborate act, Tlik-klok and Fwok-bwahk both were receiving the following telepath from Oodle-Noodle: *Tlik-klok, party of two, you are wanted on the first tee box at Pebble Beach!*

Chapter 12

Thump! Thump! Thump! Thump! Thump!

The thumping racket started not five seconds after the starship Smoke and Mirrors returned through a space-time rift. It reverberated throughout the cigar-shaped starship.

Captain Taylor and company were not back to the present just yet. Rather, they were back to Chonora's more recent history from where they had fled deeper into its past.

The Smoke and Mirrors had fled deeper into Chonora's past, in the first place, to outwit Tictoctickians. But this double-down on time travel had also been for the purpose of exploring more thoroughly the history of relations between Chonora and its sister planet, Tictoctic. Chonora shared Tictoctic's orbital path around the star, Cygnitaurus, but always remained the exact opposite side from Tictoctic.

My mind-reading suggests that the thumping originates from the planetary dragon spirit of Fafama, telepathed Oodle-Noodle. *The dragon spirit is boundlessly happy to be welcoming our return, having feared we might be forever lost. It is behaving like your pet dogs on Earth when they welcome home their keepers with out-of-control tail wags.*

"Helena- errr, Captain," Chris corrected himself for professional decorum's sake, "those lights disturbingly close to the S and M...they are zigzagging so strangely! From what Oodle-Noodle telepathed, do we gather that is the planet-sized ephemeral dragon's tail wagging? Together with the thump-thump-thumping, I mean."

"Utterly preposterous!" protested Professor Skepticus.

Professor Aquinas happily lifted and dropped, lifted and dropped his glasses on the bridge of his nose in time to the continuing thump-thump-thump barrage.

"Clearly," Skepticus elaborated, "the irritating sounds could constitute a warning! Yes, that's it! We must fear the so-called 'thumping' indicates starship hull stress approaching critical levels. The Smoke and Mirrors has made one passage too many through a rift in the space-time fabric! Think of the noise from a boat's hull straining against water pressure imposed by stormy seas!! As for those zigzagging lights: We shouldn't be wasting our time, superstitiously, positing some absurd, planet-sized spiritual agency. Rather, we must consider a far more realistic, far more worrisome possibility. The mirror arrays might be malfunctioning, possibly also the result of one time travel too many!"

FWOOOMPH!!!

"OUCH!!"

A torch-like flame suddenly seemed to flare out of nothing more than thin air, directly into the seat of Skepticus's special pants.

"'Ouch,' Professor Skepticus?" said Aquinas, pausing from his perpetual re-adjustment of his spectacles. "I thought your pants were designed specifically to protect your second most prolific bodily orifice from the ravages of Effy the ephemeral dragon!"

"Even more unfortunately, Professor Aquinas, my pants offer no protection whatsoever from your magical, non-scientific thinking! I cannot deny we are far from understanding the particular air-borne phenomenon that periodically afflicts me. But then you assume it must be some mythical creature just as well escaped from a children's fairy tale! Harrumph!"

"Gentlemen, gentlemen," Ali Magabu held out a beseeching hand towards the arguing professors. "Regardless of whatever produced your afflicting flame, Professor Skepticus, the thumping has finally stopped. And so have zigzagging motions from the conglomeration of mysterious lights which seem once again held in thrall by the Smoke and Mirrors."

"Of course," nodded Professor Aquinas.

Oodle-Noodle rustled her assent with what she mind-read Aquinas was about to say.

"I do believe the planetary dragon spirit has at last received the reciprocal greeting for which it was excitedly wiggy-wagging," Aquinas explained. "I am talking about when Effy tried to torch your pants, Professor Skepticus, on a not-unreasonable expectation. Namely, that more of Officer Olsen-Taylor's most delectable chocolate chip cookies would be pocketed away there!"

"Nonsense!"

"Nonsense or not, that *is* the question," Captain Helena Taylor stepped in, set on moving matters along. "Buddy, I know your to-do list already overflows. For starters, however, I'm pushing something else to the front of the line. I want you to perform diagnostics on the Smoke and Mirrors' hull integrity. It's only a matter of hours before we run the space-time rift gauntlet once more, to finish returning home to our present. And so, on the off chance there is anything at all to Professor Skepticus's worrisome hypothesis... Would that we could enjoy complete confidence in what Professor Aquinas has suggested..." Helena motioned towards the mysterious lights on the view-screen. They persisted in assuming the uncanny appearance of a lit-up, connect-the-dots dragon enormously proportioned. "Whatever-it-is should have no problem this time keeping up with us, since we won't need to be executing any more evasive tactics," Helena continued. "That is of course assuming we will reach the rift well before the quantum wave catches up to us again."

Buddy's to-do list included retrieval of the firefly donut "anchor" left near the drifting-apart ruins of Chonora's destroyed space station. Pursuant to that retrieval, the Smoke and Mirrors would be making for the space-time rift on the outskirts of the Cygnitaurus solar system. That rift constituted the final leg of the starship's trip back to the present.

Firefly donut retrieval proceeded at a leisurely pace, but not too leisurely. Captain Taylor and company needed that time, anyway, to digest new information acquired from Chonora. But again they were on the clock. They didn't want the quantum wave catching up with the starship before it could enter the aforementioned rift. Otherwise, starship and crew both could end up in serious jeopardy, prior to the risky business planned for after returning to Earth year 2063.

Chief Medical Officer Dr. Deborah Davis-Murphy walked in on Captain Taylor's meeting.

Taylor and company were assembling an event chronology to detail the relations of Chonora with Tictoctic. This task was taking place in the room adjacent to the decontamination chambers. That way the Chonorans and away team were brought into the conversation while still kept isolated from everyone else aboard the Smoke and Mirrors.

Dr. Davis-Murphy had deemed such isolation necessary, at least for the time being. She needed to finish her risk assessment concerning Chonoran bacteria and viruses. How would they biochemically react with

234 | David Taylor

bacteria and viruses from four other planets: Earth, Fafama, Oomb, and Tictoctic? Of course those other bacteria and viruses were already running rampant, intermingling aboard the starship.

The away team down to Chonora had consisted of Ali Magabu, Fred Frankly, Tanya Petrovsky, Wafoodle-boodle and Chris Olsen-Taylor. Wafoodle-boodle was exposed to Chonoran bacteria and viruses from the get-go since she didn't even wear clothes, let alone a spacesuit. The others took longer for their contamination. It started with Chris when he removed his helmet so he wouldn't suffocate from his own vomit. But the result was the same. They all had to be boxed up in the decon chamber adjacent to the one holding Chonorans Chig-cher and Chwerp-chee.

"No!" Deborah exclaimed, on realizing the location of newly-instated Starship Chef Ludi Perez.

Chef Perez was seated directly underneath Chig-cher, inside the decon chamber specially prepared for the Chonorans. Chig-cher hung from one of two special fixtures installed there for him and Chwerp-chee to comfortably rest.

"What are they eating?" Deborah asked in her most distressed voice. "And how did Ludi end up in there?"

Chig-cher responded with chirps that translated, "How did this kind, generous being happen to join Chwerp-chee and me? Why, I simply opened the door when she knocked, and she stepped right in, you silly! But don't worry; I thereupon shut it immediately to maintain your decontamination procedure. Mmm!! These- What did you call them, Ludi? These 'chirroz chon chanchules' are *delicious*! And look at this!!" Chig-cher indicated a sauce stain on his cream-colored canvas shirt. "They produce the most aesthetically pleasing patterns whenever I happen to spill any of them!"

"Arroz con gandules, or rice with pigeon peas in English." Ludi corrected Chig-cher's mispronunciation with a gentle pat on his hanging-down tentacle fingers. "But that's okay. I still understand."

"Like I said," chirped Chig-cher with a fluidly nonchalant wave of his free arm, "she is a kind, generous being!"

"I can only imagine how difficult it is not to chirp when expressing yourself in another language!" Chef Ludi went on, happy to offer more reason for Chig-cher's assessment of her character. "Spanish is my first language, not English. For me, is always difficult the difference between the prepositions 'in' and 'on'!"

Long before Ludi finished her digression, Deborah was trying not to hurt herself as she beat her head in frustration against the nearest wall.

"Sorry, Deb," Helena Taylor looked up to say from the conference table. She, Oodle-Noodle and Buddy Leung were seated there, busily piecing together recent Chonoran and Tictoctickian history. An irradiated Chonoran magazine, a Chonoran newspaper likewise irradiated to kill off extraterrestrial viruses and bacteria, and large post-it notes littered the tabletop. "We were so involved with constructing a timeline..."

"No need to explain, Captain." Deborah finally collected herself enough to raise her hand in "halt" mode. "The Martians who invaded Earth in H.G. Wells' *War of the Worlds* were defeated ultimately by Earth disease. Once we surrender to the Tictoctickians, maybe we can likewise defeat them with a toxic brew of extraterrestrial germs!"

"Did you have something else, Dr.?"

"I was just coming to see... I might as well go marinate myself in olive oil, prepare for our grilling not of the interrogation kind on Tictoctic." With that, Deborah spun around and left.

"Captain," said Chief Counselor Ali Magabu from within one of the decon chambers. "Truly, with Yulala's pregnancy our dear Deborah thought all but impossible..."

"I know, Ali," Helena nodded. "She's the ultimate Mother Hen, never ceasing to worry over our safety. We need to offer her extra reassurance of how much we appreciate her efforts. Right now, though, we've got to get back to this chronology. Oodle-Noodle, and you two in the other decon chamber, I want you to listen also!"

Captain Taylor's sudden plea for the Chonorans' attention took Chig-cher by so much surprise that he spilled some of the rice and pigeon peas on his shirt. But he did not hesitate from squishing and smearing them there, to enlarge the previous stain.

Helena couldn't help noticing what Chig-cher was about. She remarked, "So this intentional defacement of clothes is really such a big thing on Chonora? Good grief, Chris, you must have been born on the wrong planet! I think you might well have become a fashion idol on Chonora."

In the decon chamber alongside Tanya, Ali, Wafoodle-boodle, and Sergeant Fred Frankly, Chris responded. "But if I had been born on Chonora," he said, "Fred and I might never have met!" He batted his eyes flirtatiously at the sergeant.

Fred commented, "I might want to help those furry-assed deer devils roast you like a pig over an f-n' barbecue spit!"

Chig-cher pointed at Chris and Fred both. How much more proof was needed of their suppressed mutual attraction?

None of the non-mindreading others would ever learn what Chris suddenly found himself wondering with bottomless insecurity. Had Helena finished mourning the death of the ruler of Fafama, the Fafamafalafama?

"Okay, we've had more than enough of the gallows humor." Captain Taylor struck an especially officious, let's-get-back-to-work tone. "I'm going to run through the chronology of Chonoran historical events we've thus far been able to piece together. I leaned heavily on Chig-cher and Chwerp-chee's personal recollections of major happenings as they were reported. Also, there are some pertinent articles contained in these magazines they so generously purchased for us. There are our own observations as well. And of course Wafoodle-boodle and Oodle-Noodle might have mind-read more than a few additional details that pertain."

Chig-cher's bulbous brain lit up pastel purple with pride when Helena mentioned the "generously purchased" part.

Chwerp-chee would have taken Chig-cher's head glow down a shade, to indigo blue. He would have accomplished this by reminding Chig-cher of the consequence if he had had his own way at the convenience store. Namely, they would have ended up buying the Earthlings a home remodeling magazine and a latest fashions digest instead of news periodicals. Such purchases would likely have been of no help at all. Chwerp-chee might have gotten into this, but it was clear the Earth leader's patience was burning out like the glow of a Chonoran who had been fasting for too long.

"What I gather," went on Helena, "is that several years ago, a robotic probe launched from Chonora made an historic discovery. It found a sister planet orbiting Chonora's sun. This new planet was located the opposite side of the sun from Chonora, in Chonora's exact same orbit. Even more historic were the photos of Chonora's sister taken on its night side. Those photos clearly revealed concentrations of light across the surface. They could only have emanated from population centers of a highly intelligent species comparable to the Chonorans."

"Imagine our disappointment when we realized how absolutely un-sexy they were! Especially how there were horns growing out of their heads!" Chig-cher chirped distastefully. "Those growths might as well be fossilized bushes that lost all their leaves in some horrible blight!"

"Yeah? Well I'm guessin' none of them bleatin' devils are exactly losing any sleep, fantasizing about taking a roll across the ceiling with one of you!" Fred prided himself on making this observation without resorting to his favorite 'f' word. *Ciela would be f-n' pleased!*

"Um, to move along with what we think we know," awkwardly continued Captain Taylor, "and please... Chig-cher or Chwerp-chee, please don't hesitate to correct anything I might have misunderstood.

"So, um, something oddly serendipitous happened, concurrent to the Chonorans' discovery of the sister planet. A consortium of their top astrophysics engineers developed a spacecraft that can exceed the 'normal' light-speed constraint. It operates on the same principle as the Smoke and Mirrors. But its flying saucer design context is dramatically different.

"Anyway, Chonorans fired up their collective imagination. They asked: Why not send the newly engineered spacecraft to Chonora's sister planet for its first full maiden voyage? I gathered this correctly?" Captain Taylor nodded Chig-cher and Chwerp-chee's way.

"Most correctly," Chig-cher's chirps translated as he nodded his assent. "You could have been gathering 'chumcha' pollen for smearing most stainliciously across your woefully unsoiled uniform!"

"Um, yes, well, and so," went on Taylor, again with the awkwardness. "Chonorans and Tictoctickians developed mutually understandable pictograph communication. It went along the same lines of what we developed with the Fafamans to initiate interplanetary, interstellar contact. But a huge problem occurred."

"It was horrible," chirped Chig-cher in a most lamenting voice. He melodramatically draped a tentacle arm across his bulbous forehead. "While our brave Chonoran astronauts were space-walking over to the Tictoctic space station, every last stain got freeze-dried off their protective suits!"

"Dear Chig-cher, I think Captain Chaychor is referring to how the barbaric Tictoctickians shot at them. It is a miracle none of them were hit before they were able to return to their saucer!" Chwerp-chee accompanied his gentle admonishment with equally gentle touching. He affectionately tugged at his significant other's bald, bulbous head with suction discs on his tentacle fingers. "The smallest puncture out there in space, and death would have been instantaneous."

"Yes, well..." Chig-cher scratched at the back of his head with the tentacle toes of his bare left foot. "If I saw me approaching in such a hideously unfashionable condition, I'm not sure I wouldn't have fired on myself!"

"Okay." Helena Taylor made a measured inhale and exhale. She took double the time on her exhale as on her inhale, to keep an even temperament when she proceeded. "The Tictoctickians apologized for misconstruing your brave Chonoran astronauts were on an attack mission. Despite their apologies, however, a huge controversy broke out once the Chonoran saucer returned home."

I gathered something most significant in that regard with my extensive mind-reading, Oodle-Noodle telepathed to continue the narration. *Chonorans the world over saw video of the Tictoctickians' attack, and the impressive immensity of the Tictoctickian space station. Lots of politicians sounded the alarm from Chonora's most powerful empire, where Chwerp-chee and Chig-cher lived.*

It was an empire comparable to the United Americas Empire on Earth. Those politicians stirred panic over the possibility the Tictoctickians weren't too far off from developing their own light-speed spacecraft. If they succeeded, couldn't they, wouldn't they easily circle round their mutually shared sun to launch an attack on Chonora? What made such an attack seem even more plausible were the conclusions drawn by Chonoran scientists. From video of Tictoctic itself, together with spectroscopic data, those scientists concluded Tictoctic is suffering run-away, fossil-fuel-powered global warming. Extreme climate change is wrecking the planet. Damage goes well beyond what the Earth is currently experiencing, as terrible as that is still proving to be.

Chris, Ali, Helena and Fred nodded grimly. Even Chig-cher was taken aback. He found he could no longer dwell so disparagingly upon how unfashionably spotless these odd, upright-sitting extraterrestrials kept their clothing.

The Chonoran scientists concluded, Oodle-Noodle continued, that the Tictoctickians were probably becoming increasingly desperate. So desperate, they might want to explore the prospect for colonizing, occupying another inhabitable planet. That is, another planet not in so dire a condition as their home world. And what better planet for such a plan than Tictoctic's sister, Chonora?

A daring proposal quickly gained traction. Why not conduct a dramatic demonstration of the Chonoran Empire's military might, specially designed to intimidate the people of Tictoctic? Then Chonoran scientists could offer ways the Tictoctickians might successfully address their crisis-stage environmental problems.

More specifically, industrial contractors on Chonora had developed a magnetic pulse-beam weapon. Oddly enough, requirements for its operation made the recently constructed Chonoran flying saucer the obvious choice for its testing. To produce a pulse-beam of sufficient power for disintegrating a large building or spacecraft would be no easy thing. Something immense and circular spinning at an impossible velocity would be needed. Smaller and slower would result in a pulse-beam unable to do much more than knock an old tin can off a fence. Such a wonderful excuse, contractors privately confided to one another, for having their invention deployed aboard Saucer One as it was named originally. Saucer One was something immense and circular that spun at an impossible velocity. It could fire a demonstration shot powerful enough to put a big dent in one of Tictoctic's uninhabited mountain ranges. That would show the destruction that Chonorans were capable of wreaking.

What better way to dissuade the Tictoctickians from ever again attacking Chonoran explorers?

"Yes," Ali nodded. "I noticed something in the translation of this article about the government's response to anti-military protests." He lifted one of the Chonoran magazines off the table. "It was a propaganda mantra: 'Interplanetary peace through Chonoran strength.' I find that mantra to be a truly most haunting echo of comparable mantras that have been concocted over and over again during our own planet's history."

Correct, nodded Oodle-Noodle with a rustle of her leafy branches, however trimmed back they were to facilitate comfortable standing-about aboard the Smoke and Mirrors. *I believe the parallels to Earth history are even more haunting when you consider the bit of Chonoran history invoked to support that mantra. Chonorans experienced world war against a fascist regime like a cross between the German Nazis and the Japanese empire. During that war, nuclear scientists developed a special weapon they hoped would force the fascists' surrender.* At this juncture Oodle-Noodle started giving Chig-cher and Chwerp-chee some background history about Earth. She was able to telepath such information simultaneous to going on about Chonoran history for the Earthlings. *Chonoran nuclear scientists developed an atomic bomb. That bomb was dropped on two of the fascist empire's port cities, the same as atomic bombs were dropped on Nagasaki and Hiroshima in Japan. Even more tragically, the parallel did not end there. On Earth there is ample reason to believe the Japanese wanted to surrender prior to learning of the atom bomb's creation. However, they were unable to successfully communicate this. There is likewise ample reason to believe something similar accrued on Chonora. People high up the*

Chonoran fascist empire's chain of command also tried unsuccessfully to communicate their intent to surrender. That surrender would have included rounding up for incarceration those psychopathically deranged individuals who led the fascist empire to war in the first place.

"Okay, Oodles of Noodles," grumbled Sergeant Frankly, "we don't need your peace-and-love editorializing regarding all manner of ifs, buts, candy and nuts. Stick to the facts, and let's get this f-n' history lesson over and done with, already! Jeesh!"

Oodle-Noodle nodded her rustling acknowledgment before she telepathed, *The Chonoran congress had to decide regarding the next mission to Tictoctic. They could give peace a second chance, simply offer help for addressing the sister planet's global warming crisis. Or the Chonorans could just go ahead with the magnetic pulse-beam demonstration shot. In a close vote, the demonstration shot won out.*

Numerous anti-war protests erupted worldwide. Several pacifist leaders gave prophetic warnings. They said a demonstration shot most likely could not happen on Tictoctic without causing massive injury, death and destruction. The notion of an uninhabited mountain range was nothing more than wishful thinking. And in the long term, such a barbaric action could lead to the destruction of Chonoran civilization by vengeful Tictoctickians.

"Did you say, 'prophetic warnings'?" Chig-cher anxiously, chirpingly interjected.

In response to Chig-cher's question, the Earthlings and Oombian tree creature silently bowed their heads.

Chig-cher jumped into Chwerp-chee's lap, both of them still hanging upside down. He hung on there for dear life.

Yes, I did, Oodle-Noodle responded unsparingly. *Despite those prophetic protests, the retrofit of the magnetic pulse-beam onto Saucer One proceeded, with the mission soon to follow. After ten most suspenseful days, Saucer One returned in triumph. Saucer One's captain reported not having to wait long at all, once the demonstration shot was fired. Less than a planetary revolution later, the beings of Tictoctic responded. Exhibiting great enthusiasm, the Tictoctickians welcomed the Chonorans' proposals for their next mission. The Tictoctickians looked forward to help in reversing the course of their planet-wide environmental crisis. At least this appeared to be the case.*

Victory parades were held in every large Chonoran city. I have mind-read that Chig-cher and Chwerp-chee still remember them well. Proudly waving Chonoran astronauts were transported upside-down through the main streets. Buckets of the darkest violet inky urine were sprayed joyously on them from every rooftop, in lieu of confetti. Aside from that, the astronauts could have been riding in ticker tape parades across the United Americas.

Chonoran voices still sounded caution and warning. But they were ignored when not altogether stifled. Political pundits speculated it was possible the demonstration shot not only guaranteed peaceful future dealings with the creatures of Tictoctic. For all anyone on Chonora knew, the Chonoran show of force one hundred eighty million miles away might also have had good auxiliary effects. It might have precipitated the cessation of whatever wars were still be waged across Tictoctic. Chonoran speculation went that it didn't matter which side the Tictoctickians took in their various conflicts. They were realizing something to their extreme humiliation. Presumed Chonoran armed strength made Tictoctickian weaponry obsolete.

In yet another haunting echo of tragic Earth history, banners went up all over Chonora, proudly announcing, 'Mission Accomplished.'

"Wow," Fred Frankly whistled.

"Which brings us," Captain Taylor said, "to the fate of the first Chonoran mission for helping out Tictoctickian civilization. Chig-cher and Chwerp-chee, apparently your civilization's first light-speed saucer craft stocked up on samples of solar and wind technology. It also carried plentiful drawing board sketches. Everything was supposed to help wean Tictoctickian civilization off the fossil fuel technology that was devastating their planet."

"I recall exactly what you are talking about!" Chig-cher's animate chirping translated. "Remember, Chwerpy?" He patted on his significant other's head to lavender-glowing effect. "Remember videos of the saucer crew carrying aboard seedlings and bags of fertilizer? Remember how they chirped and chirped about replacing entire grain and vegetable fields lost on Tictoctic?"

"I also remember they reported having somehow inoculated the seedlings," Chwerp-chee chimed in. "They wanted to prevent extraterrestrial biochemistry from killing off new crops before they could take root."

"But then Saucer One disappeared, vanished, no contact. For all we know, they never had even a moment's chance to enjoy the planting process, and the wonderful dirt-staining that would have proceeded." Chig-cher shook his head regretfully.

"What we found very illuminating was an editorial in this issue of *Just Hanging*." Captain Taylor waved around the magazine.

Just Hanging looked to Sergeant Frankly, Tanya and Chris like it could have been some Earthbound periodical such as *Time* or *Mother Jones*, if not for the alien lettering. The cover displayed a photo from space of Tictoctic. The Chonoran symbol for a question mark was superimposed on the planet. That symbol consisted of a spiral one way connected to a spiral going the other way. It was like an extremely flowery capital 'S' from Elizabethan times, Chris thought.

"The editorial was entitled, 'The Price of Peace,'" Helena Taylor went on. "Basically, it argued the protestors were wrong. They shouldn't complain about the massive buildup of militarized saucers for deployment on a rescue mission to Tictoctic.

"The author didn't reach this conclusion right away. It occurred to him some while after the ominous disappearance of Chonora's first full-sized flying saucer on return mission to the sister planet. He argued that however nobly well-intended, his fellow Chonorans were irresponsibly naïve. They never should have presumed one magnetic pulse-beam demonstration would do the trick. That the Tictoctickians wouldn't need to see anything further of Chonoran military might. In other words, one demonstration shot wasn't nearly enough to dissuade an extraterrestrial civilization from war-making behavior."

And yet, Wafoodle-boodle jumped in to telepath, *we also need to consider what I learned mind-reading certain Tictoctickians. I'm sure the Chonoran military strategists thought they targeted a remote, uninhabited mountainside on Tictoctic. But again, the protestors were* correct and they were wrong. On any life-thriving planet, completely uninhabited mountainsides are rare if they exist at all. The Chonorans' "demonstration shot" actually destroyed entire villages and killed thousands of the Tictoctickians. This horrific result fed into the more militaristic thinking of some Tictoctickian politicians. It made possible their ascendance over what beforehand was becoming an increasingly popular movement to seriously address the planet's environmental degradation.

"No shit, Wafoodle-shake-your-maple-syrup-drippin' caboodle?" spat out Fred Frankly. He was unable to keep his skepticism from informing his voice with no uncertain terseness.

"No shit," Sergeant Fred-let's-be-friendly, sir. What's more is something I mind-read during our shuttle pod return to the Smoke and Mirrors. One conflicted Tictoctickian soldier aboard the co-opted Saucer One was reflecting on how things might have gone. That is, if only the Chonoran saucer hadn't launched its unprovoked attack on a populated region of Tictoctick. He was thinking what his fellow creatures' reaction to the original, unprovoked Tictoctickian assault on the Chonorans might have been without such an attack. It might have proven transformative. Their horror at that assault might have led to a popular revolt against the militarization of Tictoctickian society.

"So what you're sayin', let me get this straight, Wafoodle-bang-on-your-f-n'-caboodle," said Fred. "You believe the Chonoran peace protestors were right about everything! The Chonorans never should have lifted a finger against Tictoctic, even after they got shot at by those furry-assed f-ers!"

Sergeant Frankly, prior to Dek-Fook-Tek's seizure of the first Chonoran flying saucer spacecraft, Chonoran technology was unexcelled. It far surpassed anything Tictoctickians could possibly have developed on their own. Tictoctickian society had become too fascist, too conforming for any such achievement. But now you have had Tictoctickian seizure of the very saucers constructed to defend against Tictoctic. The Chonorans have basically armed and created the very threat they were striving to eliminate.

The Chonorans tried to avoid the hazard instead of focusing on where they wanted their figurative golf ball to fly. By so doing, they have brought to pass their nightmares instead of fulfilling their dreams, Chris thought to himself. They have sliced their golf balls, oof balls, whichever, deep into penalizing territory. Chris could not bring himself to express this aloud, for fear he would be accused of trivializing the situation. Although he was sure the tree creatures would have telepathed him props.

"After this 'Chek-Chook-Chek' snatched Saucer One, do you know, have you mind-read the fate of our fellow Chonorans? The saucer crew?" Where they were not covered by his canvas shirt, Chig-cher's arms glowed sickening dull yellow. He couldn't help his apprehension over what he was about to learn for the trouble of his inquiry.

Wafoodle-boodle and Helena Taylor exchanged troubled looks. Who would be stuck answering Chig-cher?

"I don't know how to say this in a way that expresses my full sorrow, Chig-cher. We believe your fellow Chonorans have been made part of the Tictoctickian food supply," the captain took it upon herself to respond at last.

"Our whole world has been turned downside up!" complained Chig-cher. He leapt anew into Chwerp-chee's welcoming arms.

Chwerp-chee's numerous suction discs pulled comfortingly on Chig-cher's bulbous head, to more lavender-glowing effect. Inky-dark, purplish pee spurted nervously from Chig-cher's neck, further enhancing the pigeon-pea stains on his canvas shirt.

"Once we got you both on board the Smoke and Mirrors, we made a quick time-travel departure from the vicinity of Chonora's larger moon. You were not afforded a view of the havoc Tictoctic's seized saucers wreaked on your planet. That happened in what for you is your planet's future," warned Captain Taylor. "Soon we will finally arrive back to our present, which lies even further into your future. You are going to have to brace for what you are liable to see, of what else has ultimately happened to Chonora. Then we will explain, as best we can, the tree creatures' plans for disrupting and eventually undoing the cycle of violence."

"Well," Chig-cher scanned his shirt, very much pleased with the result of so much staining. He chirped with all the brazen courage he could muster, "If we are to perish, at least I will go out on a most fashionable note!"

Chapter 13

"It would seem, Officer Rek-mek-a-nek, we have returned here none too soon!" tongue-clickingly exclaimed Captain Kek-stek of the Sixth Celestial Breath.

The Sixth Celestial Breath had dropped out of light-speed multiples, to resume reconnaissance of the Cygnitaurus solar system's outer perimeter. Captain Kek-stek was referring to what happened not ten kipektels later.

A jagged electrical bolt suddenly cut across the seeming absolute void of space. Tictoctickians were reminded of cloud-to-cloud lightning, but without clouds. The jagged bolt split into two. From the depths of that split, the cigar-shaped starship named Smoke and Mirrors emerged with a dramatic flourish. More specifically, sprays of sparkling photons, like shimmering fairy dust, issued from the vehicle's rose-shaped rear. Moreover, the Smoke and Mirrors was accompanied by what Yulala believed to be the planet spirit of Fafama. Chris would have said the planet spirit found itself thrust into exile from its cataclysmically ruined origin. And for that exile, it was tagging along with the starship like a faithful puppy dog. Yes, the planet spirit did get temporarily separated from the Smoke and Mirrors when that starship travelled further into the past from a past-time voyage. But ever since...

"Captain Kek-stek, if I might utter something about that conglomeration of twinkles. Of course, I am talking about the twinkles continuing to shadow the other-worlders' space-worthy exoskeleton. They would appear to assume the shape of one of our fiercest oskynt. However, the neck stretches to an unreasonable length, more like a limbless kissikist. And it is nearly the size of Tictoctic, rather than of a creature roaming the surface.

And you can see right through it, despite its enormity. Whereas, it is impossible to see past an oskynt's furry surface to its skin, let alone through the rest of its body. That is, unless it has fallen victim to the peculiar disease capable of making a beast lose all its hair. No. The oskynt's body is opaque. Or at least its few remaining preserved carcasses are opaque."

"In other words, you idiot," huffed and snorted Captain Kek-stek, "apart from it showing no similarity whatsoever to an oskynt, that thing out there bears an uncanny resemblance!"

Officer Rek-mek-a-nek bowed his head how most Earthlings would have characterized as sheepishly. He most humbly bleated, "There is probably more wisdom to be gained from a drop of Dek-Fook-Tek's drooled saliva than from my entire mental capacity."

A ritual litany ensued from the rest of the crew assembled on the navigation deck of the Sixth Celestial Breath. "May we someday be privileged to bathe in, be enlightened by, the Supreme Authority's spit."

"Very well," tongue-clicked the captain agreeably. "We cannot be sure how the exoskeleton's captain or that sparkle-thing is going to react when we implement Commander Kwit-Nik's orders. Officer Rek-mek-a-nek, I want our magnetic pulse-beam set on edge between diffuse and targeted!"

⊙ ⋈⊙⊙ ⋈⊙⊙ ⊙ ⋈⊙⊙

"Well hang me upside down, ankle-cuffed by a pair of your freshly woven socks, Prissy-pie, if it doesn't pour when it rains!" Michael DeFarge, commander of the compact battle cruiser, Elusive, slapped his thigh hard. He slapped it so hard, his palm stung as he squinted at the view-screen. He squinted because he was anxious not to overlook the slightest, possibly most crucial detail.

"Yes, dear, I do see what you are referring to." Priscilla didn't look up from her knitting. She had already taken in everything she believed needed taking in. "The Smoke and Mirrors is still accompanied by its dragon constellation. And it has returned from a time travel venture not thirty seconds after the saucer from Tictoctic showed up again. Doubtless, the saucer captain is resuming reconnaissance of this region of the Tictoctic solar system."

"So what, you think the convergence of these two events is no more than an accident?! No more than mere coincidence?! Good God, woman!" Pulling only a little harder on his unruly hair, DeFarge could have yanked out a fist full, down to the very roots.

"I think we will see what happens next, dear. Don't worry. I am sure you will find the perfect time to act. You will set the stage for our big battleships to permanently eliminate the most unseemly threat posed by those cervine beasts of Tictoctic. Daring to compare themselves to humanity, they have co-opted a status God never meant to be, never intended. Anyone who has read the book of Genesis must surely know this! It is the devil's work, that's for certain, when antlered creatures fly spacecraft." Michel DeFarge's wife conducted the entirety of this analysis in a most subdued voice. Where Michel was concerned, she could have been expounding on the likelihood one of her friends might win a baking contest. And once again, she accomplished her communication without lifting her head from knitting.

"Your lips to God's ear!" said Michel DeFarge. "Or rather, sounds like I've got this ass backwards! Sounds like God's lips to your ear! Whichever, better hang on tight! I'll be damnably damned if the deer demons aren't charging up that pulse-beam of theirs this very minute, for having another go at the Smoke and Mirrors! No! Not the Smoke and Mirrors! Instead, I fancy christening it the Peaceniks' Doomed Deliverer of Demented Delusions! Unless Captain Taylor retreats into that time rift once more, we might be getting our pretext for putting our God-lovin' show on the road even sooner than expected!"

What grew plainly noticeable to DeFarge was neon blue light encircling the outer rim of the flying saucer. It would glow brighter and brighter, finally separating from the saucer rim as a diffuse ripple spreading out to disruptive effect in all directions.

But then...

"What's this?! What's this?!"

Even these animate exclamations from Michel DeFarge did not concern Priscilla overly much. She took no more than the briefest glance up at the view-screen from her needlework.

"You saw that, Prissy?! Their blue light just faded away before emanating the first ripple! Did their weapon short out? Blow a fuse?! Or did our fatally naïve friends surrender before those demon stag finished ramping up, even?! Look at that! Look at that!" DeFarge pointed at the screen.

"Yes, dear," was all "Prissy" had to say after another quick glance.

"Now the saucer and the Smoke and Mirrors are steadily approaching one another! What splattering dump of moose diarrhea *is* this?!?!"

Quite simply, Commander DeFarge, telepathed Wafoodle-boodle, *the creatures from Tictoctic have readily accepted our terms. But this is merely the first stage of our alternative to the massive violence you* believe is necessary only because your fear has overcome your faith.

Priscilla also received this telepath from the Oombian tree creature aboard the Smoke and Mirrors. She shook her head in regretful disdain.

⸱⋈⊙⸱⋈⊙⸱⋈⊙⸱

What Wafoodle-boodle intentionally neglected to mention to Captain DeFarge was the nature of the "terms" expressed by Captain Helena Taylor.

Officer Rek-mek-a-nek did power up the Sixth Celestial Breath's magnetic pulse-beam, albeit on a diffuse setting. But that was when Captain and crew aboard the immense flying saucer experienced a dramatic change to what their panoramic view-screen revealed. The left half of that screen suddenly filled with an image of Helena Taylor standing on the navigation bridge of the Smoke and Mirrors. Her utterances were quickly translated into the tics and tocs of Kek-stek's first and only language. "Captain Kek-stek of the Sixth Celestial Breath," she said, "this is Captain Helena Taylor of the starship Smoke and Mirrors. You might wonder how we know your name and rank, plus the name of your starship. We can thank the mind-reading abilities of our associates from a planet other than either yours or mine. Anyway, we offer our surrender, the surrender of everyone aboard here. Long before now, we intentionally disarmed, let go every last weapon our passengers or crew might have been carrying. As a loving gesture, we came to your solar system defenseless. In return for this gesture, we hope you might allow exploration of a plan for more fully meeting your civilization's nutritional needs. That is, without your having to resort to killing higher order life forms from other planets, ourselves included."

"Cancel the charging up of the diffuse pulse-beam!" harshly urgently brayed Captain Kek-stek. His tone was also meant to communicate something else. He didn't want the slightest, meekest bleat to interfere with his hearing the rest of what this unnaturally clothed beast from a distant planet was saying.

"We have completed a time travel mission," Helena's translated message went on, "to better understand what has brought you to your present circumstances. We believe we can offer you a superior path to superior food, and a superior life overall."

Oodle-Noodle would have had the captain go even further. That tree creature from Oomb would have had Helena Taylor mention how the Earthlings wanted to time travel again. They wanted to undo the apocalyptic devastation of Chonora. But Captain Taylor vetoed this part. She thought it simply too much for the extraterrestrial deer creatures to absorb on top of everything else she was proposing. Besides which, Helena wasn't sure the Oombian didn't agree with her.

Earlier on, Oodle-Noodle brought up Chonoran history for Chwerp-chee and Chig-cher's sake, only. She admitted that the ruination of their civilization included virtually everyone and everything they knew and cherished. However, she also assured the Chonoran couple that such ruination would not stand, if there was any possible way to help it.

"Captain Kek-stek," Officer Rek-mek-a-nek took advantage of the pause in the "Akt" creature's address to humbly baa. "Are we sure this isn't some devious trick? Maybe the other-worlders want you to power down our defenses so they can have their associates attack us while we are distracted with their wild fantasies?"

"Officer Rek-mek-a-nek!" Captain Kek-stek's angry snort produced visible puffs of steam from his nostrils. "Are you incapable of taking 'yes' for an answer?! Our sensors...you know this as much as I do, you idiot! Our sensors pick up no other spacecraft within two billion lek-leks of us! That is, no other spacecraft from here to the Seventh Celestial Breath keeping guard orbit around Chonora! There is nothing save an inconsequential, aimlessly drifting bit of space junk! And of course," Captain Kek-stek went on, unaware the "space junk" was actually the Elusive, "there is that animated constellation monster producing lots of fire, but no burn! Yes," Kek-stek calmed a bit to nod reflectively, bemusedly even. "It is indeed exceedingly odd for cuts of meat to offer up alternatives to their consumption. But matters are proceeding exactly as Commander Kwit-Nik prophesized! Inspired by Dek-Fook-Tek, I am certain," Captain Kek-stek added none too soon. His crew's quizzical regard was about to gallop round the corner to suspicion. Suspicion totally unwarranted, well did Kek-stek know. The very idea, that he might be anything less than fawningly adoring of the ultimate war hero of Tictoctic! Especially since Dek-Fook-Tek was soon to be self-proclaimed the Supreme Authority of the planet, if not of the entire solar system! "Once Kwit-Nik was made Commander of our saucer defense fleet, thanks again to the boundless wisdom of Dek-Fook-Tek..."

"The furthest horizon is as a beginning, only, to the extent of his knowing." The rest of the crew ritually chanted this during the pause Captain Kek-stek correctly intuited he better allow before he continued.

"As the new commander," the captain reiterated when he finally resumed tongue-clicking, "Kwit-Nik faced distraction from multiple directions. But he immediately detected the other-world space vessel unburdening itself of an enormous payload. Cast adrift in deep space, this payload erupted in a series of explosions. Every last bit of weaponry from aboard the space vessel must have been detonated! Commander Kwit-Nik concluded the occupants of the other-world vessel were intent on offering a peace proposal when they entered our solar system. But could he have imagined their opening move would be their total surrender? No, he could not!" Captain Kek-stek rose from his captain's chair and spun around. With unbridled delight, he pounded his cloven hind hooves against the floor of the navigation deck. "Our magnificently prescient Dek-Fook-Tek could have imagined it, but not Commander Kwit-Nik! The commander's orders were that we insist the other-world vessel surrender for our immediate, unconditional boarding! But now, such insistence is unnecessary! Occupation of that odd-shaped spacecraft will be simplicity itself! Then we can safely deliver its occupants to an audience with Commander Kwit-Nik. The commander wants them for their intelligence-gathering during their purported time travel. But also, he actually said this to me, for their entertainment value! The commander wants both of these things before the other-worlders are made into a most welcome addition to our food supply!"

Raucous baaing ensued from Captain Kek-stek's subordinate officers. But it got abruptly tamped down by a new translated message from the other-world vessel, at long last.

"When you board our spaceship," said Captain Taylor, "you should find of special interest the testimony by your fellow beings. We imprisoned them after we liberated the planet, 'Oomb,' from your occupation.

What they tell you about how we have treated them should prove most illuminating of our intent. We now await your occupation of our vessel, offering not the least resistance."

❧ ✧·❧·✧·❧ ❧

"There! There!" Wildly animate, Michel DeFarge pointed at the Elusive's view-screen again. "What is that, Prissy, if it's not those furry-assed antlered demons boarding the Smoke and Mirrors?! Without a hint of fight put up by our recklessly naïve fellow humans! Ah! I've got it!" He snapped his fingers. "It's a trap! It has to be! Once our people lure enough of those what-the-f-kians-"

"Dear! Your language!" Priscilla tsk-tsk-tsked without looking up.

"Oh, sorry, Prissy-pie. I only meant to say: Once our good guys lure enough of the enemy off their accursed saucer, they can sneak aboard, infiltrate that infernal contraption. If they seize control, it's WHAM! BAM! With the demon stag's own pulse-beam, Captain Taylor threatens blowing to space dust the Smoke and Mirrors! Including most importantly those Tictoctickians who have tried to occupy it! Unless they surrender! No! Wait!" DeFarge snapped his fingers again. "Captain Taylor and company aren't capable! They must be counting on *me* to do the infiltrating!"

"Yes, dear."

No such thing, Commander DeFarge. This telepath was also shared with Priscilla. It was enough to make her look up from her knitting. *It doesn't matter whether or not the flight commander of the Sixth Celestial Breath, including his away team, boards the Smoke and Mirrors. There will still be more than enough Tictoctickians left behind. They can easily prevent you or any group of your fellow Earthlings from seizing their spacecraft. But that is* not to say we are not luring the extraterrestrials from Tictoctic into something, because we are. Only it's not a trap. It's like unto your Priscilla's lure, with what she weaves in the place of a spider web. We are intent on luring them into love, a loving relationship, to start ridding them of their hate and fear. We would lure you to that place as well, if we could.

Priscilla waved a dismissive hand, most casually. She plunged her darning needle back into knitting Michel's next pair of socks as she said, "Don't pay that voice in our heads any attention, dear; it's just trying to hypnotize us, and we can't be sure *where* it's from."

Funny, thought her husband, how the way she handled her needle, "Prissy-pie" might as well have been spear fishing.

⸙⸳⸙⸳⸙⸳⸙⸳

On the navigation bridge of the Smoke and Mirrors, Captain Kek-stek got up close to Captain Taylor. He got up so close that Taylor received an uncomfortable impression. And she was already uncomfortable enough from how he made no secret of sniffing at her. The impression was that he might actually have been about to lick her face, and find out how her sweat tasted.

Kek-stek's subordinate officers stood around the bridge with their air igniters at the ready. But they made no specific effort to coral or herd any Earthlings.

"How many calves you have aboard? Any calves?" translated Kek-stek's crisp tongue-clicks.

"Captain, I truly believe he is making reference to children; the translating algorithm ought to have picked up on that," Counselor Ali Magabu observed in his gentlest voice.

If only, Helena thought to herself with grim wistfulness, a minor mistranslation could have been the biggest of their worries.

"Look what we have here, Captain Kek-stek!" Officer Rek-mek-a-nek brayed proudly when he herded Chwerp-chee and Chig-cher onto the bridge at the butt end of his air igniter.

The two Chonorans swung along on a special cable installed for them. It hung from the ceiling throughout several rooms and corridors of the starship.

"Baa! Two Chonoran tenderloins as a peace offering?!" Captain Kek-stek's ears fluttered with excitement. He stepped even closer to Helena, close enough for her to smell his breath like cheese gone really moldy bad. His new crisply delivered tongue-clicks translated, "Captain Taylok, you've brought us these two fine-looking specimens as a peace offering? I must say, I would certainly relish sitting down with you at a common table, pulling meat off their bones. Can there be any better way to imbue me with confidence our directive has stampeded from a source of most divine wisdom? I think not! Baa!"

There were several other deer creatures on the navigation bridge of the Smoke and Mirrors who had trotted over from the Sixth Celestial Breath. They baaed along with Captain Kek-stek.

Before responding, Helena looked deep into Kek-stek's eyes. What she found herself feeling had nothing to do with the stubby bluntness of his antlers. She felt like she might as well have been looking into the gentle eyes of a stag encountered crossing an open field back on Earth. This compounded her difficulty believing these creatures were any more the heartless killers than Earth deer. Such difficulty emboldened her to respond, full of dismissive bravado, "We have far more flavorful fare to offer you than those two. If you don't believe me, believe Fwok-bwahk and Klik-klok, your fellow Tictoctickians. They rave about our chef's special arroz con gandules."

"Akkots con kankules?" A dubious tone to his voice, Captain Kek-stek strained his tongue-clicks to try pronouncing the Spanish words for "rice with pigeon peas."

"Yes," nodded Taylor. "By comparison, they will make Chonoran meat seem the foulest dung by comparison."

Chig-cher's bulbous head glowed sickly brownish-yellow in reaction to Captain Taylor's characterization. "Actually," he went on to chirp whisperingly to Chwerp-chee, "I would think that done up properly, our dung could be quite savory. But I realize you are not one comfortable with venturing into such culinary frontiers. That is quite alright. A strong relationship always requires a bit of compromise. And I am more than ready to make such compromise despite the potential I have scented after many a smooth dump."

"Shut up," Chwerp-chee tersely chirped under his breath.

☙ ﷽ ❧ ﷽ ❧ ﷽

"And they're off! Both of them! Side by side!" Michel DeFarge observed of both the Smoke and Mirrors and the Sixth Celestial Breath. Nearly simultaneously, those two starships accelerated to normal light-speed and faster. Their spiral course was set round the Cygnitaurus solar system's star, headed for Tictoctic. From Michel's perspective, they were there one moment, gone the next. Similar to what happens when someone flips off a light switch, he fancied. The sparkling photon trails left in their wake appeared like someone just flipped *on* a light switch, however. "I wonder whether Captain Taylor's crew is still working the controls of the Smoke and Mirrors, under gunpoint of course," Michel DeFarge wondered aloud. "Or maybe those unnaturally clothes-wearing critters are flying it themselves! Good God a-mighty! And damnably damned if that dragon constellation didn't appear to keep up with them both! The only question is: How am *I* going to keep up without the enemy, our quarry, realizing I'm keeping up? That comet! Yes! That's the ticket! It's a considerable bit slower than they are proceeding. No matter. I'll just scoot from behind that to whatever other flotsam and jetsam we can locate between here and wherever they're going, hopefully headed into the belly of the Tictoctic beast! It will be like scooting from behind pine tree to boulder to whatever damnably damned else! On the trail of the finest most regal elk! Only difference, Prissy, is I've got our drone attack up our sleeve. We just have to pick the best time and place to flush those antlered hornets into the open. Then our full-sized battle cruisers can carve out this section of the galaxy for *real* peace! That's the ticket!"

"Yes, dear."

Chapter 14

"I expect you to pardon what I am about to say," was how Commander Kwit-Nik's rapid-fire tongue-clicks translated. He held up to eye level a pigeon pea from his plate full of arroz con gandules (rice with pigeon peas) and ripe, fried plantains. "These 'kandulays' bear a striking resemblance to the pellets we defecate. Before any of us graze, I will require additional assurance we are not being invited to eat our own poop!"

Up until Commander Kwit-Nik's suspicion-laden remarks, Captain Taylor's surrender had gone off without a hitch. That is, where the collaborated plans of the Earthlings together with the Oombians were concerned. Nevertheless, the stress still proved so stomach-churning, the commander's ominous tongue-clicks did not add to it significantly. In fact, Commander Kwit-Nik's frame of mind had already been probed by the telepathic Oombians.

Ever since Taylor's surrender, a harsh but expected reality persisted. At any moment the deer creatures from Tictoctic could decide they had had enough of creatures from other worlds advising them on dietary matters. The Tictoctickians could go back to treating the Earthlings plus two Chonorans like any other part of their food supply. What didn't help was Chonoran meat being considered a preciously rare delicacy on Tictoctic.

"I know what you are going to bray, Officer Fwok-bwahk." Commander Kwit-Nik held up his other cloven hoof-hand not occupied holding the pigeon pea. But he was thereby urging Lieutenant Ak-keek-teek to remain silent, not Fwok-bwahk. Kwit-Nik sensed the lieutenant was full to bursting with disgust over wasting any more time on the other-worlders' idea of what should constitute a hearty meal. "You and Tlik-klok have been eating such foods as this for several days now," continued Commander Kwit-Nik. "They have been your lot, ever since the other-worlders from Akt succeeded in isolating you and fellow Tictoctickian soldiers from the rest of us. I do not want to sound insulting. However, I cannot be sure you were not hypnotized into believing your own poop makes for a most savory repast. Try as I might, to trust these creatures who addicted you with their game of 'kookf,' I must remain ever vigilant. Efforts to poison important leaders of the Tictoctickian defense, including myself, can suddenly stampede from anywhere. So before this meal proceeds, I must insist on two preconditions. First, Captain Taylok, we will switch plates."

Commander Kwit-Nik let go his pigeon pea, and it dropped back onto his pile of "arroz con gandules." Then the commander lifted Helena's plate from before her as he slid his plate into its place.

"Second, I cannot be sure you Aktlinks haven't been hypnotized, yourselves, into relishing pellets of the defecated kind. And so I must insist on the following. I know." The Tictoctickian commander held up a cloven hoof-hand anew, to ward off potential objections. "Your Chef Ludi, here, put on quite a show. She insisted she harvested consumable, nutritious seed variants from kandulay plants. Maybe it was not a show. Maybe it was real. We have an expression on Tictoctic about offering up a delectable regurgitation, but then switching it out for the undigested, grass-embedded dung of an oskynt. So this is what else I demand: Officers Tlik-klok and Fwok-bwahk, you will take leave from us under armed guard. Inside an Aktlink excretion room, you will produce at least a few pellets, each. Chef Ludi, you will prepare those pellets the same way you prepared these purported non-pellets. You will do so under Chef Glork-tek's supervision, that he might confirm there is no variance from how you prepared purported non-pellets the first time. Then you will serve them to Chef Glork-tek. Chef Glork-tek, you will conduct a taste comparison with a plate switched out from another Aktlink, no matter which you choose. To save time, you will not need to stir in the poop pellets with more rice.

"Let us assume Glork-tek can assure me the kandulay beans and the poop pellets are not one in the same. And furthermore, Captain, that you do not look to be keeling over from having been poisoned. Those two happenstances will grant me bahvek-sharpened confidence this meal is as innocently well-intentioned as you want us to believe."

Captain Helena Taylor nodded, "Very well," before she wasted no time digging heartily into the Puerto Rican traditional food on Commander Kwit-Nik's plate. Her stomach had been in continual churn over her worry whether voluntarily surrendering was the right thing. Unsurprisingly, she had gone for several days hardly able to eat. But lots of time had transpired with the alien deer creatures making no move to add any Earthling or Chonoran to their food supply. This was the case despite noises to the effect that munching on roasted arm of "Aktlink" or fried leg of "Konokan" still most certainly remained an option. Consequently, Helena's hunger finally overtook her. She was famished to such extent that she threw caution to the wind. If her stress made her nauseously ill upon giving in to her appetite, so be it. More importantly, she feared how any hesitation on her part might be taken, where going ahead and eating was concerned. It might be misconstrued for an indication she knew the food was poisoned.

Most other Earthlings followed Helena's example, gorging with abandon on Ludi's traditional Puerto Rican dish.

Meanwhile Chef Glork-tek and Chef Ludi Perez left the table after Tlik-klok and Fwok-bwahk. As per Commander Kwit-Nik's orders, they would attend to whatever pellets the two Tictoctickians could defecate on command.

Helena's starvation subsided, the more she ate. After she ate plenty, she found her thoughts drifting. She was making random reflections on particular happenstances since the Smoke and Mirrors arrived near Tictoctic under escort of the Sixth Celestial Breath.

The first of those reflections concerned the present million-mile-high orbit of the Smoke and Mirrors around Tictoctic. The Tictoctickians easily agreed to board the Earth vessel for a sampling of the culinary delights other-world plants offered. Commander Kwit-Nik said the deer creatures' continuation of their normal food-gathering operations could be put on hold for a short while, at least.

Once that was settled, another consensus was just as easily reached. The Earthling starship would maintain one-quarter light-speed during its planetary orbit. But such orbit would be at a sufficient distance from Tictoctic, meal attendees wouldn't go dizzy looking outside one of its panoramic-sized portholes. Advantage accrued, of course, from being able to enjoy a modicum of gravity while eating, thanks to the one-quarter light-speed. Nobody needed to squeeze their food out of special plastic bags, like the Tictoctickians did under weightless conditions on the Tictoctic space station. Squeeze-food was also status quo for crew and company aboard the Smoke and Mirrors whenever they were experiencing zero-gravity slow flight.

Her mouth stuffed with more rice and pigeon peas despite her satiated appetite, Helena meditated on the porthole view. Tictoctic was looking about the size of Earth's moon when observed from Earth. During the starship's two-and-a-half-minute quarter-light-speed orbit, the sunlit side of the planet Tictoctic she found especially striking, not in a good way. From a similar distance, the Earth still appeared beautifully pearl-like blue despite environmental degradation wrought of global warming. Tictoctic, however, appeared mostly a dull tan color. Helena well knew this sickly cast had to have resulted from runaway climate change even more severe than back on Earth. She guessed Tictoctic's water supply far less abundant, if far more than Fafama's. Coupled with extraordinary amounts of fossil fuel use...

The Earthlings and Oombians were proposing other-world resettlement of the Tictoctickian population. But could such resettlement truly be only temporary? Or was Tictoctic's climate so ruined, millennia would pass before Tictoctickians saw its ecosystem healthily restored, once again fit for habitation?

The two-and-a-half-minute orbit brought the Smoke and Mirrors around to the dark side of Tictoctic, again some million miles away. That is when Helena's thoughts drifted back to greeting Commander Kwit-Nik. For that first contact, she tried to engage the commander in a handshake after showing how it's done with Officer Buddy Leung.

When Commander Kwit-Nik met Captain Taylor's effort by extending his cloven hoof-hand, he triggered much braying and baaing laughter from other Tictoctickians. Kwit-Nik's Lieutenant Ak-keek-teek tongue-clicked through his foamy-drooled amusement, "Next, shall we rub snouts with a roasted oskynt carcass? Or waggle the forelimbs of a flash-frozen Chonoran?" In case any of the Earthlings had the least lingering doubt why their extraterrestrial guests found Kwit-Nik's offer to shake hands so funny...

Memory of the lieutenant's chilling remarks stirred Helena to also recall her one defensive, protective move. She made it well prior to any Tictoctickians boarding the Smoke and Mirrors. She hid the children, along with enough adults for their care, behind soundproofed barriers specially designed to act as false façades. The adults included Professors Aquinas and Skepticus, the two Marines and the Marines' wives. Chwerp-chee and Chig-cher should also have been made part of that group. But as it turned out, hypnosis from Wafoodle-boodle easily facilitated securing them away there later.

The Tictoctickians took no time noticing the sealed-off section of the starship. But Helena Taylor had a cover story ready to go. It went like this: Nothing more was concealed than the nuts and bolts of the rear-end mirror-array propulsion system.

"Stop Captain, before you gather onto your eating utensil the next morsel from your plate!" tongue-clicked Commander Kwit-Nik. Thereby he abruptly broke in on Helena's contemplative, thought-wandering chew. "First, I will require you to partake of the purportedly safe and nutritious vegetable-based food I have gathered onto my eating utensil."

The next thing Helena knew, Kwit-Nik thrust his fork underneath her nose. He nearly plugged her nostrils with the mix of rice, pigeon peas and ripe plantain he variously stabbed and scooped off the plate he had switched away from her. "You see, Captain, one could imagine you anticipating I would not trust the plate handed to me was not poisoned. Under that scenario, you would have actually dared to have had the fatally tampered-with food placed before yourself at the outset. And then you would have depended on me to insist on trading dishes."

Helena deliberately did not allow herself the least hesitation after Commander Kwit-Nik announced his suspicion-laden imagining. She opened her mouth wide to engulf completely his insistently offered forkful. Just as quickly she sat back in her chair, munched away with clear satisfaction, and swallowed.

The commander has to go through these paranoid-seeming motions with us, Oodle-Noodle telepathed from where he was standing behind Helena. *He fully trusts us, but there are enough of his fellow Tictoctickians here who do not. They number nearly as many as those others in attendance who are ready to join him in a revolt against their dictatorial leader, Dek-Fook-Tek.*

Helena already knew Kwit-Nik was play-acting. She could see it in his sad eyes, not to mention his busily twitching nostrils. She also knew she needed to respond firmly yet calmly to his expressed concern. She needed to do that for the benefit of those worrisome deer creature extraterrestrials in attendance to whom Oodle-Noodle referred. They were the ones who remained fanatically devoted to their evidently crazed leader. Among the Tictoctickians Helena suspected of such fanaticism, she found Lieutenant Ak-keek-teek especially disturbing. All of this in mind, she said, "I understand and yet I don't understand. Let us imagine, indeed, that my people had some scheme in play to poison you and your associates. Commander, your personnel occupy our starship in overwhelming numbers. I really don't see how the result of such a scheme wouldn't have been your immediately adding us to your food supply."

Kwit-Nik waited out more of his nostril twitches before responding. He tongue-clicked, "If only it were the case, Captain, that other-world species of supposedly civilized ways never behaved irrationally. Regretfully, our experience has been otherwise."

Captain Taylor avoided looking directly towards Lieutenant Ak-keek-teek. Out the corner of her eye, though, she glimpsed a ridiculously wide, bucktooth grin dawning across his countenance. That grin came complete with the wildest, untamed look in his eyes.

Helena Taylor's intuition really unnerved her. She sensed the lieutenant could have maintained his eerie visage all the way through chopping off one of her arms and roasting it over an open flame pit. Something like that. Nevertheless, she managed to at least project an outward sense of composure. She did this by preoccupying herself with wonder about the experience Commander Kwit-Nik was referring to earlier. That is, the experience regarding other-world species behaving irrationally. It finally occurred to her the commander had to be talking about the Chonoran demonstration pulse beam-attack on a Tictoctic mountainside. This attack eventually led to Tictoctickian forces seizing the bulk of Chonora's saucer fleet. Included most importantly in that seizure were all the saucers fitted by the Chonorans for interplanetary war.

"Ah, Chef Glork-tek, you have returned." Commander Kwit-Nik knocked his articulated hand-hooves together in minor celebration over this event. For Helena they sounded like two wooden blocks knocked together.

"Indeed I have returned," Chef Glork-tek's humble baaing translated as he retook his seat to the commander's left. He brought with him a dish featuring five steaming-hot black pellets.

Tlik-klok, Fwok-bwahk and Ludi returned to their own seats around the oval conference table, presently doubling as a dining table for the party of twenty-four.

"So you know what you must do." Kwit-Nik nodded towards the two plates set before Glork-tek.

"Of course," the chef brayed somewhat less humbly, more matter-of-factly. "I am to sample the purported kandulays side by side with the pellets produced by Tlik-klok and Fwok-bwahk. My goal is to confirm absolutely whether or not the other-worlders have deigned to serve us excrement."

Remember, Oodle-Noodle telepathed the assembled Earthlings, *Chef Glork-tek already knows what the result will be. But he and Commander Kwit-Nik also know what some of their fellow creatures here require. For them, nothing less will suffice than the chef having demonstrably eaten at least two of the poop pellets.*

Glork-tek began with the pigeon peas, tonguing two of them off his fork. He nodded approvingly while he chewed them. Then he commented, "Unusually flavorful and, oddly enough, meaty for plant food. They make me anticipate most favorably the rest of this." He pointed with his fleshy yet narrow tongue towards the fried ripe plantains and the achiote-colored rice. "Also," he added, "I did not taste any fecal notes. Now we try the pellets."

Glork-tek tongued two of the poop pellets directly off their plate and into his mouth, without use of a fork. Nearly triple the size of the pigeon peas, they were produced one each by Tlik-klok and Fwok-bwahk. "What I am noticing already," he baaed as he strove to suppress his gag reflex, "are the most pungent dirt notes of fecal extrusions. Cough! Yes, there are hints of the kandulays' flavor, cough! But that is as expected from a diet admittedly rich in kandulays. Excuse me." He washed down the poop with his glass of water. Fanatics in attendance expected no less from the commander's official taste tester. Spitting out any of the pellets would have put his life at risk. One of those fanatics would have endeavored to bring down on him the often-irrational wrath of the Supreme Authority Dek-Fook-Tek. Said fanatic would have fed into the Supreme Authority's paranoia via secretive communication. He would have suggested to the Supreme Authority that Chef Glork-tek was avoiding the full effect of the poison, even though poison was not at issue. At issue was whether fecal matter had been substituted for vegetable matter.

✱✿✻✱✿✻✱✿✻

"I'll be damnably damned!" exclaimed Michel DeFarge. He slapped his hand against his control console for added emphasis, to draw his wife's attention. "Those furry-assed devils are willing to literally make their own eat shit, to assure they aren't eating shit!"

"Your language, dear," Priscilla said with gentle admonishment. She continued knitting, not deigning to look up.

Oodle-Noodle and Wafoodle-boodle kept in telepathic contact with DeFarge during his evasive spiral path headed for Tictoctic from the outer perimeter of the Cygnitaurus system. They sent him a steady flow of assurances everyone aboard the Smoke and Mirrors was safe. Those assurances included details of how the children together with an ample supply of caregivers had been hidden away for their added protection. The children had been hidden away, of course, just in case. One never knew when the Tictoctickians might suddenly crave the human version of veal cutlets, to hell with vegetarian alternatives.

Anyway, the Oombian tree creatures continued giving Michel DeFarge minute-by-minute updates on the dinner party aboard the Smoke and Mirrors. But they wondered, why bother? Self-styled lone hunter Michel DeFarge made very clear to the Oombians he couldn't trust indefinitely they were telepathing reliable info. "What if you are threatened by the Tictoctickian beasts with immediate torching? That is, if you don't feed me a constant stream of pablum while they munch on the captain and crew, one by one? Sorry, trunk-o-noodles," said DeFarge. "Suppose I see or otherwise sense anything what leads me to believe your ultra-naïve peacenik jig is up. And I'm guessing that's just a matter of very short time from now. When that happens, I am moving in with all I've got, as per my original mandate! This waiting around is simply a courtesy I'm extending. If you can somehow prolong your delusion a bit longer, add a couple extra days to your lives, well I am a humane person if you do catch my drift!"

The Sixth Celestial Breath did escort the Smoke and Mirrors into orbit around Tictoctic. That is when Yoon-hee Park-Smith managed to eavesdrop on certain surveillance data. The Tictoctickian troops occupying the Smoke and Mirrors periodically transmitted this data to Commander Kwit-Nik. They also transmitted it down to a monitoring station on the surface of Tictoctic, within Dek-Fook-Tek's antler-shaped sub-arctic stronghold.

Meanwhile, there was a six- to seven-minute delay for DeFarge's reception from Officer Park-Smith of her eavesdroppings. The delay depended on which asteroid or other celestial object DeFarge had his compact battle cruiser, the Elusive, shadowing at the time. But at least DeFarge received a different perspective on what was actually transpiring aboard the Smoke and Mirrors. He didn't have to rely solely on the tree creatures with their pacifist ax to grind. Ironically, DeFarge figured that ax would most likely get them both chopped down, ultimately.

"I hate to say it, Prissy-pie," Michel was presently speaking in regretful, most somber reflection. "But after their meal ends, I don't think Captain Taylor has much else left up her sleeve to postpone the reckoning. Think I better start gearing up."

"Yes, dear."

⁙⁘⁙⁘⁙⁘⁙

"Chef Glork-tek!" Commander Kwit-Nik tongue-clicked in the most commanding tone he could muster. "Your culinary ruminations are, as always, most ground-pawingly appreciated, in both their literal and figurative sense. As for you, Captain Taylok, you have yet to collapse off your chair. You have yet to behave like an oskynt, several mini-pektels after it has been shot in the head. In other words, you haven't suddenly fallen over sideways upon finally realizing you are dead. So I think we can safely bray that everyone may proceed to sample your Chef Ludi's plant-derived food preparations. Although it has to also be said, Captain, your chairs appear exceedingly uncomfortable, exceedingly unaccommodating of our rear ends. Thank Dek-Fook-Tek I have not needed to use one. Considerable muscular discipline would have been required not to have found myself tipping over onto the floor to escape such mystifying unpleasantness. And mystifying unpleasantness would most certainly have been the case, even without the aid of poisoned food. It is wise, indeed, I thought to reflect on what our Supreme Authority, Dek-Fook-Tek, would have done in our situation. Thereby did I order our own chairs brought over for ourselves."

Helena would have responded, *Nothing mystifying at all. It's your furry little tail; our chairs aren't designed with a special hole in them to accommodate such an anatomical feature.* But they had had exactly this same conversation several times before. In fact, they had had this conversation so many times before, Helena wondered. Was an awkward lack of much else to comfortably discuss responsible? Or was dementia evidenced on the deer creature's part?

Captain Taylor had another reason for allowing the commander's remark to stand without any further comment. She wanted to avoid experiencing yet another ritual fawning over the "Supreme Authority," the Tictoctickian war hero in the plot to seize Chonoran saucers.

Her silence didn't matter, however. Kwit-Nik's remark was all Lieutenant Ak-keek-teek needed for him to rise up onto his hind hooves. He solemnly tongue-clicked, "Furniture designing suffers for Dek-Fook-Tek having too much else to attend to."

The other deer creatures from Tictoctic seated around the oval conference table rose up onto their hind hooves as well. They ritually chanted, "May our future furniture designers feed from his inspiration, like the young foal seeks nourishment from the regurgitations of the mother."

The Earthlings stood out of respect and fear.

Consequently, the lieutenant and Officer Rek-mek-a-nek couldn't help snorting through the chant. They labored to conceal their amusement. Here were future cuts of hopefully most tender, delectable meat giving their due to those intent on their slaughter!

Everyone did finally return sitting, to at last sample in earnest the Earthling-prepared meal.

Without shame, Lieutenant Ak-keek-teek latched his eyes longingly onto the bosom of Yoon-hee seated beside him. He couldn't help relishing the tender breast meat he guessed responsible for two ample bulges in her outfit.

Unfazed by his leering, Yoon-hee turned directly the lieutenant's way to pointedly inquire, "So, are any females participating in your space program?"

"*Our* females are perfectly happy to remain surface-bound on Tictoctic! They find contentment caring for our brood. And they perform another important function, as well. They screen out defective males before those misfits can become a problem further down our hoof-beaten paths. Besides, a female presence aboard any of our spacecraft would prove most disruptive. Bull fights would break out regularly over who should sire the herd of them. We do not need the distraction up here in space such rivalry would cause." Ak-keek-teek gave the Earthling males – Ali, Buddy, Pedro, Kevin, and Chris – one of his big, bucktooth smiles as in: *Why aren't you asserting more control over your females?*

I'm sure they are absolutely thrilled remaining surface-bound on Tictoctic, to get as far away from you chauvinist clowns as possible! This is what coursed through Kevin's head, at least. *For all you know, while you are terrorizing the cosmos they are developing serious relationships with the more sensitive males of your species!*

"Um, about those defective males," said Ali with detached sternness in his regard of the bucktoothed lieutenant. "May I ask what becomes of them? And just how are they found to be defective?"

"Screening by the females is not perfect; several males do survive the process. They must be grazed out later when their insufficiency is realized," Lieutenant Akkee-teek responded, answering a different question from the one asked. "But I want to assure you!" His tongue-clicking devolved, for once, into defensive-sounding braying. Ali's steady, penetrating regard was unnerving him. "Where our females are concerned, we maintain for breeding even the most irrational and subversive ones. We would never dream of consuming any of them, even in our times of greatest need."

How very civilized of you! Kevin wanted to scream in Ak-keek-teek's face.

"My lieutenant spoke of disruptive rivalry," said Commander Kwit-Nik, seeking to defuse the growing tension he was sensing. "I understand, Tlik-klok and Fwok-bwahk, you have been enjoying a different sort of rivalry aboard this spacecraft with a game... How is it called?"

"Kolfk on Akt, and koofk on Koombt," Tlik-klok responded.

"You mean golf and oof," corrected Chris.

"Yes," Tlik-klok nodded. "Kolfk and koofk!"

Close enough, Helena severely stared down her husband to express nonverbally. She did not want him to press any further the matter of the deer creature's likely unavoidable mispronunciation.

"You hit a little ball with a wood or metal object secured to the end of a long stick," Tlik-klok explained for Kwit-Nik's sake.

"And you keep hitting it," Fwok-bwahk went on, "until you push it dropping into a little hole in the ground."

"Interesting. I can think of something else I keep hitting until I push 'it' into a little hole in something else!" Rek-mek-a-nek was intending to reserve this remark for Captain Kek-stek's entertainment only, seated beside him. But he got so carried away with his bemusement, his baa rose loud enough for a translator to pick up.

Kevin snorted rice out his nose, in concert with Captain Kek-stek shooting a lone pigeon pea from his own twitchy snout.

"These... These little balls you speak of, Officer Tlik-klok," the captain of the Sixth Celestial Breath tongue-clicked, having settled down from his mirth. "Where do they come from, or shouldn't I ask?" With this question, Captain Kek-stek rose from his chair onto his hind legs and he spun around braying resumed hilarity. Officer Rek-mek-a-nek and Lieutenant Ak-keek-teek joined him.

"Ha! Maybe Chef Glork-tek needs to sample the golf balls also, before anyone plays another game with them! Ha!" Buddy made this stab at adding to the fun.

Laughter issued from many different directions, for many different reasons. Tanya, Ludi, Ali, Helena and Yoon-hee forced themselves to laugh. They hoped a jovial mood would leave the Tictoctickians less likely to contemplate slaughtering the Earthlings for their food supply. The laughter from Chris, Tlik-klok and Fwok-bwahk was more genuine. In Chris's case, his amusement easily overrode any foreboding of imminent personal peril. And there was Kevin. His chuckling busted out because ironically, he found Buddy's gallows humor beyond incredible. How could Buddy even think to go for another one of his pathetically lame punch-lines under such dangerous circumstances? He couldn't be *that* oblivious to how close they might have strayed to the edge of doom, could he?

"Some of you have made an extra effort. Not only have you sampled this meal through your mouth. You have sampled it out your nasal passages as well," Commander Kwit-Nik observed by way of transition. "So, I ask my fellow Ticktoctickians their opinion of what the Aktlinks have prepared for us. To kick off that stampede, I must say I agree with Chef Glork-tek. The food is most flavorful, and the kandulays do satisfy my meat craving. But what about the rest of you?"

What about the rest of us? You will simply have to take a bite out of a few of us to find out. Buddy Leung experienced extreme frustration, stifling himself from sharing this first response that came to mind. Especially since it struck him as much funnier than any other punch line he could remember having ever delivered. However, even he could easily grasp the jeopardous folly of such a remark under the circumstances.

"As you indicated, Commander," answered Captain Kek-stek, "the kandulays are meat-tasting. Also, the kwied kwantains provided a flavorfully sweet contrast. I could imagine surviving on a diet of this stuff myself, if I had to."

"We haven't grown tired of it yet," chimed in Fwok-bwahk.

"This plant dish might *seem* delicious for some of you," said Lieutenant Ak-keek-teek, striving to dampen where he sensed the conversation going. "Even for me, I can almost imagine it providing a minimally adequate accompaniment to the main course. But that is the whole, bahvek-sharpened point. It is incomplete without a nice, tender cut of meat." Ak-keek-teek paused to deliberately leer at Yoon-hee's bosom anew. Then he slowly lifted up his head to give her his ultra-wide, bucktooth smile before he turned away. Wherefore he directed his attention back towards his fellow deer creatures to cheerfully bray, "On the other hoof, meat can more than stand alone as a full meal."

To Captain Taylor's unnerving surprise, it wasn't just the occupying Tictoctickians who nodded at the lieutenant's remark. Both Tlik-klok and Fwok-bwahk did likewise.

Remember, Captain, Oodle-Noodle telepathed Helena Taylor, *and for the other Earthlings as well. Many of them are nodding understanding only, including your two Tictoctickian guests for this mission. They do not necessarily agree.*

"There you have it, Captain Taylok. You have our reactions to your most generously provided meal. That is over and done with. So now what, exactly, is the full, viable alternative you are offering to how we would normally be treating you?" Commander Kwit-Nik posed this question with no uncertain firmness. "You can't be suggesting the greenhouse aboard your starship could supply any more than a paltry addendum to our food resources!"

"I am not suggesting any such thing," Helena shook her head with an assuredness she struggled to more than feign. "If I can beg your patience to hear us out completely, Officer Leung and I will present our proposal in its entirety."

"I would hope your proposal will not take very much time to disgorge. Or else we must need gallop from it immediately into the source of our next meal," harshly tongue-clicked Lieutenant Ak-keek-teek. For "our next meal," he settled his eyes longingly on Yoon-hee's bosom yet again.

If only we weren't outnumbered and defenseless, Kevin thought to himself as he locked eyes with the lieutenant. *Otherwise, I would take someone else's antlers here, and use them to stuff your buck teeth down your throat! I'd stuff them so far down your throat that you'd have to poop them out your ass!*

"They have prepared plenty enough extra kwice with kandulays for our next meal, I am sure," Kwit-Nik tongue-clicked dismissively. "Proceed, Captain Taylok."

"Thank you, Commander. I am certain you and your leader, Dek-Fook-Tek, are already well aware of a grim reality. There has been increased warming of your planet coupled with accelerating environmental devastation. We believe these circumstances led to your present eating habits. Many of your plant and animal species have gone extinct, and the most habitable zones have shrunk down to a few regions only. One of those regions includes land masses near your Arctic circle. The other includes land masses down near your Antarctic circle. But I reiterate: You must already know all of this, and in far greater detail than we could imagine."

"Yes," nodded Commander Kwit-Nik. "A major contributor to our planet's deteriorating condition was Chonora's entirely unprovoked pulse-beam attack on our Kookatakook mountain range. Thousands of fellow Tictoctickians were killed."

"Such a horrific tragedy never should have happened, for certain." Helena wanted to avoid directly challenging anything Kwit-Nik said. But the truth was, the Chonoran pulse-beam attack had nothing to do with Tictoctic's climate change crisis. Helena also would have wanted to push back on Commander Kwit-Nik's assertion the Chonoran attack was "entirely unprovoked." Nevertheless, she said, "By far the largest contributor to your planet's current state has been an over reliance on fossil-fuel burning for energy needs."

"Such a horrific tragedy, as you term it, never *would* have happened had we confiscated that Chonoran battle saucer before it ever reached Tictoctic. However, Captain, your point is well taken regarding our dirty energy dependence," conceded Commander Kwit-Nik. He appreciated Captain Taylor's effort to steer clear of head-chargingly correcting him. He couldn't help the bitterness in his tongue-clicks, though, as he went on, "Okay, so Tictoctic is a ruined mess." Commander Kwit-Nik pointed out the window at his planet.

The Smoke and Mirrors was rounding to Tictoctic's sunlit half, on the starship's two-and-a-half-minute orbit from a million miles away.

Finding himself increasingly irritated, the commander waved his articulated cloven hoof-hand dismissively. "Just what *is* your proposal?" he asked. "Enough with the insulting background information we already know."

"Commander Kwit-Nik," said Buddy Leung, picking up where Helena left off, "we propose to relocate your people to another planet. Hopefully this resettlement will only be temporary. That is, until Tictoctic is put back on the path towards fully thriving life from its current critical-condition death spiral. And believe me, we do not use the term, 'death spiral,' lightly."

"Another planet, Captain?" Commander Kwit-Nik repeated the Tictoctickian translation of "another planet." Fellow deer creatures' ears joined his in rising erect like rabbit ears, as Chris saw them. "To move an entire planet's population to another," he tongue-clicked, "you cannot be talking about Koombt! Koombt is four, five light-years away! That is too far away for a relocation project of such magnitude!"

"We are not talking about Oomb." Captain Helena Taylor took over for Buddy since the commander seemed so intent on directing his tongue-clicking at her. "We are talking about a planet less than one-half light-year away."

With this pronouncement from the female other-worlder, several deer creatures' ears fluttered.

"Less than one-half light-year away," the commander repeated. "How would you know this? Have you had your own reconnaissance pellets nosing around our solar system?"

Helena had to be careful. She had to maintain her calm, steady tone, like any other truthful person would be expected to. She had to do this despite the insincere fawning she was about to undertake. She also had to be careful not to provoke the deer creature's impatience by straying into less important matters. For example, she would have loved to comment on the unusually close proximity of the nearby planet's solar system to the Cygnitaurus system. She could have easily expounded on how both systems shared the same Oort cloud. But such trivia had to wait for another time. "We do have our own interstellar reconnaissance technology," Helena said. "We strongly suspect you possess such technology as well, doubtless inspired by your Supreme Authority Dek-Fook-Tek. Would that not have been how you first learned of our planet? And of the other planet several light-years away you were targeting for interstellar conquest?"

"All in aid of our defense, Captain," curtly tongue-clicked Kwit-Nik before Helena could proceed any further. "Our proposed cattle ranches were meant to defuse the clear threat posed by other-world civilizations which have achieved space travel. That is, besides the now-defunct Chonoran civilization. Regarding the other planet several light years away you referred to, Captain, I must make a special observation. From what we gathered in Captain Gekalek's report, we were too late to prevent your civilization from destroying it."

"Actually, they destroyed themselves, though with weapons we provided," Kevin couldn't help interjecting. "Their supreme leader wanted to have our technology annihilate their terrorist threat, once and for all. Only, the result was indiscriminate destruction virtually everywhere across the surface of their planet. They used our nuclear missiles to bring down a comet we had maneuvered into orbit for adding significantly to their water supply."

"I see," Kwit-Nik nodded. "So how do we know your good intentions will not lead to a comparable disaster for Tictoctic?"

"We have not brought any weapons," bluntly pointed out Captain Taylor. She was still feeling a chill from how the translator spit out "cattle ranches" for a phrase tongue-clicked by the commander. Consequently, she added with equal bluntness, "As for the rest, you can judge for yourselves after I lay out the full extent of our proposal. But first I want to know: If you learned of other planets so much further away, you must have already detected the nearby planet as well. Was there any effort made to investigate this planet for its food source potential? Based on our reconnaissance information, it sustains a lush ecosystem devoid of any civilization with which to have to contend. Or if there is a civilization, it has a long way to go before entering the space age. No military threat should be posed whatsoever.

"Of course, there is always the possibility of lethal biochemical incompatibility between your nearby planet's ecology and your own planet's ecology. But that would not be consistent with what we have thus far discovered between other planetary ecologies, including yours and ours. The odds are heavily in favor of compatibility.

"So let us assume confirmation you can safely eat food harvested and raised on the nearby planet. Wouldn't that yield a far easier route to your nutritional security? Wouldn't that be better than trying to project your admittedly most imposing military might across several light-years? Shouldn't an exploration of the nearby planet be your first priority?"

There was something Helena was lying about, and giving Tictoctic leadership far more credit for than they deserved. This had to do with how she learned about the habitable planet in a solar system less than one-half light-year away from Tictoctic. True, Hubble 7 Space Telescope data detected such a planet orbiting at life zone distance from sun Heuvelman 3 (as named on Earth). However, everything else the Earthlings as well as the Tictoctickians knew about it stemmed from reconnaissance pellets sent out by the Chonorans. Those pellets were sent out before Chonoran civilization was attacked by the Tictoctickians. Which attack came thanks to Tictoctickian co-option of weaponized saucers built on Chonora.

"We did prioritize, Captain." Commander Kwit-Nik was responding to Helena's question concerning why no Tictoctickian exploration of the closer-in planet. "We learned something important from the completely unprovoked magnetic pulse-beam attack by Chonorans. We learned civilization-threatening danger could be posed by most any other-world civilization, once they entered the space age. This lesson in mind, we carefully examined the interstellar reconnaissance data."

Helena, Ali and Buddy exchanged significant glances over the commander choosing to say, "*the* reconnaissance data" over "*our* reconnaissance data."

"The data clearly revealed a fully operating space station in orbit around the planet you say your weapons were co-opted to unwittingly destroy, Captain. The data also revealed what I would term provocative circumstances in your home solar system. Your planet's moon was colonized, as well as the next planet further away from your star than your own. Again, we are determined not to take any chances on a repeat of what was inflicted upon us by the Chonoran space-faring barbarians. No!" Commander Kwit-Nik brought down his cloven hoof-hand to pound on the conference table. He made silverware rattle where it was left on plates. "We are profoundly inspired by the wisdom of our Supreme Authority, Dek-Fook-Tek." Commander Kwit-Nik nodded in a deferring manner towards Lieutenant Ak-keek-teek. Kwit-Nik long since figured it too dangerous entrusting the lieutenant with even the slightest whiff of rebellion plans. Presently he also sensed additional danger from testing the lieutenant's patience. Kwit-Nik couldn't safely make him wait any longer for the next feigned adulation of their mentally deranged dictator.

Unaware of the cold calculation behind Commander Kwit-Nik's glowing mention of Dek-Fook-Tek, Lieutenant Ak-keek-teek rose up on his hind limbs. He proceeded to bow solemnly forward and ritually chant, "Dek-Fook-Tek gives us direction, without which we are as the blind kookookakoo wandering aimlessly through deep caverns."

By the time the lieutenant completed this chant, all the other deer aliens, Kwit-Nik included, had risen to join in. The humans had risen as well, though keeping quiet.

Foolish creatures from Akt! Lieutenant Ak-keek-teek thought contemptuously. Unable to contain himself, he snorted with amusement as he resumed his seat. *Certainly there are animals THEY must imprison for eating, notwithstanding their fraudulent pretension of subsisting only on plants. Are we to believe the Akt animals would do anything other than flee, if they but had the chance? This farce cannot last much longer. Soon, Commander Kwit-Nik better realize the safest plan is to have the other-*

*worlders chopped up and grilled. Then they can be
served spicy hot on the same dishes where they served us
this joke of a meal!*

"We are forever in debt to Dek-Fook-Tek's inspiration,"
the commander meantime reiterated, again for the
lieutenant's sake. But back to the matter at hoof, he then
proceeded, "We have shifted space exploration away
from our neighboring solar system for the simple reason
you indicated, Captain Taylok. Its habitable planet clearly
offers not the least threat to us. Instead, we have directed
resources towards the two further-away planets, yours
included. Based on our experience, we have had to
assume the danger they pose is comparable to or maybe
even worse than the danger we formerly endured from
Chonora.

"What is more, we noticed something especially
bothersome about the planet of these two tree creatures,
the planet they call Koombt. Koombt was offensively
equipped with a laser mesh shield. When we noticed this,
we had no choice but to add that planet to our threat
list. Being prepared for war is our highest priority."

*Yes, of course. May it never be said that preparing for
peace, for cooperation, for love, ever took priority over
preparing for war.*

Captain Helena Taylor and Counselor Ali Magabu
detected a bitter note in this latest telepathed
commentary from Oodle-Noodle. Nevertheless, Helena
found herself deeply impressed by the point the tree
creature was trying to make. Pursuant to which, she
responded to Commander Kwit-Nik, "So you are telling us
your civilization completely neglected any exploration of
a known habitable planet a mere one-half light-year from
Tictoctic? Your fellow creatures foreswore such an

investigation in favor of preparing for a hypothetical threat from two other planets much further away?"

"Excuse me, Captain," Lieutenant Ak-keek-teek leaped in. "Where Chonora is concerned, the threat was not hypothetical. It was all too blood-sheddingly *real*! And far closer to us than one-half light-year! Baa!"

"No more delays, Captain Taylok! Detail your plan that would have us foregoing defensive assault on your battleships stationed near Koombt!" exclaimed Commander Kwit-Nik. "More immediately, explain why we shouldn't add you to our menu! And explain why your tree creature associates here shouldn't be chopped up into so many wood chips for barbecuing you!" Commander Kwit-Nik made these demands in lieu of any direct response to his lieutenant's heated remark.

Remember something, Captain, Oodle-Noodle telepathed Helena by way of morale-sustaining caution. *Commander Kwit-Nik is rooting for your plan to work, even before he has learned every detail. It affords the best chance for his contemplated coup against his crazed leadership. But there are Tictoctickians, most notably including his lieutenant, who continue their fierce loyalty to Dek-Fook-Tek. They would follow Dek-Fook-Tek down the mouth of an erupting volcano if he asked them. For those already suspicious regarding Commander Kwit-Nik's degree of loyalty, the commander must continue to bluster in your presence.*

Helena would have railed about how *her* side regards their battleship and laser mesh shield deployment as defensive. And that meanwhile, the Tictoctickian side prepares to launch an offensive strike with its magnetic pulse-beam technology. But Oodle-Noodle's gentle telepath successfully transported her back to keeping everything in perspective. So she said, instead, "There are multiple parts to our plan. But all of those parts share an ultimate, most profoundly inspiring goal. That goal is the implementation of safe, peaceful alternatives to hostilities on a durable, lasting basis.

"The first part of the plan involves some of our people remaining on board the Smoke and Mirrors. They will journey to that unexplored life-sustaining planet we have spoken of, less than one-half light-year away from the Cygnitaurus System. There, they will sleuth out practical, temporary resettlement areas for your fellow beings. Our expert exo-planet geologist, Dr. Carol James-Leung, will make sure those areas are safe from potentially dangerous instabilities capable of producing earthquakes and volcanoes.

"Ludi Perez, of course, is our expert chef who so lovingly prepared your delicious vegetarian meal. That meal, incidentally, replicated what she might have prepared back on Earth, on her ancestors' island named Puerto Rico. She will be in charge of an agricultural feasibility study of the unexplored planet. Her goal is to assess the potential for growing rice, beans, and plantains there, in large enough quantities to feed millions of Tictoctickian settlers. Also, she will gather and test the safety of whatever plant food resources she discovers already thriving in wild abundance. She will be working in conjunction with our chief medical officer here, Dr. Deborah Davis-Murphy. Dr. Davis-Murphy has gained tremendous expertise studying biochemical compatibilities and potentially dangerous incompatibilities. Those are issues we face, of course, when shuffling together life forms from different planets. Who knows? Maybe Ludi and Deb will even discover safely consumable animals on your nearby habitable planet. A vegetarian diet is far healthier for the long term than any other diet. But despite those definitive findings, if you conclude you are not satisfied without any meat..."

In reaction to these provocative remarks, several deer creatures brayed their amusement, Lieutenant Ak-keek-teek chief among them.

Once the lieutenant and company quieted down, Helena continued. She found herself surprisingly undaunted by the deer creatures' ridiculing racket.

In fact, she felt liberated by a strong conviction over the good sense her proposal made. There was also the nothing-left-to-lose aspect of the mortal peril into which she had placed herself and every last sentient being aboard the Smoke and Mirrors. "Officer Tanya Petrovsky will be investigating climate and weather-related issues the settlers from Tictoctic might have to deal with," went on Helena. She made no least reference to how her declaration was met, of a vegetarian diet being the best. "Lastly, there is our Oombian friend, Wafoodle-boodle. She will be working with Officer Kevin Smith-Park to study recreation potentialities for your civilization's proposed home away from home."

"'Recreation potentialities'?" Commander Kwit-Nik repeated in the tongue-clicked translation. His ears fluttered with what most of his own colleagues save for Chef Glork-tek could not have known was eager anticipation. Chef Glork-tek was one of Kwit-Nik's few fellow beings aware of his fascination with oof and golf. In any event, Kwit-Nik found his fascination fueled all the more by what he learned about those two Tictoctickian prisoners brought along by the Earthlings. They had clearly become addicted to hitting little balls with big clubs while held captive on Oomb, and aboard the Earthlings' starship as well, presumably.

Captain Taylor nodded with a wry grin; from Oodle-Noodle's mindreading, she knew exactly what was going through the commander's narrow furry head. She couldn't help her bemusement over a certain possibility, however remote its chances. Maybe golf, oof, whatever held the key to defusing cannibalistic hostilities from Tictoctic. If enough deer creatures were hooked on that silly game over which her husband obsessed so much... Anyhow, Captain Taylor nodded assertively to the commander's short, questioning plea for elaboration on "recreation potentialities." Then she said, "Our Oombian friends have very generously supplied us with thousands of freshly carved oof clubs, plus tens of thousands of oof balls. That should be plenty to start you on your way towards enjoying their game. We plan to bring most of the equipment and balls to the new planet. But we will be leaving enough behind for Officer Chris Olsen-Taylor and Oodle-Noodle to share with any of you who care to give it a try. Perhaps my officers can even improvise a small oof course layout down on Tictoctic near your Supreme Authority's headquarters."

"All the better for your people to locate the center of power on Tictoctic, Captain! They can launch an attack while we are distracted by trying to get little balls to drop down into little holes!" Commander Kwit-Nik tersely tongue-clicked.

Lieutenant Ak-keek-teek stomped a cloven hoof-hand hard against the table top to express his rare, heartfelt approval of something the commander said.

"Commander Kwit-Nik, we are here as a group of couples. Even Oodle-Noodle and Wafoodle-boodle. They have been in a committed relationship for more than two hundred of their planet's orbits of their sun. However, my assignation of duties guarantees the following: No couple will remain together during the implementation of the various aspects of the peaceful problem-solving mission I have described. For example, our Chief Counselor Ali Magabu will be staying behind, on your planet. He will help smooth over misunderstandings that might crop up between our people and your people. This while his only mate, his mate for life Tanya Petrovsky, joins us on the planet proposed for your society's temporary resettlement. Were our people to launch such an attack as you have expressed fear about, we could be certain our loved ones on Tictoctic would perish. It should go without saying we don't want that."

Lieutenant Ak-keek-teek rolled his eyes, but Commander Kwit-Nik crisply tongue-clicked his own response with a certain regard for Helena.

Helena did not know better than to read the commander's regard as expressing his deep appreciation for her effort. That is, for how logically, empathetically she dealt with the concern he had needed to express. It was concern, of course, on behalf of those cohorts less sold on trusting the other-worlders than he was, let alone willing to mount an overthrow of Dek-Fook-Tek.

"So Captain," the commander said, "I understand that many of you will be scouting out the planet one-half light-year away. You will be judging the feasibility of our society's temporary relocation there. But in the meantime, what exactly will the others do on our Tictoctic? Aside from your chief counselor who you say will mediate disputes between your people and our people?"

"My partner for life, Chris, will be accompanied by Wafoodle-boodle. During the relocation process, they plan to make various diversions available for your people.

Such diversions include Oombian and Earthling music. As for my other fellow Earthlings staying behind, they will explore how to bring Tictoctic back from the edge of its ecological, environmental crisis. For example, Officer Pedro Perez is an expert in solar electrical engineering. He will work with Tictoctickian industries to end your dependency on fossil fuels. That can happen via transition to geothermal, windmills and solar power for most of your energy needs."

"So Captain, part of your offered plan would ease our civilization's gallop through a forest of great uncertainty for resettlement on an entire other planet. But some of us would remain behind to work on reversing the course of Tictoctic's environmental degradation. That would be the other part, with your assistance and guidance, of course. And some day in the long trot, we would be able to return our civilization to a rejuvenated Tictoctic."

"Yes," nodded Helena. "That is a most accurate summation of our hope."

"But it rests on the assumption we abandon our original plans for addressing the vast shortages, the starvation we struggle to fend off on a daily basis. That is, our plans to defensively add you, your fellow creatures, to our food supply."

"As we demonstrated here, we will also work closely with you to rapidly replenish your food supplies using healthy alternatives. And fun alternatives as well, beginning from day one. You have not tasted my partner's chocolate chip cookies yet."

"Kocolat kip kookies," the commander repeated slowly. He struggled like the rest of his species did, with "ch" and certain other consonant blends. Those blends did not come easily, if at all, to him and his fellow deer creatures. Spoken Tictoctickian was primarily a binary series of tics and tocs. Only the subtlest inflections made for distinctions between many words. "What about your battleships presently patrolling these tree creatures' solar system, Captain?" Commander Kwit-Nik asked with no problem, back to his first language. "Let us presume your crew is preoccupied with the environmental rehabilitation of Tictoctic and our temporary resettlement on another planet. What will those battleship crews be doing while we ruminate on your kocolat kip kookies and learn how to play koombt or kolfk?"

"So long as there is no attack from your saucer fleet, you have nothing to fear from them. The personnel aboard those starships will spend their time entertaining themselves and thriving on a plant-based diet."

Captain, if I might telepath...

"Excuse me," Helena went on, "our friend here from Oomb, Oodle-Noodle, she wishes to add something. But first, a word of caution for those of you who might not have experienced her voice in your head before. There is nothing to fear, no mind control."

"You say there is so much for us not to fear, Captain. Okay, tell your friend to proceed," Kwit-Nik's tongue-clicks translated. "But if she has been reading my mind, she already knows this."

Thank you, Commander, and I do know this. I just wanted to add something.

Lieutenant Ak-keek-teek, Officer Rek-mek-a-nek and Tictoctickian guards anxiously turned their heads from side to side, ears aflutter.

Suppose both sides of a potential violent conflict could know what was in the mind of their supposed enemy, Oodle-Noodle telepathed further. She seemed heedless of the growing panic among those aforementioned Tictoctickians, who were finding it increasingly difficult to remain seated. *If they could read minds, they would learn most beings wish to avoid war. They would also learn the multitude of other things they share in common.*

The lieutenant and his likewise-agitated company couldn't help themselves any longer. They rose as one onto their hind hooves.

It is only those who have lost all hope of any other alternative-

That's as far as Oodle-Noodle got before the deer creatures gave full vent to their feelings, Ak-keek-teek leading the way. They were totally unnerved by the Oombian tree creature's voice in their heads. And so, they raised their air igniters and sent torch-like flames every direction. They would have literally seared away Oodle-Noodle's telepaths, if that were possible.

I'm guessing that every last one of those who have lost all hope for a peaceful alternative just happen to be gathered round this table, Kevin censored himself from expressing out loud.

"Aieee!" Yoon-hee screamed, because Lieutenant Ak-keek-teek's air igniter singed hair on her right arm. She managed to douse the smoke still rising there with water still left inside her drinking glass.

Yoon-hee's fright was not what led the Tictoctickians to stop firing away, however. Rather, it was a flame close to Officer Rek-mek-a-nek that seemed to have emitted from no discernible source.

Wow, Buddy Leung and Chris thought to themselves. *Maybe Effy thought other ephemeral dragons were trying to consort with him!*

"What was that, Captain?" asked Commander Kwit-Nik.

Meanwhile, Lieutenant Ak-keek-teek strove not to lick his chops and leer too overly long at where his air igniter singed Yoon-hee's arm hair...and Kevin Smith-Park strove to stifle his impulses. Kevin wanted to leap across the conference table. Pursuant to which, he would have clutched the lieutenant's neck in one hand for pummeling his snout mercilessly with his other hand clenched in a fist.

"I wouldn't want to bet those air igniters didn't nearly start to combust the entire air supply in here, Commander," warned Captain Helena Taylor. "Have you ever seen so many of them fired off at the same time in such a small, confined space? I'm not sure how safe those things are when you do that." Taylor figured the less these deer creatures knew about Effy, the better.

Commander Kwit-Nik nodded slowly. Captain Taylor sensed he found her analysis entirely reasonable. If he suspected she was holding back anything, the expression on his face didn't show it. After a deep inhale, though, Kwit-Nik made an exhale that reminded Taylor of a horse's snort. He succeeded this with a sweeping glance at everyone round the oval conference table. And he crisply tongue-clicked, "I hereby open a mental pasture for my fellow Tictoctickians to graze. More specifically, I want your response to the proposals by these creatures from other planets."

"Commander Kwit-Nik?"

"Yes, Officer Rek-mek-a-nek?"

"During our successful disruption of conquest plans by the Chonoran beasts, I heard them chirp most shrilly. At least, this occurred with those we seized who weren't flash-frozen by unprotected exposure to the cosmic void. Anyway, I always imagined their noises as pleas for mercy, once they realized they were becoming additions to our food supply.

"What we have been hearing from these particular beasts smells to me like the most elaborately ornamented pleas for mercy ever sniffed! It is as if long ago, something unusual happened before our ancestors chopped off an oskynt's head on the path to meal preparation. The oskynt turned to the one wielding the ax, and it said, *Here is what I will offer if you set that thing aside.*"

By the time Officer Rek-mek-a-nek concluded his explication, fellow officers were braying their amusement. The hilarity was so contagious, even Officers Buddy Leung, Gina Murphy-Davis, Tanya Petrovsky and Chris Olsen-Taylor variously snorted or busted out laughing themselves.

Lieutenant Ak-keek-teek and Officer Rek-mek-a-nek pointed cloven hoof-hands at the Earthlings. The lieutenant and officer both were in near-disbelief. How could these other-worlders be so foolish as to find anything worth laughing about in a witticism which hinted at their imminent demise? But this only added to the deer creatures' mirth.

Commander Kwit-Nik was the one Tictoctickian not so amused. Counselor Ali Magabu noticed a shocked expression casting a shadow over his face. Ali could make no better comparison than to the look on a deer caught in the headlights.

Slowly yet purposefully, Commander Kwit-Nik rose from his chair. He emanated such solemnity, the Earthlings quickly ceased what they well knew could amount to snickering past their own graves. They found the rest of the way back to seriousness at lightning speed.

"Six solar orbits ago," Kwit-Nik tongue-clicked with lecturing earnestness in his voice, Chris thought, "I sat beside our Supreme Authority, Dek-Fook-Tek. I watched him heroically lead the charge to neutralize a fleet of Chonoran saucers armed with magnetic pulse-beams. One fact had already become mountain-water clear. The Chonoran Empire was preparing for an all-out invasion of Tictoctic.

"Anyway, during Dek-Fook-Tek's most impressive defense actions, an unidentified flying object mysteriously appeared and then disappeared. That object's immensity, if not its design, matched the largest of our saucers. Captain Taylok, that object was your own spacecraft, the one on which we are presently gathered together. This is entirely consistent with the account Captain Kek-stek passed on from you, Captain. According to Kek-stek, you reported travelling into the past for a better understanding of our circumstances. And that you desired this knowledge prior to surrender.

"My fellow Tictoctickian soldiers, such a side trip had to have come at great personal risk for these other-world creatures. But suppose it didn't. Suppose that for them, time travel is accomplished as securely, as routinely safely, as galloping across a narrow stream. Suppose that. And then suppose they are here to deceive us, entrap us for the purpose of our enslavement or worse. If that is the case, why didn't they send their warships back in time as well? Why didn't they make common cause with the Chonoran outer space military to execute our destruction? Perhaps even make us *their* additional food supply?"

Helena wouldn't have been surprised if Secretary of Defense Spinner asked Captain Entroper and company something similar. Namely, why weren't they planning a past-time sneak attack on the Tictoctickians? For all

Helena knew, such a plan was well underway. Although without Buddy Leung's guidance...

Ali Magabu found himself focused on something else. He was struck by how the commander neglected any mention of Tlik-klok and Fwok-bwahk. After all, they were seated right there at the oval conference table. Those two deer creatures had allowed themselves to be used by the Earthlings. They threw Dek-Fook-Tek off the scent long enough for the away team down on Chonora to safely make it back to the Smoke and Mirrors. Commander Kwit-Nik remembered seeing the Smoke and Mirrors near Chonora all those orbits of Cygnitaurus ago. Didn't he also remember seeing Tlik-klok and Fwok-bwahk? Wasn't the commander standing right beside Dek-Fook-Tek when that particular Tictoctickian addressed them? Didn't the commander see Tlik-klok and Fwok-bwahk pretend they were operating the shuttle pod, even while it was being flown out of the Chonoran atmosphere by Tanya?

"Now I want to pass along a particular rumination for my fellow Tictoctickians," humbly baaed Commander Kwit-Nik. "It is a rumination I want you to chew on, yourselves. Taste what you can make of it, as though I were a mother passing along a predigested morsel to her baby fawns. I will set the stage: Let us suppose there *is* a secret, insidious plan by these other-worlders. Suppose they are tricking us into ambush, or some other such devilry. If that is the case, I don't get it.

"But this is my rumination: How accurately do they represent the intent of their fellow beings back aboard the warships in the Koombt solar system? And what can we be confident about in that regard, when it comes to these tree creatures who joined them from down on the surface of the planet Koombt? In other words, assume their fellow beings aboard those warships near the planet Koombt are up to no good. Still, is it not possible these other-worlders in our presence are sincere about wanting a peaceful resolution?"

"Commander Kwit-Nik!" harshly brayed Lieutenant Ak-keek-teek. There were hints of panic and disbelief in his voice. "Are you really, really, no joke, considering actual acceptance of the other-world creatures' proposal? It is not feeding outside my designated grazing area to advise you that such acceptance cannot be made, without first seeking the consent of Supreme Authority Dek-Fook-Tek! You were specifically ordered by Dek-Fook-Tek to launch the defensive assault on Koombt within two more revolutions of Tictoctic! The other-worlders' proposal would involve a delay of that timetable many times over, at least!"

"Captain?" Commander Kwit-Nik turned Helena's way to sternly tongue-click.

Chris, Yoon-hee and several other Earthlings round the conference table were struck by the same notion: Commander Kwit-Nik had suddenly made it Captain Taylor's burden to address the lieutenant's concern.

"Commander Kwit-Nik, we are talking about a big change of plans from what was apparently already agreed to with your superior," Captain Taylor admitted. "So I can see where you would indeed be expected to gain his approval before charging forward."

Lieutenant Ak-keek-teek gave Helena one of his unnervingly ridiculous-looking, slowly dawning, buck-tooth grins.

Helena had to wonder what was going through the lieutenant's mind. Was he thinking on the comicality of negotiating with who were otherwise destined to become cuts of meat? Helena felt sufficiently spooked to focus on a particular something for Oodle-Noodle's mind-reading benefit. *We might have to gamble on our escape plan sooner rather than later.*

"Captain Taylok," Commander Kwit-Nik assertively tongue-clicked while reaching to pull down a flat-screen TV. He turned it on a diagonal for everyone there gathered. "As you know," he said, "when we boarded your spaceship, we assumed full responsibility for its subsequent functioning. That involved linking your communication equipment to Tictoctickian resources. So here are my orders for our officers staffing what used to be your navigation bridge!" Kwit-Nik raised his voice, intent on those officers' full attention over the two-way intercom. "They are to connect the navigation deck view-screen directly with Dek-Fook-Tek's command center down on sub-arctic Tictoctic! I am also ordering our proceedings be received by the captains of the six saucer craft encharged with heading up our defensive assault!"

Over the course of several torturously tense minutes, the conference room view-screen went from "snow" to color bars. Then finally, a transmission revealed Dek-Fook-Tek's royal reception chamber. The chamber looked well familiar to Commander Kwit-Nik; that's where he and Chef Glork-tek were first brought before Supreme Authority Dek-Fook-Tek. Prior to this audience, languishing confinement had been their lot. It was the best they could have hoped for, upon return from a disastrous mission to the Oombian solar system. That was where other-worlders tricked the Third Celestial Breath's entire crew into deserting her.

The Third Celestial Breath's ultimate fate was what Captain Gekalek discovered in another solar system, seven light-years distant. Somehow, the Third Celestial

Breath made it all the way there, only to face total destruction on a planet the Tictoctickians did not know was named Fafama.

An aide to Dek-Fook-Tek stood up close to a monitor in the royal reception chamber. Buddy Leung had the feeling that aide would have enveloped the entire screen with his short-furred face if he could have. As it came to pass, however, he did not succeed in totally blocking from view certain events behind him. Those events remained more or less plain to see for audiences aboard six flying saucers as well as the Smoke and Mirrors.

Insensible to his imminent ineffectiveness, the aide sharply tongue-clicked, "Commander Kwit-Nik! I find nothing on our schedule about your seeking communication with Supreme Authority Dek-Fook-Tek at this time."

To the bristly aide's rear, a doe stripped half-naked could be observed galloping past, down on all fours.

"What peculiar scent has led you on such an impromptu antler charge into our Supreme Authority's supremely busy schedule at this particular moment?" the aide asked haughtily, oblivious to what transpired behind him.

That was when the Supreme Authority himself could be seen strutting along most pompously on his two hind limbs, so Kevin Smith-Park thought. The Supreme Authority's antlers were held high on transparent cords by his frantically crawling-about antler handlers. The antler handlers were stationed in the ceiling above him like multiple puppeteers for the same marionette. Anyhow, Dek-Fook-Tek swelled out his chest, his lower half stripped naked like the doe's lower half. He calmly swaggered towards where the doe galloped at a panicky pace. Several viewers could have reported this aboard the flying saucer fleet as well as aboard the Smoke and Mirrors. Fearing reprisals, none of them did.

Yes, Commander Kwit-Nik's fellow deer creatures didn't dare voice aloud how at least a portion of Supreme Authority Dek-Fook-Tek's "busy schedule" was taken up. But the commander hoped an important impression was made upon many of them, nevertheless. Especially so for those captains and officers who had already hinted they could be herded into action against Dek-Fook-Tek.

"We have a serious proposal to ruminate over," the commander said finally. "It would involve a delay of the defensive assault for several days, perhaps as long as a dekpek."

"A dekpek delay of the defensive assault?" the aide repeated, the one trying to block from view whatever might be happening behind him. Nostrils aquiver, he could have been a rabbit sniffing at a carrot on which he was about to nibble, Chris thought. "That *is* serious. One moment," said the aide. He backed off from his intimate closeness with the television monitor.

Just then, noises were emanating from a seeming struggle. Intertwined grunts and moans intensified to a climax. Kevin would have snickered it didn't take a Sherlock Holmes to figure out what happened.

I can hear those deer critters now, in one of their innumerable ritual chants which seem made up as they go along, Kevin went on to imagine. *"His love-making induces such unsurpassable heights of ecstasy! If only there were clones of the mighty, all-powerful Dek-Poop-Deck! In such happenstance, it would be cruelly insensitive for any of us not to have them service our significant others, rather than doing that ourselves. Only one thing keeps us from pining away for his lackeys to pin* us down so he can gang-rape us. After such an experience, there would be nothing left to live for, no greater pleasure to ever be anticipated."

"What is this I hear, Commander Kwit-Nik?" Dek-Fook-Tek filled the screen with a deer-in-the-headlights look of perplexity, Chris thought.

"Supreme Authority Dek-Fook-Tek, it is about the captain of the other-world starship, the starship she peacefully volunteered to surrender to us. She has made a most curious proposal."

"'Peacefully volunteered to surrender to us'?" Dek-Fook-Tek repeated mockingly. "Remember, Commander, accounts of female oskynt behaving docilely while being led inside a holding pen? Where they would await the butcher's knife? And then all the sudden biting off someone's arm most neatly at the joint?"

"I do," responded Kwit-Nik matter-of-factly. However, he also made a point of swelling out his chest. Tictoctickian tradition dictated he offer himself for disemboweling impalement upon Dek-Fook-Tek's antlers. That would have proven impossible through the view-screen, but still...

Dek-Fook-Tek actually stepped back from his television monitor. He felt intimidated how he would never admit, by the firmness Commander Kwit-Nik's matter-of-fact response conveyed. The commander's aforementioned ritual offering-up for impalement made no difference.

"Okay," Dek-Fook-Tek finally, most crisply tongue-clicked. It was as though his mental and emotional control over the situation had not been usurped for even the briefest moment. "So what is this proposal by the surrendered starship captain? Does she know an especially enticing recipe for her corpse's preparation she wishes to recommend? Baa!" he brayed most bemused.

Snickers broke out both where Dek-Fook-Tek was located, and in the conference room aboard the Smoke and Mirrors. Not to mention bleats of laughter aboard the Tictoctickian flying saucer battleships. Even the two deer creatures Tlik-klok and Fwok-bwahk joined in.

Helena and several of the other Earthlings struggled to remain calm, keep their exhales longer than their inhales for fending off hyperventilation.

"That is not what her proposal is about," Commander Kwit-Nik shook his head, after he waited long enough for the expressions of mirth to die down. "And actually, there are several parts."

"You mean, Commander Kwit-Nik, there are several parts to her proposal like there are several cuts to her meat?" asked Dek-Fook-Tek.

The snickering brays and bleats resumed.

Counselor Ali Magabu sensed the Supreme Authority Dek-Fook-Tek was feeling imperiously flattered by his newfound talent for standup comedy. And that he was working it accordingly.

"Very well, then," Dek-Fook-Tek went on. He judged adequate time had been given over for appreciation of his wit. "Let us sample her cuts, I mean those parts, for their appeal."

Kwit-Nik might have been amused by Supreme Authority Dek-Fook-Tek's clowning around. But if he was, he didn't show it, or even acknowledge what Dek-Fook-Tek was about. Instead, Kwit-Nik most earnestly seriously tongue-clicked, "For one part, the starship captain is offering a vegetarian alternative to relieve our food shortage, at least temporarily."

"You mean the condiment becomes the main ingredient?" Dek-Fook-Tek actually paused after he asked this question, before continuing. He wanted to allow enough time for more snickers. With which his fellow deer creatures obliged him, whether their additional amusement was real or feigned. "Tell me then, Commander," he continued finally. "Do we get to garnish these plant-filled dishes with shavings of the captain's hair and skin? Plus sprinkles of her sweat?" The Supreme Authority found himself so bemused, so self-entertained, he dropped down onto all fours, and he pawed at the slate floor with his cloven hooves.

Pedro and Ludi reached behind Tlik-klok's seat to grab one another's hands and hold on tight.

"The captain did have their chef prepare a plant-based meal for us. She is over here," Kwit-Nik nodded Ludi's direction.

"And how was it, Commander?"

"Not baaaad," Commander Kwit-Nik baaed with the same intently earnest delivery with which he said everything else. That was as far as he got, though, before he couldn't hold it in anymore. His shoulders started heaving, and he joined his fellow deer creatures in snickering bleats and brays of amusement.

Commander Kwit-Nik quickly felt ashamed, especially given what he strongly suspected was at stake. Nevertheless, another humorous line occurred to him. But he disciplined himself not to utter it aloud, not contribute any further to his fellow creatures' merriment...plus what he easily sensed was the other-worlders' growing discomfort trending towards terror. *On the verge of its consumption, food does not normally so articulately protest, "No, wait!"* Rather than indulge such an observation, Kwit-Nik finally resettled into his more usual earnest demeanor. He said, "The other-world captain assured me members of her crew will help us grow the crops from which her chef derived our sample meal. She expressed confidence we can produce enough of them to fully satisfy our nutritional needs. This goal is easily attainable, so her claim goes, on the nearby planet only one-half light-year away. Whatever arable land still remains on Tictoctic would provide a surplus, if anything. The main idea is for most of us to resettle on the nearby planet until Tictoctic is rejuvenated."

Dek-Fook-Tek reared back up onto his hind limbs. By that time they had been amply re-clothed by his servants. His ears twitched with his bafflement over what the commander detailed. He baaed, "Which planet? Her planet?"

"No, Supreme Authority," answered Commander Kwit-Nik. "She was referring to the planet we discovered less than one-half light-year away. From our research we know that planet thrives with life. Yet at the same time, it is not inhabited by potentially threatening, space-faring creatures as we have located elsewhere." The commander knew better than to bleat a word of the actual truth regarding who did what. No way did "we" as in "we fellow Tictoctickians" discover, let alone research, the nearby planet. Everything the Tictoctickians knew about it had been gathered by Chonorans before their civilization was genocidally subjugated by the Tictoctic Empire. "The Akt captain proposes a mission in her starship to the planet of interest," Commander Kwit-Nik continued. "The mission would involve a feasibility study on our resettling there, again only as a temporary arrangement."

"'A temporary arrangement,' you bray? You mean temporary until the other-world beasts can escape,

Commander Kwit-Nik?" Dek-Fook-Tek's recent clowning around was quickly forgotten as he tried to decide what tic-toc-ticked him off more. Was it the sheer audacity of the other-worlders? Or was it the commander's appalling willingness to air their ridiculous, obviously mercy-begging proposals?

"Actually, Supreme Dek-Fook-Tek, some of the other-world beasts would be left behind on Tictoctic. They would serve you more of their culinary preparations, because your approval of the vegetarian food replacement aspect must reign above all else." Having sensed his crazed superior's ire, Commander Kwit-Nik made a point of bowing most humbly.

"That our hearts will continue to beat without His daily input is not something we would ever bet on," Lieutenant Ak-keek-teek ritually chanted.

The commander gave his lieutenant as slight a deferential nod as he thought he could get away with before he continued. "In addition," he said, "they wish to share the music of three different planets, and a special game unique to two of them. That game has very much intrigued Officers Tlik-klok and Fwok-bwahk. And this has happened during what they claim the other-worlders have made a most considerate confinement."

Upon this mention of them, deer creatures Tlik-klok and Fwak-bwahk leaned their heads approvingly towards Helena, Chris, Chief Medical Officer Deborah Davis-Murphy, and Ludi Perez. These four Earthlings reciprocated with *What-can-we-say* shoulder shrugs.

Dek-Fook-Tek waved a scoffing cloven hoof-hand. "Why can't their music be heard simply by listening to them whinny, bray, maybe rustle their leaves in the tree creature's case... whatever it is they do inside their holding pens? While they are at it, will they also want us to sample their excrement?"

Renewed deer creature snickers met Dek-Fook-Tek's remarks. His nostrils twitched proudly regarding his successful return to standup comedian mode. *Certainly, he mused, a new ritual chant, a ritual chant that celebrates my supreme sense of humor, must soon be herded my way!*

"Their excrement is not considered by them to be a delicacy, oh Supreme Authority," answered Kwit-Nik.

"Baa! What a surprise!" snorted Dek-Fook-Tek. "It is the first reasonable thing you report about them! And this peculiar game you bleat of? Is it a chase where they run away from us?"

"You hit a ball with a stick. And you keep hitting it until you get it into a hole."

"Baa, what kind of 'it' would someone be hitting to get into what kind of hole? The stick? And what kind of stick would that be? And what ball are you bleating about? Only one ball? Not two? Baa!" Dek-Fook-Tek completely cut loose. Down on all fours he galloped around in a circle with his self-entertainment. As a result, he came in and out of view on the video monitor aboard the Smoke and Mirrors.

From off monitor, Helena and company at the oval conference table heard what they could not know was Dek-Fook-Tek descending into a lunatic rage. He beat to splinters one of the special walls set up for this purpose, punching at it with his forelimbs. Earthlings might have likened him to a prize-fighting boxer deluded into thinking his main opponent was the side of a barn.

By a minute into this off-screen spectacle, the Supreme Authority's handlers had shut off the audio portion of the feed. But Commander Kwit-Nik hoped his partners in the overthrow plan heard enough to strengthen their resolve. Perhaps they would even be inspired to try recruiting others supportive of Dek-Fook-Tek's forced descent from the throne.

Unaware of Kwit-Nik's thoughts, Helena feared the worst. She feared there was no way presently that her group's proposal had a chance. Just around the corner, probably, she and her fellow human beings faced imprisonment on a slippery slope to their slaughter. They would find themselves added to the deer creatures' food supply sooner rather than later. So Captain Helena Taylor focused again on encouraging Oodle-Noodle to read her mind. She wanted the tree being to telepath Sergeants Frankly and Hanson immediately. Her message was for them to initiate the escape plan, however dim its prospect for success.

The escape plan reprised Buddy Leung's escape plan months earlier. Buddy placed a fake bomb device with a digital readout countdown underneath a food prep table in Chef Glork-tek's kitchen. Thereby were the Tictoctickian deer creatures frightened into abandonment of the Third Celestial Breath.

For the reprise, Sergeant Fred Frankly would stealthily leave the living quarters that were sound-proofed and otherwise masked to appear devoted to solar-propulsion-related equipment. He would accomplish such a feat by slipping out through an air vent.

Step two, Frankly would hide a new phony explosive where the deer creatures were likely to stumble across it. In the best case scenario, Commander Kwit-Nik would order the Earthlings and Oombians kept aboard to be blown apart while the Tictoctickians were ordered to abandon ship. Once all the deer creatures took leave,

Buddy would crank up the Smoke and Mirrors to depart the Cygnitaurus system at top speed.

The plan's success hinged on Chef Glork-tek and Commander Kwit-Nik not wanting to share crucial information with their fellow beings. At issue, of course, was what they remembered of how they had been scared off the Third Celestial Breath.

The Earthlings also had to hope that once the Smoke and Mirrors was free and clear to escape, a sympathetic Kwit-Nik would actively help. He would do what he could to avoid or at least postpone what would have proven an easy enough pursuit by Tictoctickian saucer craft. An unhindered pursuit would likely mean the end of the Smoke and Mirrors. The starship would be blasted apart by a targeted magnetic pulse-beam, long before it got back anywhere near solar system Callaway X Centra.

The ultimate question: Would Commander Kwit-Nik reciprocate the risk taken by the Earthlings when they completely disarmed the Smoke and Mirrors?

"Well there, Oodle-Noodle," Fred spoke aloud after that tree creature telepathically passed along to him Captain Taylor's thinking. "You could have knocked me over with a slap from one of your freakin' leaves. I am sorry, for sure, the rest of the galaxy isn't all sweetness and love-conquers-everything like you have back on Oomb. But this is what some good people from Earth were trying to warn you! It's exactly what they were trying to get through your thick trunk! Hell! Now we have to hope plan B will work!"

Not yet, Officer Frankly. You please must wait for the captain's final go-ahead.

"Dek-Fook-Tek's sense of humor makes the ground quake from his audience's amusement." This is what Lieutenant Ak-keek-teek meantime led his fellow deer creatures to ritually chant, back over in the Smoke and Mirrors conference room.

A medically sedated Dek-Fook-Tek returned into view on the conference room's flat-screen monitor. A splinter had been removed from where it lodged in his ample upper lip. His "Grrr!" of pain accompanying the splinter's removal was concealed from earshot. "Lieutenant Ak-keek-teek, Commander Kwit-Nik," the Supreme Authority soldiered on, if bleating meekly. The aforementioned sedation had taken its toll. "I need to talk with you both in private. You must temporarily leave the presence of those other-world animals who would dare attempt negotiating with us."

"Supreme Authority Dek-Fook-Tek?" the lieutenant made so bold as to bleat without first seeking permission. This happened soon as he and the commander withdrew to a smaller side room containing a smaller television monitor. That Dek-Fook-Tek uttered his name prior to uttering the commander's name had gone to his head. "Can we presume the parts of their plan we will sample are parts obtained by skillfully wielding a knife? Baa!" Ak-keek-teek laughed at his own wit.

"No. Not at all." Drugged-out Dek-Fook-Tek shook his oversized antlers slowly. Once more, he was assisted by his antler handlers to an extent he could never admit. "I want the other-worlders' plan implemented exactly as you, Commander Kwit-Nik, claim that Captain Main Course and her Officer Appetizer described it!" Dek-Fook-Tek went on sluggishly. "And you *will* postpone the defensive assault until after we have seen that plan through. Commander Kwit-Nik, Lieutenant Ak-keek-teek, you must understand. Going ahead with their desperately ridiculous ideas, we are bound to thereby learn critical new things about those dumb beasts. Inevitably, such things will help us when we launch my saucers for the pre-emption of their inevitable hostilities. Besides, we can only imagine what further, absolutely comic relief they have in store for us! Baa!" Despite his drugged-out drowsiness, Supreme Authority Dek-Fook-Tek's shoulders heaved with his renewed, uncontrollable amusement. Quickly thereafter he went down on all fours, and sank on bending knees until his belly touched the floor. What he did next only added to the ever-high stress of his antler handlers, who continued to manage his antlers like puppeteers managing a marionette. He rolled over onto his back and kicked his legs in the air, helplessly mirth-stricken.

Counselor Ali Magabu commented after Oodle-Noodle telepathed what she sixth-sensed had transpired with the deer creatures during their private conference. "Truly," Ali said, "I am reminded, most curiously, of a quote from our great, historic leader of nonviolent conflict resolution, Mahatma Gandhi. He said, 'First they ignore you, then they laugh at you, then they fight you, and then you win.' Only in this instance, it's 'First they want to eat you, then they laugh at you,-"

"Sure," interrupted Kevin, "and then they *still* want to eat you!"

Chapter 15

Captain's Log, Earth date November 10, 2063

I am seated on the navigation deck of the Smoke and Mirrors, gratefully encompassed by colleagues who have long since felt like family. I am just as gratefully unencompassed, at least for the time being, by deer creatures from Tictoctic.

The Tictoctickians do follow alongside us in their massive flying saucer I have learned is named the Sixth Celestial Breath. The Celestial Breath part refers to exhalations of their "Supreme Authority," Dek-Fook-Tek. It is meant to suggest he is the ultimate butterfly. His breaths rather than flapping wings have significant impact light-years away. That is just another of the ever-more-ludicrous conceits by which his minions labor to exalt him.

Yes, the Tictoctickians are shadowing us; they are monitoring our every action. But apparently, the concept of giving sentient beings enough private space to operate has the same cachet here that it has back home on Earth. And so, as I alluded to at the outset of this log entry, there are no Tictoctickians in our immediate presence. Maybe it is just a matter of their finding us even more malodorous than we find them.

For the record, Helena would have gone on to write how she assumed the deer creatures bugged the starship for covert surveillance. And that this was the reason she kept the children and their ample caregivers still stowed away in a concealed location. However, there was more than an off chance her log tablet might fall into the wrong hands, Tictoctickian cloven hoof-hands to be precise. Then the translation capability provided by the Earthlings would reveal far too dangerously much. A more thorough documentation of the mission would have to wait for later, assuming there was a later.

We are fast approaching a special planet in the solar system less than one-half light-year from Tictoctic. It is where a probe has provided strong evidence for the existence of thriving ecosystems. Yet there are no signs of space-age civilization, or any civilization for that matter.

Helena Taylor continued overly careful with what she committed to typing in her log. Again, if her entries were ever scrutinized by Tictoctickians utilizing the shared translation technology... As far as Helena and Buddy knew, the probe she mentioned in her log wasn't just any old probe. It was a probe of Chonoran origin. This meant the information garnered from it came thanks to Chonoran initiative. As with the saucer starships, it had been co-opted by the Tictoctickians.

When Captain Taylor stopped to think on this circumstance further, she wondered at why the Oombians hadn't already weighed in. Why hadn't they already credited futurist philosophers back on Earth with having been vindicated, after all?

Secretary of Defense Michael Spinner, among others, argued that the militarized space-faring forces of Tictoctic rested his case. Such forces provided convincing proof an armed civilization could indeed survive long enough to project its might for an interstellar war agenda.

The futurists, however, predicted something very different. They said that any extraterrestrials discovered having progressed well into the space age would necessarily be of peaceful, unarmed intent. Otherwise, the futurists argued, they would have done themselves in with their own advanced weapons capability.

Where Secretary Spinner was concerned, Tictoctickian militarism had proved those futurists dead wrong.

Presently, though, the Earthlings learned that the deer creatures' space-age achievements were not actually their own. Those achievements were stolen, co-opted from another civilization. And exactly as the futurists predicted, that other civilization got itself destroyed for having projected military might off their home planet Chonora. True, the Tictoctickians did turn Chonoran weaponry against Chonoran civilization, probably not what the futurists had in mind. Nevertheless...

Something else occurred to Helena as she continued pondering the prospective fate of civilizations, rather than resuming her log entry. If the tree creatures' peace plan didn't succeed, an interplanetary war between Earth and Tictoctic looked increasingly probable. Maybe their respective civilizations would wipe out one another, yet fulfilling Earthling futurists' consensus expectation. On the other hand, say one side did triumph, and triumph in a surviving sort of way. Helena was not clear how that one side, be it Earth or Tictoctic, wouldn't spread its influence further throughout the galaxy, on a full militaristic footing. In the final analysis, the futurists would be proven wrong, after all.

On this particularly grim thought, the starship captain welcomed her attention becoming increasingly drawn to the destination planet. When she looked up from her contemplations, she found it taking up nearly the entire panoramic view-screen.

Helena resumed typing into her log, a continued departure from her usual voice entries. She did this in order to keep picking her words extra carefully. What we know of this planet, her log entry went on, is that it's the closest we've come, yet, to an Earth-like world. As if Oomb and Fafama were not close enough. There is less water than on Oomb, but far more than on Fafama. Its mass is nearly identical to Earth's, about a millionth of a percent more. One of its continents has Florida-sized peninsulas extending from its south flank, side-by-side like five equal-length fingers. Those peninsulas might well turn out not to have been the massive remnants from a long-gone civilization. In which case our resident geophysicist, Cathy, is going to have a field day!

There are odd, brownish patches polka-dotting the continent of the five "fingers."

I see those patches on another land mass as well. That other land mass extends snake-like from the north ice cap nearly all the way south. Maybe it runs along their version of our Earth's Mid-Atlantic Ridge.

Wherever those brownish patches are located, they are surrounded by richly verdant areas. And the oceans are shaded deep blue. Clearly, this is a planet with a thriving ecology. But no greetings have issued from there to, among other things, supply us with a name so we don't need conjure one up. This feels, by far, like our most mysterious port of call, yet.

Captain Taylor, Oodle-Noodle intervened to telepath, *my mind-reading is not picking up anything indicative of technologically advanced creatures. There are creatures on the order of pigs and dolphins with a high intelligence, yes. But they have not evolved like we have seen from the deer creatures of Tictoctic.*

"Thank you, Oodle-Noodle." Helena noted down the Oombian's first sixth-sense findings regarding their new destination. Then she went on to speculate in her journal, What if this planet is at a stage comparable to the Earth one hundred million years ago? How will we make it suitable for safe habitation by the deer creatures if fearsome beasts roam about, comparable to our extinct dinosaurs?

"Uh-oh, Captain." This time it was Tanya Petrovsky interrupting. Her tone of voice chilled Helena as much as anything she had heard translated from deer creatures during the vegetarian meal prepared for them by Ludi Perez.

"Let's have it, Officer Petrovsky." Helena surprised her own self at the defiant tone she took with Tanya, if tainted by weariness.

"Of course, Captain. Our spectroscopic scan is picking up concentrations of radionuclides in seemingly random areas on this planet's surface."

"You mean, such as strontium 90?"

"Strontium 90, cesium 137, traces of plutonium and americium..."

"Signature remnants from one or more nuclear explosives," Helena said to no one in particular. Rather, she was thinking to herself out loud. Although she did keep quiet about the irony of having contemplated, just minutes earlier, predictions from futurist philosophers. Again, she had been thinking about how those predictions were faring in the face of evidence accumulated from other solar systems.

"Oodle-Noodle, you've picked up no signals of intelligence down there comparable to ours?"

None, Captain.

"So if there was a nuclear war on this planet, there were no survivors. Tanya, anything you can postulate from your analysis, on when those radionuclides were released?"

"Approximately two hundred fifty years ago. But that is preliminary, until I can gather more data from planet's surface. It might have been much more recently, or up to a thousand years ago."

"So this is the question, people. Are there enough safe zones for the size of the Tictoctickian population we envision accommodating? Or is the planet still too contaminated from, um, whatever happened. Tanya, Cathy, I want you to take a shuttle pod on a reconnaissance tour. Thing one: With your closer-in spectroscopic readings, try to determine definitively whether we've arrived at an extraterrestrial Garden of Eden. Or is it a Garden of Eden in the middle of reclamation from Paradise Lost via nuclear holocaust? Thing two: Give us a fair guesstimation, either way, how much land mass and sea is safely, live-ably usable by the Tictoctickians."

From the conference room window, Captain Helena Taylor watched the egg-shaped shuttle pod's departure. Micron-thin stabilizer fins electrostatically materialized about its hull, thus lending the proximate appearance of a metallic dolphin. Tanya was preparing for descent through the planet's atmosphere, a deep dive to achieve low-cruising altitude.

The shuttle pod continued on its way, flaring out oranges and yellows from its first contact with wisps of upper air molecules.

Helena found herself reflecting on the crew's goodbyes, days prior.

Married partners had been about to travel separate directions, one partner down to the surface of Tictoctic, the other nearly one-half light-year away. Helena was part of the latter group, once more assuming command of the Smoke and Mirrors. Although she well knew that the starship could be seized from her yet again, at any time, by Commander Kwit-Nik. The commander was shadowing her mission in the Sixth Celestial Breath.

Helena inadvertently overheard Cathy and Buddy doing their farewells outside a washroom where she just happened to be cleaning up.

"Buddy, my Buddy," said Cathy.

Helena easily imagined what she would have seen in addition to overheard, if only. Namely, geophysicist Cathy with her hands entwined round Buddy's neck.

"I *know* how much I care for you," Cathy was going on, "because this first real possibility we won't see each other ever again is...is...sniff!"

"You're too pessimistic, my shmaltzy-schmootzy. Isn't that right, Oodle-Noodle?!" Buddy raised his voice as though wherever the Oombian was at that particular moment, she would have more easily mind-read his subsequent request. "While I am gone, I am counting on you to telepath sweet nothings of hope in Officer James-Leung's ear! Also, ha! Remind her that while she fears for my life, more likely than not I will be helping the deer creatures with their putting and chipping!"

It would be an honor, Officer Leung.

A slap ensued that Helena was certain landed on the seat of Buddy's pants. "You're just trying to make me want you out of my sight!" Cathy groaned tearfully. "You're doing a miserable job!"

Captain Helena Taylor also overheard Chief Medical Officer Dr. Deborah Davis-Murphy with her wife, Third Engineer Geena Murphy-Davis. Helena was about to enter the ship's infirmary, but she paused well outside to shamelessly eavesdrop.

"We have to promise ourselves," said Deborah. "After this latest fools errand, no more missions aboard the Smoke and Mirrors!"

For Geena's response, the captain thought she detected a whimper. Whatever it was got followed by a stiff-upper-lip from Deborah. "There *will* be another mission of the Smoke and Mirrors! For us to decline our participation! *Both* of us!"

Helena could not have known what Deborah did next, despite her final note of bravado. She stealthily handed over some cyanide capsules to Geena. If it ended up that the deer creatures were going to slaughter her... Deborah gave Geena enough to share with fellow Earthlings down on Tictoctic in that grim happenstance.

Where Ali, Tanya, Kevin and Yoon-hee were concerned, Helena did not stumble into any such accidental-turned-purposeful listening. But she easily conceived how their partings went. Kevin put on a bold face. He tried to laugh off the situation with something about how at least he would be tickle-free for a while. So Yoon-hee dug her fingers deep into his armpits as she mock-snarled with fierce determination, "I better stock up enough tickles to hold you over!"

As for married Officers Ali Magabu and Tanya Petrovsky, Helena heard Ali most clearly in her imagination. He was whistling past the graveyard, as it were. That is, he was saying to his wife Tanya, "Truly, Tanya sweetie, I find myself more worried for me than for you, as for the thousand ways I am sure they can find to prepare me."

Helena conceived Tanya responding something to the effect of, "Nonsense, Dr. Magabu! They will find you far too unappetizing to come anywhere near, let alone slice and dice. Ah! But as breeding stock..." In Helena's imagining, this was as far as Tanya got with her own show of false bravado before she teared up, overwhelmed...not too dissimilar to how Helena teared up again, just re-conjuring this fancied bit of conversation.

Then there were Ludi and Pedro Perez. They were Chris's two relatives who so profoundly embraced an alternate course to their lives, sixty years into the future. Oodle-Noodle telepathically facilitated their goodbye conversation with two-year-old daughter, Alexita. Thereby the deer creatures were still kept from realizing anyone was concealed in a closed-off part of the starship.

Helena Taylor saw Ludi and Pedro speak into thin air what they wanted the Oombian tree creature telepathing their daughter, Alexita. They used Spanish so any eavesdropping Tictoctickians would have no idea what they were saying. Anyway, Helena also saw them listen quietly to Alexita's response as conveyed by Oodle-Noodle. Oodle-Noodle's telepath seeped gently into their heads.

Helena could only hope the Perez family's young daughter was lulled into a durable feeling of safety, security by her parents' version of fearless bravado.

As the remote conversation concluded, however, Ludi and Pedro gave one another a plainly clinging-to-one-another-for-dear-life tearful embrace. The starship captain was moved to say, "I think we have left enough significant others behind on Tictoctic, separated from their special ones aboard ship. The Tictoctickians should already feel as confident as they ever will about our intent. That we aren't just going to take the Smoke and Mirrors and speed out of here, never to return nor check out the nearby planet. So I think an exception could be warranted in your case, to keep you both together. I'm sure we can do this without raising any more doubts than the deer creatures would have about us, regardless."

But Helena did not get even halfway through these remarks before both Pedro and Ludi were determinedly shaking their heads "no."

As soon as the captain finished, Ludi was quick to respond, nevertheless remaining in her husband's desperate embrace. "Captain, this mission is so deeply important for, um, for our family back on Oomb. I cannot see my staying behind on Tictoctic with my Pedro unless you order me. Ay Dios mío, who else will be better able on that new planet to test for the viability of growing gandules and plantain bananas? Also, who else is better prepared to investigate that new planet's plant life for other nutritious and delicious foods?"

How clever, Helena still marveled presently as much as she had marveled those couple days ago. *How ingeniously Ludi reframed my proposal! Her mention of "family back on Oomb" could have ignited the Tictoctickians' suspicion. They might have wondered whether that family was actually stowed away hidden on the Smoke and Mirrors. But talk of remaining on Tictoctic should have diverted their thinking away from any such prospect. That is, assuming Tictoctickians were covertly listening in!*

And then there's the amazing situation with Chig-cher and Chwerp-chee. That we could seize a moment to tuck them away beside the children was incredible enough. But even more incredible was that Oodle-

Noodle's hypnosis apparently worked, causing the Tictoctickians to forget their very existence!

Chris was standing well within earshot of Helena's offer when Ludi and Pedro turned it down. Helena realized this as the Perez couple strode away arm in arm for their final goodbyes. So her very next order of business involved a most hurried rush over to her husband's side. The words started to spill out before she got there. Chris imagined her carrying them piled atop one another in a precariously high pile. "You know I can't make an exception for us." By Helena's final word of this sentence, she had come close enough to grab Chris by the wrist.

"Of course we have to set the example, 'len- uhh, Helena." When Officer Olsen-Taylor responded, he patted Helena's hand clenching his wrist. He barely managed to stifle his "'lena hon'" pet name for her.

"I am the world's worst communicator." Helena looked into Chris's eyes with a wan, teary smile. But before he could offer a kiss or anything else, she let go his wrist, and shook free of his patting hand to spin around and walk away.

Chris was left to speculate on what Helena wasn't good at communicating. Maybe it had to do with the, for her, far-from-satisfactory state of their relationship?

He could not have imagined her thoughts the very same moment she strode off. They concerned one additionally awful, terrible aspect of the planet Fafama's destruction, albeit trivial when compared to the destruction itself. The pendant the first wife, the Varalawa, had been preparing for Helena to share with Chris must have been lost. Perhaps the first wife hadn't even gotten to complete its engraving.

I apologize for barging in on your mental processing like this, Captain Taylor, Oodle-Noodle abruptly telepathed. *I thought you needed to know that Sergeant Hanson and Yulala might be having their baby sooner rather than later.*

Helena made sure she didn't lift her gaze ceiling-ward, like she usually did when she was telepathed by an Oombian not in the same room with her. Moreover, she grabbed the nearest maintenance log, and pretended to be conducting a routine review.

Helena's dissembling behavior was prompted by a precautionary assumption. Namely, the Tictoctickians were keeping her under constant surveillance, maybe even conducted directly by Commander Kwit-Nik.

Again, the Oombians and Earthlings were left unchaperoned aboard the Smoke and Mirrors for the mission to the unexplored planet, but no matter. Kwit-Nik and company tagged along beside the Smoke and Mirrors in the Sixth Celestial Breath. *Maybe our odor proved as unpleasant for them as theirs proved for us. Maybe they complained they felt cooped up in a barn with a herd of unwashed cattle,* Helena mused.

Excuse my new intrusion, Captain, Oodle-Noodle gently, telepathically insinuated herself on Helena's mental landscape presently. *Sergeant Hanson has made a fascinating observation available for mind-reading. Yulala's belly already appears distended to the proportions of an Earthling mother's belly some eight months into pregnancy. Moreover, Yulala noted that the typical Fafaman mother's fetus comes to term in about a third the time of an Earthling fetus.*

It is most fortunate that Ciela is also hidden away with the expectant couple. She has had experience on

Oomb assisting the midwife for two sisters' childbirth there.

Over the past hours, I have been acting as telepathic intermediary for Chief Medical Officer Davis-Murphy. She is reviewing delivery procedure and possible complications with Ciela, Sergeant Hanson and Yulala. The doctor speculates there has been a synergistic interaction between Fafaman and Earth biochemistries. As a result, the gestation time table has accelerated to an even faster rate than the typical Fafaman fetus's three months. I just thought you should know, Captain.

"And," Helena almost proceeded to respond aloud, as had been her habit for Oombian telepaths. Instantly, though, she stifled herself, to rather focus on making available for Oodle-Noodle's mind-read, And I thank you for that, Oodle-Noodle. Don't think twice about any future barging-in on my contemplations you might believe is necessary.

Chapter 16

"There goes their puny shuttle pod, Commander," derisively tongue-clicked Lieutenant Ak-keek-teek. The lieutenant was standing beside Commander Kwit-Nik to gaze out the panoramic view-screen of the Sixth Celestial Breath. They both enjoyed an unobstructed view of the shuttle pod leaving the Smoke and Mirrors.

The pod was on a descent path into the mysterious planet's atmosphere, less than one-half light-year away from Tictoctic. This egg-shaped vehicle flamed reddish-orange due to friction with the unexplored world's outer layer of mostly nitrogen and oxygen.

The lieutenant went on, "All too soon, they will be making a survey to discover the best staging areas for establishing ground support of an orbiting invasion command center."

"Oskynt excrement, Lieutenant!" Commander Kwit-Nik pounded at the floor with one of his cloven hind hooves. "You heard what they said about detecting pockets of radioactivity! Perhaps those pockets are indicative of this planet having bred a civilization after all, a civilization that wiped itself out in some enormous conflagration! For all intents and purposes, it would appear to have been a conflagration well beyond the one by which we vanquished our homegrown foes on Tictoctic, prior to our suffering Chonoran aggression!

"No, Lieutenant. No invasion command center. Rather, the Akt creatures are simply seeking enough safe areas for their proposed resettlement of our fellow beings."

"With all due respect, Commander Kwit-Nik, you are likely to discover regions of naturally occurring radioactive substances on many planets. It makes no difference whether there be any especially intelligent species to exploit them, or not!"

"But Officer Ak-keek-teek, the Akt creatures claim those substances appear on this planet in proportions only to be expected from spent radioactive material."

"Baa! I am certain if we were to waste our time attempting to verify their findings, we would find they were deceiving us!"

Kwit-Nik took in this complaining speculation quietly, not deigning to offer any further rebuttal.

Lieutenant Ak-keek-teek snorted with frustration and tongue-clicked, "Whatever the true situation, this is crazy! We already know everything we need to know about these beasts! We ought to be confiscating their spacecraft, and placing them in a holding pen! Chef Glork-tek can determine which we raise for breeding, and which should go to immediate slaughter!"

Commander Kwit-Nik didn't know whether Ak-keek-teek was aware that Tictoctic's best minds still didn't understand very much about Chonoran technology. They certainly did not understand enough to "waste our time" running the element scan the "beasts" ran, even if they wanted to. For sure, Tictoctickian technology had not yet progressed anywhere near that far along.

But no matter; Commander Kwit-Nik's chief, and least trustworthy, officer just opened another route for Kwit-Nik to easily put him off balance. The commander took no small amount of pleasure in a strong push-back response coming to mind so quickly. "So Lieutenant Ak-keek-teek," the commander tongue-clicked tersely, "do you mean to imply our Supreme Authority Dek-Fook-Tek was crazy for letting these beasts from Akt proceed with their plan? Do you blaspheme against Dek-Fook-Tek?"

Lieutenant Ak-keek-teek swelled out his chest, how lower-ranked officers swelled out their chests for their superiors. This was the way of the military culture of Tictoctic. Soldiers routinely made their chests available for antler slashing or goring by those up the chain of command. Naturally, they secretly hoped such an offer would not get taken up. That the humiliating submission it embodied would suffice. This is what Ak-keek-teek made to look like he was about. Nevertheless, he responded brazenly to the commander's question. As to whether he, the lieutenant, blasphemed against their Supreme Authority, he said, "And what if I do?"

Commander Kwit-Nik locked eyes with Ak-keek-teek. After considerable ear twitching, he responded, "Lieutenant, I am going to do you a big favor. I am not going to make you eligible for becoming another 'Officer Appetizer' by sharing with anyone else what you just said." With that, Kwit-Nik turned around, got down on all fours, and stompingly trotted away. Well he knew the lieutenant was baiting him. The lieutenant was trying to goad him into saying even one word about, making the slightest reference to a planned insurrection against Dek-Fook-Tek.

It would have been another matter altogether, had Kwit-Nik believed Ak-keek-teek was anything less than blindly, fiercely, fanatically loyal to the "Supreme Authority."

Chapter 17

"Baa, their game! Their game is what has me most curious!" Dek-Fook-Tek knocked together his cloven hoof-hands in eager anticipation.

The sound issuing from Dek-Fook-Tek's hooves reminded Chris Olsen-Taylor of the sound from wood-block chimes, though not nearly so musical.

Dek-Fook-Tek was presenting himself before Chris and Ali, in an open field not far from his command post just south of Tictoctic's Arctic Circle. And there was another curious thing about him: the management of his antlers.

Under different circumstances, the two Earthlings might have been amused. But they remained worried that any second, they could suddenly find themselves headed for a slaughterhouse, added to the deer creatures' diet.

Clearly, nevertheless, Supreme Authority Dek-Fook-Tek's antlers were ridiculously oversized.

The Earthlings first saw Dek-Fook-Tek on a video monitor several years into the past, close to Chonora. Back then, his head growths were similar to a typical stag's on Earth. They appeared immense, yet still manageable.

The second time Earthlings saw Dek-Fook-Tek was on the video monitor in a conference room aboard the Smoke and Mirrors. This was during crucial negotiations with the deer creatures after Captain Taylor surrendered her starship to Captain Kek-stek. Dek-Fook-Tek's antlers looked impossibly overgrown. Supreme Authority or not, how did he keep them lifted so erect? How didn't they tip his head all the way over to one side and break his neck, even?

Chris was especially puzzled. He remembered what he learned years ago at a natural history museum. Deer-type creatures on Earth typically shed each successively larger antler growth. Shouldn't the Supreme Authority's antlers have fallen off before they became so out-sized? *What, has he been ingesting a special steroid?*

The field where Earthlings improvised a demonstration golf course was where they got to see how Dek-Fook-Tek accomplished his antler-balancing feat. Although, Wafoodle-boodle telepathetically warned them they needed to pretend total unawareness. They mustn't allow themselves more than fleeting glimpses out the corner of their eye. Otherwise they risked being dragged off for meal preparation, over the Supreme Authority noticing what they were noticing.

Dek-Fook-Tek's antler handlers stood securely strapped to ladders on wheels. From those elevated positions, each handler held on tight to a steel cross. From those two crosses depended lengths of transparent string possessing the tensile strength of deep-sea fishing lines. They were tied to Dek-Fook-Tek's antler prongs.

For Chris, the antlers might as well have been two especially large bushes, mirror images of one another. And seen during winter with their leaves fallen off.

Anyway, two more handlers pushed the ladders along beside wherever Dek-Fook-Tek moved. That allowed his antler puppeteers, as Ali would have termed them, to keep up.

The model golf course was the last stop on Dek-Fook-Tek's tour of Earthling activity. It was established by Ali and Chris in a fenced expanse of several acres. A sign posted on the fence translated, most eerily morbidly where the Earthlings were concerned, "the ranch." As in cattle ranch.

First stop on Dek-Fook-Tek's tour was Geena and Yoon-hee's greenhouse. Despite the northern hemisphere's long, sunny, summer days, weather stayed generally cool and dry. A bit too cool, a bit too dry, Yoon-hee's estimation went, for pigeon pea plants to do very well outdoors. The pigeon pea plant seeds sowed by Yoon-hee had been harvested from humid, semi-tropical conditions along Puerto Rico's north coast.

But no problem. Yoon-hee and Geena came equipped with the makings for a ten-by-ten-foot greenhouse. They strove to demonstrate small-scale what could be accomplished large-scale.

Similarly, Ali and Chris hoped their one-hole golf course would thrill the deer creatures with how much fun could be in store on a full-size, eighteen-hole layout. They mowed their exemplar course into a field of subarctic tundra grasses.

Yoon-hee ran up to Dek-Fook-Tek and Chef Glork-tek, just outside the entrance to the semi-transparent tent-like greenhouse. That entrance was neither wide enough nor high enough for the Supreme Authority's antler handlers standing on mobile ladders.

"Further south," said Yoon-hee, "you will be able to grow huge fields of bean-bearing plants without the need for such an edifice as this. But that will have to wait until climate patterns return closer to normal."

Dried mud caked on her fingers from pulling weeds, Officer Geena Murphy-Davis accompanied Yoon-hee Park-Smith. She added, "There is no reason you cannot construct warehouse-sized versions of this greenhouse up north here. Take a peek past the entry flaps. Look at how the seedlings have emerged over just a few days. By the time our starship returns, the first crop might be ready for harvesting."

"Observe them both." Dek-Fook-Tek turned Chef Glork-tek's way to tongue-click with persisting amusement. He did not deign respond to the Earthlings directly. "They are nearly the size of two oskynt calves, yet their industriousness rivals a colony of pebble-sized niki-niks! They put oskynt sloth to shame, were any oskynt still left alive in some remote, unexplored area!"

"Your perceptiveness puts professionally trained naturalists to shame as well, Supreme Authority Dek-Fook-Tek." Chef Glork-tek bowed, thus prompting Geena and Yoon-hee to do likewise.

"But there is even more," the Supreme Authority continued, wishing to enlarge upon his chef's compliment. He was oblivious to how he was being patronized. "The way those two busy beasts rushed to our side, they could have been two kokatoks scampering over to greet us. Before we had to add it to our diet, I used to delight in my niece's pet kokatok. Its name was Tickity. Such fun, how it showed excitement over seeing me! Its tail flattened against the ground lifted its body wagging from side to side! Its drool sprayed everywhere! My niece loved that too! Baa!" On his second mention of his niece, Dek-Fook-Tek stamped a hind cloven hoof hard against the ground. He strained to contain his still-raw grief over her untimely death from something comparable to leukemia, several solar orbits earlier. Wafoodle-boodle had shared this personal tidbit with the Earthlings well prior to their present encounter. She had gleaned it, of course, from her mind-reading rummaging about Dek-Fook-Tek's head.

"Everyone knows how much she loved her Tikity." Chef Glork-tek offered a comforting snout wiggle against Dek-Fook-Tek's own snout as he bleated softly. "Her untimely loss still scars all Tictoctickians, even to this day."

"I am not sure how long our amusement and entertainment can be allowed to last before inevitably yielding to our appetite, sniff!" Dek-Fook-Tek sniveled to Chef Glork-tek. He gave Yoon-hee and Geena a watery-eyed, chop-licking regard that chilled them both to the bone.

"I know, Supreme Dek-Fook-Tek. Let us see in what manner the others are using their time," said Chef Glork-tek. He most gently led Tictoctic's ruler to turn around, and-

"Did the chef actually wink at us?" Yoon-hee kept her question for Geena to a whisper.

"If Wafoodle-boodle is right about Commander Kwit-Nik planning an insurrection, we don't know that Glork-tek isn't in on it," Geena whispered in response.

After leaving from Geena and Yoon-hee's presence, Dek-Fook-Tek approached the corner of the "ranch" where Buddy and Pedro were working.

Ahhh, so that's how he does it, Buddy Leung would have spoken aloud and nodded with dawning understanding. Again, that could have proven fatally dangerous.

Sí! Incredible! was all that Pedro would have coaxed from his mouth while nodding in near disbelief, if only. He wisely shared Buddy's fear of expressing himself.

What Buddy and Pedro just learned, Geena and Ludi had become aware of only a short time before. No less than four handlers labored to keep Dek-Fook-Tek's ridiculously oversized head growths held high. Two stood on ladders, two wheeled the ladders either side of Dek-Fook-Tek.

As noted earlier, the handlers atop the wheeled ladders maneuvered their leader's antlers like they were two puppeteers controlling marionettes. However, their manipulations were dictated by where and how Dek-Fook-Tek decided to comport himself. The puppet was actually controlling the puppet masters.

The other handlers were assigned to push the ladders along. They likewise worked nonstop to keep up with every last nuance of their leader's movement.

"Well, they picked a good time," said Buddy Leung. He stood back to admire the solar panels and miniature wind turbines assembled by him and Pedro after they hauled everything over from the shuttle pod. "I think we are ready to put on a show."

"And what show would that be they are ready to put on, Chef Glork-tek?" Dek-Fook-Tek asked the deer creature beside him when he strutted up closer to the Earthlings. The same as with Yoon-hee and Geena, he did not deign address directly what he heard translated from Buddy and Pedro. "Do these other-worlders always have to construct such an elaborate display of shiny surfaces, plus metallic flowers with their petals spinning? Is that what they have to do when they wish to lure females closer? And are we about to witness even more from them? Are they about to warble like extinct tictekkers, or otherwise make some far-carrying sound in the hopes of convincing females they are suitable for mating?"

"Supreme Authority Dek-Fook-Tek, your power of imagination is exceeded only by the strength of your conviction," Chef Glork-tek bleated with calculated meekness. He wanted to respond instead with an acid edge, *Not quite.* But he feared that would have made him suspect, not to be trusted. As a result, perhaps Dek-Fook-Tek would have had him gored for his disloyal impertinence, then roasted using one of his own recipes.

"Supreme Authority, your conviction looms tall as the tallest peaks of the Tickakaytas," Dek-Fook-Tek's antler handlers baaed in unison. The two handlers encharged with pushing along the ladders on wheels ritually bowed down. The other two handlers, the ones Chris might have likened to puppeteers, didn't bow down. They couldn't very well leave off from their task of holding up the mighty one's antlers. Nevertheless, they joined in for the rest of this particular litany as well, to utter, "It is far too steep for us to climb past its lower elevations, but we can stand back and observe with awe."

Ah, yes, Chef Glork-tek thought to himself while he also joined in. *We haven't had one of these absurdly adulatory litanies in a while.*

"Supreme Authority Dek-Fook-Tek," said Officer Buddy Leung from down on one knee alongside Pedro.

Both Earthlings figured they better ape the deer creatures' reverential poses, even if they couldn't tongue-click along.

"We are ready to demonstrate this power base's potential," Buddy went on. "It can provide your royal command center with all the electricity needed, simply from wind and sun. No burning of coal or other fuel will be required. And no wires will be necessary from here to there." Buddy gestured towards Dek-Fook-Tek's immense military headquarters. That building rose from the subarctic plain less than a half mile away, in the shape of antlers. Or more accurately, in the shape of antlers constructed of strictly rectangular shapes like Lego blocks, Pedro mused.

"Electrical energy transported from here to there! No wires necessary!" brayed Dek-Fook-Tek with amusement. He went down on all fours and jumped about as though, Pedro thought, he were some sort of bucking bronco. But nobody was mounted on him to buck.

Chef Glork-tek feared Supreme Authority Dek-Fook-Tek might be in need of a fresh tranquillizer injection.

None too soon, Dek-Fook-Tek at last eased off his frantic behavior. He reared back up onto his hind limbs, and crisply tongue-clicked, "How amazing nature can be, Chef Glork-tek! Before we needed them added to our diet, there were the web-winged flip-flaps. Ridiculously oversized radar ears guided their flight through pitch-black caves. Now we have these new animals with extraordinarily elaborate working-out of their own instinctive patterns!"

Yeah, ridiculously oversized like your ego and your antlers! Buddy easily imagined Kevin venting. That is, if Kevin were there to hear this translation of Dek-Fook-Tek's tongue-clicks.

"So let us see what happens, Supreme Authority," nodded Chef Glork-tek. Then to Officer Leung, "You understand the chronology we have agreed upon, inspired by the wisdom of Dek-Fook-Tek?"

Buddy Leung didn't affirm immediately what Chef Glork-tek baaed. He was checking how Dek-Fook-Tek's antler handlers were behaving. He wanted to make certain he wouldn't interrupt them offering up another ritual chant in the Supreme Authority's praise. "At the pleasure of Dek-Fook-Tek, of course, we will switch on our array first," Buddy answered at last. "We need to establish we are successfully converting the voltage output from wind and solar, alike, into 'spooky action at a distance' quantum-space-leaping current. Once we have done that, Chef Glork-tek, we will have you communicate with the royal command center. You will ask them to please temporarily take all systems off line. However, one never knows when some unforeseen complication might develop. So obviously, the royal command center will want to double-check beforehand that nothing critical could be impacted."

Pedro replicated Buddy's what-will-be-will-be shrug, both resigned to their fate.

⸎⸎⸎

"Baa, I am going to require a grass-bundle's-worth more of proof." Dek-Fook-Tek shook his head like he was shaking away nuisance flies, Pedro thought. Made no difference the text confirmation sent him by a trusted officer inside his royal command center. The text reported that everything remained up and running despite disconnection from the local power grid.

On a paper-thin computer screen handed him by Chef Glork-tek, the Supreme Authority brought up a live camera feed. It originated near the power station some twenty Earth miles away from Dek-Fook-Tek's subarctic stronghold. An unobstructed look was afforded, at smoke plumes issuing from a smokestack to the power station's rear. "This!" Dek-Fook-Tek tapped his cloven hoof-hand on the computer with such force, Buddy feared he would crack the screen. "I want the power station itself turned off completely! I want to see the smoke stack stop spewing its gray filth! Only this way can I know for sure there was not some trickery keeping our power connected! That the instinctive labors of the outer space beasts didn't provide us with any more energy than a niki-nik hill or takookpeet burrow!"

"Of course," nodded Chef Glork-tek in what he knew could be nothing less than full assent. "To assure we are not being duped, a temporary outage would be a small price to pay, including for neighbors dependent upon that power source."

"Neighbors feeling any less than most profoundly honored will be considered treasonous!" Dek-Fook-Tek's angry tongue-clicks emerged so loudly, they could have been firecracker caps popping off, where Pedro was concerned.

During the slow minutes taken for smoke-stack shutdown, Buddy and Pedro pretended to busy themselves. They kept making unnecessary adjustments to solar panels' slow but steady tracking of the sun's course across the sky. Both men feared that standing around lacking industriousness for even the briefest while might not be in their best interest. Tictoctic's dictator given any chance to ponder the Earthlings in respite from work might lead him dangerous directions. He might dwell on how Chef Glork-tek could have them roasted for dinner.

Chef Glork-tek was also intent on distracting Dek-Fook-Tek from culinary considerations regarding the other-worlders. He tongue-clicked with delicate softness, "Such tranquility and peace, watching those otherworldly beasts on their instinctive ministrations as you so brilliantly term them, Supreme Authority..."

"Yes, their silly animal ways do bring me as much peace as amusement," Dek-Fook-Tek conceded.

"Exactly! Exactly!" Chef Glork-tek baaed in a forceful whisper. "We know this from research on kokatoks before the great famine. Many of us had them for pets. They lowered people's blood pressure, thereby resulting in longer, happier lives."

"Okay," said Dek-Fook-Tek, "let us suppose the Akt beasts' all-plant diet *does* satisfy our nutritional needs. Let us also suppose the components of that diet can be harvested in quantities adequate to feed everyone. And by everyone, I mean both here and on the planet they urge for our temporary resettlement while Tictoctic is revived. What are you braying about exactly, Chef Glork-tek? Are you suggesting that in such eventualities, we should keep the Akt beasts as pets rather than consuming them?"

"Aren't they the cutest things?"

"BAA!!" Dek-Fook-Tek returned down on all fours for his bucking bronco thing again, in wild abandon with his merriment. "Maybe I should retain you as my permanent court jester, Chef Glork-tek! You produce absurd comedic notions as effectively as you prepare gustatory masterpieces! BAA!!!"

"Look! The smoke is extinguished!" excitedly brayed Chef Glork-tek. He called Dek-Fook-Tek's attention back to the computer screen view of the power substation.

Buddy and Pedro dared jog over beside the two deer creatures to confirm Glork-tek's report with their own eyes.

"I also just received email confirmation that everything remains up and running," Glork-tek added.

"Imagine if you will, Supreme Authority," said Buddy Leung. "Imagine putting a stop to smoke stacks like this all across Tictoctic. Imagine them no longer dirtying the air and heating up huge portions of your planet to unlivable extremes. And then imagine the credit you will be able to most justifiably take for bringing Tictoctic back to life! This can start to happen within a few orbits of your sun!"

Dek-Fook-Tek gave Buddy a special regard, focused on his legs rather than making eye contact. He sent his tongue sliding slowly across his thin upper lip.

"I am imagining something else instead! But the game! Yes! You are also beasts who play games! Chef Glork-tek, take me over to the game quadrant of the cattle ranch!"

"Well, this is good enough timing anyway," commented Chris Olsen-Taylor.

The Supreme Authority and company were headed Chris's direction. Good enough timing, indeed; he, Ali Magabu, and Wafoodle-boodle had just finished setting up a demonstration golf hole.

This was when Dek-Fook-Tek expressed curiosity over "their game" to Chef Glork-tek. And his cloven hoof-hands knocking together reminded Chris of sounds from wood-block chimes.

While the deer creatures continued approaching, Chris and Ali sought to pique Dek-Fook-Tek's curiosity even further. That is, his curiosity as it had been revealed to them through Wafoodle-boodle's mindreading. They did this by melodramatically stepping back to admire their handiwork.

The golf hole, the first of its kind ever sculpted from Tictoctickian soil, ran about two hundred fifty gently undulating yards across the subarctic tundra. Its wide fairway narrowed gradually to a small, flat green. That green featured a six-foot-tall pin set snuggly into a four-inch-wide cup. The pin's small, red, triangular flag fluttered picturesquely in the gentle breeze.

A mountain range featuring two deep passes carved by glaciers provided an impressive backdrop. The glaciers themselves had completely melted, shrunk away several solar orbits ago on account of global warming.

Next to the tee box, golf clubs were left leaning against special stilts installed for that purpose.

The Supreme Authority's ears fluttered excitedly from his contemplation of the entire situation.

Chef Glork-tek was reminded of how Dek-Fook-Tek would survey an especially ambitious culinary preparation set before his royal countenance. "Baa," Glork-tek baaed to gain the Earthlings' attention. He saw they were clearly entranced, and somewhat terrified, by Dek-Fook-Tek's looming antlers. "Your game is ready to play?" Glork-tek said. His tongue-clicks conveyed encouraging enthusiasm that informed what the Earthling-provided translator emitted.

"Supreme Authority Dek-Fook-Tek, Chef Glork-tek, we are honored," Counselor Ali Magabu responded with a deferential bow. "Truly, we are honored you would take the time to examine our most fascinating game."

Dek-Fook-Tek clip-clopped closer to the clubs. He sniffed at them with his nostrils in a twitchy commotion. His short furry tail wagged most rapidly where it protruded from a triangular aperture stitched into the rear of his pants. His tightly fitting pants, themselves, reminded the Earthlings of speedos or leotards.

"Umm, would you like Officer Olsen-Taylor here to demonstrate?" Ali ventured to proceed.

Dek-Fook-Tek just kept sniffing away. He transitioned from the clubs to a down-on-all-fours inspection of the fairway.

"I truly believe my fellow officer is the better one to show you how this game works," Ali added. "He has played so much more often than I have had the pleasure of doing."

Dek-Fook-Tek froze in his tracks, and looked up. With the continued help of his antler handlers riding the mobile ladders, he turned towards Chef Glork-tek to ask, "I wonder how they cut the grass so uniformly short?"

As before, the Supreme Authority did not deign direct his query the Earthlings' way. Rather, he might as well have been asking a fellow deer creature how beavers in a zoo built their dam. This is what Chris Olsen-Taylor made of Dek-Fook-Tek's behavior.

But Chris and Ali both believed they best not answer Dek-Fook-Tek's question about the grass themselves. They left the Oombian tree creature Wafoodle-boodle to fill Chef Glork-tek's head telepathically with that information.

As expected, Glork-tek passed it along to the Supreme Authority.

"You see the device over there, Supreme Dek-Fook-Tek, left amidst other equipment brought down from their spacecraft?" said Chef Glork-tek. "I believe it functions like mowers of old in our more temperate climes, before extreme warming died off the lawns. Our other-world creatures appear to have cut most of the grass on one short setting. But in that circular area around the flag-pin, they used an even shorter setting. I have no idea why."

"Chef Glork-tek, do these other-world beasts understand when I hereby order them to show how their game is played? And the consequences most extreme for them but savory for us if they do not?"

"I believe they do, Dek-Fook-Tek. One of the beasts is trotting over to their equipment for that very purpose, even as we tongue-click."

Chris Olsen-Taylor already had a seven iron in one hand, and a dimpled golf ball in the other. After propping up the ball on a tuft of grass, he took a few practice swings.

Chef Glork-tek realized he had seen such swings before. They were similar to the Earthling's, though without a club. Kwit-Nik. Ever since leaving Oomb, Glork-tek had had occasion to happen across Commander Kwit-Nik all alone. On every one of those occasions, Glork-tek found Kwit-Nik with his hoof-hands locked together forming a triangle. His chest became one side of the triangle while his outstretched forelimbs provided the other two sides. With that triangle, Kwit-Nik always made an odd back-and-forth motion.

Chef Glork-tek considered Commander Kwit-Nik more his actual leader than Dek-Fook-Tek. He just had to hope the commander's judgment wasn't clouded as from an especially thick early morning fog. Glork-tek feared that Commander Kwit-Nik had developed too much empathy for the creatures from outer space. Kwit-Nik's obvious affinity for one of the other-worlders' more popular sports certainly couldn't be helping.

At the same time, though, Chef Glork-tek did admit to himself a mysteriously drawing attraction, where "kolfk" was concerned. He loved the idea of launching a small ball across long distances, high through the air. Plus there was the equally intriguing goal of knocking that ball rolling into a small hole in the ground.

"There!" exulted Chris. The deer creatures of Tictoctic needed to be peacefully persuaded of an alternative to their interplanetary, meat-gathering conquest of space, or else. But for a blessed moment, Chris was able to stop thinking about the "or else" part. What facilitated his moment of grace was striking a golf ball near-perfectly with his seven iron. The iron's clubface compressed the ball so that it was launched skyward on a trajectory straight down the fairway. Chris left himself with only a short wedge into the green.

"Great shot, Officer! Truly excellent!" applauded Ali.

Wafoodle-boodle rustled her leaves in likewise enthusiasm.

"I want to hit the ball onto that circular area of shorter-cut grass, called a green. I will use this club called a wedge," Chris explained to Dek-Fook-Tek.

Dek-Fook-Tek had come close behind Chris on the fairway. He had come so close behind, Chris experienced an uncomfortable feeling the Supreme Authority might sniff at his butt, or bull his way into it with his antlers. Chris knew the ruling deer creature could only move so fast if his antler handlers were to keep up. But still...

Towards the conclusion of Chris's narrative about what he was going to do next, he became aware of a gallop growing steadily louder. Was another Tictoctickian approaching? The gallop sounded slower than what the Earthlings were used to hearing from other deer creatures. It included heavier thumps against the ground, as well.

But Chris put it out of mind to focus on successfully executing his wedge shot. Pursuant to which, he lined up his four-foot putt.

Wafoodle-boodle telepathed, *Very good, Chris; keep focused on your game. Counselor Kootlek has arrived to observe and comment. He is Dek-Fook-tek's closest adviser when Commander Kwit-Nik is not around.*

"Crappadoodledo, I missed!" exclaimed Chris. His ball rolled way wide of the hole, to the left. For all the frustration he expressed, though, he was faking it. He actually felt quite pleased with how he appeared to be trying for the one-putt, but couldn't.

Wafoodle-boodle planned a telekinetic intervention to give Dek-Fook-Tek a shorter putt while pretending it was the same length as Chris's. Hopefully the Supreme Authority of Tictoctic would succeed where Chris intentionally failed. All the better to get him hooked on the game, if that were possible.

"No boldness is required to guess our Supreme Authority will most likely surpass your performance, Officer Olsen-Taylok," ventured Chef Glork-tek.

Where Ali and Chris were concerned, Glork-tek played the situation perfectly. They might as well have coached him.

Counselor Kootlek brayed, "Chef Glork-tek, you sound like you are insulting our illustrious Dek-Fook-Tek! 'Most likely'?!?! I would bleat at the very top of my lungs from the very highest mountaintop, 'Most certainly'!" The Tictoctickian counselor literally slobbered over Supreme Authority Dek-Fook-Tek. Kootlek's fierce braying blew bits of his prodigious drool onto Supreme Authority Dek-Fook-Tek's face, but no problem.

Dek-Fook-Tek nonchalantly licked them off.

Ali and Chris strained not to do a double-take, nor ogle for too long or too closely at Kootlek's proportions. Counselor Kootlek was by far the most overweight deer creature they had ever seen, there or on Earth. When he dropped down on all fours, his belly hung low enough for its concealing, beige, tight-fitting shirt to scrape the ground. And when he stood erect on his two hind limbs, that same belly assumed the appearance of a classic beer belly. The Earthlings could tell he strained to catch his breath after he finished galloping over where they were assembled. Ditto after every small bunch of words he subsequently brayed. Clearly, this particular counselor was out of shape.

These fools probably don't comprehend the impracticality for me, trying to swing those 'kolfk' clubs. Wafoodle-boodle telepathed gently enough to trick Dek-Fook-Tek, she hoped. She wanted him to believe he was contemplating his own thought, not someone else's planted in his head. Ditto for what came next. *I could probably use that putter with no problem. But here is my idea for the other shots: Down on all fours, I will charge at the ball with my antlers, sending it forward until it reaches the green!*

"I would join you for that shouted declaration, Counselor Kootlek," Chef Glork-tek finally responded, thereby addressing the counselor's breathless insinuation he might be something less than loyal.

Ali was pondering worriedly, *How will Dek-Fook-Tek...I can see how his handlers might manage his antlers for putting. They should be able to help him succeed where I suspect Chris intentionally missed the cup. But as for wielding any of the other clubs for even a half-swing...*

"I have an observation to make that clearly has evaded the rest of you!" Dek-Fook-Tek suddenly announced with a moisture-laden snort. His nostrils emitted two puffs of steam. "The magnificence of my antlers usurps any possible use to me of those kolfk clubs upon which you lesser beings must rely! But this can only mean one thing concerning that ridiculously small ball, smaller even than one of my testicles when I was new-born. My elevation of it skyward will need be executed by my charging into it!"

Counselor Kootlek gaspingly baaed, "Such insight – Huff! Puff! – was surely as distant from our grasp – Huff! Huff! Puff! – as the planet Chonora before the Supreme Authority's supreme intervention! Huff! Huff! The other-world beasts – Huff! Puff! – they must set up a ball – Huff! Puff! – for your charging into, Supreme Authority Dek-Fook-Tek, – Huff! Huff! Puff! Puff! – with all due haste! Huff! And let us most fervently hope, Chef Glork-tek – Huff! Puff! – the dumb cattle will set up that ball most properly, as though upon a niki-nik hill! Huff! Puff! We cannot have our Supreme Authority's exacting ground-gouge against it – Huff! Puff! – result in a trajectory far inferior to the one he has already richly earned, – Huff! Puff! – even had he not deigned to demonstrate how he instantly masters games he has never played before! Huff! Huff! Puff! Puff!"

It was clear to Chris Olsen-Taylor that Counselor Kootlek was treating him and Ali Magabu the same as

Dek-Fook-Tek treated them. The out-of-shape counselor wouldn't lower himself to addressing the "dumb cattle" directly.

Chris worried, as did Officer Magabu, about Dek-Fook-Tek's plan to launch the golf ball. What reaction would follow a result less impressive than his tee shot? Especially if it turned out far less impressive? *Charging into a ball with his antlers can't go well,* feared Chris. *But just how much worse a shot can he make than I made, that his devotees could still get away with praising it as far superior? Couldn't the Supreme Authority's shot turn out so badly, even his own powers of egotistical self-delusion would be stretched to the breaking point?*

The Earthlings ended up not having to really worry on this account. Dek-Fook-Tek's handlers managed to push his accompanying ladders on wheels fast enough for him to gallop charging into the golf ball. They had had plenty of practice at this when he was goring the entrails of someone suspected of being disloyal. Anyhow, the flat side of one antler prong did blade against the golf ball so as to lift it above the mown tundra grass.

The ball climbed to an altitude of only inches. That is when Wafoodle-boodle exercised her telekinetic powers. She exercised them as no Oombian tree creature had ever previously dared to cheatingly exercise them during a round of oof. They were weak telekinetic powers the Oombian tree creature was pushing to their limit, but they still got the job done. The ball changed course, taking a trajectory far higher than Chris's tee shot. It flew so high and so far, in fact, it bounced onto the green and rolled within two feet of the cup.

The tree creature gave Chris Olsen-Taylor an oh-that-explains-it wink, but Chris enthused nonetheless. "For your first encounter with a golf ball, Supreme Dek-Fook-Tek," he said, "you have made an unconventional swing work astonishingly well! Should you sink this putt..." Captain Taylor's husband was able to emote with some genuine sincerity. Assume Wafoodle-boodle had not intervened with her telekinesis. Chris could tell that even then, Dek-Fook-Tek's use of his considerable antlers would have produced an impressive enough tee shot. For sure, the ball would have bounced and rolled at least halfway towards the green.

Even better where the Earthlings' plans were concerned, Dek-Fook-Tek was easily able to make the nineteen inch putt. His handlers' deft manipulation of his oversized antlers was essential to that effort, of course.

"It took you two strokes to get the ball in the cup, Supreme Authority. But it took me four strokes," said Chris. "And in this game, low score wins. So congratulations!"

Earthlings' applause ensued together with Wafoodle-boodle's celebratory leaf rustle. Chef Glork-tek plus the two ladder-pushing servants knocked their cloven hoof-hands together to produce the sounds of wood block chimes again.

It was a different matter for Dek-Fook-Tek's two other servants. They had their hands full, holding up their ruler's antlers on marionette strings, essentially. They had to hope their approving brays would be considered sufficient tribute.

Dek-Fook-Tek reacted by tilting his antlers from side to side, and kicking out his hind limbs. Had he been indoors he would have sought one of the drywall boards to destroy, set up for that explicit purpose. Drooling profusely, he baaed, "Baa! Such a ridiculous game! In any other game, the ball is already in motion when you are trying to address it! But with this kolfk, the ball just sits there and awaits its fate! Baa!"

"Supreme Authority Dek-Fook-Tek, - Huff! Puff! - a word with you in private, please! Huff! Puff! It must be out of earshot of these beasts from space," Counselor Kootlek tongue-clicked. He was the only deer creature other than the antler handlers not knocking together his hoof-hands.

Ali Magabu sensed the Tictoctickian counselor intent on tamping down the reverie. His previously expressed awe did not matter, over Dek-Fook-Tek's proposal for how he would strike the golf ball.

"You are my counselor, Officer Kootlek! I scent no good reason not to accommodate your request, this time," the Supreme Authority baaed. He protruded and curled down his tongue as low as it would go. He was licking up whatever of his own drool did not drip completely off his chin.

Look out. Counselor Kootlek is about to object over you and the other Earthlings not supplementing their food stocks immediately. He is going to argue that your continued survival is a complete travesty. Especially since the supplies of flash-frozen Chonorans and chopped-up dissident Tictoctickians are starting to run low, telepathed the tree creature to Ali and Chris. *I will provide you as accurate a narrative of their conversation as possible from my mind-reading.*

The private word took place inside Dek-Fook-Tek's subarctic compound. Counselor Kootlek said in crisply staccato tongue-clicks, ever interrupted by his huffing and puffing, "Supreme Authority Dek-Fook-Tek, - Huff! Puff! - my unflinching loyalty compels me to report – Huff! Puff! – something most ominous happening with several of your subjects. Not just those assigned to give of the sinew of their bodies – Huff! Puff! Huff! – so the rest of us might make it into a new pastoral age where such sacrifice will no longer be necessary. Huff! Puff! It is also happening among troops secure from fear of the slaughterhouse. Huff! Puff! Several of them are expressing grave concern. Huff! Puff! Huff! Puff! While Tictoctickians wait to be roasted, - Huff! Puff! - the beasts from another planet are allowed to prolong their lives! Huff! Puff! Huff! They are allowed to delay their own visit to the slaughterhouse! Huff! Puff! Huff! Puff! There is something especially notable about the ones making this complaint while held in transition pens. Huff! Puff! They are not the barbarous dissidents who try to escape, - Huff! Puff! Huff! Puff! Huff! - who must have the bolt hammered through their skulls earlier than scheduled! Huff! Puff! No! Huff! Puff! The complaint comes from those who mill about - Huff! Puff! - awaiting their noble sacrifice, amply comforted by their loyalty to you, Supreme Authority Dek-Fook-Tek! Huff! Puff! Huff! Puff! We do not want to see a situation, I am sure, - Huff! Puff! - where concerned troops unite with voluntarily self-sacrificing meat providers to initiate a blasphemous revolt! Huff! Puff! Huff!"

"'Revolt,' Counselor Kootlek?!" harshly brayed Dek-Fook-Tek. "Please, Counselor, I would not want to think you are projecting onto others what is beating in your own heart! Your value would literally boil down to how successfully you could sate my appetite!" Dek-Fook-Tek made a show of intently pondering the counselor's over-sized belly. He languidly passed his extended tongue about his lower and upper lips, licking his chops.

Counselor Kootlek broke a sweat that beaded up on his nervously twitching snout. He nevertheless swelled his chest as vulnerably outward as his tummy would allow. And he meekly bleated, "Nobody can dispute the fact, my Supreme Authority, - Huff! Puff! – nobody, that you have always possessed a keen sense of those really loyal to you. Huff! Puff! *Really* loyal to you! I have nothing more to gain from saying what I said to you, about a possible revolt, than one simple truth. I have remained resolutely devoted to your service, and intend continuing in that manner! So be it if you make such of my remarks, you conclude I am of more service to you deliciously dead than - Huff! Puff! – unappetizingly left alive! Puff!"

Supreme Authority Dek-Fook-Tek bowed his immense antler array. To the frantically nostril-twitching Kootlek, the Supreme Authority looked like he was seriously weighing his choices. Should he drive that array deep into his counselor's chest?

But Chef Glork-tek intervened. "Supreme Authority Dek-Fook-Tek," the chef said, "I feel your frustration with Counselor Kootlek. He seems unable to grasp the full potential you have directed us to explore. You have worked so hard at this already; might I at the very least relieve you from having to trot out every last most obvious thing for the counselor?"

Dek-Fook-Tek lifted back up his antlers. His handlers helped considerably, of course. Pursuant to which he nodded those head growths most deferentially the chef's way. Then he returned his attention to Kootlek. He pompously tongue-clicked, "As my counselor, Kootlek, you cannot also be expected to understand all my many machinations on behalf of my subjects. That is, of course, unless those machinations are properly explained to you. Your role comes galloping to the forefront afterwards, not before. Now is the best time for Chef Glork-tek to fully detail what I am talking about. Chef?"

"Of course, Supreme Authority." Glork-tek bowed most humbly. He was certain the "Supreme Authority" had not the slightest idea what he was going to say, but whatever. "Dek-Fook-Tek originated a scheme, Counselor Kootlek," Glork-tek went on. "He originated it with the same boldness he brought to the historic co-option of the Chonoran saucer fleet. It is a scheme whereby sooner rather than later, not one more Tictoctickian need bravely allow their blood to be shed on the slaughterhouse floor. Although we must admit such bravery is lost in the long shadows cast by our Supreme Authority's own immense courage.

"First, there is a truth, a reality about the other-worlders' meat with which we must reckon. I had the misfortune of sampling that meat on the planet Koombk. It tasted terrible, nearly inedible. My most inventive culinary efforts failed to make it the least bit palatable. I might as well have been spicing up voluminous oskynt droppings, were oskynt still extant."

"Wo," whistled Chris after Wafoodle-boodle relayed to him and Ali this portion of what she mind-read the chef telling counselor and Dek-Fook-Tek. "Glork-tek is making stuff up! He's pulling it out of his furry little ass! I know for a fact not one human has been eaten yet by the deer creatures!"

It does portend well for our safety and our plans that Chef Glork-tek is going to such deceptive lengths, offered the tree creature as a hopeful, encouraging salve.

"I have not given up on the other-worlders' gustatory, palatable potential by any means," Chef Glork-tek was meantime continuing. "It is quite possible that stress hormones were released into the sample specimen's system by the circumstances of his demise. Those hormones would have fouled the particular cuts I prepared. That is a principle reason for this free-range environment we have created for them."

"What about those particular alien beasts being allowed to explore another planet?" Counselor Kootlek strove to keep the strong skepticism he felt from tempering the tone of naïve, marveling inquisitiveness he feigned to convey. "Is this 'free-range environment' to extend for trillions of lek-leks? Huff! Puff!"

"They are exploring that other planet for us, Counselor," gently bleated Chef Glork-tek. The chef play-acted he was controlling himself to remain patient with someone far more ignorant of circumstances than he was. But in reality, he was covering over the fact he was basically making up excuses as he went along. "Any dangers those beasts come across, they will be dealing with on our behalf. They will be making such sacrifice so they can investigate the potential of that other planet for our temporary resettlement. And by temporary, I mean at least until Tictoctic can be ecologically rejuvenated.

"Several thousand solar orbits ago at the dawn of Tictoctickian civilization, our ancestors forced the steekees to haul great loads for construction from place to place. Counselor Kootlek, do you agree that was the best plan, or do you believe that untold multitudes of slaves should have been breaking their backs instead?"

"Your point is nearly as sharp as an antler prong sharpened personally by Dek-Fook-Tek's bahvek," Counselor Kootlek conceded. He felt in a rare expansive mood, having finally caught his breath.

"There is more," went on the chef. "To entrap its tiny prey, the ten-legged tintakutak weaves webs with a self-generated substance. That substance is so strong, we use it to weave our finest clothes. For another example, niki-niks keep chambers full of tickywickies for milking their sex attractant glands. Similar to such activities by Tictoctic's lowliest creatures, these space beasts grow and harvest a special grain and a special bean. When they cook them together with spices, they produce a meal as flavorful and meaty as any from the most tempting Chonoran leg or cut of butt I have ever sampled. Presently these beasts, these other-world cattle, are working under the strict surveillance of Commander Kwit-Nik. They are working on the unexplored planet one-half light-year away, as we have already mentioned. The commander is seeing what else he can learn about them for the inevitable conquest and taming of their planet of origin. Once the commander conducts their return to our fair realm, Counselor, you will be able to try the meal I have described, and judge for yourself."

"But what will we do with so many other-world cattle?" asked Counselor Kootlek. "Surely, - Huff! Puff! - not every one of them will be required in order to raise our new, alternative food supply. What to do with the excess? Especially – Huff! Puff! - if they do turn out unpalatable, whether or not contaminated by stress hormones?!?"

"I have contemplated closely their various activities," Supreme Authority Dek-Fook-Tek literally stepped in between the chef and the counselor to tongue-click. With the crucial assistance of his antler handlers, he held his antlers regally high. "I have concluded they could make the most excellent pets, thanks to their plentiful silliness. They could mean less stress, better health, for the more important of my subjects. But this is assuming no means are found by which they can be transformed into most tempting dishes. It is way too early to give up hope of that! Snort!"

Chapter 18

"I was missing my husband plenty enough already!" Cathy James-Leung shouted to be heard above the stiffening breeze in otherwise idyllically bright and sunny mid-morning conditions. "But even more so, now that I've got a crazy new idea about this region to vet with him!"

"Which is..." Helena waved her hand in a circle as in, *Hurry it up, already!* With what they had just experienced, she was anxious to head back to the shuttle pod pronto. She really wanted to say, *Save it for later, Cathy!*

"Captain Taylor, imagine a microscopically sized singularity, a miniature black hole, went splat against this planet. Then imagine the result was like a stone sending out concentric circles where it plopped into the water. So that the south coast of this planet's largest continent was split into-"

WHUMPF!!

"-five, perfectly parallel peninsulas..."

"Excuse me please, Cathy," interrupted Tanya Petrovsky. She brushed hair out of her eyes for a better look around them. "I am not sure whether I heard something, or felt minor tremor. Captain?"

If I might, telepathed Oodle-Noodle to interject, *there was definitely noise accompanied by a vibration through the ground.*

"Couldn't it simply have been an especially large wave crashing against the shore?" asked Cathy. "The breeze is blowing from the same direction. There! You hear and feel that?"

"Yes, that is surf! But that is also nothing like the other," insisted Tanya.

"I'm afraid Tanya is correct. Very afraid," said Helena Taylor to agreeing leaf rustles from Oodle-Noodle. It was all Helena could do to express even this much. Sheer dread sent her life passing at breakneck speed before her eyes. Or rather, the part of her life she had lived on the unexplored planet less than one-half light-year from Tictoctic.

Days earlier, Captain Taylor and company made their first low-level reconnaissance flight across Kakifika's surface. Kakifika was the name Taylor had provisionally given the mysterious planet, how she supposed the deer creatures might pronounce 'Pacifica.' Anyway, the Earthlings' flyover proved hauntingly sobering. On its conclusion Helena remarked, "This feels too much like the space-age equivalent of Charles Dickens' ghost of Christmas future."

The Earthlings recorded unusually high radioactivity in an arid-looking brown region. As they somberly anticipated, there was every indication of nuclear holocaust having lain ruin to an advanced civilization. At the brown region's center, a vast crater measured one mile in diameter. That crater was covered over by a dense network of mossy vines. Bits of bright green speckled its otherwise dull, faded shades of olive.

"This vegetation must be continually dying off within days of its growth," commented Dr. Cathy James-Leung. "Apparently, though, the dead stuff takes forever to decay. That's probably due to preservative effects from the presence of excessive radionuclides. People found the same situation in Chernobyl, Russia after its power-plant meltdown. Whatever, one would expect the vegetation here to eventually better adapt so you can see more patches of bright green. Obviously, though, the two centuries or more since an extinction-level war on this planet still hasn't been enough time for such adaptation."

Just outside the crater presumed ground zero for a nuclear device was where Captain Taylor and company spotted some most haunting ruins. Included was an obelisk shape leaning over like the Tower of Pisa in Italy. More dull-colored mossy vines flecked with green sparkles covered this edifice to its peak.

"To what hero of a dead nation's history, or to which one of its most cherished ideals, was that monument dedicated?" Tanya wondered aloud.

Immense rectangular-shaped structures loomed near the obelisk. They were set close together and also completely enrobed by the struggling-yet-blanketing vegetation. Those structures would most certainly have been business and habitation skyscrapers.

This particular urban ruin shared a most curious characteristic with other urban ruins discovered by the shuttle pod away team. None of them were located beside large bodies of water. Rather, each of the mysterious planet's former centers of civilization adjoined slender rivers. The same could not generally be said for major cities back on Earth.

Especially astounding was the lack of urban development anywhere along a unique area in Kakifika's northern hemisphere. As already mentioned, it featured five parallel peninsulas clearly outlined by endless miles of wide, white, coral sand beaches. The Earthlings thought such a region should have featured ghost town remnants of at least one city equivalent to Miami or New Orleans. But no, and no elevated levels of radioactivity there, either.

Consensus rapidly grew unanimous for where Captain and company should initiate an exploratory settlement project. There had been numerous viable-looking candidates. None of them included those five parallel peninsulas dangling like a cow's Lego-built udder from the planet's largest continent, as Chris would have suggested. However, most of them were found within central regions of that same enormous land mass. Radionuclide levels registered a bit above normal, but were found by Dr. Davis-Murphy to measure well within safe limits. Moreover, plenty of vestigial evidence remained for the selected option having been an agricultural center. At least a few centuries must have elapsed since grain crops there were last harvested. However, they still blanketed the land in artificially neat rectangles. A crazy quilt to tuck in the planet every evening, Helena unexpectedly found herself fancying.

Again, the Earthlings thought the five parallel peninsulas along the largest continent's south coast ought to have evidenced vacation activity. And yet most unaccountably, no indications remained of any such thing. Consequently, Captain Taylor delayed checking out that region at ground level. Top priority had to be exploration of what could be done in a presumed breadbasket of the vanished civilization.

The Earthlings were dealing with an extreme time constraint. They worried Dek-Fook-Tek's patience might wear thin awful fast if they didn't return to Tictoctic within a couple weeks. This concern gnawed away at them despite Commander Kwit-Nik transmitting frequent progress reports back to his Supreme Authority. And it explained why Dr. Deborah Davis-Murphy acted so precipitously.

Those intrepid, long-lived mice Magellan and Christopher, as well as a pot of pigeon pea plants, were exposed to samples of Kakifikan soil and atmosphere. Normally, the subsequent incubation period for something to go wrong would last for days. This time, though, Deborah rushed to give the all-clear after a mere twenty-four hours. Nobody had to push her. She pushed herself in hastily declaring unprotected exposure to the Kakifikan atmosphere safe enough.

Nevertheless, within minutes of Tanya nestling down the shuttle pod in a wheat field, Helena already feared the worst, at least initially. Despite low radiation levels, something happened which led her to believe the selected location might prove far too dangerous. No matter whether Earthlings, Tictoctickians, or anybody else were the ones looking to reboot society there.

From off in the distance, the away team heard animal grunts and snorts rapidly growing louder and louder. Then there they were, leaving flattened trails of golden grain in their collective wake. Two very pig-like creatures loomed into view. Both were bright pink and both were the size of sperm whales, seventy feet long apiece. They romped ever closer on six legs, causing rumbles underfoot. Although those rumbles were nothing compared to quaking the Earthlings experienced presently after a sudden, previously mentioned WHUMPF!

Helena was about to cry, *Back to the pod! Get us out of here, Tanya!* But that's when the two monster porkers skidded to a halt. They came to full stop some hundred yards away. Otherwise they might have stomped on their other-world visitors. Very placidly, they proceeded to nibble at wheat-like plants.

At least this gave the Earthlings an explanation for the trails of trampled-down crops they noticed during shuttle pod flyovers. Tanya had been thinking crop circles gone berserk.

I don't believe we have anything to worry about regarding these creatures, telepathed Oodle-Noodle. With her branches outstretched, she left the Earthlings' side to approach the whale-sized grazers. In no time one of the behemoths was nosing about the tree creature's leaves with its piggy snout the size of an oil barrel. Oodle-Noodle gigglingly telepathed, *Ooh! That tickles! But how gentle! Like one of your whales back on Earth when not hunted for its blubber!*

Cathy's embarrassingly loud fart caught the two pig monsters' attention. One looked up from its grazing with a puzzled-sounding snort, and the other did likewise from its sniffing about Oodle-Noodle.

Uncontrollable farting was the biggest biochemical-related downside the Earthlings experienced from not wearing decontamination gear on Kakifika. Helena mused to herself that maybe she should have renamed the place Fartifika. Chief Medical Officer Deborah Davis-Murphy quickly sleuthed out the whys and wherefores. Eating beans grown on this planet, whether pigeon peas brought from Earth or garbanzo-type legumes discovered already thriving, didn't matter particularly. Inhaled bacteria easily interacted with whatever the Earthlings ate to produce vast amounts of methane impossible to control expelling.

Even more curious, if thankfully less disgusting, was what the porcine giants emitted from their business end. The Porkzillas, as they came to be affectionately nicknamed, produced an alternative gas that gave off a most pleasing scent like honeysuckle.

Anyway, both Porkzillas turned Cathy's direction. They went up close to her and the other three women.

The Oombian tree creature counseled telepathically, *Do not run away from these gentle creatures. Allow them to become familiar with your scent. This is like dogs on Earth giving newly encountered humans the sniff-over.*

The whale-sized, pig-like beasts finally focused solely on Cathy, the source of the rapid-fire noise. One Porkzilla prodded her with his behemoth snout to turn around. Then both went sniffing most approvingly at the seat of her pants, snorting the whole time.

"Hey, I'm just thinking out loud here, ladies," Officer Kevin Smith-Park's voice erupted in the women's earpieces. Kevin spoke to them from the starship Smoke and Mirrors, in geosynchronous orbit above where the away team flew down to Kakifika's surface. "Maybe we should slice and dice those two King Kong Pig Pongs. Then we can hook the Tictoctickians on mountains of bacon as an alternative to human barbecues!"

Only if you want to turn these docile creatures into monstrous killers, Officer Smith-Park. That is what happened on Earth, back several decades ago when certain whales realized they were being slaughtered to produce oil and soap!

Further exploration revealed segments of wire fencing erected centuries earlier. But it wasn't nearly massive enough to have kept out the Porkzillas. In fact, Cathy and Tanya unearthed evidence of it having been trampled down, broken through in places. Cathy speculated things were different prior to the nuclear holocaust. The peaceful, carnation-pink monsters might have been more the size of pigs as they were known on Earth. Which meant radioactive fallout induced a form of gigantism. Only then would the fences have lost their effectiveness.

Whether or not that was the case, Helena and company soon established the practicality of a crucially important part of their plan. They demonstrated how rapidly the small area where they landed could be transformed into a self-sufficient settlement.

Officer Ludi Perez had the first pigeon pea crop sprouting within days. Moreover, she discovered other naturally occurring legumes. And she had no trouble producing baking flour with grains harvested from the abandoned fields. For those tasks, Cathy, Tanya and Captain Helena Taylor worked under her direction.

Meanwhile, Cathy also worked to confirm the region was geologically stable. The nearest fault-lines of any consequence lay hundreds of miles distant in whichever direction. Actual tectonic plate boundaries were located even further away, along the vast continent's east and west coasts.

Kevin made a couple of forays to the planet's surface near where fellow officers were conducting their agricultural and geological research. He constructed a model home in the style found popular among many Tictoctickians. It featured an extra-thick interior wall for kicking and antler-charging. Such a structure could take years of abuse before needing to be replaced.

Perhaps most important, Cathy located enough ground water to supply a town of thousands.

The biggest problem concerned the Porkzilla who came to be affectionately named Pigmalion. Pigmalion interrupted Officer Kevin Smith-Park's home-building multiple times. Right where he was working, she would roll over on her side for a tummy rub.

The spookiest situation involved golf, or oof. Along the southeast corner of the abandoned grain fields, Oodle-Noodle happened across archaeological remains of a comparable sport. She counted eighteen suspicious-looking fields overgrown with zoysia-like grass. Those fields meandered about the gently undulating landscape. Moreover, the Oombian tree creature discovered a small building halfway-buried beside what made sense would have been the first hole. In case there was any doubt. The same combo of vines and moss ensnarled it that Captain Taylor and company found blanketing ruins of Kakifika's urban centers. Oombian and Earthlings alike easily ascertained the small building was a clubhouse. People would have checked in there before they played.

Kevin covered hands and arms with rip-proof arm-length gloves made of space-age, foil-like material. Thereby he protected himself against all manner of potentially poisonous, praying-mantis-proportioned twelve-legged bugs. He could safely pull away vegetation covering the clubhouse roof.

After Kevin cleared a mess of vines, he dug through the roof itself and shined a flashlight within. If anyone died there during the nuclear war, the remains turned to dust. Indeed, piles of dust were scattered about the floor.

A granite counter featured a web-enshrouded laptop-type computer, presumably used as a cash register in its heyday. Piled beside the laptop were lots of boxes turned beige with decay. They were the same proportion as boxes Kevin knew held a dozen golf balls each, back on Earth. When he poked at the top one with a long stick, it dissolved into a small cloud of dust. Its contents rolled off the counter, bouncing on the floor. They were twelve golf-ball-sized balls with the dimples smoothed away, assuming they ever had dimples.

There was something else, just in case any least doubt remained. Rusted-over metal shafts sported various-lofted club heads. Those shafts stuffed age-faded bags that fell over on their sides untold years earlier.

I will mow these eighteen fields, Oodle-Noodle announced to Kevin Smith-Park, *to resurrect this course.*

Where Kevin was concerned, his uncontrollable fart right after the tree creature's telepath could not have been better timed.

In any event, exemplar farming, cooking, housing, infrastructure and recreation projects were completed quickly. The away team could return to Tictoctic, ready to make their do-or-die sales pitch for resettlement over interstellar war.

But before they did, Helena was set on one final task. She believed they should inspect more closely the five, oddly configured parallel peninsulas. They could assess whether those peninsulas offered beach vacation potential. Or whether, on the other hand, there were good reasons they had apparently gone undeveloped, avoided even.

Helena and her away team required no time at all to discover why the peninsular coastlines simply wouldn't do for a seaside resort. This happened once they parked the shuttle pod on a beach along one of them. Their attention was drawn immediately fifty yards offshore, out past fifteen-foot breakers. The Earthlings and Oombian spotted the long, frilly crest of a sea creature that would have dwarfed the Porkzillas.

"Even during calm surf," Tanya commented, pointing, "no person who values their life would want to swim in same water as that whatever-it-is."

Putting an exclamation on Tanya's comment was something that looked very similar to a sea turtle. It seemed to plop down from out of nowhere, on the white coral sand beside the away team. After the creature took a few clumsy lurches forward, wings unfolded from its two front flippers. It flapped those wings with the blurry speed of a humming bird, to take off airborne towards the surf.

That was when a crocodilian head the size of a young hippo reared out of the nearest-to-shore line of crashing surf. Presumably, that head belonged to the sea beast with a lengthy frill down its back. Lunging skyward, its cavernous maw opened wide with a thunderous roar. The sea monster was obviously intent on catching the flying turtle, but moved not quite fast enough.

The flying turtle reacted with instinctive instantaneity. It retracted first one flipper wing then the other into its shell, followed by its head and hind flippers. The result being that the small creature suddenly spun like a Frisbee. It propelled itself out of harm's way well before the reptilian beast's mouth clamped shut.

A shark-like creature did not succeed in getting out of that same harm's way when it dramatically breached. The crocodilian sea beast even more dramatically gulped it down whole.

Meanwhile, the flying turtle executed an additional maneuver. Still spinning like a Frisbee with its head and limbs retracted into its shell, the turtle landed exactingly on the crest of a tall wave. It rode that crest like a surfboard. Then close to shore, this amazing creature suddenly poked its head and flippers back out, just in time for a commotion of foam and splashing surf. But it was quick to emerge from that commotion, waddling safely up the beach. Retractable long, sharp claws from its front flippers tore apart a hapless crablike creature.

"Captain, the sea monster bears a striking resemblance to one of our own prehistoric reptiles, the Mosasaur," noted Cathy. "Only it's about three times larger. Witnessing so much, um, wild creature activity on casual first inspection would suggest to me this beautiful beach is full of peril, whether on shore or off shore."

"Yep," Helena nodded regretfully. "Well," she sighed, "let's reconnoiter inland a bit before we head back to the S and M."

The Earthlings and Oombian tree creature climbed over the sand dunes, through tall grasses there. They remained ever on the alert for other monsters. However, Tanya's wrist sensor wasn't detecting the presence of anything very big. Scurrying patterns suggested species of rodent or small lizard.

A few yards down the inland side of the dunes, Cathy knelt to scoop a fistful of soil. "Captain," she said, "I'm pretty sure we are traversing a limestone formation very comparable to parts of Florida and Texas. That makes it susceptible to sinkhole formation, especially during rising sea level which they might have had here prior to their catastrophic war. I'm assuming, of course, that the vanished civilization also was dealing with global warming. Anyway, prolific sinkhole formation might have posed an additional obstacle to resort development on the five-finger peninsulas."

"I'm listening, Cathy. No I'm not. Look!" Captain Taylor pointed further inland. She directed attention towards a portion of the grassy, weedy coastal plain where a water mirage was forming.

The mirage came complete with funhouse-mirror quivering distortion of the air above it. Suddenly, however, the illusory water upended itself. The Earthlings were faced with a silvery, shimmery, convoluting amoebic presence at least one hundred feet across.

That is when the Oombian and Earthlings alike heard, and felt, a thundering gallop as of a cattle stampede. Heads emerged from the shimmery presence, complete with horned nostrils. A bony frill surrounded each head like a lion's mane. Each frill was lined by several, long, talon-like spikes, forward-facing rather than swept back.

The three Earthling women were observing a seeming variant on such ceratopsian dinosaurs as the Triceratops or the Styracosaurus. They found themselves too spellbound to react. So it was a good thing the approaching creatures abruptly halted their stampede, for casual grazing on what little tufts of vegetation they could find. Otherwise, the Earthlings would have been trampled for sure, well before they could have gotten out of the way.

Captain Taylor and company hardly caught their breath by the time a few of the dinosaur-like animals lifted their heads. They behaved as though they heard an alarm, Tanya thought.

And then, as abruptly as they halted their stampede, every last one of those horned animals did a "one-eighty" and headed back the way they came. They disappeared through the shimmering whatever as hastily as they first emerged from it. Lastly the shimmering whatever, itself, dissipated.

Helena was reminded of a fading rainbow.

Something else appeared immediately thereafter, also reminding the women of a dinosaur, in this case the ostrich-like Struthiomimus. It seemed to materialize out of thin air and zoom past them. And it dissolved away just as quickly.

The galloping herd of horned, spikey-frilled beasts left trails on the coastal plain. Off-terrain vehicles might as well have been doing spinouts there, Cathy imagined. The ostrich-like creature, however, left not the slightest discernible indentation or track in any of the bare sandy patches of soil along its path.

"This happened too fast for me to know for sure, Captain," remarked Tanya. "But I thought I was seeing through phantom creature's body, like it was semi-transparent."

"Of course. A Ghostasaur," quipped Captain Taylor. "The bottom line is," she proceeded on a far more serious note, "we have seen enough. More than enough. Back to the shuttle pod ASAP."

The away team headed for the dunes. On the other side of them was where Tanya landed the shuttle pod.

At the start of this short trek, that's when Cathy initiated her speculation about some teensy-weensy black hole. Maybe such a phenomenon impacted the planet to produce the five parallel peninsulas. Cathy was going to go on, about how therein might lie an explanation for the bizarre creature sightings. But then the ominous WHUMPF was both felt, and heard.

The immediate past having finally finished passing before her mind's eye, Helena said firmly loudly, "The faster we get out of here, the better! Everyone, run! Oodle-Noodle, I know your locomotion roots tend to-"

Not to worry, Captain. You go on ahead. I shouldn't be too far behind, telepathed the tree creature. Oodle-Noodle casually toppled herself over to one side; she was intent on using her arm branches for rolling herself along.

"Captain Taylor, please stop!" Tanya stopped herself when she said this, looking down at her wrist sensor. "Just up ahead, over that dune, we are running directly towards-"

That's all she could utter before another gator-type head, this one at least fifteen feet long, loomed up from behind the sand dune. Raising his enormous snout towards a sky clouded only by light wisps of cirrus ice crystals, he gave off a low growl. The growl was so deep and so protracted, Helena Taylor felt her inners mulched into ground beef, were that possible. Still, she managed to scream, "Like I said, run! Away from the dune!"

Oodle-Noodle reversed direction too, on her wobbly-yet-fast log-roll.

The gator monster scampered over the dune, splitting it down the middle. With his elephantine weight, he might as well have been a glacier carving a mountain pass. Once reaching the flat coastal plain, he reared up onto his extra-thick hind legs to achieve greater pursuit speed. All the while he continued his deep, terrorizing growl.

As the monster steadily gained on the away team, they felt his foot stomps make the ground shake. They experienced increasing difficulty keeping from falling over, from having to resort to Oodle-Noodle's log roll themselves. Then they realized they were experiencing far more ground tremor than should have been produced by the reptilian monster, however immense his weight. Helena and Tanya wondered whether there was an earthquake also at work.

But Cathy didn't wonder. She realized they had come across what she warned about: a limestone layer susceptible to collapse. It had leached too thin and too weak for sustaining the monster's bounding mass. This occurred to Cathy just as the ground gave way.

Oombian, Earthlings and whale-sized gator monster alike were swallowed by an enormous sinkhole.

Chapter 19

"This looks really bad, Commander. Even worse than expected," is how Lieutenant Ak-keek-teek's emphatically ominous tongue-clicks would have translated. The lieutenant was referring to Oodle-Noodle and Kevin's handiwork.

Oodle-Noodle and Kevin had recovered what looked to have been a golf course, or something very much like a golf course. But that transcended Lieutenant Ak-keek-teek's imagining.

Commander Kwit-Nik was flying Lieutenant Ak-keek-teek in a scout saucer at a low altitude, above where the Earthlings carved out a new settlement on Kakifika.

"By 'really bad,' Lieutenant, are you suggesting this particular kolfk layout might prove especially challenging for achieving a good score?"

"Clearly, Commander Kwit-Nik, the barbaric other-worlders' ridiculous game holds a special fascination for you. This fact has not gone unnoticed by me, nor by any other of our Supreme Authority Dek-Fook-Tek's most loyal subjects. And I am not convinced it even started as a game! More likely it is some instinctive, vestigial relic of a long-ago, now-obsolete, totally irrelevant survival mechanism. But trust me! With every nob of my antlers, I agree with you. How wonderful life would be! If only we could accept what these outer space creatures are offering as trustingly as our children accept the pre-chewed ruminations of their mothers. However, I know you are most wisely inspired by Dek-Fook-Tek to yet doubt what they are about. Correct?" Lieutenant Ak-keek-teek gave Kwit-Nik another of his slowly dawning, ridiculously wide, buck-tooth-dominated smiles.

Lieutenant Ak-keek-teek brayed about himself and other deer creatures as "Dek-Fook-Tek's most loyal subjects." The implication was not lost on Commander Kwit-Nik, that he might not be one of them. For that, Kwit-Nik would have happily, hoof-stompingly impaled Lieutenant Ak-keek-teek directly through what he considered his inane grin.

In truth, of course, Commander Kwit-Nik seriously was plotting Dek-Fook-Tek's overthrow. Moreover, he did have to concede the lieutenant got one other thing correct. As much as the commander wanted to fully trust the creatures from a distant planet, he just couldn't bring himself there, yet.

Over recent six-day units of Tictoctickian time, Kwit-Nik made terrific progress with his coup plans. He assembled nearly enough covert support. He gathered nearly enough of the sworn allegiances he required for deposing the demented, egomaniacal, psychopathic Dek-Fook-Tek. What a tragic waste, were he to throw that all away on faith in the good will of interplanetary visitors who turned out to be duplicitous. Especially since they were interplanetary visitors who, it could not be argued, faced a most onerous task. They were desperate to be removed from consideration for replenishing the Tictoctickian food supply! What a tragic waste, again assuming the interplanetary visitors' good will proved a total sham. "I respect your counsel, Lieutenant, and want to hear out your apprehensions once we land," Commander Kwit-Nik consequently tongue-clicked with a nodded acquiescence. Nothing more. Nothing less.

"So what do you really make of this? And of the seventeen others similar to it, scattered about such a wide perimeter?!" From a subtle ground elevation, Lieutenant Ak-keek-teek made a sweeping gesture with his forelimb. This gesture encompassed one of the shorter fairways and its accompanying green, complete with flag pin.

"I make of this, Lieutenant, an especially low-cut field sculpted into the terrain. A small ball is meant to be hit there on its journey to that circular area of even lower-cut grass. And I make of that circular area a place where one must strike the small ball with a special implement. The ball is impelled rolling towards the hole marked by that stick waving a red, triangular flag on top. The ultimate objective is for the ball to drop into that hole." Commander Kwit-Nik snorted a visibly condensing exhalation from his nostrils. He wanted to most harshly bray in addition, *Idiot!!*

"A plausible narrative to accompany photos of this odd landscape," Ak-keek-teek nodded. "But what if that narrative is only what the other-worlders want us to *believe* is the purpose for such a transformation of this region? What if," the lieutenant shifted from boisterous tongue-clicking to conspiratorially soft baaing. "What if this landscape and all the others are actually landing platforms for an invasion force of alien spacecraft? What if the flag pins are a code system for indicating which sort of attack vessels need to go where? Put succinctly, what if the other-worlders have turned this planet into a staging area for their invasion of Tictoctic? And they take special pleasure fooling us into believing completely otherwise?" Again with the ridiculous, slowly dawning bucktooth grin.

The commander strained not to snort anew his displeasure, as that would have made it too obvious. Nevertheless, he responded, "Assuming you have discerned the reality, why platforms of grass on not the hardest ground, and not the flattest ground, either? What sense does that make? Consider all the slopes, all the contours! Plus, we saw from the air how no two 'platforms' are alike! I might be more impressed with the staging area scenario if these fields were paved over by hard macadam, and were more uniformly proportioned. Instead, each one is different!"

"No two niki-nik hills are exactly alike, either!" Ak-keek-teek snorted. And he stamped his hind hooves against the ground, himself lacking Kwit-Nik's self-control. "They are far from uniformly proportioned! And you have seen the other-world beasts' space vessel! It looks uprooted from a garden of the ultimate giants! Maybe Dek-Fook-Tek can spare some of his most valuable time to consider the matter. Otherwise, how can any of us know for sure, have even mistiest notion, the manner in which their flying craft touch down? What landing platforms they require? We must remember these beasts are dumber than us, inferior to us in such ways that what we face, actually, is as a plague of outer space tikkykas!"

"Beasts who clothe themselves like we do?"

"'Clothe themselves like we do,' Commander? Really? I would say they are maybe more comparable to kwappataks poaching fellow crustaceans' shells for shelter. Surely you know how kwappataks move from smaller shells to larger ones as they grow bigger. Or, what you consider the other-worlders' clothes might actually be peculiarly soft exoskeletons in place of the tikkykas' rigid calcium secretions! Here is a most fascinating experiment: Strip these creatures of their misnomered clothing, to see how long they take for secreting new ones! Have you ever gotten a peak at exactly what they do inside their metallic burrow networks aboard their instinctively wrought space-faring vessels? Unless you have, how can you be sure those other-worlders actually clothe themselves? I will grant that their clothes mimicry of us was impressive during their ridiculous vegetarian meal! But look! That edifice!" The lieutenant pointed towards the recently exhumed clubhouse. His furry little tail wagged excitedly, out the specially woven slit in the seat of his pants. "That would be the control tower for directing the landing of their warships! Please tell me, Commander. Of what possible use would such an enclosure be for the game you have described? Especially sitting right out there in between two of these crafted landscapes?"

"I wouldn't know, Lieutenant. Let's see if we can open it, or kick in its door."

The clubhouse for the resurrected golf course had been left unlocked by the Earthlings. The deer creatures quickly figured out how to turn the doorknob, in aid of trotting inside.

"So this explains the enclosure's possible use, Lieutenant," authoritatively tongue-clicked Kwit-Nik as he literally sniffed around, down on all fours. "These are the sticks with angled hammerheads that they use for striking little balls. What we have here is simply a storage area for them."

"Are you absolutely certain, Commander?" Ak-keek-teek extracted two irons from a golf bag, for carrying outside.

In the clubhouse darkness before they emerged, Commander Kwit-Nik could still make out the whites of Ak-keek-teek's oversized buckteeth. They shined brightly, if anything.

"You see this, Commander?" Ak-keek-teek brayed excitedly. He held one golf club straight skyward and the other out to his side, as though they were semaphores. "Clearly these are for signaling their attack vehicles into safe landings! The idea is beyond belief, that so many of these metal sticks were manufactured for the sole ludicrous purpose of pushing little balls into holes in the ground!"

"Yes? Then why is the enclosure also piled high with boxes of little balls?" The commander took the lid off one of them. He had picked up that box while the lieutenant was grabbing the two clubs. He tilted it so Lieutenant Ak-keek-teek could easily view the contents.

"Careful!" Ak-keek-teek let go his clubs so he could warningly wave his forelimbs at Kwit-Nik. "You don't know that those spherical objects aren't set on a hair trigger! They could go off if they hit anything with the slightest impact!"

"Yes? Then why are they stored twelve-each in this box? So they can regularly risk an explosion bumping into one another whenever they're moved?"

"The wisdom of Dek-Fook-Tek!" Lieutenant Ak-keek-teek excitedly knocked his hand-hooves together. "You imply a correct understanding, Commander Kwit-Nik! Doubtless you are inspired by ripples of strong common sense that emanate across the vastness of outer space whenever our Supreme Authority opens his mouth! What actually happens must go like this: Those little spherical explosives are manufactured to most unique specifications! When they are struck by these clubs, it is only the force with which they land that causes them to detonate! Gathered close together inside a box, they can bump against one another endlessly without any of them going off!"

Just then, both deer creatures heard a distant yet distinct grunt, followed by another and another. Each grunt sounded louder than the last, until the Tictoctickians finally realized it was issuing from a fast-approaching

"Porkzilla". The pig-like beast left a muddy trail in her wake, on her direct heading for the clubhouse.

"You see, Commander Kwit-Nik?!?! We have been led into a trap by the other-world creatures!"

"Yes," Kwit-Nik baaed grumblingly, "I am sure that was their plan. They knew if they could just destroy the two of us, the rest of the Tictoctickian Empire wasn't going to respond in full force! Dek-Fook-Tek was going to tuck his tail between his legs and run off!" The commander couldn't help his sarcasm.

"BAA! It is a good thing I carried along an air igniter!"

Ak-keek-teek was going to fire his weapon, literally ignite the air to blowtorch effect. But the whale-sized creature who Earthlings had affectionately dubbed Pigmalion suddenly lurched over on her side. The full force of her multi-ton body made a quaking thud against the ground.

Once more resisting the temptation to append *Idiot* to his remarks, Commander Kwit-Nik said, "That common sense rippling across the trillions of lek-leks from Dek-Fook-Tek suggests something else to me. It suggests this brightly colored beast wants one of us to rub its tummy. It might as well be a pet kokatok. At least, I don't *think* it is about to explode! Or, maybe it is like an oskynt after having given birth. It is awaiting the suckling of its teats." *Suckling by your own self perhaps, Lieutenant Ak-keek-teek, were I to command it!*

"Commander, I am receiving an urgent communication from back aboard the Sixth Celestial Breath." Lieutenant Ak-keek-teek was holding a hoof-hand to one ear to better hear over grunting sounds from the monster anticipating a belly rub. He missed Kwit-Nik's most sarcastic remarks, as they were uttered when his earpiece received the transmission. "From our surveillance drone," the lieutenant went on, "we have determined that the other-worlders have apparently gotten themselves into serious trouble with a different monster. This has just happened on the central of five parallel peninsulas along the southern coastline." What the lieutenant self-censored was his thought, *If that monster eats them, what a waste of potentially most delectable meat! Stupid beasts for putting themselves in such peril!*

Chapter 20

Helena, Tanya, Cathy and Oodle-Noodle landed softly on a large tract of mud-cushioned turf. It remained largely intact when the gator monster's bounding weight opened a sinkhole.

The members of the Smoke and Mirrors away team were able to quickly scramble back onto their feet, or cilia-covered roots in Oodle-Noodle's case. Not so for the enormous extraterrestrial reptile. He was still struggling to get off his back. The monster's extra-wide hind legs and relatively lean forelegs were thrashing about helplessly, at least for the time being.

Upon further reflection, Captain, there is something I regret most apologetically, Oodle-Noodle telepathed Tanya and Cathy in addition to Captain Taylor. *I should not have trimmed my helicopter fronds so much, simply to alleviate feeling cramped aboard the shuttle pod. Had I left them only two feet longer, I could have facilely airlifted us out of peril. We could have already made our safe return aboard the shuttle pod. Those fronds came in most useful on Chonora; why would I have assumed-*

"Stop peeling your bark in frustration, Oodle-Noodle, over what might have been," Captain Taylor impatiently cut her off. "You had no way of knowing. I'm partly to blame for pushing you to that decision, and we don't have time for-"

"Captain," Cathy interrupted, "sneak a peek between this magic carpet we landed on, and that other patch still hanging down from the surface. Do you see? A cavern!"

"Then let's hurry up and move, before our friend who wouldn't mind nibbling on us raw finds his footing!"

Helena pointed where Cathy pointed, towards the dark slit between two large patches of turf. One patch lay flat on the ground, and the other was hanging down as Cathy had mentioned.

Once the three humans stepped in between the two turfs, and Oodle-Noodle carefully toppled herself there, they felt a cool dankness. Where Tanya's flashlight illuminated the floor, they also noticed fragments of stalactites. The stalactites doubtless crashed there when the sinkhole formed.

"This is consistent with the readout from my instrumentation when we were above ground," said Cathy. Her voice echoed down a long chamber. "We are inside an enormous limestone formation leached through and through."

"ROAARRRSISSSS!!!"

Even Oodle-Noodle was focused so intently on Cathy's analysis, she joined the others in being caught by surprise. That is, when the gator monster inserted its fifteen-foot-long snout through the gap between hanging and fallen turf. Cavern echoes amplified its roar to such extent, the Earthlings sealed their hands over their ears. But they still feared their eardrums could burst.

RUN! RUN NOW! Oodle-Noodle telepathed as forcefully as possible. *I will hold off the creature as long as I can with this broken-off stalactite!*

The Oombian tree creature was already poking at the monster's nostrils. Stalactite and snout, both, could have been weapons wielded in a fencing match, complete with thrust and parry. So Tanya thought as she spun around and heeded Oodle-Noodle's urgent orders.

The three Earthlings retreated deeper into the stretch of cavern uninterrupted by surface collapse.

Do not concern yourselves, Oodle-Noodle's telepath went on. *I am taking every possible care not to inflict a wound on this precious creature only following through on its instincts.*

"Believe me, Oodle-Noodle!" Helena shouted despite awareness the Oombian tree creature would have just as easily read her mind, had she whispered or said nothing at all. "That concern does not make even the bottom of my list! I'm much more worried about your leaving an 'out' for yourself!"

By that time, the gator monster had had more than enough with Oodle-Noodle's broken-off stalactite holding him at bay. With one sudden, giant lurch, the monster ramrodded his body forward. As a result, the hanging-down turf burst into a shower of clumpy dirt.

Oodle-Noodle read the monster's mind non-too-quickly, to cease her fending-off efforts. She dropped the broken-off stalactite, and heeded Captain Taylor's advice about leaving an "out" for herself. But she didn't roll across the cavern floor, like she had done across the surface in retreat from the gator monster. Instead, she took advantage of the slippery-slick conditions of the cavern wall, made even more slippery by blotches of olive moss. She rolled herself away upright at far greater speed than possible, floating along on her cilia-covered roots.

Unfortunately, by the time Oodle-Noodle caught up to the Earthlings, so did the gator monster. The cavern ceiling hung too low for him to stand fully upright. Bent partway over, though, he still succeeded in stomping forward on his two hind legs. If he had had to bend over completely, his weight distribution would have brought him down on all fours, thereby slowing down progress.

The gator monster managed to maintain his new posture despite knocking into occasional stalagmites randomly situated along the cavern floor. They broke off as easily as thin, dry, brittle twigs when someone is running through underbrush, Tanya thought. She noticed what was happening to the stalagmites when she looked back, even as she continued her retreat.

All three Earthlings could feel the pursuing monster exhale warm acridness down their necks. Even worse, they as well as Oodle-Noodle took the wrong turn at a fork in the cavern. They came to a dead end just when the gator's long snout was almost hovering over them.

"I do understand your concern for creature's welfare, Oodle-Noodle! But I can't help wishing the vibrations from his stomping would shake free one of those stalactites from the ceiling, and knock him out!" complained Tanya. She looked around desperately for any rock she could throw at the beast, any last sharp object to hold him off.

The monster gator was making that low, deep, rumbling grumble the Earthlings had heard before his first appearance.

"What you described only happens in movies, Tanya!" said Helena Taylor. "But I did have a film fantasy of my own! I was hoping Effy snuck aboard the shuttle pod with us so it would have been here to torch off the monster!"

"We needed those two sweet young boys to shove some chocolate chip cookies up its ass!" tearfully laughed Cathy. She shared Helena and Tanya's grim apprehension the gator monster was simply deciding who to eat first. That any second, he would suddenly scoop one of them into his vast maw, whole. Just like that, one of them would be gone despite Oodle-Noodle heroically stationing herself in between the women and the creature's enormous snout.

Which snout was slowly swaying from side to side with the creature's continued low, rumbling grumble.

Helena was ready to have Kevin prepare the Smoke and Mirrors for departure. Irrational from fear, she wished her fellow Earthlings aboard ship would forsake the mission. That they would take the children somewhere safe, assuming somewhere safe even existed.

Adding to Helena's already growing angst, Oodle-Noodle telepathed, *Captain, I know this comes under the heading of: Why does everything have to happen at once? Nevertheless, as of course you are well aware, I have not only been laboring to protect us. I have also been acting as telepathic intermediary between Ciela and your medical officer Davis-Murphy. Apparently Yulala is experiencing birthing contractions mere minutes apart. And her distended belly is glowing like a flounder mouse's belly at night. Nobody knows what that means exactly, not even Yulala. But Ciela has turned off the lights in hope of speeding up the birthing process. Dr. Davis-Murphy speculated that in Fafama's prehistory, the glowing belly might have acted as camouflage.*

"Oodle-Noodle, I'm not sure we have time for- Oh-oh!"

Helena, Cathy, Tanya and Oodle-Noodle looked ceiling-ward the same time the gator monster did. No harm done by the women, but the monster's long snout accidentally broke off a stalactite. The sword-shaped, three-foot-long calcite formation narrowly missed impaling Cathy through her shoulder, instead crashing against the cavern floor.

What led to everyone looking ceiling-ward the same time were noises from a stampede directly overhead. When they stopped, after a brief pause they picked up again, going the opposite direction. The monster gator's curiosity got the best of him, and he returned from where he came. He appeared to be trying to keep up with whatever was producing the stampeding noise above ground.

"Of course," whispered Helena. She was careful not to snap her fingers in celebration of her realization, as much as she wanted to. "That shimmering water mirage rift through which those dinosaur-type creatures herded themselves: It must have opened again."

"Maybe gator monster has seen them enter through rift before," speculated Tanya, also in a whisper.

"They might constitute a big part of his food supply. If he has experienced their stampede enough times before, he might be able to recognize it, even when it's muted and happening over his head," chimed in Cathy.

Helena motioned for them to move on out, down the other prong of the cavern complex's fork. She hoped they could emerge, resurface somewhere past the dunes and towards the beach where they left the shuttle pod.

"Captain, I just wanted to let you know. Ludi and I haven't forgotten about you." This was Kevin's voice in Helena's ear. "After what Oodle-Noodle telepathed us, we didn't want to distract you from, errr, just surviving. You are in our prayers."

Again, Helena had to stifle her impulse. She was tempted to order departure for the Smoke and Mirrors, have Kevin do everything possible to at least make sure Ludi reunited with Pedro. And of course his own self with Yoon-hee.

I've let Kevin know we are still okay, Captain, Oodle-Noodle telepathed. *The less noise any of you produce here, the better.*

The away team moved carefully slowly so as not to slip on smooth, wet, calcite-encrusted patches of cavern floor. Taking Oodle-Noodle's advice to heart, they also strove to avoid making any sounds that could be magnified by their de facto echo chamber. The gator monster needn't bother tracking an inter-dimensional dinosaur-type herd when there was fresh meat available so close by. But there was no sense reminding him of that.

And then Tanya farted, a prolonged, staccato rip.

Helena, Cathy and even Oodle-Noodle froze. Tanya couldn't freeze. She suddenly shook uncontrollably, tearfully.

The fart reverberated through the cavern network for what seemed an impossibly long time. It even gave the illusion of growing louder.

Finally there was a moment of quiet, disturbed only by a single plop of water on the cavern floor, dripped from a stalactite.

Sure enough, a thunderous roar erupted. Tremors underfoot from the stalking gator monster had faded away when he tried to follow the herd's course overhead. But presently they resumed, and were rapidly intensifying. The gator monster was retracing his steps, back towards the away team.

"I'm so sorry, Captain!" shouted Tanya as the Earthlings and Oombian made reckless, slipping-and-sliding panicky haste down the alternative fork in the cavern complex.

"It's not your fault!" Helena had to really shout to be heard above the monster's roaring, stomping din which echoed after them along with the monster itself. Helena well knew they were all dealing with the same issue ever since their first inhale of Kakifika's ironically fragrant air. Extraterrestrial bacteria were interacting with human digestive tracts to produce an overabundance of too-easily-expelled methane. The captain only hoped Tanya wouldn't feel obligated to try something heroically stupid if- *Of course she'll try something heroically stupid!*

THUMP!! "ROAR!!!"

Between minor earthquakes and the monster's most thunderous complaint yet, Earthlings and Oombian alike were nearly knocked off balance. Helena suspected the gatorsaur might have slipped and fallen. If so, they would gain a little extra time for returning to the shuttle pod, maybe the difference between life and death.

"Oh, another fork, but this is weird," commented Cathy.

The group halted where there was a pitch-black hole on the left, of smaller diameter than the tunnel they had thus far traversed. It glistened with presumed wet calcite layered about the entrance.

To the away team's right, a large cavity looked recently dug into the sandstone. Daylight shined there from just round a corner.

"Eww, must be rotten fish stench emitting from hole!" Tanya held her nose and waved her hand to fan away the foul odor, most unsuccessfully. "I assume that's not from what I did!"

Cathy crouched down on her knees to inspect the floor. "Very curious, Captain," she commented. "We must be close to shore, as the ground here is sand-covered. But at the same time there are these stalagmite formations poking through. They are spaced apart with unusual regularity, and unusual sharpness at their tips."

"Look directly above them," Helena pointed. "Those stalactites are their mirror twins. OH NO!! RUN!!"

CHOMP!!

For Oodle-Noodle, it was too late. The cavernously enormous mouth had clamped down on her, lodged her firmly in vertical position.

The rest of you leave; I remained upright intentionally so this creature's mouth couldn't close completely on you. Now he can't gulp you down his gullet which is that stench-filled cavity there. Oodle-Noodle pointed towards the dark abyss Tanya "ewww"ed about. *I realized what we had stumbled into only moments before you did, Captain. Go! Get out of here!*

"We can't leave you alone for this beast to snap in half like a toothpick!" shouted Helena. She and Cathy climbed atop Tanya. They scraped their arms and legs on Oodle-Noodle's splintery bark as they clutched tightly at her trunk. The women hoped they could make impossibly difficult the monster biting down completely on Oodle-Noodle.

There was a deafeningly shrill screech. Carbon dioxide blasted from the monster's throat, nauseatingly fetid with the half-digested rot of meals past.

The next thing the women knew, they could feel themselves lifted high. A moment earlier, they were piled atop one another beside Oodle-Noodle, holding her tight. But presently, they were swinging from her trunk. They were hanging on for dear life as the Mosasaur-type sea monster shook her head furiously from side to side. She was in a panic over the tree trunk having lodged her mouth stuck wide open.

The sea monster had waddled partway up the beach, where she worked her immense tapered head into the sand dune beside a cavern entrance. She camouflaged herself as a faux cavern. Any unsuspecting creatures that might wander in never wandered out again.

Anyway, the sea monster's head shaking finally proved too much for Tanya, Cathy, and Helena. They lost hold of Oodle-Noodle, and found themselves hurled several yards away onto mercifully soft sand.

Please tell Wafoodle-boodle I love her, and want what is best for her, whatever brings her joy, when I am gone.

No sooner did Oodle-Noodle complete her telepath than the gator monster loomed up behind the come-ashore sea monster. With his own behemoth maw, he tried to sink his teeth deep into the oversized Mosasaur lookalike's neck.

The immensely proportioned sea-going reptile felt mortally wounded. As a result, she stretched her jaws even wider apart, thus finally releasing the tree creature.

Oodle-Noodle fell onto the beach, where she strove to roll herself away from the battling monsters.

Tanya and Cathy were waiting with open arms.

"No celebration yet, people!" Helena shouted above the collective din of crashing surf and combatting reptilian behemoths. "We need to board our shuttle pod, and- NO!" Captain Helena Taylor sprinted forward with wild abandon.

The incoming tide had lifted the shuttle pod and started it floating toward the crashing breakers.

Helena made a mad dash into the water, heedless of what looked like a shark fin darting through the shallow surf between her and the egg-shaped vehicle.

Said vehicle was bobbing up and down like an oversized bathtub toy, so Cathy thought while Helena found she couldn't run any further. She had waded in where the surf was too deep for lifting her boots fully out. So she dove into a furiously wrought swim. She kicked her legs so thrashing fast, the shark-like fin of whatever-it-was steered a wide path around her.

Not so for the seagoing creature with a turtle-like body and a long, snakelike neck. It noticed Helena's strong breaststroke, and subsequently mistook her for some seal-like animal in distress.

Helena latched on to one of the shuttle pod's landing struts the same time a mighty crashing wave engulfed her. Her adrenalin surged all the more from a sense she was being watched and likely pursued by something intent on taking a bite out of her. Consequently, she easily found enough strength to hold on tight until her head re-emerged from the drowning surf. Then she pushed her hi-traction boots against the landing strut that was her anchor during the breaking wave. Helena thought on the good fortune both struts were collectively keeping the flying vehicle right-side up. That in turn kept its hatch well above sea level. As a result, she did not expect much water to splash inside when she and others entered, except in the case of more crashing waves. The Earthlings and Oombian simply had to time their boarding in between the breakers.

There was another problem, though, while the hatch slid open via Helena's remote control. A snakelike head the size of a motorcycle broke surface behind her. It remained hidden until the last possible moment, thanks to waters made opaquely olive-colored by roiled-up sediment off the ocean floor.

No! Not when I am so close to safety! This was all Captain Taylor could think when she felt a warm, moist, sulfurous exhalation on her neck. She turned around just far enough to deliver a punch with her fist. She made a direct hit between the sea monster's nostrils. It paused to puzzle, cross-eyed, at the strange sensation on its snout. Helena thereby gained the moments necessary for hauling herself through the open hatch, safely into the shuttle pod. Two more people and one tree were left to go, as she saw it.

The long-necked sea creature looked very different from the other two monsters still battling one another on shore. All the same, it tried again and again to ram its head through the too-small shuttle pod opening. This monster was ferociously determined to seize the small creature inside who punched it in the nose.

On each additional battering of the shuttle pod, the long-necked sea creature extruded its forked tongue as far as possible.

Meanwhile Tanya and Cathy sat horseback on Oodle-Noodle. Oodle-Noodle's effortless floating ability came in handy, or branchy, for ferrying them over to the shuttle pod.

"Oodle-Noodle?! Tanya?!" shouted Cathy. "You have any idea how we're going to get past those jaws?!"

"What about *these* jaws?!" Tanya responded. She pointed to a large, shark-like fin that loomed out of the surf beside them. She shuddered from presumably the body of whatever-the-fin-was-attached-to making sliding-past contact with the soles of her boots.

"We've got to believe it's more interested in local fish! That we are too unfamiliar for it to mess with us!" Cathy felt no less terrorized despite her suggestion.

"Lack of familiarity doesn't appear to be diminishing the long-necked monster's interest in Helena and the shuttle pod!"

"I'm sorry, Tanya!" Cathy screamed, her tears becoming one with the sea spray. "It looks like a lack of unfamiliarity doesn't matter for Mr. Shark-Fin, either!"

"Mr. Shark-Fin" had taken to swimming circles around her and Officer Petrovsky while they straddled the floating tree person, Oodle-Noodle.

"But if sea monster sees it has a choice... HEY MONSTER!! OVER HERE, MONSTER!! CHECK THIS OUT!!" Tanya rose up on her knees as high as she could atop Oodle-Noodle, waving her arms about wildly. She was trying to gain the attention of the long-necked, turtle-bodied sea monster still laying siege to the shuttle pod. The trick was to not lose balance, not allow swelling waves to wash her off Oodle-Noodle.

"What are you doing, Tanya?!" Cathy screamed initially. But then she thought better of it. In a voice far too quiet to be heard above the din of hissing surf and sea monster, she told herself, "If at least Helena can escape..."

By that time, Tanya's tactic had worked. She had drawn the long-necked creature's attention away from the shuttle pod. What helped was that the potential meal within the pod was proving impossible for the creature to extract.

Tanya and Cathy feared the long-necked sea monster didn't notice the shark fin, and was eyeing them instead. That it was only debating who to seize first by its poison-dripping fangs. They were wrong. But they were not to comprehend that reality until the last possible moment.

The monster's snake-like head loomed closer and closer, its jaw set in a permanent grin. Its python-sized forked tongue flicked in and out of its mouth, exuding mounting anticipation. Both women were paralyzed with fatalistic fear there was nothing more for either of them to do. They were both hopelessly doomed.

Cathy and Tanya actually missed what happened next, because they closed their eyes to await a bone-crushing bite that never came. The sea monster suddenly surged diving after its real prey. By the time both women could screw up enough courage to reopen their eyes, the monster's head was already reared sky high atop its twenty-foot-long neck. A pale-bellied shark-like creature the size of a Great White writhed desperately in the grip of its powerful jaws. That was, until it went limp from poison injected by the sea monster's sword-sized fangs.

"My hypothesized outcome, believe it or not," Tanya told Cathy.

Meanwhile, Oodle-Noodle's branches acted in concert to paddle them hastily over beside the shuttle pod.

Captain Taylor was already poking her head back out of the pod hatch.

"We must bring you on board as well!" shouted Tanya Petrovsky at Oodle-Noodle. The tree creature provided Tanya a most wobbly floating platform for climbing into the shuttle pod, but a platform nonetheless. Helena reached down to help while Tanya continued, "It will be no problem for three strong women to pull-"

Hurry! Talk later! Oodle-Noodle telepathically interrupted. *Our long-necked friend is nearly done consuming that poor shark!*

"Tanya's right, Oodle-Noodle! We're not leaving you behind!" insisted Cathy James-Leung when her turn came. She went from straddling Oodle-Noodle's trunk to stepping atop it. Cathy used Oodle-Noodle the same way Tanya did, as a stepping stone to board the shuttle pod. But she shared Officer Petrovsky's creepy feeling about the Oombian tree person. Did Oodle-Noodle have other, self-sacrificing plans? Her gentle nature could almost make the women feel guilty over surviving at the shark's expense.

Once Cathy reached safety, she, Helena and Tanya hastened their attention to hoisting aboard Oodle-

Noodle. But they were barely in time to look on helplessly as their Oombian rescuer pushed away. How she used her arms and few remaining other branches reminded Cathy of how certain squids used their tentacles for darting backwards. Very quickly, the last remaining sight of Oodle-Noodle was lost in the murky, roiled-up waters.

"NOOO!!!" the three women cried hysterically until feeling, sensing something watching them. They looked up to see, not more than one hundred feet away, the long-necked sea monster staring down at them. It had reared up its head to a twenty-foot height again. That was when the Earthlings also realized the monster's long neck was attached to a whale-sized body. Four flippers were treading the surf to keep the creature anchored still, despite the tide's ebb and flow.

"NOOO!!!" the women shouted anew. They scrambled to seal shut the shuttle pod's hatch.

"How are we going to enable shuttle pod lift-off directly from the surf, Tanya?"

"We can't, Captain! I have retracted the landing struts. Now we're going to have to wait for tide to push us shoreward! I would nurse that process along by turning on impulse engine! But that would flood the entire non-solar flight system component! And of course, the solar will do nothing for us until we are free of significant gravitational pull!"

Suddenly, the shuttle's intercom system erupted with static-y clicking and its equally static-y translation. "Attention! Attention! Beings inside the water-marooned flight vessel! Are you hearing this?"

"We are hearing this!" Helena shouted as she held on tightly to the back of the pilot's seat to keep from losing balance. The shuttle rocked from side to side ever more violently with the landing struts retracted and the sea monster closing in.

"Commander Kwit-Nik here! Perhaps you will be noticing two pings against the roof of your vessel! That will be our electro-magnetic cables when they find their mark! We are lowering them now from our reconnaissance saucer! The next step will be to attempt lifting you to safety!"

"Thank you, Commander!" responded Helena. She simultaneously thought to herself, *Oodle-Noodle, if you are okay, please please telepath us!*

Ping! Ping!

As the shuttle pod was slowly but surely extracted from the surf, Helena brought Kevin and Deborah up to date on what was transpiring. Both of them, of course, were aboard the Smoke and Mirrors in orbit around Kakifika.

Free of the sea's clinging embrace, the shuttle pod swung about wildly. That is when Tanya broke in on Helena's update. She urgently said, "Please excuse me, Dr. Davis-Murphy! Do you know whether Oodle-Noodle's physiology can allow her to survive underwater for long period of time with no air?!?"

"Oodle-Noodle does occasional self-pruning. That way she remains compact enough to comfortably move about the Smoke and Mirrors and the shuttle craft. We know from this that she can survive quite easily on the respiration from only a few leaves. But as to whether-"

THUNK!

The shuttle pod felt to Tanya and company like it bumped into a firm yet not entirely rock-hard mass, and then stopped swinging. Something was holding it still.

"Commander Kwit-Nik, can you see what's going on? Our view-screen tells us nothing!"

"Your craft has been wrapped in the coiling neck of a sea monster! The monster's appearance is not dissimilar to a creature long since digested by catastrophic volcanic eruptions in Tictoctic's prehistory! I am talking about tens of millions of solar orbits ago!"

Just when Commander Kwit-Nik completed his remarks, a snakelike motorcycle-sized head came into shocking view on the shuttle pod's panoramic cockpit dome. Its fangs continued dripping with venom.

The sea monster proceeded to ram itself against the dome with jolting force. The three women couldn't help screaming. Helena and Tanya gathered that the oversized reptilian-like beast must have caught sight of them moving about the shuttle pod. This would have been thanks, of course, to easy interior viewing provided by the inch-thick cockpit dome. Captain Taylor and company cringed with fear that the dome might develop hairline fractures, regardless of its strength and thickness.

"We are sorry, beings from Akt!" translated Kwit-Nik's resumed tongue-clicks. "Our reconnaissance craft is experiencing difficulty maintaining altitude! We have failed to lift you away from that unthinkably enormous creature's extraordinary grip! To avoid crashing, we must disengage our electro-magnetized cables, effective now!"

With that, the cables let go.

The three Earthlings experienced another jolt. The cause this time was the sea monster losing balance, not having to fight the clinging and pulling from above. Yet it maintained an iron grip around the shuttle pod, not lessening that in the least. In fact, on a surging muscular spasm the monster temporarily increased the force of its neck's squeeze.

The hybrid flight vehicle's hull made an ear-piercingly sharp creaking sound.

"Heaven help us, Captain!" cried out Tanya. "This monster's head might not be able to compromise window's structural integrity! But its neck might succeed in crushing our only remaining protection like empty drink can!"

"Tanya!? The electro-magnetic spark-plug system for turning on the anti-matter drive! Remember when you-"

Crreakk!

"-borrowed from it?! Didn't you send a current through the hull to electrocute those giant ants so we could make our getaway from Fafama?!"

"That would electrocute us as well, Captain! Do you feel around this cabin?! There is wet film of sea spray from when we were reboarding!!"

The shuttle pod made that awful creaking noise again. The long-necked sea monster was dragging it underwater, into the far deeper sea much further off the coast.

Chapter 21

"What's this, Prissy? One of our good guys' firefly donuts *did* make it through safely?"

"It's been skirting this solar system for the past hour, dear," Priscilla DeFarge answered matter-of-factly. She leaned over her sewing work to casually depress various keys on the Elusive's control panel. "Its transmission was cloaked as gamma radiation. But an accompanying decoding function automatically triggered our receptor's download program."

Michel DeFarge was inspecting his hunting rifle barrel for any slightest trace of caked-on burnt gunpowder he might have missed during previous cleanings. He looked up and shook his head in wonder. "Well," he said, "makes no difference if I understood all that, just as long as you do, Prissy most perfect! Okay, let's see what we've got."

The compact battle cruiser, Elusive, was lingering in the shadow of an asteroid some two hundred million miles away from the planet Tictoctic. Panoramic views of that asteroid filled the cruiser's window on the universe. However, when Priscilla DeFarge tapped on her control panel's lone blue button, they shrank over to the left half. The right half filled with a close-in look at Secretary of Defense Michael Spinner, Chair of the Joint Chiefs of Staff Sandy Warlor, and explosives design physicist Dr. Magdalena "Maggie" Wang. The way they stood beside one another, Michel DeFarge fancied they could have been some TV network's news team.

"I picked the short straw for getting this party started," Secretary Spinner said with a snort and a belly thump. "So here goes. Hope you remember I'm Secretary of Defense Michael Spinner and not, contrary to rumor, one of the three stooges. Must admit, though, it still feels like I skipped over a couple levels whenever I stand in the company of these two heavyweights here." Spinner indicated Warlor and Wang with his thumb, hitch-hiking style. "I'm sure you remember General Sandy Warlor and bomb-maker extraordinaire, Dr. Magdalena Wang."

Warlor and Wang shook their heads. They were thinking, *What are we going to do about him?*

"Anyhoo," Spinner went on, "I have been told *I'm* the real heavyweight, but that was referring to something else, ho, ho, ho!" Secretary Spinner patted his rotund chest to complete his Santa Claus imitation with a feigned lack of calculation, as he was often wont to do. "To get down to the nitty-gritty," he said on a more serious note, finally, "we thought you and the little lady, both, might appreciate receiving a fresh look at us fellow human beings. You know, a little something extra to accompany the confirmation your updates have been making their way our end as dependably regularly as- Well, I don't want to gross out my two esteemed colleagues here."

"Too late, Mr. Secretary!" With a bespectacled blend of grimace and grin, Dr. Wang slapped at the air. "You already have!"

"Like I said before: I'm waaay out of my league beside these two. Okay, one more thing before I turn this over to Sandy. I'm counting on your safe return, Captain DeFarge, for that stag hunt you promised me up in northern Alberta! Won't it be refreshing, not to have to worry about the stag firing back?"

"It's damnably damned unnatural, that's what it is!" Michel shouted at the view-screen as though Secretary Spinner could hear him instantly across the light-years.

"Commander DeFarge, Priscilla DeFarge... I should call you First Officer Priscilla DeFarge," Sandy Warlor corrected herself. "We deeply appreciate the unflagging toughness and integrity you both bring to this extremely crucial and potentially dangerous mission. We know you must be every bit as anxious as we are to put the operation underway. And yet you have demonstrated an almost superhuman patience. Indeed, your wait must seem to have gone on forever. But the long history of human civilization tells us what we might inevitably need resort to when that wait is finally over. And no one, neither Captain Helena Taylor nor anybody else, can say we did not give peacemaking alternatives a chance. The Oombian tree creatures have had a more than fair opportunity for making their dream world into reality.

"I want to remind you about something regarding future updates from the Smoke and Mirrors. The longer this drags out, the less reliable those updates. What they tell you, even what the Oombian tree creatures telepath you, is increasingly likely to be provided under duress. Or in the Oombians' case, under wishful thinking increasingly detached, increasingly divorced from reality. Put another way, it will stand in reckless denial of the evil with which they are dealing. As you weigh such updates, Commander DeFarge, exercise the utmost caution. Do not allow anyone, especially those tree creatures with their anomalously unique history, to get in your head. For any action you judge necessary, you should not be troubled with the notion your decision has been arrived at the least bit too hastily. Here on our end, we have total trust. When you conclude you must act, a second's delay will be to err on the side of waiting too long!"

"This is what I have been telling you, dear," commented "Prissy" back to her knitting. She didn't even deign to look up when she spoke.

"We've established a special connection for you with someone back on Earth, Commander DeFarge. He's another fan of yours who jumped at the opportunity to put in his two cents." Warlor stepped aside for DeFarge to enjoy a clear view of the flat screen behind her. "Ned Mercer, CEO of WESAFU: Weapons For A Safer Future," she announced. "He led the design team responsible for inventing the piggyback drone we put at your disposal."

DeFarge excitedly leaned forward in his pilot's seat and loudly declared, "I love this guy, Prissy!"

"Prissy" stopped knitting.

"His commercials are great! Greatly great! 'I want to see those quarantine barriers come down as much as the next guy,'" Michel quoted, imitating Mercer's nasal twang. "'One day, I believe they will. We at WESAFU are working hard to hasten that day's arrival. Isn't that right, Clarissa?'"

"'That's right, Daddy,'" Priscilla DeFarge answered in falsetto. She was imitating the response of Mercer's daughter in the commercial, while riding a swing.

"Commander Michel DeFarge, what an honor!" Ned Mercer presented himself in an old white tee shirt frayed round the neckline. No uniforms for him. He swept unruly strands of hair from his eyes. "About a certain stag hunt, I also want in," he continued. "And maybe your commanding officer named Priscilla can knit me a pair of her famous socks? Anyway, just a few words the Chair of the Joint Chiefs was kind enough to let me add to this message in a space-age bottle. At WESAFU headquarters, obviously we are not out there manning the barricades with you, putting our asses on the line.

However, with our 'piggy-backer,' we feel like we have sent our most beloved older son off to battle. Yeah," he nodded for extra emphasis. "And we can't send any other sons off to battle until we receive confirmation this one was well-enough prepared, if you catch what I'm saying.

"So, General Warlor and Secretary Spinner tell me they have learned a whole lot more about the threat from aliens who want to put us on their *menu*! God in heaven! I'm told those antlered cretins are wielding an extraordinarily powerful new weapon called a magnetic pulse-beam. How I wouldn't want to get my hands on the design for *that*! In the meantime, the sooner we can ramp up production here on Earth, the sooner our 'piggy-backers' can be deployed in the numbers you will need out there to get the job done! Yeah!" Ned Mercer did his extra-emphasis nod again. "Now I've also heard talk about shaking up the antlered cretins' hornet's nest. Flushing them away from their home planet before they can finish with their preparations for interplanetary conquest, oh yeah! You might want to consider it! That's all I'm saying!" Ned slapped his hands down on a table set before him, his fingers splayed far apart.

Michel DeFarge fancied that the piggyback drone's inventor could have just put the finishing touches on a gourmet meal. Roasted venison, perhaps. Now others had to decide what next.

"Those Tictoctickian demon deer *do* got some of their saucers moving in nearer to their home planet. That much even *I* can tell by studying our long-range radar. And there can be no doubt about it. Tictoctic is where they are keeping our very own lambs who have maybe led themselves to slaughter," Michel DeFarge muttered at the view-screen. Again, it was as though he could talk in real time to Secretary Spinner and company, rather than their speeches having been recorded hours earlier.

DeFarge's mutterings were by way of convincing himself General Warlor was correct. Imagine him deploying a piggyback drone the very next minute, even. Still, nobody could fairly accuse him of acting rashly, of being anything less than overly cautious.

The recording concluded with Dr. "Maggie" Wang speaking about Ned Mercer. "There is no question he invented the piggyback drone," she said. "But before the hostiles can respond, I will invent the piggybacker on the piggyback. This is how we will win!"

"Hmmm," hmmmed Michel. He was continuing to entertain thoughts of attacking sooner rather than later, despite the inevitable telepathed pushback he knew was coming. Whether minutes or hours hence, inevitably one of those tree creatures with the silly Dr. Seuss names would be preaching nonviolence, again.

"Hmmm, indeed, dear."

The saucers moving nearer to their home planet are nothing to be concerned about, Commander DeFarge.

Priscilla received Wafoodle-boodle's telepath as well. But she made a show for her husband of going about her knitting, totally unfazed. She meant to communicate two possibilities. Either she was cut out of the telepath loop, or if she was still in it, whatever the tree creature wanted to express deserved ignoring.

The captains of those saucers are in the thrall of misinformation soon to be corrected, Wafoodle-boodle went on despite Priscilla's behavior. *Your fellow creatures and I remain able to go about our peace mission safely.*

"Yeah? And how long do you think *that* is going to last?"

"Why argue with them, dear?" But right after saying this, Priscilla pointedly dwelled on something. Intent on the Oombians mindreading her, she thought, *Thousands of years ago, back on our planet Earth, food was scarce, and our ancestors faced threats from all sides. If they had not taken up the bow and arrow, they would have gone extinct. It wouldn't have mattered whether they were killed, or starved to death.*

I hope you would decide wisely, Wafoodle-boodle proceeded to telepath, nevertheless. *That is, if the scenarios came down to these: Profits could be assured from the mass production and sale of the piggyback drones. But also assured would be war with no clear end in sight. Or, there could be no sales, the drones left untested. But then there would be a better chance at peace from a well-defined plan for getting there. Yes, preparing for peaceful conflict resolution does risk being unprepared for war. It is also true, however, that preparing for war risks being unprepared for peaceful conflict resolution, making war that much more likely.*

Priscilla blurred any focus on Wafoodle-boodle's message she might otherwise have been unable to avoid, given its telepathed nature. She managed this by humming "God Bless America" to herself. Incidentally, she also hoped to thereby distract her husband from the tree creature. What she could not have known was what transpired light-years away. That is, on the conclusion of Captain Entroper recording the video they had just watched from the starship Barak Obama.

It happened before Sandy Warlor and company parted company to review various aspects of the plans to defeat Tictoctic. Sandy emptied her thoughts to Michael Spinner and Magdalena Wang. "Look," she said, "I know I can air something without you guys taking me the wrong way. Um, I think there is an observation we can safely make about people in general. Given the choice, most human beings agree. On whatever side of a conflict they find themselves, they would rather not fight wars. We saw a dramatic example of this before the quarantine barriers went up, as we know they needed to. Of course, we kept having these floods of refugees. But they weren't just the women and children. There were lots of men as well. Heaven knows the bad guys would have wanted the men especially to stick around and fight on their side. But here's the thing: On our side, which we know has the high ground, there were many of these people we could have really used to help tip the balance. Yet they wouldn't fight for us either. The vast majority of them just didn't want to go to war, period. What if it's the same with the general population on Tictoctic? Plus, I think if you asked most of our troops, they would tell you they don't really want to be fighting, either. I remember an interesting if brief conversation with Sergeant Hanson. He is one of the two Marines who joined what we already know, regretfully, is going to be a doomed effort led by the tree people. He explained how he'd become interested in the writings of Gandhi. And he gave me the understanding he wasn't the only Marine with such interest. What if something similar is going on among those extraterrestrial deer soldiers? What if a couple of them are interested in the writings of some Tictoctickian pacifist?

"Maybe I'm playing devil's advocate here. However, if everyone who didn't really want to go to war, on both sides, just decided they weren't going to fight, um…"

"So, so," Secretary Spinner laughed congenially sympathetically, fairly bursting with good-natured camaraderie. He gave Sandy light touches on her shoulder. "You just need someone to talk you down off that cliff ledge where you've climbed way out on. We get it don't we, Dr. Wang?"

"I have such thoughts all the time, General Warlor," bomb maker Dr. Wang affirmed. She moved in close to provide a comforting arm around Sandy's shoulders.

"You see, this is what I admire the most about you, if I may, General Warlor," said Spinner. "You bring an unsurpassed level of care and thoughtfulness, of humanity, to every situation. But it's also tempered like forged steel by certain razor-sharp understandings of the world as it is, not as we'd wish it to be. One of those understandings I know you of all people don't need reminding about. On the enemy side, on the side of the antlered aliens, we can rest assured. If there are any Bambies, all gentle peace and love, they've either been eaten, enslaved, or are hiding out somewhere. Those demon deer in charge, they're just waiting for us to let down our guard.

"That brings us to something else bad about how the tree people have inspired Captain Taylor and crew. As a result of those beings' intervention, our folks aboard the Smoke and Mirrors will likely have their lives literally eaten away. But there's even more. This, this ultra-naïve inability to imagine, to comprehend that not everyone else out there wants to live in peace and harmony, exploring the universe...phew! For certain, that inability has the extraterrestrial baddies all excited over the prospect maybe the rest of us are just as naïve. We have to hope such a huge misjudgment will ultimately prove their downfall!"

There was something Secretary Spinner could not have known. And talk about an inability to imagine, it was the furthest thing from his present state of mind. It was what Commander Kwit-Nik articulated within hours of the secretary's discourse on his conception of the real world.

From the safety of his reconnaissance saucer, Commander Kwit-Nik pondered the Earthlings' shuttle pod being pulled underwater. A sea monster did the pulling, with its neck coiled around the pod. That horrific spectacle moved Kwit-Nik to make a particular assertion aloud. He felt beyond caring how Lieutenant Ak-keek-teek would react. Especially so, since Kwit-Nik well knew that anything they might fire at the monster would for sure kill everyone aboard the other-world shuttle craft as well. "The terrible fate of the other-worlders on this strange new planet makes something mountain-spring-clear to me, Lieutenant," the commander edgily tongue-clicked. "What these odd beings from two different planets said they were about was *exactly* what they were about. They have sacrificed their lives simply to investigate whether our resettlement on this planet could safely include seaside locations."

"A waste for sure, Commander," Ak-keek-teek baaed as though in full agreement. But the waste *he* referred to was actually the waste of perfectly fine meat.

"I have enjoyed random private discussions with some of our indisputably most loyal troops, Lieutenant," Commander Kwit-Nik went on. "In those discussions, I have found few soldiers who would not rather some alternative to war, were that alternative demonstrably feasible. Plus we know something else from back during the wars of consolidation. Among the war refugees there were lots of males, nearly the same number as females. They didn't want to fight for our side any more than for the side they were fleeing. They wanted no war, period, end of that oskynt pine cone sniff." The commander was grown increasingly certain he could not herd his lieutenant towards joining a revolt against the madness of Dek-Fook-Tek. That in fact, woe be it were Lieutenant Ak-keek-teek to catch the faintest whiff, scent of what was happening right under his own snout. Most likely, he would think nothing of turning in Kwit-Nik as a traitor. Subsequent to which, Ak-keek-teek would happily nibble on the then-former commander's barbecued thighs.

But there yet seemed to Commander Kwit-Nik a chance he could antler-prod his lieutenant to deeper thought. Granted, that chance could prove as faint as the moss still growing on a boulder in one of the more polluted and overheated regions of sub-equatorial Tictoctic. It would be a chance, nevertheless. And so Kwit-Nik went on, gently baaing, "I realize this might sound crazy, Lieutenant. I might as well wonder how oskynt would do for pets, if we could only resurrect, de-extinct them. However, imagine most of the other-worlders out there are like these who sacrificed their lives for us, despite our having threatened to make them part of our diet. What if their distaste for war is comparable to ours?"

"Commander Kwit-Nik, I trust it is not too close to heresy, to suggest your wishful thinking achieves nearly the grandeur of Dek-Fook-Tek's antlers. Thankfully, though, your ruminations are tempered by that other grandeur which is Dek-Fook-Tek's wisdom. I am certain of that.

"And what does Dek-Fook-Tek's wisdom tell us? I quote: 'Do not become distracted by purported good intentions of a suspect few!' The other-world leadership is most assuredly waiting for us to let down our guard. We can make a comparison to how the oskynt behaved as cuddly as a pet kokatok, way back when. But it was only waiting for intended victims to let down *their* guard. At the first opportunity, the oskynt charged forward, goring chests until the entrails spilled out. In that same way, we well know the other-worlders would seize the first chance we gave them. They would seize that chance to attack us with who-knows-what-unheard-of weapons with which they armed their battleships. Maybe they have even developed some death ray to make our magnetic pulse-beam seem the bluntest of worn-down antlers by comparison."

'A suspect few'? Really? Commander Kwit-Nik wanted to ask as he discerned both the sea monster and the shuttle pod vanishing into murky Kakifikan seas. In case I required any further reminder why Ak-keek-teek can't be trusted! I wish that buck-tooth grin could be sanded away by a special 'bahvek.'

While fevered thoughts raged through the commander's head, he could not have known what the lieutenant was thinking. Kwit-Nik's remarks such as this have to make me wonder how truly loyal he is to Dek-Fook-Tek. With no other troops in our immediate presence, he has not thought to initiate, even once, a ritual litany. Nor has he brayed to my attention, by way of any admonishment, that neither have I. This experience only goes to reconfirm certain wisdom, doubtless rubbed off on me from Dek-Fook-Tek. Indeed, flower pollen might as well have been rubbed off on my snout by nibbling at Chonoran jerky spiced with kakaykumt petals. The wisdom is of having so boldly taken one particular matter into my own hooves without seeking the commander's approval!

Chapter 22

Wafoodle-boodle urged Chris to request an audience with Dek-Fook-Tek right away. And she argued that it should include all the Earthlings plus herself, an Oombian tree creature. She intentionally neglected mention that the Supreme Authority of Tictoctic was about to call for such an audience in any event. She knew Dek-Fook-Tek's purpose was to advise the Earthlings they would be sent to the slaughterhouse. Wafoodle-boodle hoped their fate could be forestalled through a pre-emptive change of subject.

Dek-Fook-Tek's heart would have to be melted enough for him to at least temporarily delay the executions.

Wafoodle-boodle saw no sense in Chris and company becoming terrified any sooner than absolutely necessary. Wherefore she didn't share with Chris what she knew of the Tictoctickian dictator's plans. Moreover, she figured the Earthlings should enter the meeting exuding confidence over what they could accomplish. Far better that, than trembling visibly over the possible imminence of their fate. And visible trembling was sure to ensue, she feared, if she did admit what might be in store.

"Such an unexpected pleasure! By their meek, docile behavior, our other-world acquisitions have already made impressive auditions to become our first new pets in over fifteen solar orbits. As though that were not enough, they have now also resorted to begging for an audience with me! Unclothed, they could have been most loyal, obedient kokatoks!" Chris, Yoon-hee, Ali, Geena and Wafoodle-boodle heard this translated from Dek-Fook-Tek's tongue-clicks when they entered his royal reception hall under armed guard.

The Earthlings' latest encounter with the Tictoctickian ruler was taking place inside his antler-shaped northern stronghold, not far south of Tictoctic's Arctic Circle.

On their first look around the Supreme Authority's royal reception hall, something became quickly obvious to the Earthlings and Oombian tree creature, alike. The northern stronghold's exterior was not the only thing designed to pay tribute to Dek-Fook-Tek's oversized head growths. Scattered lamps took the form of miniature antler facsimiles. Tapered light bulbs topped the six most elevated prongs of each lamp. Chris and Ali were reminded of Jewish menorahs.

The antler-shaped lamps didn't do a very good job of keeping the windowless royal reception hall very well lit. There were too few of them, spaced too far apart. Yoon-hee guessed Dek-Fook-Tek's subjects were loath to point this out, on account of the fatal personal risk that might entail. And she suspected such dim lighting was intentional. Better illumination might have made the antler handlers' marionette strings more conspicuous, left them less camouflaged.

"I look forward to savoring, at a most leisurely pace, what the other-worlders have brought us!" Dek-Fook-Tek tongue-clicked by way of an additional welcoming remark. He pretended to ignore the tray wheeled in by Chris. Yet he couldn't help noticing a velvet cloth concealing something piled high there.

Curiosity over what Chris wheeled in did not stop Dek-Fook-Tek, however, from proceeding with an additional nerve-wracking survey of the Earthlings. His regard lingered on each one just long enough for him to lick his chops with a commotion of snout wrinkling.

"Mmmm," Counselor Koot-lek nodded approvingly. He patted his hoof-hands against his beer-belly-proportioned tummy.

"Esteemed Dek-Fook-Tek!" Chris bravely stepped forward, finally, to plunge right in. "Esteemed" was how he and the other Earthlings had learned was wise to address another authoritarian ruler, the Fafamafalafama. Further steeling himself, he went on, "After your typical meal," Chris Olsen-Taylor said, "do you ever receive a special treat?"

"Counselor Kootlek?"

"Baa, yes, my Supreme Authority, a special treat of course." Kootlek made like he was going to pat his belly again. However, he abruptly clutched at his upper chest instead. A grimace crossed his face. If Ali and Geena didn't know better, they would have sworn he was suffering from angina, heart pain. Not at all surprising, given his obvious overweight condition and what the Earthlings knew of Tictoctickian diets.

Dek-Fook-Tek and his other aides also noticed the counselor's episode. They required considerable restraint not to lick their chops, not to behave as Dek-Fook-Tek had just behaved when contemplating the other-worlders.

Once more Wafoodle-boodle made the clear call, the clear decision, not to share with, not to telepath the Earthlings what was going through Tictoctickian minds.

The Tictoctickians suppressed any show of their growing glee over the prospect one of their own might suffer a fatal heart attack sooner rather than later. They recalled from past experience with deceased colleagues that out-of-shape bellies were among the very tastiest.

"After our major meal of the day, yes," Counselor Klootlek continued when his discomfort finally subsided.

"The special treat is usually a sphere of salt-enrobed fat on a stick. Huff! Puff! Pleasure is most delectably prolonged when the sphere is licked with careful, lingering deliberation, - Huff! Puff! - rather than bitten off and chewed all at once."

"Fascinating, truly," nodded Ali Magabu. "But our Officer Olsen-Taylor refers to something rather sweet, not meat-related."

Counselor Kootlek's ears fluttered quizzically. "Sweet?" he tongue-clicked with puzzlement. "There is honey from the kuzzkuzz, used to glaze Konokan butt slices. Which incidentally we have needed to produce synthetically in recent times since reserves have become so depleted. But of course that is usually the main course of the day. Huff! Puff!"

"Interesting. Again, however, we are talking about a nonmeat item. It is sweet through and through, and partaken after the main course," Chris gently explained. "We even have a special name for it: dessert."

"Dekkekt?" Dek-Fook-Tek tried his best to repeat.

"Yes," Chris nodded. He half-expected to be cut off by another ritual adulation of Tictoctic's ruler. Maybe there would be swooning over Dek-Fook-Tek's linguistic prowess despite his inability to correctly produce certain sounds. However, no interruption came as he said, "And for many of our desserts, a prized ingredient is something named chocolate. Chocolate is made from a seed produced by the cacao tree."

"Kokolat," repeated Dek-Fook-Tek.

"Baa," Counselor Kootlek nodded. "I hope everyone was giving their full attention – Huff! Puff! – when you spoke, supremely wise and brilliant authority! Not that they shouldn't always be giving you, Huff! Puff! full attention when you grace us with the pleasure of your utterance! Huff! Puff! But, what a difficult word the other-worlder from Akt does have for their most-prized sweet-food ingredient! Huff! Puff! It is a word of such impossible pronunciation requirements, I would not dare attempt even its first syllable. But if I had closed my eyes when you repeated it, Supreme Dek-Fook-Tek, - Huff! Puff! - I doubt whether I would have been able to tell you were the one speaking. Most likely, I would have assumed your profoundly precise articulation issued from one of the other-worlders' plump-lipped mouths! Huff! Puff!"

Dek-Fook-Tek could become violently unbalanced when not receiving frequent enough over-the-top adulation. Blissfully unaware of this, Chris marveled incredulously. He couldn't believe the ridiculously patronizing lengths to which Counselor Kootlek went regarding the Supreme Authority's miserable pronunciation of the word, "dessert."

But it worked; Dek-Fook-Tek nodded totally satisfied acknowledgment of Kootlek's praise, oblivious to its dishonesty.

That's when Chris Olsen-Taylor continued, "What our chefs do, they stir together the following ingredients: ground-up grain from a particular long grass; eggs laid by one of our flying creatures; a special fat we process from the milk of one of our animals; a plant-derived liquid extract we call 'vanilla'; baking powder; and yet another plant-derived substance, a substance that could be labeled sweetness itself. But we call that one sugar."

"Kugahk."

"Um, yes. And finally we embed this mix with chunks of chocolate. After that, we spoon out spherical clumps onto a baking tray, and cook them until-"

"Baa!" Dek-Fook-Tek pawed impatiently at the slate floor with his hind hoof. "I do not need to hear the entire recipe! Simply tell me this: The thing you are describing, is that what we will find underneath this cloth?" The Supreme Authority directed his snout at the velvet material assuming a mountainous shape draped over the rolled-in tray.

"They are called 'chocolate chip cookies,' and there are enough here for everybody," said Chris confidently. Far as he knew, Effy the ephemeral dragon was trillions of miles away, in Tictoctic's closest solar system. Aboard the Smoke and Mirrors, that amazing creature was keeping special company for the only other known survivor of catastrophic events on Fafama: Sergeant Hanson's wife, Yulala. So Chris trusted he needn't worry about any of the cookies suddenly being disastrously charred down to dust, what Effy liked to do with them. "The first cookie is for you, of course, esteemed Dek-Fook-Tek," Chris said after he dramatically unveiled the pile of dessert by pulling off its concealing cloth with lightning speed. He used a napkin to gently lift one cookie packed full of chocolate chips from the top of the pile. And he ever-so-carefully lowered it down onto a most fancifully designed dessert plate.

"No," Dek-Fook-Tek shook his head. "The first one will be for Counselor Kootlek. He is my taste tester."

Kootlek accepted the plate. Without actually lifting the cookie, he made a production of sniffing at it, his snout and ears in a commotion. Proceeding from which, he started to lick it.

Chris visualized Counselor Kootlek as some wine connoisseur swishing fermented liquid about in a glass for sniffing the bouquet.

Kootlek's licking rapidly intensified until finally, he took a bite out of the "special treat." Standing back from the plate, this deer creature ruminated on the bit-off piece.

Chris was reminded of a cow munching on grass, though with frenzied nostrils like a rabbit munching on a carrot. Nevertheless, he also continued to picture that aforementioned wine connoisseur furiously working his first sip about his tongue.

Initially, the look on Kootlek's face worried Chris. It was a look of total perplexity, capable any moment of tipping over to complete disgust. Chris feared Kootlek might argue he needed to take a bite out of an Earthling, fast, to wash away the awfully weird flavor.

Counselor Kootlek suddenly froze in mid-munch.

Chris thought, *Okay, this is it; he's about to love it, hate it, or keel over from a coronary.*

Rapidly, the deer creature's mystified expression metamorphosed into a wide, happy grin of unbridled joy. His eyes were blinking rapidly. And if the Earthlings could but somehow have politely glimpsed his rear end, they would have discovered something else. Counselor Kootlek's furry tale was become a blur of wagging, fast as a hummingbird's wings where it poked through the specially stitched hole in his pants.

With a swallow, the counselor lowered his snout to nibble off more of the chocolate chip cookie. But before he could, Dek-Fook-Tek brayed most harshly what translated for the Earthlings as, "Wait! Are you feeling okay?!"

"I am feeling beyond okay, Supreme Authority. In fact, I am not sure but that my first bite of this extraordinary food is not addressing my chronic pain disorder at its source!"

Chocolate IS good for the circulatory system, Geena thought to herself. *But that pain disorder he is referring to might be associated with the angina episode we observed. In which case he's going to require a lot more than a little chocolate! Like maybe some open heart surgery!*

"Dek-Fook-Tek," continued Kootlek, "your merciful caring makes a mother oskynt's nursing of her calves seem the cruelest neglect-"

"Hand over the rest of that kokolat kip kookee!" Dek-Fook-Tek interrupted the counselor's ritual fawning praise to harshly bray. He leaned forward from his throne. Then with one lightning-fast swipe of his forelimbs, he seized the elegantly designed plate where the rest of the nibbled-at cookie rested.

"There are plenty of cookies for everyone," Chris said in his meekest voice.

"I was not unaware of how carefully the Akt beast selected this kookee for our ingestion. Perhaps he anticipated I would use a taste tester, Counselor, and so this is the one *not* poisoned!" Yet again, Supreme Authority Dek-Fook-Tek avoided dignifying any of the other-worlders with a direct address. Plus, they had to wait longer than usual for a translation because the Supreme Authority spoke with his mouth full. Thereafter he strained to conceal his visage, inasmuch as it might reveal how his own taste buds were reacting to the chocolate chip cookie. Once he finished swallowing, he tongue-clicked in his haughtiest tone, ever, "Counselor Kootlek?!"

"Yes of course, Dek-Fook-Tek, from whom all blessings flow as from the most savory and fragrant blood spurts of a mortally wounded os-"

"TRY ANOTHER!!! AND THIS TIME, YOU CHOOSE!!! NOT THE AKT BEAST!!!"

"Of course," humbly baaed the counselor. He made all due haste to secure another chocolate chip cookie from atop the pile of them.

Dek-Fook-Tek finished off what remained the second cookie. That is, after Counselor Kootlek bit off a part he made sure contained several 'kokolat kips.' The Tictoctickian ruler licked every last crumb from the plate. With renewed poker face, however, he said to Kootlek, "Have these creatures from Akt turned over their kookee recipe to Chef Glork-tek?"

"Um, yes we have. I have," Chris nervously added to be more precise. He spoke before Wafoodle-boodle could warn him telepathically to fudge the answer.

In response to Officer Olsen-Taylor's response, Supreme Authority Dek-Fook-Tek rose off his throne. He got down on all fours and broke into what Ali and Geena could only think of as some crazy soft-shoe celebratory dance. His hooves clicked rhythmically against the slate floor. He made a shrill bray, drool dripping in long strands from the corners of his mouth.

Once Dek-Fook-Tek was done, he remounted his throne. One aide hurried to wipe clean his mouth and snout, both, with a napkin the Earthlings provided. Then the Supreme Authority lifted his antlers, stretching his neck high as his antler handlers could facilitate. He regally tongue-clicked, "Counselor Kootlek, these other-world beasts' kookees are far from unappetizing, it must be admitted. However, there are two problems of enormous import that made this audience necessary in the first place, whether they wanted it or not. And I am afraid that for them, the adequate new addition of kokolat kip kookees to our diet does nothing for mitigating those two problems."

On this declaration, the Earthlings exchanged looks that could not have evidenced greater worry. And they didn't know even half of what Wafoodle-boodle knew.

"One of those problems," Dek-Fook-Tek went on, "has been called to my attention by such true patriots as Officer Kook-kank-tank and Lieutenant Ak-keek-teek. Those patriots have been asking the ultimate question. They have been asking it ever since Captain Rek-mek-a-nek brought us the other-worlders' inefficiently oversized, bizarrely designed spacecraft. Incidentally, let us not forget we have seen comparably strange, instinctively rendered artifices on our own planet. For example, there are precariously tall and narrow niki-nik mounds on desert wastelands in the tropics. Anyway, our indisputably loyal members of the Tictoctickian armed forces have charged their heads forward early and often with an important question.

"Almost daily, without resistance, fellow beings allow themselves to be sacrificed for sustaining the common food supply," Dek-Fook-Tek pointed out. "Meanwhile, why should lower beasts such as these be permitted to roam cage free? Why should they go on making their music like the kliklets at night rubbing hind legs together? And why should they be able to continue playing that admittedly most nibble-enticing game of trying to place a little ball into a hole in the ground with the fewest possible strokes?

"My indisputably loyal commander of our armed space forces, Commander Kwit-Nik, joined me in seeing the situation a bit differently. We believed there was much to be gained from keeping these other-world creatures alive for some while longer. We would learn more about their weaknesses, their vulnerabilities, to help in the larger conquest. I thought we might even discover significant value to this plan of theirs, for us to resettle in a nearby solar system. That is, until such time as Tictoctic could be brought back to its full, forested glory.

"My toleration of the other-worlders' stay of execution would still end, eventually. However, it did not seem the most preposterous thing in the world to honor their unwitting contributions by goring them personally. After which, their meat would be served to only myself and my top advisers.

"But NO!" Dek-Fook-Tek rose from his throne anew. He galloped over in front of a recently installed kicking wall so quickly, his overhead antler handlers strained to keep up. With several puffs and snorts, down on all fours he kicked out his hind hooves repeatedly at that wall. It split apart, splinters flying everywhere. "NO!" he brayed screeching loud.

Again, one aide wiped drool from the corner of Dek-Fook-Tek's mouth. Another aide had him sip from a tranquillizer-laced cup of water.

"Lieutenant Ak-keek-teek has communicated a most dire report to me from the Sixth Celestial Breath," Dek-Fook-Tek went on, spraying saliva everywhere. "It concerns the other half of this other-world herd! They have been up to no good, down on the surface of the habitable planet less than one-half light-year from us! Those beasts have exploited their privacy to landscape several landing areas for fellow beasts' warships! There are eighteen landing areas in all! YES!"

Back down on all fours, Dek-Fook-Tek turned away from his audience to charge at the split-apart kickboard. His antlers pushed so far in that three aides were needed to help him shake free. The tranquillizer taking effect didn't help.

Eighteen landing areas?! Chris exclaimed to himself. *He's talking about a golf course!*

"The meaning of this couldn't be clearer than if one of them had lifted his hind leg to pee on Tictoctic's highest mountain! They might as well have been male oskynt marking off the territory where they kept their harems!" raged Dek-Fook-Tek. "That nearby planet is their staging area for an all-out attack on Tictoctic, like a plague of scout-saucer-sized niki-niks!

"And so, Counselor Kootlek, we must punish these other-world beasts for their deceit, for their murderous intent regarding my most magnificent civilization! The ones assembled here are to be taken away immediately! They will face ignominious, dishonorable slaughter on the slaughterhouse assembly line! After which, they shall be barbecued on the flames produced by burning this absurdly mobile tree creature! Then they shall be fed to some extra-special Tictoctickians among us, as a final treat on their own way to patriotic goring! These pests, clearly they deserve to be eaten on no higher level than that! I would have had them fed to oskynt instead, had any of those still been left alive! As soon as the other half of their herd returns, the same fate awaits them! Guards! Take the other-worlders away!"

Five deer creatures armed with air igniters seemed to the Earthlings to materialize out of the shadows in Dek-Fook-Tek's royal reception hall. Chris, Geena, Yoon-hee, Ali and Wafoodle-boodle all joined hands and branches, respectively. Soon, too soon, though, they were roughly separated apart.

An air igniter's cold, hard muzzle pushed painfully into the back of each one save the tree creature. Wafoodle-boodle actually found the burrowing of an air igniter muzzle into her bark to have massage-like benefits. But that wasn't why she hesitated to telepath an objection to Dek-Fook-Tek. Rather, she feared the severity of his pathology despite his feeling the full effects of the tranquillizer. Her telepaths welling up in his mind were liable to send him into another paroxysm of rage, his drugged-out state notwithstanding.

"This is a huge mistake! Those aren't landing areas! They are fairways for a golf course! Remember the game we showed you?! This is a huge mistake!" Chris repeated helplessly as he was led away.

Ali, Geena and Yoon-hee had torrents of tears streaming down their cheeks. "Can we at least wait for the others to return?! To say goodbye?!" Yoon-hee finally calmed herself enough to ask through her grief.

The guards had already reached the exit with Yoon-hee and the other hapless beings from "Akt" and "Koombt" in tow.

That was when an enormous flat-screen television suddenly slid down from where it hung on a ceiling track. It locked into place at a slant to Dek-Fook-Tek's left.

"Supreme Authority Dek-Fook-Tek!" excitedly brayed Counselor Kootlek with a hoof hand to his fluttering left ear. "I have word we are receiving a highest priority communication from Commander Kwit-Nik aboard the Sixth Celestial Breath!"

"Halt, guards!" Dek-Fook-Tek demanded with a stamp against the slate rock floor with his hind hoof.

"Supreme Authority Dek-Fook-Tek," was how the commander's first words translated. His kindly visage, so Chris thought, lit up the center of the flat-screen. "Your patience awaiting word from me deserves a special monument in your honor, in and of itself."

"Suppose it should take extremely long for word from our Supreme Authority. So extremely long, our unbrushed teeth would fall from our mouths. Our mouths would appear as the mouths of oskynt skulls discovered still decaying in the barren field. We can rest assured that nevertheless, the wait would have proven more than worthwhile," Counselor Kootlek led aides, handlers and guards alike to ritually chant. Made no difference to Kootlek that the Supreme Authority was who had been the one doing the waiting, not anyone else.

"There is no need for such a monument, Commander," the exceedingly tranquillized Dek-Fook-Tek lazily shook his head.

"His modesty-"

"Grrr," snarled the Supreme Authority. Despite his drugged-out state, he was growing anxious about making his full response to Commander Kwit-Nik. He was growing too anxious to have that response delayed another moment longer, more ritual praise or not. He went on, "Fortunately, Commander, Lieutenant Ak-keek-teek behaved satisfactorily enough to send me the alert. Don't worry; we will deploy two other saucers, fully armed for helping you destroy what those deceitful creatures have fabricated. We will decimate their warship landing areas as easily as rain storms wash away niki-nik mounds! Snort!" Snort, yes, but too sedated for another hoof stomp.

"Alert?! What alert?! And what deceit?!"

Dek-Fook-Tek pushed down on the arms of his throne to lift himself back up onto his hind hooves. He would have resumed kicking the wall to splinter it apart some more. That is, if he weren't feeling so mellowed-out from the tranquillizer. "I have no time for jokes!" he brayed groggily. "We are talking about a species of other-world beasts trying to set up an ambush of our great civilization! Their behavior might be likened to an oskynt sneaking up behind a baby kootoofek lost from its mother in ancient days past! Certainly, Commander, you have read how the oskynt used to shovel that hapless creature into a bathtub-sized maw before it could cry for help! Well, imagine that kootoofek infant armed with nine attack saucers plus uncounted numbers of smaller battle shuttles!"

With a sideways glance Lieutenant Ak-keek-teek's way, Commander Kwit-Nik finally managed to size up the situation, and how he would handle it. Forthwith he unflinchingly, both ears perfectly still, swelled out his chest. And he tongue-clicked most firmly crisply, "I know of no such deceit, nor plans for ambush, by the other-world beasts. On the contrary, this is what I do know about these albeit strangest of creatures. They have galloped great lengths, studying the feasibility for our kind to temporarily resettle on the new planet. Which planet we have named, contingent upon your approval, Kakifika. Anyway, the other-worlders' study nearly resulted in several of them sacrificing their lives. They took such a risk, just to confirm one region of this planet will prove too dangerous for our habitation.

"If I am proven wrong, my Supreme Authority, please instruct Lieutenant Ak-keek-teek to fatally impale me upon his own antlers. But he should wait until he has made them as sharp as possible, employing my bahvek.

"We are returning home now with the other-worlders. I hope we can join you in your subarctic command station compound to celebrate our success clearly inspired by your supremacy. With your all-important blessing, the celebration will include sampling specially prepared foods easily harvested on Kakifika. They are foods meant to bring our fellow creatures way back from the precipice of starvation where we have all had to graze for nearly fifty solar orbits."

Dek-Fook-Tek's nostrils flared with his sedated effort to grasp what the commander was saying. After long seconds of silence, he finally responded, "Commander

Kwit-Nik, are you aware what your lieutenant transmitted to me yesterday?! That he claimed the other-world beasts have landscaped military staging areas on, okay, let us call it Kakifika? That those areas can accommodate several of their warships landing there? Complete with a control tower for directing air traffic?"

Ah-ha! Kwit-Nik thought to himself. It was just as he had supposed.

Lieutenant Ak-keek-teek kept his eyes fixated on the view-screen, at Dek-Fook-Tek's long snout and considerable antler display. The lieutenant's own bucktooth visage was in full gloat, not deigning to return the commander's glance his direction.

Of course, Kwit-Nik thought to himself. *Lieutenant Ak-keek-teek expects to gain Dek-Fook-Tek's full commendation for grasping what his immediate superior, namely me, refused to perceive. Then he expects orders to take my bahvek, and sharpen his antlers for my fatal impalement. Pursuant to which he, Ak-keek-teek, will be pronounced most brayingly loudly the new commander of Tictoctic's outer space battle fleet!*

Lieutenant Ak-keek-teek anticipated Commander Kwit-Nik answering Dek-Fook-Tek with a correction. Even worse, that it would be a correction implying the Supreme Authority was duped by the lieutenant. Such a response would indeed have led most speedily to Kwit-Nik's death sentence.

Ak-keek-teek could not have imagined what Kwit-Nik concocted, instead. The commander began his response by implicitly complimenting the Supreme Authority. "Supreme Authority Dek-Fook-Tek," Commander Kwit-Nik tongue-clicked while forcing himself to project chest-swelled-out boldness. "My lieutenant has clearly forgotten one of your very finest pieces of wisdom, to be found of course in a feeding trough stuffed full of them. And it is all on me, certainly, for not having reminded him often enough."

Ak-keek-teek's gloat turned suddenly glower Kwit-Nik's way. "What is this 'finest piece of wisdom' with which you would presume to saddle our Supreme Authority?"

"The magnificent Dek-Fook-Tek should not have to waste extra of his precious breaths explaining, so I will explain instead. I remember it word for word, thanks to the flame-searing impact it had on me: 'Do not waste bullets on an oskynt until you are certain it is an oskynt, and not an oddly shaped mossy boulder.'"

"May we be eternally shamed if ever we forget the wisdom of Dek-Fook-Tek, once it is imparted to us," Counselor Kootlek solemnly, ritually suggested. He was quick to come down on a forelimb knee.

The other deer creatures in Dek-Fook-Tek's immediate presence followed suit lightning fast. Woe faced anyone accused of the least memory lapse over the multitude of wise sayings attributed to Dek-Fook-Tek. How especially nerve-racking for them, not recalling having ever heard what Commander Kwit-Nik attributed to Dek-Fook-Tek.

No wonder. Kwit-Nik just made it up.

After the Tictoctickian ruler's sedative-subdued approving acknowledgment of Counselor Kootlek's ritual warning, the commander continued. "The truth is this, Supreme Authority Dek-Fook-Tek," Commander Kwit-Nik tongue-clicked with new confidence. "What Lieutenant Ak-keek-teek mistook for other-world warship landing runways are actually fields of play for their curious game. And by 'their' I am referring to tree beings and bony-limbed animals alike. It is the game they call either kolfk or koofk."

By this time, Ak-keek-teek's hind limbs were quivering too much to remain standing. He had had to go down on all fours. From there, he went completely prostrate on the cold slate floor, front limbs tucked in, folded under his body.

"About that 'control tower,'" Kwit-Nik added, intent on as much ridiculing reality check as he could heap on Ak-keek-teek. "It was only one story tall, hardly suitable for directing air traffic. And all we found inside were playing utensils and tiny balls for the other-worlders' game. They hope the amusement their game provides will ease temporarily resettlement on Kakifika."

"Yes, that silly game," Dek-Fook-Tek nodded knowingly, if still groggily from continuing sedative effects. "Well, Lieutenant Ak-keek-teek, it would appear you have earned ignominious disembowelment from Commander Kwit-Nik's antlers. After they have been specially sharpened by his bahvek, I meant."

"If I might, Supreme Authority Dek-Fook-Tek," the commander dared demur. "Clearly, Lieutenant Ak-keek-teek is beyond exhaustion from misplaced concern. Nevertheless, I am sure he would be more than willing to unblinkingly take that punishment with his stripped-bare chest swelled all the way out. But sheer loyalty compels me to share a deep conviction, regardless of the possible consequences you might judge I must suffer as a result. It is a conviction that errors such as Ak-keek-teek's deserve the mercy and forgiveness only you, Dek-Fook-Tek, can provide. After all, it is an error on the side of over-zealous caution to protect your empire."

The lieutenant's ears and spirit perked up at Commander Kwit-Nik's remarks, despite his simmering rage. The commander's suspect allegiance was bad enough. Perhaps it was more dedicated to that stupid other-world game than to interplanetary conquest. But Lieutenant Ak-keek-teek's anger knew no bounds over how Commander Kwit-Nik had managed to outflank him. It galled the lieutenant no end, having to depend on the commander's powers of persuasion. If Kwit-Nik didn't convince Dek-Fook-Tek to spare Ak-keek-teek's life...Grrrrrrr! *It is Kwit-Nik's fate that should be hanging in the balance. Not mine!!*

"You have assessed the reality well, Commander," Dek-Fook-Tek nodded in a circular head motion safely accomplished despite the continuing effects of the sedative. Of course, this was thanks to the skillful manipulation of his ever-ridiculously oversized antlers by his handlers stationed above-ceiling. "Well enough, in fact, to save your own self from disembowelment. As I said before, it *appeared* the lieutenant earned that particular death. But as we know, appearances can be deceiving, especially when overzealous fealty to me, my safety, is misunderstood as a fault.

"I look forward to this celebration you brayed about, Commander, whereupon we may begin a whole new relationship with our other-world visitors." Dek-Fook-Tek turned Chris's direction specifically, to add, "Your introduction of the kokolat kip kookees has been something special! You might have earned an honorary, nonlethal chest-slashing from me, after all! We shall see!"

Chris wanted to respond, *That is an honor such as I do not deserve.* But the whole matter of who did or did not deserve chest-slashing, and to what extent, had shifted back and forth remarkably easily. Helena's husband wouldn't want to risk venturing a communication consciously, intentionally fraught with double meaning. So he kept his mouth shut and merely nodded.

Meantime, Lieutenant Ak-keek-teek's bucktooth grin reappeared as he rose back up on his hind hooves, on the navigation deck of the Sixth Celestial Breath. He tongue-clicked at Dek-Fook-Tek's sedated visage on the left half of the view-screen. He said, "I also eagerly anticipate a whole new relationship with the other-world visitors."

Commander Kwit-Nik knew, as assuredly as did the mind-reading tree creature, what both his lieutenant and the Supreme Authority really meant by "a whole new relationship." The old relationship had been one of allowing the "other-world visitors" to live and move about with their various plans and schemes. Perhaps many of those plans and schemes were instinctive patterns as of a niki-nik colony building a niki-nik tower. Perhaps the other-worlders only mimicked higher intelligence, civilized behavior. In reality, they were little more than dumb beasts ruled by a complex pattern of hormonal discharges. Anyhow, the commander well suspected that the "whole new relationship" would be the same as Tictoctickians' relationship to Chonorans. Despite what the other-world creatures had tried to do for the Tictoctickians, their thanks was still going to be getting added to the deer creatures' food supply.

But Commander Kwit-Nik knew something Lieutenant Ak-keek-teek and Dek-Fook-Tek could not. The primitive, underdeveloped state of their mental telepathy could not help them to anything more specific than a general unease. Kwit-Nik knew what the saucer captains plus most officers under their orders were more than willing to do, once the celebration meal was concluded. Namely, they were prepared to prevent the intended herding-off of the other-worlders to the slaughter house. They were prepared to do that in tandem with the overthrow of Dek-Fook-Tek, placing Kwit-Nik totally in charge.

The fear generated by the lieutenant's misleading report of warship landing platforms on Kakifika had proven wonderfully provident. Such fear had led to many saucers being relocated, defensively repositioned on close-in geosynchronous orbits of Tictoctic. Every last one of those saucers was captained by devotees to the coming revolt. How ideal for overwhelming Dek-Fook-Tek's subarctic command post with reconnaissance vehicles!

Tictoctickians imprisoned for disrespecting the Supreme Authority would be released, every last one of them. Peaceful negotiations with the other-worlders would gallop the way for wholesale transition to a vegetarian diet.

Also as a result of such negotiations, resettlement on Kakifika would be launched in earnest. And if anyone of Kwit-Nik's kind were still desperate for meat in their diet, real pure meat not of the composite, synthetic kind...*baa*, there was that oversized creature that rolled over on its back on the new planet. If Kwit-Nik didn't know better, this was its invitation for him and the lieutenant to rub its tummy. Might its meat not prove as tasty as the yummiest oskynt meat described in the legends of yore? Although for himself, Kwit-Nik wasn't sure he could kill such a gentle beast without serious qualms. Better to focus on landscaping wherever farmland was not needed. Soon he could be playing that most intriguing game of little ball struck by long stick into various holes in the ground, scattered about the countryside!!

Chapter 23

Earthlings gathered with Tictoctickians around an enormous dining table inside Dek-Fook-Tek's subarctic command station.

The two Oombian tree creatures, Oodle-Noodle and Wafoodle-boodle, situated themselves back away from the table. They stood beside one another in special tubs transported off the Smoke and Mirrors. Those tubs featured mud for the Oombians to sink their roots. They were otherwise filled with water clouded by algae.

The Earthlings took a different tact. Rather than sitting next to their respective mates, or standing next to them in mud, they mixed it up with the Tictoctickians. They were careful to have Commander Kwit-Nik, Counselor Kootlek, Chef Glork-tek and others sit in between them. They feared how the psychopathically erratic Dek-Fook-Tek might react if he saw hugs breaking out. And hugs breaking out among Earthling couples was for certain, should they have gotten anywhere near one another. Ali and Tanya were not sure they would have been able to peel themselves apart. Especially after what Tanya had endured on Kakifika.

Kakifika's perilous seaside lay trillions of miles distant. Nevertheless, Helena couldn't keep what happened there from replaying in her head, over and over.

Once the scout saucer commandeered by Kwit-Nik freed the shuttle pod from its electromagnetic cables' grasp, the sea monster had free rein. Its serpentine neck remained securely coiled about the egg-shaped vehicle that flew down to Kakifika's surface from the Smoke and Mirrors. And so, this whale-sized likeness to a Plesiosaurus lost no time dragging said vehicle under water. It pulled the shuttle pod down deep, down very deep.

Just when captain and company trapped inside thought they couldn't become any more terrified, BAM! Something rammed the shuttle pod's cockpit dome. It was a three-horned, frilled head like a ceratopsian dinosaur's, but attached to a shark's streamlined body.

The far larger monster constricted its serpentine neck tighter and tighter, causing ever more hull creaking. Helena and Tanya, especially, wondered how much longer they would have before water leaked spraying inside. Would their shelter soon turn into an undersea tomb?

"What did you say, Tanya?! About why can't you electrify the shuttle's hull to shock away the monster?!?!" Carol cried, desperate beyond desperate.

"Remember sea spray that got in here? We would electrocute our-"

BAM!

"Officer Petrovsky, I think we have to take a chance with electrocution-"

That's as far as Captain Taylor got with her new order, when the shuttle pod suddenly lurched over to one side. The next thing the Earthlings knew, the sea monster loosened its death grip, and the shuttle pod floated surface-ward.

"Okay!" shouted Captain Taylor while the three women strapped themselves down, finally. "Tanya, can you rev up the anti-matter drive soon as we're topside??!"

"We're there *now*, Captain!" said Tanya. Her fingers were a blur of motion across the control console.

The shuttle pod bobbed out at the water's surface, and went surfing on the crest of an especially mountainous wave. At that wave's highest loft, on the verge of breaking and curling into a thunderous collapse, the pod's engine roared to life. Escape velocity lifted the vehicle forward. None too fast, as that put it mere inches beyond reach of a whale-sized, Mosasaur-type sea monster's lunging emergence. The monster's wide-open maw was intended for what it mistook as a fellow sea creature.

The shuttle pod circled around, high above the violent sea. It flew at an altitude the Mosasaur monster, not yet ready to give up, couldn't quite achieve despite spectacular breaches.

Hundreds of yards over to the breaching monster's side, the Earthlings spotted the Plesiosaurus-type creature that nearly dragged them to their doom. It was engaged in the oddest, most unexpected behavior, chasing its tail around in a circle like a baby puppy dog, so Helena thought.

"Captain, what's that, that just washed ashore?!" Tanya pointed away from the long-necked sea monster, despite its continuing to bite at its own tail for some unfathomable reason. "That wouldn't be-"

"Can you bring us down lower, Tanya, hover mode? Keep us a safe distance out of sea monster reach?" Captain Taylor despaired of the washed-up object being anything more than a large piece of driftwood. Its proportions certainly looked correct for Oodle-Noodle. But there was only one major branch visible, not the two that would have been the tree creature's arms. More important was what Helena couldn't bring herself to mention to Tanya and Carol. If their Oombian tree creature friend were still alive, wouldn't she have telepathed them by then? To assure them she was okay?

"Oh, great, someone else's attention has been attracted as well, Captain!"

Tanya didn't bother pointing, it was so obvious.

The same alligator-type monster that chased them earlier had climbed back over the sand dunes from further inland. It was sniffing and pawing at the washed-ashore object of interest.

As despairing as Helena yet remained of the object being Oodle-Noodle, she still cringed. Was the gator monster going to behave like a dog fetching a bone?

No. As it turned out, the monster finally grew tired of the washed-ashore object. He reared back up onto his extra-thick-and-powerful hind legs to lumber off.

"Maybe the inter-dimensional herd of Triceratops knock-offs is beckoning-"

That's as far as Cathy got with her speculation before a voice filled her and her associates' heads with a comfortingly familiar cadence. *Captain and officers, I have only recently regained consciousness. And I have had to lie here totally still while the monster prodded and poked at me. But there is good news-*

Cathy, Helena and Tanya were already cheering.

Wait, I haven't even told you what the good news is!

"We can see you there sunning yourself on the beach after your swim, Oodle-Noodle! That's all the good news we need! We'll be down to retrieve you in no time!"

But there's other good news, Captain. Yulala and Guy's baby has been born safely. Yulala and child are resting well.

"Extend them our congratulations, Oodle-Noodle," Helena said while she was unbuckling her seat belt, the shuttle landed already. "However, our focus is on getting you out of here safely. I also want to know just what was going through your head when you swam off! Why didn't you let us haul you into the shuttle pod in the first place?! You really thought it would be easier to retrieve you from here on shore?" For her questions, Captain Taylor looked down directly into Oodle-Noodle's eyes.

The tree creature's bark had just finished crinkling even more than usual, to reopen them.

I was facing a grim certainty, Captain Taylor. Neither you nor the shuttle pod was going to make it if I didn't do what I did. Or let's assume your "last ditch" desperation order to Tanya had worked to save you. Several sea creatures were going to be electrocuted.

"Oh?"

What I did was this: I propelled myself like one of your planet's squids. I used my branches and under-trunk cilia in the place of tentacles. I propelled myself to the very rear of the monster with its neck coiled in a death grip around your shuttle pod. I made an assumption upon which the practical effectiveness of my plan was completely dependent. My assumption was that any force applied to the tip of the sea creature's tail would critically weaken it. That the result would be comparable to how pressure applied to a typical snake's tail impairs the snake's coiling ability. There was one problem, however. No way could I actually get a good grip on the sea monster's tail. It was lashing about too violently fast in the water, creating its own turbulent surf. But a sharp object placed in its path became embedded just deep enough, much like a wood splinter, to produce the full weakening effect.

Cathy paused from helping lift Oodle-Noodle up into the shuttle pod on a medical stretcher. She snapped her fingers and exclaimed, "So that's why our Plesiosaur lookalike was chasing its tail!"

I sensed the creature releasing its grip on the shuttle pod almost instantly. But no need to worry about its health; it should have successfully extracted the splinter by now. Unfortunately, I was unable to get out of its way after performing my deed. That is, I was unable to get out of its way soon enough to avoid being knocked unconscious by one of its flippers.

"Wait." It was Tanya's turn to pause from their rescue effort. She alone, since Cathy and Helena had already figured out the answer to what she proceeded to ask. "What did you use exactly, Oodle-Noodle, for 'splinter'?"

First let me assure you it was no big deal. Little pain resulted from the procedure, and my limbs have amazing regenerative abilities. To obtain the sharpest possible object for penetration of the creature's skin, I simply snapped off my left arm at the trunk joint.

"'Simply'?" Helena Taylor shook her head in amused disbelief. Despite the Oombian tree creature's plentiful peace-and-love talk, she was yet willing to inflict a little pain on the sea monster. She was unable to imagine any other way around- *Yeah, yeah, yeah,* Captain Taylor nodded. Oodle-Noodle didn't need to telepath any rebuttals because they were already occurring to the captain. *It was far more merciful than electrocution; a splinter under someone's skin isn't the worst thing in the world, especially if it saves lives...* "Well, Oodle-Noodle, I don't know how we can possibly thank-"

"SISSSSSSS!!"

The Earthlings were so happily excited with Oodle-Noodle's survival, the shadow suddenly cast upon the white coral sand didn't register at first. And when it did register, captain and company assumed a lone cloud was temporarily blocking direct sunlight, nothing more.

However, a distinctly reptilian sound issued from over and behind the away team's backs. A snake's hiss might as well have been amplified several-fold. Captain and company also noticed the sea air become oppressive, weighed down by moisture-laden stench.

The stench emanated from strands of flesh wedged between the gator monster's teeth. They remained there from when the monster bit into the neck of a Mosasaur-type creature the away team had inadvertently walked into.

The three women turned around slowly to look up. That is when a large drop of blood splattered against Helena's face. The blood was shed by one of the aforementioned flesh strands.

What ensued was a roar so loud, the fear-paralyzed Earthlings wondered how it didn't burst their ear drums.

Quick! Snap off my other arm!

"Snap off your other arm?!?!" Tanya cried in disbelief at Oodle-Noodle.

The panicky humans had already dropped Oodle-Noodle back lying prostrate in the sand like a huge piece of driftwood.

The gator monster left off from roaring to make a deeply rumbling grumble.

Its sports-car-sized snout came lower for the selection process. Which of the three trembling Earthlings would the gator monster want to gobble up first?

Cathy thought on how one year ago, an especially loud bass guitar at a rock concert caused her entire body to vibrate.

I can't snap my arm off myself with the other gone! One of you needs to snap it off for me! Then you need to insert the jagged end into one of the creature's nostrils. This is a strategy we learned on Oomb. It minimizes the violence during those rare occasions a comparably enormous ooktook sneaks up on us in the higher elevations of Boombeeno. Ouch! Very good!

Tanya pulled off Oodle-Noodle's remaining arm none too soon. Pursuant to which, she brought it up before her like Luke Skywalker in *Star Wars* wielding his light saber, Helena fancied.

The gator monster had already lowered its snout nearly to the ground, for choosing from among the three women.

An adrenalin rush eliminated any hesitation on Officer Petrovsky's part, so that she wasted no time lunging forward. On first try, she succeeded at inserting the splintery end of Oodle-Noodle's second sacrificed arm into the gator monster's right nostril.

"We have a folk tale about a lion with a splinter," Helena commented while the gator monster turned away from the Earthlings to deal with its unexpected discomfort. "Wo!" she exclaimed immediately thereafter. She just missed getting sideswiped by the dinosaur-sized reptile's long tail lashing from side to side, thanks to raging frustration over the stick up its nose. Nevertheless she went on, even as she joined the other two women hustling to lift their tree creature savior back aboard the shuttle pod. "In that folk tale," she said, "a mouse comes along and removes the splinter from the lion's paw. So the mouse and the lion become really good friends."

Captain Taylor, as much as I would long to see that story play out here, I am a realist, Oodle-Noodle telepathed.

Tanya and Cathy were strapping Oodle-Noodle against one wall of the shuttle pod. Her trunk roots and cilia had already been lovingly carefully set down into a bowl full of moist, loamy soil.

I would not recommend you attempt relieving that creature from its discomfort, the Oombian tree creature went on. It will figure out how to extricate my arm soon enough. Besides which, the dictates of its hormones are overriding its spirit's love and empathy. Sad to telepath what of course you already know. The reward any of you would receive for trying to remove its splinter would most probably include a trip down its gullet. But as with any other carnivore, we must remember that somewhere deep inside, it grieves every bite taken out of another creature.

"AHHHHHH-CHOOOOO!!!!!"

Helena would never forget the gator monster's thunderous sneeze just before she finished closing the shuttle pod's airlock. She found herself actually feeling something for that brutish animal despite what its sneeze accomplished.

The gator monster's sneeze ejected Oodle-Noodle's arm splinter from its nostril like a launched rocket.

Crackly electrostatic deployment of the shuttle pod's micron-layer wings scared off the gator monster from any further assault. Equally important, Tanya was able to verify the sea monster's neck constrictions did nothing to seriously compromise the pod's hull integrity. Still, the Earthlings donned their spacewalk suits for returning to the Smoke and Mirrors, just in case. Those suits included one specially designed to convenience Oodle-Noodle.

The shuttle pod ascended rapidly out of Kakifika's atmosphere. Blue sky briefly tinged by orange-ish friction flashes darkened to star-filled black firmament within seconds.

"So, how are the new parents doing, Oodle-Noodle? They have a name yet?" asked Captain Helena Taylor during the mercifully predictable return towards the Smoke and Mirrors.

The childbirth aboard ship was Helena's second order of business. Her first order of business was checking in with Commander Kwit-Nik. She thanked him for the rescue attempt using his scout saucer's electromagnetic cable.

But back to her second order of business, the captain well knew the constraints she would face once she got back to the starship. That is, where communication with the hidden-away adults and children was concerned. This included the two Chonorans, Chig-Cher and Chwerp-Chee. Oodle-Noodle had somehow managed to hypnotize the Tictoctickians into forgetting they were aboard. Anyway, Captain Taylor's contact with the lot of them would have to be indirect, wholly dependent on Oodle-Noodle's mindreading and telepathy.

Helena and company presumed the Smoke and Mirrors under constant Tictoctickian surveillance, auditory as well as visual. It had to be expected wherever known-about passengers and crew were located. Any slightest slip-up... Not so for the shuttle pod, however. The Earthlings still needed to lean on Oodle-Noodle's telepathy. But the shuttle pod was not bugged by the deer creatures. At least the Earthlings could speak unguarded inside there.

Captain, I am afraid Yulala and Sergeant Hanson are feeling most upset, Oodle-Noodle went on to answer Helena Taylor's question. *Their baby girl, both of her eyes are over to one side of her face like on the flounder mouse of Fafama. Those few who are aware of the situation have been trying one consolation or another, but thus far to no avail.*

"What sort of consolation? I hope Dr. Davis-Murphy knows better than to say to Guy and Yulala, 'I told you so.'"

The doctor most certainly thinks that, Captain. But she has not actually asked me to convey any such sentiment to the couple. Instead, she has been emphasizing the blessing that their child appears to be in good health.

"What have those few others been saying to try to help?"

Captain, for explaining how one of the Chonorans tried to help, I need to elaborate on the childbirth itself. Yulala warned her husband and Ciela what to expect if it turned out anything like other Fafaman childbirths. They were told not to be surprised if she found herself squeeze-launching the baby from her birth canal.

"'Squeeze-launching'?!" Helena, Tanya and Cathy repeated together in perfect unison.

It was believed by Fafaman biologists to have been an evolutionary adaptation from their prehistory. Baby and mother alike were thereby protected against certain predators. The placental material shot out first. In the distant Fafaman past, shot-out placentas might have acted as bludgeon force against an animal attack, usually from some giant insect. They also might have provided cushions for newborn safe landings.

"Just when I thought I had heard it all," Helena shook her head. "Okay, so what happened with Yulala? I assume her 'launch' was successful?"

Ciela prepared for making the sort of delivery common to Earthlings. She had equipment for a Caesarian section at her side, just in case. Dr. Davis-Murphy would have walked her through that particular scenario had it proven necessary. Again, I would have acted as the telepathic intermediary.

Anyway, while Ciela was ready for an Earthling-style birthing, the two Chonorans volunteered to hold a comforter between themselves. They were to catch the baby in the event of a Fafaman-style projectile birth. Sergeants Hanson and Frankly would have acted in that capacity, as baby catchers. However, Yulala wanted Guy to keep patting down her forehead with a wet cloth, and to coach her breathing regimen.

Anyhow, as I'm sure you already guessed, the Chonorans did have to make the catch. They both got their canvas shirts stained, which in their culture is always a good thing. The one of them who is sillier than the other – I believe his name is Chig-Cher –

"He is sillier by far," confirmed Helena.

When the new parents started to become upset, Chig-Cher made his own unique effort to console them. He fussed over how lovely the placental stain looked on his shirt. He said he would wait long enough before cleaning that he wouldn't be able to completely wash it out. He would always have a souvenir of the happy occasion.

Yulala burst into tears again, and Chig-Cher's significant other, Chwerp-chee, wrapped a tentacle arm round Chig-cher's neck to pull him away. Chwerp-chee could have been back on Earth, yanking Chig-cher offstage by a cane because he was performing badly.

For my own part, I'm not sure that what I telepathed Yulala and Guy was really any more useful. I advised the couple it was too soon to know the maturational changes their newborn might undergo. Those changes could result in a more symmetrical face. Not to mention the cosmetic surgery the chief medical officer or physicians back on Earth might be able to perform.

For certain, when Sergeant Guy Hanson tried his own hand at courageously providing Yulala with a comforting thought, it totally backfired. He said that for another person born of mixed Earthling/Fafaman descent, their baby daughter could grow up to be the person of his or her dreams. On this remark, Yulala sobbed inconsolably. She got so upset, Ciela had to temporarily remove the baby from her presence.

Sergeant Hanson quickly realized what was wrong, without his wife having to explain. Of course there can be no such mixed-descent birth into a different family. Far as anyone knows, no other Fafamans are left alive besides Yulala, since an enormous ice comet plowed into Fafama. So another mixed marriage of Fafaman with Earthling is impossible.

Oh, wait. Some real comfort at last.

"What's happening, Oodle-Noodle?" Tanya was unable to contain herself before the tree creature's telepath could continue.

Those two boys Ciela and Fred adopted, the mischief-makers, they went up beside Yulala's bed. They have just told Yulala and Guy they want to be like two big brothers for their daughter. Oh! Alexita, the daughter of Ludi and Pedro, she's joined them to give the baby a kiss. The mother and father are laughing through their tears!

"What are the other adults up to?" Helena asked as the shuttle pod's electrostatically held-together stabilizer wings were dissolving apart on its final approach to the starship. The pod was to dock inside a compartment along the starship's "asparagus stem" hull. "By the by," she added. "We will have to make this the last part of the conversation for now, our out-loud portion of it in any event."

Sergeant Fred Frankly has just stomped away from the delivery room. He's extremely frustrated with the lack of information from outside their hiding place, despite my telepathed updates. He's also not happy with having been unable to lend his support to our survival efforts in the decidedly more dangerous region of Kakifika. To his credit, he keeps reminding himself he can't go renegade. He can't just contact Kevin or another Earthling presently presiding over "official" living areas of the Smoke and Mirrors. That is, not without Tictoctickian surveillance finding out where the children are tucked away. He well knows what crucial roles he and his fellow concealed adults might have to play to keep the children safe. In the event circumstances don't go favorably for the rest of us, Sergeant Frankly will need to lend more support than he could ever dream about, or dread.

As for Professors Aquinas and Skepticus, they have been irritating one another no end over what precisely Yulala has been going through. But at least Professor Aquinas had the foresight to tow Skepticus away from the new parents' presence. Whatever they have had to say, Skepticus especially hasn't been given the chance to upset the new parents more than they already are.

"You must at least admit, my dear Dauntilus Skepticus, that wasn't some thunderous flatus emission!" insisted Aquinas. "So much for your severely bloated hypothesis! Severely bloated in more ways than one!" Aquinas moved his spectacles up and down on the bridge of his nose with his agitation, nearly enough to make himself dizzy.

"I need to admit no such thing, my dear Thomas Aquinas!" Skepticus roared back. "Yes, yes, the flatus emission isn't everything! But it is a part of the thing! The other part has to be some especially enormous bowel evacuation. Of course, those two hopelessly idealistic young people cannot admit the truth! They cannot admit to themselves anything less than what they were so cruelly led to believe would be a child! However, the genetic incompatibility of two different ecosystems lorded over by two entirely different genetic codes makes a child impossible!"

"What?! What?!" Aquinas nearly flipped his glasses backwards off his head with his perturbation. "Did you not notice the baby kicking about its arms and legs?! Did you not look into her eyes?! And did you not hear her cries exactly like a baby, BECAUSE THAT IS WHAT SHE IS?!?!?!"

"And you would expect a newly dumped amount of excrement to just sit there quietly, Professor Aquinas? Would you expect it to not move so we might take its picture or something?! And, and..." Skepticus was determined not to allow his colleague to respond until he made his final point. "...you have never, ever heard a lifeless tea kettle whistle once its water started to boil?! Or heard a steaming pile of the thickest tomato sauce start to pop bubbles for the same reason?!"

"I do believe, Professor, I am hearing from a steaming pile of miraculously enspirited-"

FWOOMPH!!

"Ouch!" screamed Professor Skepticus, grabbing at the seat of his pants. For the umpteenth time, a torch-like flame seemed to flare out of nowhere there. "What?! What?!" the professor exclaimed. "The atmospheric anomaly is still wandering about the starship?! And how could it have produced such a chemical reaction close behind me, yet again?! I know for a fact that not the merest crumb from a chocolate chip cookie is to be found there, or from anything else flammable for that matter!!"

"It is a no wonder, Professor Skepticus! In its own inimitable way, Effy is expressing a shock equal to mine over your absurd characterization of the newborn!"

"A newborn whose existence very simply cannot happen, Professor Aquinas, if only for the sheer incompatibility of the Fafaman biology's genetic sequencing with-"

FWOOOMPH!!!

"Ouch!"

Oodle-Noodle provided this detailed update on the professors' conversation while Captain Taylor and company exited the shuttle pod to reboard the Smoke and Mirrors.

Captain Taylor's recall of Oodle-Noodle's role somehow jolted her attention back to the present.

Ludi was announcing the next course to be served in Dek-Fook-Tek's Great Gathering Trough.

As peacefully benign as the situation appeared, Captain Taylor couldn't stop worrying. Sure, Effy the ephemeral dragon was keeping Professor Skepticus humble. But Taylor well knew its fire-breathing would probably do no good if matters turned deadly sour with the Tictoctickians.

As already recounted, deadly sour is exactly how matters had developed for Chris, Ali, Yoon-hee and Buddy Leung. This happened in the minutes before Commander Kwit-Nik called out Lieutenant Ak-keek-teek's poisonous misinformation. And again as already recounted, Kwit-Nik defused the potential crisis in a manner that saved face for Supreme Authority Dek-Fook-Tek.

Captain Taylor had to hope Chef Ludi's meal would conclude on a far more productive, less perilous note than after her husband served up his chocolate chip cookies.

"Next, we have for you a meaty, Kakifikan fungus. It is similar to your pakakapa mushroom, and the Portobello mushroom found on Earth," explained Chef Ludi Perez. Ali set down the fungus dish before Dek-Fook-Tek's taste tester, Counselor Kootlek. "The fungus has been smeared with an olive oil and garlic marinade, then soaked in pomegranate juice," Chef Ludi added.

Dek-Fook-Tek's taste tester appeared to enjoy a knifed-off bite of the fungus preparation so much, his ears folded straight back. He closed his eyes in full, enraptured focus on the flavor.

Abruptly, Supreme Authority Dek-Fook-Tek drew the dish away from Kootlek, rather than waiting to be served his own.

"Baahhmmm," yum-yum-yummed Commander Kwit-Nik. He tongue-clicked, "If I did not know better, I would have guessed this was an oskynt liver. And that it was prepared from one of our few remaining frozen meat reserves, then drenched in even rarer defrosted oskynt blood. To think we could be enjoying a meal such as this on a daily basis, with plenty for all!"

"Baa, I am not sure." Lieutenant Ak-keek-teek pretended much difficulty swallowing his first bite. His act convinced many Earthlings he was struggling not to vomit or spit it out instead. "I do not feel this rises to the flavor level of, um..." The lieutenant paused to make a production of leering at Helena Taylor seated beside him, down at her hips more specifically. "This is worse than the least savory actual liver I've ever eaten, or imagined eating."

"About this particular dish, I am none so sure, myself," Dek-Fook-Tek mumbled, barely translatable with his mouth full from his slow ruminations. "Although between its juiciness and red color, I can almost imagine it is blood-soaked. *Almost.*"

Given the power of the placebo effect, Ludi couldn't help wondering. How would the lieutenant and Supreme Authority have reacted had she lied? What if she had claimed this particular dish was indeed some extraterrestrial beast's bloody liver? She well appreciated the danger attendant to such a stunt, though. Were Dek-Fook-Tek to ever have learned of her deception, he would likely have become dangerously unhinged. Again.

Chef Glork-tek was most favorably impressed by the extraterrestrial fungus's fleshy texture and garlic flavor, its uniqueness. He also imagined what some comedian could have trotted in and tongue-clicked, assuming he didn't care whether he lived to make another joke. *No liver could ever approach the deliciousness of Dek-Fook-Tek's liver. Once the smallest morsel was tasted, it would make all other livers seem the foulest oskynt excrement by comparison! Demand would rise to an insufferable level. As a result, our Supreme Authority would have to be chopped to pieces immediately so everyone might feast upon his regal tenderness!*

"Supreme Authority Dek-Fook-Tek!" crisply tongue-clicked Commander Kwit-Nik. He was intent on sharing aloud his own response to Dek-Fook-Tek's evident distaste for the particular vegetarian dish in question. "Mention was made earlier of a peculiarly pinkish, flat-snouted creature roaming the grain fields of Kakifika. It is far more impressively proportioned than the largest known oskynt to have ever roamed Tictoctic. On our first settlement mission to officially claim that planet as part of the Tictoctickian Empire, we should surely slaughter one of them! What delights might await us from feasting upon its liver, and on so many other parts of it as well?"

You know how murderous your sea-going kayfafas turned when sailors took to slaughtering them for lamp oil. Those creatures remained that way until they were hunted to extinction, Oodle-Noodle telepathed Commander Kwit-Nik as per her usual sixth-sense communications. But she put that reminder of Tictoctickian history into the mind of Dek-Fook-Tek in a far less intrusive manner. Hopefully, where Oodle-Noodle was concerned, the Supreme Authority could be easily fooled. He could be made to believe her reminder, as well as the rest to come, was the product of his own unaided thought process. *But the kayfafas were, again, water-bound,* went on the Oombian tree creature. *The enormous flat-snouted beasts, however, are land-bound. And they might be populating Kakifikan pastures in large numbers. Were they to feel under deadly threat, they could pose an extreme danger to your settlers. Why not preserve them as the gentle creatures they are? Why hunt them, especially given the new reality made possible by other-worlders? The Earthlings have introduced you to a variety and quantity of vegetarian foods harvested so easily, meat in your diet should no longer be necessary.*

"Commander Kwit-Nik, your powers of reasoning did bring you half-way up the mountainside." Dek-Fook-Tek paused to swell out his uniformed chest. The dark brown outfit was emblazoned with his oversized antlers stitched in gold-plated silken threads. He burst with pride, on the verge of unwittingly claiming an Oombian tree being's thoughts as his own. "However," he finally continued, "we need to reach the summit. In aide of that goal, we learned something important from our history. Before certain short-antlered sailors started slaughtering the kayfafas for lamp oil and soaps, those sea beasts behaved like the most submissive kokatoks. Hunting them on the path to extinction, though, brought out their murderous inner nature. Thank me, they could not come ashore to wreak havoc on population centers.

"But gallop forward to the present. We have this temporary resettlement program for a lush nearby planet. True, it is instinctively proffered by these other-worlder creatures seated and standing in amongst us at my feeding trough. All the same, we do not want to jeopardize that program by bringing out the monstrous potential of newly discovered, land-roaming beasts there. But that is exactly what we would do if we set about hunting them! Smaller proportioned beasts more the size of the oskynt, of course, would be another matter!"

Commander Kwit-Nik made haste to rise from his chair and lead his fellow deer creatures in yet another ritualized praise. "Without the wisdom of Dek-Fook-Tek," he said, "we would be as blind oskynt lost inside a cavern labyrinth."

"Yes you would," Dek-Fook-Tek nodded approvingly while his supposed loyal subjects variously retook their seats or resumed standing guard. "Anyway, Chonoran livers sautéed and served up on a bed of fried belly fat crisps are by far the tastiest! It is most unfortunate the reserve supplies are lower than that of oskynt liver even! And that the breeding experiments with the few Chonorans of good stock, kept herded for that purpose, failed to yield results. Results, that is, before we at last needed to add them to those shrinking meat reserves! One has to wonder what perversity of *their* inner nature made them suddenly so unwilling to copulate. Indeed, we might never know what caused their one-hundred-percent abortion rate after artificial insemination. But that is what it is. Temporarily, we have to make do with certain alternatives for our chief food sources. And the best venue for making do is another planet until Tictoctic can be revitalized."

Ak-keek-teek gave the Earthlings a chop-licking, drooling regard. He meant to communicate they were his idea of "certain alternatives."

In a rare show of self-restraint, Dek-Fook-Tek resisted joining the lieutenant with his own ravenous regard of the other-worlders. He didn't resist for long, however, after Ludi and Ali served the next course: Rice with pigeon peas plus a garbanzo-type legume discovered growing like weeds on Kakifika.

Oodle-Noodle and Wafoodle-boodle spared the Earthlings from learning telepathically what Supreme Authority Dek-Fook-Tek subsequently imagined.

Dek-Fook-Tek went "mmmm," ruminating over a mouth full of the rice mixed with various beans. But in actuality, that "mmmm" was about the prospect of Captain Taylor's skinned corpse. The Supreme Authority could see her turning slowly over a roasting spit, with rice spilling from her mouth. At a Hawaiian luau, an apple instead of rice would have been holding open a roasted pig's mouth.

The tree creatures also spared Helena and company the stress from knowing of an intense conversation in progress. Wafoodle-boodle was pleading with Michel DeFarge to stop readying a drone attack.

Commander DeFarge, the deer creature commander of Tictoctic's flying saucer invasion fleet has assembled a broad-based coalition. They are intent on the forcible yet peaceful removal from power of their crazed ruler, Dek-Fook-Tek. They also plan to remove his most fervent close advisers who share in his extreme mental instability, telepathed Wafoodle-boodle to Michel DeFarge and Prissy DeFarge alike.

Wafoodle-boodle's telepath happened simultaneously to one of Dek-Fook-Tek's servants receiving an under-the-breath bleat. Dek-Fook-Tek ordered the servant to dislodge a rice grain uncomfortably stuck between two of his supreme molars. A golden royal toothpick was to be employed with zero amount of fanfare.

Commander Kwit-Nik is convinced his leadership's madness can be handled, or hoofled in the deer creatures' case, more as a law-enforcement issue. Civil war should not be necessary. This is how Wafoodle-boodle went on explaining Commander Kwit-Nik's overthrow plot for the DeFarges. *There is near unanimity of agreement regarding Dek-Fook-Tek's recklessly bloodthirsty, unhinged, most erratic behavior. And here is additional good news: After removing Dek-Fook-Tek from power, the commander will focus on brokering a peace treaty with Earth and Oomb. His contemplated treaty features two elements. Element one, we help temporarily resettle most of the deer creatures to the newly explored planet less than one-half light-year from Tictoctic. Element two, we also help pull Tictoctic out of its global warming death spiral. What you Earthlings have learned from trying to terraform Mars should come in quite handy, or branchy in our case. Commander Kwit-Nik is just waiting for the next irrational outburst from Dek-Fook-Tek, which shouldn't be long in coming. Meanwhile, your planned drone attack would accomplish nothing more than unnecessary death and destruction.*

"Well I'll be damnably damned, Foodle-Strudel or whatever your name is!" Michel DeFarge slapped his hands together at the navigation controls of the Elusive.

The battle-ready Elusive presently shadowed an asteroid about three times its size. That asteroid was passing between Tictoctic and its lone moon about half the diameter of Earth's moon.

"If what you're putting in my head, whispering in my ear is true, we can support the coup! That's right!" Michel affirmed with a fist pump. "It's still wicked unnatural for stags anywhere to be parading around in uniforms, flying spaceships and acting like they are superior to other forest critters! Even so, I'm all in on supporting their good guy commander! Just telepath, do your telepathing dingie to him! Tell him we're ready and willing to assist with our piggyback drones! We simply need the coordinates where we can precision-target our hijacking of their magnetic pulse-beam technology! We'll get those pulse-beams operating more efficiently than the Tictoctickian rebels could ever hope to make happen on their own! For damned sure, we will take down their mad leadership before that Dek-Fook-Tek guy knows what hit him!"

I can assure you, Captain DeFarge, even the most precise targeting will still result in completely unnecessary death and destruction. Why not see the commander's plan through to what potentially promises being a peaceful resolution?

"You can name yourself whatever silly name you like, tree being," Prissy DeFarge looked up from her knitting to declaim into thin air. It was as though the Oombian were standing right there for her stern questioning. "How are you trusting anything, anything these demonstrably murderous beasts tell you?!?"

But they didn't tell me; I mind-read their intent. So it becomes a matter of whether you trust what I am telling you. You ought to be able to do that since you know how accurately I have mind-read your intent imminently to launch a drone attack. But you are under extra pressure to move up the timetable, aren't you? Isn't the drone manufacturer anxious to learn whether his "piggy-backers" work under actual battlefield conditions? Doesn't he anticipate enormous profits from selling them in large numbers? Ask yourselves: What will those profits be worth, if your attack only confirms the deer creatures' worst fears about Earthlings? And results in the undermining of the coup, plus a certainty of all-out interstellar war? But an attack was what you were assigned to travel out here for in the first place, wasn't it? How does that expression go? "Stir up the hornet's nest"?

Michel DeFarge pounded his fist so hard against the navigation console that he put a dent in it. "Oh! So we're the problem! *We're* the bad guys! Forget about those furry-tailed bastards plundering our peaceful settlement on Oomb! Forget about them drawing up plans to cattle-rustle all the sentient beings from here to the North Star! We're the problem! No, I won't stop, Prissy!" This comment referred to his wife shaking her head at him as in, *it's not worth the energy and high blood pressure to argue with an invasive voice in your head.* "Time to speak some damnably damned real world sanity to this throwback to the antiwar hippie era! I don't know, Foodle Strudel, whether all your mind-reading is letting you in on *this* little factoid: Reconnaissance spacecraft are streaming out of the Tictoctickian battle saucers, and they are descending closer to Tictoctic's atmosphere. Do you really suppose that's for having a little picnic after the crazies are led away in handcuffs? Perhaps you're expecting an Alice-in-

Wonderland tea party, even? Isn't it more likely the demon stag are making certain none of you can escape when they lower the boom? Pretty soon, won't they be tossing pieces of your trunk on a big old campfire to make sure Captain Taylor and company get good and roasted for a feast?, a feast to celebrate the impending launch of their interplanetary invasion?!?"

Your assessment could not be more inaccurate, Captain DeFarge. I have mind-read what's actually going on. Many Tictoctickian deer creatures are indeed preparing for something. But that something is not interplanetary invasion. Rather they are worried over the possibility that resistance to the coup will prove greater than expected. They are concerned there might still be too many of their fellow deer creatures unwilling to haul the mentally imbalanced leadership into custody. But happily, I have sixth-sensed that is not the case.

"Yeah?!? Well, how do you know them Tictoctickians aren't playing some mind game trick on you? Pah!" DeFarge turned away from his wife to use his spittoon. He'd had it installed so he wouldn't risk unintentionally causing any function-compromising corrosion of the navigation console. "You're right, Prissy!" he added. "I shouldn't trust a thing that Waffle-Strudel puts in my head!"

My extrasensory capability makes such a "mind game" exceedingly difficult, Commander DeFarge. Please. I ask you, I beg you to reconsider. You must know of the apocalyptically unintended consequences over on planet Fafama. The Fafaman ruler thought he could have violence pinpointed to destroy the rebels. But he ended up producing a planet-wide extinction event instead! And besides, you and Priscilla consider yourselves of the Christian faith. How do you reconcile that faith with

Jesus's Sermon on the Mount, when He urged people to love their enemies? To turn the other cheek when they are struck on one cheek?

Wafoodle-boodle persisted with her argument despite an unnerving, profoundly disturbing perception about Michel and Priscilla DeFarge.

Priscilla shut out any least consideration of the Oombian tree creature's informed reasoning. She achieved this mental feat by focusing most willfully on her sock knitting, on all the trivial details pertaining thereof. She even mumbled to herself, "I cannot listen to this."

As for Michel, he might as well have slammed a door in the Oombian's face, how his full attention went to the details of piggyback drone operation. There were the no small matters of cloaking the drone, then maneuvering it over to the Fourth Celestial Breath. Then Michel had to have it latch onto the battle saucer's underbelly.

⁕ ⳾⳾⳾⳾ ⁕ ⳾⳾⳾⳾ ⁕ ⳾⳾⳾⳾ ⁕

A servant labored mightily to wipe Supreme Authority Dek-Fook-Tek's mouth clear of any remaining chocolate chip cookie crumbs. He was the same servant who toothpicked the rice grain out from between two of Dek-Fook-Tek's rear molars. For the mouth-wipe, he used a napkin made of oskynt fur brought before the self-proclaimed ruler of all Tictoctic upon a gold platter. After that, he swiftly, quietly, unobtrusively withdrew from Dek-Fook-Tek's presence.

"And so," regally crisply tongue-clicked Dek-Fook-Tek, "we have experienced a most impressive display from these other-world beasts. That display has doubtless come about on account of their instinctive imperatives. I am reminded of the male keekakook. He used to spread open his hind feathers in a most colorful rainbow display. Then he alternated between bouncing upside down on his head and dancing on his three-toed feet. All of this, just to attract a female for mating! That was, of course, before we had to consume the remaining keekakooks to fend off our starvation. For my own mating needs, incidentally," the Supreme Authority added in a baaed aside, "such effort is unnecessary." He raised his eyes to direct everyone's attention to his unwieldy set of antlers. It was as though his fellow deer creatures didn't already know, and the other-worlders hadn't already guessed.

"All women tremble with delight before his towering sex organ, the same as they bow before his royal scepter." Lieutenant Ak-keek-teek beat Commander Kwit-Nik to lead the other Tictoctickians in offering up this ritual praise. Not that the commander really tried. The lieutenant made a sweeping arm gesture Dek-Fook-Tek's way as though he were introducing the Supreme Authority, or his sex organ, for the first time.

"And I thought adulation for the Fafamafalafama went to ridiculous lengths," Kevin commented to Dr. Deborah Davis-Murphy, back aboard the Smoke and Mirrors.

"We have their non-meat food, their special curious game, and even their various most elaborately constructed mating calls. Incredibly, those calls are recorded for playing over and over again for purely entertainment purposes," Dek-Fook-Tek was going on. "What the creatures from Akt have bestowed upon us, with the assistance of the mobile trees from Koombk, bespeaks a certain instinctive imperative. For sure, it is an imperative far different from the urge to copulate. It is an imperative that must have set in when special migratory hormones caused them to leave their original nesting planet.

"Well, for their efforts, we must remember when our immediate ancestors used to spare certain oskynt to perform in the circus. Those beasts delighted children by balancing one-legged on a seesaw. And now, I believe the other-worlders from Akt have earned special treats for how they have delighted *us*. Our original plan, of course, was to have most of this particular herd prepared for our culinary pleasure. Only scant few were to be spared the slaughterhouse nail through their skulls, so that we might test their breeding potential. But this would seem an especially undeserved fate to be visited upon so many of them."

Oh-oh; is he going to suggest it might not be so cruel for "the slaughterhouse nail" to be "visited upon" only one or two of us? This same question occurred simultaneously to Chris, Helena, Ali and Pedro. It made them all feel like a two-hundred-pound weight had been suddenly placed on their chests.

"What I order instead is that just one of them be sampled at this time. They can choose which one, but there is no need for worry. Whoever they choose may rest assured he or she has richly earned, and will most definitely receive, an honorary chest-goring. Even better, it will be conducted at the point of my very sharpest antler prong."

"The mercy of Dek-Fook-Tek frets over the slightest tear that might be inflicted upon the wing of the smallest klitflickity, on its daily nectar-gathering mission amongst the flowers." This was the ritual praise Lieutenant Ak-keek-teek led his fellow deer creatures to chant. Yet again, he usurped the commander's role in this endeavor.

But Kwit-Nik couldn't care less. He was too preoccupied formulating his protestation to Dek-Fook-Tek's decision, plus mustering up the courage to deliver it.

⟨≈ℋᵍ°⟨ℋᵍ°⟨ℋᵍ°

"This makes no sense!" Rek-mek-a-nek baaed at the top of his lungs. Captain Rek-mek-a-nek, that is, reassigned to the Fourth Celestial Breath. For the umpteenth time, he had rechecked his reading of a display screen on the navigation console. He still wasn't able to believe his eyes. "Who could possibly be firing up the magnetic pulse-beam from anywhere else but here?!" continued the captain with his complaint. He had long since become heedless of his droplets of stress-induced foamy drool. They were splattering the pulse-beam-activation monitor.

"Nays" of denial were bleated round the navigation bridge by other Tictoctickian officers. Earthlings with their eyes closed might have thought they landed amidst a flock of complaining sheep.

"Someone here has to be lying! Someone here knows something!" the captain insisted. Captain Rek-mek-a-nek brought down his forelimb, and stamped a cloven hoof-hand to denting effect against the control console. For him, it was an uncharacteristically violent display of anger and frustration. "Confess now, and succeed in aborting pulse-beam preparation, and the antler-slashing you receive will be reined in. It will be kept just short of fatal, I assure you." The captain strained to tongue-click without sliding into another shrill bray, lest his message's delivery belie its embedded promise of mercy. Also, he worked his finger-like articulated cloven hooves across the console keyboard in a flurry of tap-tap-taps. He was intent on aborting whatever attack was in the works.

The readying pulse beam reached an audible hum. It sent a vibration through everyone aboard as though they were receiving a mild electrical shock.

Captain Rek-mek-a-nek's furied effort was to no avail. "Impossible!" he tongue-clicked to himself more than anyone else. "Someone is overriding the circuit! But who?! Who?!" He looked up and around, only to find everyone regarding one another with nostril-twitching, ear-fluttering suspicion. None of them dared engage in any other activity. They didn't want to take a chance on something being construed as having the least thing to do with the magnetic pulse-beam activation. *This unauthorized attack preparation must be coming from somewhere other than the navigation bridge!* Rek-mek-a-nek concluded.

"Captain!" urgently tongue-clicked Officer Klik-Klak from the operational parameters console. "Our hull integrity monitor has just detected something the appearance of an oversized robotic klikityklak! Its eight legs are holding it attached to the Fourth Celestial Breath's underbelly!"

By then, the immense militarized flying saucer was glowing bright neon blue all the way around its rim. The magnetic pulse-beam was fully charged-up for firing on who-knew-what selected target.

Described by Officer Klik-Klak as a mechanical version of one of Tictoctic's most common and fearsomely large spiders, the drone was providing remote control.

Incidentally, that Tictoctic spider was a midget compared to the ahtpah of Fafama, but still...

⟡·⟡⟡·⟡⟡·⟡⟡·⟡

Officer Kekkekalek found himself twenty Earth miles south of Dek-Fook-Tek's sub-arctic command center. He was on planetary surface leave from duty aboard the Fifth Celestial Breath. And he had just taken his family into a fast food restaurant.

The restaurant's title would have translated as "Oskynt Meadows." A flashing-red, neon image of the legendary extinct beast was depicted shoveling a bite out of that title. Ali Magabu would have marveled at the slash-like lettering. It bore a striking resemblance to ancient Sumerian inscriptions back on Earth.

"You can play with your new toy later, Kookas," Officer Kekkekalek impatiently baaed at his five-solar-orbits-old son. The officer and his wife-for-the-day were being seated at a feeding trough.

The feeding trough was automatically antiseptically rinsed and superheated mere moments ago, in preparation for the next meal.

Officer Kekkekalek referred to the plastic toy oskynt every child received with the family meal. Press a button on the toy's belly, and its head flew off courtesy of spring action. The rest of the brown- and purple-mottled plastic body could be hung upside down on a small plastic likeness to a slaughterhouse meat hook. The toy meat hook travelled around on a hand-cranked toy conveyor belt. The conveyor belt was part of a toy slaughterhouse sold separately at participating clothes shops.

Officer Kekkekalek managed to snatch the flown-off plastic oskynt head from the floor before his son-for-a-day did. He secured it inside his pants pocket despite his son's bleated complaints. The officer's wife-for-a-day, Kootahtah, assured her son he would get back the toy oskynt head once he ate his fair share of supper.

Chunky slurry filled the trough to the level for a medium-sized-family meal. The slurry consisted of ground-up bits of Chonoran cartilage; a blood-and-fat mixture from sacrificed Tictoctickians both honorably slaughtered and punished for rebellion; real bits of oskynt hair; crushed herbs and spices; and artificially flavored milled grains incorporated as meat extender.

Officer Kekkekalek tore open the special flavor packet of desiccated klakkloptek body parts. They were harvested from Tictoctic's version of the palmetto cockroach. He was going to sprinkle them evenly like parmesan cheese atop the slurry when a strange rumble began.

At first, Officer Kekkekalek and everyone else in the restaurant, even his son-for-a-day, dismissed the rumble as nothing out of the ordinary. It had to be just another jet or hybrid space vehicle. Obviously it was leaving from or coming in for a landing at the Supreme Authority's command center, several lek-leks north. But then that rumble grew louder and louder. Very quickly, everything and everyone in the Oskynt Meadows franchise was shaking as in a strong earthquake. Windows blew in, pelting customers and restaurant workers alike with shards that left them covered in streaks of blood.

Most first reactions were to hungrily lick and lap at one another's wounds. But that only lasted until the realization fully set in of glass shards cutting up tongues.

All Officer Kekkekalek could do was wonder at the telltale flash of blue light. He knew it had to have originated with a targeted magnetic pulse-beam attack from outside Tictoctic's atmosphere. The officer asked himself what monsters could have done this.

The massive hospital and soldier-rehabilitation complex across the street was reduced to a smoldering ruin.

Someone ran from the devastation, whether a doctor or a patient. He was completely engulfed by flames, save for his uppermost antler prongs.

◦ ┌⊙◦ ◦ ┌⊙◦ ◦ ┌⊙◦

462 | David Taylor

"Supreme Dek-Fook-Tek," Commander Kwit-Nik boldly rose to say. Thereby did he put fellow deer creatures on notice the coup was about to begin. Of course, Lieutenant Ak-keek-teek and Counselor Kootlek were left out of that particular loop. "I appeal to your sense of reason," the commander went on. "Consider what you have ordered from the perspective of these other-world visitors. I am braying about your proposal they choose 'only' one of their own for addition to our food supply, as opposed to several. Expecting the other-worlders to regard that proposal as generous is highly unrealistic. I am no mind reader, unlike the tree creatures they brought along with them. However, it does not require mind reading to imagine what they are thinking. I suspect they don't care how much you might sharpen the fatal prong with your bahvek. They still regard even one of their own being subjected to slaughter as horrifically cruel. Else why would they go to such lengths to try persuading us we should adopt a non-meat diet? Why else would they argue that going vegetarian will prove far more beneficial for our health in the long gallop?"

"Buuurrrrrrrpp!" Dek-Fook-Tek's counselor Kootlek couldn't hold back his belch any longer.

"On this same theme, Dek-Fook-Tek," Kwit-Nik went on even further, "I must also address the notion of 'honoring' some other-worlders with your personal chest-slashing. Excepting the other-worlder to be slaughtered, you assure them it will remain shallowly non-fatal. For certain, many of your subjects dream of you bestowing such wounding upon them. Some even want you to refreshen their scars. But it is not difficult to imagine other-worlders bringing a different perspective. That they cannot see past the likely painfulness. There is also the potential danger for something to go deadly wrong, as it sometimes admittedly does. Remember, the other-worlders did not grow up in our culture."

"Commander Kwit-Nik, your empathy for lower animals is nearly as charming as it is ridiculous," Dek-Fook-Tek hee-hawed.

Lieutenant Ak-keek-teek bared his buck teeth in agreement.

"About the 'lower animals' part," Kwit-Nik nodded in acknowledgement, only, of the characterization the Supreme Authority gave.

Dek-Fook-Tek and Ak-keek-teek froze still, save for a commotion of snout wriggles and ear flutters evidencing their agitation.

"You said something about the kayfafas, Supreme Dek-Fook-Tek." Commander Kwit-Nik spoke deferentially anew. He was giving Dek-Fook-Tek every last opportunity *not* to become irrationally unhinged.

When Dek-Fook-Tek finally did lose self-control again, any remaining doubts the coup must proceed would be trampled upon as by a herd of stampeding oskynt. At least, that's how a fellow Tictoctickian would have put it.

"What you pointed out, Supreme Authority, was the kayfafas were transformed nearly overnight," observed Kwit-Nik. "They went from docile and peaceful creatures to becoming killer sea monsters. That is, once we started hunting them. Imagine the kayfafas had possessed such weapons and space vehicles as our visitors use. Imagine the havoc they would have wreaked upon us."

Dek-Fook-Tek's nostrils flared wider and wider, exactly as expected.

Undaunted, Commander Kwit-Nik tongue-clicked as crisply as ever, "But I submit to you something even more profound we must dare to face, dare to realize. These creatures here with us today," he turned to Tanya

Petrovsky at his one side, then Chris Olsen-Taylor at his other. "We must recognize they are sentient beings on equal hoofing with ourselves. They offer us peace, a kind, gentle peace. We should seize the opportunity they are bestowing upon us."

Dek-Fook-Tek abruptly reared up from the dining table onto his two hind legs. He rose to his full, imposing height. He did this as swiftly as his antler handlers could facilitate, pulling on marionette-type strings from up above the ceiling. With his fore-hoof, he pounded down hard on his dessert plate. Only minutes earlier, he had been lapping up the last remaining crumbs there of his chocolate chip cookie. He pounded down so hard that he shattered the plate into several shards. And he brayed at the top of his lungs, "COMMANDER!! TELL ME WHAT SPECIAL MIND-PARALYZING SECRETIONS THESE OTHER-WORLD BEASTS HAVE CAUSED YOU TO INHALE, TO SO TWIST YOUR THOUGHT PROCESSES!! I REMIND YOU WHAT THOSE CHONORAN ANIMALS DID WHEN WE WELCOMED THEM TO OUR PLANET!! THEY ATTACKED US!!"

Commander Kwit-Nik nodded at various guards. Dek-Fook-Tek was in too much of a mouth-frothing rage to realize they were taking their positions for the imminent coup. Only then, just as determinedly calmly as before, did Kwit-Nik respond. "Actually," he said, "to welcome the Chonorans to our planet, one of our own renegades unilaterally fired most ineffectual pellets at them. That is what happened in our first encounter with the Chonorans. Yes, their response proved disproportionately aggressive. However, the fact remains-"

"BAAAEEEEEEEEE!!!!!" Dek-Fook-Tek shrieked uncontrollably, so piercingly that the Earthlings covered their ears. He lunged at the dining table. Aided as always by his antler handlers, he swung his head wildly from side to side. The resultant wide sweeps of his oversized antlers sent dishes and cups flying shattered apart in all directions. They also shredded the light-olive-colored tablecloth made of finest kooptapook silk.

Commander Kwit-Nik's purposefully understated response sent the coded message for initiating the coup. "Dek-Fook-Tek would appear to be out of control."

With this, the antler handlers up above the ceiling started to rein in the Supreme Authority's destructive behavior. They fancied themselves cattle rustlers of old. They could have been pulling a male oskynt out of the mating pen to be returned to his own.

That is as far as anyone got with the coup, when two messengers entered the Great Gathering Trough at full gallop. "Urgent! Urgent!" they brayed in unison. Then they brought themselves down to bow beside Dek-Fook-Tek where he had just finished so destructively clearing the table.

"YES!?!?" Dek-Fook-Tek snorted, sending globs of frothy drool splattering against the messengers' stubby antlers. Once more, he pounded his hoof-hand hard against the dining table. He pounded so hard that eating utensils as much as the rubble from broken dishes and cups danced up and down. Thereby was produced a multiplicity of incongruously delicate-sounding tinkles. "WHAT NOW??!!??!!??"

"Supreme Authority, the most Supreme Authority ever, Dek-Fook-Tek..." The messenger who answered was unnerved by Dek-Fook-Tek's evident anger over he had no idea what. He feared looking up as he mustered the courage to continue humbly baaing, "The Dek-Fook-Tek Hospital for the Care and Rehabilitation of the Sick, the Elderly and- and our Wounded Soldier Heroes has been attacked. A magnetic pulse-beam made a direct hit resulting in its total destruction. And- And that beam issued from the Fourth Celestial Breath."

"The Fourth Celestial Breath?" Dek-Fook-Tek repeated. He baaed faintly, for once overcome more by bafflement than rage. "That was assigned to the newly promoted Captain Rek-mek-a-nek."

"Correct as always, Supreme Dek-Fook-Tek." The messenger did not expect such a muted reaction to his awful news. So he allowed himself a fleeting glance at the Supreme Authority before continuing, "Captain Rek-mek-a-nek has ascertained something most horrific with one hundred percent confidence. A device with the appearance of an enormous, metallic bug latched on to the Fourth Celestial Breath's underbelly. From there, it hijacked the operation of the magnetic pulse-beam weaponry. Best as the captain can tell, an as-yet-unidentified entity of unknown origin was behind this."

"Baa! Baa!" bleated Dek-fook-Tek triumphantly. He pounded on the dining table with sudden, joyful zest. "Do you understand now, Commander Kwit-Nik?! Does it penetrate your thick skull how these inherently devious small animals of monstrous intent have deceived you?! How they have distracted you from their actual plans?! You would have been wiser to have taken Lieutenant Ak-keek-teek's warnings more seriously!"

Ak-keek-teek bared his buck teeth anew in one of his absurdly oversized smiles.

Commander Kwit-Nik rose from his seat, chest swelled out vulnerably for an antler slashing. He gave Captain Helena Taylor a fleeting look expressive of ultimate betrayal before tongue-clicking, "The moments I stay alive past this most dramatic proof of my too-naïve nature are moments I do not deserve, my Supreme Authority Dek-Fook-Tek."

Tictoctickians everywhere had already long since concluded they needed to cancel the coup. Their planet's single most powerful entity might be completely crazy. However, his unparalleled judgment was still needed. It might be the only thing keeping them safe from what had proven time and again to be most dangerous other-world species. That's how the prevailing thought went.

Some Tictoctickians did persist with their belief they would be better off not led by such a mentally imbalanced fellow deer creature. But they took the commander's offering himself up for immediate execution as the clearest possible stand-down.

"I have to say something!" Helena Taylor interjected as she also rose to her feet, not bothering to ask permission. She figured there was nothing to lose. And besides, what needed to be pointed out was better coming from her aloud than from one of the tree creatures attempting another telepathic intervention. This time, sixth sense messaging was most likely to get blown off by Dek-Fook-Tek as some personal inner demon set on undermining himself. That was, if his paranoia did not move him to suspect a mind-poisoning process that originated with the other-worlders. He had already suggested Kwit-Nik might be succumbing to just such a malady. "We have travelled here from our far, far distant home world," went on Helena. "We have put our lives in jeopardy for peace. But there are others of our kind who have been long set on war against you. They believe that is the only practical choice. We had hoped those people would give us enough time to finish exploring an alternative. Now, maybe the pulse-beam attack on your hospital did originate from some other source. More than likely, though, it seems our war believers have gone ahead and tried to accelerate a violent confrontation. Still I plead with you, Supreme Dek-Fook-Tek. Do not give up on the peaceful alternative! We have come so far! Please don't allow this stupid, barbaric act by some of our own to ruin everything! I am not sure that all-out war between our two planets will result in anything other than total destruction, everywhere, on both sides!"

Once more not deigning to address any Earthling directly, Dek-Fook-Tek turned Commander Kwit-Nik's way. He curtly, crisply tongue-clicked what translated as, "I wonder. Why does she not mention her species have destroyed one of our other planets of interest? Foolishly not even thinking to salvage any of its inhabitants' bodies for helping maintain their food supply?"

"The ruler of that other planet put our weaponry to an unintended use! Our weaponry was supposed to protect them from extraterrestrial threats! But he misused it to try and eliminate a domestic terrorist threat! He did that rather than addressing the domestic threat's root causes! The result only proves my point!"

This time, Supreme Authority Dek-Fook-Tek turned Lieutenant Ak-keek-teek's way for his response to the Earthling's desperate protestations. "I suppose I allowed it to go on at this length because the behavior of cornered animals always fascinates me. Undoubtedly millions of solar orbits were necessary for such deceitful behavior to evolve.

"In any event, we must realize something in order to avoid the fate of the other planet. We have to meet instinctively programmed cunning with intelligently designed cunning, the superior cunning by far.

"I wasted too much time contemplating those other-world beasts going about their supposedly generous labors on our behalf. But most fortunately, I did not stop at hoping for the best. No!" Dek-Fook-Tek shook his head imperiously slowly from side to side, enormous antlers and all. "Exercising my military strategizing, I simultaneously planned for the worst. Keepers of the crypts!" He knocked together his two cloven hoof-hands. Again, the sound they made reminded Helena and the other humans of two wooden blocks being knocked together.

Two sets of doors swung wide, like two sets of French doors. Four other deer creature Tictoctickians entered. They bore a pair of long, sleek, rectangular, aluminum boxes.

One solid thud after the other, both boxes were lowered to the floor. Then the Tictoctickians unfastened special latches to open them.

They might as well have been opening the tops of two coffins, the humans thought with a collective shiver.

"One for each of their tree creatures," Dek-Fook-Tek explained.

Already, two Tictoctickians tipped over Oodle-Noodle and Wafoodle-boodle. They would lift the ends closest to the Oombians' eyes, which were welling up with maple-syrupy tears. The other two Tictoctickians would lift the Oombians by their ciliated root bottoms.

"An element of surprise is critical for my tricking into the open the perpetrators of barbarism! And let us not forget it is not just barbarism! It is barbarism inflicted without provocation upon my fellow beings!" Dek-Fook-Tek explained while the tree creatures found themselves lowered into the metallic boxes. "Surprise is also critical," he went on, "for proof of the tree creatures' connection to these beasts and their instinctively constructed starship. A starship, I might add, of awkward, inefficient design. It is exactly as to be expected when animal behavior mimics that of authentically intelligent beings.

"Anyway, for the element of surprise to actually happen, there is something we cannot allow. Mental telepathy from these outrageously mobile tree creatures of Koombk simply has to be stopped! That's where the boxes into which they are being lowered come into play. They are lined with material we have found supremely effective not only for safely containing plutonium and other radioactive materials. That material also works extremely well for closing off, shutting down weak-force telepathic powers we have discovered among a few of our fellow Tictoctickians."

This is okay, Earthling friends, Oodle-Noodle started to telepath Captain Taylor and the other humans. She was not only addressing people in the meal hall. She was also directing her telepaths nearly a million miles away, towards the Smoke and Mirrors in high orbit around Tictoctic. *We are capable of suspending our respiration for-* That's as far as Oodle-Noodle got before the lid was sealed on her box with a deep thud!

"The next time those crypts are opened will be to set their contents aflame, for roasting the Akt creatures! That is the price of doing business with deceitful beasts of the interplanetary wild! Guards, seize the other-worlders from Akt! Take them away to the slaughterhouse! Chef Glork-tek, for my evening meal I want to see a choice cut of the self-professed captain served to me upon a silver platter!"

"From our past experience, Supreme Authority," humbly baaed Chef Glork-tek, "I must warn you about the stress hormones these creatures are doubtless presently secreting throughout their system. It could seriously compromise their flavor profiles. Given a little additional time-"

"If you are not prepared to serve up the so-called captain most deliciously this evening, I will find someone else who is!"

Chapter 24

"This looks to be going far better than any damnably damned thing I could fairly have expected, Prissy! So much for Oodles of Strudels' last telepath before she abruptly left us with *nothing*! She's probably figured it ain't worth arguing with us anymore. Either that, or for all we know, this very moment them demon stag are chopping her up into so much kindling wood! They really had no way to verify what she was putting in our heads. Oodles of Strudels could have assured them she had ceased all communication with us, but then gone ahead and told us whatever she wanted! I doubt they would have been so dumb as not to realize that!"

"Yes, Dear."

"Prissy, you've got to set down that sock long enough to take in this spectacle! Just look at it! Bigger saucers firing on littler saucers! Littler saucers firing on bigger saucers! Now you tell me: Were they really going to just randomly turn on each other? Was that really going to be a thing if some mysterious outside force – that's us – hadn't blown up one of their military bases?!?!"

"Of course not, Dear."

Michel DeFarge had taken the Elusive into geosynchronous orbit around Tictoctic a mere hundred thousand miles above the planet's surface. This was down much closer than DeFarge dared go before. He was trusting that the Tictoctickians wouldn't figure out any time soon how wildly their space station radar tracking got misdirected. Nor that the subtle star-field distortions the Tictoctickians were already noticing were the result of the Elusive's cloaking·technology. That this technology was bending light from one side around to the other side of the Elusive as it cruised along.

Michel DeFarge had his economy-sized battleship hiding out in the open. And he was using a magniview function for a better look at the seeming chaos, transpiring not far from the outermost limits of the Tictoctickian atmosphere.

And seeming chaos it was. DeFarge put the Elusive into orbit too distant from the main action to notice something important, despite the magniview. None of the various Tictoctickian spacecraft, whether large or small, was actually inflicting damage. The captains were careful to just miss their supposed targets. They were striking harmless, glancing blows at worst, yet still providing a maximum amount of detail-obscuring fireworks. All the better to flush the bad guy out into the open. The bad guy being, of course, the one who operated the drone found attached to the Fourth Celestial Breath. He was probably directly responsible for the entirely unprovoked terrorist attack on the hospital, as the Tictoctickians saw it.

"There we go, Prissy! There we go!" DeFarge pointed excitedly. "Weave those socks directly onto my feet, if that's not one of our shuttle pods lifting away unnoticed from the melee!! One guess where she's headed!"

"Back to the Smoke and Mirrors."

"The same! But we're not going to attempt direct contact! Not yet! First we have to make good and sure our too-naïve friends have been able to dock safely, without incident! Then we'll reveal ourselves, and hopefully all skee-daddle outta...Well I'll be damnably damned!" Captain Michel DeFarge slapped hand against forehead. A question had been nagging him. Namely, why wasn't one of those tree creatures re-establishing sixth-sense communication with him? Shouldn't that be happening if the shuttle pod approaching the Smoke and Mirrors was full of good guys? However, a sudden realization temporarily overrode that concern. "Think I understand now why the demon stag have a circular firing squad going on!" DeFarge exclaimed. "It was just sitting out there in front of me, so obvious I nearly missed it! Don't know, can't tell, whether the crew aboard that saucer discovered our drone clutching at their underbelly like some damnably damned barnacle. You'd think they would have by now! I couldn't very well reel it back in without their tracing it back to us, in any event. Which is why, of course, it was programmed to permanently scramble its circuit boards after it attacked. The point is this. The rest of those furry-assed critters, blasphemously weaponed-up in all contradiction to what should accrue with the natural order, they must have spotted the drone. Then they must have concluded the attack on their military installation issued from the saucer where it was attached! So they retaliated against the saucer, the saucer fired back, and it all went up shit creek from there!"

"Dear, your language."

"Oh, sorry Prissy." As DeFarge apologized, he also found himself drawn back to fearfully wondering: Why the telepathic blackout from the tree people? Maybe Oodle-whatever-her-name had to be left behind for the others to escape. Or maybe she was too preoccupied helping with the escape. To that end, perhaps she was busy putting sabotaging thoughts in the demon stag's heads, such as, *Captain So-and-so has such a big set of antlers, he's thinking about dueling it out with the supreme furry-ass!* Or, and this explanation struck DeFarge as more plausible. *Oodle MacStrudel is royally Tictocticked-off at me for my military action! For hijack-firing that magnetic pulse-beam to blow up some stuff and probably a couple of bad guys into the bargain, as well! With all her peace-*

and-love candies and nutty nuts, she is just too damnably damned pissed to telepath me, ever again! Sorry 'bout my language, Prissy, if you've learned how to mind-read also. Anyhoo, maybe I'm getting the ESP version of the silent treatment! Yeah! That has to be it!

Michel snapped his fingers in frustration. Despite the varied explanations he conjured, his unsettled feeling stubbornly refused to let go. It didn't help that those explanations just provoked more questions. For example, how could the demon stag not have become aware of the drone attached to their saucer's underbelly? Once they did become aware, wouldn't they have alerted their fellow stag aboard other spacecraft? And then wouldn't those fellow stag have foregone blaming them directly for the pulse-beam attack on land-based targets? Which would have also meant no space war of the kind that appeared to be unfolding just outside the Tictoctickian atmosphere? These new questions only compounded Captain DeFarge's anxiety over why the telepathic blackout from the tree creatures.

"Well there we have it, Prissy." DeFarge waved his hand towards their spacecraft's panoramic view-screen.

The "there" DeFarge was referring to had to do with the Smoke and Mirrors. Its lengthy cylindrical hull, the "asparagus stem," was studded at regular intervals with pointy stabilizer "thorns." In between two of those "thorns," a landing bay had neatly opened out of the hull. That was DeFarge's "there," presumably to receive the shuttle pod.

"Their scout vehicle will soon be tucked inside, snug as a bug in a rug, Prissy. Soon as it is, I say we reveal our presence," said DeFarge. "They should recognize us from the Elusive's design, like a pint-sized Smoke and Mirrors. Then we see if they have room for us. If not, of course we'll skee-daddle out of here the same way we made our entrance, along a parallel path with the S and M. Meanwhile, hopefully the enemy continues their self-inflicted wounds. The longer they do, the weaker they'll become before they can launch their invasion. And mind you, it's an invasion for which we will be more than ready! Especially now, since we have the piggyback drones for turning their weapons against them! You with me, Prissy?" *Help me strangle my pesky nagging doubts?*

For a rare occasion, Prissy set aside her knitting to look up at Michel. "Dear," she said, "don't you think we should re-establish some form of communication with the Smoke and Mirrors before we decloak? Just to make certain?"

"Wo!" DeFarge shook his head as in, *This can't be! You can't be siding with my inner nag!* "Let's suppose we signal them, dear Prissy, or they signal us. Either way, there might be one of those Tictoctickians not too busy lobbing pulse-beams at each other to monitor transmissions. He will receive a 'heads up' about someone else here from outta town, besides the Smoke and Mirrors!

"Look, Prissy, how about this? After we decelerate enough, we are going to automatically decloak. But we're going to *have* to decelerate if we're going to enter their docking bay. So how 'bout we delay re-establishment of communication with our naïve friends aboard the S and M for when we decloak, and not a moment sooner? If they don't give us some positive sign immediately thereafter, we don't take any chances! No! We speed outta here fast as this contraption can carry us! How's that?"

"You do what you think is best, Dear." Prissy had already resumed her knitting.

Confound that woman! I hope this isn't going to go how it often goes when she crosses me. Not only is she proven correct, but my face is rubbed into the mud with how correct she is, and how wrong I was! This went through Michel DeFarge's head while the Elusive's deceleration gradually decloaked it.

For any observer, the Elusive would have seemed a sudden mist exhaled into the dark emptiness of space from an invisible source. Pursuant to which it would have consolidated as a blurry mass assuming ever-sharper focus, glinting in the starlight.

"You see that, Prissy?! There!" Captain DeFarge was pointing excitedly at the view-screen again. "They've rolled out the red carpet for us! They must maintain an extra landing bay for spacecraft besides their shuttle pods! That's the positive sign we were looking for!"

"Yes, Dear."

DeFarge maneuvered the Elusive drifting into the newly opened hangar, near where he saw the shuttle pod enter the Smoke and Mirrors. He accomplished this feat most comfortably. However, his wife's noncommittal response haunted him. It aggravated his queasiness over the lack of any further signs of life from the immense starship. That is, other than the aforementioned revelation of a second parking spot.

When Michel DeFarge executed a similar maneuver to dock inside the Barack Obama, he got to enjoy a little banter with the docking attendant. But there was no banter this time. Instead, Michel had to keep rationalizing for his continued duel with his nagging doubt.

Yes, the fireworks show proceeded unabated near Tictoctic. The Tictoctickian space fleet still seemed at war with itself. Yet that's where Michel's rationalizing came into play. Say he'd followed his wife's advice. In other words, say he'd initiated contact with the Smoke and Mirrors before the Elusive had flown anywhere near it.

Wouldn't such contact have drawn the demon stag's attention away from their self-destruction? Wouldn't that have been the only thing necessary to redirect their fireworks towards the good guys?

⸎⟒⟊⟒⟒⟒⟊⟒⟒⟒⟊⟒⟒⸎

"Prissy? You're going to want to come out here for this! Officer Kevin Smith-Park is conducting the official greeting! Um, I remember him on the news, an interview after the S and M's first mission!

"Hey, Officer Smith-Park!!! I recognize you! You're something of a celebrity, aren't you?"

Kevin smiled wanly. He was unable to force himself to open his mouth for fear if he said the wrong thing...

"Um, pardon my saying this, Officer. But, umm..." DeFarge couldn't help prattling on nervously. His inner nagging had crescendoed to a steady scream.

Kevin Smith-Park had long since rounded a corner to meet Michel DeFarge. He already stood at the bottom of the exit ramp from the securely docked Elusive. And what he offered Michel was nothing more than an eerily silent handshake.

Michel double-checked his pants. Maybe, he wanted to believe, he forgot to zip them all the way up after he unstrapped himself from his navigation seat. "Umm," he repeated once he finished his fruitless self-inspection. "Pardon me, like I said. But this feels like you're welcoming us to someone's damnably damned funeral w-"

"I am Lieutenant Koostookalek and this is Officer Keekteek," the lieutenant's harsh braying translated. He and his fellow Tictoctickian rounded the same corner Officer Smith-Park had rounded, to come into full view for Michel DeFarge. Each deer creature held an air igniter aimed directly at DeFarge.

"P-Prissy, honey, I'm sorry! You're going to *have* to come out here, now!" DeFarge raised his hands to surrender, but he still found the wherewithal to think to himself, *Well I'll be damnably damned! Maybe for the last time, my nose has gotten rubbed in Prissy's being correct again, after all! And this one is a real, fatal doozy!*

"Oh, bother," Priscilla DeFarge could be heard complaining from inside the Elusive. She gathered together her knitting supplies while Officer Keekteek stormed past her husband to yank her out.

"Under the direction of Supreme Authority Dek-Fook-Tek- Wait, why am I bothering to formally address a lower species?"

"We've found the rest of them, Lieutenant! You were correct!" erupted Officer Kykeetot. His tongue-clicking crackled from Koostookalek's wristband. For Michel, those tongue-clicks sounded near-simultaneous with their English translation via Kevin's waistband-bound translator.

"Where there is one niki-nik you will always find several more," went on Officer KyKeetot to Koostookalek. KyKeetot was reporting from deep inside the Smoke and Mirrors. "The Akt beasts lied to Captain Rek-mek-a-nek about certain compartments of this instinctively wrought, space-faring exoskeleton," the officer added. "They claimed those compartments were storage rooms. Or that they were the internal organs which organically facilitated surpassing light-speed.

"Those compartments are nothing of the sort! Rather, they are like the maze of hidden compartments within a typical niki-nik hill. We all know about the niki-nik maze, how it protects a colony from the probing, vacuuming nostrils of the serpent-snouted kahkvakt. In this case, the maze concealed enough other-world beasts, Lieutenant, to keep the entire crew of a Celestial Breath well-fed for twenty days."

"I hear you, Officer KyKeetot! Please remember, though, we are under explicit orders from Commander Kwit-Nik. However great the temptation, we are to postpone such an indulgence as you suggest until Chef Glork-tek gives the all-safe go-ahead. That being re-masticated, exactly what size concealed herd are we talking about?"

"Well, Lieutenant, surprisingly it includes two Konokans."

"Two Konokans?!" Lieutenant Koostookalek lifted his head high with his shock. His antlers scraped the low ceiling in the starship's shuttle pod exit corridor.

"Not only that, but they have been with the Akt beasts long enough for the Akt translator to actually function three ways. It translates our language, the Akt language called Kenklist (English), and what we had previously assumed was sheer gibberish issuing from the beaks of the KonoKans."

"Well that is another surprise, Officer!"

"Another surprise indeed, Lieutenant! However, the Konokan who calls himself Kig-kek is a special case. I will grant that the Akt translator is correct. I will accept there is more to Konokan utterances than mere flikity chirps. But again, in the case of Kig-kek, what issues from his beaked orifice is total nonsense! The translator might as well be reading shapes into clouds! And it is not simply nonsense, either! It is irritating nonsense! It is nonsense so irritating that his fellow Konokan literally wrapped one arm round his fat head! He did that in order to seal a suction disc directly over his mouth! Otherwise, I was ready to commit an act of insubordination by roasting Kig-kek right there on the spot with my air igniter, no permission asked of you. My goal would have been to ingest his tongue before all else. I feared the off chance it might yet be able to make a noise from beyond death if it wasn't chewed and swallowed out of existence!"

"And what exactly did the Kig-Kek creature say that was of such irritation, Officer?"

"There were several details, Lieutenant. His basic message was that he didn't want to be led to slaughter in any apparel too fancy. He was hoping to wear something simple, yet elegant, something that demonstrated-"

"I get the idea, Officer! And must commend your powers of restraint! They surely issue straight from Dek-Fook-Tek himself, considering!"

"Esteemed Lieutenant, do you think we might be able to go ahead and help ourselves to that nuisance Konokan? From his bulbous head alone, I would guess one of our chefs can produce a batch of morale-boosting jerky snacks for an entire saucer crew. Besides, his fellow beast won't be able to keep his beak sealed forever. Who knows when he might express something even more antlers-scraping-a-granite-wall irritating than we have already endured?"

Michel DeFarge was able to understand every word exchanged by the lieutenant with the officer elsewhere in the Smoke and Mirrors. The officer's disembodied voice variously brayed and tongue-clicked from the lieutenant's wristband communicator. But Kevin's translator crackled with the English translation near-instantaneously.

DeFarge could have done without it. He wouldn't have had to suffer through the Tictoctickians discussing consumption of sentient beings. Their tone was casual, but the content of their conversation made Michel's beating heart feel like a hammer in his chest. It made no difference that the meal preparation of a Chonoran, not a fellow Earthling, was what had come under consideration. Regardless, for Michel there might as well have been a sharp spike of hopelessness. And that spike was driven down deeper and deeper, ever deeper into the core of his being.

Poor Prissy! Usually so cool and reserved, presently she trembled visibly. She was hanging on for dear life to her knitting project gathered up most awkwardly in her arms. Michel wished he had listened to her like he had never wished he had listened to her before. Yes, he really should have sought better confirmation all was well aboard the Smoke and Mirrors. He should have done that prior to having the Elusive make a beeline for one of its shuttle bays.

Michel tried to inch closer to Prissy, for comforting her. However, he received immediate pushback from the muzzle of Officer Keekteek's air igniter.

"I wouldn't think that would be an issue, Officer KyKeekot." Lieutenant Koostookalek was responding to KyKeekot's famished request to at least be allowed to transform Chig-cher into so much chewable jerky. "But I better check with Commander Kwit-Nik. Before we take a bite out of any of those relic Konokans, he might want to find out more about them. For example, just exactly how were they still left alive, to end up aboard this other-worlder space-worthy exoskeleton? Speaking of which, my original question about the number of other..."

"Yes, Lieutenant, of course. The rest of them are from Akt. There are two males of older-looking flesh. They will likely pose a special culinary tenderizing challenge, even for Chef Glork-tek. There is one other adult, in addition to the one we caught originally. A female. The flesh from both of them should tenderize perfectly. But, about that adult male we caught originally. He was trying to make his way back through an air vent to the hidden-away area. Which led us to find the other-worlders' secluded chambers in the first place. The only other Akt creatures we discovered there were two young males, and lastly, one even younger female."

"Lieutenant Koostookalek," said an armed guard just returned from checking around inside the Elusive.

"Thank you, Officer Kykeekot!" said Lieutenant Koostookalek into his wristband device while motioning for the armed guard to hang on. "I'll have to get back to you in a few mini-pektels. In the meantime, let me repeat: No snack-making until I update the commander."

"Inspired by Dek-Fook-Tek," were the last words Lieutenant Koostookalek heard issuing from his wristband device, from Kykeekot, before he shut it off. Then he turned to the officer who had just barged in from his inspection of the other-world smaller spacecraft. He crisply tongue-clicked to him, "Officer Kookytook, what have you learned of significance?"

"Lieutenant, I have learned there are three other drones stored aboard the miniature space-worthy exoskeleton. They are of the same kind as the one that latched on to the Fourth Celestial Breath."

"Baa, yes," nodded Lieutenant Koostookalek knowingly. "You mean to say they are of the same kind of drone that hijacked a magnetic pulse-beam for destroying Dek-Fook-Tek's hospital complex."

On hearing this translation, Priscilla looked up to meet Michel's dumb-founded stare. Both humans knew they were thinking the same thing.

A hospital complex! The tree creature's worry over the drone's degree of accuracy was not unwarranted.

Although Michel went on to think, all by himself, *There's a problem with the drone-hijacking technology, for sure. Now we'll never know the result, had we made a precision hit on the demon stag's military command center. Would that have allowed our damnably naïve fellow Earthlings trapped in there to have actually escaped? Still, we succeeded in stirring up the hornet's nest! Only, we need some way to alert our folks back near Oomb! They also need to know that the demon stag confiscated the rest of our drones! Thank God their programming will automatically scramble like eggs once someone fiddles with them who is unfamiliar with their operation! I hope!* Michel DeFarge's heartbeat pounded stronger than ever with his off-the-charts anxiety.

"Lieutenant, we are receiving a high priority call from Commander Kwit-Nik!" suddenly blared tongue-clicks from an overhead intercom while Kevin's translator continued its impressive job keeping up. "Shall I patch through?"

"Officer Klunkatunk, *all* calls from Commander Kwit-Nik are high priority calls! Patch through fast, before any more of the commander's time is wasted than has elapsed already!"

"Lieutenant Koostookalek," said Commander Kwit-Nik, "you have secured the terrorist, *and* the vehicle he used for executing the hospital attack?"

"Commander Kwit-Nik, I am happy to report: Thanks to Dek-Fook-Tek's divine inspiration, we have secured not only the spacecraft and the terrorist, but his female companion as well. She was found busy knitting something. I believe our biologists would explain she was as a kikpik weaving a web. Maybe like a kikpik, she instinctively planned to entangle the male terrorist for mating, during which she would have lopped off his head."

"Baa, maybe this is the same story for all animals from Akt," the commander speculated. "In which case, it could prove a more merciful way we can have their males slaughtered. Plus, there might be the added benefit of suppressing their bodies' expression of flavor-compromising chemicals." Commander Kwit-Nik didn't actually believe any of this himself. He was indulging such speculation for the sake of misdirection.

"It is a pasture full of pleasure to operate under your direction, Commander, as inspired as you clearly are by the bountiful compassion of Dek-Fook-Tek."

"You are welcome, Lieutenant," said Kwit-Nik. But he brayed inside his head at how mischievously he made himself sound like the inanely egotistical "Supreme Authority." Then he went on, "I can guess Dek-Fook-Tek's inclination. He will want the two other-world animals *and* their miniature space vessel brought down here to the surface of Tictoctic as soon as possible. Baa," Kwit-Nik baaed with affected nonchalance. "A last thing for now: Did you happen to discover any other of those drones? I mean, like the one used to hijack operation of the Fourth Celestial Breath's magnetic pulse-beam?"

"Three drones in all, Commander! The terrorist vessel that is carrying them, I will personally pilot it back to the Fourth Celestial Breath. Also included, of course, will be the terrorist and his female companion bound and tied under armed guard. From the Fourth Celestial Breath, we will make galloping haste for delivering the entire lot to the royal command post. But what should we do with the other other-worlders? Baa." It was Lieutenant Koostookalek's turn to affect disinterested nonchalance. "Many officers here have been making noises they want to sample this herd. Officer Keety-Kooty is something of an amateur chef, baa. Could you possibly grant permission for him to test-snack just a forelimb off one of the Konokans or younger calves? We are well aware of the danger. That such an indulgence could induce an adverse reaction. So we would be careful to exclude any essential personnel from our tasting experiment."

"As reasonable as you make it sound, Lieutenant, permission denied. Chef Glork-tek prepared a sample dinner course from an Akt specimen secured during the too-temporary liberation of Koombk. Unfortunately, though, the flavor was found so distasteful as to induce projectile regurgitation after a single bite. As for the Konokans, before we slice and dice them, we need to learn a lot more. How did the Akt creatures come into their possession when they were thought to have already gone extinct?"

"I did not know about the projectile regurgitation, Commander."

"It is not something anyone in the high command wanted to have in general dissemination," Kwit-Nik went on to further embellish his total fabrication. "Chef Glork-tek is convinced the main issue lies with those pesky stress hormones. We have to find a way to gently ease these animals into slaughter. But once we do, there will be no reason to hold back. Their flesh should prove every bit as appetizingly flavorful as the most tenderly marinated and roasted Konokan butt cheeks."

"Yum."

"Yum, indeed. So where have you herded the additional other-world beasts you discovered on board? And are you certain you have secured all of them? Are you willing to bet your life there are not any more in hiding? Could there be some as-yet un-searched nook or cranny of the other-world starship?"

"Excellent questions, Commander Kwit-Nik. Not only have we thoroughly searched and re-searched every possible hiding space. On one of their navigation bridge control consoles, we have discovered a life sign monitor. That monitor reconfirms the exact location of every creature, no matter how small, aboard this space-faring, colony-sized exoskeleton. Included are our own selves plus a few other-world insects. And as for that herd from Akt, we have every last one of them rounded up inside one of the larger chambers. The air vents there are sealed off with extra wire mesh. None of those beasts can sneak away, how we discovered there were places for them to sneak away to in the first place."

"That is good, Lieutenant. But you should also have them bound and tied, in such a manner they will be unable to nibble through their ropes. We know from past experience how sneakily resourceful they can most assuredly prove."

Chapter 25

Only Officer Pedro Perez had a recollection of the slaughterhouse assembly line to draw from. His experience came prior to the alternate reality where, and when, Buddy Leung rescued him and a group of Marines.

Pedro's prior experience happened while captive aboard the Third Celestial Breath, departed from Oomb. That immense flying saucer was flown by deer creatures from the planet Tictoctic. They intended to sample human meat for its viability as a supplement to the perilously low Tictoctickian food supply. However, Buddy time-travelled a shuttle pod to catch up with them before they could leave solar system Callaway X Centra. And then he foiled their scheme.

Presently, the slaughterhouse assembly line that triggered Pedro Perez's déjà vu was located down on the surface of the planet Tictoctic. Pedro hung by his bound wrists, side-by-side with fellow Earthlings in the same predicament. Yoon-hee hung to his left, last in line. His wife Ludi hung to his right.

The conveyor belt to which Pedro's manacles were attached was dragging him between two high walls. He was being brought ever closer to a semi-transparent curtain of thick plastic strips. Past this polystyrene veil, the other humans were disappearing one by one. A thunderous BAM sounded after each sentient creature travelled beyond the veil. Each BAM was succeeded by something reddish splattering, spraying against the opposite side of the plastic strips.

For Pedro, this looked hauntingly familiar. It was the stuff of his occasional nightmares. Buddy had long since explained those nightmares. They were the lone remnants, mercifully, of the other far crueler reality from where Pedro was delivered courtesy of the wonders of time travel.

I hope they have this straight, Pedro thought to himself anxiously, despite what he knew. *Sure looks like blood. Although, I suppose the whole point is to make this appear as real as possible, not create any suspicion.*

"It is most astounding, how stoically they are taking their fate," baaed one armed guard to the other. The guards' vantage point was an overhanging railing.

"Baa," agreed the other guard. "I remember the Konokans in days of old, their frantic chirps as they sensed their imminent doom. Maybe they were begging us to release their relatives. Or maybe they were praying to some fancied all-powerful Dek-Fook-Tek of the entire universe. They were asking Him to assure them a place in paradise after they die."

"Instead of a place on our plates or in one of our feeding troughs, baa!"

"Baa!" the other guard joined in the first guard's baaed laugh.

The din from the guards' amusement provided cover for Ali Magabu's advice. He whispered as loudly as he dared in order to express his heightening concern. "You heard what they said above us? Truly, we need to kick up more of a fuss." Ali demonstrated what he meant. "YOU GUARDS?!?!" he shouted at the top of his lungs. "OUR TRANSLATORS ARE STILL WORKING!! YOU CAN UNDERSTAND US!! PLEASE!! PLEASE!!" he shouted ever more loudly.

Tanya was next in line to vanish behind the plastic strip curtain. Evidently, she would soon receive an iron bolt hammered through her skull.

"NO!! NOT TANYA!! YOU HAVE ME AND THE OTHERS!! YOU CAN SPARE MY TANYA!! AYEEEEEE!"

BAM!

The Earthlings knew Counselor Magabu was putting on an act. Still, they found the shrillness of his concluding scream mighty unsettling. Especially so, experienced in conjunction with what happened next.

A red liquid, presumably from Ali's wife, spattered the inside of the cloudily transparent plastic strip veil.

What also didn't help was the comparably shrill, high-volume intensity of the braying translation of Ali's protests. It sounded to Tanya like a sheep suffering sheer agony.

"Te quiero siempre, mi amor (*I love you forever, my love*)." Ludi turned her head Pedro's direction as much as her arms strung up and manacled over her head would allow. "Por si acaso...(*just in case...*)"

BAM!

"Ay, Dios," Officer Pedro Perez sighed with relief after his turn came finally to be dragged past the plastic strip veil. He found everything as Oodle-Noodle promised. But he had to keep his voice low when he sighed, so the guards wouldn't overhear. They were situated on a second floor balcony where their angle of vision blocked observing the farcical quality of what really took place.

Waiting beyond the veil was Chef Glork-tek. He stood to one side on a mobile staircase. It was the same kind of staircase Supreme Authority Dek-Fook-Tek's antler managers used when the Supreme Authority was out and about. Pedro remembered a boarding ramp he descended off a small plane after it landed on the island of Vieques. That happened especially long ago, when he was only eleven.

With practiced, lightning-fast efficiency, Chef Glork-tek disconnected Pedro's wrist binder from the slaughterhouse assembly line manacles. As Pedro stumbled free, he unavoidably stomped on a sleeping-bag-sized container. The container squirted more, red-dyed water against the veiling plastic strips. This event was timed perfectly with the iron bolt going BAM as it once more hammered harmlessly at thin air.

The next thing Officer Perez knew, he was out a side door, in Ludi's tight embrace.

Ludi held on for dear life.

"Thank you, as always, officers," Chef Glork-tek tongue-clicked most officiously. He emerged from behind the plastic strip curtain after smearing red-dyed water here and there on his apron. Dried blood stains from prior actual slaughters helped enhance the desired effect. "Others might mistakenly take your efforts for granted," the chef continued. "In the spirit of our great Dek-Fook-Tek, however, I would not dare leave your least action unacknowledged. That includes even your most cursory glance at those other-world animals as they were led to their most merciful fates. But we are short on pektels. And so, to make up for any negligence in that respect, I assure you each a most tempting morsel from my next preparation. I am thinking to make Akt eye the star of the show."

The guards looked to one another. They lazed their tongues round the corners of their mouths and bleated, "Baahhmmmm..."

"For now, you may take your leave early," the chef went on. "The evening shift is due here any moment. Between now and then we are not expecting any food deliveries, especially after this bonus of Akt beasts. Incidentally, I drugged the other-worlders insensible before their dispatch. Hopefully that will prevent their flesh from becoming spoiled by unsavory stress hormones."

"We did notice decidedly less protest from them than from the usual cattle, most honored Chef Glork-tek."

The chef nodded agreeably. He thought to himself, *It helped for the other-worlders to learn in advance they were going to experience the slaughter that was not a slaughter.*

⊹ ⋊⊤⧊°⊹ ⋊⊤⧊°⊹ ⋊⊤⧊°

Happily unchained and able to hug at will, the Earthlings were led away from the slaughterhouse vicinity by two deer creature guards. The guards were armed with air igniters like any other Tictoctickian guards. But in this case they were protectively showing the other-worlders where to go, not threateningly herding them forward.

On their reunion past the plastic strip veil, Helena had given Chris a hug. Too brief a hug where he was concerned. And during that rare show of public affection, Helena kept looking over his shoulder. She didn't devote her full attention to him. Rather, she anxiously double-checked other persons' lot as they crossed the veiled threshold. She wanted to see them actually freed from their manacles before the iron rod could be hammered through their skulls. So Officer Olsen-Taylor certainly understood. Helena Taylor was the captain, duty-bound to stay ever on guard for fellow officers and, in the case of Chig-cher and Chwerp-chee, passengers. Like she wouldn't have been automatically playing Mother Hen, regardless, Chris suspected admiringly.

Anyway, the Earthlings were led ever further through a naturally occurring, unnaturally reinforced cavern network. Soon as they left one passage for the next, sensor-triggered light shut back off behind them. This made them feel like they were constantly re-emerging from pitch-black darkness.

To hold lingering insecurity at bay, Captain Taylor and company had to keep reminding themselves of the same thing, over and over. The deer creatures wouldn't have gone to such lengths for their rescue, only to have them slaughtered elsewhere. It helped that around one bend they were reunited with Oodle-Noodle and Wafoodle-boodle.

The Earthlings already knew their tree creature friends were safe. That they must have been sprung safely from those specially lined crypts where they'd been placed. This, because Oodle-Noodle and Wafoodle-boodle had long since resumed reassuring telepaths. Obviously, both Oombian tree creatures had not been chopped into firewood.

Regardless, anxiety still ran rampant when the motley entourage from multiple planets arrived at what looked like a dead end. It could have been a boulder-strewn cave-in. No further movement forward appeared possible...

...until one of the guards grabbed with his cloven hoof-hand at an especially tall and fragilely thin stalagmite, apparently. This guard surprised the Earthlings, how he was able to work around the supposed calcium carbonate formation. Buddy Leung was reminded of someone operating a clutch on an antique, fuel-powered automobile.

In response to the guard's handling of the faux stalagmite, the supposed cave-in slid neatly aside. A rebel command center was revealed.

There to greet the recently liberated creatures was-

"Commander Kwit-Nik," Helena Taylor sighed, equal parts relief and ah-ha moment. The relief was that Oodle-

Noodle had called it correctly; they weren't getting thrown from the proverbial frying pan into the fire. And the ah-ha moment? Of course! Commander Kwit-Nik's deep involvement in their deliverance from a grisly fate made perfect sense!

Captain Taylor had had enough encounters with the commander to recognize him anywhere. His humbly proportioned yet still needle-sharp antlers were distinctive among his fellow deer creatures. However, what really set him apart was his unusually large number of worry wrinkles. They were furrowed deeply into his white-speckled, down-covered forehead.

"To thank you for saving us from certain death seems woefully inadequate. Doubly so, Commander, under these circumstances," Taylor said finally.

"Captain, of course you are aware of the cold, calculated attack by two of your fellow beings on one of our primary hospitals for wounded soldiers?"

"I am painfully aware, Commander. Of course," Helena Taylor nodded. "I was in the room when you and Dek-Fook-Tek received word."

"Then you must also be aware of the senseless death and destruction. But what you might not yet realize is that it sabotaged our efforts, so carefully herded together over such a long period of time. The attack sabotaged them on the verge of near-certain success." The translation of Kwit-Nik's tongue-clicks pierced the Earthlings' consciences with sharpness comparable to how his antlers were capable of goring their chests.

"I know." Captain Taylor couldn't have freighted those two, simple words with more regret if she had tried. "So it *is* true," she went on nevertheless. "You did have a plan to, um, offer your fellow beings a kinder alternative."

"We had gained the overwhelming majority consensus we required. Even the ruler's antler handlers were successfully corralled."

Not unexpectedly for Captain Taylor, there were no laudatory adjectives attached to the commander's mention of "the ruler," Dek-Fook-Tek.

Commander Kwit-Nik reserved the use of such an adjective for characterizing someone else. "The great spirit of our long lost pastures," he went on, "knows the truth. It knows the absolute insanity with which Dek-Fook-Tek's antler handlers have gotten to see him behave. It also knows what we were about to achieve.

"We were about to have Dek-Fook-Tek and his likewise-unstable adherents, such as Lieutenant Ak-keek-teek, put under arrest. To this end, we had retained the services of several world-renown psychologists. They were more than ready to officially declare the entire herd mentally unfit to continue in their present capacities.

"The guards who led you off to the slaughterhouse were originally going to be taking away Dek-Fook-Tek and the lieutenant. There were others not in on the plan, such as Dek-Fook-Tek's most corpulent, out-of-shape counselor. We were confident they were too weak-willed to push back. There was no chance they would start any kind of a stampede against our most carefully ruminated actions. Moreover, we had recruited co-conspirators on military bases and aboard virtually every battleship saucer. Their actions were going to simultaneously complement our actions in this location.

"As you might have already guessed, there were many, many fellow beings we needed to corral into our confidence. Some of them were already feeling mighty conflicted. Without their support, with, instead, their active resistance, our duty would have turned into an unsuccessful suicide mission. That is, had we been able to fulfill that duty. Again, what your fellow beings, what those two terrorists did...

"When the first report came in, we knew what to expect. The terrorists' horrifically senseless actions would instantly stampede many of our conflicted fellow beings away from our plan. We can only hope their disenchantment will not prove enough for any of them to betray us. Since we did cancel the coup, you would think that is enough."

Not that it matters; the violence accomplished by the Earthling terrorists was still foolishly awful, Oodle-Noodle seized Kwit-Nik's pause from his explication to telepath. *But they weren't planning to destroy a hospital. They thought they had targeted a weapons storage depot of Dek-Fook-Tek's subarctic compound. They were expecting to create chaos there that would ease escape by Captain Taylor and company.*

"You may be correct, tree creature." Commander Kwit-Nik gave Oodle-Noodle a regard wherein his snout wrinkled busily with his distaste. "Whatever they intended, their greatest achievement, I fear, was something else. They convinced several Tictoctickians that Dek-Fook-Tek is not so crazy, after all. That his plan for what he terms defensive conquest of other inhabited planets actually makes sense. In the context of a far larger peril, what does it matter if their leader is given to bouts of irrational rage? Yes, maybe his bizarre behavior requires the installation of new drywalls every ten days for kicking and shredding apart. As long as he keeps them safe from enemy attacks, so what?"

"You mentioned the criminal behavior of our two fellow Earthlings, Commander Kwit-Nik. Please believe me when I say their behavior shames the rest of us. But you are suggesting that what they did hasn't changed your fundamental assessment." Helena made this more statement than question, despite how Kwit-Nik had her wondering ever more nervously. Was he almost talking himself into going along with Dek-Fook-Tek, after all?

"Captain Taylok," Commander Kwit-Nik nodded, "you and your fellow beings took great risks for us on Kakifika. You almost got yourselves killed, investigating the feasibility of our temporary resettlement there. Clearly, your selfless efforts are not of a kind with the evil of these other beings from Akt. They hijacked our magnetic pulse-beam and, whether by design or by accident, they bombed our hospital complex. That cannot be brayed too often. But there is more."

Commander Kwit-Nik inclined his antlers towards a side room in the underground complex. Its location put it well out of earshot from various, air-igniter-armed sentries standing about. Once the Earthlings and Oombians gathered there with Kwit-Nik, he baaed softly, "What I am about to tongue-click might be considered heresy, even among my strongest supporters. Yes, it might be ridiculed by those who still regurgitate my coup plans to ruminate approvingly upon them. Nevertheless, I cannot help finding myself increasingly convinced that you creatures are every bit our intellectual equals. You might even be our superiors." He nodded Oodle-Noodle and Wafoodle-boodle's way. "Where the attack on one of our hospitals is concerned, well," Kwit-Nik shook his head plaintively. "We did some pretty awful things on Koombk. There was really no reason for your fellow beings, Captain, not to respond the way they have, as much as that response sabotaged our plans.

"And so, my goal not only is to facilitate your escape back to your starship. I also want to give you plenty of lead time for returning to your staging area near Koombk. Plenty of lead time, that is, to warn of the inevitable, irrationally violent onslaught forthcoming from our militarized saucers."

"And you will be going along with that onslaught, Commander?" Helena sidled up so close to Kwit-Nik, his snout became a commotion of wriggles, expressing his discomfort. He had to suppress an instinctive urge to flee bounding away from the other-world spaceship captain. It was an urge not helped by her foul odor.

Something Commander Kwit-Nik could not have known, unless Oodle-Noodle telepathically clued him in. Captain Helena Taylor had to work hard, resisting her own urge to pet him. Helena felt certain he would have found that most insulting.

And so, Captain Taylor did not stroke the downy fur on Kwit-Nik's longish neck, as though she were to soothe some agitated horse. Instead, she asked him, "Is all hope vanished for your original plan, thanks to the terrorist attack?"

"Chef Glork-tek and I agree," Commander Kwit-Nik continued to baa softly, even as he backed off from the "Akt" creature. "The plant-based foods you have provided, we find delicious in a most profound way. They seem to reach into our prehistory when our anthropologists tell us our ancestors nibbled on berries and grasses for the bulk of their diet. Moreover, there is our big, excrement-encrusted secret. It is a secret which has had to remain baaed in hushed tones amongst our medical and nutritional experts. Namely, the stampeding prevalence of heart disease has coincided closely with our increased reliance on meats in all their processed forms. This coincidence has been too strong not to have a causal link. And yet, that increased reliance has proven absolutely necessary. Our pollution from fossil fuels, as you so quickly diagnosed, has not only caused dramatic warming of our planet's climate. It has also decimated entire plant ecologies, and led to massive animal die-offs.

"But again, you have found us a way out, a dramatic new path. Kakifika offers us the chance at a whole new start.

"There is also your game of koofk which has so corralled my interest, and the interest of many other Tictoctickians. Plus there is your elevation, your ennoblement of mating calls to – what is that term you use? Kusik? (*Music?*) It is so entrancing, so thrilling. It might be listened to, and pranced about to, without a thought necessarily given over to sexual intercourse.

"This brings me to humbling deliberation upon one particular aspect of all three of your civilizations' cultures. It is a commonality which suggests to me every last one of you has transcended Tictoctickian society. It is the matter of your pairing up on apparently a long-term basis. Here on Tictoctic, such behavior has prevailed only among some outcasts. We think those might have included the two fellow Tictoctickians who absconded with one of our saucer scout vehicles. Our best guess is that they were on a mission to warn the rest of the galaxy about us. In any event, some of our outcasts have insisted on committed relationships, one to one. Meanwhile, for the rest of us, females are kept in child-rearing herds. We males must visit them regularly to noncommittally hook up, as our saying goes, for species propagation only."

Buddy, Chris, Ali, Yoon-hee, Helena, and Tanya, every Earthling but Cathy strained not to exchange significant looks. This happened when Commander Kwit-Nik mentioned the couple who made off with a scout saucer. Little more than eighteen months earlier, two deer creatures from Tictoctic crashed a small spacecraft on the planet Fafama. Before they perished from their injuries, they warned of their fellow beings' plans for interplanetary conquest. It didn't seem a far stretch to believe that this couple and the couple to whom Commander Kwit-Nik referred were one and the same.

"And so, Captain, there is a large herd of reasons neither I, nor Chef Glork-tek, nor many others of us can give up hope, just yet. We still have to believe there is a chance our bloodthirsty, mentally-crazed leaders can be stopped. Assuming the worst, though, a phrase plays through my head. I share it with you now, before I send you on an escape trajectory. 'Don't become us.'"

Buddy Leung recalled, *Those are the exact words of that deer creature couple back on Fafama. They spoke it in harmony on their dying breaths. "Don't become us."*

Helena seized Commander Kwit-Nik by the shoulder to hold him back from turning away yet. She did this despite full well knowing he was about to lead them into whatever escape plan he had concocted. "When we return to our people, we will not give up hope, either, on staving off war," she firmly asserted. "The hurdles we will have to clear are probably not dissimilar. I gather there was a special invention our terrorists used to temporarily seize control of one of your saucer's weapons. That's how they attacked the hospital, again whether intentionally or inadvertently."

Commander Kwit-Nik nodded.

"One of our arms manufacturers is probably looking to profit from a high demand for such an invention by our military. We call that, 'making a killing.' So I am not sure I shouldn't be saying, 'Don't become us,' as well."

Commander Kwit-Nik lowered his antlers Helena's way. At first, she feared he might have been enraged by what she shared with him. That he might have been moved to try goring her. But then he made clear he was bowing them in humiliated embarrassment, for he baaed in his softest voice yet, "I wish I could tell you we do not suffer from greed-herded weapons manufacturers of our own. Each one of them rationalizes. They say that if they don't produce the bombs and magnetic pulse-beam technologies for the wars of the future, others will. Others will take their place on Dek-Fook-Tek's most-favored list. Also, they repeatedly argue we have to be prepared to militarily dominate over civilizations on other planets. Otherwise, those civilizations will dominate over us."

An overwhelming number of our "us" are just like an overwhelming number of your "us," Commander Kwit-Nik. Oodle-Noodle interjected with her telepath, not bothering to seek Captain Taylor's permission. *They want to live in a peace-loving, playful world. But they are very vulnerable to fear, to a lack of faith imposed upon them by a tyrannizing few. It is a lack of faith that ultimately, there will be enough resources to go around for everyone. Plus, they are overly susceptible to another fear. It is fear of evil being a conscious presence rather than a faithless void. But on my planet, Oomb, faith has long since triumphed most overwhelmingly. It is upon such a strong foundation that Wafoodle-boodle and I, plus several other of our fellow tree creatures, will construct our strategy. We will strive to build a restraining influence on the political and military power projected from Earth. As you seek to revive your original scheme on your end, know that this is happening back our end. And moreover, in our very worst case scenario, well...* Oodle-Noodle paused to glance Wafoodle-boodle's way. She gave Helena the impression she was seeking Wafoodle-boodle's permission, her approval before continuing...to which her companion did nod, however subtly. *We are seeking a most special other-world intervention. It might be forthcoming in any event, but, well, that is all I can telepath for now.*

Commander Kwit-Nik's rabbit-like ears twitched with his perplexity over that last remark.

Helena formulated the simple, one-word question she dared not voice aloud. *Intervention?*

Wafoodle-boodle's consent for me to "go there" was not without reluctance. It is reluctance I share so strongly, I felt moved to gain her approval in the first place, Oodle-Noodle went on to telepathically explain for Helena only. *Perhaps the possibility ought to have remained not communicated. This is especially so since Wafoodle-boodle and I might fail in our petition. However, deep is the despair to which we intuit Commander Kwit-Nik has lowered his antlers, to use his species' own parlance. His despair is deep enough, we fear what senseless tragedy he might end up committing otherwise. It might be of so much more consequence if, well...*

Helena held up a hand Oodle-Noodle's way to nonverbally express, *No further explanation is necessary.*

⋆⟡•⟊⟊•⟡•⟊⟊•⟡•⟊⟊•

"Lieutenant Ak-keek-teek." Dek-Fook-Tek made a gracefully slow, head-tilted sideways acknowledgement of the lieutenant's visage appearing on his royal view-screen. Just how gracefully, the Supreme Authority was only able to accomplish thanks to the skillful manipulations of his antler handlers. As always, they were posted like marionette puppeteers up in the ceiling directly above him.

"Supreme Authority Dek-Fook-Tek, I am not sure a reprimanding chest-slashing would not be preferable to the discomfort I feel from having to interrupt you. No one can doubt that your focus has been on matters of priority unimaginable for a fool such as me." Ak-keek-teek reared up on his hind limbs, and he swelled out his chest, ever resigned to his fate as custom dictated. "But let it also be noted," the lieutenant went on, tongue-clicking assertively. "What I have to report confirms your most prophetic concerns over the real purpose of the other-worlders' visit."

On hearing this, Dek-Fook-Tek motioned with one forelimb at the young doe brought naked before him. She needed to prance off with all due haste. Pursuant to which, Supreme Authority Dek-Fook-Tek's clothes handler labored nervously to pull underpants and pants back up over the supreme legs. Forbidden from the handler's view were the sacred lone antler spike of procreation and its two accompanying magma chambers full of molten, golden, life-giving nectar. At least, that's how the supreme genitalia were supposed to be regarded by Tictoctic society. Even the most unintended glimpse of them could be enough to get the clothes handler executed on the spot.

"Continue, Lieutenant Ak-keek-teek," said Dek-Fook-Tek.

Ak-keek-teek relaxed his posture to go on, relieved, "Supreme Dek-Fook-Tek, our sensors have confirmed what eyewitnesses posted beside the launching runways have reported. It is something most ominously unusual. There was an unscheduled departure of the shuttle craft that brought down the other-worlders from their exoskeletal starship. It would appear they found a way to escape the slaughterhouse, and are now trying to escape their richly deserved fate altogether."

"Does Commander Kwit-Nik know about this?!" Dek-Fook-Tek stomped one of his hind-hooves against the floor with such sudden fury, he threw his clothes handler off balance. That handler just avoided accidentally knocking his castrated stump of a servant's antler against Dek-Fook-Tek's royal crotch.

On Dek-Fook-Tek's question, Lieutenant Ak-keek-teek reacted with one of his ridiculously wide, buck-toothed grins. But before the lieutenant could bleat the merest response, his share of the Supreme Authority's view-screen abruptly shrank to the left side. Filling the right side was Commander Kwit-Nik crisply, most officiously tongue-clicking, "Forgive my bypassing customary procedure and charging in on this conversation, Supreme Dek-Fook-Tek. Rapidly stampeding circumstances do not afford us the usual formalities."

The lieutenant found himself torn. His disgust mounted even further with Commander Kwit-Nik for so blithely disregarding protocol. And yet he delighted over the prospect Dek-Fook-Tek might take Kwit-Nik's words and actions for a seriously personal insult.

"I can verify everything that I am confident Lieutenant Ak-keek-teek has reported about the other-worlders and their shuttle craft. Moreover, from our saucer radar feeds I am now carefully following the exact flight path of the runaway shuttle. Extrapolation data suggests the other-worlders are pursuing an indirect, roundabout course back to their mother ship. Perhaps they are operating under the delusion they have thus far escaped our notice."

"Two points if I may, Supreme Authority Dek-Fook-Tek."

"You may, Lieutenant."

"It is an-ever inspiring honor to relieve you of having to expend energy belaboring for others what is so very obvious for you, whenever I can. That is, so you may redirect your supreme energy to far better use," Lieutenant Ak-keek-teek concluded.

"Indeed it is," Dek-Fook-Tek agreed. He nodded for the guard at the door to bring back the naked doe. Also, he writhed and twisted himself with such furious urgency as to make clear his clothes handler needed to reverse course.

Dek-Fook-Tek's clothes handler had just finished zipping back up the supreme pants. This task had proven supremely difficult, thanks to a certain bulge which had appeared to be pitching a miniature camping tent using the supreme underpants. Nevertheless, he wasn't about to complain over having to undo his work.

"Point one, Commander Kwit-Nik," the lieutenant went on, ever willfully oblivious to aspects of Dek-Fook-Tek's behavior. "We know the mind-reading abilities of the two tree-person other-worlders. Must we not assume they escaped their specially insulated, anti-telepathic tombs? So that now they are already well aware of our being well aware of their escape? And-" Lieutenant Ak-keek-teek held forward an articulated cloven hoof-hand. He wanted to stave off an unexpected, unwelcome sense regarding the contemptible commander. He could feel Kwit-Nik more than ready to address his first point. "Point two, Commander: Surely you do not intend to take down the runaway Akt vessel by launching missiles from the surface of Tictoctic?"

Commander Kwit-Nik had easily anticipated both of Lieutenant Ak-keek-teek's points. But he did something in place of a direct response to either one. He removed himself from Dek-Fook-Tek's view. In its stead, he gave Dek-Fook-Tek a look onto the navigation bridge of a full-sized saucer. From there, he and Lieutenant Ak-keek-teek alike got to hear, "This is Captain Rek-mek-a-nek of the

Fourth Celestial Breath, Supreme Authority Dek-Fook-Tek. In hot pursuit, we have successfully locked onto the fleeing shuttle craft about which Commander Kwit-Nik alerted me. We have managed this singular feat despite the shuttle craft's evasive maneuvering. The commander's solution to their irregular course algorithm is doubtless crucially inspired by your superior leadership, Supreme Authority. It has made possible what you are on the verge of witnessing. I am now going to feed you our magnificent view. Pending of course your final approval, you can watch personally as our targeted magnetic pulse-beam obliterates this security threat." Captain Rek-mek-a-nek considered adding a qualification. Namely, that compared to a look at the Supreme Authority's antlers, the "magnificent view" might as well have been of someone's anal region. But the captain decided that would be laying on the phony reverence a little too absurdly thick. Thick enough to garner suspicion.

"So many bodies, Supreme Authority, so much food going to waste," wistfully brayed Lieutenant Ak-keek-teek. But what he really wanted to say was that this had to be some sort of traitorous trick by Kwit-Nik. That he, Ak-keek-teek, should have been made commander instead. He was the true devotee of Dek-Fook-Tek, perhaps the truest devotee anywhere on or off the planet.

"Not that many bodies, Lieutenant," Dek-Fook-Tek shook his head. Meanwhile the naked doe was brought back before him, down on all fours presenting with her rear end. "I appreciate your concern," Dek-Fook-Tek went on. "But there are plenty enough other such beasts, an entire planet's worth for us soon to feast upon. These particular ones have demonstrated such dangerous levels of murderous deceit that we simply can't take the risk. We can't allow them to live a moment longer than is necessary, on the small chance we might yet be able to secure their flesh for Chef Glork-tek's kitchen."

"And do we know," Lieutenant Ak-keek-teek leapt in before Dek-Fook-Tek could give the final, official go-ahead, "that this is not another evil trick? That the tree-creature other-worlders are not using their telepathic powers to somehow still turn this situation to their co-conspirators' advantage?"

"If I might answer the lieutenant's question, Supreme Authority Dek-Fook-Tek..."

Supreme Authority Dek-Fook-Tek did not get to see Captain Rek-mek-a-nek making his request in response to Ak-keek-teek's last-ditch objection. Rather, the feed to Dek-Fook-Tek's view-screen from the Fourth Celestial Breath was displaying something else. It was displaying a star-strewn view of a shuttle pod originally from the Smoke and Mirrors. The pod was continuing on a course by turns spiraling and zigzagging.

Assuming Dek-Fook-Tek's lack of objection meant his approval, Rek-mek-a-nek proceeded. He said, "Commander Kwit-Nik anticipated exactly the dire possibility Lieutenant Ak-keek-teek has indicated. As a consequence, he has ordered Chef Glork-tek to promptly incinerate both tree creatures within the crypts where they were placed. Any telepathing they would be doing now would have to arrive from beyond their ashen graves, if one were to believe in such a thing!"

Commander Kwit-Nik could not have enjoyed swinging an oof club more than he enjoyed the lieutenant's buck-toothed smile. That smile no longer expressed unmitigated glee. Rather, Ak-keek-teek's oversized front teeth looked more clenched, gritted, than revealing any real pleasure.

There was no doubt in Kwit-Nik's mind what Lieutenant Ak-keek-teek was hoping. Ak-keek-teek was hoping the other-worlders' getaway further diminished the commander's esteem and dependability in the eyes of the Supreme Authority. But presently, Commander Kwit-Nik appeared to be handling the crisis so well, too well!

How much longer can Kwit-Nik continue to shield from our Supreme Authority's view his own deceitfulness and gullibility? The lieutenant wondered this to himself. *Kwit-Nik was only too willing to go along with the other-worlders' other-world resettlement project in the first place. And then, to rub more pine needle sap into our eyes, he made excuses. They were ridiculous excuses for those cleared-out stretches of land on the newly-explored planet! Those artificial clearings can only be landing platforms for the other-worlders' invading strike force! But Kwit-Nik insisted they are the mere play areas of some stupid game!*

"Commander Kwit-Nik has recovered well from his perilous state of untenable naiveté," Dek-Fook-Tek nodded approvingly. Off-camera, the naked doe backed ever closer to him. "Proceed with the other-world vessel's complete destruction, Captain Rek-mek-a-nek."

A flashing neon blue light glowed brighter and brighter along the rim of the militarized flying saucer named the Fourth Celestial Breath. It glowed ever brighter on each flash. A pulsating hum permeated the entire spacecraft until finally, a whitish-blue beam issued towards the shuttle pod, and locked onto its rear. Thereby was the entire space vessel caused to shudder with such rapidity, it was literally shuddered explosively apart.

"BAAAAAA!!!" Dek-Fook-Tek exhaled deeply. Nobody outside his royal command center chamber was ever supposed to learn the reality. That his exhalation was as much from his climax with the young doe brought before him as from his exultation over successful destruction of the enemy vessel.

"It only remains for us to determine how the other-worlders could have escaped the slaughterhouse in the first place," hee-hawed Lieutenant Ak-keek-teek.

Commander Kwit-Nik ignored the return of pure joy to the lieutenant's ever-ridiculously wide, buck-tooth grin, as seen on his view-screen. "Before that, Supreme Authority," Kwit-Nik said, "I would argue there is one other thing."

That's as far as Kwit-Nik got when an interruption occurred right on schedule, where he was concerned. Half of the view-screen had given Dek-Fook-Tek a clear look at the shuttle pod's destruction. But now that half was showing something else. It was occupied once more by a feed from the navigation bridge of the Fourth Celestial Breath, presided over by Captain Rek-mek-a-nek. "Supreme Authority Dek-Fook-Tek," somberly spoke Rek-mek-a-nek, "we just received an ominous report from our troops posted on the other-world starship exoskeleton. They have located a strange device in the kitchen area. That device is implanted with an active digital countdown. We think it might be a bomb placed there by the other-worlder we caught sneaking about. Of course, he was the one who led to discovery of the secret chambers where his fellow beasts were hiding."

"Very well!" Dek-Fook-Tek would have made a show of stomping around in a circle on his two hind hooves. However, his clothes manager was still finishing zipping up his royal pants. "What do you say, Commander Kwit-Nik? I assume you are still with us even though gone from my view-screen?"

"Yes I am still with you, my Supreme Authority."

"Well this is a simple matter, yes?" said Dek-Fook-Tek. "We make sure every last other-worlder is tied up aboard the awkwardly shaped other-world exoskeleton. Then we evacuate our troops, and leave those beasts from Akt to be blown to pieces by their own device. They are a strange herd, indeed. Not even I would know what their plan could possibly be that would involve destroying what safely got them all the way out here to our fair realm."

"The modesty of Dek-Fook-Tek makes even the tender young oskynt, suckling away at its mother's teat, appear a braggart by comparison," went the ritual praise. Captain Rek-mek-a-nek was joined in offering that praise by every fellow deer creature assembled on the Fourth Celestial Breath's navigation bridge; every deer creature assembled with Dek-Fook-Tek in the royal reception hall of his subarctic command post; and Ak-keek-teek and Kwit-Nik where they were individually situated. But only a few Tictoctickians actually remembered how the entire saying went. The others mumbled nondescriptly along.

"Supreme Authority, I richly deserve your baiting me, your testing my willingness to fall for the naïve solution. Niki-niks are known to have brought sweetly flavored poison back to their niki-nik hills, only to end up killing off entire colonies. Inspired by your fathomless wisdom, I expect to easily rise above them." Commander Kwit-Nik bowed his head contritely for the benefit of Lieutenant Ak-keek-teek.

The lieutenant was still receiving a video feed from Kwit-Nik's underground headquarters, while Dek-Fook-Tek was receiving audio alone.

"As I have no doubt you remember," Kwit-Nik continued, "we have seen this plot before. It was a bomb threat these other-worlders wielded to most shamefully trick us off the Third Celestial Breath. We must admit early and often: Our evacuation never would have happened had we welcomed enough of your inspiration into our minds. We would have realized that bomb was a fake.

"But I hope to have learned from such an onerous mistake, and hereby offer up this plan. Supreme Authority Dek-Fook-Tek, it is a plan born of having felt most rightly severely chastised by your profound wisdom, of course. It is a plan for which I have already long since laid the groundwork. I did that in anticipation of the particular deceit the other-worlders are foolish enough to be repeating.

"So here we go: When our troops evacuate their starship, I am ready to launch one of our scout saucers from a nearby staging area on Tictoctic. It will look just as though another breakout escape from Tictoctic were happening. Only minipektels ago, of course, we witnessed what happened to the actual away team from the full-sized other-world starship exoskeleton. They were blown asunder together with one of their miniature exoskeletons, in the ultra-frigid depths of space. However, the other-worlders who we forced to remain on board the full-sized other-world starship exoskeleton will not know that. They will think their away team has finally hijacked one of our vessels to make safe leave from Tictoctic. What they will not expect is what the scout saucer will actually be carrying. No fellow beings will be on board. Rather, the supposedly hijacked vessel will be carrying a bomb, a real bomb. It is a bomb powerful enough to utterly destroy the other-world starship plus everyone on board! Here is the genius of it, of course animated by the celestial exhalation of your genius, my Supreme Authority.

Listen while I make contact with the scout saucer programmed for liftoff from the launch pad.

"Hello? Is Captain Taylok there?"

"This is Captain Taylor."

Commander Kwit-Nik could see on his view-screen Dek-Fook-Tek suddenly lifting his antlers high on his stretched-out neck. Again, Dek-Fook-Tek was aided in that effort by his antler handlers. Anyway, he looked like he'd just been roused from the verge of dozing off.

Meanwhile, glee was dawning anew, refreshed, across Lieutenant Ak-keek-teek's silly-looking buck-tooth countenance.

Kwit-Nik knew just what Ak-keek-teek was thinking. If all the Tictoctickian troops were going to be evacuated, just how was the scout saucer to land inside the other-world exoskeleton starship? Weren't the other-worlders who remained on board incapacitated, tied up? Who among them would be able to open a landing bay for the scout saucer?

Supreme Authority Dek-Fook-Tek was blithely unaware of the concern Lieutenant Ak-keek-teek literally foamed at the mouth to express. So, his focus centered on tongue-clicking in majestically crisp staccato. "Captain Taylok, of course!" he said. "That must be the voice of the other-world leader!" Dek-Fook-Tek implied he expected to hear her all along, even though he was thinking to himself, *Impossible! Wasn't she blown up in their escape pod?*

"Yes, Supreme Dek-Fook-Tek, that is the voice of the other-world leader, but not really!" announced Commander Kwit-Nik. "Rather, it is the response from a special language algorithm program. You already knew this, of course. But allow me to elaborate for those among us who need to be brought up to speed. The language algorithm separates into snippets many recordings of other-worlder utterances. It is as though those snippets were bits of spice sprinkled on a roasted Konokan butt slice. However, the algorithm can automatically rearrange them, to splice them back together in ways that still mimic intelligible communication. The only thing required to prompt its operation is a question. And if a question is directed specifically at someone by name, the algorithmic function draws from their voice for the response. That is, assuming the particular person's voice is on file. This way, we lull the other-worlders left aboard the starship into no worries over the scout saucer. Once they carry on a conversation with Captain Taylor's voice, any possible hazard will become the furthest thing from their mind. They will reopen their shuttle bay to welcome the saucer inside, bomb and all."

Dek-Fook-Tek's attention wandered already. He was considering whether a special pill would do the trick. Would it grant his system the stamina to bless yet another young doe with his ecstatically transcendent release, so quickly after his previous release? But this time, to be synchronized perfectly with an even bigger, even more triumphant explosion of a gigantic other-world exoskeleton starship?

Lieutenant Ak-keek-teek said, "Brilliant plan, Commander, except for one major problem. Every last other-worlder aboard their exoskeleton starship is bound and tied so our troops can safely evacuate. How will any of them be able to re-open the exoskeleton's shuttle bay hatch once our troops have left?"

"Lieutenant, I must commend you for raising a question sure to be on the minds of fellow Tictoctickians," said Kwit-Nik. "Except Dek-Fook-Tek, of course. We will have that our troops were in a panic to put sufficient space between themselves and the exoskeleton starship before the phony bomb could go off. They simply forgot to close the shuttle landing bay after them. At least, that is what we can safely assume those creatures from another world will conclude. They are too stupid to elevate their cognition enough to imagine anything else! They will find it more than plausible, the idea our fellow beings were so distracted by fear, they couldn't think straight."

"Supreme Dek-Fook-Tek," it was Captain Rek-mek-a-nek from aboard the Fourth Celestial Breath again. "Our troops aboard the starship report that the digital countdown is proceeding most speedily on the device in the kitchen area. There cannot be more than fifty mini-pektels left until it reaches zero."

"We cannot delay any longer, even for praise of my always correctly-leaning decisiveness," responded Supreme Authority Dek-Fook-Tek. With one hoof-hand, he nixed his rotund Counselor Kootlek's ritual chant to honor the moment. Kootlek's mouth already hung halfway open, even as Dek-Fook-Tek motioned for a guard to lead forward a different, naked young doe. "Commander Kwit-Nik," went on the Supreme Authority, "initiate your remote-controlled launch of the bomb-rigged scout saucer! Captain Rek-mek-a-nek, advise our troops aboard the other-world starship to make haste with their evacuation! As though they really believed there is a countdown to a bomb going off! Also make sure they accidentally on purpose leave open the hatch to the shuttle landing bay from where they depart! Oh, and one last item. By all means do take the time to bound up and carry with you the two Konokans! I am already salivating at the thought..." Dek-Fook-Tek licked his chops as much over the prospect of fresh Chonoran meat as fresh Tictoctickian virgin.

"Supreme Dek-Fook-Tek!" Kwit-Nik shrilly bleated.

Meanwhile a short distance away from the commander's rebel stronghold, a scout saucer spun rapidly skyward off the launch pad.

"I don't know that either the captain or our troop contingent aboard the starship is up for your test of their judgment at this time," Commander Kwit-Nik went on. "One of them might charge forward with an objection in the next quarter of a mini-pektel. Otherwise, I would let them know that of course you were not serious about the Konokans. The Konokans have spent an inordinate amount of time in the company of those most deceitful other-worlders from Akt. Who can know for sure what destructive havoc they are rehearsed for wreaking? Especially given an oskynt's eye-blink longer to live than the Akt beasts?"

"Captain Rek-mek-a-nek, you heard what your commander has said," stated Dek-Fook-Tek. "Make sure the troops aboard the exoskeleton starship understand completely, and leave the Konokans behind! And make sure they also understand the hatch for the shuttle bay is to be left open after their departure! Accidentally on purpose!" Supreme Authority Dek-Fook-Tek's frustration knew no bounds. The mere thought of having to let go to waste perfectly good, increasingly hard-to-come-by Chonoran meat...He wanted to stomp one of his hind hooves against the slate floor to vent. But he couldn't; his clothes handler was pulling down his royal pants anew.

The clothes handler kept reminding himself not to even hint at the least disenchantment over his sorry lot in life. Otherwise, he might very well face the grisly fate of his predecessor. Scant days ago, he got to nibble clean his predecessor's barbecued ribs. That meal had been a grim reminder what awaited those who treated their servitude on Dek-Fook-Tek's behalf as anything less than a bracing pleasure and honor.

"Commander Kwit-Nik!" Captain Rek-mek-a-nek suddenly tongue-clicked.

Meanwhile, the purportedly bomb-rigged scout saucer was spinning out of the Tictoctickian atmosphere. It was on a straight course for the Smoke and Mirrors in high orbit some hundred-thirty-thousand miles away.

"Commander," said Rek-mek-a-nek, "Officer Krunktunk advises me a female other-worlder prepared an impressively sized amount of kookee batter. From such batter, the claim gallops, several thousand of us might each enjoy a complete kokolate kip kookee. Given how tasty that would be, Krunktunk is wondering whether they should bring the batter with them."

"Tell them to leave the batter where it is, Captain!" warned Kwit-Nik. "It is most assuredly a trap set by the Akt beasts! Imagine if you will what I am guessing those beasts have already plotted. Imagine untold numbers of our officers falling ill, poisoned useless by kokolate kip kookees. That is, at the same time their warship exoskeletons are arriving in our solar system! Better yet," Commander Kwit-Nik pretended to have been struck by a sudden inspiration, "tell Officer Krunktunk this. Tell him to have his troops launch that batter dispersed harmlessly into space. They must do that before they board the scout saucers for departure from the exoskeleton starship!"

"Done, Commander!"

⊱⋅☾⊰⊱⋅☾⊰⊱⋅☾⊰

"Is anyone aboard the Smoke and Mirrors hearing this? Are you there, Kevin? It's okay to respond; Buddy has accessed the quantum code scrambler. He's made it virtually impossible for our Tictoctickian friends to make out anything other than excess static, should they happen upon this frequency!"

"It's great to hear you, Captain!" Kevin Smith-Park shouted towards a hallway intercom. Kevin was bound to a hand railing just outside the large meeting hall where most others, children included, were both bound *and* gagged. "But your voice sounds stilted somehow. Are you okay?"

"Just making sure my words come through clearly after the scrambler unscrambles, Kevin. Anyway, is there anything you can do about letting us into one of the shuttle bays? Oh, never mind! What luck! Looks like the Tictoctickian occupiers forgot to close the door on their way out!"

⊹⋆⊹⋆⊹⋆⊹

"I must admit something, Commander," said Lieutenant Ak-keek-teek with an effortless grin. He was enjoying himself no end, though puzzled by the passionate sounds transmitting from Dek-Fook-Tek's end. Ak-keek-teek had to assume his Supreme Authority was anxious for the plan's success. But was Dek-Fook-Tek so anxious, he might as well have been remote-control-operating the bomb-laden scout saucer, himself? If so, then no wonder he produced so much huffing and puffing! With that in mind, Lieutenant Ak-keek-teek continued, "Having that speech algorithm initiate a conversation with the other-world beasts aboard the enemy starship is Dek-Fook-Tek-inspired genius! Also, it is a deliciously fitting tribute to all those innocent lives lost in the vicious, unprovoked attack on your hospital rehab center, my Supreme Authority! How perversely delicious, the oskynt excrement about a 'quantum code scrambler' even while we are listening in! Plus, to have the other-world officer recognize certain stiltedness to his leader's speaking... One can only hope that as the bomb is detonated, he and the others will last just long enough to realize how thoroughly they have been duped, before they are explosively incinerated!"

⚜⚜⚜

"I *do* mean to rush your scout saucer docking, Captain," said Kevin with unbridled urgency in his voice. "No telling how long the Tictoctickians will wait for the kitchen device to go off before they suspect it was a ruse. Then you can be sure they'll return with their magnetic pulse-beams ablaze!"

Officer Kevin Smith-Park, as a matter of fact the Tictoctickians have already figured the kitchen device was a ruse. But you should be relieved to learn we anticipated that eventuality, and planned accordingly, telepathed Oodle-Noodle.

⚜⚜⚜

"Commander Kwit-Nik, I have thought of something. It would make the eavesdropped conversation between the other-worlder and our language algorithm program even more enjoyable. I am tongue-clicking about a video monitor of the empty bridge on the rigged scout saucer's navigation deck. Don't you agree, Supreme Authority Dek-Fook-Tek?" asked Lieutenant Ak-keek-teek.

"Yes, yes, of course," Dek-Fook-Tek tongue-clicked in perfect time to the cadence of his steadily more frantic respirations of passion.

Kwit-Nik quickly realized the source of delight clearly evident in Lieutenant Ak-keek-teek's ever-ridiculous grin. Ak-keek-teek relished the prospect of catching himself, the commander, in a lie of fatally dangerous proportions.

Ak-keek-teek was expecting the video monitor inside the scout saucer would reveal genuine other-world beasts making a genuine escape. But Kwit-Nik had anticipated even this eventuality. Before Ak-keek-teek could harshly bray, *Well, where is that video monitor view?*, Kwit-Nik flipped a switch. The lieutenant's and the Supreme Authority's view-screens suddenly revealed the scout saucer's navigation deck, totally deserted. The tape loop recorded earlier worked perfectly.

"We don't need to peer in there any longer," the lieutenant brayed finally, with unconcealed impatience and frustration. It was all he could do, not to turn his back on the view-screen and kick it shattering apart with his hind hooves. "Captain Rek-mek-a-nek, can we have the full-screen magniview of the scout saucer approaching the enemy starship exoskeleton? That is, of course, if this does not trample on any other necessary exigencies, Commander." The lieutenant strained not to allow an angry exhalation to come hissing from between his buck teeth.

"Of course, Lieutenant," said Kwit-Nik. "Captain Rek-mek-a-nek, there is no problem with that request! Satisfy it!"

۰ᵒᵗᵚᵒᵒᵗᵚᵒᵒᵗᵚᵒᵒ

The scout saucer's entrance into the shuttle bay of the Smoke and Mirrors happened uneventfully. But it was rapidly succeeded by immersion of the Smoke and Mirrors in several odd twinkles sparkling round about. The next thing Dek-Fook-Tek knew, he knew with a shrieked baa of released tension he could not control. The other-world starship was seemingly engulfed in an enormous firestorm. When that conflagration faded away, no clear evidence remained of anything having ever been there, let alone an immensely proportioned space vehicle. Only a scattering of flaring-out pinpoints of light remained. The deer creatures could only presume those flare-outs were from bits of wreckage. For the briefest while, though, they gave the impression of having assumed the outline form of some unimaginably enormous monster.

"And now, Commander," said Dek-Fook-Tek as his latest sexual conquest was led away, "it is time we launch our full-out defensive invasion of Akt!"

"Commander Kwit-Nik!" Captain Rek-mek-a-nek's voice suddenly erupted with harsh braying. This was in stark contrast to the peaceful outer space starry firmament filling the various view-screens. "Commander, are you aware three scout saucers have suddenly spun to escape velocity from near your location?"

"That information is coming up now on the monitor, Captain," answered Kwit-Nik. He checked that the three empty spacecraft were pursuing the varied tangent evasion paths with which he had programmed them.

"It looks like whoever is operating them somehow managed to delay or temporarily conceal the relevant data output. Like they were deeply familiar-"

"Commander!" interrupted Chef Glork-tek, right on schedule. "I have found some of our security guards strung to the dissembly line in the slaughterhouse!"

"LEAVE THEM BOUND!!!" Dek-Fook-Tek shrilly brayed as he kicked his clothes manager away. He tore off his pants, snatched them up by his mouth, and shook them from side to side with a deep growl like a lion. At least that is how the Earthlings would have characterized his behavior.

"There have been traitors in our midst, Dek-Fook-Tek!" Lieutenant Ak-keek-teek brayed with his own wild abandon. "They are traitors Commander Kwit-Nik did not previously detect! They must have been the ones who freed the enemy other-worlders to attempt their failed escape! Now they are attempting to escape like cowards themselves! No doubt, they are seduced by that stupid game where you hit balls into holes with sticks! And by non-meat foods surely calculated to make us weak!"

Dek-Fook-Tek finally dropped his pants from his foaming mouth, having ripped them to shreds with his sharp teeth. A tranquillizer injection by the royal physician sedated him enough to resume tongue-clicking, "Commander Kwit-Nik, the defensive action against Akt must be postponed so all battle saucers can be reassigned! I want them to pursue the three escaping scout saucers! And I want every last saucer successfully disabled, *not* destroyed! Then I want the traitors brought before me so I can disembowel them personally! And I want their disembowelment televised across our planet! Nobody will go unaware of the exacting fate that awaits those who would dare futilely act like Konokans, attempting to terrorize our society! Let me ruminate on it a bit more, but we might also need to make an example of several of our terrorist-inclined prisoners!"

Commander Kwit-Nik thought to himself, *If only there was a far enough extreme to which Dek-Fook-Tek would go, to unwittingly resurrect our original ambition. But, at least the other-worlders might hereby gain enough lead time...*

Chapter 26

Supreme Authority Dek-Fook-Tek took his time inside the slaughterhouse. He made what Chef Glork-tek could only have characterized as a self-satisfied swagger, aided as always by his antler handlers.

Usually, Dek-Fook-Tek's antler handlers remained out of sight. But this was another of those occasions when the Supreme Authority was on the move, away from his royal chambers. There was no ceiling where his handlers could hide. So instead, they stood atop stairways on wheels that were pushed along by other servants to keep pace. In plain view, they manipulated his antlers like marionettes on strings. Thereby they still prevented those ridiculously huge head growths from tipping over.

Dek-Fook-Tek's swagger informed his pacing back and forth. This is how he inspected troops. Only he wasn't inspecting troops. He was inspecting six guards strung up helplessly to the slaughterhouse disassembly line.

Chef Glork-tek accompanied Dek-Fook-Tek. He had no choice since he was the one who reported finding the guards in their present predicament in the first place.

As for the guards, they did not have to feign terror. Cold sweat beaded on their snouts. Nasal drip bubbled from their nostrils.

Prior to the guards voluntarily placing themselves in such a circumstance, Chef Glork-tek handed down assurances from Commander Kwit-Nik. But those assurances proved far easier to trust in the abstract. Once the Supreme Authority loomed in the guards' presence, not a one of them could help worrying. Might Commander Kwit-Nik have overdone his optimism?

According to Glork-tek, the commander expressed all kinds of confidence. Yes, the deadly pulse-beam attack on the hospital could not have been more horrific. But ever since the initial shock, everyone necessary was quickly coming back around. Everyone necessary was returning to acceptance of one basic fact. Namely, Dek-Fook-Tek and his closest, likewise-demented advisers needed to be declared mentally unfit to rule. Their forcible removal from power could not be avoided.

The time was approaching soon enough, Chef Glork-tek told the guards, when they would be hailed as heroes. They would garner this recognition for providing the necessary mini-pektels of delay and distraction of the dictator. During those mini-pektels, the official go-ahead for the insurrection would be re-secured from crucial elements within the government.

But what if the insurrection didn't go as planned? What if it was sabotaged again by some unforeseen event? Or what if one of the guards decided to betray the plot, fearful that if he didn't, someone else would? Which would have meant the iron rod hammered through the skulls of the five who kept the secret, insurrection or not?

Supreme Authority Dek-Fook-Tek swiveled around. But rather than swagger past the bound-up guards for the umpteenth time, he stood still. And he brayed at the top of his lungs, "Look at you!! LOOK AT YOU!!!!" Then Dek-Fook-Tek quieted down, as though he suddenly regained full command of his temper. "While you are hanging there completely useless," he baaed, "we have had to postpone our defensive retaliatory action against those other-worlders. We have had to delay our vengeance on those cowardly bloodthirsty beasts," he went on with his temper coming steadily unglued again. "They had our exemplary hospital senselessly destroyed! So senselessly, they didn't even spare a thought to collecting the resultantly grilled bodies for a feast! But now, those loathsome creatures are able to fly their light-speed exoskeletons a while longer! And why do they get to do this?! Why?! Because Commander Kwit-Nik has had to redirect our battle fleet! He has had to have them track down and destroy as-yet unnamed renegades who made off in *three* of our scout saucers! THREE! They lifted them from under our very snouts, NOT FIVE DEKALEKS FROM HERE!!!" On this shouted bray, Dek-Fook-Tek lowered his antlers and charged them into a portable drywall other servants brought along for this very purpose. After splintering apart the drywall, he shook away pieces of it left impaled on his antlers. Pursuant to which he tongue-clicked, "So tell me how this could have happened! YOU!" Dek-Fook-Tek suddenly swung around towards the chained-up guard closest to him.

That particular guard hung like the other five, manacled by his bound wrists. He was the one nearest the plastic strip veil beyond which awaited the skull-crushing bolt.

"Tell me how this could happen!" Dek-Fook-Tek repeated. "And do not bother me with the worthless trivia of your name!"

"You-you can see the bruising on the backs of our necks," the questioned guard bleated tearfully. Those mentioned bruises came thanks to a makeup job by Chef Glork-tek. Nevertheless, the guard feared a new wave of uncontrollable rage from the Supreme Authority. Dek-Fook-Tek might suddenly charge at his chest, treat it to the same fate as the drywall board. There was nothing that guard had to fake where his emotional reaction was concerned. "The officers who did this, we know who they are," he finally added. It was only then that he and the other five bound-up guards strained to twist their heads.

Thereby they gave Dek-Fook-Tek a look at Chef Glork-tek's cosmetically rendered injuries.

Chef Glork-tek himself was grateful Lieutenant Ak-keek-teek hadn't tagged along. Glork-tek wouldn't have put it past the lieutenant to prod and poke at the faux bruising with his cloven hand-hooves. By such close examination, he would have been sure to have discovered the makeup job.

"We recognized them as fellow guards. We thought they arrived at the land-based scout saucer staging area simply to relieve us of duty. Or- Or maybe they were going to apprise us of some unexpected exigency," the trembling guard continued, the guard on whom Dek-Fook-Tek focused. "But the next thing we knew, they trotted behind us and we found ourselves strung up. Chef- Chef Glork-tek told us we needed to remain like this because you would want to see what happened with your own eyes. Baa, maybe- m-maybe those traitors who knocked us out are operating those runaway scout saucers. I am glad your battleships have been deployed to destroy them!" the guard concluded on a forced tone of defiance.

Dek-Fook-Tek's quiet, motionless, steely-eyed regard was unrelenting.

"Baa, my Supreme Authority Dek-Fook-Tek," the terrified guard brought himself to bleat, figuring he had nothing to lose. "Your mercy makes the mother oskynt's care for her suckling brood seem cruel by comparison."

The other five strung-up guards, Chef Glork-tek, and the dictator's antler handlers and stairway movers joined in the ritual adulation. As usual, they moved their lips quietly if they didn't quite remember this particular litany.

Dek-Fook-Tek nodded acknowledgment of the compliment directed his way. That didn't necessarily mean he felt at all appeased. But it was enough for the guard on whom he remained focused to gather his wits about himself, and go on. "Again, we assume the operators of the runaway scout saucers are the same traitors who did this to us," he brayed. "That makes me all the happier to share their names with you, Supreme Authority Dek-Fook-Tek."

"Baaa, more useless trivia," Dek-Fook-Tek waved his forelimb dismissively. "They will be incinerated soon enough, and their charred remnants will float away harmlessly in the cold depths of outer space." He said this despite having given Captain Rek-mek-a-nek quite different orders from incineration.

Rek-mek-a-nek was to bring back the scout saucer hijackers alive, for the Supreme Authority's personal goring. But suppose anyone there had been aware of Dek-Fook-Tek's previous directive. Would that deer creature have valued his life so little as to point out the contradiction?

"There is something I want to know from *you*, Chef Glork-tek," Dek-Fook-Tek suddenly tongue-clicked. Most abruptly, he finally turned his attention away from the guard to whom he had been giving unnerving regard. The Supreme Authority's new focus was on Commander Kwit-Nik's most trusted adviser in the plan to overthrow the dictatorial regime. "How do you think we should deal with this, Chef?"

"Supreme Dek-Fook-Tek," the chef made pretense to baa most meekly humbly, "I think we should launch a full investigation, guided by your immortally brilliant counsel. That investigation should continue, and I quote from you, 'until the guilty have been rooted out, even as a poisonous tuber is rooted out by a hapless, mouth-shoveling oskynt.' Virtually everyone who is *not* Dek-Fook-

Tek must be carefully ruminated upon as a suspect. Such suspicion overshadows even my own self. So, I would most respectfully submit that the investigation needs to start with me." For extra emphasis, Chef Glork-tek swelled out his apron-covered chest. He made himself available for an immediate, fatal slashing if not full disembowelment by the Supreme Authority.

The bluff worked.

"Chef Glork-tek," Dek-Fook-Tek tongue-clicked most crisply, "you have just saved yourself from being strung up in the place of these- I am not sure what we should call them now. Either they are co-conspirators with the ones who made away in the scout saucers. They are trying out a story on us, as bluntly ineffectual as their stumpy antlers so long neglected by bahvek sharpening. Either that, or they are too incompetent to be of any further use to us. The answer herds us correctly one direction, or the other. It really does not matter which. So please activate the disassembly line so I can at least have the pleasure of hearing the iron bolt hammered through their skulls."

That was more than enough for guard officer Kikass. The chef had given them his assurance. Before it came to this, the word would go out from the commander. Herds of other guards would stampede against Dek-Fook-Tek to haul him away. And so, with as much volume as he could muster, Officer Kikass opened his mouth in protest. He was intent on spilling the entire plot in the hope of saving himself. But he didn't even get to complete the first two syllables, even.

Three other guards galloped into the slaughterhouse down on all fours, evidencing their urgency. Clip-clopping to a halt before Dek-Fook-Tek, one of them reared back up onto his hind legs. He officiously tongue-licked, "Begging your pardon, my Supreme Authority Dek-Fook-

Tek. We have just completed our inspection of the terrorist spacecraft housed not three dekaleks from here."

"You are baaing about the spacecraft that hijacked a magnetic pulse-beam from the Fourth Celestial Breath?!" carelessly brayed Dek-Fook-Tek.

"And employed that pulse-beam for the barbaric attack on your hospital complex," the guard nodded. "There are certain artifacts we have discovered inside it. We believe they require your immediate attention. Doubtless, Supreme Authority, you will want to contemplate them prior to your audience with the two other-world beasts who operated the spacecraft. You might want to start with this." The guard handed over a lamp removed from the navigation deck of the Elusive.

"What is it?" the Supreme Authority tongue-clicked in near disbelief. He kept turning the artifact every which way by his cloven hoof-hands. "It cannot be- What manner of monster could do this?! I order you to disseminate photos of this horrific item as widely as possible! Make sure every single breathing Tictoctickian sees this! Everyone must learn what manner of monsters from another world we are dealing with, in case there is any least remaining doubt!"

The base of the lamp featured a small pair of deer antlers.

Chapter 27

"Well dress me in a bikini for the swimsuit competition at the Miss Universe Beauty Pageant, if it isn't Captain Taylor and her crew back safe and sound from the heart of interstellar darkness!" Secretary of Defense Michael Spinner slapped his knee.

Helena, Buddy and company could see Spinner's knee slap in the right half of their panoramic view-screen on the navigation bridge of the Smoke and Mirrors. In the left half of the screen, the starship crew could see the starship Barack Obama coming up alongside, at a safe distance of course. Both starships were still travelling at close to standard light-speed. The fairy dust of sparkling, particle-favoring photon exhaust was steadily emitting from their rear-mirror-array "rose blooms."

Helena intuited something especially rotten from the defense secretary, as assuredly as Oombian tree creature Oodle-Noodle could mind-read it. He had to check himself against sputtering, *You're still alive* as in, *We were not expecting any of you to survive.*

"We need to talk, Mr. Secretary." After what Captain Taylor processed from their awful experience, she could not bring herself to grant Spinner the least pleasantry.

"I'm sure we do need to talk, Captain. I don't doubt that. Harrumph!" Secretary Spinner cleared his throat to express his disapproval of the curt way Taylor addressed him. Subsequently it gave him no small delight to say, "I hope you understand something, Captain. Before we can allow you to set a course back to Oomb, we are going to need to confirm, establish you *are* you. And if you are, that you are not proceeding under any kind of duress. Again, Captain, I hope you understand that."

"I understand that, Mr. Secretary. You need to confirm the Smoke and Mirrors hasn't been transformed into a Trojan Horse, with us taken hostage. Or worse, that you aren't watching an ingenious videotape while the Tictoctickians are literally picking the meat off our bones. Chris, Officer Chris Olsen-Taylor, he will take you on a camcorder tour of the entire vessel. You can check in on everyone, ask anything you wish. Will that suffice?"

"We will need to do all of that, Captain."

The Barack Obama met the Smoke and Mirrors on the outer fringe of solar system Callaway X Centra. The unarmed starship had just completed its two-week journey back to there from the Cygnitaurus system some four light-years away. Fifteen days of relative tranquility gave Captain Taylor full opportunity to reflect on her experience. What exactly had come of trying to drag the tree creatures' peacemaking dream into reality?

The escape from the vicinity of Tictoctic went off without a hitch. Yoon-hee found Commander Kwit-Nik's instructions easy to follow, for operating the scout saucer. Once it was successfully docked in a shuttle pod bay, Tanya and Ali were the first officers to re-board the Smoke and Mirrors. They made a mad dash for the kitchen because of what spectroscopic sensors detected.

As planned, a mountain of chocolate chip cookie dough batter prepared by Ciela had already been dumped into space. But that was not all of it. Tanya Petrovsky and Ali Magabu discovered plenty of large cookie dough clumps still floating weightless about the pantry. There were enough clumps to fill two large, plastic bags. Officers Petrovsky and Magabu quickly hauled the bags away to one of the airlocks along the photon exhaust shaft. There, they tossed them out.

Chris and Buddy came up right behind them with another giant bag. That bag was full of light-sensitive mirror array material, hammered to bits and pieces. They unloaded their deliberate mess into the exhaust shaft as follow-up to the already rapidly dispersing cookie dough.

Mere seconds later, the direction the Earthlings ejected the bags' contents worked out well. The cookie dough and mirror array debris drifted in its entirety from the rear end of the photon exhaust shaft of the Smoke and Mirrors.

The rest depended on the planet-sized version of the ephemeral dragon, the spirit of Fafama where Yulala was concerned.

Whatever it was, it quickly came through. It issued a fiery blast to incinerate the cookie dough. This was the large-scale version of what its far tinier counterpart did regularly aboard the Smoke and Mirrors. Effy, however, usually waited for fully baked chocolate chip cookies.

Anyway, the fiery blast was magnified to monstrous proportions by reflections off the scattering-apart mirror array shards. A most convincing show was provided for the Tictoctickians. The Smoke and Mirrors looked to have been blown to pieces by the bomb Commander Kwit-Nik claimed he planted aboard the scout saucer.

The commander told the Supreme Authority the scout saucer was remote-controlled by him. But again, it was actually operated by navigation engineer Yoon-hee Park-Smith.

The explosive spectacle proved plenty large enough to distract from what transpired just beyond it. Instead of being destroyed, the starship accelerated at maximum pace to one-hundred-fold conventional light-speed.

On the return flight to the Callaway X Centra solar system, Captain Taylor would have held her breath the whole way if she could have. *Please, no other unanticipated incident requiring the use of spare mirror array parts we no longer carry!*

Buddy Leung assured Taylor if worse came to worst, they could always have the starship hitch a ride, piggyback a firefly donut. They already did this, of course, on the way home from Mission One. Dirty comet debris had shattered apart significant portions of both the fore and aft mirror arrays, thereby making firefly donut assistance crucial.

Thankfully, there were plenty of situations to distract Captain Taylor on the journey back towards Callaway X Centra. In particular, she wanted to see how adults and children alike were holding up. She welcomed chief counselor Ali Magabu to her side for this task. At the top of the captain's priority list, by far, was to check on Sergeant Guy Hanson and his Fafaman wife, Yulala. How were they doing with their newborn child, Goolafala?

Chief Medical Officer Deborah Davis-Murphy confided the bad news to Helena within the first hour of their escape from the Tictoctic vicinity. Deborah feared Goolafala's "decline into nonviability," as she put it, was imminent. The child's DNA naturally blended gene pools from two different planets. There had been no artificial genetic tinkering before the moment of conception. Even with such tinkering, the odds for success would have been vanishingly low. So without such tinkering, the best anyone could hope for was that Goolafala would pass away peacefully in her crib. To prevent her suffering too much, she could always be given pain medication, drugged senseless for her final breaths.

Thus far, however, the baby girl appeared to be doing well enough. That made so much more difficult reminding Yulala and Guy of the all-but-inevitable outcome. No matter how gently, there was no easy way for either Deborah or Helena to broach the subject.

Before Goolafala's birth, Wafoodle-boodle had repeatedly advised the young lovers to brace for the worst. The Oombian tree creature telepathically forwarded this warning from Dr. Deborah Davis-Murphy, instead of Deborah giving it to them directly. They were hidden away during the Tictoctic mission, behind walls resistant to life monitor intrusion while still allowing mind-reading intervention.

By Deb's own admission, the successful childbirth was a miracle, Captain Taylor thought to herself, early and often. *Maybe the miracles won't stop there. Although Goolafala does have that bizarre face only a mother could love, as the saying goes. Why did both her nocturnally large eyes have to migrate over to the same side of her head? Yes, yes, I know why. But still…*

For sure, Goolafala was eating well. When the captain could finally spare a few minutes to check in personally on the family, she had just finished bottle-feeding herself to sleep.

The Chonoran humanoid-octopoid, Chig-cher, hung from ceiling supports at Goolafala's bedside. After Yulala used a breast pump, she took advantage of the opportunity Chig-cher excitedly afforded her to catch up on rest.

When Captain Taylor entered the family's quarters, Sergeant Hanson was just about to slip out and go reconnect with other people aboard the starship. "Don't stay here on my account," she whispered softly, patting him on the shoulder. "It's Goolafala I've come to see."

"She's the star of the show, Captain. Yulala and I are just the hired help."

"So long as you remember that," with which Helena pushed Guy Hanson on his way.

"Welcome, Captain," Chig-cher's chirps as well as their translation came out quietly. His translator was set on extra low volume, unsurprisingly. What people unacquainted with life on Fafama might have found very surprising, however, was what else the Chonoran did so mother and child could continue their slumber unabated. He turned the room's brightness knob to a high setting.

Goolafala herself was buried out of sight in her crib, beneath a layer of Styrofoam packaging peanuts.

Shortly after Goolafala's birth, Guy and Yulala had the worst time figuring out how to get her to sleep. At first, the young inter-species couple thought it was a matter of Goolafala taking after her mother's nocturnal nature. Their expectation was that simply turning up the lights, rather than turning them off, would do the trick. Goolafala would easily slip off to slumber. She did not.

Goolafala had no difficulty closing her eyes. And especially on the tail end of nursing, she would appear to drift off like any Earth baby or, as Yulala reported, any typical Fafaman baby. But then, it didn't matter whether Yulala continued holding her, even rocking her in her arms. Or Guy could give it a try, or they could just set her down in her crib. None of that made any difference. The baby would cry inconsolably for hours. And when she did finally succumb to exhaustion, it was not for long. Her parents could leave the lights on, or turn them low, or turn them off altogether. Goolafala always woke up an hour later, cranky as ever, ready for a new feeding.

Even more distressing was Goolafala's other behavior. Didn't matter whether in one of her parents' arms or down in her crib. It was all the same. She would kick and claw away at the mattress, the parental clothes, the parental flesh, whatever. Dr. Davis-Murphy feared a lethal interaction at work, of Earth-originated stomach bacteria with Fafama-originated stomach bacteria. Ultimately, the resultant colic was going to kill off the poor little thing.

Yulala and Guy were beyond exhausted from this most dire-seeming situation. For hours, they desperately shifted Goolafala from their arms to her crib and back again. Both parents were about ready to finally allow the chief medical officer to inject their love child with a powerful, potentially dangerous sedative. Then the deathwatch would officially begin.

But before it could get to that, Sergeant Fred Frankly happened on an idea. He had been checking Goolafala's status frequently, unable to rest once he learned of her suffering, and what it was doing to her parents.

Fred took Guy out in the hall so they could both hear themselves think while he tried to explain. "Sergeant ET Daddy," he barked, "now I don't know if you've read about the Fafaman flounder mice. Both their eyes were on the same side of their head like with our flounder fish back home, or like Goolafala. Well, I've been stuck hiding in the belly of the Smoke and Mirrors, unable to target practice on the torch-wielding deer demons. That's given me more time than I ever wanted for pondering those eyes."

"So that's how you've been passing the hours?" Sergeant Hanson asked, sniffing with tearful sorrow.

"Nothing better to do, good buddy. Okay, I lied. I've had much better to do. I've been gettin' it on with Ciela to try and produce some pint-sized trouble of our own. That, plus I've been chasin' around those two, young punks-in-training to stick some chocolate chip cookies up their own devilish asses. But the truth is, neither one of those pleasurable pursuits has allowed me to get away from worrying over Goofoffalot or whatever her name is."

Hanson couldn't help smiling, albeit wanly.

"As an f-n' result, I've also been readin' up on what we learned about Fafaman biology. That is, Fafaman biology before Fafama was destroyed by the dirty comet we put in orbit to shed them an additional water supply. Okay, then," Sergeant Fred Frankly slapped his hands together and rubbed them hard. "Did you know that to sleep during daylight, the flounder mouse has to shiver itself down below the soil's surface? Is it possible your pajama-full of Goolafala Poopalotama needs to do something similar?"

"We've tried putting a blanket over her, but she just shakes it off."

"No," Fred shook his head. "I mean, what if she was able to burrow herself into her crib, somehow?"

Sergeant Frankly would never forget how his Marine buddy's eyes grew nocturnally large before he answered. "I think the packing materials for the mirror array spare parts include Styrofoam peanuts!" exclaimed Hanson. "It's the same for some of Deborah's medical supplies! Maybe a layer of those...!"

The very first time Yulala set down Goolafala on the two-foot-thick bed of Styrofoam peanuts, she buried herself effortlessly. She buried herself so effortlessly, she appeared to her parents and Sergeant Frankly to be simply sinking. A rowboat taking on water from a big leak is how Guy would have characterized it. Seconds thereafter, the three adults heard Goolafala's sigh of relief, of total surrender to her exhaustion. She fell into a deep sleep from which she was not to awaken for nearly ten hours.

"You see this stain covering my shirt?" Chig-cher pointed proudly for Captain Taylor's sake. He made this spectacle of himself after he turned the lights brighter to assure Goolafala stayed asleep under the layer of Styrofoam peanuts. "This is from Goolafala spitting up all over me! Isn't it beautiful?"

"It is something," the captain nodded.

"I tell you," Chig-cher made an uncoiling slap at thin air with his tentacle arm. "I'm going to let this stain dry for a good long while, long enough to assure it never comes out fully in the wash!"

"My special other is such the sentimentalist," explained Chig-cher's husband, Chwerp-chee.

Speaking of sentimentalism, a new tradition was begun aboard the Smoke and Mirrors. It happened spontaneously, right after Captain Taylor and her away team finished untying Dr. Davis-Murphy and the rest from where they were bound captive. It consisted of group hugs whenever two or more entered one another's presence anew.

"I am only going along with this because none of you are cats trying to rub your dander off on me," Dr. Dauntilus Skepticus made a point of saying, before even he surrendered when arms were outstretched to embrace him. "And I am warning you, creatures from Chonora! No ink stains for me, whether squirted from your necks or elsewhere! I like to keep my shirts in pristine condition. If only there were a way for me to insert my upper torso into them while they remained folded up in their original packaging! That would be the ticket! As for you two little boys: Stuff just one more chocolate chip cookie down my pants, and- oh, that's right; we are running something of a cookie shortage after dumping all that batter off the ship, aren't we? How unfortunate. YOW!!"

To the boys' giggly amusement, Skepticus was torched in the rear for the umpteenth time by Effy, the ephemeral dragon.

"Truly, Professor," said Ali. He tried to maintain a straight face when he noticed the thin wraith of smoke rising anew from behind Skepticus. "That must be your atmospheric anomaly. It's having a purely nonliving chemical reaction to so many sentient beings gathered together in such close proximity."

"Yes, well..."

Halfway back to the Callaway X Centra system, Helena staged a big group-hug meeting with officers plus tree creatures. In tranquility, she wanted to afford them a voicing-aloud of their reflections. More specifically, Helena wanted them to discuss the tree creatures' peace-and-love dream. How did it really go, trying to drag the Oombians' scheme into reality with the Tictoctickians?

"I will get the ball rolling here," said Captain Taylor once the small talk dissipated.

All eyes turned on the captain.

"Let's assume we make it back safely to the Callaway X Centra system," she went on. "Let's also assume the collected military force from Earth is still camped out there in high orbit around Oomb. That it hasn't been set loose on the warpath yet. Whatever we assume, I have something to say to the Secretary of Defense and the Chair of the Joint Chiefs of Staff. For sure, they will want to know what happened to that couple flying their own small-scale armed vessel. Oodle-Noodle here is under the impression from her mind-reading that the couple was sent out to Tictoctic to stir up trouble. Well, we all know the bad news I must break to Secretary Spinner and company. There was no choice but to leave that couple, whoever they are, captured by the Tictoctickians. Otherwise, the rest of us were not going to make it out of there alive.

"And, please correct me if you think I've got this wrong. But it looked like our Oombians' peace plan was working more or less. It actually had a chance for success, before the piggyback drone sent from the small-scale vessel got in the way. To review once more, the drone caused a magnetic pulse-beam to destroy a Tictoctickian hospital and rehabilitation complex. Oodle-Noodle gathered that the real target was a military command post. I'm guessing the idea was that a surprise attack there would have provided us with ground cover to escape, but..." Captain Taylor found herself at a loss for what more to say.

"The peace plan did seem to be working at least somewhat, Captain." Officer Kevin Smith-Park picked his words carefully.

"Go ahead, Kevin," said the captain. "Nobody's going to bite. Unless, um... Anybody here persuaded by the Tictoctickians that perhaps we have sold cannibalism short?"

"Yes, Captain, we can laugh about it now," Deborah Davis-Murphy bristled. "But from what Yoon-hee tells me, their Grand Wazoo with the out-sized antlers thought he deserved plaudits for mercy and kindness. After all, his proposal was for only one of you to be selected for prime time. Prime rib time, that is. Apparently, the Tictoctickian deer creatures are cannibals. They eat their political dissenters and other outcasts to help sustain their food supply. To prevent wholesale revolt over you so-called other-worlders receiving special treatment, they were going to slice and dice at least one of you!"

Captain Taylor, if I might, Oodle-Noodle intervened telepathically. The tree creature was standing relaxed in a large, shallow pan of moist soil. Officers seated in front of her craned their heads around to look her way. That really wasn't necessary, though, for fully understanding what she was "saying."

"Of course, Oodle-Noodle. Please proceed."

Thank you, Captain. Officer Kevin Smith-Park, it is exactly as Officer Davis-Murphy indicated about the Tictoctickians' "Grand Wazoo." He did indeed believe it would have been an act of mercy if only one of you were slaughtered for adding to their food supply. But there are other facts Wafoodle-boodle and I learned, with which we strove to assure the away team. One of them was that the commander of their entire flying saucer fleet had big, noble plans in mind. He was on the verge of triggering an arrest, an enforceable arrest of the "Wazoo." Those of "Wazoo's" minions found to be equally, psychopathically demented were also to be taken into custody. These actions were to have occurred at the "Wazoo's" subarctic outpost and several other locations. Arrests were also to have been made aboard two of their largest, militarily equipped saucers.

Several of the away team members made nods conceding Oodle-Noodle's claim. The tree creatures did indeed telepath them this mind-read information about the commander's intent.

Once this coup was accomplished, Oodle-Noodle continued, *the fleet commander named Kwit-Nik was going to temporarily assume power. He would only remain "Supreme Authority" until a more democratic arrangement could be made. Admittedly, such an* arrangement would have fallen far short of representative democracy. Or at least it would have fallen short, even of what you pretend to have in the United Americas. Yes, Earthlings, we Oombians cannot overlook how so many of your people remain disenfranchised and powerless behind the so-called quarantine walls.

Regarding the editorial aside by the tree creature, Dr. Davis-Murphy wanted to object. She stifled herself, though. All she produced was an exhale of exasperation.

With his temporary power, Oodle-Noodle continued, *Commander Kwit-Nik was going to take three important measures. The first measure concerned imprisonment. All Tictoctickians who did not commit any acts of violence against the empire were to be released from jail. The ones left "behind bars," as your Earthling expression goes, were to be granted pardons from facing slaughterhouse death. No longer would they be added to the deer creatures' dwindling food supply. As for the few remaining Chonorans whose very existence was top secret, they were also to have been spared the iron bolt through their heads. During peace negotiations, there was to have been an eye towards having those Chonorans relocated to Oomb. Their home planet was rendered more uninhabitable than Tictoctic, even. And of course, it would have gone without saying that the rest of us would have been free to come and go as we pleased.*

For the second measure, the Tictoctickians' entire flying saucer fleet was to be put to work. They were to be mounting a massive relocation migration of Tictoctickians. Most Tictoctickians were to have been transported from their home world to Kakifika, to build upon our trial run settlement. With help secured from you Earthlings, they were to rely entirely upon renewable energy resources, primarily wind and solar.

The same would have applied for the rejuvenation of Tictoctic. The course of its runaway global warming was to have been reversed by shutting down most dependence on fossil fuels. Accelerating that reversal would have been large-scale efforts to repopulate decimated plant populations.

Tied closely to the second measure, the third measure was going to involve a rapid transition away from a meat-based to a plant-based diet. And to rephrase a popular song from Earth history, buckets-full of chocolate chip cookies were going to help that particular medicine go down.

The Tictoctickian rebels discussed all these measures and more, dear friends, including liberalizing their mating culture. Particular males could have remained together with particular females on a long-term basis. The same would have gone for particular males and females who wanted to remain together with members of the same sex. And males could have become more directly involved in child rearing. There were going to be all these measures and more, dear friends. And do you have any idea why? Can you imagine what became Commander Kwit-Nik's conclusive motivation? Too few of Oodle-Noodle's branches had yet regenerated their leaves. And so, no flourishing rustle issued from her when she turned side to side. But with her densely ciliated roots, she stirred up the moist soil in which she stood.

Dawning realization opened Kevin's eyes out of squinting perplexity. He shook his head to say, "No. Oh, hell, no! You're not going to tell us Commander Nitwit, whatever his name is, was going to reshape his planet's

history just so he'd have more time to practice oof, golf...
I'm not even sure now which game is which! Oh, hell, no!"

One of the commander's insistences was going to be that we continue providing his species with more oof clubs and oof balls. We would also have needed to offer lessons, and help with oof course designs on Kakifika. By the way, Officer Smith-Park, whether you call it oof or golf doesn't really matter. The two games are practically identical, down to eighteen holes of play for a full round.

Sergeant Fred Frankly squirmed about in his seat.

Chris mused to himself it was like Frankly were trying to gently writhe himself free from someone's embrace.

Finally, Fred spit out, "So what you're telepathin' us, Oodly-Noodly, is that drivin' this Commander Nitwit-"

"Kwit-Nik," corrected Captain Helena Taylor.

"Beg your pardon, Cap'n, but I prefer Smith-Park's name for him. What our leaf-growing friend here is telepathin', it seems, is that for Commander Whatever-you-call-him, it doesn't just come down to one thing. I mean one thing aside from not having to wonder where their next meal is coming from. So like I was yappin', it's not simply about some among his herd wanting to have a special sweetie pie out of their entire, unnaturally clothed bunch. They also want plenty of f-n' holes in the f-n' ground, to play whenever the mood strikes them!

"Well let's just say both those wishes are granted. Do you really, *really* expect us to believe that would be enough to put the skids on his fellow deer demons' designs for interplanetary conquest?!"

Sergeant Frankly, telepathed Oodle-Noodle, *the notion is not as unlikely as you might think, nor so unreasonable. We have been filtering your starship's vast historical archives through our ever-probing curiosity about your planet. From that, we have ascertained a* most fascinating tidbit. Centuries ago in Great Britain, a king made special haste on peace treaties with his neighbors. Why? Simply so he could devote more time to golf. Look it up. His name was James the Fourth, of Scotland.

"Okay," Fred Frankly inhaled like just thinking about what Oodle-Noodle telepathed made him lose his breath. "So our lone wolf vigilante, playin' like he's Han Solo runnin' the f-n' Millenium Falcon in *Star Wars*,-"

We have learned all about Star Wars.

"-you really believe he screwed up the whole f-n' enchilada with his piggyback drone attack?"

That attack resulted in the deaths of hundreds of innocents. In minutes, it sabotaged the good will we were accumulating with our constructive efforts both on Tictoctic and Kakifika. We have to hope the commander can still bring his fellow creatures back around to supporting his plan, despite the notorious destruction of their hospital. Again, it cannot be overstated how much damage that attack did to our peace plans. The piggyback drone gave the deer creatures good reason not to trust us. Many of them returned to supporting their psychopathically crazed ruler's plans for war with us. Their concerns persist over the state of his mind and that of his closest allies. But if they believe he can keep them safe from outer space threats...

At least Commander Kwit-Nik has been able to buy some time. He has remote-controlled some of their empty scout saucers to make it appear they have gone rogue. Thereby has he led their ruler, Dek-Fook-Tek, to believe they are a renegade threat he must destroy. And that they must be dealt with before the formal, full-out invasion is launched our way. Incidentally, Dek-Fook-Tek is characterizing that invasion as a defensive response.

Wafoodle-boodle here, Oodle-Noodle motioned Wafoodle-boodle's direction, *has mind-read the Celestial Breath saucer captains. Many of them are still maintaining allegiance to the commander and his peaceful vision. They are purposely having trouble targeting the saucer scouts for obliteration. They are delaying achievement of that objective for as long as they believe they can. That is, before fellow officers blindly loyal to Dek-Fook-Tek suspect something. Or Dek-Fook-Tek himself starts to doubt those saucer captains' fitness, their competence, for their assignments.*

Sergeant Guy Hanson slapped his hands against the same oval table where only a month earlier, Earthlings and Tictoctickians sat down together for a vegetarian meal. Ali Magabu and Helena Taylor nodded alike, in recognition this was the sergeant signaling nonverbally he was ready to "weigh in."

"Sergeant Hanson? Your thoughts?"

"Thank you, Captain. As the only other person here well-versed in military strategizing, aside from Sergeant Frankly, I am not sure what to think. But as I suspect he probably wanted to do, I would at least like to play devil's advocate. And I would like to do that on behalf of the renegade who wound up getting that hospital destroyed with the piggyback drone. He along with his wife is now in the hands, hooves, whatever we should call them, of the Tictoctickians, correct? Captain Taylor," Guy turned to Helena, "what if Commander Kwit-Nik's proposed coup doesn't succeed? In fact, what if it wasn't going to succeed, even if the drone attack didn't take place? Leave aside the question of whether the deer creatures were actually going to slaughter and consume one or more of us. What if their ruler planned to go ahead with the saucer invasion, regardless? In that case, isn't it a good thing the piggyback drone was tested out? Otherwise, didn't we really have nothing to put up against their magnetic pulse-beam?"

If I may, Wafoodle-boodle telepathed to approving nods from both Oodle-Noodle and Captain Taylor. *Sergeant Hanson, you seem to be asking whether not preparing for war risks being unprepared for war. That is a tautology, the truth of which I would be the first to admit. However, you fail to ask whether preparing for war does not also risk destroying the prospects for peace. Lots of innocent deer creatures were killed in their hospital and rehabilitation center. "Whoops! Wrong target!" might now lead inexorably to interplanetary war. But you seem to be saying that at least now we know the piggyback drone works. At least its manufacturer can make a fortune for themselves. You might even be able to win the war by using piggyback drones to destroy their saucers with their own magnetic pulse-beam weapons. Thousands of deer creatures aboard those saucers might be blown up in the process. However, we all know that war is hell. I am sorry to sound so bitter, but, congratulations.*

The ensuing quiet was total. So total, the sentient beings in attendance could easily make out an ever-mysterious tinkly-tinkly. It issued from light particles bouncing about on their turbulent way through the photon exhaust shaft. Somehow, those particles were being forced to decide. They were being forced to choose their physical over their wavelength existence. And the starship's rose- and tulip-shaped mirror arrays bathed in electromagnetic fields were enabling the result.

And resident physicist Dr. Timothy Aquinas was really no closer to understanding this process than when he first boarded the Smoke and Mirrors for its second mission.

"Well one thing I feel compelled to concede," shuttle pod flight officer Tanya Petrovsky finally broke the silence to say. "Those sociological futurists like Chandry Malek, they look vindicated to me. They predicted we are not going to discover any extraterrestrial civilization fully mastering space travel, if it hasn't set aside violence as means to conflict resolution."

"Say what, Tanya?" Kevin did a double-take. "I thought we've seen just the opposite established!"

"Sorry, Officer Petrovsky," added Sergeant Frankly whilst rubbing the back of his thick neck. "I have to agree with your fellow outer space explorer. You nearly gave me whiplash with your f-n' concession! Methinks you've got this ass-backwards!"

"Wait," said Tanya. "Hear me out. What I thought we learned was that Tictoctic civilization didn't actually invent those saucers or their magnetic pulse-beams. Rather, they literally hijacked that technology from the Chonorans. No? What do I have wrong?"

"Officer Petrovsky, if Professor Skepticus were seated here, he could explain to you." Dr. Deborah Davis-Murphy couldn't help a hint of condescension, such was her frustration. "But since he's not, I'll try my best," she added with a huffy sigh. "What the deer-like species have done with Chonoran technology is not unlike what the first, primitive life forms did, eons ago back on Earth. Those life forms absorbed certain bacteria that became the mitochondria. Mitochondria have been a critical part of Earth-life cellular structure ever since. However, let's say a saucer never went anywhere near Tictoctic. Still, it would have been a case of the Chonorans having developed an armed spacecraft easily fit for deep space exploration. Who knows what would have happened then? Maybe the Chonorans would have wanted to be the ones who invaded our Earth or some other already-inhabited planet. In addition, if the Chonorans had never gone to Tictoctic, that wouldn't have meant the Tictoctickians would never go to Chonora. I think you could make a case the Chonorans ought to have been more militarized than they already were, to fend off a possible civilization-ending attack from Tictoctic."

I don't understand your scenario, Dr. Davis-Murphy, jumped in Oodle-Noodle telepathically. She was unable to contain herself, even if a big pot full of muddy water did. *What "civilization-ending attacks" on Chonora would the Tictoctickians have been able to make without the magnetic pulse-beam? And please remember how their theft of that weapon came about. Again, it was a reaction to the Chonorans' precipitous violence. And of course that violence was a response to the precipitous violence with which the deer creatures met them on their first journey to Tictoctic.*

Moreover, Dr. Davis-Murphy, there is something crucially important regarding the future of Chonoran civilization, even were Tictoctic not involved. Wafoodle-boodle and I happen to have mind-read all about it.

You remember that awful glimpse we first had of Chonora, frozen in past time? You remember those thermonuclear explosives going off in the Chonoran atmosphere? You remember how it appeared the Chonorans launched those air-to-space missiles? That they were trying to defend themselves against the attacks from the saucers stolen by Tictoctickians? But that the magnetic pulse-beams from those saucers were setting the missiles off before any of them could get anywhere near them?

Well, Wafoodle-boodle and I both mind-read something most disturbing. We mind-read it in the moments before the Smoke and Mirrors breached a space-time rift to travel even further back into the past. This particularly brief exercise of our sixth sense was made possible by the quantum consciousness wave. As we all well know, that wave caught up to our location before we could make our temporal departure. Anyway, what we both ascertained concerned one of those thermonuclear detonations. It was the one that happened down closest to the surface of Chonora. We ascertained that it was NOT launched for defensive purposes. It was launched by a terrorist group intent on gaining vengeance for a portion of the Chonoran population's impoverished conditions. In other words, it was intended to go off inside the Chonoran atmosphere!

But we mind-read another plot from back even earlier into Chonora's past. This plot was developing while Dek-Fook-Tek headed up the mass-hijacking of the Chonoran space fleet. And of course, nobody here needs to be reminded how that mass-hijacking led to his assumption of supreme rule over Tictoctic. Anyway, the other plot was led by a small group of Chonoran nihilists. They had worked their way into the Chonoran space program. Those nihilists were going to do some hijacking of their own. They were going to seize two saucers. Then they were going to land one of them on Chonora's smaller moon, and have both of them direct a magnetic pulse-beam at each other. The resultant collision of such powerful electromagnetic charges was calculated to produce an incredibly strong force. The head nihilist expected that force would be strong enough to actually dislodge the smaller moon from orbit, and send it crashing into Chonora.

The dead silence that ensued from this remarkable claim lasted a full minute.

"So you're saying the odds weren't good for the survival of Chonoran civilization, Oodle-freakin'-Noodle?" Kevin grumbled finally. "It didn't matter whether or not Tictoctic entered the equation?"

On Oomb, we have garnered reason to suspect some universal directive at work. Spacefaring civilizations have to renounce war. Otherwise, they wipe themselves out before they can travel for very far or for very long, if at all, away from their home planet.

Another full minute of silence ensued. A follow-up question hung in the air, a question to which every Earthling there assembled feared to give voice. Did the tree creature mean she believed the Earth was doomed also? None of them, not even the Oombians, had any way of knowing what was in store mere weeks later back on Earth. Namely, a pair of other nihilists was intent on detonating an explosive in the Canary Islands. The detonation was to send the side of a dormant volcano sliding into the Atlantic Ocean all at once. Thereby would a massive tsunami be triggered, headed for the east coast of the United Americas.

And that was only the beginning.

"So Captain," finally went on Kevin. He had at last worked up the gumption to move beyond the question on everyone's mind, without having addressed it. "You really think the better part of Tictoctickian society could get by well enough on Kakifika? Even with the coastlines taken out of play due to sea monsters and the like?"

"If I may, Helena."

Cathy James-Leung received a you-may-proceed gesture from Captain Taylor.

"Yes, Officer Smith-Park," said Cathy, "the coastal wild life does detract from the viability of seaside development. Also, the weakness in the space-time fabric we found on one of the five parallel peninsulas makes that particular region even more hazardously unsuitable. It allows a herd of creatures remarkably similar to ceratopsian dinosaurs to stampede about on an unpredictably random basis. Nevertheless, we have found plenty enough geologically and temporally stable inland areas. They could support the entire Tictoctic population, if need be."

"Do you have any idea, any idea at all what happened to the Elusive, Captain Taylor?" By this urgently intoned question, Secretary Michael Spinner brought back Helena from the daydream upon which she had nearly drifted off to sleep. Induced by recollecting Cathy's dismissal of Kakifika's seaside resort potential, that daydream concerned a certain beach on North America's east coast. "We aren't keeping you awake, are we, Captain?"

"No, no, Mr. Secretary." Helena Taylor shook her head at the Smoke and Mirrors view-screen, where General Warlor and Secretary Spinner's intent visages were projecting.

General Warlor and Secretary Spinner themselves both remained aboard the battle-ready starship, Barack Obama.

Helena stifled a yawn to go on, "Far as we know, the Elusive was confiscated by Tictoctic troopers. We didn't stick around to find out for sure; we left lightning fast when the opportunity presented itself."

"Going in there totally defenseless like you did, Captain, we would have expected nothing more." Secretary Spinner shook his Santa beard emphatically. "That much, at least, was sensible on your part. But please tell us," his forehead furrowed most worriedly. "What happened to the piggyback drone?"

"Its programming self-destructed before they could peel it off the underbelly of the Tictoctickian battle saucer. That's what Oodle-Noodle here ascertained with her mind-reading and remote-viewing. Same goes for the unused drones packed aboard the Elusive. So you can tell the drone manufacturer not to worry, Mr. Secretary. Their precious cash cow in the event of interplanetary war did not fall into the deer creatures' cloven hooves. Oh, and sorry we didn't get ourselves destroyed. Sorry we didn't give you the perfect pretext to go out there laser cannons ablaze and drones swarming like locusts. Why don't you just assume that the couple aboard the Elusive has been converted into so many gourmet meals? That way, you can prosecute your damned war regardless of our having emerged unscathed!" Helena Taylor was convinced the drone attack did damage to the Oombian peace plan commensurate with the deadly damage it did to the Tictoctickian hospital. So she had lost all taste for diplomacy, where dealing with these particular government superiors was concerned.

Secretary Spinner and General Warlor exchanged looks of what-are-we-going-to-do-with-these-nuts? Then Spinner took a deep inhale and exhale to at last respond, "Tell us how you *really* feel, Captain; no need to hold back. First, though, would you mind explaining something to us? Would you mind explaining how you expect that if we do nothing, those unholy, by your own admission blood-craving beasts will leave us alone??! Harrumph!" He cleared his throat like asking this question was dislodging a big wad of congestion, coughing it up from his chest.

"Correct me if I am wrong, Oodle-Noodle," said Captain Taylor. "Think I know what our friends from Oomb here would say, Secretary Spinner. They would say you are conflating doing nothing with doing anything other than some kind of military action. But we were doing a lot, Mr. Secretary, General Warlor. We were establishing the practicality for the deer creatures relocating themselves to a wilderness planet away from Tictoctic. We learned their home planet has become an increasingly hostile habitat due to runaway global warming. As for the wilderness planet, it has not yet experienced the re-evolution of apex, highly intelligent predators such as our selves or the deer creatures' selves. That is, since their previous version of highly intelligent predators essentially committed mass suicide. Anyway, to elaborate further our accomplishments back on Tictoctic,-"

"Captain," interrupted Spinner, "if this is about greenhouses and solar panels, we've already heard and read about them."

"And you heard and read how it looked like we were defusing the potential for interplanetary war? You heard and read how a powerful, disgruntled faction was about to take over? And that they would have nixed Tictoctickian plans for a meat-gathering, other-world invasion?"

"So you really, honestly believe love and peace were about to break out on Tictoctic?"

"Mr. Secretary, I am not sure what I believe. All I know for certain is how well our military scheming went for Fafama."

"Oh, you're going to play *that* card again!"

Captain, allow me, Oodle-Noodle telepathed for Helena Taylor's reception only.

Helena nodded assent as she hugged herself tightly. Buddy Leung could tell she was trying to chill, keep from leaping forward to pound her fists against the view-screen.

Secretary Spinner, General Warlor, allow me to share with you what I mind-read before we fled the Tictoctickians' solar system. Their Commander Kwit-Nik was still trying to reassemble his coalition to overthrow their psychopathic leadership. He was still hoping to have that leadership put away in a mental institution while he prosecuted our planetary resettlement plan. Plus, he was intent on pushing for wholesale diet transformation. His fellow beings would no longer need to cannibalize their own, nor go hunting after you. Of course, we cannot know one way or the other how well his efforts are succeeding presently...

"But while we await the results, you would have us do nothing. No. I will humor you by putting it: You would have us do nothing, militarily."

Correct, Mr. Secretary, Oodle-Noodle nodded with a rustle of leaves from her newly rejuvenating branches. Those branches included both her arms. Her previous arms were snapped off in the service of escape from various reptilian monsters along the coast of a Kakifikan continent. *Nevertheless,* Oodle-Noodle continued, *agree with me or don't. I am not advocating you do nothing, period. For example, I believe we could help Commander Kwit-Nik further prosecute his case for détente between his civilization and yours. We would require access to an unmanned, enormous container ship designed for light-speed multiples. We could load up such a vessel with food supplies, various seeds and fertilizer, additional oof club sets, oof balls, and flag pins. We could also add boxes full of your amplets. They would be programmed with a vast variety of music from both our planets. Plus, Officer Chris Olsen-Taylor could add the few songs he was able to salvage from Fafama before the holocaust there. And of course, we wouldn't want to forget boxes full of chocolate chip cookies and cookie batter.*

"Chocolate chip cookies and more oof clubs. Yes, let's not forget any of those," Secretary Spinner nodded sarcastically.

For Helena Taylor, General Warlor's raised-chin countenance appeared interchangeable with that of a cold stone statue.

"The only problem is this," Spinner continued. "We have already more than broken the budget on rush completion of two additional starships fully outfitted for war. And a third one is in the works. Even assuming Congress was persuaded as to your scheme's value, where would they find enough money to borrow for it?"

About our proposed container ship for sending a care package with love to Tictoctic: It could have been constructed instead of one of your two other battleships. Or the third one you said is "in the works." And I'm guessing something when it comes to ordering multiple piggyback drones. Since you now know they succeed in what they are supposed to be doing, money will be no object. "Ditto," as you also say, were the decision to be made that a fourth battleship is necessary. No. In civilizations such as yours, there never appears to be a financial issue with preparing for more war. It's the stuff of peace-making where all the pennies have to be counted.

"I am able to mention something about the oof clubs and the cookies?" Nutrition Officer Ludi Perez raised her hand for permission to speak.

Secretary Spinner opened his arms wide, and said, "Hit me with all you've got, Officer. Unless you object, Captain."

"Mr. Secretary, Officer Ludi Perez has had to adjust to a lot here. It's so different from her life a half century ago. Considering that, she has been doing amazingly well," observed Captain Taylor. "I could not be more delighted for her to take an active part in this dialogue."

"Thank you, Captain. Mr. Secretary, what I hear from you, I think you need to know something. You need to know what I experienced serving the extraterrestrial deer some variations on our Puerto Rican rice and bean dishes. And also how I saw them reacting to lessons in playing oof, or what you call golf. Many of those creatures, they were pleased to eat our 'arroz con gandules.' And many of them were practicing their golf swing, even when they were not holding a club in their hands. Sí, some of them, especially the one named Dek-Fook-Tek, they frighten me. But if their people who are reasonable can put those scary ones in a mental institution...The idea of Oodle-Noodle is not so loco."

"Well, Señora Perez, I thank you, what is it you say? Muchas gracias? As opposed to grassy ass? Thank you for giving us your perspective as a time-travelling immigrant.

"But Oodle-Noodle, I want to address that warehouse-sized container ship notion of yours. You see, say we do send out that thing unmanned. But also say the Tictoctickians are still up to no good. Your Commander Kwit-Nik, think I finally have his name right. Let's imagine he's over-ruled, tossed into an insane asylum himself or worse. Even if we rustle up the funding for your container ship, what's to keep those antlered demons from permanently detaining it? How do we stop them from using it to learn more about our vulnerabilities and capabilities?"

It could be rigged for self-destruction in case it is not immediately returned to you after its contents have been unloaded. Throughout this telepath, something else was weighing on Oodle-Noodle and Wafoodle-boodle both. Oodle-Noodle couldn't bring herself to make any reference to it. But she feared it might be the only thing capable of saving Earth and Tictoctic from imminent self-destruction.

By way of reaction to Oodle-Noodle's response, Secretary Spinner silently shook his head with what struck Helena as a pained grin. Then he looked down before he looked right back up to speak. "Well," he said, "it might surprise the lot of you to learn we haven't quite concluded, ourselves, what we're doing next, and when. All we know is that President Carey has left these surpassingly important matters to General Warlor. But whatever she does decide, we're not sure there will be any role for you to play from here onwards, Captain Taylor. We have to consider the tenor of your remarks. There's also the no small matter of your completely disarming the Smoke and Mirrors. Not to mention the willful setting-off in outer space of every last weapon you were carrying, before you left for Tictoctic. That is, if we're going to entertain any lectures about wasteful spending.

"Meantime, I don't know whether one of your Oombian associates has mind-read this or not, put two and two together. But guess what: Officer Olsen-Taylor, your mother is down on the surface of Oomb. She wants to see both of you, you and the captain. Somehow, she talked her way on board the Eisenhower to come out here. She has something to share with you, what looks like has Fafaman hieroglyphics engraved all over it."

Chapter 28

"My Supreme Authority Dek-Fook-Tek, I am sorry to have wasted my time confirming what you already knew." While meekly bleating this Tictoctickian truism for Dek-Fook-Tek's pleasure, Tictoctickian biologist KeGasskee kept peering through his microscope. He wouldn't want Dek-Fook-Tek to think he was trying to avoid looking at him, yet he was. KeGasskee believed Dek-Fook-Tek should have been renamed Supreme Idiot over Supreme Authority. Nevertheless, he feared direct eye contact might enable the psychopathic leader to sense what he really thought of him.

Blithely ignorant of the biologist's sentiment, Dek-Fook-Tek nodded for him to continue.

"The matter comprising that lamp is unmistakably an antler taken from a species of creature similar to ourselves," said KeGasskee. "But it is not actually related to us. Nor is it related to any other extinct creature on Tictoctic, whether of recent demise or uncovered in the fossil record of Tictoctic. It most likely originated on another planet."

Dek-Fook-Tek did his best not to wriggle his ears in surprise. Standing fully erect on his hind limbs, he swaggered closer to the biologist. He swung his oversized antlers from side to side with the ever-present assistance of his antler handlers. "You are welcome for my bringing this to your attention, Professor KeGasskee.

"Lieutenant Ak-keek-teek?"

The lieutenant rose back up onto his own hind limbs from where he had been down on all fours following behind his Supreme Authority. He had been licking bits of royal excrement off Dek-Fook-Tek's tail where it protruded out the usual hole stitched into Tictoctickian pants. He

558

was assuring the excrement wouldn't stick there as it dried. "You have an order, my Supreme Authority?"

"You will join me for viewing a film retrieved from the captured enemy spacecraft. I am told it is a film I simply must see."

"Of course, Dek-Fook-Tek." Ak-keek-teek bowed. "What you have just so humbly revealed is yet one more indication of your immeasurably deep mercy. I assume whoever spoke to you was not fatally gored for insisting you simply must do anything!"

"Clearly, Lieutenant, his impertinence was cattle-driven by a sincere, if over-panicky concern for our greater good. A certain horror was regurgitated from what I suspect he actually did discover during his viewing. But I reserve the right, the duty to change my entire judgment on the matter. We shall see, once I behold the film with my own two eyes. Depending, I might need to revisit his future. He was the same officer, incidentally, who led confiscation of the puny-sized enemy military vessel in the first place."

"Of course, my Supreme Authority. All our fates lie in your mighty cloven hoof-hands." By this juncture, the biologist named KeGasskee had joined Ak-keek-teek to complete the ritual praise. "They are as the fates of an oskynt herd that would dare challenge lava's onward flow from an erupting volcano."

<hr/>

At the film's start, a single word flashed silently on the screen in big, capital letters: *Bambi.* The other-worlders' translator wouldn't have mattered, even had it worked for text as well as speaking. *Kambki* still would have meant nothing more than gibberish to either Dek-Fook-Tek or Lieutenant Ak-keek-teek. That is, not until it was identified later on as the name of the main character.

"What is this?? Do we have a children's cartoon full of wee little woodland creatures from Akt?!" Dek-Fook-Tek rose out of his seat to tongue-click in protest not two minutes into the Disney film from Earth civilization's twentieth century. For another minute he impatiently snorted. He looked around, wondering at which wall to lunge his antlers in a molten rage. He was just about to order the film turned off. The officer who said he "must" see it would be told he "must" appear before him, chest bared and swelled out most vulnerably...,

But then those aforementioned woodland creatures gathered around a naked mother deer with her naked child. And this pastoral tableau was accompanied by a translation into the tongue-clicks of Dek-Fook-Tek's language. "A new prince is born."

"What?!" Dek-Fook-Tek brayed as he retook his seat, however animate he remained. "Now we have a royal mother with child, both shown completely naked for all to see??!! Is this some propaganda movie from Akt meant to ridicule and humiliate us??!!"

"Or to ridicule our kind still living on Akt," suggested the lieutenant. Ak-keek-teek was selecting his words most gingerly. Naturally, he wanted to avoid becoming the target for any of his Supreme Authority's unhinged invective.

"No, wait. You heard it did you not, Lieutenant?! That older little creature has lectured that younger little creature not to insult the young prince who is named Kambki!!"

"I heard that indeed, my Supreme Authority. Though most likely, I did not hear it with the level of clarity afforded by your ultra-sensitive ears."

"Perhaps a rebel among the Akt aliens made this film! Perhaps he was sympathetic to the humiliating persecution of their resident Tictoctickians who had somehow made it all the way there from our planet! A persecution, I might add, doubtless to assure that those precious creatures will not take their rightful place! That they will not dominate over Akt's inferiorly evolved animals with no antlers of their own! Not even the shortest, stubbiest of stubs upon their foreheads! But no, wait again! What is *this*?!" Dek-Fook-Tek leaned forward in his chair. "How can they have that small creature named Tumpet teach the prince?! Is this a mockery of me after all??!!"

"Supreme Dek-Fook-Tek, thank you for finding such a gentle way to remind me what the producer was really about with this film," tentatively bleated Lieutenant Ak-keek-teek. "That he was illustrating how royalty such as your own self behaves, even at a tender young age. They are willing to humor the lowliest creatures, if need be. Woe to anyone who would dare deny your long history of kindness to your fellow creatures! It simply cannot be denied, how you have allowed us to think we have made important offerings, so we wouldn't feel totally useless!"

"Baa, you're welcome," Dek-Fook-Tek responded with imperious nonchalance. He settled back in his seat, to the lieutenant's considerable relief. But no sooner was the Supreme Authority relaxing than he leaned forward yet anew. His snout was dripping nasal run-off with his agitation. "Nude??!! All nude??!! A virtual security detachment of males wearing nothing at all??!! WHAT SORT OF PORNOGRAPHY IS THIS?!?!?!" Dek-Fook-Tek brayed at the top of his lungs. He came down onto his front limbs to kick the backrest of his seat with his hind legs. He kicked so violently hard, he snapped the backrest off its adjustable hinges. "Baa! At least now they are giving proper respect to the Great Prince. He must have been modeled after their own real-life leader. Of course!" The supremely agitated deer creature, Dek-Fook-Tek, settled back in his seat for the umpteenth time; the lieutenant lost count. He couldn't settle back all the way, though, with the backrest broken. "They were stripped of their clothing! Every last one!" he complained anew. "That must be what this film is communicating! Those deceitful demons from Akt with which we have had to deal, they tried to humiliate them!"

Bang!

On the sound of gunshot, Dek-Fook-Tek and Ak-keek-teek both craned their heads high as they could. They did a visual sweep of the entire room before realizing exactly what happened: That sudden noise had issued from the film.

The next tongue-clicked translation into their language came from the narrator saying, "Man was in the forest."

"You heard that, Lieutenant?! You heard that?!?!" Dek-Fook-Tek brayed with a new wave of agitation washing over his unstable-enough-as-it-was temperament. "The word, 'kmank,' did not translate!! And it is like another name we heard the deceitful aliens use for themselves that also did not translate! 'Kumank'!! Those must be special Akt names for monster! The Akt beasts were taunting us! They figured we would not know what 'kumank' meant! Yes! It explains why we are seeing a cartoon! Now we know why this courageous rebel filmmaker depicted stripped-naked, humiliated kinfolk in such a manner! Now we know why he resorted to a medium normally reserved for the amusement of children! He couldn't hire actual kinfolk for this depiction, set in actual epic surroundings on Akt! The chance for the Akt monsters to have happened upon where he was filming would have been too dangerous! Far safer to go the animation route!"

"Supreme Dek-Fook-Tek, the profundity of your analysis takes my breath away," Lieutenant Ak-keek-teek baaed most meekly, with a submissive bow.

"No! NO!!" Dek-Fook-Tek harshly brayed anew as he realized the monsters shot Bambi's mother.

So it went for the movie's hour-long duration, or at least for the part Dek-Fook-Tek allowed to play out. The forest catching fire prompted more speculation from him. He suggested that in the real, non-animated world, the Akt aliens deployed their own version of an air igniter. "They must have done this for mindlessly destroying their idyllic fields and pastures!" he ranted. "Their air igniters were certainly not deployed for usefully destroying wilderness areas like we do, in the service of industrial development!"

When Bambi was shot at last, Supreme Authority Dek-Fook-Tek rose from his seat in his greatest fury, yet. "Turn it off! TURN IT OFF!!" he brayed harshly, and tearfully, short minutes before the film would have ended anyway. He came down on all fours to gallop for the nearest window drapery. He bit at that drapery, growling like a dog, and then he shook it from side to side until he ripped a hole in the fabric.

By this time, Dek-Fook-Tek's personal physician had been rushed there for administering tranquillizer. The physician injected the extra-strength medication into the Supreme Authority's hip.

"Lieutenant Ak-keek-teek," Dek-Fook-Tek tongue-clicked finally, in an ultra-subdued, quieted state. The tranquillizer brought him down from his foaming-at-the-mouth rage. "I want this video to go out across the land. I also want it broadcast aboard every saucer in our fleet, complete with the translations."

"Of course, my Supreme Authority."

"And tell Commander Kwit-Nik to call off the search-and-destroy mission for the scout saucers. Let those cowards flee, if they must!" Dek-Fook-Tek's panting resumed again, despite the medication. He rose on his hind limbs to his full height. "Not another moment's delay before a full-out, defensive stampede against the monsters from Akt! But Lieutenant..." Dek-Fook-Tek clip-clopped close to Ak-keek-teek. He practically rubbed the lieutenant's anxiously wriggling snout with his own, which was slimy with nasal discharge continuing to bubble out and pop from his nostrils. "Make sure the commander understands he is not to waste any time going after the monsters' military outpost in the Koombk solar system. He is to have the full force of the celestial breath blow with the fury of an exploding star on the Akt itself! If any of our brothers and sisters are still left alive there, not already hunted into extinction, they are to be liberated!"

"We can only hope every last one of them hasn't been slaughtered yet, supremely merciful Dek-Fook-Tek."

"Baa," the Supreme Authority nodded. "Regarding the monsters themselves, make sure the commander understands that as many of their bodies are to be trawled as possible. However, he should not allow such a consideration to impede the utter decapitation of their military and space-flight complex!"

"For that, my Supreme Dek-Fook-Tek, we must also guard against... How to trot delicately through such a garden so as not to trample on any of its flowers? We must warn off the commander from being taken in by any other deceitful schemes the Akt monsters might offer."

"Yes, Lieutenant," nodded Dek-Fook-Tek again, his snout still up close to Ak-keek-teek's. "In the past, Commander Kwit-Nik has demonstrated an unfortunate susceptibility to the wiles of other-worlder instinctive reasoning patterns. Baa. I shall need to ruminate upon the possibility that you, Lieutenant, ought to be appointed the new commander, instead. Perhaps you ought to be the one in charge of this massive operation to protect the Tictoctic Empire from other-world monsters."

"What has been said before, my dear leader, bears repeating for not having been said often enough. How exceedingly unfortunate you cannot be cloned to become the commander, as well as to assume other critical functions in the workings of our glorious civilization. I know what would happen, were I to be assigned the role of commander. I would only be of any use at all on account of your inspiration shining with the ever constancy of the sun. I solemnly pledge that in such an eventuality, every last keempt of my willpower would be given over to the mission. Excuse me." Lieutenant Ak-keek-teek turned away from Dek-Fook-Tek as though to sneeze. He did simulate a big "Ah-choo!" But he was really about avoiding Dek-Fook-Tek getting a look at his ridiculously wide, buck-toothed grin. He couldn't help it playing across his long, narrow face. *My added prestige, my pick of the most arousing fawns...happiness as I have never experienced before shall ultimately be mine!*

⋅ᴴᵍ°°ᴴᵍ°⋅ᴴᵍ°

Soon-to-be *former* Commander Kwit-Nik turned away from his own private screening of *Bambi* with tears streaming down his face. But they were not tears for the main character in the animated Disney film so much as they were for the anticipated fate of his effort to revive the peace plan. It was evident to him that on "Akt," the likeness to his kind must be a lower species. Those creatures must live on a level comparable to the all-but-extinct, often-invoked oskynt that used to roam the Tictoctickian wilderness in large herds. Clearly, the film's producers tried to see life empathetically through the eyes of a whole other species. They tried to imagine how their own selves might be regarded as a destructive force of nature. Clearly, the movie evidenced a kind streak Kwit-Nik was long since convinced ran through these other-worlders. It was a kind streak only a little less pronounced than the one running through the sentient trees of "Koombk." But Kwit-Nik well knew that was not how others of his species would see this cinematic work from over a century ago, and several trillion miles away. No. The soon-to-be-former Commander well knew that untempered panic, terror and anger would break out. It would spread across Tictoctic and on board the immense battle saucers like an out-of-control niki-nik infestation. Deer creatures everywhere would be calling for defensive retaliation, and more. The abuse of their brothers and sisters made to wander homeless and naked across the wilderness of a planet in another solar system: that could not go unavenged.

There is no telling what Captain "Taylok" and the rest will do now, once they have returned to their own kind. The troubled deer creature thought this to himself as he flipped on the light switch in his personal viewing room. But as for my fellow creatures, their destructive ways cannot be allowed to spread any further! Kwit-Nik concluded. He had to re-steel himself for the tasks ahead, as well as to reaffirm his grim commitment to what he had already accomplished. It is time for me to assume the captain's chair of the Fourth Celestial Breath, with Chef

Glork-tek plus the other most loyals at my side. To make this happen, I will initiate what I suspect Dek-Fook-Tek has already sent Lieutenant Ak-keek-teek to advise me of in any event. For the sake of launching an all-out attack on Akt, the Supreme Authority will change my directive. He will insist I cease the search-and-destroy mission against the remote-controlled scout saucers he has been fooled into believing are runaway renegades. Soon as I've done that, I will tell Dek-Fook-Tek what needs to happen next, in my humble estimation. I will suggest that one saucer needs to remain behind. Thereby will the throne be protected from a sneaky rear guard action by the very other-worlders we are set on defeating. And then I will suggest I should be the one put in charge of that operation, with Lieutenant Ak-keek-teek promoted to take my place as commander. Let Commander Ak-keek-teek send the rest of the battle saucer fleet to Akt, all magnetic pulse-beams firing. With them gone from the immediate vicinity of Tictoctic, I will be free to execute a most crucial part of my plan.

The magnetic pulse-beam device I clandestinely built on the dark side of the moon, it is ready for operation. A targeted pulse-beam will be fired at it from the Fourth Celestial Breath. At the same time, I will remote-control operate the moon-based device to return-fire a targeted magnetic pulse-beam. That is all it should take. The force from those two beams colliding head-on with like charges should prove ample to knock our moon out of its orbit. It will be headed on a direct course for Tictoctic. That should become the beginning of the end to our pestilence, before it can spread any further! All that will remain will be for the captains of the other saucers to order their pulse-beams fired at Akt targets. Hacking remotely into their on-board computers, I have set the stage for what should happen next. Their beams should fire internally, bursting apart their respective spaceships. Ever after, may a kind, benevolent spirit inspire the creatures of Akt in everything they do, as they populate Kakifika to make it their own!

⸎⋊⊤⍟°⸎⋊⊤⍟°⸎⋊⊤⍟°

"One last thing before you lead the defensive charge, Commander Ak-keek-teek," crisply tongue-clicked Dek-Fook-Tek. "Bring the crew of the miniature enemy battleship before me!"

Chapter 29

Crack!

With a perfect swing of his wooden ass, Boodle-Roodle sent the softball on a high arc towards center field. Don Típico's underhand pitch put it over home plate at an ideal height for clobbering.

"I've got this!" called out Samantha Santiago. She waved off Angel Ramirez, who was sprinting over from left field.

"Ay, caramba! Don't let it hit you on the head, chica vieja! *(old girl!)*" Don Típico cried in his raspy voice.

Focus on what you expect to do with the softball, not on what someone else might fear will happen, gently telepathed right fielder Poodle-Shnoodle...

just as the ball flew into, against the webbing of Sammy's mitt.

Sammy brought down her outstretched hand to look at what she caught. The expression on her face dawned with joyful surprise, but only after she confirmed her mitt was cradling the fly ball Boodle-Roodle hit. That it was not some bird or bug creature of Oomb who didn't pay enough attention to where it was going.

Far as Poodle-Shnoodle was concerned, Sammy's happily crinkled-up bustle of age lines gave her face the beautifully arousing allure of mature tree bark.

Chris and Helena might not have seen Sammy's face the same way Poodle-Shnoodle did. But they arrived at the Oombian baseball field in time to witness her epic catch.

Chris wore his Oombian Ootzies hat, as much about protecting his scalp from the no-see-um, hair-eating fripe as it was about showing team spirit. Whichever, it certainly didn't create any problem for Samantha when she looked his direction. She instantly recognized her son and his starship captain wife, wherefore she dropped the softball from her mitt.

For Don Típico, it looked like Chris and Helena had hypnotized Samantha into neglect of anything or anyone else other than themselves.

The same time Chris recognized his mom standing in the outfield with her trademark Baltimore Orioles cap, he also noticed something else. There was a thunderous commotion of running feet, a virtual stampede. But he soon realized he and Helena were not the ones being swamped, overwhelmed by admirers and curiosity seekers. Rather, that fuss centered on Pedro, Ludi and their toddle-waddling daughter Alexita bringing up the rear.

Laughter interspersed cries of joy over the Perez family's return. But all of that seemed faded into the distant background for Chris as he and Helena steadily approached Sammy.

"Helena. Captain Helena Taylor," said Samantha. Samantha hugged her daughter-in-law first.

"It was a surprise as big as anything, you can be sure, when we learned you had arrived here," Captain Taylor prattled on anxiously. The welcoming hug from mother-in-law Samantha was drawn out longer than she found comfortable. "But it was a surprise Chris thrilled over, believe me. That we both thrilled over."

Sammy's embrace of Helena Taylor might have lingered into unease. However, the way she tightly wrapped her arms around Chris's neck felt to him like she never wanted to let go. During which she responded to Helena's awkwardly expressed sentiment with, "The genesis of this reunion goes back some sixty years ago.

For what it is intended to be, I am surprised, too, that it's finally going to take place."

"You made an awesome catch, Mom!"

"Indeed. If your uncle were here, he wouldn't have believed it. He would have given it the same long odds of happening as someone ever hitting another baseball through the warehouse window at Camden Yards!"

"I remember Uncle Ed arguing with you over that," commented Chris. Tears welled in his eyes. He became uncertain he wasn't the one who never wanted to let go, once his mom did at last loosen her grip.

"I wish your uncle were still here to see the starships and all the peculiarities of Oomb. He was such a big science fiction fan!"

"I know, Mom."

"So what is it, exactly, that's going to take place that had its start over a half century earlier?" Helena tried to sound nonchalant. She tried to sound like she was merely attempting to move matters along despite the clearly powerful emotions Chris and his mother were experiencing. But that sixty-year time frame Samantha Santiago-Olsen mentioned sent chills down her spine. The start of it coincided too closely with when the time-travel "rapture" took place of a Philadelphia neighborhood, facilitated by the Smoke and Mirrors.

All the same, Helena, Chris, and Samantha ended up taking seats on a sofa in the living room of an Oombian-built log cabin. Chris sat between his wife and mother.

The log cabin was where Pedro and Ludi had originally taken up residence in the settlement named Oombinquen on the island named Boombeeno.

Samantha patted a dark velvet cloth wrapped around something. She was nestling it in her lap.

"So, what exactly do you have there, Ms. All-Star Center Fielder?" Helena was careful to simply point towards the velvet cloth, rather than reaching for it.

Sammy nevertheless grabbed Captain Taylor's wrist. She said, "What is enrobed by this cloth was entrusted to me back in 2002, with an understanding of what I would do with it sixty years later. I would hand it over to a loved one after he underwent an awful adventure. Only months ago did I receive full insight regarding who that loved one, or those loved ones, were going to be."

"Let me guess." Helena made a gesture for Chris's mother to hold off her next utterance. "Either there was simply a voice in your head, or there was an older woman of a diminutive yet very feisty nature, not unlike yourself. If the latter, she materialized before you to convey the information. As for an awful adventure, I suppose how close we came to becoming part of some extraterrestrials' diet qualifies."

"Oh my." Sammy lifted fingers to lips. "Well, you have certainly done a good job of keeping the press in the dark about how bad things were going out here. But we do know back home of a possible extraterrestrial military threat. People are still remaining calm. They figure if we've got warships traveling seven light years to deal with that threat, it's going to have a tough time getting anywhere near our solar system."

"Otherwise there might be awful adventures for everyone," Helena couldn't help warning.

"That feisty old woman you mentioned, Captain Taylor, not unlike... I hope I'm feisty, yes," nodded Samantha. "So you are saying, Captain, I am not the only one she has haunted."

"The first time *you* were haunted, Mom," said Chris, "was that those sixty years ago, before you had even met Dad?"

"Mmm-hmm." Sammy had to mumble to keep her voice from cracking at the mere mention of her deceased husband. "It was the year after 9/11, the terrorist attack on the Twin Towers in New York City."

Helena and Chris easily tolerated an ensuing moment of quiet for Sammy to collect herself. They could hear the distant collective belch of some Oonzy-Ootzies waddling back up the shore from their mid-day feeding.

"Your grandparents, Chris," Chris's mother went on, finally, "they took your Uncle Edward and me to see some relatives up in Philadelphia, including your great uncle Pedro. I have been able to reconstruct the timeline from what your great aunt Ludi's grandma Norma told me. Based on that, we must have arrived at the residence only minutes after they were spirited away to the future by you."

"Well that explains one thing, anyway," said Chris. "To this day, I still have the occasional dream about you and Dad bringing me to see my great uncle Pedro and his family...fading memories, I'm now guessing, from an alternate universe before we 'raptured' them."

"I have my own occasional dream," Sammy nodded down at her lap. "It is a dream of having actually gotten to see my cousins and aunt Rotonda and the others, instead of an empty home with the beans left simmering on the stove. And now they are all younger than I am!" Sammy tugged down on the brim of her security blanket Orioles cap before she continued. "Back then in 2002," she said, "there was one person I did get to meet, upstairs alone in my cousins' bedroom. Norma has told me her name is Doña Galleta, or Cookie Lady."

"Cookie Lady," Chris repeated. He gave Helena a telling look as in: *Cookies have played an inordinately large role in what we have been going through.*

"It might have been more fun for me if she were Homerun Lady, but...She handed over what's inside this cloth, to pass on to you once your awful adventure is done."

"We hope it's done, Mom."

"Yes, oh my, well..." Sammy wasn't sure how to respond exactly. But then it did finally occur to her to remark, "Cookie Lady didn't say there couldn't be a new awful adventure. So I think we're okay." On that note, Sammy finally released Helena's wrist to gently, most carefully unfold the velvet cloth.

Even with the mid-day sun shining through the windows, Helena and Chris could discern a faint, greenish glow against the dark purple. That became evident well before Chris's mom had unfolded the cloth enough to reveal what was actually concealed there.

Helena's eyes grew bigger, and bigger still, nocturnal owl eyes big, Chris mused. That happened when the unwrapped object came into plain view on Samantha's final unfolding of the velvet material. It was a golden pendant. Helena and Chris were well familiar with its aforementioned greenish glow. But in addition there were hieroglyphic-type engravings.

"Cookie Lady handed you *this*?" As Helena expressed her surprise, she couldn't help diving in to lift the pendant from its velvet cradle.

"You know something about it?" asked Samantha, mildly stunned by her daughter-in-law's haste to grasp at the mysterious graven object.

"What *do* you know about it, Helena?" Chris chimed in, though keeping his hands to himself. He was too worried his wife would push him away if he tried to touch the faintly glowing pendant. And he was unable to avoid thinking most jealously, *Was this a piece of jewelry given you by the Fafamafalafama? And it got lost in the chaos of events leading to the destruction of Fafaman civilization?*

"Did Doña Galleta tell you how she acquired this?" was Helena's non-response to Chris and Samantha's questions.

"Don't you know by now, Captain? Pedro and Ludi Perez said it fell from cloud-to-cloud lightning. They handed it over..."

Helena looked up from pondering the pendant into Samantha's face. Dawning awareness dropped her mouth wide open.

Chris's mother was struck with an absurd notion regarding Helena's mouth. Namely, that it could have been the aforementioned cloud-to-cloud lightning made flesh, a second pendant about to emerge from it.

"This is the object they were discussing?!?!" Captain Taylor exclaimed as much as she asked.

"The same, Captain. So, what does it mean to you?"

"Deep in the heart of Fafama's city-sized pyramid, I met the Fafamafalafama's first wife, the Varalawa. She showed me this or its twin." Helena held up the pendant by one end, turning it from side to side to watch its green-glowing, bronze-like surface catch the Oombian sun's glint. "The Varalawa said she was personally engraving one of them for me, for us. She was going to share the other one with the Fafamafalafama." Helena turned Chris's way. "When the dirty comet crashed into the pyramid at its base, the explosive force must somehow have done the unbelievable. It must have propelled at least this one of the two pendants through a space-time rift torn open close to the planet's surface. And, well..."

"That explains why the hieroglyphic lettering is Fafaman," Sammy nodded with understanding, however astounded she found herself.

"You already knew about the lettering?!" Helena shook her head in more disbelief.

"An Oombian linguist gave me a full translation. She was able to do that, thanks to a Fafaman children's picture dictionary brought to her aboard the Smoke and Mirrors," Samantha explained. She kept holding onto the brim of her O's cap for dear life. The moment was nearly upon her when she would fulfill the final part of a task assigned to her some sixty years earlier.

"The Varalawa told me she was engraving a poem composed by an ancient mystic," Helena felt moved to further offer. "Apparently, that mystic was regarded on Fafama the same way we regard Jesus or Buddha. Little was said in public, the Varalawa told me. The worship of, or devout reverence for, anyone other than their steady succession of Fafamafalafamas was considered heresy. It was punishable by exile into the hostile wilderness way west of the Great Pyramid, where there were not even the rebel forces to help one survive. But... I have forgotten the mystic's name. However, the first wife told me a legend about her. Supposedly, one of the early Fafamafalafamas had her thrown into an ahtpah nest. He did this because she was drawing too much attention with her poetic insights."

"'She'? So this mystic was a woman." Sammy nervously licked her lips. She really wanted to have her role over and done with, in whatever this drama was that had taken so long to unfold. Especially now that she learned it might have actually begun, in a certain sense, many centuries earlier.

"A woman," Helena nodded. "The Varalawa told me that after her death, she was purported to have reappeared. She became a ghostly presence for certain of her closest family and other admirers. She was somewhat like Doña Galleta has been for us, or Jesus was for the disciples after the crucifixion."

"So, um, didn't the Varalawa get herself in trouble, wanting to engrave this mystic's words on jewelry?" asked Samantha.

"She told me that as long as people only discussed the mystic's poetry secretively, well... Clandestine behavior of that sort was tolerated at all levels of their society."

"I gather we don't have to be secretive here, so let me go ahead, please," said Samantha. She readjusted her O's cap to help herself stop quivering.

Helena surprised Chris by firmly grasping one of his hands in hers. She squeezed it how he could only read as affectionately, passionately hard, before she said, "Okay, I'm ready." Then she sought his eyes to add, "We're ready."

Preceded by clearing her throat to try and avoid raspy-ness, Samantha recited by heart. She had no need to review the hieroglyphics for any least reminder.

"'From every single awareness, no matter how minute,

the universe spreads out an infinite distance, all directions.

For this fact, every awareness dwells at the center.

Its import ripples out everywhere, forever,

as from a pebble dropped into a never-ending sea.

A couple honors that import with their devotion to one another.

I want to honor that import with you.'"

Helena squeezed Chris's hand again, tightly. This time he squeezed back as they searched one another's watering eyes.

"I am," Helena choked out, haltingly, "the world's worst communicator. Including with myself."

Chris shook his head protestingly "no" as Helena Taylor laughed through her tears.

Helena went on, "The first wife actually recited these lines for me." She indicated the hieroglyphic inscriptions. "They described perfectly how I have come to feel about you, Chris, and about us after all these years. I knew I couldn't keep them straight, though. I knew I was going to require this pendant, plus a Fafaman dictionary to boot. But then with the destruction of Fafama, all seemed lost. I couldn't imagine what was going to unfold. I didn't dare dream this oddly glowing piece of jewelry would have survived. Rather, I assumed it was buried under tons of rubble, and then melted back to formlessness like Frodo's ring in *The Lord of the Rings*. A super volcano caused by the comet apocalyptically crashing into the surface of Fafama was certain to have destroyed it. There was no possible way it could have stayed intact, let alone found its way into our hands..." Helena kept shaking her head in disbelief until Chris finally collected her into his arms, heedless of their audience. He kissed her forehead and eyelids all over.

Helena decided she would never need pain Chris by ever informing him about her attempted sacrifice back on Fafama. She had tried to seduce the Fafamafalafama in hope of distracting him from his apocalyptic plan. For sure, she could have explained that her effort came to naught. The Fafamafalafama had been hell-bound to bring the comet crashing down on Fafama's terrorist stronghold, with well-known most tragic results. But still, in the wake of such an admission, how would her husband have ever been able to trust her, ever again? How would he have ever been able to believe their love for one another was what she held dearest?

Helena also decided she never need bother Chris with tales of her parents' nit-picking criticism despite her considerable accomplishments.

What Helena *did* decide she needed to share with Chris was which of his music she really enjoyed. She had to stop playing poker face to nearly his entire collection.

But Captain Taylor wasn't alone in her critical self-examination. Chris had some of his own. Again, he did shake his head "no" when Helena termed herself the world's worst communicator. But that wasn't enough. Chris resolved he needed to do something about it. For starters, he needed to stop burdening Helena with his insecurities. He needed to put aside worrying over how Helena regarded him. His insecurities had festered from his own past. He held his parents' achievements in such awe that he often doubted the worthiness of his music distribution business. His doubts festered despite the encouragement he received from so many directions, including of course from Buddy Leung.

But now it was time to enjoy the wild adventures Helena's accomplishments had made possible, and to express his joy over that with her. *And*, to keep a little secret of his own, about how he had become infatuated with the first wife of the Fafaman ruler.

"I should tell you what Cookie Lady whispered to me in a daydream," Samantha said with great happiness. She loved seeing her son and daughter-in-law as they were presently behaving. She sensed myriad wonderful things going through their minds. "Cookie Lady whispered that in our infinite universe, events conspire sooner or later to provide this moment of love and grace for every single entity, no matter how teensy." As Samantha said this, she thought to herself, *I feel like I don't really know or understand more than a little of what is going on here. But it was well worth the sixty-year wait! It gives me hope...*

"Captain! I'm truly sorry, Captain, to be barging in like this. Truly sorry." Ali Magabu panted as he took stock of the situation, not having even knocked at the door.

"They need me back in the outfield?" Sammy tugged down on her O's cap; the split second the words left her mouth, she felt guilty for her mischievously intentional misreading of the very serious urgency she sensed.

"Truly, I wish," Ali laughed through his continued panting. He had needed to cross way too much distance for reaching Captain Taylor's location. Moreover, he feared there could not possibly be enough time left. And during his sprinted trek, it puzzled and irritated him wondering why neither Chris nor Helena left their ear implants turned on. They could have been apprised instantly of the news without his having had to strain himself so much. But all was forgiven, far as he was concerned. To catch Helena and Chris in one another's arms like he'd never seen them before... "Captain, one of the Callaway X Centra Oort Cloud firefly donut patrols has detected a virtual squadron of large, saucer-shaped UFOs. They are doing what Officer Leung terms skipping-stone, time-space curvature-hopping from the direction of the Cygnitaurus system."

"Where Tictoctic is located."

"Precisely, Captain. But they aren't headed this way. They are on a trajectory that only makes sense if they are headed for our solar system."

Chris, Helena and Ali exchanged looks where they each knew what the other two were thinking. *Was the squadron led by Commander Kwit-Nik? Or did he get himself deposed, slaughtered even?*

"Um," Helena bit her upper lip. "Officer Magabu, do we assume the Secretary of Defense and the Chair of the Joint Chiefs are both intent on giving chase?"

"The Barack Obama and the Eisenhower are already in hot pursuit."

"Then we have no time to lose." With one fluid motion, Captain Taylor bolted to her feet and pocketed away the pendant in Chris's pants.

"Captain, we also have no weapons, and any kind of retrofit would take a month, at least," noted Ali. He rushed alongside Chris and Helena, to try keeping up.

Samantha wasn't far behind.

"Officer Magabu, we do have two Oombians on board with a long, successful history of peace-making."

"Exactly what I was hoping to hear you say, Captain, truly! Huff! Puff!" Ali Magabu was back to panting while Helena broke into an out-and-out sprint.

<hr />

They are not satisfied yet. Or at least, not enough are satisfied for them to proceed. Tempted as they clearly are by the extent of their dramatically upgraded powers...

So Wafoodle-boodle, in whom you know I feel so deeply rooted,-

And I in you, Oodle-my-only-Noodle, even when you are beating me by ten strokes or more in oof.

-is it not enough for the Watchers, what they have gathered from among one of the entangled species? If not from among all four of them, perhaps? That oh so clearly, there was someone willing to dedicate her life to

honoring the enigmatic wish of an apparition experienced when she was a child? Moreover, that a vast majority of the four populations want to live, to thrive in peace? And that this is the reality, no matter how many of them might briefly succumb to the twisted logic of a faithless, mentally-impaired few?

Oodle-Noodle, you well know I am not the one with whom this argument needs to stick like sweetest sap. I am already there. It has already prevailed for me. It is like a Croopee-moortee's branch sinking roots into new soil half a year after it has been transplanted there.

I know, Wafoodle-boodle. I know. It is just so frustrating that- With all their wisdom well beyond ours, can't the Watchers fully appreciate the magic in how the vast cosmos works? How the caring heavens assured that a message of love would be delivered out of the chaos of the self-destructing civilization on Fafama? To be handed to a troubled couple of the civilization whose weaponry made that self-destruction possible?

Again, Oodle-my-only-Noodle, I am not the one with whom you need to debate. Consider carefully what you have just telepathed me. Again, I am totally persuaded to your point of view. Nevertheless, I can also certainly appreciate the Watchers' fear, their apprehension. Such intervention as they are now capable of experimenting with, it could disrupt the universal imperative's assurance. And that assurance bears reiterating: When civilizations do not completely renounce war, they self-destruct before they can travel to the stars. The universal imperative must always kick in so those civilizations' violent ways cannot seriously infect other planets besides their own.

Perhaps Captain Taylor's blind faith effort...

And what is most ironic about that, of course, my Oodle-est of all Noodles, is how she exudes more confidence than either of us feel.

So let us assume the Watchers **don't** intervene, my Wafoodle-est of all boodles. The plan would be for our voices to infiltrate the heads of the Earth's political leaders? We would try persuading them to surrender to Tictoctickian forces before a shot was even fired?

That is quite grimly so, Oodle-sweetest-Noodle. And continuing on a grimly theme: If our persuasion succeeded, we would anticipate an indeterminate number of Earthlings being consumed by the deer creatures,-

-despite our telepathic peaceful pleading, and despite the voiced-aloud peaceful pleading by those kept for mating. We would beg their extraterrestrial overlords to stop treating Earthlings as cattle,-

-and go vegetarian, instead.

Our argument would be buttressed by scientific evidence of the health benefits from abandoning a meat-based diet.

But again, our argument would inevitably fail. The cruel consumption would continue, unabated, Oodle-my-butt-swinging-Noodle, until there grew an uprising. It would be a nonviolent uprising powerful enough among the deer creatures,-

-and supported by their law enforcement officials,-

-to overthrow a government over-lorded by paranoid psychopaths,-

-and free the human beings to live as equals among the deer creatures,-

-to share, exchange their music, their games,-

-and most importantly, perhaps, the best Earthling recipes for chocolate chip cookies!

If only.

If only.

Both Oombian tree creatures' limbs wilted, their fresh leaf blossoms as well, over their dejected feelings. Both of them well knew what was actually in store, thanks to the universal imperative. It was only a matter of time before Tictoctickian as well as Earthling civilizations self-destructed. The Tictoctickians weren't going to last long enough to occupy Earth. And the Earthlings weren't going to last long enough to resist, or to see an internal Tictoctickian rebellion succeed. There was no good reason for the tree creatures to telepathically whisper sweet somethings in any of their heads.

There is nothing left for us to do, Oodle-Noodle still ran enough sap through her trunk to telepath, *than to continue our argument with the Watchers.*

⟡⟡⟡

Captain Helena Grace Taylor took determined strides onto the navigation bridge of the starship, Smoke and Mirrors, hand-in-hand with Chris.

Counselor Ali Magabu followed close behind. He was feeling like the race hadn't finished yet that started back on the surface of Oomb, when he went searching for the captain's whereabouts.

A round of applause greeted the captain. It issued from far more people than she expected or even wanted to see on board the entire vessel, let alone within that one specific area. She feared the new mission would turn out to be her most reckless mission yet, the one that would "truly," as Ali put it, prove totally self-destructing. She stalled out on her way over to the captain's chair, standing arm-in-arm with Chris. And she shouted, as much to squelch the reception she was continuing to receive as to actually ask, "Pedro and Ludi Perez!?! Can I trust you didn't bring your little Alex on board as well?!"

"Misplaced trust, Captain!" laughed Pedro.

"Ay, sí, Captain," chimed in Ludi. "Alexita is helping with the baby so Yulala can have some more rest!"

"Well, I appreciate that sentiment. But to be honest with you...Sorry, Sergeant Hanson; I'm not happy about the only remaining flesh and blood survivor from Fafama travelling with us on this fool's errand, either. I want to know: What were any of you thinking??"

"Por seguro, for sure, Captain," Ludi stepped forward with an assertive clomp! clomp! of her magboots. "It is because of my respect for you that I disrespect your unhappiness with us being here! Sí!" She nodded insistently, almost angrily. "Remember when you took the Smoke and Mirrors into the past, to send our lives on a new trajectory? How many people said you were on a, what you call it, 'a fool's errand'?! Pedro and I want to be here for you, for all you have done for us and our amazingly rejuvenated families! But one other thing, one piece of advice: I know you love your husband, but you two might want to 'cool it' so you can focus more on the mission!"

Chuckles mixed with sporadic clapping as Chris and Helena sheepishly untangled from one another to establish a more "professional" distance.

"Okay, Officer Ludi Perez," the captain went on to say, "you've come in handy already.

"Now Geena Murphy-Davis, you and Deborah are two others. You also had to suffer through so much. Monsters chasing after us on Kakifika; not knowing our fate for certain in the slaughterhouse on Tictoctic, until we each disappeared one by one behind a plastic strip veil..."

"Captain, excuse me," spoke up Dr. Deborah Davis-Murphy in a mock-admonishing tone. "There's no time for you to ask every last person why you're still stuck with them on this next mission. We're just going to fall further and further behind in the race for Earth!"

"Another point I am going to have to concede, Deb. Wait." Helena suddenly darted her head from side to side in evident panic. "Where's Buddy? Cathy, is he trying to miss not missing you again?" *He's the one person I need to make sure DOES tag along!*

"Captain! Sorry, Captain!" Buddy Leung rushed in fast as he could, encumbered in the near-zero gravity by his magboots. "Captain," he was huffing and puffing much like Ali had been, "I've figured it out! Completely!"

"Then it's-"

"It definitely is, Captain!"

"Yoon-hee," said Helena, "a change of plans. Set us on a direct course for Fafama."

"Fafama, Captain?" Yoon-hee repeated to a flurry of gasps.

"The third planet in the Alpha Centauri C system, Officer Park-Smith. Otherwise known to its residents as Fafama."

"Nay, Captain," Yoon-hee nodded. She sent her fingers flying in furious tapping across her console.

"Fafama? Oooo, that sounds so exotic," is how the Chonoran Chig-cher's chirps translated.

"Yeah, it's exotic, alright," grumbled Sergeant Fred Frankly while he joined everyone else making their way to strap themselves down. "From what Proud Papa here tells me," he practically pounded on Guy Hanson's back, "it's been transformed into a smoldering hell. I can say that since Yulala's off tendin' to their baby, or else sleepin' off her exhaustion from caring for same, like Ludi said. But don't worry, Chig-cher; you ought to get your most stained-up shirt yet, just standin' out in Fafama's runaway volcanic shit-fest! Better yet, you probably want to have your wardrobe hangin' outside the shuttle pod rather than goin' out there yourself. Make sure the poisonous fumes and roasty temps don't get to you!"

"Oooo..."

"Captain, I don't understand," said Kevin from down beside Yoon-hee. "Why make a detour to Fafama? If there is anything we can do to help thwart the alien invasion headed for Earth, isn't that going make us arrive too late? What do you expect to accomplish anyway? Or is that another surprise?"

"Officer Smith-Park, let's just say that the beauty of what we will attempt, one beautiful result is this: We will find ourselves coming up closer behind the saucer-starship race than were we to leave directly for Earth."

Kevin craned his head around to look up at Helena seated behind him. "Captain, we're not...No way!"

"Yes way," Helena nodded with a grin.

"Ahh, I gather where you are going with this," said Professor Timothy Aquinas. "It's about our planet-sized dragon spirit. It's about the big, fat mama to our 'petite' little Effy prowling the starship's corridors in search of his next chocolate chip cookie. The soul of Fafama, if you will, is finally to be reunited, made one again with the flesh."

"That is such utter nonsense, Timothy Aquinas, sir!" Professor Skepticus rose from his chair to face his contentious colleague. Indignation was written in bright red all over his face. So bright red, Chris half feared it might suddenly pop like a balloon. "This is how it ought to be phrased," Skepticus went on. "That is, if indeed the captain has a plan to repair Fafama's magnetic fields, no doubt seriously disrupted by the comet cataclysm. It ought to be phrased that such a repair might finally shake off the anomaly which has shadowed us, admittedly to some beneficial effect!! In fact- OUCH!!"

Chris reached for a nearby fire extinguisher. Once again he accepted what had long since become a routine task. After all, someone needed to deal with Professor Skepticus's pants getting torched in the rear, whether they were packing a chocolate chip cookie or not.

Her husband's quick response freed Helena to remain focused intently on the panoramic view-screen. It was crowded with stars of the Milky Way, as well as with tiny swirls of incomprehensibly distant galaxies. Professor Skepticus could not have been further off the mark regarding her plans. But she wasn't going to bother correcting him. There were far more immediate, urgent priorities. She asked Officer Park-Smith, "Yoon-hee, fore and aft mirror arrays are in full bloom?"

"Full bloom, Captain, on a course heading for Alpha Centauri C."

"Four-quadrant, advance-guard fireflies deployed?"

"Deployed, and already a good point eight light-year ahead of us, Captain."

"Then power up the electromagnetic fields, and let's save Fafama!"

The Smoke and Mirrors disappeared from its hundred-thousand-mile-high orbit around Oomb, lost in a haze of fairy dust twinkles.

That's when Oodle-Noodle telepathed anew to Wafoodle-boodle. *The irony is what these Earthlings and Chonorans might have said, were they to have been aware what else is at stake in this mission. They might* have expressed hope they are providing us with more ammunition with which to persuade the Watchers,-

When we would have put it that they are providing us with more chocolate chips with which to sweeten up our cookies for the Watchers!

Chapter 30

Shelly Taylor wondered why so many people crowded the snack bar on an Amtrak train headed for Cocoa Beach near the Kennedy Space Center. Under other circumstances she might have mused, *Certainly they can't be fighting over Oreo candy bars well past their expiration dates.* But anxiety inexplicably rippled through Shelly well before she finished washing her hands in the restroom facility, well before she began her unsteady trek back to her seat.

Shelly reached a confident conclusion, just from seeing the snack bar crowd blocking her way. Something of momentous importance was afoot. Such momentous importance, in fact, that her unsettled state from out of seeming nowhere would prove comparable to when a stone is dropped into a still pond. Whatever she was about to learn sent concentric circles in all directions, including back in time before she actually experienced it.

People's attention was glued to a flat-screen television mounted above the snack bar.

"What's going on?" Shelly asked an easily approachable woman.

"There's just been an enormous landslide in the Canary Islands. They think it's going to set off a tsunami, really bad news for somewhere."

"How awful!"

The approachable woman strained to hear every word from the television, despite one of the snack bar attendants having turned the volume high. Nevertheless, she had reacted with a pleasant disposition when bothered.

But Shelly didn't want to press her luck. So she focused more intently on the flat screen. She still suspected her unsettled feeling was rippling back in time from something she was about to learn. And that feeling had intensified to full-out anxiety.

A scroll across the bottom of the television identified the speaker as Dr. Jayray Robertson. Dr. Robertson was a geology professor from Harvard, and also a chief consultant to the United Americas Geological Survey. "-reports of an explosion prior to the landslide are tremendously disturbing. This is especially so because seismograph readings did not reveal any unusual activity within the Cumbre Vieja crater itself."

"Dr. Robertson, are you saying the landslide might have been triggered by someone?"

While the reporter quizzed Robertson, an amateur body cam video played out on the television screen. The picture bounced around due to filming from aboard a seagoing vessel, Shelly surmised. Nevertheless, it clearly revealed what happened to a picturesque mountainside that rose dramatically steep behind an oceanfront harbor. One moment to the next, that mountainside collapsed. Hillside villas and forests left nothing more behind than bare dirt and rock face.

"We know that in past millennia, ground water has seriously weakened the dead or dormant volcanos. Some of them have been so weakened that portions have slid below water. Or they have extended the Canary Islands' meager coastal plains. But there is no record of such a geological event having ever happened here on this scale. So yes, to answer your question, I am concerned the Cumbre Vieja landslide might have been triggered by someone. And by someone, of course, I mean by an explosive device."

"I'm sorry, Doctor, but if you can stay with us a while longer... There's breaking news from Annelise Jackson back at our New York desk. Annelise?"

"Thank you, Larry," said Annelise. "We've just received word on two related fronts. Professor Jorge Porfirio is a seismologist at the University of New Madrid on La Palma Island, where the landslide occurred one hour ago. He is reporting unusually high Geiger counter readings. He says they are consistent with what you would expect from setting off a shallowly buried thermonuclear device. What make Professor Porfirio's findings so disturbing for terrorism experts are claims of an explosion only minutes prior to the landslide.

"On that other related front, international shipping authorities told us the freighter, Philadelphia Freedom, never made arrival to Lisbon, Portugal. And there's more. Weeks ago when the freighter was due, sightseers on La Palma allegedly noticed a mystery ship weighing anchor some distance off the coast."

"Wait, Annelise, this is important. The freighter went missing weeks ago, and that is only now coming to light?"

"Larry, shipping authorities tell me there was a theory about the freighter's fate that required intense detective work to pick apart. Originally, the Philadelphia Freedom was feared to have been caught in what is termed an Atlantic storm maelstrom. Such a phenomenon would have sucked the entire ship to the ocean floor. There was even an SOS received from what appeared to be the center of that storm. But after it blew itself out, deep-water submersibles picked up nothing on sonar. At least nothing that could be construed as the freighter having come to rest on the ocean bed. Also, a review of satellite imagery placed the freighter at a location several miles distant from the apparent source of the SOS signal."

"You say the 'apparent source'?"

"That's right, Larry. I am told the best guess is that special equipment on the freighter induced an artificial inversion layer. Then the SOS was bounced off that layer so it seemed to emit from a far different location. Meanwhile, whoever is aboard the freighter managed to cloak its actual whereabouts."

"Any indication from authorities what the freighter's present location might be?"

"Satellite imagery from half the Atlantic Ocean has been reviewed and re-reviewed, Larry, and they have come up empty. Terrorism experts are concerned that whoever this is might have found a way to keep their movement hidden from satellite view. And search ships can only cover so much sea at once. It's turned into a large-scale cat-and-mouse game."

"Annelise, you said the ship is named Philadelphia Freedom?"

"Yes, Larry, and therein lies yet another disturbing part to this story."

Shelly Taylor grabbed at the snack counter for support. People crowded all sides made it virtually impossible for her to keel over onto the floor, even if she fainted. But that made no difference where her upset was concerned.

"The Philadelphia Freedom began its journey from Philadelphia dockyards located inside the Philly no-zone," reporter Annelise Jackson continued. "Larry, this is what terrorism officials say might have been the big warning sign not taken seriously enough. In a recent census dragnet of the entire Philadelphia no-zone, there were adult males from the previous census who could not be located. And they were not showing up on any of the death registrars, either."

"Were there enough missing people to be capable of overcoming the heavy security on a full-sized freighter?"

"One official told me it's not impossible. Most large freighters, including this one, are so automated that they don't require a large number of personnel. But until now, security requirements were thought adequately stringent. Surely, it was assumed, they guaranteed that this job access for no-zoners wouldn't become an Achilles Heel of the whole quarantine zone concept. Remember, Larry, these freighter hauls have provided one of the few means for people to work themselves out of the no-zones."

"Annelise, have any of the names been released-Excuse me." Reporter Larry Savage cupped his left hand over his left ear. "We'll come back to you, Annelise. Right now, I'm receiving word from the head of the Federal Emergency Management Agency, FEMA. FEMA is going to hold a press conference at the White House. I have been advised that FEMA has just posted a tsunami warning. FEMA has posted a tsunami warning for the east coast of the United Americas. The warning zone starts in Savannah, Georgia and ends in Miami, Florida. There is supposed to be a mass evacuation inside the warning zone. Wait. Now FEMA is saying the evacuation extends from Hilton Head, South Carolina all the way down to Cutler Bay well south of Miami. We are also being told- My God, people are being told to evacuate as far west as possible, and wherever they can to leave the Florida peninsula, period. I repeat, FEMA is advising people to leave the Florida peninsula, period, if they are able to."

"Those offshore floodwalls completed in the 2040s, Larry, won't those be enough?" Annelise reinserted herself to ask.

But Shelly didn't catch that. There was considerable, agitated commotion round about her in the passenger train car. One woman was screaming tearfully into her cell phone, "You have to leave there right now, Angie! Right now! The traffic is going to be awful over the intercoastal! Hija! I'm praying for you!"

Soon after the near-hysterical woman made her urgent recommendation, the train decelerated dramatically.

A voice came on the intercom saying, "Ladies and gentlemen, we have received word that FEMA is ordering an evacuation of the east coast of Florida and Georgia. There is a tsunami warning that officially takes effect in three hours. We will be stopping near St. Augustine, and switching tracks to bring us on a westward path that should get us over the border into central Georgia within two hours. We ask you to not disembark at our St. Augustine station, and we also ask everyone to remain calm. I repeat,-"

⋅⊱⋅⊰⋅⊱⋅⊰⋅⊱⋅⊰⋅

"Excuse me, Miss; you should return to your seat. It's recommended-"

The Amtrak conductor completed his warning as a scream after Shelly. By that time, she was already well past the train station platform on her way over to the car rental lot. Waving her any-car-in-the-lot voucher in their faces, she sprinted past a pair of car rental agents. But as she hopped behind the wheel of the closest compact she could get to, those agents received word from the outside world, finally. They came running after her shouting, "There's a tsunami warning! Everyone here is to board the Amtrak for an evacuation!"

Shelly pretended not to hear as she drove out the exit gate at a steady acceleration. She was headed for the main road leading to I-95 South.

When Shelly boarded the train originally, she wasn't sure exactly what she was going to do once she reached the Cocoa Beach station. She had some vague notion of driving over the inter-coastal bridge down to the shore. She wanted to lose herself in the ever-soothing ebb and flow of the surf. She found that surf as spiritually renewing as she used to find beach-hopping by bike down the west coast towards Monterey. But presently, she was realizing that the dream she thought she experienced the night before was really more than a dream.

Shelly's supposed dream centered on a woman as diminutive as she was spry. She was the same woman who had appeared like an apparition on Shelly's last desperate search for Flamboyo Sanchez in the Philly no-zone. Clearly, that woman really did try to communicate with her. In the dream that was not a dream, that woman advised Shelly she must get to the Kennedy Space Center shuttle pod launch area, ASAP. That is, if she was to have a last crack at reasoning with Flamboyo before he assisted in fulfilling some awful scheme...

Chapter 31

Fafama grew steadily larger in the panoramic view-screen of the Smoke and Mirrors. The starship from Earth had already decelerated well below light-speed on approach to the third planet in orbit around Alpha Centauri C.

Captain Helena Taylor and her crew were braced for their return to the land of the ahtpah and the nocturnally adapted humans, the land where they first arrived more than a year ago in answer to an extraterrestrial distress call. Nevertheless they couldn't help their horror, beholding the smoldering orb still mostly enshrouded by thick layers of roiling black smoke. A few breaks in the apocalyptic overcast did present themselves where Earthlings and Oombians could catch glimpses of surface features. But high-altitude ejections of cinder and molten rock persisted. The ice comet's collision with Fafama had buckled some of the planet's tectonic plates, thereby resulting in widespread, sustained super volcano activity.

Back when the Smoke and Mirrors made first arrival, Fafama boasted two great seas, each the size of Australia. Shades of sandy brown mottled with enormous olive-colored patches encircled them. The overall suggestion was of a somewhat arid planet nevertheless thriving with life.

Defining Fafama's ever-advancing boundary between night and day used to be a commotion of dust storms combined with thunderstorms. The Fafamans termed that commotion the sunset storm line, and said it had been going on for at least fifty million years.

The first time Chris Olsen-Taylor saw the storm line from aboard the Smoke and Mirrors, its steady advance reminded him of a yeast bloom in sugar water.

Even before the recent comet cataclysm, Fafama's night side was not lit up in its few high population areas. That is, not in ways the starship crew was used to seeing the night side of Earth from space. This was due to the resident intelligent species having evolved a nocturnal life style, which the Earthlings were quick to learn more about on their first, face-to-face encounters. However, bioluminescence did cast large areas of the planet's night side in a faint, phantasmally greenish glow, including its few waterways and seas.

Presently, there was neither greenish glow nor olive-colored mottling to be espied anywhere on Fafama's surface. At least this was the case where plumes of coal-black smoke from super volcano eruptions were not obscuring the view. More than anything else, shades of gray predominated across the landscape, from the copious amounts of ash settled out of the atmosphere. And no longer did a sunset storm line usher in nightfall.

The way the "dirty" ice comet had come crashing into Fafama's crust, the entire planet took on a subtly lopsided form. This resulted in a slow yet distinct wobble of its axis rotation. Consequent unevenness in its gravitational pull was causing the Smoke and Mirrors to rock like a canoe on a windblown lake, Chris was thinking. Moreover, Fafama used to have only two polar ice caps, albeit smaller, more circumspect than Earth's polar ice caps. But presently, a third, even teensier ice cap surmounted what remained of the comet rubble.

Perhaps the single most astounding, most dramatic feature of all, of Fafama as the Earthlings first came across it, had been its pyramid city. Like the Great Wall of China back on Earth, the Fafaman Empire's Great Pyramid was the one intelligently constructed feature clearly visible from outer space. And its lighthouse tower extended all the way up through the stratosphere. Presently, though, not a trace of that amazing architectural achievement remained discernible from any distance off the planet. Doubtless, most of its collapsed ruins were covered over by massive lava flows.

"Humor me, Buddy." Captain Taylor gestured towards the jury-rigged setup littering Yoon-hee's navigation console. An underbrush's worth of variously colored wires hung down from the ceiling. Suspended amidst that mess was a big tube like some bug caught in a spider web or an ahtpah web, Chris mused to himself. "How exactly is this going to work, again?" the captain asked.

As the captain alluded to, Buddy Leung had explained his eureka moment before. I.e., the moment he realized they could time travel far more precisely. Probably.

For successful time travel in general, there was a narrow margin of error for the angle and speed at which the starship needed to approach a rift, a wound in the space-time continuum. Such wounds were ripped open by painful deaths, the more deaths the bigger the wound.

Within the margin of error for entering a space-time rift, of course any angle and speed would do. What Officer Leung realized, he realized from the admittedly small number of occasions he had gotten away with the time-travel feat. It was quite simply this: The steeper the entry angle, the less time they travelled. The shallower the angle, the further back they travelled. Years of difference were incurred over thousandths of a degree of angle. And velocity was an additional contributing factor. Buddy Leung saw parallels to skipping stones across water. The shallower the angle at which a stone first struck the liquid's surface, the further it was likely to skip. And added speed also added to the number of skips, thereby increasing the distance the stone travelled even more.

For what the Earthlings would be about on their return to Fafama, Officer Leung detected what he had expected. Enormous space-time rifts enveloped the planet. Were those rifts visible, they would have made most of Fafama's surface, excluding its north and south poles, appear to have been clawed at mercilessly. Yulala could have mistaken those claw marks for having been inflicted by the dragon spirit of Fafama.

Officer Buddy Leung determined that most of Fafama's space-time rifts posed too much danger. Sending the starship headlong into any one of them ran the risk of entombing it deep below the planet's surface.

Buddy did detect one large rift, however, in the upper atmosphere. He presumed it resulted from the coalescing of several small "nicks." Those "nicks" doubtless stemmed from heroic efforts of numerous jet pilots, plus the shuttle blade crew off the Fafaman space station. They got themselves killed when they tried to break apart the descending comet into smaller bits that would not apocalyptically harm Fafama. They employed a futile variety of missiles, bombs and out-and-out suicide runs directly at the immense celestial object.

They might as well have been hurling chocolate chip cookies at it.

Of course the Fafaman space station, itself, was long since gone to its own flaming death. Once its power finished draining, it inevitably descended into the Fafaman atmosphere, and friction did the rest.

"That tube in amidst the nest of wires, Captain?" Buddy was going on to explain. "It's like a leveler for construction. You see the floating bubble and the ruler lines?" He seized the tube in one hand, and pointed at it

601 | Centers of the Universe

with the other. "The instant we start rifting, we want to keep that bubble in between these two particular marks I've made."

"There's more, Captain," added Yoon-hee. "Since we're going to be skimming the Fafaman atmosphere, I need to deploy the protective front-end umbrella. It is like what we did way-back-when, descending through the planet's atmosphere to have Tanya haul you into the photon evacuation chamber."

"And there was nothing to that," Helena sighed sarcastically. "Okay, let's do this."

ᴇ.ᴙᴊ﹪ᴇᴙᴊ﹪ᴇᴙᴊ﹪

Yoon-hee may have been tacking the Smoke and Mirrors two billion miles away from Fafama, on a tangent to the planet's calculated orbit. But Guy and Yulala already had plenty to worry about.

Dr. Deborah Davis-Murphy collected something special in her test tube: a sample of the unusual mucous leaching from Goolafala's pores, all over her body. Mother and father were drawing that substance from their daughter's nostrils virtually nonstop. Their effort to keep her nasal passageways clear felt increasingly useless.

Hours earlier, Yulala realized Goolafala's pajama suit and pastel-pink beanie knitted by Chig-cher were soaked through. At first, she thought her baby experienced some sort of feverish night sweat. But the mucous secretion, not additional sweating, kept coming. And her temperature remained normal, or what Dr. Davis-Murphy had had to assume was normal. It matched her mama's steady hundred and one point seven degrees Fahrenheit, as it had been doing ever since her birth. And she wasn't complaining at all.

"Have you been able to breastfeed her?" Deborah asked as she plugged the mucous-filled test tube.

"No, naht sahnce weah notahced thahs (*No, not since we noticed this*)." Yulala gently rocked her baby while unsuccessfully straining to wipe away her own streaming tears with her shoulder.

The darkness maintained for Goolafala's awake time was tempered by faint, greenish, fluorescent tubing. Buddy Leung had installed that tubing along the floor molding. But of course, this accommodation made no difference in her distressingly curious condition.

"Yulala, Sergeant, I don't want to sound callous... Okay, I know this *is* going to sound callous. I have to warn you like I have been warning you before. Prepare for the worst. Afraid I already know what my analysis of this substance is going to reveal." Dr. Davis-Murphy held up the test tube before her. "Something bad is happening to Goolafala's biochemistry, something I will be totally incapable of handling. If someone forced me to guess, this is what I would say: On the cellular level, the blending of chromosome sets from two entirely different lines of evolution is finally getting around to being rejected. Whether that is the case, or something else equally dire, makes no difference. I will do everything within my power to make Goolafala comfortable, to minimize her pain for..." Deborah bowed her head and shook it sadly; she couldn't bring herself to complete that sentence. "It would be far crueler to give you false hope. Okay, blast away."

"But Doctor," said Sergeant Guy Hanson while Yulala sobbed into his shoulder. Her own shoulders were heaving with grief even as she still tried to gently rock Goolafala. "Why would our daughter have gone this far in her maturation from an embryo? Why would she have even bothered before the rejection you spoke of? It doesn't make any sense!" Guy tearfully concluded. His own effort to avoid succumbing to grief finally failed him.

The chief medical officer lifted her head. That's when stray photons from the muted fluorescent lighting caught a telltale watery glisten in her eyes.

Guy wanted to make up for whatever little bit of anger tinged his sad exclamation. So he added in as grateful a tone as he could muster, "Thank you, Doctor. We really do appreciate your effort."

"Please don't thank me," Deborah muttered, nearly under her breath. She turned away to take leave, exuding shame.

Once Deborah was gone from the nursery, Goolafala started to squirm restlessly in Yulala's arms. She made an "mmm" sound close to an angry dog's snarl.

"Guy?" Yulala looked up at her husband with alarm in her voice.

"It's okay, Yulala. Nothing new, you must know by now. This is what she always does when she wants to go back to sleep."

"Should weah aht leahst dryah heahr ahft?" (*Should we at least dry her off?*)

"She'll be wet again before we know it! Besides, we've run out of clothes that aren't already soaked from her secretions. And her being like this doesn't seem to really bother her."

"So youah thahink weah shahld jahst paht hah dahown in hahr criahb..." (*So you think we should just put her down in her crib...*)

"And see if she wants to re-submerge herself beneath the styrofoam peanuts for a nap? Yes, I do," Guy said assertively. "Here; I'll turn up the illumination."

The same as Yulala, and other Fafamans when they were still alive, Goolafala required bright light to sleep. She required bright light even though she burrowed herself into the Styrofoam peanut bedding so far, precious few photons could have been seeping through.

Guy raised the lights to their highest setting. Then Yulala ever-so-gently laid her precious baby to rest in the crib. Goolafala effortlessly wriggled below the top layer of pastel-green-colored Styrofoam peanuts.

Sergeant Hanson was reminded of a certain small crab in Ocean City, Maryland. It always burrowed its way back down into wet sand after crashing surf exposed it to the surface.

With most tender affection fueling her despair, Yulala clung to the bars of the crib. She pondered the Styrofoam layer under which her baby daughter reburied herself. Guy came up behind her and wrapped his arms around her waist. She sank back into his welcome embrace. He nuzzled her raven black hair and whispered softly into her ear, "When was the last time you rested, my sleek owl?"

What Yulala struggled to say in English was, "That will happen when we know Goolafala is going to be okay." She suddenly stiffened, less amenable to her husband's attention. "Didn't you say they need you soon in the shuttle bay?"

"They do." Guy reluctantly relaxed his hold on Yulala. "But in the meantime, I want you to get some rest. I don't understand how you will ever accomplish that, remaining here by Goolafala's side in all this brightness."

Yulala suddenly spun around and faced Guy with a smile through her tears. "Ah ahm youah 'sleeak owl,' remahmbah?" *(I am your 'sleek owl,' remember?)*

Guy closed his eyes and shook his head at his stupidity. "And I am your blind bat, Yulala." It still thrilled him to say her name aloud.

"Yahs, Ah know!"

"But my point remains. Allow me please to take you somewhere else to rest. You have my promise I will return here to keep watch over our sweet little bundle of cookie dough until I am called away. And when that happens, you also have my promise that Ciela or someone else of her dependability will take my place."

Later on, the two young lovers would come to regret they had left Goolafala alone for even the briefest while. But not for any reason they could possibly have ever imagined.

᛫ᚺᛟᚷ᛫᛫ᚺᛟᚷ᛫᛫ᚺᛟᚷ᛫

Sergeant Hanson did bring his wife Yulala next door from their daughter's nursery, to their bedroom. Meantime, the Smoke and Mirrors nearly finished tacking two billion miles away from Fafama. It was about to swing around for a hyper-fast, twenty-light-speed plunge through a rift identified on the outer fringe of Fafama's upper atmosphere. Centripetal force from the starship making the hundred-and-eighty-degree, wide-angle turn at one-tenth light-speed was expected to provide plenty of gravity. Untethered objects such as kelpydoodle snacks would be kept from floating, drifting all over the place. There was nothing to worry about in this regard, anyway, where Goolafala in her crib was concerned. The Styrofoam peanuts had been treated with a plant-derived substance which acted like Velcro. It prevented the peanuts from spraying everywhere in zero or low gravity. This same treatment was given to the exterior of Goolafala's clothing, and the crib mattress cover. The

Earthlings did everything they could for Goolafala to remain safely tucked in.

Anyhow, when the starship did finally make the turn for its mad dash at the space-time rift, Chris was reminded of something lower tech. That is, a jet jockeying around on an airport runway to prepare for its racing leap off the ground.

"Captain, our mushroom cap deployment to protect the fore mirror array won't be necessary. And it wouldn't work in any event," said Officer Leung.

"Now you tell me, Buddy!" Helena was on the verge of motioning Yoon-hee to ramp up the electromagnetic field.

"Sorry, Captain. My computer only just now completed a review of calculations. It confirmed what I was already finding with pencil and paper. The short version of the explanation comes in two parts. Part one: Friction will literally be unable to keep up with our speed. If the Smoke and Mirrors were slim enough, we could probably pass through a wall without perturbing more than a handful of the wall's molecules, just like Superman. Part two: The extent to which the mushroom cap did decelerate that passing-through-a-wall effect wouldn't be a good thing. Air molecules most ironically would then be more likely to inflict serious, light-speed-compromising striations on both the fore and aft mirror arrays!"

"You're sure you've got this right, Buddy? Because I don't understand a word you said! Should we obtain a third form of verification?"

"That will be unnecessary, Captain. And you know if the computer results didn't fit my own, I *would* have said hold it to the entire operation."

"Okay, you've got that, Yoon-hee? No mushroom cap."

"I'm recalibrating our trajectory now, Captain, for no mushroom cap. And, we're ready."

"Let's make like *The Cat In The Hat*, and see if we can pick up after our own mess; electromagnetic fields back on full, Officer Park-Smith."

"Nay, back on full, Captain."

"Say Captain, supposing we *are* the cat in the hat." Despite the extreme seriousness of the situation, Kevin Smith-Park couldn't help the snark in his voice. As he saw it, this was Helena's fault for choosing to make such a ridiculous reference in the first place. "If we're the cat in the hat, who's the mommy for whom we are rushing to clean up before she returns home?"

Quiet met Kevin's question. As a result, the ever-mysterious tinkly-tinkly of photons rushing through the photon evacuation shaft seemed that much tinkly-tinklier.

From the outer reaches of the Callaway X Centra system, the Smoke and Mirrors was accelerating towards the space-time rift near the Fafaman stratosphere.

"That might be the mommy entering the driveway," offered Chris finally, referring to the tinkly-tinkly. He was continuing to feel ebullient over what he learned about Helena's true regard for him. Thank goodness for his mother's intervention with the engraved pendant from Fafama!

"F-n' ridiculous," Sergeant Fred Frankly muttered under his breath.

Helena Taylor noticed Oodle-Noodle and Wafoodle-boodle leaning into one another. Though she could not mind-read what they were telepathing back and forth, she easily intuited something unsettling, something else to be unsettled about. The tree creatures were commiserating over the fact that in a certain sense, there *was* a mommy. In case Helena required any confirmation, Oodle-Noodle glanced towards her...*Good God, could there possibly be anything more on the line with this mission than there already is?!?*

⋅✻⋅✻⋅✻⋅

The Smoke and Mirrors continued on its accelerating course headed for a space-time rift. Once again, Fafama appeared to grow from being an especially bright star, getting brighter and brighter, to clearly being the day-lit side of a planet.

Those on board the starship who knew what to expect from time travel braced themselves for a wave of tingles, not entirely unpleasant. Those tingles would soon be washing over them from passage through the selected wound in the space-time continuum.

Helena figured that anyone aboard who didn't know, or didn't remember, were better off not being told or reminded about the tingles. That might have made them panicky with anticipation, especially the children.

As it turned out, the familiar tingles were accompanied by something new, a minor shudder. But the results were exactly as hoped for.

The Smoke and Mirrors decelerated from light-speed multiples, down to a mere one-tenth light speed. Then it swung back around towards Fafama, yet again.

The ripples set off by the starship "crowding" past space-time resulted in a blurred view of the planet.

The cylindrical-shaped vessel with a half-closed "rose bloom" to its rear and "tulip bloom" at its fore returned to within a half-million miles of Fafama. As it did so, the comet came into blurred view also, the comet destined to crash into the planet's surface, causing a global extinction event.

When the Smoke and Mirrors achieved a desired high-altitude orbit, the sunset storm line was revealed on the navigation bridge view-screen. The storm line was frozen along the sunset interface, on its perpetual advance around the world. Chris was again reminded of a yeast bloom.

Also evident were splotches of olive green and an Australia-sized sea. Again, the Fafaman name for that sea translated into English as "the Grand Basin."

To the Grand Basin's west loomed the crowning achievement of Fafaman civilization, their Great Pyramid. As mentioned previously, that structure loomed with enough immensity to be spotted from way out in space.

"Captain, shall I bring Yulala to the bridge?" offered Tanya.

Helena shook her head. "I don't want to get her hopes up, in case our stunt fails. And I understand from Deb they are having, um, their baby might be experiencing some difficulty. Wish we didn't need to call Sergeant Hanson away."

"Beg your pardon, Captain." Fred bowed towards Helena from where he was seated up behind her. "But there's no good reason I can't go this one alone."

"I want both of you out there, Sergeant. Redundancy." Helena shook her head with finality. "I would have one of us in for Sergeant Hanson. But nobody else here, besides yourself of course, has had his level of stamina and strength training except for Tanya. And she has to remain ready at the shuttle pod's helm. You never know. She might need to perform one of her Houdini maneuvers to bring you both out of there. So Sergeant, please save your pardon-begging for the next time you drop the f-bomb in public."

"Yes, Captain. F- you, Captain."

"That soon? Okay, start begging."

"Well, Captain, it looks like we have good news, and some bad news." The bad news was so bad that Buddy Leung did not feel like joining in or even acknowledging the repartee between Helena and Fred.

"Think I'm seeing the bad news, Officer Leung." Helena was leaning forward in her chair, squinting at the panoramic view-screen. "Unless it's something else, some optical illusion reflection, I think I'm seeing those two missiles a little closer to the comet than we bargained for."

"A lot closer, Captain. We will have to decouple them from their momentum to a much greater degree than we wanted to have to attempt. As much more precisely as we were able to zero in on the past time-frame, it still wasn't precise enough."

"So, can't we just return to the present, and keep coming back here until we hit the sweet spot?"

"Captain, the good news is we made it back before those missiles hit the comet to send it on its downward trajectory. And we made it back not so long ago that they weren't even fired yet. But there is other bad news besides our arriving here too close to the event we want to delete. Uh, remember that small shudder we experienced on this crossing of a space-time rift?"

Helena saw, most disturbingly, an imploring, pleading look on Buddy's face.

"Captain," he went on, "that was due to accumulating micro-striation damage to the mirror arrays. They've built up from all the other occasions we have leaped back and forth in time. What that shudder tells me is we are pushing our luck. We couldn't possibly expect to make one more go of it to the past after our next return to the present. Not without risking another serious, possibly also fatal mess *no one* will be able to clean up. Both sets of mirrors require complete overhauls."

Helena nodded slowly in accepting, if grim, acknowledgement. "Okay, so we go with what we've got."

"As quickly as possible, Captain, especially regarding what I told you about the conundrum."

The past-time Smoke and Mirrors hung on the outskirts of the Callaway X-Centra solar system. It hung motionless there in completed space-time suspended animation, mere hundreds of billions of miles away from the Smoke and Mirrors as it was arrived to Fafama presently from the future. Moreover, perfect duplicates of Helena, Chris, Ali, Yulala, Guy and Buddy were housed somewhere in the Great Pyramid's base, "only" hundreds of thousands of miles distant. Buddy Leung had already alerted the captain what might happen if the quantum wave managed to catch up to them before their return to the present. The conundrum of being in two places simultaneously might not work its way out as conveniently as it had on previous time travel occasions.

Chapter 32

Heavy evacuation traffic crawled north on I-95. But Shelly Taylor had a clear shot down I-95 south from the Jacksonville, Florida train station. However, she didn't get any further than the St. Augustine area before she hit a police roadblock. She was waved over for a U-turn to join the mass exodus.

Sizing up the situation, Shelly determined her best plan was to get herself detained. That in fact, law enforcement officials could do her a favor. Wasn't her original destination likely to be swamped by the tsunami well prior to her arrival?

Shelly stopped her car at the base of the cloverleaf where she would have been guided to merge with the traffic returning northbound. There, she rolled down her window and said to the two policemen who sprinted over, "Officers, my name is Shelly Taylor."

"Ma'am, I don't care if your name is Mickey Mouse, and you were rushing to the Magic Kingdom for lunch with Cinderella. You're going to have to-"

"I am the daughter of Captain Helena Taylor of the starship, Smoke and Mirrors!"

After one officer called in her I.D. to confirm her claim, he said, "Okay, Ms. Taylor, what is this about exactly?"

"You heard about a freighter that vanished in the mid-Atlantic? The same one spotted near where a mudslide set off the tsunami? A person of my acquaintance could be on board. I was going to warn people at Cape Kennedy I know from my mom's work. Not all of them were evacuating, correct?"

Within minutes, Shelly found herself under armed guard. She was being brought to the interrogation room of a police station some sixty miles further west, a safe distance away, hopefully, from the tsunami flood zone.

Meanwhile, there were big doings not twenty miles off the coast of Daytona Beach. The tsunami's mound of water nearly tipped the freighter named Philadelphia Freedom over on its side. That mound of water had already easily lifted the vessel across a protective seawall. Thereby did reconnaissance aircraft finally gain visual as well as radar readings.

Prior to the Philadelphia Freedom surfing on the tsunami, a special reflective cover draped over the vessel prevented any such detection. That cover, provided by the mad physicist aboard, Morel Engeling, was partially knocked off by the tsunami.

"We've located the ship!" suddenly erupted in a static-y burst from a com-link set up at the interrogation room. "It breached the offshore breakwall, carried by the tsunami! Now it's on a west, southwest heading that will take it towards Cocoa Beach! Please advise!"

Someone of massive build, also wearing a uniform, lumbered into the interrogation room; Shelly figured he must have just flown there. Shortly before his arrival, she heard a familiar whup-whup-whup of helicopter blades. Anyway, he wasted no time turning to her and saying, "Shelly Taylor?"

Clinging to the edge of her seat with both hands, Shelly bit at her lower lip and she meekly nodded.

"I need to understand exactly how you knew the vessel of interest would be targeting the space center. And who it is you think might be on board."

Ever since the police officers had called in what Shelly told them, they were instructed not to ask any further questions. They were to wait for the massive guy to arrive who was presently interrogating her.

"It- It was a vision that came to me." Shelly couldn't bring herself to admit more specifically the vision was of a little old lady speaking to her. "The person who might be on board your vessel of interest, I met him during my investigative reporting in the Philly no-zone. His name is Flamboyo Sanchez."

"Flamboyo Sanchez," Massive Guy repeated. "You're sure he wasn't the vision that came to you? Look, Ms. Taylor, maybe you're having second thoughts about being a silent partner to whatever these people are plotting. Maybe your conscience is getting to you. Why not confess the whole way? Tell the entire story right now! Make things easier on all of us, your mother especially. I'm guessing she has her hands full enough out there in some other solar system, without worrying over your allegiances."

"You have to believe I have told you everything I know! Everything! I wish I knew more so I could help stop whatever is going on! But I don't! However, I do have some acquaintance with Flamboyo Sanchez, as already mentioned! If he is on board, which is what my vision suggested, maybe I can talk sense into him, somehow!" Shelly gave her interrogator an unflinching, pleading look. It unnerved him for what he intuited was the depth of its sincerity.

"Vision," one of the police officers scoffed with a dismissive head shake. "Look, man," he said, addressing Massive Guy, "I'm sure you know your business better than us." He lifted his hands like he was surrendering. It was his I'm-staying-out-of-this-and-respecting-your-authority gesture. Nevertheless, he added, "But I have a tough time putting any credence-"

"We have worked over the years with individuals who possess the ability to perform- Are you familiar with the term, 'remote viewing'?"

"We are still waiting to be advised!" the com-link voice crackled anew. "The freighter is practically surfing the tsunami bulge at a velocity that will carry it to shore in minutes!"

"That gives you seconds for talking this Flamboyo into changing the ship's heading straight east, before we will otherwise change its heading to thirty feet underwater." On saying this, Massive Guy interrogator handed Shelly a special cell phone. "Push this blue button for a general, multi-frequency all-call, but be advised," he added as he drew a pistol from his side belt holster. "I better not notice anything sounding like code language, or see any manipulation of that device indicative of same. If I do, you know the consequences. Captain Taylor's daughter or not, this gun will go off in your face!"

"Flamboyo Sanchez?" Shelly wasted no time reflecting on the nameless official's warning before she spoke into the phone. "Flamboyo, if you hear this, I'm Shelly Taylor. Remember me? Or, if someone else listening knows Flamboyo Sanchez, please put him on the phone! There is not much time, only a matter of minutes before they are going to destroy you!"

"He's not here," a voice finally responded. "They left on a helicopter before we jumped the sea wall!"

"Who are 'they'?!" the unnamed official yanked the phone away from Shelly to bark into it. "Flamboyo and who else?!?!" But then the official held the phone at arm's length, and shook his head. More for his own benefit than anyone else's, he muttered, "There is no helicopter; they're delaying!" On that dawning guess, the official barked over the com-link, "You are authorized to terminate the Philadelphia Freedom, with extreme prejudice!"

"There's a helicopter in the area we just realized wasn't a part of our reconnaissance mission!" was the instant response. "What are our priorities? Still the freighter first?"

"At least give the freighter captain a chance to agree to change his heading!" Shelly implored tearfully. She felt somehow to blame for not having intuited what was fermenting when she interviewed Flamboyo those several months ago.

"*You* give him a chance." The unnamed official tossed the cell phone Shelly's way.

Shelly told whoever was on the other end what they need to do to avoid being "terminated." They had to change course, then vocalize an assurance they were changing course while sonar verification was awaited.

During which time, the unnamed official responded to the question from over the intercom about priorities. "Blow that damned copter out of the sky!" he barked.

"Flamboyo?!?! FLAMBOYO!?!?!?!" Shelly shrieked into the cell phone, having overheard the order to destroy the helicopter. "If you are listening, you have to respond RIGHT NOW, or they are going to shoot you down!"

"Tell them it's going to be very dangerous for them if they try that," warned Flamboyo. *On the other hand that might make them the lucky ones. They'll be "checking out of here" before having to experience the end with everyone else.* Flamboyo bitterly told himself this.

By then, Massive Guy had again swiped the cell phone from Shelly's hands. He was telling her, "This Flamboyo has made his choice; we stop negotiating when there are threats. Also, once we have a handle on the extent of the tsunami impact, we will bring you to a more secure location. You must tell us more about your exact involvement with him, and any other 'visions' you might have had!"

"He said it's going to be dangerous for your people to try shooting down the helicopter! He sounded nearly nonchalant!" was all Shelly could think to respond.

"So what do you know specifically about his warning?!" The official stomped in front of Shelly to loom over her while he asked this.

"I don't know! Honest I don't!" She shook her head in a panic.

While Shelly was telling the truth, an interceptor jet was firing two "smart" missiles at the helicopter flown by Morel Engeling.

Flamboyo Sanchez accompanied Engeling in the cockpit.

For the jet's final minute, its crew saw bluish flashes pulse out from the helicopter, like ripples from a stone dropped in still water. In addition, a most jagged lightning bolt forked from the helicopter. The two "prongs" of that "fork" each struck a missile.

Both "smart" missiles nevertheless continued towards their target. They got to within a hundred feet of the copter, on its steady course toward the coastline about to be engulfed by the tsunami. But that is when both missiles suddenly bounced backwards, askew and turning end over end. It was as though they had run up against an invisible trampoline.

One of those missiles slammed sideways against the interceptor jet. It detonated with such force, the wingtips and tail fins were sent spinning away three different directions from the main explosion.

None of the jet's hapless crew had any idea what hit them.

Both missiles were magnetized with the same charge as a device secured aboard the copter. This caused a dramatic repulsion effect, once they came too close to the copter. It was the same effect by which Dr. Engeling planned to send the moon on a collision course for Earth.

"We've got a problem, boss!" crackled over the com-link set up at the interrogation room way west of St. Augustine.

Meanwhile, the first line of fifty-foot breakers from the tsunami broke with demolishing force against seaside resort buildings.

"The two missiles fired at the copter... This is crazy," the voice continued crackling over the com-link, "but on radar it looks like they reversed course just as they reached impact range! And one of them hit the jet that fired them!"

"Did the crew eject safely?"

"Doesn't look like they had enough time! My God! The tsunami! The east coast is disappearing!"

"I know it's horrible, but you guys have to focus! Focus! Where is the copter headed??"

"It's continuing on a course that will take it right over Kennedy Space Center! Well that's a relief, boss! The water's not quite reaching the I-95 corridor, and Space Center launch platforms are holding up well! Also, Space Center personnel had the good sense to lift one of those platforms well above flood level! It's the one hosting a shuttle pod!"

Boss's eyes bulged as he processed this report. He responded, "Have everyone unload all they've got on that damned copter! But while they're at it, they need to take evasive maneuvers so there are no further unnecessary casualties! And call Space Center to put up a firewall of ground-to-air missiles. If those missiles are also repulsed by the target, maybe at least they'll come crashing down on the shuttle pod! Gotta keep those f-n' bastards from getting hold of our spaceship! Roger that?!?!"

"Roger that, boss!!"

"And YOU!!" "Boss" aka Massive Guy pivoted around to stare down Shelly.

Her eyes couldn't have grown any wider with her terror, even had she been a nocturnally adapted Fafaman.

"Keep talking to this Flamboyo! Distract him! Get in his head!"

Shelly didn't need to be told twice. "Flamboyo!" she cried desperately into the cell phone. "You have to stop this, or they're going to kill you! They're going to keep firing at you until you run out of whatever you're doing to shield yourself!"

"We're not going to run out, chica!"

"Flamboyo!?!?! Why are you doing this?!?!?"

"Does your boyfriend know you're talking to me?!?!" Flamboyo shouted back. He had to shout. Otherwise he wouldn't hear himself above the racket from whirring helicopter blades. But hopeless desperation over Shelly was what he really wished he could drown out.

"We broke up! His values are not mine!! And now it would appear your values are not really mine, either! I thought you cared about those children!"

"It was all a front, chica! I am a very bad guy! You should not feel anything for me!"

"I don't understand why, but you're lying to yourself! Lying! And that will only get you killed!"

Not just myself. Flamboyo couldn't help thinking about what he couldn't bring himself to say aloud.

"Boss" paced the interrogation room like some caged beast in flight-or-fight mode, frustrated beyond words.

Over at Kennedy Space Center, the two guards posted atop the launch tower that contained a shuttle pod were no longer alone. They were met by guards from other launch towers. Those guards had boated over on their powered dinghies.

The tsunami encroachment was receding from its highest level. But choppy floodwaters still flowed at a level not three stories below the helipad atop each tower.

Bazookas slung across their backs, guards fresh off the dinghies scaled the launch tower trestle beams. They made it onto the helipad, teaming up with other guards already there. Cursing prevailed in regard to how anyone could have unleashed such an apocalyptically horrific disaster, for whatever reason. They couldn't take shots soon enough at whoever was responsible.

But the guards might as well have not bothered lifting a finger.

As the helicopter came whup-whup-whup within bazooka launch range, it sent out another blue flash.

Well before any of the guards could aim their weapons, they didn't know what hit them. Electrical discharges passed from weapon to weapon, and finally to the launch tower trestle work. Subsequently induced polarities sent the bazookas flying out of the guards' grasp. They landed plop-plop-plop in the ocean water on its eastward retreat offshore.

Every last guard received a temporary shock, stunned unconscious. The first few of them were roused back awake by high-pitched whining from the shuttle pod's anti-matter engine charging up. But they were already way too late. Electrostatically produced micron-layer stabilizer wings were aiding the pod's steep ascent.

"No more attempts at stopping us," counseled Flamboyo. "Or we will pause to destroy Space Station 2 on our way to the moon! We need time out there to think!"

"About what I said??!!" Shelly asked angrily, well past bothering over how carefully she ought to pick her words.

There was a brief pause into which Captain Taylor's daughter feared reading anything. Yet she couldn't resist freighting it with the teensiest bit of hope.

"Maybe that," Flamboyo answered finally, "and maybe to ponder how the moon could lead to a fresh start."

"Ah," "Boss" paused from his pacing to stab at the air with his forefinger. "Utopia on the moon: That's something to keep them talking until we can figure a way to neutralize them, and then discover what this is really all about!"

It sounded to Engeling like Flamboyo successfully misdirected the pestilence. And yet, Engeling still couldn't help worrying over his untrustworthy partner's reaction simply to hearing the woman's voice. Where Morel Engeling was concerned, Flamboyo was ultimately going to become a needless hindrance. He would have to be disposed of soon, lest he get in the way of total pestilence eradication. Human pestilence, that is.

Chapter 33

"She's deep down under there, somewhere." Guy Hanson pointed at where the thick layer of Styrofoam peanuts in Goolafala's crib had swelled to produce a small mound. "And that stuffed animal your husband won for her at the amusement park on Chonora? She was hugging it when she buried herself."

"Yes, yes," Ciela nodded anxiously, impatiently. She patted Guy on his back as in: Get out of here!

"I wanted to give her a kiss, but there would have been lots of commotion moving aside the Styrofoam. I was afraid I might wake her too soon. You see, she hasn't slept this soundly since before she started in with her sticky sweat."

"We know all about that, Señor Sergeant Hanson." Ciela's back-patting evolved into back-pushing, towards the door. "We also know how much she means to you and to Yulala. Don't worry; I will care for her as though she were my own! Now go! They need you pronto!"

"I am sure Yulala deeply appreciates this time she is getting to rest..."

"We know all about that too!" Ciela made shooing-off gestures until Hanson was out the door and out of sight.

It was when Ciela thought she finally succeeded in chasing him away that the doting father ducked his head back in, one last time. He asked, "Am I forgetting anything?"

"You're forgetting to leave! Scoot! Vamoose!"

At long last, Guy Hanson was gone for certain.

Ciela marveled anew at the love child miraculously produced by the union of an Earthling with a Fafaman. That is, she marveled at how for sleeping, Goolafala required burying herself, and the lights left on most brightly.

Ciela was about to rest her hands on the railing of Goolafala's crib. She was going to try discerning a gentle inflation and deflation of the Styrofoam peanut mound, from the baby's inhales and exhales. But that is when she noticed something even odder than normal. The floor was sticky well beyond the customary traction of her mag boots. With a shrug, she went to secure a mop. Somewhat worriedly, Ciela wondered at the amount of peculiar sweat the "chiquitita" must have been producing. How much could there be for it to drip off her crib?

⸱⟫⸱⟫⸱⟫⸱

Flight officer extraordinaire Tanya Petrovsky activated the egg-shaped shuttle pod's electrostatically maintained micron-layer wings. Then she set the pod itself on autopilot descent into Fafama's upper atmosphere, the stratosphere. She utilized the autopilot function so she could attend more carefully to Sergeants Hanson and Frankly. They were donning their oxygen-supplied envirosuits, fitted with mini-jet-engine backpacks.

As the three Earthlings went about this preparation, the shuttle pod's cockpit dome filled with a panoramic view of the multi-mile-wide ice comet. The comet was suspended in space, temporarily frozen during a moment of its past-time orbit of Fafama. Also come into clear view were the two nuclear-tipped missiles, designed and manufactured back on Earth. They had been intended by Fafama's supreme ruler, the Fafamafalafama, to bring down that messy bundle of ice and rock on rebel territory. Ultimate vengeance would be secured against whoever planned the terrorist attack on the Great Pyramid. And no wonder. That attack resulted in deaths of some of the supreme ruler's wives and children.

The two missiles hovered stationary one hundred feet apart from one another. They were located not more than a thousand feet behind the ice comet's upper portion.

The Smoke and Mirrors had lassoed the comet out of deep space, and then corralled it into orbit around Fafama. The original intention was to have the comet shed away its copious amounts of liquid into the Fafaman atmosphere. The Earthlings were trying to address Fafama's water shortage. They hoped to thereby lessen tensions between the Fafaman Empire and a rebel society that chose to live an alternate, literally underground lifestyle.

Again, missile impact against the comet had been meant by the Fafaman ruler to bring it down most calamitously on rebel areas. That event would have proven disastrous enough for the entire Fafaman ecosystem, planet wide. But an unforeseen variable occurred. Magma chamber activity heated the air above ground just enough to alter the missiles' flight paths, and consequently where they hit the comet. On the comet's unanticipated new trajectory after missile impact, it crashed into the base of the city-sized pyramid.

The plan for Fafama's rescue was concocted by First Officer Hyper-physics Engineer Buddy Leung. Both missiles' trajectories were to be altered so they would fly out into space where they could explode harmlessly. For such an adjustment, exceptional strength would be required, the sort of strength two guys with Marine Corps training might provide. That of course was where Sergeants Frankly and Hanson came in.

Were both missiles manifesting with their original, multi-ton weight, such an operation would have proven virtually impossible, even for two musclemen or musclewomen. But traversing a wound in the space-time fabric made a big difference. What Fred and Guy would be dealing with were actually two mere threads of that fabric, only. Each missile, including its respective, frozen-stiff contrail, would behave like the lightest Styrofoam possible. They would be so light, even Pedro and Ludi's daughter Alexita could have moved them about. That is, after each missile was dislodged from its "slot" in "completed" space-time. Wherefore the need for muscularly built assistants.

Buddy Leung explained as best he could. The faster an object was "caught" moving in the past, the more force would be required to "unstick" it from its momentum. And only then could it be repositioned heading a different direction.

In the gymnasium aboard the Smoke and Mirrors, Guy confirmed that Fred and Guy were the only two people aboard ship who were strong enough to succeed. But even so, their muscle would still most likely need supplanting by the additional power that jet packs strapped to their backs could provide.

By the time both missiles' positions were changed, the quantum wave would have "sensed" alterations to the past, and backtracked to experience them. Both nuclear-tipped devices would then fly directly away from Fafama, on their newly set course. The comet would not be pushed into a catastrophic descent, and the planet Fafama would be saved. Maybe.

Buddy Leung wasn't certain some unforeseen complication wouldn't arise. He termed one such possible complication "major event inertia." With "major event inertia," if there was such a thing, Buddy feared that any significant rerouting of history might prove impossible. It was possible that only relatively small changes to the past were actually ever achievable. The deliverance of two hundred people sixty years into the future, for example. Or the rescue of an even smaller group than that, so they wouldn't become culinary experiments at the hoof-hands of a Tictoctickian chef.

Tanya Petrovsky could not allow herself to fret over the "major event inertia" what-if. She needed to focus on proper adjustment of the spacewalk suit jet packs for Sergeants Frankly and Hanson.

The egg-shaped shuttle pod was auto-piloting itself into hover mode at the desired altitude. The upper half of its transparent cockpit dome continued to reveal a spectacular view of the ice comet, freeze-framed into an eye-blink of time. Also freeze-framed were little meteors and water vapor mists shed by the comet. An equally spectacular view, of Fafama's surface in dawning light, filled the lower half of the shuttle pod's window on the universe. There were several olive shades of green, some bioluminescent, interspersed with brownish patches.

Like a car's sunroof, the ceiling section of the shuttle pod's cockpit dome faced directly into the depths of outer space. If only Tanya and company had been able to study that particular view closely enough! Amidst plentiful stars, they would have espied the dragon-shaped collective of flickers evidencing the presence of the planetary spirit. That spirit had successfully followed the Smoke and Mirrors into the past. It was still drawn irresistibly wherever the starship went, yet usually kept its distance.

The planetary dragon spirit sensed special difficulty ahead, were people aboard the starship to succeed in their brazenly ambitious mission. Once the quantum wave finished backtracking, that spirit would be finding itself in two places at the same time. It would have to resolve the conundrum of both already embodying the planet, and having returned there from after the planet had been wrecked.

Presently, Tanya was about to learn that the two Marines on whom so much depended were puzzling over a related concern.

Officer Petrovsky guided both suited-up men into the shuttle pod's airlock chamber. "You go on along," she said. Thereby, she incidentally double-checked the spacesuit intercom systems were working properly. "I will keep shuttle pod stationary here, at this altitude. In unlikely event your jetpacks fail, you've got foolproof parachutes you can deploy. Either you can land back atop shuttle pod, or down on Fafama's surface, where I would descend to retrieve you. Your choice..."

Tanya was about to shut the airlock on the two Marine Corps sergeants. But that's when Sergeant Frankly turned clomp-clomp-clomp back around to ask something. With the intercom setup, he could have waited to do this until after they exited the airlock into the upper stratosphere. Nevertheless... "Can you explain to me once again about that quantum whoozy-whatzy we are racing against?"

Tanya made a most pronounced inhale and exhale with her anxious impatience. Yet she managed to rein in that emotion. She knew how exceedingly important it was for Fred to understand the conundrum. Especially if the worst case scenario played out, of the mission taking too long. "Buddy Leung says there is possible problem very unique to our task," she started to answer. "On our other time-travel projects, we were situated safe distance away from our past-time selves. There was no chance, really, we would accidentally come anywhere near those selves. Are you following, Sergeant?"

"Weird, but I am following, Officer. Of course, weird has been the f-n' rule ever since I first boarded the Smoke and Mirrors. The real weird has become when it is not weird!"

"Truly, as my husband would say, Sergeant," agreed Tanya. "So here is more of your real weird. There are you, your wife Ciela, Officer Ludi Perez and her daughter, and we must not forget those two mischievous boys you and Ciela have adopted."

"Yep, you're right. All of us are weird!"

"No, Sergeant, that's not what I'm saying!" Tanya shook her head emphatically. "I'm saying that all of you, a version of all of you is back on Oomb during this time frame to when we have returned. However, this is not the case for me and Sergeant Hanson. Sergeant Hanson's past-time version is close by, down on this planet. And my past-time version is aboard past-time Smoke and Mirrors, approaching here rapidly. Shortly after the quantum wave backtracks to digest what we are changing, the Smoke and Mirrors will be arriving. And then that other version of me will be descending through the atmosphere in this very same shuttle. I will be on rescue mission for Sergeant Hanson as well as for the captain, my husband Ali, Officer Leung and even Hanson's then-future wife, Yulala.

"Officer Leung has explanation for the quantum physics involved. You know about atoms, yes, Sergeant Frankly?"

"Atoms, sure. Two hydrogen atoms and one oxygen atom, they do a three-way and kaboom! You've got your f-n' water molecule!"

"That's one way of putting it." Tanya couldn't help smiling as she nodded. "So single atom is like entire solar system. The nucleus is sun at its center, and electrons are planets, because they are in orbit around nucleus. But from quantum physics, we know something very strange happens with those electrons. We know that until they are detected, until they are perceived by an intelligent entity, they are, effectively, everywhere at the same time, forming an electron shell. It is only when they are detected that they 'choose' to be in one particular location."

"Okay, kind of like if I could be playing poker and doing guard duty simultaneously. When Ciela comes looking for me, I would 'choose' to have been behavin' my ass-f-n' self, all about the guard duty. Yeah, I got that part."

Time was running short, well Guy Hanson knew. And Tanya wasn't saying anything he couldn't continue to hear her saying from inside his spacewalk suit while he jetted about the stratosphere. But he had had trouble himself, fully grasping physicist Leung's "oh, by the way" heads-up about "a possible conundrum." Consequently, as Officer Petrovsky went on explaining in her creamy Russian accent, Hanson returned clomp-clomp-clomping beside his fellow Marine Corps Sergeant. He gave up pretending he was giving anything less than his full, rapt attention to Tanya.

"This brings us to where our good friend, Buddy, says we have possible what he calls, 'conundrum,'" went on Tanya Petrovsky. "He says we are each like one of those electrons encircling the nucleus of atom. He says imagine your whole life, from birth to death, is an electron shell. You could be anywhere in your life. However, the quantum wave always chooses for your awareness to be at a particular point in your life. It is just like how an intelligent being unwittingly chooses, by its detection of an electron, for that electron to exist at one particular location."

On a whistle of astonishment, Guy Hanson exclaimed, "This sounds like the quantum wave is the mind of God passing across our lives!"

"Perhaps, Sergeant Hanson" nodded Tanya. "I have had such thought myself. But here is the problem, the dilemma. Imagine you have two versions of yourself standing beside one another when quantum wave is 'passing across,' as you put it. Which version of you does quantum wave choose? Or do you choose? Officer Leung has made a guess, based upon calculation that not even Professor Aquinas can grasp. He guesses your earlier, younger self is favored very quickly in such a situation. And say the two versions of you are located far apart, as you are now from yourself on Oomb, Sergeant Fred Frankly. In that situation, Officer Leung guesses the choice takes much longer time to be made. During which, what Albert Einstein termed 'spooky action at a distance' gives both versions of you some strange dizzy feeling."

"So that's why I received the instructions for hauling the Smoke and Mirrors' light-propelled ass outta here! That's for if we do get hit by that f-n' conundrum prior to makin' our f-n' exit!" Fred blustered with his pride over finally comprehending the potential situation. "I'll function better, even dizzy, than any one of you! That's because my other f-n' self is light-years away, while your other selves are much closer by! You'll be the ones getting frozen shitless like that big-ass comet out there, thanks to the quantum wave choosing the younger version of yourself from last year! But I'll still be more or less okay, leastwise until that f-n' quantum shwantum catches up to me as well!"

"Thanks, Tanya, Officer Petrovsky." Sergeant Hanson corrected his informality with a sheepish if clumsy bow, constrained by his spacewalk suit. "Now I think I really understand. We must hurry!"

"We sure as hell *must* hurry!" Fred agreed. He turned and pushed Guy ahead of him, for the airlock exit out of the shuttle pod. "I want to complete our planet-rescuin' task fast enough to skip the two-places-at-once stuff. Can easily go the rest of my f-n' life without ever learning how that f-n'-ass conundrum actually resolves itself!"

⊹⁖⊹⊹⁖⊹⊹⁖⊹

Ciela was seated beside Goolafala's baby crib, trying to immerse herself in a phonetic English-Fafaman bilingual picture dictionary. The more she became friends with Yulala, the more she wanted to learn how to communicate in her native language. Ciela thought it must be bad enough to suddenly lose your whole family and other past associates, everyone you knew. But she couldn't imagine how it must have been for Yulala to lose the entire planet where she grew up!

What remained of Fafaman civilization and ecology boiled down to not all that much. There were a few articles of clothing. Recordings of some songs Chris Olsen-Taylor, Captain Taylor's husband, had collected. Some Fafaman literature and history books Chief Counselor Ali Magabu had obtained. And of course there was Effy the ephemeral dragon along with, who knew? Maybe the planetary spirit was Effy's mother that kept shadowing the starship, to protect her child!

Ciela was also thinking what she would do if she picked up enough of the Fafaman tongue. Maybe she would teach classes for both adults and children, of

Fafaman as a second language. She would help Yulala prevent the Fafaman tongue from going completely extinct.

Again, Ciela wanted to deep-dive into the extraterrestrial language, but there were just too many distractions. They went well beyond fretting over Yulala. There was more than just wondering whether Yulala allowed herself to succumb at last to her own exhaustion. Yulala finally enjoying some much-needed rest wasn't the only thing. No. Ciela still couldn't get over how Goolafala had to have the lights left on, bright lights at that, for sleep. Clearly Yulala's nocturnal nature dominated over what Goolafala's Earthling father brought to the gene pool. Not only that, but there was this other bizarre business with little baby Goolafala. She had to submerse herself in a layer of Styrofoam peanuts as an additional condition for her successful slumber! But looked at a certain way, such behavior wasn't really that strange. Indeed, it was comparable to that of a creature found all over the place on Fafama, as Yulala explained it. That creature was named the namalumina, or flounder mouse where Earthlings were concerned. Ciela had to agree with Yulala. It couldn't be a coincidence that both Goolafala and the typical namalumina required self-burial before they could sleep. And there was another characteristic the baby shared with the namalumina. Her one eye was migrated over to the same side of her head as her other eye, identical to how they were located on Earth's flounder fish.

Pondering Goolafala's preciously endearing uniqueness left Ciela feeling unaccountably desperate. She needed to confirm the continuing stable condition of that miracle child born of parents from two different planetary evolution lines. And of course, she wanted to succeed in that confirmation without disturbing Goolafala from a slumber the little girl required as much as her mother.

Ciela gave up trying to focus on the bilingual picture dictionary generated by Ali Magabu. Instead, she went to stand over near the crib, even closer than she had been sitting beside it. She clutched at the crib's railing to peer down deep. Once more, she tried to make out a subtle rise and fall in the Styrofoam peanut mound. Success at such an endeavor would have assured her Goolafala was breathing normally.

But what was this?

Ciela lifted her hands off the railing soon as she placed them on. The railing was coated in some especially sticky, slimy material.

Of course, claro que sí, Ciela thought to herself. *It's that strange substance they told me pobrecita Goolafala is sweating. Hopefully she is sweating out una maldición, an extraterrestrial curse from her system so she can enjoy better health! That has to be what I have discovered here! No problem. I can get a damp cloth to wipe it off. Ay! It is shed all over the floor also!* The last part shouted in Ciela's head. Turning around to leave the room to go secure the damp cloth, she found even more stickiness under foot. There was no confusing it for the Velcro-like material which gave the magboots their extra-adhesive traction. That is, whenever the Smoke and Mirrors was travelling too slowly for gravity generation.

Fred Frankly's wife lifted her legs to exaggerated heights on every step she took, in reaction to the stickiness. What didn't make any sense was that she was sure she had already mopped it up. *Ay, chica, wait!* Ciela cautioned herself. *The floor is not actually sticky where I* mopped close to the crib. But how far away from the crib does the stickiness extend?

When Ciela reached the nursery room door, she found herself still having to deal with sticky floor. She halted, crouched down, and patted the floor beyond where she had already been cautiously stepping. To her frightful astonishment, she discovered that the sticky trail continued. But how? How could Goolafala's odd sweat have spread such a distance from her crib?

To try keeping calm, Ciela recalled Goolafala's parents carrying her all over the place. Doubtless that was when the baby dribbled her sticky stuff everywhere on the floor. Ciela recalled something else from much longer ago. She recalled gardening back on the planet Oomb. Pellets had dribbled from a leak in the fertilizer bag she carried for Ludi Perez. The answer was as simple as that, wasn't it? Besides, Goolafala couldn't possibly have gotten out of bed and crawled on the floor fast enough to escape notice, could she? Could she??

Ciela tried from the bedroom entrance to discern a subtle rise and fall of the mounded area of Styrofoam peanuts. That would have evidenced Goolafala still safely buried away, exhaling and inhaling.

Nothing.

An observer would have seen the woman's almond complexion turn pale. Despite her magboots, she rushed back over beside Goolafala's crib. She probed below the Styrofoam peanut surface to locate the baby girl. But her probe turned up nothing more than the stuffed animal won by Ciela's husband, Fred, at a carnival on Chonora.

Ciela pounded the intercom attached to her uniform, and she cried, "Help! We need help in Goolafala's nursery! She has vanished! Help!"

Sergeants Frankly and Hanson quickly realized how easy it was to maneuver around in the stratosphere with their jet-powered backpacks. They might have been sore-tempted to do a little high-altitude sightseeing. However, they needed to get down to the pressing business of re-positioning two nuclear warhead missiles.

Those missiles were frozen on a horrifically destructive path, bound for impact with the upper quadrant of the ice comet orbiting Fafama. Fred and Guy had arrived from the future to forestall such an event. But they didn't have much time before the missiles unfroze to continue on their apocalyptic way.

But even were Sergeants Fred Frankly and Guy Hanson to have had several hours, it wouldn't have mattered. Both were experiencing nausea from the ripple effect of flying about in already-completed space-time.

The Smoke and Mirrors and the shuttle pod had set off similar ripples. However, Fred and Guy got to watch those ripples' effects on a panoramic view-screen or through the shuttle pod's cockpit dome. That wasn't nearly as stomach-churning as actually being outside engulfed by them.

Nausea or no nausea, though, Fred and Guy still had to persevere. They still needed to perform their task ahead of the quantum wave backtracking. And there was no way the quantum wave wouldn't backtrack after it sensed time-line tampering.

The two men jetted with all due haste further skywards. They brought themselves to a hover beside one of the missiles.

"You take this cone-head we're closest to, Mr. Extraterrestrial Dad?" asked Fred. "And I'll scurry over there?"

"You scurry over there." Guy felt the awkwardness of lifting his spacesuit-encumbered arm for pointing towards the further-away missile frozen in mid-flight. That awkwardness together with his persisting nausea amplified his anxiety over the task ahead. He had been led to believe it should prove simple and easy, only brute strength required. Nothing too intricate involved. He would not have to manipulate the various tools built retracted into the spacesuit itself. More muscle might become necessary than either he or Fred could bring to bear individually, aided by their jet packs. But there was a straightforward fix for that. They could join forces to dislodge the missiles one at a time from their space-time momentum 'locks.' Yes, there shouldn't be any real problem. And yet...was Guy Hanson's upset tummy really just about the ripple effect?

No real surprises, where Buddy Leung was concerned. Both missiles proved too "locked in" tor yielding to no more than the force of the men's arms. However, Fred and Guy were able to supplement their strength with the added oomph from their jet packs.

The jet-pack thrust working well for them, Fred and Guy pushed anew against their respective warheads. An observer might have wondered whether they were two superheroes who had flown in to save the day.

Fred Frankly and Guy Hanson applying extra force finally did budge the missiles, with unexpected suddenness. Well before Fred and Guy could back off from their successful efforts, both missiles went spinning end over end. They knocked the men far from them as they spun on axes that maintained them in their respective locations. Those missiles could have been suddenly become two pinwheels.

Dazed but not confused, Fred and Guy reduced jet-pack power to the minimum necessary. They maintained altitude where they were located in the stratosphere. Then each Marine approached his still-spinning, self-assigned missile with trepidation.

Back in real time, back in perfect sync with the quantum wave, both Marines well knew what would have happened. Making the slightest effort to touch either of those two missiles, spinning or not, would have proven fatal. The missiles' weight combined with their extreme high temperature would have quickly ripped and melted off Fred and Guy's spacesuit gloves. Resultant leaks would have killed them within seconds, while escaping oxygen propelled them aimlessly away from one another. Moreover, the missiles' exhaust trails would have cut across them on each end-over-end spin. One missile exhaust "cut" alone would have been plenty ample for scalding them to death.

Fortunately, each missile's pinwheel spin slowed dramatically quickly. Soon enough thereafter, Fred and Guy mustered the courage to reach out for stopping the missiles' movement altogether. To their relief, they found the force of the warheads slapping against their spacesuit gloves to be no big deal. It was no stronger than the force from a typical hi-five.

Fred and Guy repositioned the missiles at angles diagonal to the ground hundreds of miles below. They accomplished this with relative ease, prompting the same confident thought. *We might as well have been turning the steering wheel on an ancient car.*

Buddy Leung, Captain Taylor and others had assured Fred and Guy of how easily the task should go. Their assurances had been based on their own experiences. During a previous time travel jaunt, they had gathered up

Ciela and nearly two hundred other people like so many paper dolls. Thus far, it looked like they were correct, to the sergeants' incredulous relief.

All that remained was for both missiles to continue harmlessly skyward. Of course that would have to wait until the quantum wave caught up, or rather backtracked to that instant of space-time.

Certainly the most challenging aspect for Sergeants Frankly and Hanson remained the avoidance of succumbing to nausea. Both suits were outfitted with motion sickness bladders for the vomit contingency. But knowing that didn't help. Propelling their selves a safe distance from the repositioned missiles inadvertently sent Fred and Guy into a slow spin, more stomach churning. The planet Fafama seemed to rotate from under Fred and Guy to over their heads and back again. The ever-present rippling and blurring effect made matters even worse. Fred and Guy's very presence kept displacing "completed" space-time in ways that couldn't be avoided.

"Hey Petrovsky?! Let's move it before I dump a load both ends!" Fred Frankly blustered. He did his best to motion his right arm like he was thumbing a ride.

That is when Guy Hanson blinked his eyes repeatedly since he couldn't rub them. He was trying to convince himself the nuclear-tipped missiles were not shifting position of their own volition. Rather, he wanted desperately to believe his view was distorted by his watering eyes. There was also the aforementioned ripple effect from him, Fred, and the shuttle pod "crowding" past space-time. Could that be contributing to the illusion?

Finally, though, Guy had to admit the truth. A pit formed in the bottom of his stomach while Fred gagged on the verge of puking.

Both missiles were slowly yet inexorably lowering their trajectory, until they both came to a stop. They returned to the same position where the two men had found them in the first place. Once more, they were headed for impact against upper portions of the comet.

"Oh, hell, no! HELL, NO!" Fred's realization lifted him out of his nausea.

⁂

When they rushed into Goolafala's nursery, Ali Magabu and Deborah Davis-Murphy found Fred's wife Ciela in full desperation mode. With frantic arm sweeps, she was spraying Styrofoam peanuts out of the crib all over the floor. Counselor Magabu figured she might as well have been thrashing about in a pool, on the verge of drowning.

"Ay! Ay! How could this have happened?! How?!" Ciela sobbed. She shook her head inconsolably into Deborah's shoulder. But this only happened after the Chief Medical Officer finally managed to pull her away from a vain search of the crib.

By then, the crib was down to the mattress. Only a few bits of peanut-shaped Styrofoam were still left scattered atop it.

Tears streaming from her reddened eyes, Ciela shook her head, as much in disbelief as in defensiveness. She sobbed, "I was awake the entire time! The lights were left on like they are now, because of Goolafala's nocturnal nature inherited from her mother! Sí," she nodded animatedly, answering a question nobody had yet asked. "I was out of the room to get a mop! But that took only two seconds! How could she have crawled away so fast??"

"Ciela, please, you must lower your voice." Ali held out a cautioning hand. To him, she seemed on a crescendo towards a shrieking wail. "Truly, you don't want to disturb Goolafala's mother from her much-needed rest. At least, let's ascertain first exactly what's going on here. We already know one thing for sure. Don't we, Dr. Davis-Murphy?"

Deborah nodded.

"We are sure that truly, most truly, you are entirely blameless. Entirely blameless," Ali repeated and shook his head for extra emphasis. "Now just tell us, if you can: I think you are absolutely correct. The moments you took securing a mop were too brief. Goolafala would have remained safe for that interval. However, was there any other occasion she might have been left unattended? Maybe it was the transition over to your most tender care from her father's own loving vigilance?"

Ciela's eyes suddenly widened out from their grieving slits. "When Sergeant Hanson came to get me, for some minutes I think there was nobody here..."

"That's it!" Ali Magabu snapped his fingers.

"But who on board would have wanted to make off with a baby?" asked Deborah. "Were there a deer creature from Tictoctic still around, hiding in the air shafts..." She suddenly swung her head from side to side, searching for the nearest ventilation grate.

"No, I don't think so, Doctor." Ali waved a forefinger. "Not that. Our mindreading tree friends would have picked up on a stray Tictoctickian, and alerted the captain. Not to mention the life-sign sensors.

"Ciela," went on Ali Magabu, directing his attention back to the distressed woman. "I did notice the stickiness on the floor leaves off not too very far beyond the entrance to this room. You told us there was also stickiness on the crib railing, yes? Did you find any such gunk continuing down the side of the crib, by any chance?"

Ciela's puzzlement over where the counselor was going with this line of inquiry nearly lifted her out of her upset.

But Ali didn't wait for her answer before he checked the crib himself.

"Ah, yes, truly remarkable," he commented, even before finished sliding his fingers down one of the pink-painted bars from the crib railing. "Gentle ladies, this can mean only one thing. Nobody has made away with her. Our dear little Goolafala has made away with herself. Somehow, she has descended from her crib and crawled out of the nursery. I suggest we search the hall outside this particular room, including a look-see on our other child passengers."

"Counselor Magabu, the slimy mucous Goolafala has been shedding, any ideas why its trail leaves off just past the threshold to her nursery?" Even as Deborah asked this, though, she was thinking to herself what she could not bring herself to admit out loud. Most likely, Guy and Yulala's love child dragged herself off to some secluded location, to die.

"I obviously could not know, Doctor," replied Ali. "Perhaps she simply stopped producing any more sticky discharge."

Ciela tried the door to a storage room just outside Goolafala's room. She found it locked.

Ali and Deborah walked well ahead of Ciela, on their own search for Goolafala's whereabouts. Ali was thinking he would summon an Oombian to help if they didn't find her soon.

Ciela got held up wondering why she wasted time with the storage room. Open or locked made no difference. How would Guy and Yulala's baby daughter have ever been able to reach up high enough to turn the door knob? Soon as Ciela posed this question to herself, though, she noticed something. It protruded from under the storage room door, in the half-inch slit between the bottom of the door and the floor. It was a telltale wisp of hair that glistened with the same, raven black color of Yulala's hair.

⋅ ⟨⟨ ⟩⟩ ⟨⟨ ⟩⟩ ⟨⟨ ⟩⟩ ⋅

"Buddy Leung and I have discussed this. Sergeants, Officer Petrovsky, you need to bail out of there, now. Sometime in the future, after the Smoke and Mirrors has been refitted with new mirror arrays, we will certainly give this another go..."

"Sorry, Captain, but I repeat what I said before: Oh, hell, no! HELL, NO!! After this little detour, we might be headed smack into Armageddon against those furry-assed antlered demons from Tictoctic! Then we will be lucky if the Smoke and f-n' Mirrors doesn't get destroyed, so much for having its freakin' mirrors refitted!" Sergeant Frankly's arms and legs were in a commotion that further amplified the ripples of completed-space-time. He was throwing this tantrum not more than fifty feet from the closest nuclear missile.

Both missiles had long since returned to their originally come-upon positions. They were headed at the orbiting ice comet's upper quadrant again. The sergeants' efforts had come to naught. Dislodging the missiles from completed space-time and re-aiming them harmlessly headed for outer space had done no good.

"I have an idea," Sergeant Frankly said upon finally calming down. "I am going to give it a go, no matter what! You can court-marshal the ass-pukin' shit outta my hairy butt afterwards for all I f-n' care! Sergeant Hanson, you just stay put and watch. Better yet, plant your own hairy butt safely beside Officer Petrovsky, down below us inside the shuttle pod, expeditiously! There! How's that for another one of your f-n' ten-dollar words?!"

Guy Hanson couldn't look inside Fred's helmet to see how beet-red flushed his face had become with what he was about. But clearly, his improbable buddy of so many years wasn't wasting any time.

Sergeant Frankly had already jetted himself back over beside one of the missiles.

Guy stayed put; no way was he going to obey Fred's "better yet" order. No way would he return to the hovering shuttle pod. At least, not until he understood what Sergeant Frankly was trying to do.

Everyone else watching through Guy's spacewalk suit-cam was stunned silent, from Tanya in the shuttle pod to crew aboard the Smoke and Mirrors.

Fred found the missile not as difficult to dislodge the second time as he did the first. Buddy sensed this; he wondered whether the missile hadn't quite finished "locking" itself back into its original momentum trajectory.

Sergeant Frankly finished repositioning the missile to be headed safely heaven-wards, once more. Pursuant to which, he raced flying over to the other missile, closer to where Guy was looking on. There, he repeated the repositioning procedure. No sooner was that done than he was hurrying his return to the missile where he started. He caught it beginning its slow regression to its original trajectory for the second time. "You see, good buddy, semper fi and all that, I've got this covered! Now you haul your sweet ass to the shuttle pod! You have a family to take care of!"

"So do you, Sergeant Frankly! Two little boys who look up to you! And Ciela! Remember her? Your little piece of heaven?" responded Sergeant Hanson. He met Fred on his second go at the closer-by missile.

"Those boys need someone who's not a cussin' piece of work like me! Someone with the patience those two little runts need! And Ciela deserves far better than someone so uncouth – how's that for yet another prize-winning word? Surely she can do better than someone who the fates randomly threw her way! Someone whose biggest claim to f-n' fame was that he didn't rape her when those Tictoctic bastards gave him the chance! Of course I'm talkin' about when they treated us like a bull and a cow! In case you didn't know, those deer demons tried to force us to mate! They wanted us to produce some little cutlets for them to roast! Again, she deserves better than me!"

Fred and Guy found themselves pushing awkwardly at one another. They wrestled as best they could, given the constraints of their spacewalk suits.

"No she doesn't deserve better than you! Wait! That didn't come out right!"

"Sergeant Hanson and Sergeant Frankly!" Captain Taylor's voice erupted in harsh, lecturing tones inside both men's helmets. "We appreciate profoundly your willingness to give this your all! But heaven forbid if you are anywhere near those nukes when the quantum wave puts them back in real-time motion! Their blasts of heat will kill you both! As the captain of this mission, as *your* captain, I order you to stand down and return to the shuttle pod! NOW!! BOTH OF YOU!!!"

What Helena heard in return were grunts. They accompanied Fred and Guy's struggles against each other which she was able to gather from Sergeant Hanson's body cam.

The two Marine Corps Sergeants fought in vain to achieve an advantage. The victor would kick the loser into a tailspin, sending him far, far away. So far away, by the time he managed to right himself and return to re-engage the battle, he would be too late. The quantum wave's backtracking would already be putting the two nuclear warheads on a path headed for outer space, nowhere near the comet. For sure, the exhaust from one if not both missiles would roast to death the victorious sergeant. But at least they would proceed to explode harmlessly in the cosmic void. And sealing one's fate in aid of such an accomplishment was far preferable to having lived while the other sergeant made the ultimate sacrifice.

"All you're going to do is get two young wives widowed, and their children fatherless!" Helena shouted helplessly.

Below where the shuttle pod hovered, Tanya Petrovsky realized she was looking directly at another potential problem. A parachute ahtpah, one of Fafama's cow-sized spiders, was frozen in mid-air. Vast webbing for its propulsion also hung still there. *But is this really another problem?* Tanya asked herself with sudden hopeful excitement. *Or is this a big opportunity?*

⁂

"Not good, Captain." Buddy Leung was shaking his head in unconcealed despair on the navigation deck of the Smoke and Mirrors. "You see that distant dragon-shaped star cluster? The one we are figuring is the disembodied planetary spirit of Fafama?" Buddy pointed at what looked like a constellation among constellations shining brightly in the panoramic view-screen. Only unlike those other bunches of stars, it was in fast-enough motion for discerning. "It's started to come closer. I don't know how to keep from sounding cliché, but there really isn't much time left. Soon we will be facing a space-time conundrum like we have never faced before."

"Captain," added navigation officer Yoon-hee Park-Smith from her control console. Her dire tone suggested she was about to amplify Buddy's concern.

"I am picking up an object on the outer fringe of this solar system with the exact spectroscopic signature of the Smoke and Mirrors."

"We hold tight, people," said Helena. She gave her husband's hand an extra squeeze.

Chris was standing faithfully beside the captain's chair.

⸱ ⸲⸱⸲⸱⸲⸱⸲⸱⸲

Tanya Petrovsky succeeded in lifting the parachute ahtpah to a higher altitude. She simply used the shuttle pod to push upwards on its hanging, spindly legs. The monster spider's entire network of parachute webs went with it. They remained unbroken like Tanya hoped they would.

Seconds later, via her own jet-propelled spacewalk suit, Tanya left the shuttle pod. No sooner did she exit the pod's airlock than she noticed Fred and Guy's wrestling match over who would sacrifice his life. Their struggle, which she would have characterized as ridiculous, was taking both men down further away from the nuclear-tipped missiles.

The two sergeants were approaching ever closer a spray of rock fragments shed by the comet as its ice melted. The way those fragments burned up in the atmosphere gave them the appearance of fireworks to Tanya, albeit fireworks frozen in a sliver of "completed" space-time. Tanya didn't want to warn Guy and Fred they could get their suits ripped on tiny meteorites. That would have alerted them she was up to something. However, if they drifted any closer...

⚜ ⚜ ⚜ ⚜

"Tanya,-"
Leave her be, Captain.

⚜ ⚜ ⚜

Oodle-Noodle needn't have bothered waving off Helena Taylor from distracting Tanya Petrovsky with challenging questions. Tanya was already too committed to her plan of action for any amount of arguing with her to have mattered. She busily tied ahtpah web filaments around the rear stabilizer fins of the nuclear missiles. She also kept checking Frank and Guy's ongoing wrestling match, to make sure they didn't drift too near the jagged-edged comet or any of its sliver-in-time attendant fireworks displays.

Fortunately where Tanya Petrovsky was concerned, her surmise proved correct. Thanks to its past-time state, the ahtpah web lacked its usual stickiness, making it easily manageable for what she imagined doing.

Officer Petrovsky quickly finished tying one last carefully chosen ahtpah web strand to the tail fins of the second missile. That is when she noticed Fred Frankly had untangled himself from Guy long enough for descending to a far lower altitude. Fred was obviously intent on zooming back up high, away from his friend. There, of course, he would reposition both missiles just before the quantum wave hit.

Tanya made her own descent, but for returning to the shuttle pod left in hover mode. That's when she realized both men were coming over to join her.

"I see what you've got going, Officer Petrovsky!" Sergeant Hanson's deep voice erupted crackling from Tanya's helmet intercom.

"Yeah! It's f-n' brilliant!" chimed in Sergeant Frankly. "Push Spiderzilla to a lower altitude, and its web strands tied to the missiles will be pulled taut! They'll be pulled so taut that they will pull down on the missiles' tail fins! And when the tail fins are pulled down, the warheads are aimed upwards! Next thing you know, both missiles are pointed away from the comet, towards outer space! Am I correct, Petrovsky?"

"You are correct, Sergeant Frankly."

"Okay, then, I should be the one giving the old heave-ho to Spiderzilla! Only wish I had my AK-51 along for the ride, so I could punch a hole through that- Hey!"

Guy had just lunged at Fred to push him far from the parachute ahtpah.

"No more fighting!" screamed Tanya. She expelled so much air that she momentarily steamed up the inside of her helmet. "Even with your jet packs on their highest settings, you won't succeed! Neither one of you, nor both together, will be able to produce enough force to dislodge everything that requires dislodging! The ahtpah, its parachute webbing, the two missiles tied to that webbing...only the shuttle pod can exert enough force to handle them all, simultaneously! So both of you must join me! Let's return inside shuttle pod! NOW!!"

Tanya felt both men's sheepishness when they preceded her into the shuttle pod's airlock. That brought a faint grin to the corners of her thin-lipped mouth. She imagined Sergeants Frankly and Hanson as the two mischievous little boys aboard the Smoke and Mirrors. Of course, those were the boys Ciela marched into a small side room. She had to severely reprimand them for stuffing Professor Skepticus's rear pockets with chocolate chip cookies, in aid of getting the seat of his pants burned by Effy.

Presently, there was no time for reprimands or lectures; Tanya kept her mind racing to juggle all possible eventualities.

"Hey, Petrovsky! Wait! We haven't taken off our spacesuits yet!" complained Fred.

Heedless of Fred Frankly's complaint, Tanya didn't hold back. She pushed both sergeants directly through the airlock into the body of the shuttle pod. "And we are not going to take them off, either!" she responded. "Just in case I lose consciousness, Sergeant Frankly, I want you strapped into pilot's chair! I am taking co-pilot's chair, and leaning across you to control shuttle pod operation while I am still able to! Sergeant Hanson, you take a seat behind Frankly!"

Tanya had good reason for her no-argument-will-be-tolerated orders. She already felt a familiar tingle coming on from the approaching quantum wave. She was fiercely determined, though, that her efforts would not be in vain. To that end, she had already taken the shuttle pod out of hover mode when she heard the sergeants' seatbelts click.

Much clumsiness attended Tanya leaning over Fred's lap, and having to work the control console with her spacesuit gloves left on. Despite this, in less than another minute she had the shuttle pod nosing down at the ahtpah's bulbous rear end. Via the shuttle pod, Tanya pushed against the monster with just the right amount of pressure. In no time, both nuclear missiles were aimed heavenwards away from the comet. The same as Sergeant Frankly explained, web strands from the ahtpah were tugged taut. In turn, those strands tugged on the missiles where they were tied to the missiles' tail fins. What the sergeant did not notice was that Tanya had selected web strands for this feat that were still issuing from the ahtpah's rear end. That is, during the moment of completed space-time to where the Earthlings had returned.

Anyway, the missiles remained aimed towards deep space the necessary seconds.

The blurring ripples from displaced space-time dissipated like so much morning fog, Tanya fancied. Such dissipation happened, of course, because the quantum wave had arrived.

Next thing anyone knew, the two nuclear-tipped missiles were powered into the starry firmament on billowing-out plumes of spent hydrogen fuel. They went nowhere near the comet. And searing heat from the plumes dissolved the tied-on web strands instantly.

The enormous ice comet proceeded on its dazzling, meteorite-shedding orbit. There was no longer any danger of a changed trajectory putting it on a collision course with Fafama. The comet would continue gradually making a great contribution to the planet's water supply.

"F-n' 'a,' you did it, Officer Petrovsky! Officer Petrovsky? Tanya?" Fred quickly grew aware that Tanya Petrovsky was behaving like she had lost consciousness. Both her arms were flailing about randomly in the near-weightless conditions. "You see this, Hanson?! Good thing she taught us to fly this f-n'- Not you too! Oh, hell, no!" Fred twisted around in his seat only to find Guy Hanson in the same condition as Tanya. His arms were drifting loosely, in a manner reminding Fred of how seaweed drifted in the ebb and flow of surf. "Damned f-n' conundrum," he muttered under his breath while he fought to pull the shuttle pod out of an accelerating free-fall broken only by-

Ping! Ping!

"What the f- was- Oh-oh!" Fred beheld the bulbous rear of the parachute ahtpah that had been pressed into by the shuttle pod. Its protruding venomous barb curled threateningly, poised to strike like a scorpion.

Fractures quickly radiated from where the ahtpah's barb stabbed into the shuttle pod's cockpit dome. Jagged pieces of the shuttle pod's window on the universe were soon falling away, into the cockpit. From the same ahtpah barb which had managed to pierce through that inch-thick glass-aluminum alloy, out spewed a web strand. It was sprayed with an especially sticky fluid ejaculated from pores on either side of the barb. As a result, it clung strongly to Tanya Petrovsky's floating-about arms.

Next thing Fred knew, Tanya got yanked out of her strapped-in seat by the ahtpah. With its hindmost spindly legs, the monstrous spider was reeling in its shot-out web filament.

The filament could have been a fishing line, Sergeant Frankly collected his wits enough to imagine. Frankly grabbed Tanya's limp body, and clung as tightly as possible. But he was dealing with the awkward constraints of his spacesuit. He couldn't cling tightly enough, and removal of his spacesuit was not an option where clinging more tightly was concerned. Again, the parachute ahtpah had broken through the cockpit dome. And so Fred's spacesuit was the only thing protecting him from fatally low oxygen levels in the Fafaman stratosphere. Besides, say he could have removed the spacewalk suit without experiencing any personal harm. Suppose he could have done that, in aid of achieving a better grip on Tanya in his tug-of-war with the parachute ahtpah. By the time he freed himself from such an encumbrance, she would already have been long since taken into the ahtpah's fatal embrace.

To make matters even more horrifically worse, a second web strand was shot into the cockpit. It pulled the limp Guy Hanson out of *his* seat, also despite seat belt restraints.

FWOOSH!! Flames as from an invisible torch suddenly rent the thin air between Fred Frankly and the partially shattered cockpit dome. What was left of the web strands consisted mostly of char-black cinders crumbled to dust, thus letting go both Tanya and Guy. Foot-long strand remnants that were not charred undulated lazily in the thinned-out air. They undulated similarly to how Tanya and Guy's suited-up arms were undulating where the remnants remained attached.

"Effy! You whatever-the-f-n'-hell you are, well thank sweet Jesus you are that!" exclaimed Fred. He managed to refocus on pulling the shuttle pod into an ascent out of Fafama's outer atmosphere, bound for the Smoke and Mirrors.

Ping! Ping! Ping!

"Sonofabitch!" cussed Sergeant Frankly anew. He furiously sought a rear view from the shuttle pod's navigation console screen monitor.

Ping!

Sure enough, there was that same parachute ahtpah again, firing more web strands at the shuttle pod. It labored under a mistaken impression the pod was just another of Fafama's monstrous-sized insects.

"Now's about the time when I wish my consciousness would escape to someplace else, to join my brother-in-arms and foxy lady here!" Fred muttered. He was referring to Guy and Tanya in their out-of-it state. He tried to contain his fear while the enormous, air-borne spider succeeded in stalling out the shuttle pod's ascent. The parachute ahtpah had enrobed the shuttle pod in a spun cocoon, to save for when her babies hatched.

WHOOSH! Blazing yellow flames engulfed the flight vehicle. The next thing Fred knew, nothing but cinder filaments were left of the cocoon. And the shuttle pod was easily breaking free to resume its ascent out of the Fafaman atmosphere.

Temporarily stunned, the parachute ahtpah drifted down and away on its previous web production.

What Sergeant Frankly did not get to see was that his deliverance came courtesy of the planet's dragon spirit. That spirit was in the process of reuniting with its past self. This was made possible by the salvation of Fafama, the dramatic redirection of the otherwise doomed course of the planet's history.

Frankly could feel the chilling presence of Effy the ephemeral dragon. It slid past him and back again, like a cat prowling closely enough to rub affectionately against one's legs.

⋅⟩⊰∘⋅⟩⊰∘⋅⟩⊰∘

Several minutes earlier the ruler of Fafama, the Fafamafalafama, stewed with fear and anger. At a reinforced stronghold deep within Fafama's city-sized pyramid, he was losing patience with missile flight engineer Naratama. "I actually understand very little of what you are about with your control panel, Naratama!" the Fafaman ruler raged. He stood looming over Naratama seated at the launch guidance console. "And yet, I understand enough to know there is desperation and panic to how you are pounding at those keys!"

Naratama bowed down ever lower over his control panel. He reckoned it would not be the worst thing in the world if the Fafamafalafama were to take advantage of this opportunity to most swiftly, mercifully slice off his head.

"I wish," Naratama mumbled his fa-la-las most despairingly, "I wish I could personally place myself in the path of both missiles, to have them detonate harmlessly against my otherwise worthless-"

"BUT YOU CAN'T!!!" The Fafamafalafama roared his fa-la-las in unbridled contempt. And with a swirl of his bioluminescently lit cape, he stepped away from Naratama. "So save us at least from your idle dream of undeserved martyrdom! Especially since you can save us from nothing else!!" he continued raging, though for more general consumption by other Fafamans present within the stronghold. "And rest assured! You will remain here to perish as you most deservedly are meant to! That will be your fate if nothing can be done to thwart the most disastrous scenario you say has been so stupidly, stupidly unleashed! Guards! Chain him to his post!" Then more specifically at Naratama again, "I can only hope you come up with something! Or that you are simply incorrect in your projections so that ultimately, we are safe by virtue of your incompetence!"

"No! Wait! Most esteemed Fafamafalafama of whom I am completely unworthy! It's a miracle! Allow me to replay this for you!" Naratama pointed excitedly at his console's radar screen. He was practically hopping up and down in his chair with excitement despite two guards having already seized him for chaining there, as ordered.

"It will go even worse for you, I assure you, if this is a delay tactic! If all you are doing is trying to trick me into some foolish misperception, hoping for a reprieve!" the ruler raged again. With a swirl of his flowing, bioluminescently lit cape, the Fafamafalafama pivoted back around. At least temporarily, he short-circuited his intended storming-out from the command center. Belying his bluster brewed an urgent desire to believe Naratama actually was on to something.

"Watch this replay if you would, dearest most supreme ruler Fafamafalafama." Naratama cringed in expectation that any second, the supreme ruler might lose what was left of his clearly diminished patience. That before he even watched anything, he might rain down blows upon the missile flight engineer. And perhaps those blows would be delivered by the blade of the Fafamafalafama's always-present sword. "The large blip, of course it is the orbiting ice comet," Naratama finally went on as it became clear the Fafamafalafama wasn't going to go violent, yet. "Those two pinpoint blips coming up behind the comet, those are the missiles tipped with nuclear warheads."

The two pinpoints came steadily closer to the much-larger blip. Then all of a sudden, they made impossibly sharp right angle turns and headed straight up off the radar screen.

"Soooo, ho, ho, ho!" The Fafamafalafama exulted with a cavernously low chuckle of relief. "It would appear there is no limit to how our extraterrestrial visitors can intervene in our affairs! WHICH MAKES THEM ALL THE MORE DANGEROUS!!" he abruptly bellowed with yet another dramatic swirl of his bioluminescently glowing cape. He reared back up to his full height, and spun around headed for the exit once more. "Naratama, you are free to do whatever. Guards, follow me!"

⸙⸙⸙⸙⸙

Fred Frankly burst onto the navigation bridge of the Smoke and Mirrors to Yoon-hee and Kevin's applause. They were seated side-by-side operating Yoon-hee's navigation console.

"Yay!" Yoon-hee shouted.

Fred, a bit light-headed, lurched for the closest empty chair to strap himself in.

Kevin remarked, "So it came down to Tanya to literally save the day, did it?"

"Hanson and I were too busy fighting to realize any possible alternative. Yep!" Fred waved a don't-bother-lecturing-me dismissive hand. "I know there's a lesson there for me, somewhere. But man oh man am I glad you two at least haven't slipped off into Never Neverland!"

"I didn't think the sunset storm line could ever look so beautiful." Kevin pondered Fafama spread out in all its epic glory on the panoramic view-screen.

The ice comet continued high-altitude orbit round the rescued planet. Imbedded course-adjustment rockets made intermittently timed blasts as the comet shed more water and sparkling meteorite clusters in its wake.

Far below the comet, and travelling the opposite direction, the sunset storm line persisted as impressive as before. It kept redeveloping along the steadily moving boundary between night and day. Doubtless, Chris would have once more likened the storm line to a yeast bloom in water.

"So you left Sergeant Hanson and Officer Petrovsky in the shuttle pod after you parked it?" asked Yoon-hee while she strained to keep her primary focus on what still lay ahead.

Fred nodded. "They're both totally zoned out from that f-n' conundrum. Figured the priority had to be on my hustling here pronto. Wanted to make sure I was in time to take over the controls, when and if you two also succumb to that f-n' quantum who-zy-what-zy. Oh, whoops!" Fred looked down at his seat belt. Then he looked past Captain Helena Taylor slumped unconscious in her captain's chair. He was checking where Yoon-hee and Kevin were stationed. "Guess I buckled up too far away from- Hey, Ciela's okay?"

"Ciela and the kids are fine, as we expected. Her past-time self plus those kids' past-time selves are stationed trillions of miles from here, back on Oomb. Ludi also. Their present selves are playing in a room isolated from everyone else. They won't have to watch other people going blank one by one," explained Yoon-hee. "Although I'm not sure that will keep them from becoming scared if it starts happening to them!"

"If the kiddies do zone out before we're through," added Kevin, "we hope they will zone out all at the same time."

Having unbuckled, Fred Frankly came up behind Kevin and Yoon-hee to take a seat beside them. But this did not keep him from noticing Fafama shrink down to a hauntingly magenta orb. That was how he had grown used to planets appearing when the Smoke and Mirrors accelerated away from them at light-speed and beyond. "So we're already on our way?" he asked.

"Welllll...." Yoon-hee wasn't exactly excited to explain. And she knew if she hesitated, dragged out what she had to say for long enough... "Umm, we did auto-pilot for a U-turn back into the space-time rift. But since we, um, took care of the problem which led to that rift in the first place-"

"There's no longer any rift to head back through! We're stuck! Got it! So now what?! Yoon-hee?! Kevin?! Sonofa quantum bitch!!" Fred suddenly realized those two officers had joined Helena in a trance-like state. Their spirits had chosen for their presence to continue back aboard the steadily approaching past-time Smoke and Mirrors.

Fred Frankly tremblingly made his way back to strap himself into the nearest empty seat.

By then, the present-time Smoke and Mirrors had already rounded the bend, so to speak. It was resuming light-speed acceleration towards where the space-time rift had been.

Fred felt the strangest sensation pass over him. Initially, he feared it might be a wave of nausea on the way to becoming some twenty-four-hour stomach virus. Nevertheless, out the panoramic view-screen he noticed the two redirected nuclear missiles exploding harmlessly in space. He also saw the past-time shuttle pod followed close behind by a large flying saucer.

What Fred could not have known was that Guy, Buddy Leung, Pedro Perez and company were inside the shuttle pod. They were being "chased" by the Tictoctickian spacecraft, thanks to Pedro's remote control.

But Fred Frankly had a more immediate concern. That strange sensation was coming over him again as his spiritual presence was being swept out of the Smoke and Mirrors. And his was the last presence that still could have done something to maneuver the immense starship.

No matter.

Tanya Petrovsky succeeded in redirecting two nuclear warhead missiles so they wouldn't bring an ice comet crashing down on Fafama. Thanks to her quick thinking, the Earthlings would not need time-travel back to Fafama for saving it in the first place. So the Smoke and Mirrors wasn't really there.

Oh, and Fred didn't think to wonder where Oodle-Noodle and Wafoodle- boodle had gone off to, why they weren't still holding court on the bridge.

⁂

"Halt, the most esteemed Varalawa, and the Farasarala, the eleventh wife! I must ask where you are going with these prisoners!" This translation of the Fafaman security guard's fa-la-las was what Helena heard deep inside the city-sized Great Pyramid of Fafama. At the same time, she felt herself coming out of the most curious daze she didn't quite recollect having entered in the first place. She looked around to see Chris by her side, and Tanya plus Tanya's husband Ali up ahead. Yulala and Guy were also present. *Weren't they married? No! Impossible!* Helena told herself, confused.

The Fafamafalafama's first wife named the Varalawa, plus the Farasarala, the eleventh wife, were bringing up the rear. Both wives brandished pistols to herd the group along.

The hauntingly dark hallways were lit only by light-green bioluminescence smeared randomly across the rough-surfaced granite walls, decades ago.

Everything looked familiar. For Helena Taylor, it was proving a classic déjà vu experience.

From how Helena's companions were looking about, she had the distinct impression they were sharing her déjà vu. They were emerging from the same daze.

"Most faithfully dedicated guard, here we have the twenty-third wife, Yulala." The Varalawa waved her pistol threateningly towards Yulala. "I can no longer even dignify calling her by anything other than her original name. We ascertained she has committed the heresy of falling in love with this Ahthlahn." The Varalawa went on to wave her weapon at Sergeant Hanson. "Their romance was aided and abetted by the rest of these other-worlders. In addition, they would like nothing traitorously more than to allow the terrorists' barbarous murders of members of the royal family to go unavenged! And so has come to pass a special desire by the Fafamafalafama, himself. He wants me to bring Yulala and her other-world co-conspirators to a special corner of the pyramid. It's the corner the kamakala are always trying to undermine! We are to let the kamakala determine their fate!" Varalawa gave the guard one of her rivetingly beautiful, unflinching, steely, wide-eyed stare-downs.

The first wife's imperiously fa-la-laed explanation took a long time to finish echoing down the granite-lined hallway. Nevertheless, the guard made with some unflinching steeliness of his own. He responded, "That might well have been the case, most esteemed Varalawa. But the Fafamafalafama is now demanding you and these Ahtlahns remain stationary until-"

"Ah! There you are!" The Fafamafalafama's cavernously deep fa-la-las thundered to accompany his urgently paced stomping forward. Shielded only by its scabbard, his excessively long sword accidentally knocked against the rock wall. "My Varalawa, I assume you have Cahptahn Taylah rounded up with the others?"

"Right here, my Fafamafalafama," the Varalawa answered with a diagonal downward slash of her left arm. That was the arm not burdened carrying a weapon. With her right arm, she kept her gun trained on Helena.

"Ahhh, Cahptahn Taylah! Maybe you can help me understand something! How have you and your fellow magicians once again succeeded in thwarting the will of the Fafaman people in matters that are none of your business??" Unsheathing his sword, the Fafamafalafama whipped it around with a distinct swish!

Helena could feel the air stirred.

"Not sure I understand, esteemed Fafamafalafama," responded Helena. A spooked-out part of her, though, was feeling that maybe, somehow, she *should* have understood.

"'Not sure I understand, esteemed Fafamafalafama'!" the Fafaman ruler repeated mockingly, as his fa-la-las translated. He made another arcing slash of his sword that this time inadvertently clanged against the hallway ceiling. Chipped-out bits of granite pelted the Earthlings' and Yulala's shoulders. "I am not sure I understand either, Cahptahn! How did your people take control of our two peace-maker missiles? You must know what I am talking about! Don't pretend otherwise!! Those missiles were going to send the giant ice rock crashing down on the rebel beasts! They were going to end rebel violence once and for all, in a final solution!! But that's not what happened, as if you're unaware! So tell me how you did it!! Tell me how both those missiles suddenly made impossibly sharp ninety-degree turns!! And then flew out into space, at no target at all!! Although who knows they were not intended to hit our space station instead?!?!?!"

Helena Taylor was not the only one to experience a shiver down her spine, hearing this translation of the Fafaman ruler's fa-la-las. *My God,* more than one Earthling besides the captain thought to his or her self. *Buddy must have used time travel to thwart an apocalyptic event our intervention made possible in the first place!*

"There is only one thing of which I am certain," Captain Taylor at last responded. "We would never have tried to target your space station with those missiles, either in the present or time-travelling to the past. But it might well be that your intention to exact revenge against the terrorists resulted in a widespread catastrophe here. Um, maybe even your own destruction was included, Sir."

The Fafamafalafama flinched in absolute surprise at the "Athlahn" former starship captain daring refer to him in the way "Sir" translated.

"Under such circumstances," Taylor went on, "I can easily imagine our having tried to redirect the course of your history, away from such an event. Time travel probably would have been involved."

"I cannot take any more of this toxic namanacasa flatulence," the Fafamafalafama shook his head as he re-sheathed his sword. He feigned too much impatience to bother offering or soliciting any further explanation. "Tell me, my Varalawa, where were you headed with these criminals?"

"My Fafamafalafama, we were headed to the corner of the pyramid where the kamakala labor at undermining our monument to Fafaman greatness. We were going to leave it to them to finish off these other-world beasts. Also as you can see, we were going to include Yulala for her betrayal of you! What you of course already know, it bears repeating! Most unfairly, most blasphemously, Yulala has lost her heart to this one!" The first wife pointed her pistol anew at Guy Hanson. "All that I am doing, I am doing as per your orders, my Fafamafalafama." This last part the Varalawa intoned with meekness shading her imperious bluster. She had long since decided, *Should he want to have me sacrificed too, for putting words in his mouth, so be it!*

"Oh?" The Fafamafalafama labored hard not to betray his feelings. The first wife's mention of the forbidden romance warmed his heart. And her insistence on referring to the twenty-third wife by her original name, Yulala, absolutely tickled him. Yulala was the Varafafafa's name before the Fafamafalafama recently married her. Anyway, what did not exactly temper his reaction was a yearning to call the Varalawa by her original most deservedly beautiful name, Sasamara. "Guard!?" he said. "I am speaking to you as well, my dedicated eleventh wife, the Farasarala!"

The Farasarala cringed at the Fafamafalafama's use of that word, "the," in front of her married name. Not exactly the tender, endearing way she wished to be addressed.

"You have both done your duty in supremely exemplary fashion. But now you will leave me and Sa-Varalawa, for me and Varalawa to personally deliver these creatures to their fates. I must personally witness the sealing of their doom with my own two eyes! Yes! Only then can I return to figuring out how I shall deal with their starship! That is, when and if its occupants ever seek to recover their co-conspirators here! Also, I must determine how we shall resume the plan to bring down the ice rock on the terrorist demons!"

"It is never for me to question my most esteemed Fafamafalafama." The nameless guard made a downward diagonal arm-slash. "But, you are sure you would not wish my further assistance? Could I not at least unburden the first wife of this unpleasant task?"

"No more for the task than the task requires!" the Fafamafalafama thundered in response.

"Of course, of course," the guard bowed repeatedly. He was as fearful as he was embarrassed. He quickly backed away, grabbing the eleventh wife just above her elbow to pull her back with him. He also found himself thinking, resignedly, *How soft her skin, how tender, how beautiful as well as feisty; if only, in another reality…*

⌘◦⌘◦⌘◦⌘

Yulala bolted upright in bed aboard the Smoke and Mirrors. A recurrent nightmare roused her suddenly awake. For the umpteenth time she relived her escape alongside her beloved Guy plus other Earthlings. It was her escape from the pyramid city of Fafama. Yulala found that bad dream no less disturbing for the bedroom lights having been left on to shine brightly, as her nocturnal nature required for her sleep.

But this particular nightmare differed from the others. This nightmare had the Fafamafalafama, himself, joining her and the Earthlings. The same as Guy and the rest, he was rubbing clay all over his body so a monster ant termed the kamakala would carry him through its labyrinth tunnels, to eventually emerge outside the pyramid.

"Oh! Goolafala!" Yulala gasped breathlessly. How could she have dozed off for even the briefest moment? she asked herself. Especially when the condition of her daughter was so uncertain? Yulala quickly donned her glare-reducing spectacles, to make squinting unnecessary. Before she could swing her legs off her bed to go check the nursery, though, her husband entered, cradling something in his arms. Whatever it was, it appeared enrobed in straw.

"Yulala? You're awake?" Guy asked tentatively as he approached the bed with his curious bundle.

Dr. Deborah Davis-Murphy followed close behind.

"Youah ahre bahck safely!" Yulala struggled as usual to practice, exercise her English. She had already propped herself up on multiple pillows to remain seated in bed.

Sergeant Guy Hanson's forehead furrowed pronouncedly. *Back safely?* he puzzled as he picked up his pace to bring what he was carrying over to his wife. *Back safely from where?* "I was discussing evasion maneuvers on the navigation bridge. That's all." By the time he completed this remark, he had handed his bundle to Yulala for cradling.

Yulala engaged that task most enthusiastically. And she gave Guy an extra wide-eyed look he found all the more bewilderingly beautiful for how her anti-glare spectacles shaded it. Then, in her poorly pronounced but still-understandable English she said, "Whatever you were doing, are we somehow not supposed to still be upset by this?" Yulala nodded down at what Guy handed over to her. She was remembering, finally, that it was their precious little Goolafala concealed by the straw-like substance.

"Yulala, I think you and Sergeant Hanson are both about to be very pleased with your daughter's condition." Scant hours ago, this was the last thing Dr. Deborah Davis-Murphy expected to be saying. That was when she discovered the bundle inside a storage room just outside the nursery. Deb found it tucked into a corner of the floor underneath the lowest shelf. She didn't notice it there at first because the shelf was covered in boxes full of medical research equipment.

The doctor deduced an amazing truth from what Ciela noticed stuck to the storage room door. After forming a cocoon, Goolafala had somehow managed to squeeze through the half-inch-wide slit between the floor and the bottom edge of the door. She had behaved much like a mouse finding its way through an improbably small hole in a wall.

Dr. Davis-Murphy worked gently to extract the entire weird mess from beneath the storage shelving. Nevertheless, she expected to find Goolafala already dead. That it was official: The poor creature had become the tragically unviable product, ultimately, of her parents' interspecies love-making.

What the chief medical officer did not expect to find was the cocoon-like covering continuing to emanate warmth from deep within.

Deborah Davis-Murphy was still not convinced, though. Surely Goolafala couldn't be progressing towards anything more than her early demise. Harboring that assumption, Deborah subjected the baby girl's cocoon to an MRI-type scan. What the scan revealed, Deborah feared as much as expected. There had been a total breakdown of Goolafala's body into a shapeless biochemical stew. This finding even left Ali Magabu resigned to the worst outcomes' inevitability. But most ironically, this finding also led to a thrill of unexpected hope on the chief medical officer's part. It made her hairs stand up on the nape of her neck.

Dr. Davis-Murphy recalled reading a theory about the ever-mysterious metamorphosis of the typical caterpillar into the typical butterfly. Back in the low 2000s, a little-known science writer named Frank Ryan offered a most peculiar explanation. He wrote that perhaps hundreds of millions of years ago, during the early stages of life's evolution on Earth, two entirely different organisms had blasphemously succeeded in mating. This led to a situation where a creature could be born one way, then rearrange its entire body to conclude life another way. Essentially, the creature lived childhood as one parent and adulthood as the dramatically different other parent.

What's more, Dr. Davis-Murphy noticed a significant change already, by the time she removed the cocooned Goolafala from the body scan. Rather than persistent shapelessness, she felt and saw a more-defined underlying form in the process of becoming. A second scan confirmed this. Goolafala's biochemical stew was well on its way, reorganizing into her new body.

"Whatever is going on with your daughter is proceeding very rapidly," Deborah said presently. She tried to sneak her head in between mother and father for a better look before she added, "Goolafala should be pushing her way out of there any moment now. Judging from my last scan, I think you are both going to be delighted by the results."

Just as the doctor finished speaking, a tiny fist punched through the straw-like substance.

With sheer joy, Yulala contemplated that wee little appendage clenching and unclenching in fierce determination. Cheerily, she said, "Weahll, aht leahst this coahnfahrms ouahr Goolafala is noaht tahning intah an ahtpah!" *Well, at least this confirms our Goolafala is not turning into an ahtpah!*

By the time Yulala completed her remark, a second tiny fist and a lower left leg had also punched through. Then Goolafala's entire body went into a mad frenzy, until at the last she shook off her autonomously secreted enclosure. Yulala and Guy assisted by tossing aside fragments of the cocoon as their daughter rent them apart.

Goolafala let out a healthy shriek. "WAAAAHH!!" Her large eyes squinted shut against what any Fafaman would have characterized as a harsh glare.

They were two large eyes, perfectly most beautifully symmetrically positioned. But that wasn't essential where

Goolafala's parents were concerned. Well prior to her metamorphosis, Guy and Yulala had grown to find a certain special beauty to those eyes' flounder-mouse-lopsided location, both on the same side of her face.

Goolafala's delighted parents noticed something else after Dr. Davis-Murphy scaled back the room lighting to dim, light-green iridescence. Goolafala's body glowed pale violet, with her nocturnally large eyes the deepest blue when she at last opened them wide.

"There is something I have always marveled at about my species' embryonic stage," Guy Hanson spoke softly while he enjoyed Goolafala giving his forefinger the strongest grip possible. "We go through a strange if brief phase. Our bodies sport gills, the evolutionary relics of when our distant ancestors were fish. What Goolafala went through with both her eyes on the same side of her head...that would suggest your evolutionary ancestors include the flounder mouse, my sweetest."

"Yes it wouahld," Yulala agreed, though far more focused on Goolafala's purred coo than anything her husband was saying. Guy could have also gotten her to agree their daughter owed all her good looks to him, had he suggested it. What did get more of her attention, though, was when he said, "And that explains why you pull all the blankets to your side of the bed; you're trying to bury yourself like a burrowing flounder mouse!"

"Yeahss?" Yulala nearly hissed as she finally looked away from her daughter into her husband's cherishing if also mischievously grinning regard. "Ahnd your fish ahncestahs explain why your snore sounds like you ahre drowning!" On this, she gave him a playful, loving shove with her shoulders.

"Guess I deserved that."

"Who deserved what?" It was the Fafamafalafama arm-in-arm with the Varalawa- no, Yulala corrected herself. Her name was now Sasamara.

"Fafamafalafama?! You're here?!" Yulala exclaimed in her first language, in deference to the man she couldn't help recalling was at one time the ruler of her civilization.

"Sasamara and I, when we heard about this joyful miracle taking place, we did not want to miss it," the Fafamafalafama's fa-la-las translated. "We wanted to be the first, after Doctah Davahs Muhphy here, of course." He gave Deborah a bow imbued with total, deferential sincerity. "We wanted to extend our congratulations."

"And also offer up our babysitting services," added Sasamara. "We have done this previously for Sahjahnt Frahnklah and Ciela, as we have not succeeded in producing any children of our own." She gave the Fafamafalafama's waist a tender squeeze.

"Yes, yes," the once-ruler nodded. "But the way you welcomed us, Yulala, most curious. One would have thought we had just boarded the Smoke and Mirrors, and not been here the entire trip!"

"I am so sorry, esteemed-"

"No, no," the Fafamafalafama waved off what Yulala was about to say. "I am the last one who deserves an apology, from anyone!" He was about to reach for his sword, to unsheathe and lift high in a show of his forceful assertion. Old habits were hard to break. But still, he quickly realized the weaponry was part of his most shameful past. His sword and scabbard both had long since been retired from use. He was about to reach for thin air.

"Well, anyway," said Yulala while Goolafala was holding on to one of her forefingers with her tiny hand not already busy clenching Guy's forefinger. "Prior to Doctah Davahs-Muhphy sharing our good news, I woke from the strangest nightmare! Things were turning out very differently from what I remember!"

This wasn't quite so. Rather, her dream had been of matters having gone as they actually did go. Yet there was a certain, creepy sense that how they went constituted a rerouting of history, an alternate course. In Yulala's dream, the Fafamafalafama stormed at Captain Taylor. He complained to her about the missiles mysteriously changing course. That is, the missiles fired at the orbiting comet with the intent of bringing it crashing down on rebel strongholds.

Presently, the Fafamafalafama and Sasamara were competing for who would receive the most attention from metamorphosed Goolafala.

Yulala took advantage of the distraction provided by her beautifully transformed daughter, to recollect in more detail the rest of what seemed to teeter between dream and reality...

The Fafaman ruler joined the Varalawa to herd Yulala and the Earthlings to their doom. The disgraced twenty-third wife and her traitorous new friends would meet a cruel fate, crushed to death between the pincers of ant monsters named the kamakala.

Yulala remembered how silently the journey proceeded down to the corner of the Great Pyramid where the kamakala dug their burrow network. Little did she know, then, what she would learn later. Among other significant occurrences, the first wife had given Captain Helena Taylor an everything's-going-to-be-okay gentle squeeze on her shoulder. And Helena had managed to pass that squeeze along to everyone else except Yulala.

What was really at play could not be safely admitted aloud until the Varalawa and company were certain no other Fafamans were around. Especially since orders to evacuate the pyramid never actually happened, in the fortuitous rerouting of Fafama's history.

Finally, everyone reached the edge of a pebbly downslope roped off with warnings about the kamakala hazard. Those warnings were printed in Fafaman hieroglyphics, of course.

Dramatically, the Fafamafalafama let fall his pistol to the mud-packed floor. It was the pistol he seized from a guard when he took over for him, with the idea he would help the Varalawa march the Earthlings and Yulala to their doom.

Anyway, no sooner did the pistol hit the ground than the Fafamafalafama himself fell to his knees before the Varalawa. He supplicated tearfully, "Allow the Ahthlahns and Yulala to run from us now, wherever they would go! I even understand enough about the ways of the kamakala to assist their quick exit from the pyramid! I assume they are the main reason other Ahthlahns risked their lives to gain access past the laser mesh, back into our atmosphere. Those Ahthlahns want to rescue them! They want to return them safely to their grand starship that rides on beams of light!"

The Varalawa, the first wife, might have been expecting something like what the supreme ruler prostrated in front of her to say. Still, Yulala would never forget how the expression on the first wife's face evidenced nothing more than gasping astonishment. And how also, the first wife lost hold of her own pistol as well.

"Maybe you will want to hand me over to the authorities! Sniff! I have certainly earned that indignity as the ultimate betrayer of everything I have stood for my entire life!" the Fafamafalafama went on. His phrases randomly lapsed into falsetto high pitches with his unabated tearfulness.

The Earthlings exchanged astonished looks with one another...and Guy with Yulala.

"But I don't care!" the Fafamafalafama continued. "Not one hundred nininanas ago, I was facing a horrific likelihood! It stemmed from my vengeful intent to have the rebels killed, terrorists and innocents alike! But no matter! I was almost certain to bring down the water-shedding comet on the pyramid, and end Fafaman civilization in one cataclysmic blow!

"When I was able to be honest with myself, I had to admit something else as well. I did not know with any confidence what would happen if the original plan, targeting the rebel bases only, succeeded. I still feared that Cahptahn Taylah would have her worry yet vindicated. In other words, I wasn't at all sure that life across Fafama, even life within the protective confines of the Great Pyramid, wasn't going to meet a premature end! My mind burned in the crucible of this fear over what I might be bringing to pass!

"This fear brought me to face a truth that tradition always had me fleeing from facing. And fleeing from facing truth was what I was used to doing. Many were the times I sought peace of mind in my sexual conquests with my ritually granted wives. It was peace of mind those conquests were never ever to bring me.

"If I might call you by your name, Sasamara, that far more honors you, your beauty. What I came to face, Sasamara, was that I always really loved you, only you. I have always wanted to find the courage to throw everything else away, if that is what I needed to do in order to confess this!"

Yulala, not to mention the Earthlings, might have been shocked beyond shocked by the Fafamafalafama's contritely delivered testimonial. But they were absolutely floored by the Varalawa's response.

Except for Helena, in whom the Varalawa had long since confided.

The Varalawa sought the Fafamafalafama's hands. She pulled him back up onto his feet to softly, tearfully fa-la-la in return, "You do not know for how long I have waited, waited hopelessly, for such an admission from you! I considered it an admission not at all reasonable for me to expect I would ever receive. But to explain how I felt, I engraved two pendants with words from our ancient mystic, Sarissa. One was intended for the Cahptahn and Offisah Taylah. The other pendant was intended for us, however useless I expected that gesture would prove. But both pendants are now forgotten. Both are left inside the wives' quarters where it would not be safe for us to return under these circumstances. The inscription on them... Please understand, Cahptahn and Offisah..." The Varalawa turned away from the Fafamafalafama. She faced towards the Earthlings while yet holding on to her beloved's hands, and leaning her head into his shoulder. "I wanted for our own selves what I imagined you have had for yourselves a good long while. The essence of the inscription was this." She returned her gaze deep into the Fafamafalafama's nocturnal eyes for her paraphrased recitation.

"'The universe radiates out an infinite distance from each spirit,

So each spirit lies at the center of the universe.

I desire to honor that truth by making you the center of my universe,

And wish I were to be the center of yours.'"

On completion of this short- What was it? A poem?

Yulala would never forget how the Varalawa and the Fafamafalafama collapsed into one another's arms. And the Fafaman ruler nevertheless protesting as tearfully as ever, "I do not deserve to be any more than a frozen cube of urine and feces, flushed from the space station and accidentally sent into orbit around Fafama."

Guy squeezed Yulala's hand lovingly tight, and she reciprocated.

Ali and Tanya, and Helena and Chris, were having a likewise reaction with one another.

The Varalawa pushed gently on the Fafamafalafama's shoulders. She pushed him far enough away for everyone to hear her fa-la-la. "Now, how about we join our extraterrestrial guests to escape from here? You think that perhaps they might allow us to seek asylum on their planet?"

"Really?" Where the Fafamafalafama was concerned, those were the sweetest words he had ever heard. They were second only to Sasamara's confession of reciprocating his desire for a special, exclusive love.

Guy Hanson's own most beloved shook her head like she was clearing her mind. That is how she returned herself to the present from her recollection of an oddly alternative-seeming past. Her heart filled with joy over a certain special prospect she realized for the first time. "So when Goolafala grows a little older," Yulala fa-la-laed, "she will be able to experience my home planet, Fafama, in all its glory. The sunset storm line; the looming magnificence of the Great Pyramid; the nights filled by the soft, bioluminescent glow of surfacing flounder mice;

the Fafaman trees curling up in advance of star-obscuring blinding light; the cleansing of her bowels so neatly by a tralalafa;...and, and if she looks upward at the right time, she can also view the giant space rock crossing the sky. She can see it shed water in its wake with a shimmering contrail of meteorites. As well, maybe she will catch a glimpse of the parachute ahtpah looking to ensnare a blinding-light prowler. All the wonderful as well as terrible things that go into making Fafama such a special place..."

"Dear Yulala," the Fafamafalafama gave her a quizzical regard, "you talk as though much of what you are saying has only now occurred to you..."

"Or like she was just realizing her home planet didn't get wiped out, after all," added Guy Hanson. He eyed the former Fafaman leader with a look that spoke volumes.

"Deborah told us the good news!" exclaimed Captain Helena Taylor with no preamble. She asked no pardon for bursting in on the tender scene so abruptly. "I'd love to cuddle your metamorphosed bundle of joy, Sergeant Hanson. But we've gained enough ground now on the Barack Obama and the Eisenhower. I need you on the bridge to help us strategize how we get them to stand down! At least until we can see what this 'intervention' might be about, to which Oodle-Noodle keeps alluding!"

⟡ ⟡ ⟡

Captain Taylor could not have known what was happening at the very minute she pushed Guy Hanson back to work. Secretary of Defense Michael Spinner was speaking into thin air in a conference room aboard the battleship Barack Obama. "Out of our heads, Oodle-Noodle!" he growled. "And tell Captain Taylor to stay back! She has absolutely nothing to contribute to our situation! Especially with the Smoke and Mirrors willfully, completely disarmed!"

Very well, Mr. Secretary. However, far more is about to be accomplished than you could ever imagine! And it will ALL be accomplished peacefully! Nonviolently!

Chapter 34

"Baa, Commander Ak-keek-teek," Captain Rek-mek-a-nek of the Fifth Celestial Breath baaed with studied meekness. He was addressing the new commander of all Tictoctickian outer space military forces, presently stationed aboard the Sixth Celestial Breath.

Yes, former Lieutenant Ak-keek-teek had finally gained his long-coveted promotion. But Rek-mek-a-nek suspected that still wasn't enough. Ak-keek-teek might require nearly as much ego massage as Dek-Fook-Tek, not to gallop into his own irrational rage. Informed by such concern, Rek-mek-a-nek continued, "This is a special honor, your pre-emption of the communication I was about to hazard making a bother to you."

"The bother is this, Captain Rek-mek-a-nek," Commander Ak-keek-teek responded with his ridiculously wide buck-tooth grin, as the captain joined many others in regarding it. "We aboard the Sixth Celestial Breath have had to wait way too long! We've done nothing more than sniff at one another's tails while you and your associate captains, who are about to appear for you on a six-way split-screen...This sentence threatens to grow too convoluted, Officer Koo-ker-ni-kek," the commander turned to address someone off-screen. "You ought to have known better, Officer, than to have sat by and bleated nothing while my words became lost in the syntactical thickets!!"

"I have always thought something, Commander," a voice could be heard by Captain Rek-mek-a-nek baaing in a reprise of his own studied meekness. That voice clearly emitted from the view-screen. However, its source stood offstage out of sight, to the side where Commander Ak-keek-teek turned. "I have thought it an undeserved blessing on my part, each additional breath I am allowed to take," the off-stage officer went on. "That a steel bolt has not yet been hammered through my skull seems almost an injustice."

"Well," snorted Commander Ak-keek-teek, "don't expect an honorary chest-slashing at the end of my bahvek-sharpened antlers, any time soon!"

The flying saucer named the Sixth Celestial Breath was leading the entire fleet's way, headed from Tictoctic for Earth. One by one, the flying saucers had "descended" onto the orbital plane of Earth's solar system, having successfully "skimmed" the comet-infested Oort Cloud surrounding it.

A variation was at play of the same physics that made faster-than-light travel possible for the Smoke and Mirrors. Light beams were accelerated beyond the usual hundred eight-six thousand miles per second. Then in that accelerated state, they pushed along saucers and cylindrically shaped vessels, alike. Maybe. Even beginning to understand the details continued to stump the guest theoretical physicist aboard the Smoke and Mirrors named Professor Timothy Aquinas. And as the unwitting mastermind of the mirror arrays, First Officer Buddy Leung's own thoughts on the matter were evolving a different direction.

Anyway, as Commander Ak-keek-teek announced, Captain Rek-mek-a-nek soon found himself facing a six-way split-screen. One screen, of course, displayed the commander's buck-tooth countenance, slowly re-dawning into his silly wide grin. With an uncontrollable shiver, Captain Rek-mek-a-nek sensed the new commander's mirth revealed sadistic bloodlust. Etched into his grin was joyful anticipation of death and destruction soon to be visited upon the other-worlders from "Akt." This was the punishment planned for those beasts. This was what they had earned for wiping out a hospital complex on Tictoctic via hijacked magnetic pulse-beam.

Three of the five other screens displayed the captains of the three other saucers. And the remaining two screens supplied fore and aft views of outer space. The view towards the center of Earth's solar system showed the sun as no more than an especially bright star among stars. The Tictoctickians were still over eight hundred fifty billion miles away.

"As I was saying," the commander haughtily tongue-clicked, "we have been waiting as long as we reasonably could. That is, we have been waiting for the rest of you to have your astronomers do their job! To make the discovery important enough for you to hazard bothering me, as Captain Rek-mek-a-nek put it!"

Actually, Captain Rek-mek-a-nek and his astronomer noticed what Commander Ak-keek-teek was referring to a significant while earlier. This happened when the saucer fleet started making its "descent" from "up over" the Oort Cloud "down onto" the orbital plane.

But Captain Rek-mek-a-nek held back sharing the astronomer's important finding with the commander. The captain wanted to give Ak-keek-teek ample time to make it his discovery first, to be able to complain about having had to wait on the rest of them. And the captain suspected more than one of his fellow captains guilty of the same kowtowing behavior. Captain Rek-mek-a-nek also suspected what he could not have known was indeed the truth: Commander Ak-keek-teek garnered the discovery in question from his astronomer later rather than sooner. Astronomer Koo-ker-ni-kek shared the news scant niki-niks before Ak-keek-teek initiated the present communication to boast he was first.

"I turn this over to my astronomer, Officer Koo-ker-ni-kek," crisply tongue-clicked Commander Ak-kek-teek, yet he still didn't allow his fellow deer creature to share the camera with him.

"This is an honor I do not deserve," a faint voice could be heard baaing even more meekly than Captain Rek-mek-a-nek had affected to baa.

Captain Rek-mek-a-nek mused to himself, *That is true; you do not deserve to have to address us without even your snout allowed into view!*

"Yes," the faint voice went on, "what I have discovered... No, it is what the commander has permitted me to confirm would have been his discovery! Ever inspired by our supreme Dek-Fook-Tek, it goes as follows. We are still several billion lek-leks distant from the solar system proper, including the Akt plus seven additional planets. However, the intervening vast stretches of outer space are far from devoid of measurable substance. Rather, they are befouled, similarly to how Tictoctic fields of yore were befouled with hoof-sized balls of oskynt excrement. Those vast stretches of outer space are befouled by small herds of planetoids. Planetoids are much smaller than regular planets, and they travel on irregular, elliptical paths which only bisect the orbital plane. But there is one exception, where smaller size is concerned. We were lucky enough to identify that exception not only thanks to Dek-Fook-Tek's inspiration. Such inspiration would have been more than plenty enough. But in addition, the exception's path most fortuitously took it directly in between us and this solar system's star. When the star disappeared from view for a mini-pektel, we knew exactly what we had. We had a rogue planet five times larger than Tictoctic!"

"We only just confirmed the rogue planet's existence, Commander, mere niki-niks before you initiated this conference call," Captain Rek-mek-a-nek lied. His confirmation took place much longer ago than "mere niki-niks."

"Our astronomer was starting to inform me of the rogue planet's existence when you called, Commander," chimed in Captain Keek-konk of the Seventh Celestial Breath. He followed up his bleated lie with a licking-away of the anxiety-induced foam at his mouth.

"Our astronomer just announced to me he had something special to report, about planetoids. No mention at all of a rogue planet," Captain Dooky-mek-a-toot of the Eighth Celestial Breath whinnied. His lie struck Captain Rek-mek-a-nek as boastful.

Indeed, Rek-mek-a-nek was not insensible to the strangeness of the ongoing untruthful competition, over who took the longest to notice the rogue planet. But the winner had not brayed in, quite yet.

"Astronomer Kyko-teet, were you preparing to tell me something? Or are you still wondering when sunrise will return, a new day dawn in outer space?" Captain Tweet-Kweet-a-tek of the Ninth Celestial Breath brayed harshly. He was essentially accusing his astronomer of being too stupid to realize day and night were planet-bound features.

Commander Ak-keek-teek's chest swelled with bursting pride. He remained totally oblivious of how deliberately the Tictoctickian saucer captains catered to his ego. Displaying his buck-tooth grin anew, he regally tongue-clicked, "It is very good, indeed, that we have *my* astronomer, Officer Koo-ker-ni-kek, to assure we are all feeding off the same carcass, as it were." The commander made a deferential nod Koo-ker-ni-kek's way. He was careful as before, though, to keep himself standing the center of attention. This meant the captains were still not going to catch even a glimpse of the astronomer aboard the Sixth Celestial Breath. "So I ask you, Officer Koo-ker-ni-kek," continued Commander Ak-keek-teek. "Please elaborate further for these captains, as well as for the edification of their astronomers. Their astronomers were perhaps not as alert as you; they lacked my direct presence to provide the necessary stimulation."

"Only with the most profound apologies can I elaborate, dear Commander Ak-keek-teek. My elucidation probably amounts to that of an uninformed drunk compared to what Dek-Fook-Tek would have offered. Let alone yourself, Commander, but of course," humbly bleated Astronomer Koo-ker-ni-kek from off camera.

Ak-keek-teek nodded approvingly at Koo-ker-ni-kek's insertion of his snout up his anus. That's how Rek-mek-a-nek would have likened the astronomer's self-abasement. *Suppose Commander Ak-keek-teek really could speak so much more eloquently than his astronomer,* Rek-mek-a-nek went on to think to himself. *Why wouldn't the commander relay the information himself? Oh, I know. He's too busy looking stud-ly for the camcorder!*

"As Commander Ak-keek-teek would have so observantly indicated," proceeded the unseen astronomer, "besides the large rogue planet there are, I repeat, several far smaller objects, or planetoids. Those planetoids are taking similar paths to the large planet. They are behaving in defiance of the normal routes for planets on the typical orbital plane of most any solar system. Within our immediate vicinity are no less than seven such objects. In other words, there are more than enough for our purposes. Their sizes range from one-half to one-tenth the size of Tictoctic's moon. But even the smallest planetoid is still plenty large enough for our entire battle saucer fleet to hide on its dark, shadowy side, were we to so choose. And we are out here many billions of lek-leks away from Akt's sun. Nearly every side of these planetoids is a dark, shadowy side.

"Incidentally, we made an additional discovery closer in to this solar system's most outlying planets. Thousands of icy objects make a ring around the Akt sun, on the traditional orbital plane. But most of those objects are far too small to provide even one battle saucer with adequate concealment. They are more likely to pummel than protect us. Once we resume our stampede for Akt, we should take a brief detour above the orbital plane to avoid them."

Commander Ak-keek-teek made a short bow, towards where Captain Rek-mek-a-nek guessed the astronomer just completed his off-stage, out-of-sight exposition. The captain also guessed that the astronomer reciprocated with a far lower bow.

"When we arrive to Akt," the commander imperiously tongue-clicked, "we will not want to be bothered with worry over an attack on our rear flank. However, we know what follows less than one-half light-year behind us. Those odd, cylindrically shaped starship vessels of so much irritation are in full pursuit. There are three of them, as best we can gather. So, what do the newly discovered planetoids mean?"

Obviously the commander wanted to believe he alone realized what those planetoids meant. Not one of the five saucer captains dared challenge him on that count. Instead, they presented with the most quizzical, perplexed looks they could counterfeit on their narrow little faces. Of course, there was not a one among them to whom it didn't occur exactly what the planetoids meant. Moreover, that realization happened long before Commander Ak-keek-teek ever broached the subject.

The commander gave his wait for a response enough time for the humiliation to sink in. He could rub the captains' snouts in what he had deluded himself into assuming was their profound ignorance. That is when he finally brayed most gleefully, "These planetoids mean we have the perfect hiding places! We wait in their shadows, spread out in five different directions from our present location."

The Sixth Celestial Breath had long since gone into a one-thousand-lek-lek-diameter holding pattern, not in any celestial object's shadow just yet. The other four saucers had followed suit as per previous orders.

"We will act like our ancient ancestors did," Commander Ak-keek-teek continued. "Back on Tictoctic, they crouched hidden behind boulders to both sides of the anticipated migration route of an oskynt herd. Once sufficient members of that herd wandered in between those boulders, our ancestors leapt out and fired on them with bow and arrow! From every direction! Those brute beasts had nowhere to run, nowhere to hide! Snort!" Commander Ak-keek-teek couldn't help long strings of nasal discharge hanging from his nostrils with his excitement. "It will be the same with the other-world starships! Our battle saucers will leap out from behind the planetoids to ambush them! Our targeted magnetic pulse-beams will come at them from all directions! And then we will disintegrate to pieces those clumsily, instinctively rendered exoskeletons! Subsequently we will gather up a bounty of specimens freeze-dried by the near-absolute-zero cold of deep space. They will comprise a celebratory feast on our way to defensively conquering the Akt beasts' home planet!"

The captains of the four other flying saucer battleships brayed with feigned astonishment. They had surmised the plan long before Ak-keek-teek's six-way conference call even began.

Captain Dooky-mek-a-toot put on his show first. "A plan of unsurpassed, chest-impaling ingenuity for sure, Commander," he said. "It could only have been regurgitated for rumination by one such as your own self, so divinely inspired by our Supreme Dek-Fook-Tek. But, please explain something for this lesser mind, here. I understand the other-world beasts will most likely be taken too much by surprise when we launch our defense. They will be unable to respond with weaponry they might have otherwise secreted like krakky shells secreting nature's version of a laser cannon. But their special drone worries me, comparable to how I fear the venomous bite from a kleenkelket. What happens should those bloodthirsty hostiles deploy more of them? Like the one that hacked into Captain Rek-mek-a-nek's saucer for its pulse-beam to incinerate one of our hospital complexes?"

"Baa, their special drone," nodded the commander with another of his slowly dawning, ridiculously wide buck-tooth grins. "I actually rather am hoping they *will* deploy them against us. Captain Rek-mek-a-nek knows what I mean!"

The eyes of the other saucer captains focused on the section of screen where Rek-mek-a-nek's visage was inserted for their six-way conference call.

Captain Rek-mek-a-nek thought to himself, *I know that our previous commander, Kwit-Nik, originated the plan for dealing with those drones. He figured out how to turn them against any other war-mongering beasts from Akt. And he made the necessary preparations.*

But he claimed the Akt beasts risked their lives for us during exploration of a planet in the solar system next door to our solar system. While assessing that planet's suitability for colonization, they encountered several fearsome monsters from which they had to make miraculous escapes.

Anyway, I also know all about this fool, Ak-keek-teek. He exploited Dek-Fook-Tek's psychopathology to get himself elevated to be the new commander. He is shameless about pretending he developed the drone scheme, himself. Yes, Commander, I know exactly what you mean!

"What I know, Commander Ak-keek-teek, is that you are a military mastermind," is how Captain Rek-mek-a-nek actually responded. But he marveled to himself at what the commander's own astronomer had missed. There was a planet-sized chunk of ice accompanying the smaller chunks in that previously mentioned ice belt. The commander was too stupid in his arrogance to dissect the star-chart readouts and consequently realize his astronomer failed to catch this. No matter.

The conference call concluded with the saucers peeling off one by one from the holding pattern. Each saucer took up a position in a new, separate holding pattern, one saucer for each of five planetoids. They hid behind those planetoids, relative to the predicted course of the other-world starship fleet.

Talk of ancestors hunting oskynt with bows and arrows brought yet another happy thought to the commander's mind. This thought produced a new dawning of his buck-tooth grin. It was simple remembrance of the last message he'd received from Tictoctic. That message was relayed via unmanned mini-saucer sensors comparable to the firefly donuts, if he but knew. The mini-saucers and their sensors, both, had been co-opted, like the full-blown saucers themselves, from Chonoran technology. But Commander Ak-keek-teek didn't care to ever dwell on that, if he even admitted its reality. What he did care to dwell on was the message concerning Supreme Authority Dek-Fook-Tek. Reportedly, Dek-Fook-Tek had completed preparation of his bow and arrow hunt. It was to be a hunt of that captured couple who, in their compact warship, launched the drone attack on the Tictoctickian hospital. Doubtless, they were aided and abetted by the other-world crew on the starship fortunately already obliterated, so everyone assumed.

⁂

For Dek-Fook-Tek's bow-and-arrow target practice, the oskynt-eye needed to meet certain requirements. It needed to be mounted on wheels set into a track greased for extra-smooth gliding from side to side. The oskynt-eye also needed to be what equaled roughly ten feet in diameter. And finally, it needed to be set what equaled roughly a twenty-one foot distance from where the Supreme Authority of Tictoctic wielded his antique bow. Under these tightly controlled circumstances, aides with special training were able to fulfill their assigned task. Nearly one hundred percent of the time, they succeeded at placing the oskynt-eye in the way of arrows launched by Dek-Fook-Tek.

"There is something many of our fellow Tictoctickians still fail to understand, Counselor Kootlek," Dek-Fook-Tek remarked presently. He was basking in the ego-licking afterglow of his latest target practice. His arrow had landed close to the very center of the oskynt-eye, with a minimum of its moving-about required of the oskynt-eye managers. "Back in the days of the oskynt hunts, few were the beasts remaining perfectly still, so our ancestors could enjoy an easy shot at them. Usually, the oskynt caught the scent of the approaching hunter, and went lumbering off before anyone could even raise their bow."

"If our ancestors had only had your visionary foresight, my Supreme Dek-Fook-Tek, to practice on moving targets," Counselor Kootlek baaed most admiringly with a gentle pat of his too-prominent belly. It was as though his leader's foresight was what he somehow kept stored inside there, rather than mounds of fat. Also, the counselor took care not to bring up an indelicate matter. During those hunts of yore, the oskynt always lumbered out of harm's way rather than into it. This was opposite to what the aides were doing with the ten-foot-diameter oskynt-eye. The aides were always moving the oskynt-eye into the guesstimated path of Dek-Fook-Tek's erratically aimed arrows, to give them better chances of striking it. "I repeat," brown-nosed Counselor Kootlek. "Our ancestors ought to have been possessed of your vision. They would have practiced launching arrows into a moving target rather than a stationary one. As a result, they could not have helped but to have seriously decimated entire oskynt herds thousands of solar orbits earlier than actually happened."

"Exactly," Dek-Fook-Tek nodded agreeably, with the assistance of course of his ever-present antler managers. "That is why it remained for the invention of the shotgun to bring the oskynt closer to extinction."

"Their extinction could have occurred so much sooner, even, my Supreme Authority. If only the universe had been possessed of sufficient wisdom to have had you born earlier than you were! For certain, you would then have invented the shotgun in a far timelier manner. We would not have had to wait so long for some lucky fool to finally stumble on the idea." With this assertion, Counselor Kootlek shook his head disdainfully.

Dek-Fook-Tek nodded in appreciation of what he was too narcissistic to understand as anything less than a carefully considered surmise.

"I must bleat further, your most bahvek-sharpened horniness," the counselor went on with another deferential bow. "We are profoundly aware of the shotgun's well-established efficacy. Especially in that context, your selection of the bow and arrow for stalking the terrorist couple is a most fascinating choice."

"I need to share something with you, Counselor," Dek-Fook-Tek crisply tongue-clicked after rising to his full height on his hind legs. "It is a text about the history of hunting on Akt. I discovered it aboard the terrorist attack vessel."

Actually, a subordinate officer made the discovery, though a trivial distinction where Supreme Authority Dek-Fook-Tek was concerned. Certainly that young buck would have failed miserably, if not aided by the Supreme Authority's divine inspiration.

"A translation of the text makes clear the bow and arrow technique was utilized by hunters on Akt. They favored the bow and arrow in their ruthlessly relentless persecution of our other-world brothers and sisters. For all we know, those brethren flew to Akt from Tictoctic eons ago. They arrived there before our legendary lost civilization of Kakatik sank beneath the waves due to a cataclysmic volcanic eruption."

"A most tragic event which again, my Supreme Authority, you were not born soon enough to forestall."

"Exactly. But here is the thing with the bow and arrow hunters of Akt. Here is the especially barbaric thing in which we can be sure our terrorist quarry took great, savage delight to participate. They would, so the text translates, wound our brothers and sisters in such a way that they would have to wander for long pektels suffering great pain. Such wounds inevitably became infected. And that infection inevitably made its way to still our brothers' and sisters' hearts in the most painful, terrifying deaths imaginable. All the while, the hunters followed just out of view. They chased away any winged creatures comparable to our near-extinct klafflaks. Otherwise, those creatures might have descended upon our brothers and sisters to pick at their still-living flesh and thereby, ironically, shorten their agony!"

"What manner of monster are these animals?" Counselor Kootlek asked rhetorically. The way he rubbed his vast belly, an observer might have thought he was trying to console it. That his belly could experience the horror he was feeling.

"It gets worse, Counselor," Dek-Fook-Tek nodded. "Among other things the beastly Akt hunters do with the corpse, they take the head, and they mount it on a plaque for display. This is far more than merely an imagined horror written for certain demented readers' perverse amusement. I know, because I have seen such a plaque mounted aboard the terrorist vessel! And there is an empty one beside it obviously meant for a Tictoctickian!"

"Baa!" Counselor Kooklek baaed in horrified astonishment.

"Concerning our brothers and sisters on Akt awaiting liberation, Counselor, maybe it is already too late. Maybe they have already been hunted to extinction like so many oskynt. So, enough of this target practice! The terrorist couple has been forced to shed their clothes! Now those other-world monsters will feel to their core what they have forced our brothers and sisters on Akt to endure!

"The Akt terrorists have been given plenty of time to try hiding themselves away in the subarctic forest! If preparations have not been adequate to guarantee my aim is true, the better for only partially wounding them! Thereby might they experience the pain and terror of growing, spreading infection before their demise! And after that demise, after that proud result of our royal hunt, we feast upon a gourmet preparation of the terrorist couple's remains. During that feast we can contemplate with great delight their two heads mounted together on the plaque they meant for one of us! Let the hunt begin!" On this proclamation, Dek-Fook-Tek lifted a hollowed-out oskynt horn. He blew into it, producing a deep sound that echoed off into the wilderness around the target range.

Counselor Kootlek licked his chops and rubbed his formidably proportioned tummy anew. He thrilled over the prospect of tasty morsels of exotically flavored other-world meat.

⁂

The starship battle cruisers Obama and Eisenhower rode light beams some two thousand miles apart from each other. They travelled essentially side by side.

The completely unarmed Smoke and Mirrors brought up their rear, trailing them by several hundred thousand miles.

All three starships were nearing "descent" from "above" the Oort Cloud, "down" onto the orbital plane of their home solar system. That is when aboard the Smoke and Mirrors, Navigation Officer Yoon-hee Park-

Smith reported, "Captain, we are receiving a two-one conference call from the Barack Obama."

"Split screen, Yoon-hee." Captain Helena Taylor reckoned Secretary Michael Spinner would appear. But she wanted to keep one eye on the cosmic view ahead, especially since they were nearing home.

A two-one conference call meant the starship where the call originated would enjoy look-sees at the other two starships. It wouldn't matter whether that look-see was into their conference rooms or onto their navigation decks. However, the other two starships would only receive one view, from inside the originating starship.

"Captain Robertson, Captain Taylor..." Secretary Spinner, sure enough, was the one nodding acknowledgement of both starship captains on his view-screen aboard the Obama. This while Taylor and Robertson only saw Spinner, not each other as well. "Do you want to hear the good news first? Or the other good news first?"

Spinner craned his smirking bearded face so close to the camera, Helena Taylor could have counted the individual pores on his nose. Buddy Leung mused that the Secretary of Defense's head might as well have been some planet the starship was entering orbit around. With the secretary's Santa Claus beard being its mysterious geological feature.

But Captain Taylor sensed a conscious intent meant for her specifically. The defense secretary wanted to literally get in her face with his "good news." Pursuant to which he could better perceive, make out, her reaction to that news. Maybe Secretary Spinner wanted a ringside seat to her concession that yes, his news made undeniably clear what a fool she had been. She never should have allowed herself to come under the sway of those outrageously naïve pacifist tree creatures from Oomb.

Incidentally, one of those creatures, Oodle-Noodle, presently happened to be rooted into a soil-filled pot next to the captain's chair.

"Shall we have the good news first, Captain Taylor?" asked Captain Robertson.

"Sure," nodded Taylor, "unless the Secretary of Defense expresses a preference to share the other good news first, Captain Robertson."

"Oh heavens no!" Spinner shook his head most vigorously, like he had in times past. His jowls could be espied in turmoil despite his ample white beard. "The one proceeds from the other as logically, as reasonably mind you, Captain Taylor, as all-out retaliation proceeds from an unprovoked attack by hostiles!"

When you say unprovoked attack, Mr. Secretary, what do you mean? Are you talking about the unprovoked attack on the Tictoctickian hospital? The attack facilitated by the piggyback drone hacking into one of the "hostiles'" magnetic pulse-beams? Helena bit on her lower lip to ease not asking these questions out loud. She also continued to marvel at how close Spinner kept his face to the camera. *What? Does he think if he could somehow spill his countenance all over me, I would experience some life-altering revelation of the utility of violence? I'd be like St. Paul on the road to Damascus, blinded by darkness rather than light?*

"The first good news is this: We did manage to relay back to Earth DeFarge's report on the piggyback drone's efficacy. And we did that quickly enough for mass production to have already been ramped up! Yes indeedy! And like I said before, the other good news proceeds damned elegantly from the first good news!

Production got ramped up so rapidly, the first mass-produced piggyback drones have already been launched. Most appropriately, firefly donuts piggybacked them out past the Kuiper Belt. They are now stationed one-a-piece in the darkest shadows of the ten largest planetoids."

"What's the estimated time when the piggybackers will establish those positions, Mr. Secretary?" asked Eisenhower Captain Robertson.

"It's like I just said, Captain. 'They are *now* stationed.' It's a done deal even as we speak!"

"Impressive, Mr. Secretary," conceded Robertson.

"Oh, there's more. You might even call it our third piece of good news. Those piggybackers are programmed to hitch rides on any saucer-type vehicles. The saucers just have to slow down enough for reconnoitering an area, or launching an attack. Without anyone else having to direct them like DeFarge did, the piggybackers 'know' what to do. If an attack is launched, they will boomerang it on the attacker."

Captain Robertson whistled his astonishment before he said, "So theoretically, the battle saucers could even sneak up on us, somehow. But they will still self-destruct from their magnetic pulse-beams getting reversed into themselves by the piggybackers! We won't have to lift a finger!"

"Oh, we'll hit them with everything we've got," Secretary Spinner demurred with another of his trademark jowl shakes. "We will make their rubble bounce to be absolutely sure they are neutralized. Although I guess rubble has nothing to bounce on, way out here in space, ho ho ho! But the bottom line is that yes, this whole awful mess could soon be over. Within days, our most important concern might be the exact differences between the rules for golf and the rules for oof. Captain Taylor?"

Helena had not made any indication she wanted to make the least comment. Secretary Spinner was putting her on the spot. He was fishing for a compliment, for some degree of awestruck reaction like Captain Robertson displayed. Either that, or what Spinner considered far more likely. Forced to say something, Captain Taylor would disparage the game plan. She would make an utterly contemptible remark worthy of the lecturing reaction he had long since mentally rehearsed.

"Um, do we know where the saucer fleet is located presently?" Helena Taylor said at last. "I thought our latest evidence suggested they were maintaining a steady one-half light-year ahead of us."

"Well, harrumph!" Secretary Spinner cleared his throat, flustered by Captain Taylor's studiously neutral inquiry. He found himself lost for words. "Let's see. We did receive data from our Neptune outpost, from one of those message-in-a-bottle firefly donuts," Spinner finally settled on saying. "We learned the saucer fleet has stalled out not too far ahead of us, amidst the outer-most planetoids. For all we know, Captain Taylor, they are setting up an ambush. But whatever they are about, I for one feel comfortable knowing the piggyback drones have our backs. And knowing also we are fully armed, ourselves, even were the drones to prove useless.

"Far better that than the alternative. We could have been bringing nothing more to the party than you are. Nothing more than a reception committee of tree creatures such as your Oodle-Noodle, intent on welcoming the demon stag from Tictoctic with open branches. I can just imagine how that would have gone. Your Oodly-Noodly tree creatures could have been hula dancers in Hawai'i, offering to drape leis around the Tictoctickians' necks. Then they would have been inviting the demon stag to pluck fruit off their branches that might as well have been painted there by Salvador Dali! And the thanks would likely have been total incineration by those infernal air igniters! To put it another way, Captain Taylor, I am happy beyond what I can adequately describe, *not* to be aboard your Smoke and Mirrors, flying utterly defenseless! God help you!"

Captain, Oodle-Noodle suddenly telepathed to Helena Taylor, Buddy Leung and select other crew. *I am sensing the deer creature presence at diffuse locations relative to where we are approaching. A most curious thing: There is general awareness among them of a plan, but puzzlement as to specifics.*

"Thank you, Oodle-Noodle.

"Secretary Spinner, according to our Oombian friend here, it would seem we might soon learn exactly how comfortable any of us ought to be feeling."

Before Helena could proceed any further, Michael Spinner tried to crane his head even closer to the video-cam his end, if that were possible. It was as though, the Smoke and Mirrors captain intuited, the video-cam could reveal something extra. It might allow Secretary Spinner to grasp more clearly what she was about to go on about.

"Oodle-Noodle is mindreading a widely scattered Tictoctickian presence up ahead," Captain Helena Taylor went on. "Mysteriously, that presence seems to know there is a plan for them, but not know what it actually consists of."

"Mm-hmm," Spinner nodded. He wanted to convey skepticism the deer creature extraterrestrials were doing anything other than fooling themselves. However, some faint shadow of dread suddenly, uncontrollably cast itself across his mental landscape. It was all he could do to fight off acid reflux, force it back down his throat. With a strained smirk he said, "We will see what kind of plan they can know and not know simultaneously, won't we?"

A hundred billion miles away, a hundred billion miles closer to Earth than the Earthling starships, Commander Ak-keek-teek had executed a strategy he claimed to have originated himself. In reality, he co-opted it from former Commander Kwit-Nik. Nevertheless, Commander Ak-keek-teek had himself, the four other saucer captains, and select other crew sealed inside lead-alloy-reinforced enclosures. They were the only ones privy to the full plan. And their enclosures not only didn't allow the passage of any incidental radioactivity. Kwit-Nik determined that they made mind-reading by the tree creatures a near-certain impossibility, especially from billions of lek-leks distant.

The Tictoctickians would remain tucked inside the special rooms until they could confirm all three starships from "Akt" were destroyed.

Meanwhile, Officer Kevin Smith-Park was reporting something on the navigation bridge of the Smoke and Mirrors. "Captain, that UFO we've periodically detected almost beyond reach of what we should be able to detect? Doing impossible right angle turns, at speeds that make us look like we're losing the race to a tortoise?"

"Oh, that again," Helena deadpanned with faux flippancy. "I wonder whether it's escaped the notice of Spinner and associates. If they *have* noticed it, I'll bet they are frantically puzzling over how they'll ever get one of their piggyback drones to hitch a ride."

They have detected the UFO, Captain. They have already discounted it as stemming either from minor equipment mal-function, or from some hitherto poorly understood cosmic particle interaction, telepathed Oodle-Noodle.

"Occam's Razor dictates we examine thoroughly why Spinner and his associates have discounted the phenomenon in question, Captain. We must do that before we entertain wild notions of some supreme extraterrestrial species whose facility with interstellar space travel makes us look like three-year-olds falling off our tricycles by comparison." Professor Skepticus gave this pronouncement his most imperious delivery, yet, even though he was clutching reflexively at the seat of his pants. He never knew when he might suffer yet another humiliating scorching blast from Effy, the so-called ephemeral dragon.

Spinner and his associates do not know what we know, Captain, added Oodle-Noodle, ignoring the professor.

"By 'we,' you are talking about yourself and Wafoodle-boodle?" When Helena said this, looks passed between her, Chris, Yoon-hee, Ali, Tanya, Kevin, Buddy and Cathy. There might as well have been an Oombian collective consciousness mind-read, for the same two words went through every single one of their heads.

The intervention.

On the other hand, not one of those Earthlings could bring her or his self to think about the captured couple. None of them dared imagine what the DeFarges might be enduring back on Tictoctic. That was assuming they were still alive, even.

⁊ᛋ⫯⊛°⫯ᛋ⫯⊛°⫯ᛋ⫯⊛°

"Just keep hangin' in there, Prissy; I know you can do it," Michel DeFarge whispered to his wife.

Prissy had curled herself into a fetal position on the pine needle hardpan beside her husband.

Michel was crouched behind a bush dense with hand-shaped leaves. Those leaves grew plumper than typical leaves back on Earth, yet not as plump as cacti. However, their smooth texture and silvery green sheen did remind Michel of cactus skin. And each "finger" of each "hand" was outfitted with a long, pointy, cactus-type needle. Breaking off such needles allowed easy access to the water and nutrition stored within, for both Michel and Priscilla.

The DeFarges chewed on the moist, tender leaves, though finding them too stringy to actually swallow. They were Priscilla DeFarge's main source of nourishment. She couldn't handle the occasional grubs her husband unceremoniously popped in his mouth. Michel grimaced over their too-weird taste, even as he made crunching noises while munching on their exoskeletons. Those noises gave Prissy the dry heaves without her even biting into one.

A brutal ten hours had elapsed since the DeFarges awoke from anesthetic injected by a Tictoctickian doctor into their rumps through their clothes. They found themselves naked and shivering on pine needle hardpan at the edge of one of Tictoctic's few remaining forests. They were not far from the Arctic Circle, albeit during summertime.

Between two towering pine trees, Michel DeFarge was able to easily espy Dek-Fook-Tek's northern command center. That enormous gray edifice of stone and brick assumed the appearance, so he mused, of a stag's antlers built with gray Lego blocks.

During the DeFarge couple's short audience with Dek-Fook-Tek, Tictoctickian soldiers left on the translator for only a short while. But that was long enough for Michel and Priscilla to learn they were to be hunted like deer. Then there was nothing for the Earthlings but undecipherable tongue-clicks between the stag-like creatures.

After Tictoctickians turned off the translator, they found themselves entertained no end. Michel's fierce protests and Prissy's desperate pleas sounded like so many meaningless, inconsequential animal grunts.

Once he woke up naked, Michel DeFarge well knew he and his wife didn't have much time. It wouldn't be long before the lead stag, the one named Dek-Fook-Tek, emerged from his headquarters to hunt them down.

Michel's first order of business was to slap his wife silly until she calmed herself, quit her most unhelpful moaning. "Good God, woman!" he exclaimed once Prissy's complaining subsided to a quiet whimper, no thanks to his violence. "You don't want to be giving away our location to these furry-assed demons when we move off from here! Plus, I need a little peace to do some clear cogitating!"

"But I'm so cold," Prissy said haltingly, her teeth chattering.

"Don't I know it, d-dearest Prissy. And I'll be d-damnably damned if tending to our shivers, yours and m-mine both, isn't my next order of b-business." He plucked pine cones off one of two towering trees similar to pine trees back on Earth.

"Hold me, Michel, just hold me," Prissy whimpered some more, pleadingly. "I-I-I'm s-s-so c-cold!"

"Every damnably damned instinct in me wants to g-give into y-your n-notion there, m-my P-Prissiest! But the higher order brain m-matter is s-sounding an alarm l-loud. S-Simply h-h-holding you will only k-keep us f-feeling safe for the shortest t-time. All t-too soon, those d-devilishly unnatural clothes-w-wearing creatures from hell will be t-taking shots at us! No! I've-I've g-got a m-multi-part p-plan, and this g-gives us an ad-admission t-ticket to p-part one!"

By the conclusion of his explanation, despite chattering teeth, Michel DeFarge had completed the first step. He had smeared enough sticky sap from two pine cones on his bare chest and elsewhere on his body. And he was set about smearing that sap on his wife, on her back anyway. She was loathe to uncurl from her ever-trembling fetal position in the hard pan.

Next, Michel gathered tan-colored cottony tufts of post-bloom from a nearby, abundantly growing plant. Then he labored with furious speed, well past his exhaustion point, to cover much of his wife's body and his own with them. They adhered well where he had spread the sap.

Soon thereafter, Michel was definitely starting to feel a bit insulated from the cold. In fact, he felt enough insulated to finally fight down his teeth-chattering. Clearly his plan was working as he had hoped and expected. The cottony plant material, with all its nooks and crannies amidst its tufty strands, was holding in some of the warmth shed by his body. It was slowing down heat escape.

Part one accomplished, part two required both humans get up and run deeper into the forest. Also, they needed to be on the lookout for some trap they could set to stymy the deer creatures' pursuit of them.

What they came across, they brought themselves up short of not a moment too soon. A few more steps, and they most likely would have broken their necks falling into an immense hole in the hard pan. They could not have known it was a relic burrowing nest of an extinct oskynt community, scoured out recently by a tremendous wind storm.

Michel DeFarge pulled up vines for Priscilla DeFarge to apply her knitting skills. She wove a mesh that covered the entire, perilously deep opening in the ground. Then the couple worked together to mask what Priscilla had accomplished. They hid her mesh with every loose pine cone, small branch, and fallen leaf they could locate nearby.

Priscilla and Michel completed their task none too soon. During the final minutes of preparation, both DeFarges could hear rustling noises growing louder and louder, approaching ever closer.

What loomed out of the forest, finally, were Dek-Fook-Tek's stubby-antlered servants. They were positioned much higher off the ground, even, than Dek-Fook-Tek himself. Those servants had an f-n' ridiculous job, as Michel would have put it in less polite company than his woeful wife's. They were assigned to keep the royal hunter's oversized antlers from tipping over, possibly even breaking his neck.

At ground level, other servants pushed along the ladders on wheels where their fellow servants, the antler handlers, stood. DeFarge was reminded of movable ramps at airports, for deboarding planes directly onto the tarmac.

Michel DeFarge crouched low behind some bushes. True, the elevated antler-handling servants were preoccupied manipulating the antler-suspending wires like marionette strings. But one of them might permit himself a stray look away from his task. That is when Michel ran the risk of being seen if he didn't crouch low. So that's what he did instead of continuing to spy on the hunting party.

Snuggled beside his still-trembling wife, Michel kept alert for certain noises he hoped to soon hear. Any second, he expected the ground-level servants to unwittingly send their ramps-on-wheels toppling through the false forest floor into the fortuitously located pit. Thereby would the hunter and his antler handlers topple in as well, helplessly maimed if not outright killed.

Noises did happen. There was a fwoomp accompanied by sounds of breaking branches, then a flurry of panicky bleats and brays.

Michel DeFarge remembered bleats and brays his father's sheep often made when someone sheered their wool. Thusly encouraged, he popped his head up to espy confirmation the antler-handling servants no longer stood elevated. However, he was met with an unwelcome sight. The antler handlers were still looming out of the forest, if obviously more preoccupied than ever with what was transpiring directly down below them.

Suddenly, Michel DeFarge heard harshly produced tongue-clicks above the continuing panic of bleating and braying. Which in turn was becoming interspersed by baas of pain. Without the aid of a translator device, the tongue-clicks meant so much gibberish to the two Earthlings. But Michel DeFarge assumed they were issuing from the hunter giving his servants revised commands.

"It worked, Mikey?" Priscilla squeaked in a tone as hopeful as desperate.

"'fraid not, Prissy," said Michel. He thought on how he shouldn't have been surprised to see the antler handlers still standing tall. After all, he didn't hear the clunking and grating he expected from wheeled ladders falling through a faux forest floor. *Shit, there must have been an advance guard out front of His Royal Antlerness!* "We're going to have to get our move-on, now!" Michel shout-whispered at his wife. "At least we winnowed down their numbers, I think; maybe left a few of them with broken bones!"

Confirming the urgency for the DeFarges to resume their escape from danger pronto was what Michel realized, poking his head out of the bushes again. The two antler handlers were both being moved over to one side. Of course. They were making a detour around the pit trap.

Even worse was yet another unfortunate circumstance Michel DeFarge noticed when he returned his attention to what lay ahead for him and Prissy. They were already fast approaching the final stand of pines. That is, the final stand of pines before they would reach a wide expanse of golden meadow polka-dotted by a few violet blooms. If the meadow grasses hadn't grown long enough to conceal their retreat...

⚜━━⚜━━⚜

Neither Michel DeFarge nor Dek-Fook-Tek could have known or imagined what was happening some two hundred eighty thousand lek-leks away.

Kwit-Nik had long since been demoted from commander of the entire fleet of Celestial Breaths. Presently he was Captain Kwit-Nik of only one Celestial Breath, the Fourth Celestial Breath. He was supposed to use that particular battle saucer for protecting Tictoctic from a rearguard action by the "Akt" other-worlders. Instead, though, he was conducting special maneuvers to dislodge Tictoctic's moon from orbit. Put it on a devastating collision course with his global-warming-ravaged planet. Yes, he was that desperate to protect the larger universe from his civilization's rampant cruelty.

The Fourth Celestial Breath held a steady course towards the dark side of Tictoctic's moon. From the perspective of Captain Kwit-Nik and crew, the moon was well on its way to eclipsing Tictoctic.

Lieutenant Weekwok finally mustered the courage to humbly bleat, "Please, Captain Kwit-Nik, forgive my dense skull. It is an oskynt skull's thickness for the difficulty of even the simplest, most direct information penetrating it. But, can you explain again how placing us in the shadow of the moon facilitates protection of our Supreme Authority, Dek-Fook-Tek? How does this particular maneuver save him from other-worlders? Especially from other-worlders who suppose the dispatch of so many of our saucer fleet to Akt has left Tictoctic's rear end unprotected, so to speak? Wouldn't it be far better for those barbaric beasts to have a direct view of our formidable battle saucer hovering in between them and Tictoctic?"

"My most trusted Lieutenant Weekwok, the smartest oskynt in the world would not be smart enough for awareness of its own ignorance. You should be commended for your question, not forgiven," Captain Kwit-Nik tongue-clicked reassuringly. Thereby did he confirm for Lieutenant Weekwok what many rumors hinted at. This demoted official named Kwit-Nik was one of the most reasonable Tictoctickians in a position of any significant power.

If only Weekwok knew something else knocking about Captain Kwit-Nik's mind about him. He would have felt even more confirmed in his estimation of the captain. The something else in Kwit-Nik's mind was that Weekwok had demonstrated clear superiority to Dek-Fook-Tek. Dek-Fook-Tek could never be said to have ever so bluntly admitted there was anything, great or small, he did *not* already understand.

"So," Captain Kwit-Nik went on, "our maneuver to the dark side of the moon has a two-pronged purpose. The first prong consists in the testing of a land-based, diffuse magnetic pulse-beam. For extra added concealment, the payload I am about to launch will attach itself securely to the lunar surface, lost in shadows at bottom of a crater. It is programmed to activate automatically. I have set the payload's pulse-beam at the lowest intensity; we should experience nothing more disturbing than a minor shudder. But afterwards, I will remote-control recalibrate the land-based weapon to its most lethal setting.

"Our recent other-world visitors tried to hide an interstellar-worthy exoskeleton in moon shadow near Chonora. If any of their fellow beasts attempt that same stunt here, they will have *their* exoskeleton shattered apart before they know what hit them!

"For the second prong, you noticed I said we *would* experience minor saucer shudder. In point of fact, I will also be testing this Celestial Breath's ability to entirely neutralize the diffuse magnetic pulse-beam's normal impact. Such capability, I suspect you would agree,-"

Lieutenant Weekwok was already nodding.

"-could prove most useful. This would be especially so in the event of an attack by a comparable weapon from the other-world species. Or another drone hack into one of our systems as we know the terrorists carried out."

"You have provided far more elaborate explanation than I could ever have hoped for, Captain," the lieutenant humbly baaed with a low bow.

Yes, it is as though you were channeling Dek-Fook-Tek to perform this work while you go down on all fours to relax. Kwit-Nik could imagine former Lieutenant Ak-keek-teek having brayed such a remark in a gently admonishing tone. It would have come complete with his ever-unnervingly ridiculous buck-tooth grin. That is, had he not been promoted to take Kwit-Nik's place as commander of the entire saucer fleet, for his anus-sniffing skills where Kwit-Nik was concerned.

Captain Kwit-Nik expected far different from his present lieutenant, as well as from nearly every other officer under his command. He guessed they would have fully supported the peaceful removal of Dek-Fook-Tek, together with Dek-Fook-Tek's most fanatically loyal advisers. Kwit-Nik's crew would have felt relieved to see them all locked away in a mental institution so that saner minds might have prevailed.

But Captain Kwit-Nik feared that ultimately, he wasn't any less crazy than Supreme Authority Dek-Fook-Tek. He was prone to Dek-Fook-Tek's same, ruthlessly barbaric reasoning. Ironically, Kwit-Nik thereby concluded he needed to follow through on his horrific determination. In order to spare other civilizations on other planets from Dek-Fook-Tek's unhinged cruelty, Tictoctickian civilization must be destroyed. The planet Tictoctic must be decimated. This must happen even if that meant several fine and decent beings including Lieutenant Weekwok were killed into the bargain. Again, that Kwit-Nik could think in such a manner was what seized him with the conviction he must gallop with it.

But, what was this? What incredible thing was the Fourth Celestial Breath's long-distance detection equipment suddenly picking up? No other officer on the navigation bridge understood how to "read" that equipment better than Kwit-Nik. And yet now he had trouble believing his own eyes, his own competence using instrumentation originally invented and manufactured by the Chonorans. Try as he could, though, he still couldn't get around it. The data was unmistakably clear. Something amazing was happening just beyond the Tictoctic star system's outermost reaches, on the inner edge of its Oort Cloud. An unidentified flying object was performing impossible right angle turns, even sharper than the Celestial Breath saucers were capable of executing. And that object was accomplishing such a feat at unbelievable speeds. They were speeds which by comparison made the Celestial Breaths at their maximum pace appear to be loping along like so many wounded oskynt.

⁂

"Imagine, Flamboyo. Imagine," said a tearful, imploring Shelly Taylor. It was all she could do to keep from adding, *Please, I beg of you!*

Shelly remained holed up with a security detail in a Florida police station west of Interstate Route I-95.

Flamboyo was holed up with physicist Dr. Morel Engeling on a hijacked shuttle pod headed for the Earth's moon.

"You can find it for yourself on the internet," went on Shelly. "To the northeast of Lake Huron, there is a partially thawed-out permafrost zone. We can take a group of orphaned children there from Philadelphia. All of us will have to bundle up, but on its wide open fields we can grow the food we need, plus plenty extra to share with others. I understand blueberries are among the crops harvested that far north! We will face enormous challenges, for certain. But, but, it's a more practical option than the moon! Terraformed atmosphere won't even sustain on Mars, we now know, let alone on a world that much smaller with that much weaker gravitational pull. On the moon, you would need to construct greenhouse domes enormous beyond precedent. And import voluminous supplies from Earth. Far, far more supplies than you could possibly carry there, even aboard a full-blown starship, let alone your shuttle or a solar clipper!

"Flamboyo??" The longer Flamboyo went without commenting, the more worried Shelly got that he might have tuned her out.

Nothing could be further from the truth.

Flamboyo Sanchez didn't want his partner in nihilism, Morel Engeling, to catch a glimpse of the lone tear trickling down his cheek. So he pretended his focus was centered on contemplation of the crescent moon they were fast approaching. But when he finally reacted to Shelly Taylor, his true focus was on something else. "Ay, chica," he said, "we know that thousands of people, at least, must not have been able to evacuate the coast in time before the tsunami." Flamboyo strained to maintain a level tone, somehow feign brutal callousness. He didn't want any hint of his longing regret to seep through. "You really think if we turned around and headed back to Earth pronto, I would be allowed to join you in such a project as you describe? Listen, chica, I would be lucky to escape with prison for life, not find myself strapped to the electric chair! But let us suppose your miracle occurred, and I got off with probation. How would we free children from the no-zone, just like that?" Flamboyo snapped his fingers while the moonlight's crescent went eyelash slim with the shuttle pod heading around to the dark side.

"No, Flamboyo, we don't know yet!" Shelly Taylor shouted, shaking her head adamantly. "Officials aren't certain anyone has been killed by the tsunami!" Shelly couldn't help saying this, even though she well understood the uncertainty was a mere formality, regarding carnage inflicted by the tsunami.

It was a formality soon to be swamped by reports flooding in as inexorably as the tsunami itself flooded the east coast of Florida. "Court probably won't go well for you," Helena Taylor's daughter finally conceded. "You *will* have to serve prison time. But on good behavior..."

"Damn it, woman! You *know* once they re-enter the flooded locations..." And damn it, Flamboyo thought to himself, for his inability to keep from venting with his grieving frustration over what might have been...

"So tell me, Flamboyo, *digame*," said Shelly in nothing-to-lose mode. "Whether you succeeded in hijacking the shuttle pod or not, you knew the tsunami was going to kill lots of people. You knew you were going to be marked as a mass-murderer. And that consequently, you could never, ever bring needy boys and girls up there to start their lives anew in your proposed lunar utopia. So what, exactly, did you have in mind? Or did you? Was this really Dr. Engeling's plan, and you are only along for the ride?"

"Say tell me, Ms. Taylor," Engeling interjected. He needed to derail Captain Taylor's daughter's new line of inquiry. Otherwise, it might quickly lead her and the law enforcement officers breathing down her neck to figure out his actual agenda. And that was certain to precipitate a concerted effort to have the shuttle pod "taken out." Engeling needed to delay such happenstances until well after it was too late. "Ms. Taylor," he repeated, "you getting any sleep down there? Because it sounds like all you're doing is grinding and grinding on a search for Flamboyo's ability to surrender. Your energy would be better spent looking for Bigfoot or the Loch Ness Monster.

"Oh, and you might want to pass along a message to those people who are putting you up to this. It pertains to a certain patrol vessel tailing us. To whom it may concern: That vessel needs to break off within three minutes. Otherwise, we use our like-polarity device to shatter apart its solar sails. We send it on a death spiral into deep space, where meteorite debris will make fast work of what's left of it. Unlike sound waves, magnetic force DOES travel without an atmosphere!"

Click!

Communications were cut off so Shelly Taylor and company back down on Earth couldn't explore whether Engeling was bluffing, which he was. The magnetizing equipment requisite for knocking out other spacecraft had already been packed away inside a robotic payload. And that payload would soon be delivered down to the surface of the moon's dark side.

"Ha! Look, Flamboyo! You can almost imagine their patrol vessel is tucking its solar sails between its legs. That must be one of its tightest U-turns, ever!"

Flamboyo was consumed by his own thoughts. But with his back turned on Engeling, he pretended to be trying to discern moonlight where there was none left, as the shuttle pod had finished flying around to the dark side. However, the physicist's rare moment of exultation was not lost on him. It was the first that Flamboyo could ever remember hearing from the guy.

"Flamboyo!" Engeling shouted as in, *Are you still there?!*

"I am right beside you, remember?" Flamboyo muttered with a forced bravado that fell flat.

"Okay, Mr. Sanchez, what is this?" Engeling gripped the compact hand gun in his right pants pocket; there was no question he was going to use it. What tasks remained he could easily complete on his own. But, before he ended this man's life on the path to ending most everyone else's including his own, there was one more thing. There was a last measure of vindication he sought to glean from Flamboyo, en route to The End.

Flamboyo Sanchez easily guessed what was going on in Engeling's pants pocket. Engeling was re-securing his grip on his weapon. Curiously, this emboldened Flamboyo to answer, "I was thinking, Señor Engeling, on something that has nothing to do with that f-ng woman!" Flamboyo couldn't help becoming infuriated by the physicist's dawning grin.

Where Engeling was concerned, how loudly Flamboyo protested only confirmed it had everything to do with "that f-ng woman."

"Look, mira, the Earth is doomed anyway from cruel stupidity! Why do we need to rush the process along?! Why not wait for it to play out? Especially if there is any chance, Professor Engeling, even the smallest chance we can imagine, that somehow enough decent people-"

That was it for Engeling. "'Enough decent people'?!?!?! 'Enough decent people'?!?!?" he shouted hysterically as he whipped out his hand gun and aimed it at Flamboyo's head. "I needed you in order to come this far, but I knew it! I knew it! When we got close to finally achieving my goal, you were going to torture me for my grieving!" Engeling suddenly trembled all over.

"Como? What?!" Flamboyo's perplexity nearly overwhelmed his dread of the pistol aimed at him, however shakily.

"I was told not to grieve! I was made to suffer! The ropes cut deeply into my wrists and ankles! But not this time!" Engeling shook his head with his mouth dangling half open. There was a crazed, feverish look in his eyes.

"What ropes, man? What the hell are you talking about?!"

"Not you, not anybody else can stop me this time! This time, there are consequences!" Engeling was re-experiencing his father telling him the news so long ago, that his brother was dead. The news had been related so softly, so gently. And yet, it had been succeeded by a harsh grumble rumbling from a stonily set visage. "But life goes on," Engeling's father had gone on, way back when. "We are going to put this behind us! Understand? Understand?!?!"

"No, Daddy! NO!!" Engeling's protests had become about his father tying him to the bedpost. They had already been about his denial something so horrific could have happened. That some freakishly mysterious virus could have been lying in wait to kill his brother...

"Daddy can't stop me from putting an end to a world where this could happen!" Engeling ranted presently. "AND NEITHER CAN YOU!!!" He took final aim to pull the trigger.

Flamboyo made a last-ditch lunge at the weapon. He tried desperately to push the line of fire away from himself.

The struggle was on...

But not before Engeling succeeded in pushing a lone button.

A magnetizing device payload was launched from the shuttle pod. It descended towards a dust-filled crater on the dark side of Earth's moon.

<hr />

"If you two little macho men don't stop fighting, I am going to take that thing away! From both of you, before someone gets hurt!" In the Smoke and Mirrors playroom, Ciela was warning her two little charges adopted by her and Fred Frankly. They were among the population spirited to Oomb from a Puerto Rican neighborhood in north Philadelphia sixty years earlier. Eight-year-olds Jorge and Tomás were wrestling over who would seize control of a quadruple-beam light-saber toy marketed off the umpteenth remake of *Star Wars*.

Oodle-Noodle and Wafoodle-boodle were both settled into their special nutrient pots on the navigation bridge of the Smoke and Mirrors. Had they been endowed with the least vestigial remnants of mouths, Captain Taylor and company could not have failed to notice their smiles. The tree creatures' contented amusement stemmed from the synchronistic appropriateness of the situation mind-read unfolding in the children's playroom. As it was, when they opened their vertically slit eyes along the corrugations of their thick-barked trunks, Tanya Petrovsky noticed extra-shiny glints. Their sleepy-looking affect didn't matter.

But no time for questions, whether vocalized or telepathically laid open by the Earthlings for the tree creatures to mind-read.

"Captain, looks like we're going to have to slow it down considerably, well before we even reach the Kuiper Belt," reported Yoon-hee Park-Smith. "The Eisenhower is receiving firefly donut data which suggest that random, variously sized asteroids are going to be crossing where we're headed. They will be like ducks in an amusement park shooting gallery. Only this time, we're not going to win any prizes for hitting them!"

"Yeah, or like we're the ducks, and those asteroids are the BB pellets the uncaring cosmos is launching at us," grumbled Kevin Smith-Park.

"How very folksy of you, Kevin," said Helena Taylor. "Yoon-hee, is there anything unusual about the asteroids' behavior?"

"Most unusual, Captain, but I can't put my finger on it," Yoon-hee nodded. "Had Captain Entroper anticipated this situation, I am sure she would have set a different course. She would have wanted our three starships maintaining especially high altitude above the orbital plane until we passed the Kuiper Belt."

"Too late for that," said Chris. "Guess we're just going to have to 'tiptoe through the tulips.'"

"Nay, and here's what suggests something highly suspicious," Yoon-hee added. She was too focused on her console's data output to process Chris's allusion to a 1960's song by someone named Tiny Tim.

"Like maybe 'most unusual' was 'most intended'?"

"Exactly, Officer Leung. I'm receiving curious info from randomly situated firefly donuts not a part of our starship caravan's advance guard. Anomalous flashes of light have gone off in areas from where the asteroids appear to be originating."

"Split screen, Yoon-hee. I assume that up ahead of us aboard the Obama and Eisenhower, Captain Entroper and company are noticing what we're noticing."

"They must have, Captain," Yoon-hee opined as she swiped a stray wacamacaglobule snack tidbit out of its free-floating state. Gravity had dropped to nil since the Smoke and Mirrors decelerated out of light-speed to a relative crawl.

"Hmm," hmmed Captain Taylor, forefinger crooked contemplatively under her nostrils. She was pondering the remote video replay fed from randomly situated firefly donuts onto half the panoramic view-screen. "Thinking what I'm thinking, Buddy?"

"I observed a circular ballooning-out from each of those flashes of light, Captain. If you're thinking that probably indicates Tictoctickian magnetic pulse-beam emissions set on diffuse, the answer is yes. And those emissions must be sending nearby space rocks hurtling off every which direction, wherefore our shooting gallery."

"Bingo, Buddy!"

"So the Tictoctickians *want* us to slow down this much; they must be preparing an ambush," Captain Entroper was meanwhile remarking aboard the battle saucer, Barack Obama. Of course her conversation also had to do with the light-burst phenomena.

"Here is good news we should keep in mind, Captain Entroper," advised munitions expert Maggie Wang. This is how she bluntly wedged her way into the back-and-forth between Secretary Spinner and Entroper on the Obama's navigation deck. "I have confirmation that five piggyback drones obtained hosts."

"Five piggybackers," repeated Entroper. "Five!" She squinted in a vain effort to discern anomalous moving pinpoints of light on the live-transmission deep-space view. As per captain's orders, that view took up half the panoramic split-screen, transmitting from the rear of the Obama. "We detected the exact same number of objects bypassing Oomb on their exit from the Cygnitaurus system. Not including of course the UFO..."

"Which we're all but certain can't be nothin' more than some meaningless physics peculiarity," blustered Spinner in full jowl-shaking mode. "That is, unless we're going to posit there's some extraterrestrial civilization what makes us seem like kiddies playing with our Lego blocks by comparison! No, Captain, I would say we are looking to ambush the ambushers. Wouldn't you agree, Dr. Wang?"

"I would strongly agree, Mr. Secretary."

"Oh, count me in too," Captain Entroper shook her white mop-top side-to-side despite her agreeing. "I just think it's going to be prudent of us to charge up our rear laser cannons, put them on standby. We want to remain ready, just in case the magnetic pulse-beam redirectioning wrought by the piggyback drones isn't one hundred percent successful."

"You'll get no argument from either of us, Captain!" affirmed Spinner.

Dr. Wang's fingers pranced across her control console to implement Entroper's gently rendered command that the rear laser cannons be put on standby.

"Only it's a damned regrettable matter," Spinner went on. "I can't help coming back to Captain Taylor's insubordinate decision to totally disarm at the outset of her last mission. As we've said so often before, the Smoke and Mirrors has got nothing to defend herself. Should the piggybackers fail to do the trick, we have to assume those demon stag will be staging a rear guard ambush. The S & M will be their first target, since she's now trailing a full two hundred thousand miles behind us."

...which Captain Taylor was ordered to do if she was intent on tagging along. But the Secretary of Defense left this little detail out of his lament.

Captain Entroper sighed with exasperation. So much went the wrong way back on Fafama; she didn't want anyone able to place a new guilt-trip on her doorstep. Namely, that she didn't do what she could where protecting the Smoke and Mirrors was concerned. "Skip," she said, directed towards Navigation Officer Skip Hamilton. "Skip, let's see if we can fall back behind Captain Taylor's 'love train.' We will make every effort to protectively keep them in between us and the Eisenhower."

"Shit! No time for that, Captain!"

Five objects suddenly careened out and around from behind five coal-black asteroids. Two came from the Smoke and Mirrors' aft left and three came from her aft right. All five were making a beeline for the defenseless starship.

"Captain Taylor-"

"Five UFOs of likely Tictoctickian origin are converging on us! Yes we have that, Captain Entroper!"

"They are saucer-shaped as I think we are already seeing on the magniview, Captain," Yoon-hee was reporting to Taylor on the navigation bridge of the Smoke and Mirrors.

"Daaaaaammnn! Each one of them do got themselves one of those piggybackers, Louisa!" was exclaiming Skip back aboard the Barack Obama. He noted this from a firefly donut magniview.

"Fly below us, Helena! Clear the way!" barked Captain Entroper at her own magniview. Her magniview revealed five pinpoints of light converging on the Smoke and Mirrors. "We need an unobstructed look-see in case we have to deploy our laser cannons! Skip, pedal to the metal on the mirror arrays!"

"That blue light ringing their rims, Helena!" shouted Buddy aboard the Smoke and Mirrors. "That has to be their magnetic pulse-beams charging up! They might still be set on diffuse, like they used for scattering random space debris every which way! Nevertheless, so many of them converging on us at the same time could prove just as legal as a single concentrated pulse beam!"

We have to hope the piggyback drones perform as expected. Otherwise we are doomed. This is really it; we don't look to be shaking them with our course adjustment ordered by Entroper! Yoon-hee and Kevin's quick implementation didn't matter! These were thoughts too grim for Helena to vocalize. She gripped Chris's hand ever tighter.

Chris used his other hand to hold on to Helena's chair, maintain himself standing beside her during Yoon-hee's maneuvering.

Yoon-hee was lurching the starship from side to side, trying to make targeting trickier for the Tictoctickians.

"Oh, no!" Captains Entroper and Taylor gasped simultaneously.

A diffuse magnetic pulse-beam encircled each of the five saucer rims. Then they started to expand out like ripples expanding out from a pebble dropped in a pond. This was how Chris would have described them.

Chris, and his wife too for that matter, had often been of the same mind where the eeriness of interstellar space travel was concerned. Actually feeling a trip through the cosmos could rarely be a good thing, or even a less-worse-than-fatal thing. This was as opposed to how you could safely feel jet flight through the atmosphere, or an ocean cruise even on calm, glassy-smooth waters.

And now, possibly far more impactful than the roughest seas possible, there were five magnetic pulse-beams rippling directly for-

But no. All five "ripples" dissolved away as one by one, explosions appeared to blossom deep within the flying saucers from where they issued. One by one, those apparent spacecraft apparently burst apart into five debris fields. After those debris fields flamed out, the debris itself was too small to be spotted, even on the magniview.

"That's what I'm talkin' about!" bellowed Secretary Spinner. "Hooray for the piggyback drones!"

Cheers, applause, and hi-fives broke out on the navigation bridges of both the Barack Obama and the Dwight D. Eisenhower.

It was a different story on the navigation bridge of the Smoke and Mirrors, though, situated closer to where the fireworks occurred. Reactions there remained cautiously muted.

Captain, this isn't over yet. Should I warn your colleagues aboard the starships up ahead of us? Oodle-Noodle telepathed for Helena's consideration only.

Coincidentally, Buddy Leung's intent study of the firefly sensor readings led him to report, "Something doesn't make sense with these debris fields, Captain. They cover much smaller areas than they ought to, based on what we know about the size of the Tictoctickian battle saucers."

"Yeah," nodded Kevin studying a different data set. "And my review of the magniview video is only re-confirming the impression I had the first time. There was something, couldn't quite put my finger on it, something ghostly-looking about... Oh, shit!"

Every human on the bridge of the Smoke and Mirrors found themselves transfixed with horror. They realized that just behind where the five debris fields faded away, there suddenly appeared to have materialized five flying saucers. They were all more solid-looking, less like apparitions, than the previous five. And they were huge.

Oblivious to the latest development, people aboard the Obama and Eisenhower continued celebrating the apparent success of the piggyback drones. They still believed those drones turned the magnetic pulse-beams inward, to destroy the saucers.

However, Wafoodle-boodle and Oodle-Noodle mind-read, to their horror, confirmation of the outcome having been dramatically different. Although they were pleased to learn that countless deer creatures did not get blown to pieces, after all. Anyway, what the tree creatures mind-read was that the deer creatures, Commander Ak-keek-teek and the rest, were celebrating as well. They were whooping it up over the success of their deception, how it distracted the "Akt" creatures from the real ambush.

Events transpired just as former Commander Kwit-Nik would have anticipated. And which the new commander had long since deluded himself into believing was his own conception. The piggyback drones latched onto Tictoctickian space vessels, alright. But those vessels were scout saucers sent out from the five Celestial Breaths. Moreover, they were retrofitted with holographic image projectors. The image projectors made the scout saucers appear they were their mother ship Celestial Breaths. That they were multiple times larger than they actually were.

Those particular scout saucers were also equipped with bombs. The bombs were set to detonate when the holographic films got to the parts when the Celestial Breaths juiced up their magnetic pulse-beams. The detonations were meant to sucker the Earthlings into believing the drones did their dirty-work. Namely, that the drones turned the pulse-beams against the saucers that emitted them, boomerang style. The Tictoctickians expected the flashes of light from the detonations would blind the other-world creatures to their arrogance. Those "Akt" beasts would get so caught up in celebration, they would realize too late what was headed their way.

"Captain, we're receiving a face-to-face translated by our own technology left behind on our mission to Tictoctic," Yoon-hee reported to Helena Taylor.

The battle starships Obama and Eisenhower found themselves in receipt of the same face-to-face.

Meanwhile, the five Celestial Breath saucers loomed ever larger on the Smoke and Mirrors' panoramic view-screen.

"Four-quadrant screen, Yoon-hee. I want Entroper and Robertson on the remaining two."

"Nay, Captain."

Ak-keek-teek's visage, his buck-tooth grin wide as ever, filled the lower left quadrant. His haughtily rendered tongue-clicks translated, "This is Commander Ak-keek-teek of Dek-Fook-Tek's defensively deployed Celestial Breath interstellar forces. I order all three of your exoskeletons to relax such musculature as might have been instinctively tensed to attack us. Otherwise, we will have no other recourse than to incinerate them with our targeted magnetic pulse-beams! Once you have made it explicitly recognizable you have suppressed your weaponry, we will only visit upon you diffuse pulse-beams. They will assure permanent disabling of your exoskeleton's attack anatomy. Then we will board to seize defensive control."

"Commander, maybe you will recognize me. I am Captain Taylor. I headed up our peace mission to Tictoctic."

"'Peace mission,' baa!" Ak-keek-teek went down on all fours and kicked to his rear so hard, he splintered his command throne's backrest. *Dek-Fook-Tek would drool with pride over this demonstration of my rage*, he thought to himself. *That is, if I don't assume power as the new Supreme Authority, myself. Well, I must leave that for our triumphant return to Tictoctic. First, we have to make sure "Akt" is transformed into the slaughterhouse of endless culinary delights it deserves to become! One thing at a time!*

Helena made a seat-of-her-pants calculation: It was better not to argue with Ak-keek-teek over his violently dismissive reaction to her characterization of the mission to Tictoctic. No way, probably, was he going to be persuaded that she and her crew had absolutely nothing to do with the attack on their hospital. Especially since the commander was clearly so intent on "defensive control." She went on, instead, with, "Commander, exactly how can we make explicit to you that we have shut down our weapons capability?" Again, Helena could have demurred that the Smoke and Mirrors itself was entirely disarmed. There was nothing to shut down. She could have reminded Ak-keek-teek that he must already know of the starship's defenselessness from the demoted Commander Kwit-Nik. That Kwit-Nik had learned a long while back of the Smoke and Mirrors cleanly separating off from its weapons retrofits. And that those retrofits subsequently were exploded harmlessly in deep space. Captain Helena Taylor could have gone into all of this and more. However, she made an assumption about anyone who would splinter apart their chair in a rage. Most likely, that person was not available for assumption-altering reasoned discourse. So she wasn't going to try reminding the commander what he must have learned from Kwit-Nik.

"How can you prove you disarmed, Captain? It is simple. Retract the fore and aft mirror arrays of your three exoskeleton starships in their entirely. Tuck them neatly inside their respective casings. Leave all three of your warships floating impotently adrift. After that, wait for the time to elapse I deem sufficient for there to have been no further discernible exoskeletal commotions. When, and only when I am completely satisfied, will we honor you with the permanently disabling force of our diffuse magnetic pulse-beams."

"Uh, no," Captain Entroper shook her head firmly. "I am going to tell you what *you* need to do, Commander! That is, if you don't want the debris from all five of your saucers joining your decoy debris!"

Cheers erupted on the navigation decks of the Obama and the Eisenhower, but Helena couldn't help looking on aghast. She thought to herself, *This woman wants to prove something! She wants to vindicate herself, vindicate the military logic she has bought into, even if she gets us all destroyed!*

"You are going to have your fleet head back to Tictoctic, and stay there," Entroper continued. "That way, you leave us alone, we leave you alone."

Commander Ak-keek-teek shook his head with another of his slowly dawning, notoriously wide buck-tooth grins. "You mean, Captain, you leave us alone until you decide it is time to bomb another one of our medical facilities under the guise of coming to help us. I don't think you understand yet; we are the ones not giving you a choice!

"Engineers on all Celestial Breaths, power up our magnetic pulse-beams, targeted against the other-world space-worthy exoskeletons, and await my final order to discharge!"

Helena could hear a bustle of brays and baas Commander Ak-keek-teek's end. It was accompanied by clunky noises from what she could not have known was exuberant, celebratory antler-butting. The overall ruckus reminded her hauntingly much of the approving cheers aboard the Obama and the Eisenhower. Those cheers, of course, broke out over Captain Entroper's blustery refusal to stand down when faced by the deer creature's threat.

Anyhow, for the entirety of Captain Entroper's response, Entroper maintained her eyes fixed unflinchingly in a stare-down of Ak-keek-teek's own beady black peepers. She said, "Fighter pods on standby for swarm formation. Pilot fish and tapeworms on standby for launch, one-per-saucer targeting."

Fighter pod docking bays rotated open around the midriff bulges of the Obama and the Eisenhower. The so-called peacock displays unfolded along each starship's far-more-pronounced bulge towards its rear. From there would issue the so-called pilot fish and tapeworms.

The pilot fish were to latch onto the battle saucers and send magnetic resonance vibrations through each one. Presumably, those vibrations would prove powerful enough to gradually disintegrate them.

To hurry each saucer's disintegration process along, the tapeworms were to burrow into them. Once a saucer's hull was fully breached, producing catastrophic air leaks, the tapeworm would automatically explode.

Meanwhile, the fighter pods would pepper each flying saucer with a laser cannon barrage. They would also try to defend the Eisenhower and Obama from any fighter spacecraft the Tictoctickians might send their way.

Helena focused her thoughts, intent on gaining the tree creatures' telepathic mind-reading attention. *Oodle-Noodle, Wafoodle-boodle, there is something, anything you can telepath both parties to help defuse this showdown before they get everyone killed?*

Captain, responded Oodle-Noodle, *what is about to transpire goes beyond mattering anything Wafoodle-boodle or I could possibly communicate to them.*

The tree creatures might have mind-read Secretary Spinner, but nobody heard him frantically whisper Entroper, "Wang here has just given me a heads-up. The antlered demons' pulse-beams might actually repel our laser cannonballs, boomerang style, right back where they came from!"

"Consider carefully, Commander," Captain Entroper said to Ak-keek-teek. It was as though she might not have been paying any attention to the secretary of defense. At the same time, though, her nose twitched, thrice.

Commander Ak-keek-teek's trademark buck-tooth grin was still plastered on his face. After he finished processing Entroper's twitches, however, he crossed a short bridge of horror-filled realization to grim, panicked foaming at the mouth. He brayed at the top of his lungs what translated into, "Now! Now! Discharge!"

Thanks to Entroper's nose-twitched command, fighter pods were already swarming out of their docking bays. Producing laser cannonballs the appearance of red-tinted ball lightning, those pods blasted away at the five enormous flying saucers.

Meanwhile, the so-called pilot fish reminded Chris of tadpoles wriggling their tails. Their irregular movement allowed them to avoid being hit by magnetic pulse-beams as they rapidly approached the Celestial Breath saucers.

The so-called tapeworms were on likewise approach to the immense Tictoctickian spacecraft. For Chris, their sideways evasive writhing invoked a sea snake he had once caught sight of during a glass bottom boat ride.

Neither the laser cannon fire nor the destructive devices reached their marks, however, before magnetic pulse-beams rippled out from the battle saucers. Those pulse-beams were targeted on the three, massively proportioned Earthling starships, rather than being employed to fend off the pilot fish and tadpoles.

Had Kwit-Nik been present, he would have been the first to realize something remarkably strange afoot. Via remote-controlled access, he had long since reprogrammed the Celestial Breath pulse-beams to ripple inward rather than outward. They were supposed to destroy the saucers that activated them, rather than beaming at the targets intended by Commander Ak-keek-teek. But they weren't.

Kwit-Nik would have had no way of knowing what Oodle-Noodle and Wafoodle-boodle would have guessed. That is, what those tree creatures would have guessed had they mind-read his awful scheme to protect the rest of the galaxy from his civilization's savagery. They would have guessed the coming intervention was so powerful, its effects were rippling back in time well before its arrival.

Unaware of this, Helena Taylor expected to experience a blinding flash as the Smoke and Mirrors was disintegrated by one of the pulse-beams. Her terror could not have been greater. She thought to herself, horrified, *Entroper is going for martyrdom! If the saucers are destroyed before they can reach the Earth, she will see this as her ultimate sacrifice to vindicate the value of militaristic violence!*

During those final moments before the anticipated worst, Chris hugged Helena for dear life. He had lots of company. Hugs broke out all over the one unarmed starship.

⁑ӝ∘⁑ӝ∘⁑ӝ∘

"Lieutenant Weekwok, loyal officers, I have just charged up the lunar-based magnetic pulse-beam on the lowest possible diffuse setting," announced Captain

Kwit-Nik. He had trotted down from the captain's chair to sit strapped in at a control console. From there he could operate the Fourth Celestial Breath's weapon deployment. "Nevertheless," he continued, "until I've activated my experimental counteracting defense shield, I suggest you brace yourselves for minor turbulence."

No sooner did Kwit-Nik speak than the enormous flying saucer was sent by the lunar-based magnetic pulse-beam into a stomach-churning wobble. The former commander lied about the low setting. For what he was about to attempt, he required a mid-strength setting.

From outside the Fourth Celestial Breath, it appeared Captain Kwit-Nik was simply charging up the saucer's magnetic pulse-beam. A familiar, neon-blue light was encircling the saucer's rim, and growing ever brighter. Pursuant to which, that light was "shed" in an ever-enlargening concentric circle away from the saucer. An experienced Tictoctickian would have guessed Kwit-Nik had simply fired off a diffuse magnetic pulse-beam. More was to follow, however. From all around the saucer's rim, a second blue circle of light rippled out, and then a third and a fourth. They kept emanating, which quickly smoothed out the saucer from its wobbling.

"Baa, great success, Captain!" Lieutenant Weekwok brayed fawningly over the result. Little did he realize that however slowly, the Celestial Breath was spinning its way on a direct course for Tictoctic's larger moon. Nor that in response, the moon was coming dislodged from its stable orbit around Tictoctic.

Diffuse magnetic pulse-beams were continuing to emanate from the land-based weapon's crater location. As they did so, they were repulsing and being repulsed by the likewise diffuse beams rippling out from the approaching flying saucer.

"Captain Kwit-Nik!" suddenly bleated Officer Kweeklefwak. He was in a panic over his careful study of data displayed on his redundancy console.

"I would not be so arrogant as to second guess your incomparable grasp of this technology." Kweeklefwak didn't make even a perfunctory attempt to bring up Dek-Fook-Tek for more ridiculously embellished ritual adulation. He belonged to that considerable herd of officers more than willing to have supported Kwit-Nik's defunct rebellion. He still would have happily joined Kwit-Nik in putting Tictoctic's ruler under arrest, then having him relocated to an insane asylum. "However," he went on, "my instrumentation suggests our approach to the moon has caused it to disengage from orbit, and take a new path certain to collide with the homeland!"

"My eternal spirit!" Kwit-Nik feigned shock. He feigned to only just then be realizing the truth in what Kweeklefwak anxiously bleated. Genuine horror over what he actually managed to accomplish fueled Kwit-Nik's performance to make it seem authentic, not a performance. He had long since convinced himself his awful deed was necessary. It might be the only chance for saving other-world planetary civilizations from the ruination he feared Dek-Fook-Tek would otherwise wreak upon them. Still...

"Your experiment, Captain, it seems to have given the Fourth Celestial Breath and the moon the same magnetic charge! They are repulsing one another! Can you halt our saucer's steady creep forward, and somehow reverse its polarity? Maybe it's not too late to stop the moon's crash course for Tictoctic?!?! Maybe we can even herd it into a new, safe orbit?!?!"

"I am trying! I am trying!" Kwit-Nik danced his fingers across his console's keyboards as though he *were* trying.

He put on a show intended to paralyze any other officer who might think about attempting to wrest control away from him of the immense flying saucer. Who knew that there wasn't enough time still left to save Tictoctic from complete disaster? Maybe someone could blast apart the moon with repeated, targeted pulse-beams. Anyway, Captain Kwit-Nik might as well have been dancing his fingers across one of Dek-Fook-Tek's dry-wall kick-boards. Tears were streaming down both sides of his long, narrow snout...

when he noticed something beyond extraordinary in the saucer's view-screen. High above saucer and moon, alike, streaked an impossible rainbow.

⋇⋇⋇

"Keep running, Prissy! Keep running! I can see the leading edge of another forest just up ahead! We have to keep on keepin' on, only a short time more!" huffed and puffed Michel DeFarge. He continually broke and re-broke his stride so his wife wouldn't fall too far behind him. And he was lying, where that leading edge of new forest was concerned. There wasn't even a lone bush for them to secure temporary shelter behind, for at least the next mile or so. But the meadow grasses grew way too short. Michel and Prissy couldn't possibly lose themselves from Dek-Fook-Tek's steady pursuit by crawling around in them, down on their hands and knees. There was no other choice. They had to run.

Already, the Supreme Authority's sporadic arrow launches at the two Earthlings were landing even or just a little ahead of them.

Damn! Michel thought to himself as he had to slow more and more, not to leave his pitifully whimpering wife behind. *Damned beyond damned! How can their Supreme Pain in the Royal Ass keep up such a rapid pace* at the same time he's firing off his f-n arrows?! How does he do that, especially with his insanely oversized set of antlers that his henchmen have to hold up like marionettes on a string?! Wait! That's it! There must be something besides those wheeled ladders! He must be getting pushed along on his own, low-lying wheeled platform! No damned wonder, then!

Whizz!

That latest arrow, Man, too damned close! One good thing anyhow, their f-n' damned ruler has what must be the worst damned aim...

Whizz!

...in the whole f-n' galaxy! He's like those bad guys in the action adventure movies! They can never get off even one good shot at the escaping good guys! Twenty of them can fire away with their damned machine guns, and still completely miss their targets!

Whizz!

Damn! But this is no f-n movie! The closer they get, the more likely-

"Michel!" wailed Prissy. Her right foot wedged stuck in a burrow hole, and sent her sprawled out on the ground in an ankle-twisting motion.

"No! NO!!" Michel DeFarge cried tearfully. He spun around and reversed course to his fallen wife. He reached her just a minute before Dek-Fook-Tek's hunting entourage did.

Earthling and Tictoctickians alike were too focused on their immediate circumstances to fully process a growing darkness from the moon eclipsing the sun.

Michel hurled himself atop Prissy. He braced there for an arrow to pierce his back. He could not imagine anything better than for such an arrow to strike through his rib cage and into his heart. Maybe that would minimize the duration of his pain before death. Also, somehow, could this sacrifice spare Prissy's life?

"Oh, Michel!" cried Prissy as DeFarge became cognizant of two things simultaneously. There was a distinct twang from Dek-Fook-tek's bow, and a trick of light where he thought he caught a flash of multiple colors.

The next thing Michel DeFarge felt was accompanied by bleated gasps from Dek-Fook-Tek's servant contingent. What Michel felt was far from what he expected to feel with an arrow into his back at such close range. Rather than extreme shooting pain well beyond anything he had ever experienced before, he was reminded of something from childhood. There was the sensation of a water balloon thrown at him by a playmate, when that balloon splattered against his leg. Michel DeFarge reached his right hand behind him as even Dek-Fook-Tek produced a baa of puzzlement. That is when DeFarge touched something moist. *Well, here we go*, he told himself. *This is going to be blood, tons of my blood. The arrow must have struck... I've read about some guy shot in the head who didn't feel a thing because the bullet entered in just the right, damnably damned location.*

"Damn!" Michel couldn't help exclaiming. He saw his palm covered in something the consistency of water, colored variously purple and green. "What the f-k is this?! Have I been an alien my whole life, but I just never got around to cutting myself to check my blood?!?"

Michel DeFarge stood up from his yet-trembling, sobbing wife. She was clearly in far more pain from her sprained ankle than anything he was feeling, which was nothing. "So what the- Oh, hell, no!"

Dek-Fook-Tek had re-armed his bow, and was aiming for Michel's chest.

"Even *you* can't be that bad a shot!" Michel said as he lunged at the deer creature. But he made his move too late to prevent the Supreme Authority from releasing the arrow on its way, headed straight for his upper chest...

...where it transmogrified into more splattering liquid colored variously purple and green. The arrow struck entirely harmlessly. It didn't even penetrate the insulating cottony fibers Michel had glued onto himself with tree sap, let alone break his skin with even the most superficial scratch. Rather, the arrow burst harmlessly apart into said splattering liquid like a burst water balloon. Again, this was the only comparison Michel could think to make.

Dek-Fook-Tek and DeFarge looked into each other's eyes. Then they looked down at DeFarge's colorfully splotched, cottony-covered chest, then back up, then back down again.

By that time, Dek-Fook-Tek was having his handlers lower his antlers for a charge at Michel DeFarge's chest. He was intent on goring the Earthling.

Servants suddenly posted themselves either side of Michel, plus behind him as well. They blocked his getting out of the Supreme Authority's bull-charging way.

Didn't matter. Dek-Fook-Tek had used his bahvek to sharpen the forward-most prongs of his mighty antlers into needle points. However, those prongs were still unable to come any closer than a foot to DeFarge's chest before they met with invisible resistance. That resistance was cushiony yet firm, absolute in preventing Dek-Fook-Tek from reaching his grisly goal.

"Well bless you God in heaven!" cried Michel DeFarge. He shook his fists skyward although keeping his eyes peeled on Dek-Fook-Tek's enormous antlers.

Dek-Fook-Tek himself remained down on all fours. He was not yet willing to give up trying to impale the Earthling on his ultra-sharpened antler prongs.

The low platform where the Supreme Authority stood was wheeled backwards by its handlers. They worked in close coordination with the servants wheeling the ladders for the antler handlers. This was preparation for a second charge forward.

The renewed assault had the same result, despite efforts to accelerate the pace of the charge well beyond what it had been before. The Supreme Authority's outsized head growths couldn't push past some invisible barrier protecting Michel DeFarge, whose shock left him vulnerably immobilized.

"And forgive me every time I ever done used your name in cursing vain!" DeFarge continued from his previous cry of gratitude. "This is some motherfu- Whoops! I mean, I mean, it's a miracle plain and simple! That's all I meant to say!! Now it's time for the onward Christian Soldiers part, since the truth has been finally revealed whose side has righteousness in their corner!"

On these words, DeFarge lowered his fists Dek-Fook-Tek's way, and he ran forward to pounce on him...

to no good effect. His intended savagery was met by the same, cushiony-yet-firm barrier to violence that the deer creature's antlers met.

"Seize him!" brayed Dek-Fook-Tek at his servants, how his braying would have translated if a translator were available.

But seizing the Earthling proved impossible for the four servants who took it upon themselves to execute their

Supreme Authority's command. They also encountered the mysteriously resistant yet gentle counter-force.

"Well f- you anyway, creator of the universe!" cussed DeFarge. He fell backwards over his wife still cowering low to the ground. But far more consequentially where his cussing was concerned, he realized the source of the too-rapidly descending nightfall.

Tictoctic's largest moon was moving directly towards Tictoctic. It had already come so close, it not only completely blocked out the Cygnitaurus sun. It eclipsed most of the day-lit sky as well. "So this is how it goes! When a moon is about to crash into its associated planet, the damnably damned rules of physics are suspended!"

⸎⸎⸎⸎⸎

Captain Kwit-Nik collapsed in his seat at the navigation console. He wanted to convey the impression he had tried everything he could think to try. He had done all he could to reverse the moon's course from its collision trajectory towards Tictoctic, with the Fourth Celestial Breath somehow irresistibly towed along for the ride.

In actuality, the enormous flying saucer was impelling the lunar object on its apocalyptic way. Kwit-Nik only feigned panic in his search for a solution, followed by his not-so-feigned grim resignation to inevitable necessity, as he saw it.

The navigation bridge filled with bleating, brays and baas of grief and terror. But not one of Kwit-Nik's crew suspected him in the least responsible for what they feared was about to happen.

Kwit-Nik pondered his home planet in the panoramic view-screen.

Tictoctic was growing ever larger all around behind the crash-coursing moon.

Kwit-Nik prayed for forgiveness for having deigned to play God. He even wondered at how powerless, ironically, he felt to control the overwhelming impulse to do what he did. *At least,* he tried to console himself most darkly, *this should not go on for long after impact. Surely, a profusion of huge chunks of planet plus lunar soil will be ejected at high velocity from the center of impact. There will be such a profusion of chunks that this saucer cannot avoid being struck by at least one of them. From that devastatingly annihilating force, death will come quickly.*

At this bleakest moment for Kwit-Nik, he noticed something exceedingly odd. It even started occurring to his crew, silencing them from their cries of anguish at least temporarily. Somehow, saucer and moon both had completely stalled out from their steady, downward descent. They got stuck with the moon's leading edge not more than a thousand miles away from the outermost reaches of the Tictoctickian atmosphere.

Moments thereafter, something amazingly hopeful happened, where the deer creatures aboard the Fourth Celestial Breath were concerned. Slowly yet perceptibly, the concentric encircling of the moon by Tictoctic shrunk more and more. The planet was on its way back to being totally eclipsed by the moon.

Of course, the saucer was situated the other side of the moon from Tictoctic. It had been impelling the moon towards Tictoctic by force of like magnetic charges on an epic scale.

"Great Supreme Spirit of the universe!" exclaimed Lieutenant Weekwok in carelessly blasphemous, joyful defiance of the general credo. No entity was ever supposed to receive more or even equal praise, when compared to the accolades accorded Dek-Fook-Tek. But so much for that! "It is a miracle! The moon and our Celestial Breath are lifting away together from Tictoctic!"

It was true. Suppose there were creatures on a spaceship located far to the side of both the planet Tictoctic and its moon. They would have seen the moon return to its orbit at a gentle pace.

Not the slightest turbulence was experienced aboard the Fourth Celestial Breath.

Meanwhile, the planet Tictoctic continued unperturbed on its elliptical path around the Cygnitaurus sun.

Captain Kwit-Nik flew the Fourth Celestial Breath out from behind the moon's dark side. He got there just in time to witness something even more amazing.

A rainbow was arcing out of the vacuum of space, the vacuum that contained too few water molecules for sunlight to create multi-color refractions. And yet Kwit-Nik guesstimated that rainbow was hundreds of lek-leks wide.

The rainbow's immense arc appeared to originate from somewhere well beyond lunar orbit. One end was headed towards Tictoctic. However, it was *not* headed for one of Dek-Fook-Tek's centers of power, such as his subarctic command center. Rather, that iridescent band of full-color spectrum was making a direct plunge amidst one of the planet's more wretched, impoverished neighborhoods.

That neighborhood was a place where some Tictoctickians were often all too willing to make a most deadly trade-off. They savored a few good meals, including rare cuts of oskynt meat priced way too high for the average citizen to afford. But in exchange for that pleasure, those Tictoctickians had to trot themselves into a slaughterhouse right afterwards. With their own flesh, they were required to help boost the empire's faltering food supply.

Other impoverished Tictoctickians supported the growing rebellion, instead, culinary pleasure be damned. However, discovery of this fact by the authorities always led to a trip to the slaughterhouse anyway, no oskynt meat allowed for a last supper.

The impossible rainbow planted its one end in the impoverished neighborhood. Soon as this happened, Captain Kwit-Nik saw the rainbow's other end shrink rapidly down to that same location from deep space. Then the entire phenomenon shut off with the instantaneity of a lamplight being extinguished. This led Kwit-Nik to suspect what a radar review confirmed.

An unknown something solid had landed on Tictoctic.

⊷⊶⊷⊶⊷⊶⊷

At the outer edge of Earth's solar system, Earthlings as well as Tictoctickians were bracing for fatal impact. They had sent all manner of ultra-advanced, ultra-destructive weaponry headed each other's way.

An enormous, impossible rainbow was the last thing anyone expected. This enigmatic phenomenon arrived with the unexpected rapidity of a lamplight switched on from a concealed location.

More impossibly still, the expected cataclysmic affects from the ultra-advanced weaponry did not occur.

Helena and company looked on in disbelief aboard the Smoke and Mirrors, from their embrace of loved ones. They looked on with as much disbelief as Earthlings aboard the other two cylindrical starships looked on from no one's embrace.

Didn't matter whether it was laser cannon-fire, the so-called tapeworms, or the so-called pilot fish. Everything deployed by the militarized Earthling starships appeared to splatter harmlessly against the five battle saucers. Everything stained those extraterrestrial vessels in a kaleidoscope of colors while their outer hulls continued to spin around, totally unaffected.

"Oooo," oooed Chig-cher. His tentacle arms were entangled in Chwerp-chee's while watching on a monitor in the children's playroom. "Fire that laser cannon my way! I have the perfect extra-long-sleeve shirt for it!"

The targeted magnetic pulse-beams from the battle saucers did no better. Tictoctickian deer creatures looked on helplessly as those pulse-beams likewise splattered harmlessly against the Obama, the Eisenhower and the Smoke and Mirrors.

Commander Ak-keek-teek's navigation officer had already charted the impossible rainbow to be on a "niki-nik" line for "Akt." Wherever it was headed, though, Ak-keek-teek convinced himself its origin must have been Tictoctic's solar system. "Baa, of course," he bleated tearfully. He felt truly moved by his fanciful imagining, though his absurdly wide buck-tooth grin dawned anew just the same. "Dek-Fook-Tek's Celestial Breath, somehow it has projected from the Supreme Authority himself! It has projected all the way here to protect us! My loyal officers, we are thereby made invulnerable to the most brutish assaults these savages from Akt might instinctively attempt!!" Ak-keek-teek's succeeding thought he decided he'd better keep to himself. Nevertheless, it made his grin become even wider, even more expansive, were that possible. *Wait, what has really happened here has nothing to do with Dek-Fook-Tek! But it does have everything to do with the deep spirit of our home planet! Clearly, that spirit is expressing profound awareness of the supreme role I, not that false prophet Dek-Fook-Tek, must play in our civilization's exceptional future! Our exceptionalism! With that awareness goes an obligation to protect my very being at all costs! Yes! It is finally coming into bahvek-sharpened focus, my most hallowed role in the grand scheme of things!*

The commander may have enjoyed wallowing in thoughts of his immortally invulnerable role in his fellow beings' future fortune. However, a few of his officers were thinking something else that seemed so obvious. And yet, not a one of them could screw up the courage for calling it to the commander's attention. Namely, suppose such protection of their well-being really was projected there from Tictoctic several light-years away. Why did it also most obviously accrue for those savage beasts from "Akt"? Why were their spacefaring exoskeletons spared the destructive force of targeted magnetic pulse-beams?

Commander Ak-keek-teek's musings couldn't keep him from finally wondering about that, himself. But his ability to rationalize was fierce. And his collective audience, tied together by a multiple-split view-screen, wouldn't have to wait long for him to share the delusional results of that ability. "Of course!" the commander tongue-clicked with a chuckle. "The protective intervention of this true Celestial Breath could only narrow its focus so much, on its long trip here from Tictoctic. We could not expect it to save us from destruction without also saving those savages from destruction as well. But now that it is here, now that its rainbow mantle spreads high above our heads, now is the time to fire at the Akt beasts again! Certainly at such close range, this divine force's focus will prove plenty narrow enough! Certainly it will be able to discriminate most easily between who is to be saved, and who should be left to the fate of all other dumb beasts akin to the oskynt!"

"None of this can be what it seems!" Professor Dauntilus Skepticus was meanwhile declaring on the navigation bridge of the Smoke and Mirrors. He stabbed his right forefinger defiantly high. And he began his pronouncement before Professor Timothy Aquinas could insert his far-more-timid assessment of the situation. Timothy's assessment was to the effect of their having just experienced a marvelously mysterious phenomenon, with perhaps even more marvelous implications.

"Employing Occam's Razor," went on Skepticus, "there is one hypothesis, and one hypothesis alone, we simply must embrace as the reigning hypothesis! The burden of proof is borne most heavily upon the shoulders of those who would dare doubt it! To that end, we have certain facts to consider! We have the bunching together of so many interstellar spacecraft, actively employing two different routes towards cheating the speed of light. There are the hostiles' saucers with their mirrors spinning. And then there are our vehicles bouncing the photons about in electromagnetically charged mirror mazes, configured to take the shapes of either tulip petals or rose petals. Clearly, the most suitable hypothesis is this: The confluence of so much disruption of normal light-speed has created an eddy in the flow of space-time physics! And within that eddy, other violations of the normal are happening to poorly understood effect!"

Buddy Leung wanted to ask Professor Skepticus a question. Just how far out and away from the "bunching together" of starships could this belligerently presumed "eddy" of his go? The impossible rainbow appeared to be stretching, arcing off hundreds of billions of miles in both directions. Buddy thought this aspect to the mysterious phenomenon posed a challenge for the professor's hypothesis. However, he had to make a far higher priority of what the other people on the navigation bridge were already noticing. "Captain," he said, "to belabor the obvious, it does look like the Tictoctickians are recharging their targeted magnetic pulse-beams!"

Helena Taylor retightened her hold on husband Chris's hand clasping her shoulder. She anxiously contemplated neon-blue rings of light glowing brightly around the rims of all five flying saucers. "Apparently, they think whatever happened to defang their first beams won't repeat for their second attack," Taylor said. "Oh-oh, here we go!" she added.

Bright red spheres of light were ballooning out from laser cannon launch apertures. Those apertures had been built into the "asparagus stalk" hulls of the battleships Obama and Eisenhower.

Moreover, scout saucers were swarming from the Tictoctickian mother ships. They were obviously set on engaging with the fighter pods that issued again from the Obama and the Eisenhower. But who knew what manner of missile the scout saucers might fire directly at the Earthlings' militarized starships? Especially given the new wave of tapeworms and pilot fish unleashed from those starships' asparagus-stalk hulls, in addition to the new wave of laser cannonballs?

"A second stab with the laser cannons does indeed make sense!" Professor Skepticus snorted to Captain Entroper's nodded approval. Entroper's image had popped up anew on the panoramic view-screen of the Smoke and Mirrors. She could be spotted in an embedded video frame on the lower left-hand corner of the screen. "This space-time eddy in violation of the laws of physics," Skepticus continued, "for all we know it is as transient, as fleeting as a double rainbow! Or any other natural phenomenon that cannot sustain itself for too very long! Not to mention subatomic particles that atom colliders can only keep revealed for one thousandth of a millisecond!"

Great! Chris thought to himself. *We're back to the precipice of getting ourselves annihilated! With all our prior effort, all our prior mind-blowing adventures for naught!*

But no. The result was the same as before. Didn't matter if they were laser cannonballs, targeted magnetic pulse-beams, tape worms, pilot fish, or whatever-that-was the scout saucers were firing. Every last one splattered colorfully and harmlessly, whether against the hulls of the saucers, the scout saucers, the cylindrical starships or the fighter pods. Not even the least turbulence, the least noticeable shudder was produced in any of the space-faring vessels. Instead, the lot of them was left more kaleidoscopically colored than ever.

Perplexity experienced by Earthlings and Tictoctickians alike became further compounded. On their respective view-screens, they saw what looked like rivulets of multi-colored water streaming across exterior cam lens. Chris recalled watching television back home on Earth, when traffic cameras were hit by sideways-blown rain.

"What makes absolutely no sense to me, Captain," offered up Kevin Smith-Park, "is how there could be even one drop of liquid out there. Let alone something that looks so remarkably like water! Deep space temps aren't that far off from absolute zero! And why is that stuff streaming any direction at all? Where is the 'up' and 'down' out here?"

"Remember, Officer," Skepticus raised a cautionary forefinger again. "The eddy I described pushes conventional physics against the general flow, as it were."

"There's a potential problem with your conjecture, Professor." When Buddy Leung inserted himself, he provoked an indignant look on Skepticus's face. It couldn't have been more indignant, Ali Magabu thought, had Effy torched his pants anew.

Skepticus's mouth puckered up, Chris mused, as though he inadvertently swallowed whole an especially sour lemon.

"We are detecting a solid object associated with the rainbow," went on Leung. "Our sensors suggest the rainbow itself is hopping from place to place, skipping millions of miles of space in between. Whoever or whatever it is, their trajectory will take them directly Earthward. Captain, if I am not mistaken, this is the same UFO we noticed doing equally impossible right-angle turns not so long ago. As you know, it's been haunting us periodically with its distant presence and bizarre maneuvers, ever since our very first mission!"

"Well there you go, then!" Professor Skepticus heartily slapped the armrests of his chair. "What one starship alone does, tweaking photon behavior, is enough to produce these chimeras!"

Meanwhile back over aboard the Sixth Celestial Breath, Commander Ak-keek-teek was also slapping his armrests. But fueled by his anger and frustration, he was slapping them so hard with his articulated cloven hoof-hands, they broke.

That gave him an idea. "Baa," he baaed with the newest dawning of his buck-tooth grin. He retrieved a long, slender splinter of busted-apart armrest from the floor. "It is so obvious," he tongue-clicked, whilst waving the splinter about like it was an instruction pointer. "The universal spirit in our favor cannot spare us from the worst those savage beasts might throw our way. That is, not without also sparing those savage beasts, themselves. However, a collision of one of our saucer rims into the side of one of their awkwardly designed exoskeleton tubes: That should get the job done. Baa! Even better! Even better!" The commander rose out of his seat onto his hind limbs. He stood tall, and held high the retrieved armrest splinter as though it were his sword for combat. "It should have occurred to me far sooner than this! Of course! Had we been allowed to succeed, that would have been no good! Our pulse-beam pulverization of their spacecraft would most likely have rendered the other-world beasts' flesh charred inedible! But, imagine collisions against their vessels, one saucer rim spinning in from one direction and another saucer rim spinning in from the opposite direction. That ought to neatly sever in two those instinctively wrought exoskeleton shells! Yes!" Commander Ak-keek-teek literally, most sloppily drooled. "That ought to split the shells wide open! Then the bulk of their flesh might be promptly, most efficiently freeze-dried by the absolute cold of deep space! Baa!"

"Such display of wisdom, it is as though Dek-Fook-Tek himself were in our very presence!" Lieutenant Kweest-Kweem stood from his own seat to make a low, sweeping gesture the commander's direction.

Back aboard both the Obama and the Eisenhower, Professor Skepticus's take on the situation had the command officers convinced the best move for the time being was no move. In fact, they hoped the entire Tictoctickian saucer fleet would suddenly make a run for it, even if they were to make that run continuing towards Earth. The Obama and Eisenhower would lag behind. As a result, the two different configurations of starships would once more find themselves at an astronomic distance away from one another. Physics normality would resume, hopefully. Thereby could a catastrophically damaging attack on the Tictoctickians be inflicted, via remote delivery of laser cannonballs. Such a delivery had already been successfully attempted months ago in the Callaway X Centra system. The only reason the target wasn't destroyed back then was that Buddy Leung maneuvered it far, far away mere seconds before the cannonball's arrival.

"That slimmer starship, the one with fewer bulges, is lagging behind the other two." Commander Ak-keek-teek pointed with his armrest splinter towards the Smoke and Mirrors, as seen on the view-screen of the Sixth Celestial Breath. "It's the one that bears an antler-butting resemblance to the exoskeleton we destroyed back near Tictoctic. I can feel it is comparable to the sicklier, weaker oskynt that used to fall far behind the rest of their herd. They were unable to keep up in hunting days of old, and now this other-world starship is also unable to keep up! We know for a fact it is the one of their vessels that was not firing ball lightning. Nor was it deploying those egg-shaped mini-vessels similar to a niki-nik pest infestation. Captain Rek-mek-a-nek, Captain Keek-konk, I hereby order your Fifth and Seventh Celestial Breaths, respectively, into fierce action! They will conduct the pincer movement on the mid-section of the other-world vessel we see lagging behind the other two. They will conduct that movement in the manner exactly as I have described it!"

"It will be an honor, Commander," nodded Captain Keek-konk of the Seventh Celestial Breath. Actually, he fretted over the danger from such an intentional collision of the rim of his saucer with the hull of the other-world exoskeleton. Might not that collision inflict significant damage on the saucer itself? But demonstrating his typical timidity, Captain Keek-konk said nothing to challenge the commander's judgment. Rather, he expressed his worry through more foaming at his mouth. But he did determine he would discuss a possibility with Captain Rek-mek-a-nek. Couldn't they keep their collision with the other-world spacecraft on the slow side, and still be following Commander Ak-keek-teek's orders to the letter?

Captain Keek-konk also tried to allay his fears with a recollection from basic physics. When one object hits another, the destructive energy from the object doing the hitting mostly transfers to the object hit. The hitter is left relatively unscathed. Hopefully.

"What are those two saucers doing, Captain?" Officer Kevin Smith-Park was anxiously asking Helena Taylor only moments later.

Their minds have proven easily readable on this matter, intervened Oodle-Noodle telepathically. *They are going to see whether they have any better success, ramming one of your Earthling starships rather than firing upon it. And they have selected the Smoke and Mirrors, which they perceive as being more defenseless. Try whatever evasive maneuvers you want, Captain, but I wouldn't worry.*

"*You* wouldn't worry, Oodle-Noodle; not so easy for the rest of us," responded Helena gripping her armrests tightly in lieu of Chris's hands. "Yoon-hee, I see two of them circling to try to get either side of us; if we can zip-"

"Not enough time, Helena!" Yoon-hee shrieked in panic. "The saucers have already come too close! They're messing up the photon acceleration! Even though their total amount of gravity is miniscule, we might as well be trying to achieve lift-off from the Earth's surface!"

In renewed horror, the Earthlings watched split-screen views of the two flying saucers drawing nearer and nearer. That horror was only tempered by the absurdly ineffectual, colorful splattering of more laser cannon fire against their spinning outer shells. Obviously, that cannon fire was a desperation move from the Obama and the Eisenhower trying to protect the Smoke and Mirrors.

"You're really certain about this, Oodle-Noodle?!?!" Helena shouted. Her eyes grew bigger and bigger.

The saucers were rapidly closing in from opposite directions on the mid-section of the Smoke and Mirrors. Panoramic views bore this out to cringing effect for everyone watching from the cylindrical starship's navigation bridge. Even Oodle-Noodle's bark wrinkled more than usual, and she couldn't quite bring herself to satisfy Helena Taylor's quest for comforting assurance. This was the case, despite only moments ago having telepathed that she wouldn't worry.

If the tree creatures' previously hopeful expectations turned out to be misplaced, they would share the same fate of everyone else traveling alongside them. There would be a force of impact as they had never experienced before…and they would surely perish before that experience could last for too very long. In moments, the extremely cold vacuum of deep space would suck out the air. Quite possibly, that vacuum would also suck out the Earthlings, the Chonorans, the Oombians, one lone Fafaman, and that Fafaman's half-Fafaman, half-Earthling baby daughter. But whether they were sucked out of the Smoke and Mirrors or not would make no difference. Every last one of them would flash-freeze like those corpses seen floating near Chonora.

Instead of such a horrific conclusion to their lives, however, everyone aboard the unarmed starship experienced a slight jolt. Chris couldn't help finding it far gentler than a jolt seventeen years earlier. He and daughter Shelly knocked bumper cars into one another at a beachside amusement park.

"Again, captains!" Commander Ak-keek-teek brayed at the top of his lungs aboard the Sixth Celestial Breath. "That was not nearly hard enough! Your saucers looked like two sleepy oskynt trying to nudge a third oskynt awake! Do it again faster! Harder!"

From what Helena could make out on the Smoke and Mirrors view-screen, the two flying saucers came spinning back in at a significantly higher velocity than before. They might as well have been two behemoth buzz-saws.

Meanwhile, the battle-equipped starships Obama and Eisenhower, as well as their deployed fighter pods, didn't hold back. They unloaded a significantly larger quantity of laser cannonballs at the saucers than the first time.

Regarding the end result of the extraterrestrial deer creatures' new assault, Oodle-Noodle and Wafoodle-boodle's confidence had resurged. So they fearlessly strove to assure every adult aboard the Smoke and Mirrors that the new assault should prove no less innocuous than the first assault.

That did turn out to be the case; everyone aboard the Smoke and Mirrors experienced merely another minor jolt.

For the second time, saucers under Ak-keek-teek's command had failed to slice through the other-world exoskeleton. His consequent frustration might have launched him into an unhinged, hind-limb-kicking rage. However, his gawking fascination overwhelmed him. "Our guardian rainbow, officers," he softly baaed. "See how the rainbow's rear end, what must have originated on Tictoctic, has contracted all the way past us? Obviously headed for Akt?! Of course!" Commander Ak-keek-teek exclaimed. "The message is clear! We waste our time with the meat potential freighted by these inferiorly designed space-worthy exoskeletons! The real herds for ridding our people's food shortage, forever, await our cattle-driving on Akt! We are bid to follow where the rainbow arcs! Off we go, then, on the rainbow's path!"

The Tictoctickian scout saucers retreated into the underbellies of their respective mother ships. They did so with a rapidity Chris would have likened to flies dodging a fly swatter. And no sooner was that retreat concluded than the five Celestial Breaths zoomed off in the general direction of the brightest star in the firmament. It was the star known on Earth as the sun.

Hi-fives and applause spread around the navigation bridges of the Obama and the Eisenhower.

Oodle-Noodle and Wafoodle-boodle, neither one could help shaking her head disdainfully. Their mind-reading confirmed what Captain Taylor and Buddy Leung suspected. The leadership of the other two starships seriously believed their second laser cannon assault was a success. They persisted with that belief, despite failing to put the least dent in any of the combat saucers. Captain Entroper and company actually convinced themselves the enigmatically color-splattering results scared off the extraterrestrials. And they tried not to let it matter that when Commander Ak-keek-teek and company fled, they fled on their original course set for Earth.

Helena had no doubt what Captain Entroper aboard the Obama was making of the situation. But just in case,

Entroper soon enough brought her bleached-white, mop-topped visage up close and personal in her navigation bridge's camcorder lens. "Captain Taylor!" she barked. "You might still inadvisedly join your too-naïve tree creature associates in disdaining the value, indeed the moral imperative, of military force! Mark this well, however: *Our* munitions specialist, *our* physicist, they both confirm what Professor Skepticus on board with you so soundly reasoned from the available data. What we have just experienced was not some hocus-pocus, kumba-yah moment arranged for those demonic beings from Tictoctic as well as for ourselves. Rather, it was a by-product, an eddy in the reality stream as Skepticus so poetically described. It was a by-product of the temporary suspension of the known laws of physics. This phenomenon was precipitated by the concentration of so much technology so close together, actively engaged in mutating the otherwise standard velocity behavior of light! But just like eddies in a stream often do, this one was rapidly eroding away, as evidenced by the dramatic diminishment of that overarching rainbow. We cannot know for sure. However, the extraterrestrials' precipitous abandonment of their efforts to slice your starship in two would suggest our laser cannon barrages were starting to take effect! Which also means that whether you noticed it or not, their ramrodding of your hull with their spinning saucer rims was about to succeed! You're welcome, Captain!"

Helena looked on silently. She was damned if she was going to offer any thanks.

Which unnerved Louisa Entroper enough, she finally broke off from her challenging stare into the cam lens. Instead, she bowed her head to say, "We'll be heading off soon. As though you cared, our plan is to maintain an ideal distance behind the Tictoctickian saucer fleet for remote laser cannonball and piggyback drone delivery. The temporary suspension of physics has most likely completely faded away by now, and that rainbow along with it. We are optimistic we will succeed in dispatching every last one of those infernal flying saucers in time to save the Earth. When that happens, Captain, just think on the crucial role played by bombs and other weaponry you sought to treat as nothing more than colorful fireworks! It will be bombs and other weaponry that will have allowed our civilization to go on fulfilling the promise of the good things we want for it. In the real world, Captain, the destruction of evil will have won the day!"

Thunderous applause could be made out erupting in response to Entroper's assertion her end of the transmission.

On Helena Taylor's end, Oodle-Noodle was thinking to herself, *No, Louisa Entroper. You seek vindication for having trusted the reasoning which led to the destruction of Fafama. Your conscience well knows such trust was in vain. Soon enough, you will learn the full value of the peaceful mission to resurrect Fafama. You will learn what that mission has accomplished atop the effort to complete a cycle by passing along an engraved pendant to its intended. You will learn that those were the two actions which tipped the balance for the life-saving intervention. Not violence.*

While Oodle-Noodle preoccupied herself with these thoughts, her forever companion Wafoodle-Boodle was sympathetically contemplating a most downcast-looking Professor Skepticus. He was downcast-looking despite the praise Captain Entroper had heaped upon him. *The way his hands are clasped together in his lap, he almost looks like he is praying. Perhaps he is praying, for the universe to offer up revelatory confirmation of its ultimate meaninglessness. Clearly, what happened with that rainbow and its attendant violation of so many known laws of physics has rattled him to his core. His protestations with his eddy analogy are beside the point. I am loathe to go mind-reading the places inside his head to where common decency forbids my entrance. And yet, the study of those peaks and valleys of his mental landscape within my moral purview makes one thing perfectly clear. Professor Skepticus is suffering from a crisis of faith in his lack of faith!*

⟡ ⟡ ⟡

With one, final lurch, Flamboyo Sanchez sent Engeling's small, chrome-plated handgun flying from his hand. The weapon spun end over end into one corner of the hijacked shuttle pod's cockpit. This happened during the pod's deceleration around to the dark side of Earth's moon.

Both men faced quite the dilemma.

Flamboyo wondered how quickly he could detour past Engeling to glom on to the handgun, and then use it for disabling the man. Could he accomplish the first part fast enough? Or would his attention return to Engeling too late? Would Engeling have already locked the shuttle pod into autopilot? So that all too soon, it would be shoving the moon out of orbit onto a crash course headed for Earth?

For Engeling, the mirror concern was how he could achieve his world-ending goal without Flamboyo stopping him. Suppose Flamboyo did get off a shot at him prior to completion of his nihilistic deed: If the wound was not fatal, did Engeling have the stamina to complete his task before he succumbed to pain? He recalled how he was able to continue functioning after a bull shark bit off his foot. That grotesque fact lent him encouragement, but not enough to let go his grip on Flamboyo.

Flamboyo and Morel were side by side at the shuttle pod's control console, clutching one another's arms. They shifted their attention back and forth, back and forth between themselves and Engeling's pistol wedged into the ceiling corner. From their struggle, both men were heaving their inhales and exhales nearly to the point of hyperventilation.

Thanks to near-zero gravity, not too many more seconds elapsed before the pistol resumed its lazy, leisurely somersault. It drifted back away from the corner to where the force of Flamboyo's lunge first sent it.

Flamboyo lingered attention a moment too long upon the shiny weapon, marveling at how it remained suspended in mid-air. His distractedness allowed Engeling to extricate himself from his clutches, and grab firm hold of the underside of the control console.

The men's struggle resumed while the pitch black of the moon's dark side grew ever larger as seen through the cockpit dome. More and more stars got blocked from view.

Flamboyo pulled and pulled at Engeling's wrists, trying to yank him away from the console again.

Engeling tried bowing his head down close to the console, to use his tongue and nose for pushing buttons and turning knobs. But his efforts were in vain.

When the handgun floated directly overhead, Señor Flamboyo Sanchez caught a glimmer of its chrome glint out the corner of his eye. He abruptly let go of Engeling, and surged from his chair to make a successful grab. But that is not where this motion ended. Flamboyo knew he had no time to hesitate, no time to recalibrate. Not if he were to succeed. In one continuous flow, he went from securing the handgun to latching onto its trigger, aiming at Engeling's legs, and firing.

The resultant flash, together with the ear-drum-jarring report, stunned Engeling. It so stunned him that he reflexively flailed his arms. As a result, his right arm not only dislodged the small pistol from Flamboyo's grasp. It sent the weapon with knockout force against Flamboyo's temple.

Flamboyo Sanchez's last memory before he slipped into unconsciousness was of Engeling letting out a piercing cackle.

When Flamboyo regained consciousness, he found himself tightly bound to a passenger seat. His mouth was sealed shut by spacewalk repair duct tape, which he well knew would tear off his skin if anyone tried to remove it.

"Ah, you are just in time! First, I should like you to know my appreciation for your kindness. You aimed at my legs rather than, say, my face, didn't you? As it turns out, you shot the leg that is my artificial prosthetic. It's the result of my little adventure with a bull shark to convince everyone I committed suicide. Anyhow, your attempt at humanely debilitating me has been fortuitously thwarted. So fortuitously, in fact, I can almost believe there is some divine plan afoot! That the Earth's premature demise was meant to happen! That the universe does indeed care! It cares enough to stop our so-called civilization from spreading such arrogantly concocted horrors any further throughout our corner of the galaxy than it already has! I can *almost* believe that! But not quite!

"My original plan would have spared you witnessing the end result of our labors. But since you tried so hard to stop me, I have decided you should *not* be spared, any more than I should spare myself!! Your death should *not* happen, not prior to the main event! After the main event, we will be waiting for giant chunks of moon and Earth to smash this shuttle pod apart. During that time, maybe you will be able to explain something to me. Maybe you will be able to explain how there can really be any rhyme or reason to the universe! How can that be, when someone like myself can even dream of committing this ultimate in horrendous acts? Let alone try to carry through with it, and find that he can succeed?! Why doesn't God or whatever stop me?!"

Engeling played his fingers across a few more keypads. Then he left the control console to climb back behind the shuttle pod's cockpit, and sit beside Flamboyo. "Oh, no," he shook his head when he realized Señor Sanchez was tightly closing his profusely watering eyes. "We will have none of that," Engeling explained as he applied tape to Flamboyo's eyelids. The madman was determined to hold them pried open, Flamboyo's will be damned.

Thousands of miles beneath the shuttle pod, on the moon's surface, the interior of one crater lit up. It glowed with the intensifying neon blue of a magnetic charging device. In a cascading effect, that device was doing something to the lunar surface's dark side. It was giving every last particle of ferromagnetic material that permeated it a positive polarity...

...and positive happened to be the same polarity the companion device was turning the shuttle pod.

"What's this you wish to tell me? Ahh," Engeling nodded. He affected a casual dawning realization, Flamboyo thought to himself all the more horrified. Under saner, more benign circumstances, they could have been sitting out on a veranda somewhere, sipping lemonade. The mad doctor would have just realized he'd forgotten to serve cheese and crackers to accompany the drinks. "How can you, indeed, share with me any astounding revelations that might have occurred to you?" Engeling asked. "After all, your mouth is sealed with tape, the removal of which would rip off a quarter-inch layer of your skin!"

Flamboyo Sanchez feared what Morel Engeling meant to do next. Flamboyo's pupils darted down towards his own mouth then back up to eye contact with Engeling, then down again and back up again. *Am I really going to have to suffer my lips being torn off by him before I die?*

"All right, enough of this!" On Flamboyo's next look up towards Engeling, Engeling grabbed his head. He forced Flamboyo to face forward, through the shuttle pod's cockpit dome. He wanted to make absolutely certain that Flamboyo would see the spectacle presumed about to unfold. "Watch! You must watch!"

Flamboyo's eyes were stingy and watery from their remaining taped open against his will. But through his tears he nevertheless thought he observed rainbow colors across the moon's dark side. They were consuming the blue glow emitted by the polarizing device set down within one of the lunar craters.

"What *is* that?!" Engeling howled, panic-stricken. He looked back and forth between Flamboyo and the unexpected light show. It was as though he might find some way his bound-up companion was responsible. "NO!" he shook his head in furious denial. "This isn't anything special, really! This must be- Yes, that's it: a trick of light from what we are attempting here, Señor Sanchez! It's an unpredicted but not necessarily surprising result, doubtless emerging from such a novel physics application! Of course!" he laughed nervously.

Tingling sensations broke out like goose pimples around Flamboyo's mouth, and across the parts of his body where he was bound to his seat. They were quickly succeeded by the space-age duct tape floating harmlessly away from him in the near-zero gravity.

In a rage, Engeling unbuckled himself to bolt from his own seat back up to the control console. "What is going wrong?!?!? How can this be?!?!?! Nothing is out of place!!! There are no under-performing magnetizing parameters!!! NOOO!!!!" Engeling screamed. When he looked up from the control console, he realized what was happening, or at least one of the significant things that was happening.

The shuttle pod was backing steadily away from the moon, rather than pushing the moon out of its orbit.

As more and more of outer space came back into view, Flamboyo rose from where he had been originally bound. He wanted a better look at Earth. His magnet boots, of course, compensated for the weightlessness. They kept his propulsion out of his seat from propelling him to hit his head on the ceiling...assuming such self-injury were still possible. Anyway, what he saw filled him with joy at the same time another aspect of his being judged that he was experiencing irrational hope.

An unfathomably mysterious, seemingly impossible rainbow was arcing on a trajectory headed directly towards Earth.

From gawking at the rapidly unfolding spectacle, Flamboyo grew slowly aware, not so hopefully, of his having regained Engeling's attention.

Sure enough.

Flamboyo looked to his side just in time to see Engeling take aim at him with the palm-sized, chrome-plated handgun.

Engeling fired.

Strange beyond strange describes what succeeded the yellowish-orange flash from the handgun's muzzle. The bullet bursting from that flash appeared to travel at an extraordinarily slow speed. It travelled so slowly, Flamboyo Sanchez could even see it turning on its cylindrical axis as it progressed towards him. But Sanchez found he could not take advantage of the bullet's unbelievably halting advance, to dodge it. He might as well have found himself trapped inside a typical action adventure movie. For such movies, the most violent scenes often played out in slow motion. This gave the audience plenty of time to gruesomely contemplate bodies being torn apart, blood gushing from ripped-open arteries, split second by split second.

Flamboyo could hardly move. He might as well have been paralyzed immobile again by more duct tape from Engeling.

At long last the bullet made contact with Flamboyo's chest, just in front of where his heart was beating like crazy. But that is when something else wondrous happened. The bullet splattered there harmlessly. Somehow, it instantly metamorphosed into a liquid variously streaked orange, green, and violet.

Chapter 35

"This is Paul Berger, reporting from the lobby of the Space Station 2 Marriott Grand Hotel. As you can see behind me," he gestured, "upwards of three hundred people are crowding the panoramic windows. They are vying for a better view of an enormous flying saucer that could have sprung from some old, hackneyed science fiction story. It's one of five that have arranged themselves at five equidistant locations around the Earth, hovering stationary. They might as well be the five corners of a pentagon. In any event, not ten minutes ago President Carey reported, and I quote, 'These saucer-shaped spacecraft are known to be of extraterrestrial origin.' Not suspected, not some secret government experiment like our own first starship, but 'known.' I quote again, 'known to be of extraterrestrial origin.' Amal Mahfouz is with us in our New York newsroom some ten thousand miles down below. Amal, this is quite an astounding admission from the president, isn't it?"

"It is a most astounding admission, indeed, Paul. But we have to remember what else the president said. Yes, five saucer-shaped spacecraft of known extraterrestrial origin have indeed gone into a hovering formation around our Earth. And they are spaced equidistantly from one another. However, President Carey also noted there is a laser mesh protection system enrobing the planet. The flying saucers can try to descend towards the atmosphere, or send out smaller spacecraft with that same intent. But lots of luck; they should not be able to safely breach the laser mesh until and unless they are programmed with the access code. Otherwise, the laser mesh will unleash ball lightning cannonballs that can rip through diamond-hard material, and *I* quote, 'like a hot knife through warm butter.'"

"The president loves his folksy sayings, Amal. However, that particular one does get the message across that we are safe. Wait a minute."

There were sudden screams and shouts issuing from behind reporter Paul Berger. Multi-colored light flooded the already well-lit interior of the hotel. Berger spun around to shove forward through the throng for a better view.

"I don't know if you can hear me over the many exclamations, Amal. But I hope you can see what we're seeing from our drone cam!"

"Paul, would that be the same, immense rainbow spotted just a short while ago arcing past the moon?! Paul?!"

"There is no reason to panic, people! No reason to panic!" Paul Berger found himself unexpectedly consumed with trying to do crowd control.

"Mr. Berger! Mr. Berger!"

"QUIET, PEOPLE!!" screamed Paul, totally out-of-character. But he followed up softly, with what drew both laughter and calm. "I want to hear the question from someone with the wisdom and respect to address me as 'Mr. Berger.'"

"Thank you, Mr. Berger. President Carey assured us nothing could breach the laser mesh safely without the pass code. But the monster rainbow looks like it's made the trip far down into the atmosphere!"

"Well, I believe the president was talking about objects, solid objects. I am not sure that light in and of its self..."

"So how do we know it's not a secret weapon fired at the Earth by the aliens?!"

"THIS IS IT!!" hollered someone else.

A woman screamed at the top of her lungs. She could have just come across a bloody corpse in a murder mystery, Paul thought. She passed out, also the same as in many a murder mystery.

"Please listen, people!" Paul raised his voice again. "I don't think it helps matters to panic until we know there is something-"

"You're a reporter!" shouted yet someone else from amidst the crowd. "Answer this! Why won't they allow any of us to take a shuttle pod outta here back to Earth??"

Paul Berger hunched his shoulders and winced, in anticipation of the reaction he was likely to receive when he responded. "I don't think 'they,' whoever 'they' are, would want to take responsibility for such an action," he said. "You're talking about launching a spacecraft out of Space Station 2 in the presence of a flying saucer of indeterminate extraterrestrial origin and purpose. I for one certainly wouldn't want to risk doing that."

"So you're admitting it might be hostile?!?!"

Before this tense dialogue could continue any further, there was a new surge of gasps and panicky exclamations.

Seeming to materialize out of nowhere, an egg-shaped object slowed to a hover. It was shedding that ever-mysterious trail of sparkling photon "fairy dust" from the firefly donut it rode in from the solar system's outskirts. It stationed itself between the space station's spherical protective dome and the giant flying saucer. No sooner this, than it split open on the side facing the saucer. Then it fired a full barrage of laser cannonballs the extraterrestrial spacecraft's way, effectively at point-blank range. For all intents and purposes, those cannonballs constituted clusters of reddish-tinged ball lightning.

The barrage splattered harmlessly, kaleidoscopically colored, against the hull of the flying saucer.

The saucer's rim turned neon blue, charging up a magnetic pulse-beam for immediate retaliation.

When the pulse-beam finally issued from along the saucer's rim, nobody watching was surprised at the target. It made a direct strike on the source of the laser cannonball barrage. Differently from how other recent attempts at space vessel destruction had gone, however, this one succeeded. It burst the split-open, egg-shaped contraption completely apart. The result provided a dramatic yet eerily quiet fireworks display for the terrified audience in the hotel lobby of Space Station 2.

"Baa! Baa!" triumphantly brayed Commander Ak-keek-teek on the navigation bridge of the Sixth Celestial Breath. He was down on all fours to splinter to pieces even further the captain's chair, courtesy of his excitedly kicking hind legs. "The outcome of this particular confrontation establishes a most profound truth, once and for all! In case any doubt remained, the universe has rolled out its rainbow carpet to direct *our* conquest, on *our* side! Once more, the savage attack by other-world beasts has splattered harmlessly against our craft! But our defensive response has utterly destroyed the source of that attack!"

"Such deep understanding of how these events have unfolded, Commander," humbly bleated Lieutenant Kak-keeket at his side, "dare I even say it? Dek-Fook-Tek himself might as well have been here to guide us. For certain, he could not have contributed anything more useful. No, wait," the lieutenant hastened to go on, fearing he might have over-reached his calculated kowtowing to too blasphemous an extreme,

But he was cut off by Commander Ak-keek-teek with razor-sharp tongue-clicking which would have translated, "No, don't wait, Lieutenant! You have, I believe, put it just right!

"Baa," Ak-keek-teek continued, "look at all those ridiculously clothed beasts, crowding about that window! I am reminded of my youth! Various fathers would sometimes take me from my nurture center to one of the last remaining seafood restaurants! For our meals, we would choose among the crustaceans and fish such as the krakalak and the glooktakook. While we pointed at our selections, they crowded about one glass pane of their aquarium, to achieve a better view of their future consumers!" Commander Ak-keek-teek found himself moved to tongue-circling, lip-smacking contemplation, what another officer saw as almost lecherous. Suddenly, though, he snapped out of fantasizing one of the Earthlings unclothed and roasted. Instead, he brayed at his navigation officer, "Lieutenant Kwak-tak, launch an unoccupied, remote-controlled scout saucer on descent into the lower atmosphere! We will test whether these beasts have set up any planet-wide defense! They might have enrobed their Akt in the same laser mesh shield they enrobed the planet Koombt, inhabited by those nuisance mind-reading trees!"

Befuddlement flashed across the lieutenant's face. Why such a test? Especially given how well the military engagement went with the egg-shaped attack vehicle obviously deployed by the "Akt" beasts?

Noting his lieutenant's befuddlement, Ak-keek-teek promptly added, "As our confidence grows ever stronger, no doubt can remain that clearly, the universe is on our side. However, we must never become lax in our vigilance! We must assure the universe does not stray from its one true course! If the laser mesh shield is activated, I have every expectation it will only do more innocuous color-splattering against the scout saucer's hull. But I insist on verification! Pursuant to which, we will proceed into the atmosphere ourselves. We will make a niki-nik line for the location of most sacred import. Of course, I am talking about the rainbow's apparent destination!"

⁕ ⁜⁛⁜⁕ ⁜⁛⁜⁕ ⁜⁛⁜⁕

"This is Amal Mahfouz back at our news desk in New York. We have late-breaking developments possibly related to what we have previously been reporting. First, I want to assure our viewers. Yes, we are cutting away from Paul Berger in the lounge of the Marriott International aboard Space Station 2. But we wouldn't be doing that if we feared anyone there faced immediate peril. As far as we can tell, though, everybody aboard Space Station 2 remains safe.

"Let's recap the historic news before we get to those late-breaking developments. Five flying saucers of likely extraterrestrial origin are hovering equidistant from each other in a pentagonal arrangement around our planet. Again let me emphasize, the one saucer sitting close to Space Station 2 has shown no hostile intent, no hostile intent." Amal shook her head. "It has maybe even evidenced a certain curiosity.

"However, as we witnessed through Paul's head cam, there was a short skirmish. It took place after a mysterious, egg-shaped object suddenly materialized in between the space station and the saucer. The 'egg,'" Amal made quotation marks with her fingers, "opened fire on the saucer. In apparent response, the saucer emitted a blue beam at the 'egg,' and that blue beam destroyed it. We don't know if anyone was aboard the destroyed 'egg.' But there is already growing suspicion among physicists and warfare engineers who have studied the video. They believe the 'egg' was an unoccupied drone of indeterminate origin."

The "egg" was indeed an unmanned military drone, launched from the starship Eisenhower.

"Now about our other updates," Mahfouz continued. "We are receiving reports from virtually worldwide that have two themes. You might be hard-pressed to decide which theme is the more astonishing. On the one hand, there is something happening to the quarantine walls, no matter whether they are new or were erected fifteen years ago. They have suddenly become ineffectual. People are exiting the so-called no-zones in droves, including right here in New York City. And curiosity seekers from outside those zones are finding themselves free to wander into them, granted authorized approval or not.

"Then there is that other phenomenon, that other theme, inundating us with fantastical stories. Put simply, there has been a widespread inability by anybody to effectively commit acts of violence. One especially amazing incident is confirmed by several witnesses. Moreover, that incident was caught on video we will share with you once we can establish its authenticity.

"The incident began with an armed gang exiting the Philadelphia no-zone. They tried to confront police. Notice I said 'tried.' During the shootout that ensued, people on both sides were ducking behind cars and- We have received verification?" Amal held her right hand against her right ear, where she was just getting word. Behind her in the news studio, there was a flurry of activity, people rushing back and forth. In some cases, they were shouting frantically. "Okay," Amal added, "we're going to show you that video now."

The very jumpy film revealed a wide street, empty save for some cars and mini-vans parked on both sides. Also, there were pops, cracks, and rat-a-tat-tats from a variety of gunfire. As the gunfire continued, an occasional person could be espied popping up from behind a vehicle to take a shot.

Viewers quickly figured out who was who. The police and their squad vehicles were parked on the left. Gang members were entrenched on the right.

Sharper ears could make out signature noises of bullets penetrating the chassis of one or more vehicles. Sharper eyes could discern those bullets producing holes in police cars and civilian cars alike. As well, there were thin wreathes of smoke from discharged weapons.

The extraordinary became very clear, very quickly. It started with what looked like an inexplicable splatter of green paint on one gang member's face. That happened when he leaned out from behind a dark-burgundy mini-van.

So, are they firing paintballs? initially wondered many viewers.

As though to provide a response, a police officer's upper chest suddenly seemed splattered by purple paint. That's what he got for leaping up from behind the hood of his patrol car.

Forthwith, those aforementioned sharper eyes were able to spot curious specks decelerate to a brief hover in mid-air. They came to a hovering halt in front of police officers and gang members alike. To some viewers, the specks gave the appearance of clouds of gnats. But soon thereafter, they fell to the ground.

They were bullets.

"What the f-n' hell?!" grumbled one of several especially agitated viewers. "Has reality turned into some f-n' Bugs Bunny cartoon?! Bullets have been trained to roll over and play dead?!"

The most dramatically bizarre portion of the video was yet to come.

Bullets kept flying. People could be made out shouting variations on, "What the f-k is happening?!" One even laughed.

More and more projectiles hit cars and vans alike, until one found its mark in a mini-van's battery packs. Penetrating all the way through one of them, this particular bullet sparked the lithium crystals. As a result, the vehicle blew up, consumed entirely by towering flames. Not an unexpected development, given how the firefight had intensified.

But then many viewers realized three gang members were hiding behind the van. And that amazingly, not a one of them was even singed, when all of them ought to have been immolated by the flames. When they instinctively jumped out from behind the exploding vehicle, they were still of enough presence of combative mind to have not let go of their various weapons. Nevertheless, they left themselves open targets for the police.

The police proceeded to fire away with absolutely no harmful effect. This made screamingly obvious what the viewer could only suspect from earlier portions of the video. Gunfire could not harm any of them, whether police officers or gang members. More and more like paintball, or something out of a silly cartoon, the bullets splattered transmogrified into harmless colors. Or they halted in mid-air, and dropped harmlessly to the ground after a one-second hover.

Ever more astounding happenstances were to follow.

One gang member who leaped out from behind the inferno-blazing mini-van quickly realized he had made himself an easy target for the police officers. He saw signature bright flashes from those officers' discharging muzzles. The flashes were accompanied by shouts for the other scared-out-into-the-open gang members to drop their weapons and put their hands in the air.

Blinded by panic, the "gangstah" in question spun around and ran straight into the roaring, crackling fire. Too late he realized his adrenalin-rush-fueled error, and he tried to halt his hurtling forward. But he stumbled over a piece of rear mini-van bumper blown off in the explosion. And then he plunged headlong, disappearing down amidst the flames.

However, "Damn!" swore one television viewer. "Is he some kind of superhero?!"

The seemingly hapless fellow managed to stagger back away from his expected torching, his expected charring to a crisp, without a mark on him. There was not even a scrape on his knees where his fall ripped a hole in his blue jeans. It finally sank in how invulnerably unharmed he had emerged from a situation he would have reasonably expected to have ended his life. That's when he stretched his arms high in the air, his right hand still holding on tightly to his assault rifle. He turned around slowly, shouting triumphantly, "How do you like this, mothahf-ers?!?!"

A couple of police officers futilely unloaded their guns the celebrating man's way.

Meanwhile, other gang members tentatively tested the limits of the miraculous. They exposed their shoes to the mini-van's flaming, billowing-smoke mess that continued issuing from more explosively igniting lithium.

Some television viewers fancied those gang members could have been testing water before jumping into a swimming pool.

Bullets splattered harmlessly like more colored water against the triumphant "gangstah's" chest. Or they froze mid-flight to drop plink-plink-plink on the crumbled-apart asphalt road. This happy survivor who had unwittingly plunged head-first into an inferno didn't see what was coming next. He was too distracted to notice a drone the police were positioning overhead, to drop a small grenade.

No matter.

The explosion from the grenade gouged out a car-sized crater in the road. However, all it did to the human target was cover him in another, harmless, kaleidoscopic array of color.

The intent was not lost on the target, though, however innocuous the results where his well-being was concerned. With a most crazed look in his face, he brought down his assault weapon before him. He cut short his rejoicing, which had consisted of him raising that weapon to the heavens. Instead, he leveled it towards an officer who remained standing up vulnerably high from behind a squad car, stunned immobile. And he fired away...

...with the exact same, harmless results as what had been delivered his direction.

Chaos ensued in this persistently surprising video. Gang members ran in and out of the mini-van flames like children on a hot summer's day running in and out of a lawn sprinkler. Other gang members and police alike eschewed their parked vehicle protection to conduct the gun battle at point-blank range. It was as though, several viewers including Amal thought, not one of them could believe they could go on like this. Eventually, wouldn't one of the bullets break through to find its fatal mark? Else why continue firing?

When the infliction of violence was actually able to resume, the audience thought they knew what to expect. Namely, both sides of the conflict would retreat back behind their respective shelters to continue the battle.

But the strangely ineffectual shootout seemed to continue with no end in sight. It only went on for so long, though, before both sides tossed away their weapons. They ran at each other, fists and batons on the law enforcement side while a few gang members also brandished knives.

Fists, knives, batons, plus all the cussing and epithets either side could think to primal-scream in frustration, none of that mattered.

One gang member lunged at a police officer with his switchblade, on course to slit his throat. However, it hit something at once rubbery soft and steely resistant, yet totally invisible. The switchblade hit that wall well before its lethally sharp point could arrive anywhere near the gruesome goal. After retrying such a lunge with the same ineffective result, the gang member whirled around. He attempted the same such lunge where there was no-one to hurt. This time, he did not encounter the rubbery firm resistance. Moreover, the officer whose throat he tried to slit took advantage of his straying attention. The officer leaped at the gang member with the intent of pouncing on his back. Thereby would he force the switchblade out of the gang member's hand as the gang member fell forward face-first. The officer would strive to secure the switchblade, and even wield it against the gang member if deemed necessary. Again, though, pouncing proved no more effective than the fisticuffs and knives had proven. Assuming this would be the case, the switchblade bearer didn't worry about turning his back on the police officer in the first place. Pouncing, punching, stabbing: all such action was met with that same, enigmatically invisible resistance.

Many television viewers thought the limit had been reached. There couldn't possibly be happenings of an even more extraordinarily inexplicable nature for the video to reveal.

But the extraordinarily inexplicable was far from finished unreeling yet.

One by one, police officer and gang member alike gave up trying to inflict violence on the perceived foe. And one by one, they looked heavenwards at the rainbow arcing high overhead.

The rainbow's immensity could not be overstated. It covered nearly the entire sky viewable from between forbiddingly tall and bleak-looking hi-rise tenement buildings. The head cam revealed all of this for a transfixed worldwide audience.

A police officer and a gang member accidentally bumped into one another, so lost had they become in contemplation of the spectacle. That was the beginning. They looked down at one another, only to spontaneously, tearfully hug. Arm in arm, they resumed contemplation of the endlessly mysterious rainbow. It didn't take long before their fellow officers and gang members also went arm in arm.

People came pouring from the apartments, some crying, "Alleluia! It's a miracle!"

That was when the person with the head cam ran over to join them.

"Scenes like this one, they appear to be playing out all over the Earth." Amal Mahfouz, tears streaming down her cheeks, struggled to keep enough composure for continued reporting. She looked around at press releases dumped on her anchor desk from every which direction. After some consideration, she lifted one in her trembling hands to say, "Here's a story concerning the civil war in Somalia. It bled out of the quarantine zone into the safe zone. But then both sides were seen to have, and I quote, 'built a bonfire with their discarded arms. The bonfire is going off like a perpetual fireworks display while everyone is dancing in celebration.'"

⸎⸎⸎⸎⸎⸎⸎

Dancing in celebration was not quite what was happening back aboard the battle-equipped starship Barack Obama. The Obama was racing the Eisenhower on their return to Earth, with the unarmed Smoke and Mirrors bringing up the rear.

"Help us out here, Professor Skepticus." Captain Entroper aboard the Obama had Skepticus on view-screen from aboard the Smoke and Mirrors.

Both starships afforded clear views of the impossible, impossibly long rainbow steadily shrinking away, headed for Earth. What could not be seen was that it had already entered Earth's atmosphere.

"You called it, Professor," Entroper continued. "When two different light-speed-tampering technologies resume distant separation from one another, the more conventional laws of physics reassert their primacy. They are no longer so flagrantly violated. According to a firefly donut relay we've just received, the Tictoctickian saucer's magnetic pulse-beam did finally succeed. It destroyed our remote laser cannon delivery pod.

"However, there is a, shall we say permutation? Before the pod got hit, nothing good resulted from the fire power it unleashed on the saucer. The firefly cam picked up more splatters of what might as well have been water color paint against the saucer's hull. Those splatters were dripping off impossibly wet in the cold of space! What does this mean, Professor Skepticus?! In your best estimate, should we fear the enemy has something going for it that we do not?"

Nothing good resulted because the saucer wasn't destroyed, its deer creatures along with it? Captain Helena Taylor couldn't tell how much this thought was her own, and how much was telepathed by Oodle-Noodle. The two seemed to merge together. She could only cross her arms and shake her head in disgusted wonder.

Here, they had on hand the mastermind of mirror array, light-speed-cheating propulsion, Buddy Leung. He was fully available for Louisa Entroper to pick his brain. Yet she was acting like he didn't even exist, and the same for hyper-physics Professor Timothy Aquinas. Captain Entroper was eschewing their expertise in favor of Professor Skepticus, who still wasn't even able to come to realistic terms with the ephemeral dragon, Effy. Not to mention Effy's planet-sized counterpart, who had been keeping the starship's helpful company until the resurrection of Fafama reunited it with itself, essentially. No, Skepticus was continuing to insist that Effy was nothing more than some poorly understood nonliving phenomenon, despite growing evidence to the contrary.

"No, no, no," Professor Skepticus shook his head. He was reacting to Entroper's fear expressed from aboard the battleship Obama, that the "enemy" might be enjoying some distinct military advantage. "What I would glean from the evidence delivered by the firefly cam is this: The smaller the payload, the faster the temporary suspension of normal physics has worn off."

"Ah," nodded Secretary Spinner. He entered the picture beside Entroper on the video frame transmitting from the Obama to the starship Smoke and Mirrors. "Well can I hear an 'Alleluia'?" Spinner went on. "I think I've got it! Our remote delivery laser cannon orb was small enough to have quickly lost its invulnerability after the laws of physics reasserted themselves. However, the enemy's dang-blasted war saucer – and I'm happy to hear us all agreed to just plain-out term them the enemy, aren't you, Captain Taylor? That hellfire saucer is just so damned large, damnably damned large like Michel DeFarge would have said, heaven help him wherever he is at the moment! What I'm saying is, that large flying saucer is like a big block of ice that takes longer to melt than a little ice cube, correct?"

Perhaps the professor is correct, Captain, Ali Magabu made mind-readingly available for Oodle-Noodle or Wafoodle-boodle to telepath Helena Taylor. *But truly, there appears to me to be another possibility worthy of our consideration. It could have something to do with this "intervention" our Oombian friends are anticipating. Besides their relative sizes, there is a second significant difference between the remote delivery pod and the Tictoctickian saucer. It's a difference of far greater import, I should think. The pod was unoccupied. There was nobody aboard who would have been killed in its destruction. However, the saucer is most decidedly full of deer creature extraterrestrials!*

⊱ ⋆˚࠹˚⋆ ⋆˚࠹˚⋆ ⋆˚࠹˚⋆

Commander Ak-keek-teek looked on in confident anticipation.

Meanwhile, the people crowding the floor-to-ceiling windows in the lobby of the Space Station 2 Marriott International looked on in angst-ridden terror.

A remote-controlled scout saucer had issued from the underbelly of the Sixth Celestial Breath. It was making zigzag moves on descent towards Earth's atmosphere...and the enveloping laser mesh shield.

Sure enough and despite zigzags, the scout saucer interrupted an invisible sensor beam without providing the requisite code to un-interrupt it. This triggered a laser barrage from every which direction. Normally, such a barrage would have burst apart the scout saucer, not to mention more largely proportioned spacecraft. But the result imitated what happened with previous laser cannon attacks on Tictoctickian craft. Seeming water color paints splattered harmlessly against the scout saucer's hull.

Earthlings in the Space Station 2 Marriott variously gasped and cried, "No!!" when they saw what followed. The scout saucer successfully made its way down into the Earth's upper stratosphere. It shrank to pinpoint size from the perspective of anyone aboard the outer space Marriott.

Celebratory braying, baaing and kicking broke out on the Sixth Celestial Breath. The kicking literally broke apart several backrests.

Commander Ak-keek-teek's kept his own reaction, though, much more subdued. That is, beyond yet another of his slowly dawning, ridiculously wide buck-tooth grins. He was just about to order one of his less-trusted, ergo more-expendable servants to occupy a second scout saucer holographically enrobed to appear as a full-sized battle saucer.

Five other scout saucers had been comparably disguised on the outskirts of the "Akt" solar system. Such hi-tech deception fooled the "Akt" beasts, as Ak-keek-teek saw them. For a short time, anyway, the "Akt" beasts believed they had managed to destroy five full-sized saucers.

Presently, Commander Ak-keek-teek worried the successful breaching of "Akt" defenses by the first scout saucer was not what it seemed. Maybe it was calculated to lull him into false trust he could safely deliver an important contingent of Tictoctickian military force down to the surface of the "Akt." Too late, they would realize they had been ambushed by the beasts' instinctively wrought, supremely deadly offense capabilities.

What better way to forestall such tragedy than to experiment with a second scout saucer disguised as a Celestial Breath? In the worst case scenario, a servant's body would go completely to waste, unsalvageable for even a few strips of jerky. But at least the "Akt" beasts would be the real ones deceived. Once again, they would be fooled into believing they had obliterated a full-sized battle saucer!

Commander Ak-keek-teek ruminated with what he considered the height of military, war-making strategizing, beyond anything Dek-Fook-Tek could have imagined. His rumination brought him to this: Wasn't there still a dreadful possibility regarding everything the commander and his fellow Tictoctickians had already experienced? Ever since entering the "Akt" beasts' solar system? The impossible rainbow most critically included? The commander wanted to believe those experiences amounted to an affirmation by the ultimate power of the universe, itself. He wanted to believe the universe was sanctifying the righteousness of their mission. But wasn't there a possibility, however vanishingly small, of something entirely opposite? An elaborate setup, perhaps, to wipe them out before they knew what hit them?

"Commander Ak-keek-teek!" erupted most abruptly, shockingly for the commander from a micro-speaker. The navigation bridge filled with a loud if crackly voice, tongue-clicking away. "Your secret plan to verify that the most fundamental workings of the universe itself are on our side has succeeded beyond brilliantly! I hope I have accomplished patching in this cam-feed to your panoramic screen-view. But whether I have or have not makes no difference! I am being pursued by fighter jets of a most primitive, instinctively wrought sort! They are as would be expected from these nonetheless potentially delectable savage beasts! Their jets are unloading on your scout saucer, to most pathetically undamaging effect! So what say you now, my Supreme Commander Ak-keek-teek? I could blast them out of the sky with the scout saucer's pulse-beam set on diffuse, if that is your pleasure! I most humbly await your final word!"

"Excellent, Officer, excellent!" Commander Ak-keek-teek effusively brayed. His enthusiasm also served to smooth over his shock, however much he appreciated the initiative taken by this particular Tictoctickian. Clearly, whoever this officer was, he snuck aboard what was supposed to be an unoccupied scout saucer for testing the "Akt" planet's defenses. "You have demonstrated such courage as only I, Dek-Fook-Tek, and maybe, maybe one or two others would ever think to surpass! So I think the doe-impregnating honor should be all yours! Yes! I grant you the privilege of announcing to my crew, plus the crews of the other four Celestial Breaths listening in, exactly who you are! Baa! I will not allow me to take that honor away from you!" Commander Ak-keek-teek said this, himself not knowing who this person was. Yet the commander was vainly slipping into an ever-deeper delusional state. He convinced himself he must indeed have known who it was, and ordered him to do what he did. But again, as commander of the Tictoctickian outer space military forces, he simply had too much else on his mind of vastly more import to remember. He couldn't be bothered remembering the name of this one lone needle on the pine tree. He might as well try to recall such trivia as exactly how many does had enjoyed his copulations with them on his last planet leave from space duty. Especially so, since he was clearly destined to become the new Supreme Authority.

The commander found himself amused at what the video feed from the drone accompanying the scout saucer was revealing.

Several heat-seeking missiles were splattering harmlessly, one after the other, against the scout saucer hull. There were more kaleidoscopic bursts of seeming water color.

"Commander Ak-keek-teek, my name is Officer Pleek-leek-geek, as I am certain you already knew. If there is anyone more loyal to you than I, well maybe they are your lucky does. They have experienced your penetration, mighty beyond anything I could imagine! Nearly enough for me to wish a sex change operation!" Pleek-leek-geek bleated blushingly from the scout saucer's cockpit. *Would that you were even half as attracted to me as I am to you, commander of my spirit! The surgery to which I alluded would prove unnecessary to bring the two of us together,* Pleek-leek-geek added to himself. This was what he dared not bleat or bray aloud.

Commander Ak-keek-teek picked up easily on underling Pleek-leek-geek's infatuation with him. The commander reciprocated, however fleetingly, with a suggestive, nostril-wriggling regard for Officer Pleek-leek-geek when he came into view for the officer on a different feed. In his state of ever-ascending greatness, the commander well knew what would literally behoove him to occasionally, most discreetly do. That is, to satisfy such lust shown for him by others, even in the case of such obvious perversity. How better to sharpen, like antler prongs worked over by the best quality bahveks, the loyalty of those with whom he must surround himself? Especially if he expected to forestall assassination attempts from Commander Kwit-Nik and others! Weren't they becoming faithless, disloyal creatures out of their own, laughable egotism? Commander Ak-keek-teek would have lingered upon such thoughts if not for a gentle voice suddenly filling his head. It impelled him with, *Please bring your spacecraft, all your spacecraft, well down into the atmosphere of this planet. Traverse to where the rainbow ends. We await your hovering presence there.*

"Officer Pleek-leek-geek! Everyone!" Commander Ak-keek-teek officiously haughtily tongue-clicked with his most ridiculously broad buck-tooth grin, yet. "You must believe what I tell you! I, and I alone, have just been made a direct conduit for the supremely divine imperative of the universe!"

"Baa!" several officers on the bridge came down on their foreleg knees to humbly bow towards Ak-keek-teek. They so behaved despite the hardship for some of them who were without the correct Velcro-like knee pads. Those without knee pads floated bumping against one another in the near-zero gravity. "I know I speak for everyone else here when I agree with Officer Pleek-leek-geek," said one of them, despite his discomfort. "Your inner beauty, Commander, your glow from being made that most supreme conduit: By comparison, it would make a mockery of the most arousingly endowed doe with whom we could ever dream to couple. She would appear as ugly as a decapitated oskynt corpse!"

"I am sure," nodded the commander. "But listen to me! And you captains aboard the four other Celestial Breaths, mark my words! Mark them as carefully as you would mark a nesting area with your most pungent urine!"

When he spoke, Commander Ak-keek-teek had no idea he was not alone. That the same, gentle voice in his head had also intruded on every single other one of the deer creatures, no matter their location or who they were.

"I will follow the rainbow to its end, to where the universe leads us, to where *I* lead us, on our triumphant path to our divine destiny," the commander went on. "While I do so, Captains Rek-mek-a-nek and Keek-Konk, you will seek high population areas. There you will stun large groups of cattle with your magnetic pulse-beams set on diffuse. By means of the trawling nets, you will reprise the defensive actions we took against Chonora. You will gather up the stunned cattle until your meat lockers are full to bursting. Then we will bring those meat lockers back to Tictoctic! We will end the food shortage in a single, awe-inspiring stampede!" *Incidentally, that will allow me to usurp Dek-Fook-Tek's power, and make most glorious ascent onto his throne!* This was the part Commander Ak-keek-teek judged intemperate to voice aloud, at least for the time being. He had no idea, it did not cross his mind to imagine, what everyone hearing his order also knew from the gentle voice permeating *their* brains. He was countermanding what he had termed "the supremely divine imperative of the universe." The gentle voice called for *all* the spacecraft to be brought down closer to the planet's surface, in the rainbow's wake, not the commander's spacecraft alone.

As the Sixth Celestial Breath went into a tilt for its spinning descent into Earth's atmosphere, Commander Ak-keek-teek rationalized. He told himself, *The universe may suggest, but I decide!* Then he said, "Captains Dooky-mek-a-toot and Tweet-kweet, you will remain in high stationary orbit, to deal with the Akt starships when they arrive!"

⋅≻≈°⋅≻≈°⋅≻≈°

Flamboyo noticed a gentle clunk! Another shuttle pod was docking with the one he helped Morel Engeling hijack. Well before then, the mad scientist gave up trying to fight him. An unknown force mysteriously rebuffed Engeling's every lunge at Flamboyo. It seemed intent on sparing Flamboyo from any least harm Engeling strove to inflict on him, let alone outright murdering him. But it also seemed intent on sparing Engeling himself from injury, the way his violent efforts were so gently rebuffed.

Law enforcement officials boarding the hijacked shuttle pod found Engeling exhausted. This was especially so, since he had been unable to do harm even to his own self. He tried hurtling his body against a wall, and stabbing his own throat with a zero-gravity ink pen. But he might as well have been hurtling himself against the softest mattress, and he couldn't get the pen's ballpoint close enough to even stain his skin. For his subsequent suicide attempt, Engeling held the gun to his head and pulled the trigger at point-blank range. The bullet splattered harmlessly all over his temple like a bursting water balloon. So finally, he tried firing repeatedly into his mouth. He hoped maybe he could choke to death on whatever mysterious liquid the bullets metamorphosed into. But the ammunition down his throat somehow became gentle puffs of air. They left a pleasant sensation, if anything...all these efforts at self-destruction proved for naught.

One officer seized Dr. Engeling while the other slapped on the handcuffs. The handcuffing officer repeated what he said to Flamboyo, who had already willingly surrendered. "We are arresting you on suspicion of hijacking a shuttle pod, and causing mass destruction of lives and property by means of a tsunami!"

Dr. Morel Engeling couldn't help wailing in his biggest fit of frustration, yet. "How is it that you can so effortlessly handcuff me when I could not even write on myself with a pen?!"

"Seems that only violence is being thwarted, *hermano* (brother). Not justice," gently suggested Flamboyo.

Both men were led through an air lock into the docked shuttle pod.

"Ti-mo-thy," Dr. Engeling moaned grievingly slowly. His face wrinkled into a show of utter despair. "Our Daddy binds me like this because he wants me to stop! He wants me to act like a man! But," he shook his head tearfully, "I'm not going to stop! However much it hurts!"

Engeling was not to be the last human Flamboyo would experience breaking apart with profound sorrow.

"Why, Flamboyo?! Why?! We only had to hang on a little while longer, just a little longer for this worldwide miracle to arrive!, preventing anybody from harming anybody else! Why?!" cried Shelly Taylor. Dark circles ringed her eyes. Red blotches covered her nose. Her hair was a jumbled tousled mess from the hours she had been distressfully running her fingers through it...when Flamboyo could have been running his fingers through it, instead.

Shelly was a portrait of heart-rending misery. That portrait came to Flamboyo via video transmission inset on the lower left corner of the law enforcement shuttle pod's view-screen.

The shuttle pod approached Earth. It was returning to Space Station 2 from a couple hundred thousand miles away, from the dark side of the moon.

"Why, Flamboyo?! Why?!"

Señor Flamboyo Sanchez could only shake his head. Nevertheless, he kept it raised to look into Shelly's eyes on the view-screen as he responded, "Too much doubting, mi amor." This was when he noticed, with a certain inexplicable thrill, something else also approaching Earth. It was bringing up the rear of those side-by-side, weaponry-outfitted starships Obama and Eisenhower.

It was the starship Smoke and Mirrors. The fairy dust photon stream in its wake had diminished to the faintest trickle from having decelerated well below light-speed.

⚬ ⟊⟊⟊⚬⚬ ⟊⟊⚬⚬ ⚬⟊⟊⚬

"Captain Helena Grace Taylor!"

Ooo, she's addressing my wife by her full maiden name, Chris Olsen-Taylor thought to himself. *She must be extra mad. I'll bet this has to do with our telepathed invite, if she received it as well. And I don't know why she wouldn't have received it, although...*

Meanwhile, Ali Magabu was thinking to his self, *I'm not sure what this has to do with specifically. Although I truly suspect it's related to that new voice in our heads. That voice was so gentle, the Oombian telepathy felt harsh by comparison. How truly pathetically sad, if Louisa is attempting anew to blunt the edge of her own guilt feelings. What happened to Fafama before we managed to rewrite its history, I wouldn't be surprised if that is still haunting her. As well it should.*

"Captain Taylor, we have abided much nonsense from your libertarian approach to... commanding is way too strong a word. But now, what is this sick joke your Oombian spiritual guides are about? At such a crucial juncture as this, why are they pretending they are not the ones supplying the telepath we've just received?!?"

"I have to agree with Captain Entroper on this one." Professor Skepticus raised a forefinger to insert himself. "It is a basic application of Occam's Razor. Once again we are assuming we haven't been victimized by some extraordinarily elaborate magic trick. Once again, we are trusting that something wasn't made to seem real that is not. We are accepting that tree creatures from the planet Oomb have been endowed with extreme powers of mental telepathy, even though the odds for that happening are vanishingly small. About any new telepathic messages we receive, we must conclude they originate from who we already know can send them, or create the mass illusion of sending them! That is the far, far, farrrr more likely explanation! Indeed, we must prefer that explanation over believing an even more incredible explanation! And what could be more incredible than the notion an additional extraterrestrial intelligence has been able to introduce themselves telepathically??"

"Captain Entroper, Professor Skepticus," Helena swung her captain's chair around to make a short deferential bow Dauntilus Skepticus's way. "I think the accused should get a chance to answer for themselves. Oodle-Noodle? Wafoodle-boodle?"

Captain Entroper as well as others aboard the starships Obama and Eisenhower, and of course Professor Skepticus and others with me here aboard the Smoke and Mirrors, started in Oodle-Noodle with most respectfully timed leaf rustles. However much I wish it were not so, surely you have noticed something most unfortunate. That by comparison to the telepath we have recently received from unknown entities, mine grates. My telepath comes across harshly. I would guess the reason is actually quite simple. Our new friends have had so much more practice, a so much longer history of telepathy, than us Oombians have had.

"'Friends'!" Entroper scoffed mockingly. "Do you mean, the kind of friends who seduce you further and further, until you realize you have been led into a trap?!?"

I mean the kind of friends who make it impossible for other entities, total strangers, to hurt one another! And that do so, no matter how hard those entities try to activate their most lethal weaponry!

"There is an analogy I would make here, Captain Entroper, if I might," intruded Secretary of Defense Spinner on Entroper's end of the conversation. "Farmers often need to prepare their harvests for shipping long distances. So they pack them with special padded lining like you have for egg cartons. They try to make sure the fruit and veggies don't bruise!"

I haven't yet experienced anyone here trying to round us up for packing, responded Oodle-Noodle telepathically. Certainly not these newly arrived extraterrestrials! I should think the implication is clear, especially if you apply your Occam's Razor again. Especially if you want to argue that the simplest, most elegantly straightforward explanation usually comes closest to the truth, even though that is often not the case. To wit, the mysterious, rainbow-wielding entities seem to have put a lot of effort into saving you and the Tictoctickians from one another's attempted violence. They must sincerely care for your well-being, period. An important assumption accrues here, of course. It pertains

*to any civilization advanced so far ahead of you as they
most obviously are. The assumption is that such a
civilization is also most advanced in their level of empathy
and kindness. Otherwise, they would have already wiped
themselves out.*

"Oh, jeez," groaned Secretary Spinner. "Let's pull out
yoga mats and fill our minds with 'namaste.'"

"Ms. Tree Person, that's a very all-or-nothing
presumption you're making about the extraterrestrial
threat," said Entroper supporting Spinner's reaction.

And your "threat" label is not presumptuous?

"Look, Captain Taylor," said Captain Entroper. "I'm
receiving confirmatory reports regarding two saucers
already arrived near Earth. Their rims are turning neon
blue again! They're charging up their magnetic pulse-
beams for another go at us! I don't have time for any
more idle, dangerously naïve speculation! You can have
all of it, do you hear?! The only thing, the one thing I ask
of you, for now, is that you hold back on coming any
closer home. Delay your acceptance of whoever's
telepathed invitation to blindly follow the rainbow to its
destination. Who knows? Maybe we get ourselves killed
wiping out both menaces, which is to say the alien stags
and the rainbow-wielders alike. And maybe the entire
Earth is destroyed into the bargain! But then you have
yourself a Noah's Ark's worth of creatures aboard your
starship. You can return to Oomb, and with a little luck
your naïve faith in a benign universe is all you will need to
get by, going forever forward! But I might as well be
addressing a brick wall; you'll still do whatever." With that
last, disparaging comment, Entroper turned her back on
the camcorder filming her from the navigation deck of
the Barack Obama. For everyone on the navigation deck

aboard the Smoke and Mirrors, the video feed suddenly went blank.

"I actually do want to hold back a while before we fly in any closer," said Helena, especially for Chief Navigation Officer Yoon-hee Park-Smith's benefit. "The destruction of the remote laser cannon delivery pod might indeed suggest that the protective thwarting of normal physics has worn off. I certainly don't want us caught in any potential cross-fire."

"Nay, Captain," Yoon-hee nodded, exuding pleasure with the captain's reasoning. She played her fingers across her navigation console to adjust the starship's course, including more significant deceleration.

"Wafoodle-boodle," went on Helena, "something to keep you busy as we await the outcome of the renewed confrontation between 'our' warships and the Tictoctickian saucers. Please ascertain just how many of us aboard want to take up the mystery telepathers' invite. This assumes, of course, we can safely proceed with a shuttle pod mission down to the Earth's surface, wherever that rainbow has landed."

"I remember an old sci-fi movie, *The Day The Earth Stood Still*," said Chris. "Klaatu and company landed their saucer on the mall in Washington, D.C. Those particular aliens were portrayed focusing on Earth's center of power."

"Don't mean to interrupt you, Chris... Okay, maybe I do," conceded Kevin. "The saucers and our starships are putting on quite a show out there!"

It was true. And thanks to the panoramic magniview from aboard the Smoke and Mirrors, Kevin and company had front-row seats.

The renewed effort by the starships Obama and Eisenhower to engage battle with the flying saucers wasn't accomplishing anything more than before. Again, accomplishment consisted in how much destruction one side leveled against the other.

Blue beams issuing from the Celestial Breath saucers splashed kaleidoscopically against the asparagus stem hulls of the starships Obama and Eisenhower. Red-tinged ball lightning issuing from the Obama and Eisenhower resulted in similar splashes, spraying out from the spinning hulls of the Celestial Breaths. Occasionally, the blue beams and ball lightning caused certain objects to actually explode blowing apart in bright orange flashes. However, firefly donut data allowed the Earthlings to quickly conclude that only unoccupied, weapon-bearing probes launched by both sides proved so vulnerable.

"I've got it!" Munitions expert Maggie Wang aboard the Obama snapped her fingers in sudden, triumphant exaltation. "Yes, vessels occupied by life forms have easily resisted all attempts to destroy them! But, BUT, we need not postulate ultra-advanced do-gooders are gumming up the basic laws of physics! By definition, what do life forms always have that non-life does not?!" The look in Wang's eyes flamed so wild, neither Entroper nor Spinner, nor anyone else on the navigation deck of the Obama dared interrupt her. Even to confirm she had their total attention. "They have biologically generated electromagnetic fields! As opposed to non-biologically generated electromagnetic fields!! Of course!! Biologically generated electromagnetic fields *must* be the cause! They must be why magnetic pulse-beams and laser cannonballs alike are collapsing into harmless splatters of color! Listen, people! That's what you get in a dynamic, physics-warping vicious feedback loop catalyzed by light-speed-altering features! All we need to do is somehow trick the enemy off their saucers! We have to fool the Tictoctickians into abandoning what carried them to our fair realm! Once that abandonment happens, we can finally blow up their spacecraft! We can strand the deer creature extraterrestrials on Earth where law enforcement can go around arresting them!"

Captain Entroper wondered, *How the hell is THAT going to happen?*

Meanwhile back aboard the Smoke and Mirrors, Counselor Ali Magabu was remarking, "Captain, I am wracking my brain to recall what I am reminded of, truly. There is something oddly familiar about all these nondestructive, indeed it would seem anti-destructive, splashes of color."

I find exceedingly fascinating your mental wrestling to recall what you are reminded of, Officer Magabu. With your permission, I should wish to telepathically dig deeper, as it were. Maybe I can help you unearth what it is, Oodle-Noodle ventured to telepath. *However, everyone, there is the much more immediately pressing business of new developments on Earth. My companion and I have mind-read some extraordinary happenings across your home planet. They rival what we've already witnessed out here!*

"Go on, Oodle-Noodle; don't keep us in suspense," nodded Helena.

There are situations, Captain, thousands of situations wherein people have been unable to inflict physical harm on one another. And about that extraterrestrial spacecraft that the mystery rainbow condensed into: It is not focusing on some center of political power as happened in that science fiction movie you recalled, Officer Olsen-Taylor. Rather, it is coming to a hovering halt near a virtually powerless, if sprawling city in the nation of

India. The city is named Varanasi, located along the Ganges River.

The whites of Ali Magabu's eyes showed clear around his irises. He said, "Someone correct me if I am wrong. Today is March 3rd, 2064, correct?"

"That's correct, Magabu," said Captain Taylor. "What of it?"

"Kevin, if you'll excuse me..." Counselor Ali Magabu leaned over where Kevin Smith-Park was seated, to pull up information on his console. When he found what he was looking for, the counselor nodded and said, "Mm-hmm, mm-hmm."

Kevin craned his head around Ali's arms to sneak a peek at the console. His reaction to what he espied was, "What the...?!"

"Helena, everyone," Magabu said after finally lifting back away from the control console. "When my parents fled persecution in Nigeria, they needed to elude certain government agents, throw them off the scent as it were. This need became an excuse for us to have a little fun. We made a whirlwind tour of other countries before we settled down in Cairo. One of our destinations ended up being Mumbai, India, formerly known as Bombay. We journeyed there in early spring, when the Hindus and people of other faiths were celebrating something called 'Holi.' For that celebration, I still remember adults as well as children running through the streets, throwing water balloons at one another. They were also shooting at one another with water guns. The water itself was dyed different colors. In addition, people were spraying people with variously pigmented powders. Very quickly, everyone including ourselves got caught in the middle of this truly silly-looking onslaught. No time at all, we were covered in a variety of bright pastels."

"Exactly like what happened when our starships tried to go to war with the Tictoctickian saucers!" Buddy Leung couldn't help laughing ecstatically.

The reports we are picking up from Earth are speaking of bullets and knives mutating into harmless water stains. The appearance is of people's clothing becoming batiked, chimed in Wafoodle-boodle.

"Listen to this, Captain," said Kevin. He had gained a clear view of what Ali brought up on one of his console screens. "'Holi is considered, by Hindus and non-Hindus alike, to be a celebration of love. People substitute harmless water color play for their usual conflicts, and make new compacts to resolve old disputes.'"

Our task, ultimately, is to precipitate a Great Healing, Helena Taylor recalled a non-Oombian voice gently filling her head to say, some year-and-a-half earlier. That same voice also urged her to transport into the future a neighborhood from north Philadelphia, to re-settle on Oomb.

"So let me guess, Officer Magabu," said Professor Skepticus, sighing wearily. "Today is the date of the 'Holi' celebration this year, a slender reed of coincidence you would labor most exhaustively to transform into an obesely fat to-mah-to of mumbo-jumbo import! Or should I say Mumbai-jumbo import?"

<hr>

Twelve-year-old Manjeeta slowly returned to consciousness inside a windowless, cement-walled room. Her more general location, the Shivdaspur district, sat on the outskirts of the five-thousand-year-old, sprawling city known as Varanasi, India, and known by various other names as well.

For Manjeeta's first few minutes of coming-to, she clung desperately, quickly more hopelessly, to a fleeting initial thought. She simply woke up from the most awful possible nightmare, safe and snug in her decrepit aunt's sparse apartment. That residence was located not too many blocks away from lengthy sets of stairs called ghats. On a regular basis, Manjeeta witnessed people descending those ghats. They set adrift the wrapped-up remains of loved ones on the Ganges River.

Manjeeta had to participate in such a ritual only the past week, for her mother and father. Both were killed in a flaming bus wreck.

Yes, yes, Manjeeta said to herself despite growing aware of no windows, and no tattered mandala hanging over her bed. Her bed consisted of nothing more than a worn, thin mattress directly upon the uneven floor of compacted cow dung. Wasn't it the same modest sleeping accommodation Manjeeta's well-meaning aunt provided? *Yes, this is Lord Vishnu's way of helping me to appreciate what I have, by presenting me in my sleep with a nightmare so much worse.*

But Manjeeta had to reluctantly conclude, finally, that she was already fully awake. She was not about to rouse a second time, from a dream within a dream. Windows and tattered mandala, both, remained stubbornly absent.

Manjeeta propped herself up on one elbow to have a better look around. She saw two other girls who appeared to be her age. Unlike herself, though, neither one had yet to regain consciousness.

Manjeeta was not alone, and neither one of who she was not alone with was her aunt. On this discovery, she could no longer hold back a virtual flood of memories of what transpired just before she drifted off unconscious against her will. And there was nothing in them of her aunt having safely tucked her to bed.

Manjeeta pulled her yellow- and green-striped sari ever more tightly around her wiry thin frame. But she trembled nevertheless from what she recollected.

She had gotten herself lost in a typically crowded market beside a pile of coconuts. The coconut seller was cutting them open with swift, swooshing arcs of his long knife for a line of paying customers, one after the other. For a blessed moment, this happy commotion lifted Manjeeta out of her grief over her lost parents. There was even a scent of roses wafting in from somewhere, temporarily overcoming the usual mix of spices with fresh cow poop.

But panic interceded, and Manjeeta looked every direction. Suddenly, she realized she was somehow separated from the only member of her family still left to her in this world, her aunt Nina.

That is when she experienced a needle prick in her shoulder. At first, Manjeeta took it to maybe have been a bee sting as she had experienced long ago, at the tender age of six.

The long ago bee sting happened in an open field one summer afternoon, while awaiting part of a performance of the Indian epic, *Ramlila*.

All too soon, though, Manjeeta realized such a bee sting was impossible, no bees around. An odd leaden feeling rapidly spread, radiated from where she was pricked. It suffused her body too rapidly for her to scream for help as it reached her neck, her mouth, her head.

Manjeeta's very last memory before losing consciousness completely was of a wool blanket thrown atop her. That happened in the wheeled cart onto which she had been tossed.

Somewhere off in the distance, there was a shriek, perhaps her aunt's...

On their own recovery of consciousness, Peenu and Numila had only enough time to share their names with Manjeeta. That is, before someone the other side of the wooden door could be heard working a lock on chains.

There he stood, silhouetted by the light of day behind him. He was a short, lean man in a red silk shirt, taking nervous rapid puffs on his bidi cigarette. He carelessly tossed the remnant butt aside as he stepped forward to say, "Dear young ladies, you will find I am far kinder than most. Just follow my simple directions carefully. Others would starve you until you were too weak to resist. But my special clients, they appreciate a certain feistiness. So please, if you will allow these fine gentlemen to induct you into womanhood. They gave me their assurances they will be gentle, the more you cooperate. A bowl of garlic naan bread, paired with the finest chai, awaits you afterwards. And then I will hand out pichkari water color guns so you can shoot one another for Holi. The entire universe would appear to be celebrating this time, because the largest rainbow, ever, fills the sky! Yes! You will see! Like I said, I am far kinder than most. Now this is where I make my exit."

Manjeeta, Peenu and Numila shivered on their worn-out floor mattresses despite the close, still air.

The silk-shirted guy was gone. In his place entered three, rotund, middle-aged men. "It is exactly as the kind man said," nodded the one wearing a blue, green and red-striped kurta. "Fortunately, while you were still catching up on your sleep, we sorted out who should go with whom. Do not worry. Only one of us will remain here for one of you. The other two will bring the other two of you to separate rooms. It is all very respectful and discreet." He bowed. "Now you," he pointed at Manjeeta, "you are with me, and we will remain here."

By this time, Manjeeta found herself enough recovered from her dizziness, just from sitting up. She rose to her feet, clenched her hands in fists, and proclaimed defiantly, however still shivering, "I am not with you! They are not with them!" She pointed down at Peenu and Numila. They were cowering into each other's arms on one of the mattresses. "I will NOT remain with you, here or anywhere! And they will not go with them!"

"It is okay," said the man in the striped kurta. He strode forward to seize Manjeeta. He wanted to assure she would not interfere when the police officer and the other guy rushed in to carry off Peenu and Numila. "These feelings are perfectly normal for the first time, but you will see it is really not that bad."

"NO!!" Manjeeta shrieked. She extended her arms to try pushing the fellow away.

"Please!" whimpered Peenu and Numila. They were embracing ever more tightly. The idea was to resist being pulled apart by the two oncoming men.

But their effort proved unnecessary.

All three girls shut their eyes. They were expecting to experience the violence of men intent on raping them, when...nothing. Only a gentle breeze.

The three men quickly realized something incredible. An invisible force was firmly yet gently making it impossible to lay a hand on, put the slightest touch on even one of the girls. The men's breathing became more labored, increasingly more hyperventilated.

The girls' breathing grew less tentative, more assertive until finally, Peenu and Numila were both on their feet, untangled from one another. They clenched their hands most defiantly into fists, like Manjeeta's still were.

Manjeeta felt emboldened to start marching herself out of the room. The three men tried to pounce on this creature with her sari draped as tightly about her diminutive figure as possible. Again, though, they met with the gentle rebuff. They were powerless to stop her. And they did no better against Peenu and Numila when those two finally worked up the courage to follow suit.

Running out into the courtyard, the three men complained, "We need to get our money back!" "What witchcraft is this?!?!" "The gods have gone completely mad!"

Manjeeta and her two new acquaintances were greeted by other girls their age plus older women as well. They were variously shouting and crying, "Our prayers have been heard!" "Praise Allah!" "Lord Vishnu has not abandoned us after all!" "It is a miracle!" "Jesus is surely on the way!" "The Goddess Lakshmi has awoken!"

"WHAT DEVILRY IS THIS??!!" screamed the guy with the red silk shirt. He stormed into the courtyard amidst a jumble of women and girls, and men unable to lay a hand on any of them. The men were in a panic, searching for an exit back out onto the street. That is, if they were not storming the red-silk-shirted man, clenched fists raised high to demand refunds. "WAIT!" the red-silk-shirted man cried. "REFUNDS FOR ALL!! BUT FIRST," he hoisted an oil container high above his head for all to see, "I MUST PUT AN END TO THIS DEVILRY!!"

The men who had been storming the red-silk-shirted man quickly, approvingly made way for him to stride past them. He approached the women and girls. When those females, young and old alike, realized what he was carrying, it was too late. He was already swinging his container forward, dousing them in its pungent, fossil-fuel contents. They froze in helpless terror.

The red-silk-shirted man lit a match, and tossed it on the oil-soaked ground.

With a ferocious WHOOSH, orange, blue and yellow flames shot up with raging intensity. The men could not see past those flames to how the women and girls were doing. But they did hear cries from what they could only imagine were fellow humans charring to a crisp.

But then, mixed in amidst those oranges, blues and yellows were greens, purples, reds and browns, with varied shades thereof. And the female cries were evolving into ecstatic shouts of thankfulness for this miracle of total invulnerability to violence.

The flames died down enough, finally, for the men to see what happened.

The women and girls were inflicted with nothing more than brightly colored stains splattered on their tattered saris, blue jeans and even some arms and faces.

"Clearly, evil Queen Halika has asserted her rule! She has transformed the burning gasoline into so many gulaal and abeer dyes!" lamented the man who had planned on deflowering Manjeeta. Meanwhile, the police officer who had entered the girls' holding cell alongside him drew his pistol and muttered, "I am not so convinced yet!"

The women and girls continued fleeing the courtyard to fan out into the street. The courtyard gate's lock offered them about as much resistance as had a piece of paper been taped across there.

The gun-wielding police officer took aim at Peenu bringing up the rear of the fleeing females, and he fired. His aim was dead on, but the result was another, harmless kaleidoscopic splattering of colors.

Peenu paused. However, when she realized she remained unharmed, she jumped about in exultation, shouting, "Holi! Holi! Holi!"

Meantime, many of the women and girls who had already run out into the street were looking heavenward. They were transfixed gaping variously at the rainbow or the enormous flying saucer, the Sixth Celestial Breath. The saucer was parked hovering near the Ganges River.

Manjeeta's attention was drawn more the opposite direction towards a forbiddingly looming gray wall. It stretched off many miles both north and south. It was the wall that separated Varanasi and its environs, as one of the larger quarantine zones, from more affluent parts of India. Descending on the Varanasi side of that wall were what Manjeeta literally took to be three giant eggs.

⁕ ⁕⁑⁑⁕ ⁕⁕⁕ ⁕⁑⁑⁕ ⁕⁑⁕

"Captain," Yoon-hee was reporting to Helena inside one of the eggs, actually a shuttle pod. "Our magniview is allowing us to spot sporadic bonfires. They are popping up on the outskirts of Varanasi, near where we plan to land. They flare out in colorful arrays. I'm guessing they represent more foiled attempts at harmful actions, but why this widespread? Are there that many people here intent on hurting others?"

The inability to inflict violence is collapsing the prostitution zone; that is what you are witnessing, Officer Park-Smith, asserted Wafoodle-boodle *reassuringly. Again, there is nothing to fear for any of your ultra-curious children who are accompanying us, or for you to fear on their behalf.*

"Captain Taylor, you are aware of that coliseum-sized flying saucer almost hovering on top of you?!?" This was Captain Entroper from way up out of Earth's atmosphere in the battleship Barack Obama. Her lecturing voice issued from all three shuttle pod intercoms. But she was mainly seeking Helena's attention. "You're not worried your luck might be about to finally run out?!"

Just then, three magnetic pulse-beams were emitted from the enormous hovering flying saucer, the Sixth Celestial Breath. They were focused squarely on the three shuttle pods, one beam per pod. No different from before, colorfully innocuous splatters resulted.

"No we're not worried," Helena responded to Entroper. "We trust our Oombian friends' assurances we can safely take up the mystery extraterrestrials' invite."

"Very well," said Entroper. "We don't trust any of them; that's why we're hanging back. We already have our magniview picking up individual steps on the- What's that they call them? – the ghats? So we've got an excellent ring-side view. Oh, and when you park, I would not leave your shuttle pods unattended. There's something Dr. Wang might have figured out about this inability to destroy flight vehicles. It is absolutely unrelated to any simplistic peace-and-love hocus-pocus your tree friends might be thinking."

"Okay," reacted Helena noncommittally.

Captain Taylor, a small detail Wafoodle-boodle and I neglected to mention, Oodle-Noodle telepathed. The people aboard the other two Earthling starships did not receive the same level of invite we did. Unlike what we were encouraged to do, they were instructed only to attend at a hovering distance. They were advised not to actually move among the crowds of irresistibly curious planet-bound Earthlings. We are guessing those same instructions went double for the Tictoctickians.

⊱ ⊰⊱ ⊰⊱ ⊰

"Captain Rek-mek-a-nek, based on our micro-saucer probes I believe we have discovered what we were looking for. We have come across a region perfectly suitable for netting us thousands of healthy Akt creatures to replenish our food stocks. But it is a very curious region, indeed." Lieutenant Keek-Kook shook his head in wonderment after he finished crisply tongue-clicking to Rek-mek-a-nek on the navigation deck of the Fifth Celestial Breath.

The Fifth Celestial Breath was hovering little more than thirty thousand feet off the ground near Orlando, Florida.

"I want to ruminate upon the curious aspect, Lieutenant," answered Captain Rek-mek-a-nek. "But first, are the Akt beasts taking notice of us?"

"One of our mini-probes has filmed many of them pointing up at our vessel. Recordings of their voices have been run through our Akt translator. We have thereby ascertained they are wondering whether our vessel is part of the incursion of other-world spacecraft. Either that, or whether instead it is some elaborate hoax that fellow Akt creatures are playing out for their entertainment. Whatever they think, they would appear as docilely oblivious to the possible consequences as an ancient herd of oskynt. In fact, we could probably panic them off a cliff with ease, if that were our goal!"

"'For their entertainment'?" the captain repeated brayingly, mystified.

"Baa, Captain. The Akt beasts have been looking up at the saucer probes, amused. And their animalistic grunting has been translating into the strangest remarks. I quote: 'This is so cool, their pretending to be spying on us!' 'Let us hope we can purchase videos at a gift shop! Maybe we should ask!'

"You ought to see what else our mini-saucer probes have filmed. Like I said, it is a very curious region, indeed. Examine closely these video clips."

Captain Rek-mek-a-nek watched as half the navigation deck's panoramic view-screen displayed a long row of people of all sizes and ages. They were slowly filing into one of the most oddly designed structures he'd ever beheld. That structure was labeled with lettering which for him might just as well have been Egyptian hieroglyphics. But for many Earthlings it read: Mr. Toad's Wild Ride. Other bizarre-looking buildings were labeled Space Mountain, It's A Small World, Avatar Tree Vengeance and Star Wars Death Coaster.

"That one," the lieutenant was referring back to Mr. Toad's Wild Ride. "Those beasts stand in line for what have to seem like a hundred pektels or more, waiting to get in. When they are finally seated inside transportation devices, they are taken on a short trip inside the enigmatically shaped construction. And in virtually no time they are returned to exactly where they started! Even stranger still, some of them, you see, they run back around to wait in line, all over again! This is true, especially for the shorter, presumably younger ones!"

"We must pity them more than anything else, Lieutenant. I remember what I read about Tictoctic's frontier days of distant yore. Female oskynt and their calves were seen to waste entire days chewing grass, regurgitating it into one another's mouths, and then chewing it again. Not the life for us, certainly, if we are more than just dumb brutes, ourselves. But something must be admitted. In our nurseries, it is a recognized healthy habit for mothers to regurgitate partially chewed food for the youngest brood to more easily digest." Captain Rek-mek-a-nek strained to officiously tongue-click, rather than allow his utterance to devolve into humble baaing. He could not help a twinge of his conscience, looking on at the line of happily excited children. They had no idea what his fellow deer creatures held in store for them.

"We must pity them?! Really?! We must pity them, when it was a pair of them that crossed untold trillions of lek-leks simply to destroy one of our hospitals?! Pah!" Lieutenant Kook-Keek's spit reached the view-screen, where it dribbled down ever so slowly.

"That certainly is an antler prong well-jabbed, Lieutenant," acknowledged the captain, without bringing up what was also knocking about his head. Namely, there was that other matter of Tictoctickians attacking an "Akt" settlement on the planet of the telepathic tree creatures. Were the "Akt" beasts supposed to simply accept such violence without any effort at retaliation? "Well, Lieutenant," is how Captain Rek-mek-a-nek's bleated sigh, instead, would have translated into English. "Now is as good a time as any for a diffuse magnetic pulse-beam. We will knock unconscious a good number of those pathetic creatures before we cast out the trawler net, yes?"

"Yes, of course, Captain. I will make it so, immediately! We don't want to wait until another assault from the Akt beasts' attack jets gets in our way! Such an assault is sure to prove as futile as previous assaults. It is sure to result in nothing more than additional ineffectual rainbow splatters against our Celestial Breath's hull! But still..."

With a few adjustments of various knobs on the lieutenant's control console, the Fifth Celestial Breath's immense rim glowed neon blue. That glow intensified until it detached from the flying saucer, which was tilted down towards the amusement theme park. The diffuse pulse-beam grew ever brighter and thicker on its rapid ripple outwards...

Some attendees were ready to scream, when the neon blue arc blew apart with a loud Poof! A billion powder-blue pieces of mysterious puff rained down harmlessly on the Fantasy Kingdom of Disney World, to loud cheers and much applause.

"Please excuse me, Captain, for my possible impertinence. If it does turn out to be no more than that, may a rainbow exhalation from Dek-Fook-Tek himself scatter me to bits like has just happened to our diffuse pulse-beam!" Lieutenant Keek-Kook couldn't help exclaiming. His chest swelled, equal parts vulnerably and proudly.

"To what possible impertinence are you referring, Lieutenant?"

"Again and again, Captain" Keek-Kook responded, "we have seen the same truth play out. Space-age weapons, both ours intelligently designed and the Akt beasts' randomly mutated into being, are proving powerless, impotent. Perhaps that over-arcing rainbow compels a return to better days of old, when simple devices such as the bow and arrow were what we required for securing our food. Perhaps we are meant to experience far more success casting out our trawl net from the start. Thereby do we draw in our catch, feisty squirmy with life. After that, we act mercifully quickly! We flash-freeze the Akt beasts on the quickest possible ascent out of their planet's atmosphere, back into the void of space!"

"Exactly that, Lieutenant!" Captain Rek-mek-a-nek feigned to enthuse far more than he was actually feeling. He remained haunted by one mini-probe video clip of the younger beasts. They were happily jumping off a train that brought them back to where they started, only to return waiting in line for a repeat. "Very well, Lieutenant. Lower the Fifth Celestial Breath about halfway, to launch the trawl net!"

Within the minute, the Fifth Celestial Breath was spinning its descent to within three miles of the surface, where it resumed a stationary hover.

"Awesome!" yelled a teenaged boy in the Space Mountain line. He pointed skywards to draw his younger sister's attention. "It looks like we're going to have a repeat performance!"

But another loud voice nearby was saying, "Should we really be assuming the flying saucer is a Disneyworld feature?! My phone shows a UFO invasion in progress ever since the arrival of a giant rainbow to India! How can we be sure that thing up above us isn't from the invasion?! Especially after that bizare tsunami that flooded the east coast?!"

Such a question shouted for general consumption was all it took to precipitate scattered exclamations and screams. They rapidly crescendoed to widespread panic. Many people ran helter-skelter. They bumped into one another, uncertain what to do yet scared silly with the notion they had to do *something*. They couldn't just continue to stand there!

From the underbelly of the giant flying saucer, several mini-rockets emerged attached to an immense trawl net. Those mini-rockets rapidly drew the net earthwards, and spread it out to blanket a portion of the Magic Kingdom in Disneyworld. But by the time they approached within a thousand feet of the surface, mini-rockets and net alike suddenly burst apart into teensy multi-colored pieces. They made floating descent like so much confetti in the biggest celebration parade, ever. Once they reached the ground, it was easy to see they looked and felt like innocent, harmless flower petals.

"Ooos" and "Ahhs" rose collectively from ground level. Adults and children, alike, scrambled to gather up the metamorphosed remains of what had been intended to haul them heavenward into the flying saucer, like so many fish hauled from the sea.

Captain Rek-mek-a-nek met with profound relief what the mini-saucer probes revealed was occurring well down below him. From the corner of his mind that suffered a twinge of conscience over the intended fate for the youth beasts, a wondrous thought insinuated itself. Somehow, miraculously, a strange force was not allowing any violence to be inflicted on anyone, no matter the means for its delivery.

"Captain," intruded Lieutenant Keek-Kook on Rek-mek-a-nek's most satisfying contemplation. "Officer Deek-Dook-Stee who you sent on northern hemisphere reconnaissance, he is reporting back on something special from a particular subarctic region. He believes you will want to know about it sooner rather than later."

"Patch in the officer on the view-screen, Lieutenant."

"Captain Rek-mek-a-nek," Officer Deek-Dook-Stee was heard to humbly baa short mini-pektels thereafter. "I will not dreary you with my blunt-antlered countenance. On your portion of view-screen you are giving over to this transmission, you will see composite videos from our low-level mini-probe. As you will notice, the topography is not too different from island areas on the planet of the mobile, mind-talking trees. Only, they are located in a subarctic versus a subtropical clime. Give special attention to the coastal regions. Are those not the special landscapes for the tree creatures' game they call koofk?"

Captain Rek-mek-a-nek rose leaning forward well out of his armchair, squinting. He wondered most unrealistically, he knew, whether he might make out a "koofk" ball in flight towards one of the special, circular green patches. He also would have wanted to be able to discern a hole dug into one of those patches. As he remembered, that was where the ball was to be pushed into, by a most peculiar hammer-head mounted to the end of one of the "koofk" sticks.

"Head-butt special attention if you will, Captain, to this particular video clip. I will replay it multiple times until you can confirm you spotted the small herd of furry-looking creatures moving across the lower right-hand corner."

"Like dwarf oskynt, Officer? Another potential food source, unless this anti-violence spell will not allow us to harm any of them either?"

"A question worthy of Dek-Fook-Tek himself, Captain. Or maybe I should say, worthy of Commander Ak-keek-teek."

"I have an idea, Lieutenant Keek-Kook and Officer Deek-Dook-Stee," crisply tongue-clicked Captain Rek-mek-a-nek. His response intentionally neglected acknowledging the officer's compliment of the new commander. The captain's thinking was galloping much more over to: What would Commander Kwit-Nik have advised under this circumstance? "Lieutenant," continued Captain Rek-mek-a-nek, "bring us on a course heading to meet up with Officer Deek-Dook-Stee. If Commander Ak-keek-teek has not allowed himself to be led into a trap, fine. We will learn later of the full glory to which he has brought us." Captain Rek-mek-a-nek could not help tainting this prediction with weary sarcasm. "In the meantime," he proceeded, "we explore other options in the subarctic lands you have described, Officer Deek-Dook-Stee. We might be able to make a deal with the koofk players there, in exchange for food they might possess. For example, we could offer not to gore their chests. Anyway, by the time we fill our stomachs,

Commander Ak-keek-teek might or might not have
achieved results. If not yet, we do have koofk sticks and
balls on board, part of the supply bestowed upon us by
the tree creatures. Maybe we could head-butt in some
koofk practice. That is, if there is any interest."

"Baa," eagerly baaed several officers on the
navigation bridge. There was plenty of interest.

⸎⸎⸎⸎⸎⸎⸎⸎⸎

"Baa! Baa-baa-BAA!!" Commander Ak-keek-teek
brayed most complainingly. He also finished kick-
smashing to bits the captain's chair on the navigation
bridge of the Sixth Celestial Breath.

Multi-colored, flower-petal look-alikes showered the
outskirts of Varanasi, India. They were like so much
confetti, akin to what the commander did not know had
showered a location on "Akt" named Disney World. As
already mentioned, the trawl net deployed from the Fifth
Celestial Breath high above the theme park had also
been reduced to flower-petal look-alikes.

"Our net did not last even long enough to gather up
those silly-looking flying eggs!!" raged Commander Ak-
keek-teek, with no more of his chair left to destroy. "The
Akt beasts must have thought they were so clever, riding
them off their weakest starship to impudently descend to
this planet's surface! But one thing we can be sure of!
They were not welcomed to any lower altitude than we
were welcomed by the telepath uniquely bestowed
upon me! That is, if their leader was telepathed at all!
Their having actually landed on the ground speaks to
their unlimited arrogance!

"Baa," the commander suddenly rose back up to his
full height on his hind limbs. Only a jagged stump
remained behind him where his chair had once been.

"Perhaps this is the whole point, or the whole opposite point!"

The officers on the bridge grew increasingly anxious. Where would Commander Ak-keek-teek direct his hind hooves kicking, or bahvek-sharpened antlers charging, next? But instead, to their relief, the commander's oversized buck-tooth smile dawned anew.

"On the one set of antlers," Commander Ak-keek-teek tongue-clicked, "let us assume the universe is indeed manifesting an imbalance tipped way far over in our favor. In *my* favor as the real intended ruler of Tictoctic and beyond! In that case, the Akt beasts might well have been telepathically directed. Or they might simply have been impelled by their migration instincts. That is, if their minds are far too underdeveloped for receipt of a telepathic message. Either way, they were compelled to make themselves thusly more vulnerable. They were compelled to leave behind the security of their giant exoskeleton, to roam like an oskynt herd upon the Akt soil. But no trawling them up into a net for us, no!" Commander Ak-keek-teek shook his head furiously. "If the universe bends our direction, we are called to a different action! We are called to supreme, divine vengeance for what was discovered from that terrorist couple who destroyed one of our hospitals!

"Here on Akt, it is clear these beasts are accustomed to barbarically hunting our otherworldly brothers and sisters. They might even have already hunted them to extinction as we have done with the oskynt! But not for their meat! No! Rather, for some psychopathically sick mounting of our brothers' and sisters' heads on plaques for wall decoration!

"We are meant to go after the Akt beasts with our air igniters, to hunt them down one by one! And we are meant to do that not only for *their* meat, but also to mount *their* heads on wall plaques! And then those plaques will serve as warnings for the rest of the other-worlders throughout this galaxy! Somehow, we will set up those plaques as grim reminders of the fate awaiting any other other-worlders who would ever dare so mistreat species like unto ourselves!!"

Every last officer in the commander's company on the navigation deck came down on all fours. They pawed stamping at the floor with their articulated cloven hoof-hands while they brayed approval.

"But careful!" Ak-keek-teek lifted a hoof-hand high, signaling his subjects to put their reverie on pause. "As I said, there is also the complete opposite possibility we must not lose the scent of, no matter how miniscule its likelihood! This massive rainbow we see before us, it has bled across the light-years to coagulate itself into some massive oblong object. And now that object is flinging off multi-colored sparks while it hovers by the edge of a large riverbank. What if, what if it is just another instinctively evolved weapon of the Akt beasts? What if the telepath I received has lured us into a trap? And what if that trap was as instinctively set as the mating behavior of our shell-bearing kwabts when they emerge at high tide along the coasts of Tictoctic? What if very soon, something surprisingly deadly – a blinding ray, perhaps – is suddenly going to emit from that oblong object? What if such a weapon is meant to vaporize the Sixth Celestial Breath plus all of us inside it?" The commander paused, and he lowered his head to continue on in a low baa. "We should evacuate the Sixth Celestial Breath, to form a hunting party down below on the Akt planet. As we pile up the bodies, we can trot close enough to the rainbow's coagulated form to see more of what it is about.

"In the meantime, let us suppose the enemy does happen to destroy our Celestial Breath. What if the Akt beasts operate on too instinctive an autopilot to realize the warship has become but an empty shell? Fantastic! The Celestial Breath's destruction will have proven for naught, because all of us will still be alive! All of us will still be able to plot with our fellow soldiers aboard the other four Celestial Breaths! We will overcome this horrid if hopefully most delectable species, to direct its fate the way of the oskynt!!

"But again," Commander Ak-keek-teek raised his formidably antlered head back up to its full height. He tongue-clicked crisply and loudly, "I command our evacuation, but only as a wise precaution! We undertake this dramatic action on the vanishingly remote chance the universe is not demonstrating its allegiance to our cause! You see, Lieutenant, true military genius entails being able to provide for two diametrically opposed scenarios, simultaneously!"

While Commander Ak-keek-teek led his ordered procession to the scout saucers, his mind wandered. He thought on how in not much more time, his antlers should proliferate enough for him to require his own antler handlers. Surely that would befit the new ruler of the Tictoctickian solar system... and of other solar systems, as well.

⊱ ⊰

"Don't blame you for your restless pacing, Captain Entroper," remarked Officer Kevin Smith-Park from aboard the Smoke and Mirrors. He was trying to draw her attention tactfully. "Those scout saucers pouring from that bigger saucer the Tictoctickians have lowered into the atmosphere over India...it's like so many wasps leaving a hive that's been hosed..."

"Hey, Officer, you leave the folksy language to me, got that? Ho, ho, ho!" butted in Secretary Spinner on Entroper's side aboard the Barack Obama. "But hell, yeah, you should be over here, my end! Captain Entroper gets any feistier, I'm going to have to remind her I'm a married man! Wait! Am I allowed to say that? Ho, ho, ho!"

"Maybe you'd *better* watch out, Mr. Secretary!" Louisa Entroper paused to say before she resumed her aforementioned pacing. The Secretary of Defense said, "Oooo!" as she went on, "I'm restless in a good way, Officer Kevin Smith-Park, over two things. The first relates to *you!* That's right! You've had the good sense to remain on board the Smoke and Mirrors, keep it from emptying out completely. That's especially important given what Dr. Wang here has so cogently theorized."

"The telepathed invite did go out to every single one of us," said Kevin. "Our Oombian tagalongs are pretty convinced it's innocent stuff. They even had the Perez family's two-year-old daughter all excited-"

"Wait, I wasn't even thinking about... That's right, the children..."

"Every last one of them is down there, Captain Entroper. In fact my better half, Yoon-hee, she expressed regret we didn't pack along our adopted son Dae-Hyun; you remember the videos we showed you?"

"Of course! So, Officer, you're by your lonesome?"

"No, Professor Skepticus decided to keep me company."

"Indeed," confirmed Skepticus. "If I may, Officer?"

"Be my guest," said Kevin.

Skepticus hove into glowering view on the Obama's navigation deck view-screen. "Anecdotes!" he grumbled. "That's the only data any of my fellow passengers are going to collect down there, assuming they survive long enough. Anecdotes! We know the enormous extent to which personal experience can mislead us, where the big picture is concerned. For that very reason, I strive as much as humanly possible to avoid it. Indeed, there are no anecdotes I detest more than anecdotes garnered from my own interface with reality!! So, let my fellow passengers be misled!" Skepticus made a dismissive gesture before he backed out of view for people aboard the Obama.

"Umm," ummed Kevin, "Captain Taylor and I *did* decide at least one person who knew how to operate the S & M ought to remain on board, just in case. We made this decision even though we're not sure exactly what form 'just in case' might take. But please explain for me, Captain Entroper, why you're glad we did this."

"Dr. Wang, our weapons expert extraordinaire, she suggests there is one thing that might be neutralizing the attacks. Whether they issue from our side or from the enemy doesn't matter. It is the electromagnetic field we each carry around as a living being. Stirred into the hyper-physics propulsion mix, maybe you can't destroy a starship. A completely evacuated starship, however, might be a different story. We are going to find out with one of the deer demon saucers hovering in the lower atmosphere over India. Intercepted communications together with our observations suggest every last Tictoctickian has been disembarked from there. So, sit back and enjoy the show! If we succeed, the plan is not to try tricking the other deer demons into abandoning their vessels, as well. Rather, we will follow up the one saucer's destruction with lots of tough talk. We will see whether we can bluff the rest of them out of here, on their speedy way back to Tictoctic! No! Wait! I have an even better idea!"

The test of Dr. Wang's theory was not going to happen. Instead, the Earthlings aboard the Obama and Eisenhower were going to try making common cause with the deer creatures from Tictoctic.

⁕⸳⁜⸳⁜⸳⁜⸳

"Amal, my body cam feed provides a good look at how matters stand currently in the lobby of the Space Station 2 Marriott International. But you tell me there is no control over what is going out on television screens, anywhere."

"That is correct, Paul. For all we know, at the moment the two of us might be having a private conversation."

"Well, since we don't know, should I proceed with what I was going to report in the first place?"

"You mean, Paul, in lieu of the scandalous level to which our discourse usually sinks when we are certain nobody else is listening in?"

"Of course," Paul deadpanned. "Okay, so we see people engaging in a variety of very non-scandalous activity up here aboard Space Station 2. Some continue to look outside the window of the Marriott International lobby. They are watching for more of those multi-colored flashes scattered about the Earth's surface. Or they are pondering how the impossibly big and mysterious rainbow appears to have condensed into something solid, hovering over India. Yet others have told me they are on the alert for the arrival of any additional extraterrestrial spacecraft."

"Paul, what you said about the rainbow condensing into something solid over India: Can you elaborate?"

"I can elaborate. I am told that ground zero for the mysterious phenomenon, even more mysterious than the flying saucers, is Varanasi, India, along the Ganges River."

"Yes, Paul, that's the word I'm also receiving. But again, you spoke of the rainbow condensing into something solid."

"Yes, that. Well, you would think we are too far away from India, up here, to be able to discern such a transformation with any clarity. But that's exactly what happened. Maybe an atmospheric inversion layer acted like a magnifying glass. I don't know and nobody has told me. Whatever happened, many people and I clearly observed the rainbow compact itself into an immense, oval-shaped object."

"Excuse me, Paul. Check your nearest television. Is it carrying our conversation?"

"I was wondering where that echo was coming from."

"But are you seeing that oval-shaped object you mentioned, Paul? Are you receiving a close-up view on your television screen?"

"I can confirm that. Wow! How did our network deliver a camera crew there so fast?"

"They didn't. We have no idea who is making the video transmission, and coupling it to our conversation. Anyway, do you see the object hovering above a vast stairway down to a river's edge?"

"I am assuming that is the Ganges River, Amal. And if I am not mistaken, the stairway you referred to is called a ghat. Wow," reporter Paul Berger couldn't help repeating. "People are climbing down the ghat, holding something wrapped up like an Egyptian mummy. It must be a cremated loved one they intend to let go in the river, to continue on her or his spiritual journey."

"But they are hesitating at the bottom of the ghat, aren't they?" asked Amal Mahfouz.

"Indeed they are. Wait. Are you seeing them lift the wrapped-up object towards the glowing egg-shaped object? Do you think they might be hoping the remains of their loved one will be levitated into whatever-that-is?"

"They already appear to be giving up on the notion," Amal reported. "Oh! They just lowered the body, what we think is a body, into the river."

"I must say, Amal, it feels like we are spinning our wheels, waiting for the next shoe to drop."

"Yes it does feel that way, Paul. We don't even know whether the United Americas government, or any other government, has the least idea how to respond. We also don't know whether they can tell us even the teensiest bit more than we have already ascertained. If they can, they sure are not admitting it. We have sent out multiple inquiries, and are receiving zero response. The situation might be totally out of any Earth person's hands."

"Okay, Amal, let's spin our wheels about another closely related matter. No news organization, including from India and certainly not our own, is confirmed to have entered Varanasi yet. So who's the mysterious benefactor granting ringside seats on televisions and computers around the world? Do we assume the occupants of that immense, glowing, oval-shaped UFO hovering above the Ganges River are responsible?"

"I don't know, Paul! You tell me!" Amal chuckled gently. "But if pressed, I would answer yes. Whoever is behind the impossibly huge rainbow, and its transformation into that UFO, is also behind the mysteriously televised coverage.

"One moment; I am now receiving reports from around the world. Our professional wheel-spinning is being automatically translated into the prevailing language, depending on where people watch us from."

"In other words, Amal, let's talk about people watching in Spain, for example. Are you saying they hear us as though we were both fluent in Spanish?"

"Ah cannae ken fur certain, whawr th' quality ay nir bletherin' is concerned," is how clubhouse managers Jim MacShank and Donnie Spriggs heard Amal Mahfouz's response. They were standing by the check-in counter of the Tinkywink Links, a golf course located on a remote northeast shore of Scotland. But Amal's response to Paul Berger's question was actually, "I don't know for certain, where the quality of our voices is concerned."

"Afair ye pit anither dent in th' ceilin' wi' yer backswing, Donnie, come over an' reckon wi' this!" Jim made a huge, circular arm gesture for his business partner, Donnie Spriggs.

Donnie was, indeed, anxiously eye-ing a portion of ceiling. He hoped he didn't dig too deep a hole up there with the practice swing of his three-wood. Splinters of varnished wood were sprayed on the slate tiles down around his feet.

Back in New York City, Amal was continuing, "But in the example you gave, Paul, apparently Spanish-speaking audiences are automatically hearing what I say in Spanish. Whether I sound fluent or not, again I wouldn't know."

"So tell me what we're lookin' at, and I'll try to resist the temptation for takin' a chunk out of our flat screen into the bargain!" is how Donnie's Scottish-English would have translated into plain English. He pondered the view offered by their fifty-inch flat-screen television set into one ceiling corner at a downward angle. Revealed there was the giant UFO over ten thousand miles away. The mystery rainbow had long since balled itself up into that kaleidoscopically iridescent, football-stadium-sized, oval-shaped object. And that object was hovering low over a section of the Ganges River running alongside Varanasi, India.

"They're insistin' it's not a clip from some science fiction movie!" responded Jim. "And that what we see happenin' in India is being shown on teles and computer screens the whole world over!"

"Not on *our* computer screen it's not!" Donnie insisted.

The Tinkywink Links laptop computer sat on the check-in counter, for taking care of golfers interested in an eighteen-hole "roon." However, greens fees and the like were not what Donnie saw displayed there when he craned his head around. That's when he cried, "Scunner! (*Nuisance!*) I would have said, 'yer bum's oot the window' (*you're not making any sense*), but just look!"

"I remember hearin' something most peculiar about those travellin' trees from another planet. They have the oddest custom. Ev'ry mid-day, their bums are quite literally out the window. That's how they celebrate when mass copulatin' broke out on their planet instead of war!"

"Yer aff yer heid!" (*You're crazy!*)

"So tell me, Amal," was saying reporter Paul Berger on Space Station 2. Paul just realized something about the UFO hovering over India. It continued visible to the unaided eye, a shiny presence even from where he was standing in the Marriott International lobby. "Are you receiving any reports on how the Indians are treating this new development? I would expect some people really fear what is happening. Although I do want to emphasize we have seen absolutely no reason for anyone to panic. However, I can imagine some very religious sorts asking: Isn't it as likely to be the work of the devil as it is to originate from some angelic, extraordinary extraterrestrial intelligence?"

"Paul, people are flocking to houses of worship the world over. Many of them are indeed praying for deliverance from what tele-evangelist Buck Speedway is already terming the second coming of Lucifer."

"Of Lucifer. Wow."

"But there are others who regard the confluence of events as a sort of divine retribution," Amal went on. "They see this especially in the sudden world-wide failure of the quarantine zone walls and fences. Their attitude is perhaps best summed up by the Pope. He has expressed fear that, as he puts it, and I am quoting here, 'the holy trinity might well be in the process of delivering Old Testament rage over humanity's callous cordoning-off of nearly three-quarters of its population. Essentially, those who are well off have been giving up on ever improving the lot of those less fortunate. Jesus can't be happy about that.'"

Amal Mahfouz's extended quote was finishing in its Scottish brogue version for Donnie Spriggs and Jim MacShank. But those golf course owners didn't catch the last part. They found their attention diverted elsewhere. They spotted two, silvery flying saucers through the wide-open French doors at the clubhouse entrance.

Both scout saucers were spinning across the partly cloudy sky, scooting in and out of especially big and fluffy cumulus clouds. When finally they came to a hovering halt side by side, they slowly lowered altitude. They kept descending until lost from view behind gently rolling hillocks. The location was somewhere on the back nine of the Tinkywink Links.

"Well what an f-n' scunner *this* is!" cursed Donnie. "Now me oon bum's oot the windae, and ah'm just a-guessin' yer's be oot der, too, Jim!"

"Aye, ah'm a-feared it is, Donnie! Should we send our bonnie Noni oot der to warn that foursome?"

"You mean ta say th' three sons wi' their father in tow? Who travelled all across the pond to check us oot based upon that five-star review I planted on 'Trip Advisor,' you're very welcome?"

"Aye, the same! They need ta know they might not 'ave th' time to finish their roon before the apocalypse!"

"There be a problem wi' that, Jimmy me fellow. I know yer maneuverin' fer sainthood or somethin'. But we will end up havin' to offer them boys a partial refund if they were not done at least the fourteenth hole when Noni catches up!"

"Well aren't yer the chancer (con man)! I suppose yer wantin' to charge 'em extra if we get wind of their experiencin' an extraterrestrial abduction!"

"Yer gotta remember, Saint Jim, they are all hazards out there, what you can't allow yerself to get distracted from our profits! Which, if we dornt make enough of, that hole on the green becomes our black hole of debt! It be suckin' us down right after the ball is putt oot!"

⋅ᚺᛟ°⋅ᚺᛟ°⋅ᚺᛟ°

Adults, children, and two Oombian tree creatures disembarked from the three small shuttle pods.

The shuttle pods landed on scrubland just inside the monolithically large and gray quarantine walls surrounding Varanasi. The scrubland was located on the edge of the Shivdaspur district.

The starship's diversely constituted entourage filed together to form a procession, two to three beings wide. They headed in the direction of the low-hovering, stadium-sized oval object by the Ganges River. That object loomed as invitingly shimmering multi-colored before them as the aforementioned quarantine walls loomed forbiddingly gloomy behind them.

Captain Taylor led the way hand in hand with her husband Chris.

At least initially, Chris expected the ever-present crowds would cower aside. Their cowering would compare to the Red Sea parting for the tribes of Israel when they fled Egypt, he mused. The resultant path would grow plenty broad enough for Earthlings, Fafamans, Oombians and Chonorans alike to make haste for their destination.

However, from Oodle-Noodle's cautioning telepaths, not to mention her own intuition, Helena knew matters would grow very messily complicated, very fast. Especially since right behind them, several Tictoctickian scout saucers were also landing.

Hovering only a mile overhead, a Celestial Breath saucer had cast out another immense trawl net. But that net was already vaporized into so much additional multi-colored, confetti-like material fluttering down harmlessly everywhere.

The real complications started with Manjeeta and her two new friends, Peenu and Numila. These fellow travelers in miraculous deliverance from childhood prostitution suddenly leapt out into the open, blocking the procession's progress.

"Sister of Goddess Lakshmi," Manjeeta said for her bow before Captain Taylor. Taylor noted the girl's sari was colorfully stained, and that the girl herself was pressing it modestly against her wiry frame on the off chance any of it might come loose. "Sister," repeated Manjeeta to Captain Helena Taylor, "you and your companions hatched from the eggs we saw descend from outer space?"

"We did," Helena responded. Joy unexpectedly filled her heart. She thought on how her own daughter, Shelly, might have behaved if she had grown up under these circumstances. "Many of us are from this planet, your planet, Earth. And a few of us, such as these two tree creatures you see here, they are visiting us from their planets, other planets. They want to be friends."

Manjeeta nodded a clipped fast nod before she explained, "Our parents are dead, and we have been taken away from what else is left of our families. Please, we want to travel to the stars with you!"

Peenu and Numila nodded eager affirmation of Manjeeta's assertion.

"You can make room for us inside your egg spaceships?" Manjeeta inquired almost bubbly with hope.

"Our egg spaceships come from much larger spaceship where yes... This is okay, Captain Taylor?" asked Tanya Petrovsky. Tanya had raced forward from way behind the front of the procession. She was irresistibly drawn by what she could overhear.

Helena Taylor tossed her hands uselessly aside to answer. "What can I say?" she asked rhetorically. "Especially as the mere sister of a goddess?"

"You heard that... What is your name?"

"My name is Manjeeta, beautiful lady, and this is Peenu, and this is Numila."

The three girls bowed.

"Well, Manjeeta, Peenu, and Numila, the goddess's sister has spoken," announced Tanya. "There is plenty of room aboard our mother spaceship, the layer of those eggs from where we hatched. We welcome all three of you into our exploration of outer space, under care and guidance of me and my husband. He is grinning over there like he just swallowed one of our flying eggs. You can call him Papa Magabu!"

After the three girls jumped up and down clapping, Manjeeta most seriously, somberly latched onto a hand from Helena and a hand from Tanya. "Do not worry," she said. "Both of you are goddesses, also."

Water balloons filled with saffron dye were tossed at Captain Taylor's entourage from random spots in the crowd. They burst apart colorfully, all over the girls and several others, including the Chonoran Chig-cher.

Chig-cher danced ecstatically, in celebration of his fresh shirt receiving fresh stains. He waved his tentacle arms very fluidly as only tentacle arms can wave.

Imitations of the stain-loving extraterrestrial's arm-waving were taken up by those in the crowd standing closest to him. He heard translated into the Chonoran tongue, "This is a new avatar, a tenth avatar by which our Lord Vishnu returns incarnated to Earth! He is the octopus avatar, with all but two of his eight tentacles shed like so many lizard tails!"

"Look over here!" someone else shouted. He was pointing towards Guy and Yulala's baby daughter.

Goolafala was gazing around from the comfort and security of her mother's arms.

"Lord Krishna has a younger cousin, violet-shaded instead of blue!"

"Ah!" cried another. "This is a Holi celebration that will require us to rewrite the *Mahabharata*, to add extra chapters! They will be the most joyful chapters we feared to ever dream!"

"Speaking of fear, Oodle-Noodle," said Helena. She noticed several telltale antlers of varying sizes and sharpness. They were scattered amidst the crowd that was filling in behind the procession she was more or less leading. But they were coming steadily closer. Their air-igniter-toting bearers, led by Commander Ak-keek-teek, were striving to catch up with the quarry. "Oodle-Noodle," repeated Helena, "you're certain it will continue to prove impossible for anyone to inflict violence?"

Captain, as in all things, there has to be a finite capacity by whoever these interveners are, to 'game' the laws of physics. However, if that capacity were running out any time soon, I am reasonably confident we would receive ample warning.

"'Reasonably confident'? Great," reacted Helena.

Lieutenant Weekwok halted his advance before a random cow. That cow looked lost in casual contemplation of the commotion round about her.

"Join us," brayed the lieutenant. He offered the woefully under-nourished, skin-and-bones bovine creature an extra air igniter. But when that creature's contemplation continued as though the Tictoctickian weren't present, he baaed, "Starve, then, dumb oskynt cousin!" and resumed his stalking of Captain Taylor's procession.

"So there's where you two runts went!" Sergeant Fred Frankly was meanwhile fuming, after worriedly back-tracking to locate the young boys he and Ciela had adopted.

Jorge and Tomás were mimicking the Oonzy-Ootzies' bouncy-waddle in and out of Oombian seas, like the surf's ebb and flow. The two eight-year-old boys had already accumulated several imitators surrounding them. They took seven steps backward, seven steps forward concluding in a harmonized, if forced, belch, seven steps backward again, and so on.

"Oh, hell, no!" the sergeant suddenly shouted in a panic.

Frankly had no idea the inspiration for his outburst was the would-be new supreme authority of Tictoctic, Commander Ak-keek-teek. But he saw the armed Tictoctickian approach very close to his adopted sons leading the Oonzy-Ootzy dance. And that coming up behind him was a small girl enrobed in a brightly colored, magenta- and orange-striped sari.

The small girl aimed her pichkari water gun most mischievously at the commander's rear end. Her target was his fluffy, white-striped tail wagging excitedly from the aperture specially woven into his Tictoctickian pants.

"Noo!!" Sergeant Frankly shouted as he literally dove through the crowd. But he was too late to stop the girl.

No matter.

The tiny creature's water pistol did cover the commander's pants and fluffy little tail in blue dye. And that together with her bemused giggle did turn Ak-keek-teek's alarmed attention her way. And then Ak-keek-teek did focus his air igniter on her. And moreover, he did pull the trigger, way too soon for either Fred or the girl's frantic parents to stop him.

However, no stream of torching fire emerged. Commander Ak-keek-teek's intended victim was not charred to what he hoped would still prove an edibly thick crisp. She was not charred at all. Rather, a harmless, gentle shower of multi-colored, confetti-like material sprayed her.

The battle, such as it was, was on.

The adopted boys suddenly found fully loaded water pistol pichkaris in their hands. Several more children variously armed with water balloons and other pichkaris convened at the same location.

Other extraterrestrial deer joined their commander to see if any of *their* air igniters would perform as they should.

Gently flower-scented water dyed in a variety of brightest blossom shades splashed everywhere. It intermingled with bursts of more multi-colored, confetti-like material from the air igniters. Chig-cher ran back and forth amidst the melee, accompanied by several people still trying to imitate the fluid movement of his tentacle arms.

Ever more amused, Chris was happily reminded of his daughter Shelly when she was a little girl. Accompanied by her friends, she would run with wild, joyful, carefree abandon across active lawn-sprinklers.

Chig-cher's goal was to see whether some of the confetti-ish material would stick to his already-amply-stained shirt, add some special glitter.

Not too many seconds later, the deer creatures tossed aside their air igniters in a super-frustrated, collective rage. They got down on all fours, snorting mad, and they lowered their antlers. They were intent on a charging gallop into the starship crew procession devolved into chaotic jumble.

Crowds pushed fearfully away from them. They gave each uniformed extraterrestrial deer creature plenty of space for deciding exactly which direction to go.

Guy, Fred, Ali, and Yoon-hee rushed to insert themselves in harm's way, in between the lowered antlers and the children especially.

Totally oblivious to any possible danger, the children were still happily spraying colored water and confetti-like bursts on one another. Whether they used water pistol pichkaris or tossed-away air igniters made no difference to them.

The air igniters should have proven way too heavy for any of the young people to lift. However, Chris saw Peenu and company handle them with ease. Formerly lethal weapons appeared to have become paper-thin light.

Nobody needed worry. This is what the Oombian tree creatures kept gently, telepathically reminding everyone. At the same time, they spread their branches wide for random plucking from their variety of bizarre-looking yet always quite deliciously tempting fruit. Anyone was welcome. But Commander Ak-keek-teek and company were absolute in declining the favor. They were too busy trying to inflict harm.

Another fact of no surprise to Oodle-Noodle was that the direction the Tictoctickians charged made no difference. They found they could not bring their antlers anywhere near touching anyone, let alone impaling or even scratching them. The deer creatures came to feel the very air itself was working against them. It became sluggishly thick in just the right places to stall out even those charges preceded by an accelerating gallop. At the same time, though, the kind yet mysterious injury-preventing force applied equally to them. The deer creatures did not suffer even the least neck strain when halted in their tracks from hurting others.

Children and adults alike continued adding to the Tictoctickians' embarrassment by splattering them with more water colors from the Holi celebration.

In fits of ever-mounting rage, the Tictoctickians began kicking out their hind legs whilst pivoting round about. Fred Frankly thought they looked like bucking broncos with nobody on board to buck. For sure, not one of them was succeeding in landing a hind hoof on anybody.

A call finally went braying from Commander Ak-keek-teek above the otherwise festive din. Captain Taylor's translator crackled, "We are wasting our time here! Back to the scout saucers!"

"Captain Taylor!" Manjeeta was tugging on Helena's sky-blue uniform stained variously purple, green and yellow. "Here are some more new friends who wish to join us."

The deer creatures broke into a collective gallop. They headed for their landed scout saucers located well behind the rear-most extent of the gathered crowd. While they did so, Captain Taylor looked where Manjeeta waved an introducing arm. That bold orphan was drawing attention towards nine other girls her age, plus a bit older. They presented in far worse condition than her, or than the other two girls who had been kidnapped with her, namely Peenu and Numila.

The nine new girls were variously emaciated, bruised up, and/or missing a few teeth. All nine were scantily clad and overly face-painted from the most recent occasion of their pimps using them for prostitution bait. And all nine were agreed on one thing. "They want to join us on your flying eggs," said Manjeeta. "They want to return to your mother chicken ship to explore the universe! This is- Please tell Captain Taylor your name."

"Captain," intervened Dr. Deborah Davis-Murphy. Deborah distracted Helena so she missed the first girl's name, anyway, if not a clear view of the first scout saucer's lift-off with a distinct whirring noise, en route back to the Sixth Celestial Breath. "Captain, many of them are probably suffering from an autoimmune illness. And those two are clearly dealing with Down Syndrome."

"Oh, my wife and I can help!" A middle-aged man eagerly pulled his burka-covered spouse out of the crowd to bring them both standing before the captain. "We certainly have the medical expertise! Yes! We have been traversing the quarantine zone for years, unsuccessfully trying to rescue girls! Now it seems, praise Allah, some powerful loving force is forbidding the bad men from laying another hand on them! If your starship's medical facility is up to date on the latest gene and hormone treatments..."

"My therapy dog will surely come in handy!" A middle-aged lady also stepped out from the crowd. She seemingly was pulled there by her hot dog on four legs, a dachshund. He wiggy-wagged his rear end so happily excitedly, he was spraying wee little sprinkles of pee.

Doggie Holi water, truly, Ali mused to himself.

"We would also like to join you on your outer space explorations, wouldn't we, Dwarf Vishnu?! Yes we would! Yes we would!" The middle-aged lady bent over to rub nose-to-snout with wiggy-wagging "Dwarf Vishnu."

"Captain." It was Chief Medical Officer Davis-Murphy again, her voice freighted with cautionary tone. "Suppose the word spreads that we are welcoming aboard anyone who asks. What are you going to do when suddenly we are besieged by droves of these people wanting to play space cadet? There must be upwards of a million people here! We are not going to be able to miraculously produce starship cabin rooms for them like the five thousand loaves of bread! Once they realize that, their celebration could turn ugly!"

"Are you talking about forcing us to board your cosmic eggs?" someone confronted Taylor and Davis-Murphy in a panicky voice. He pointed back behind them in the direction of where the shuttle pods were parked. "Climbing one flight of steps, one flight of steps I tell you, it is enough to shake my nerves, especially if I look down! Please, do not ask me to climb a stairway to the stars!" He darted his eyes from side to side, then suddenly made a mad dash to escape.

"What!?! They have come to gather us like so many hens?!? They have come to force us to curl back into fetal positions for squeezing into a giant womb?!? And then we will not be allowed to re-hatch until we are so far away from home, we will be unable to distinguish our sun from all the other stars?"

"Yeah, something like that," Fred Frankly took it upon himself to respond. He turned to Ali who happened to be standing next to him, and he asked, "What the hell was THAT about?!"

The new fellow to express alarm led a virtual stampede away from the motley entourage.

Sundry unsolicited volunteers had accumulated to join the starship crew on their next mission. And the panic of those who most definitely did not want to join in alleviated Dr. Davis-Murphy's fear over too much of a good thing. But that panic produced another helpful result, as well. The procession led by Captain Taylor suddenly gained an extra-wide swath cleared up ahead. That would ease their approaching the Ganges River.

Chris mused to himself the procession embodied a peculiar upgrade on the proverbial rolling stone. It gathered some people like they were moss, but it repelled other people as though they were the same magnetic polarity.

Anyway, Captain Taylor hoped ringside seats would still be available for her entire motley crew to see what developed next with the shimmering UFO hovering close to the river.

One decrepit old woman nearly blended in completely with the dirt-infused rags of her tattered sari. Colorful splatters from the Holi celebration hardly leavened her pathetic appearance. She cowered beside a stall where traditional savory sweets were sold. She was too weak to move, as her daughter stood defiantly shielding her and shouted into Captain Taylor's face, "My mother has travelled more than five hundred kilometers to have her body cast into the Ganges! After her long journey, you will NOT deny her the moksha! You will not rob her of freedom from successive incarnations!"

All blessings for you, your mother and the rest of your family, Wafoodle-boodle intervened to telepath. The Oombian tree creature offered the daughter her pick of whatever fruit still remained depending from her branches.

"So, Dr. Davis-Murphy, to answer your question," went on Captain Taylor. It was as though their conversation over the chief medical officer's concern had not been interrupted. "I don't think we will have to worry over too many people wanting to accompany us. In fact, let's hope these poor girls who were virtually ripped away from family will still allow our help. Not to mention the assistance of others who have stepped forward to offer their expertise."

"Cahptahn Taylah, if I might interrupt," fa-la-laed the Fafamafalafama. Sasamara clung to his side, and his translator was set on high volume so he would be heard above the chaotic din. "You both may remember an important saying we have on Fafama, 'No more for the task than the task requires.' Well, I have overheard the good you want to accomplish for these abused women and girls. It is my most earnest hope you will find yourself carrying no more burden than the burden you are able to carry!"

"Rrrruff! Rrrruff-ruff!" suddenly went the therapy dachshund; it seemed to Ali Magabu this four-legged wiener was sniffing and barking excitedly at thin air. "Ahh, yes!" Ali nodded with mirth-producing illumination. "Of course! There was someone else aboard ship who would want to join us down here, see whether there are any cookies to torch!"

After Counselor Magabu said this to Sergeant Frankly, the dachshund trotted in a wide circle. Once again, the pooch was sniffing and barking at seemingly thin air...until the children's pichkari sprays splattered magentas, bright lemon yellows, and dark lime greens against the ephemeral dragon, Effy.

What became crystal clear was that dragon and pooch, both, were going in circles, sniffing each other's butts.

Fred would have commented he was ready to die, now that he had seen a dog poking its snout around a ghost reptile's asshole. But there was no time for such levity before a noise erupted, produced by a specific set of stampeding feet. They belonged to a group of men, a very angry group of pistol-wielding men including the red-silk-shirted pimp who kidnapped Manjeeta, Peenu and Numila. The angry men surrounded Captain Taylor and Officer Davis-Murphy. They were brandishing pistols, waving them fluidly in the starship officers' faces.

Helena was of a peculiar enough presence of mind to liken the men's motions of intimidation to a priest's waving-about of an incense holder.

"We paid for these women," the silk-shirted guy spit into Helena's face, his breath heavily laden with the piercing odor of bidi cigarette smoke. "They are most deeply in our debt, so you will not take them from us! We understand perfectly: Some evil spell has been cast on this place so that now, our tools for maintaining order," he waved his pistol in the captain's face again, "are rendered impotent! But it is for the time being, only! Even the most evil spells wear off, sooner or later! We are going to accompany you until this particular spell does exactly that!"

"You have treated these girls' lives as though they constituted so much disposable dishwater!" Helena fearlessly pushed aside the pistol butt to respond directly into the pimp's face. "You owe them more than you could possibly accumulate on their behalf during several incarnations!"

There was a whoosh!

Initially Helena thought that maybe, in addition to everything else, some monster bat had appeared out of nowhere. It spread open its wings so fast, the sound she heard came from dramatic air displacement. But then she realized it was only the Fafamafalafama. In a fit of anger, he unfurled his cape worn like a security blanket ever since he fled Fafama.

"You will NOT accompany us, and you will leave the girls alone!" the translation boomed as much as the Fafamafalafama's fa-la-las. He strove to loom over the pistol-wielding men. His effort was enhanced by his extra height from growing up on a planet with slightly lower gravity than Earth's. "I was the supreme ruler of Fafama, with twenty-three wives!!"

"So- So you ought to understand the- the special needs of men!" nervously suggested the red-shirted pimp. He was cowering and stepping back. But at the same time he marveled over the bioluminescent sparkles studding the Fafamafalafama's cape.

"I understand I caused a lot of pain for a lot of people!" the former Fafaman ruler bellowed. "This included my own self! Now there is only one star I orbit! Sasamara! However, a part of me wishes I still bore my sword, to lop off your heads for having stolen even a glimpse her way!"

"Oh, no!" one of the other pistol-wielding men protested, shaking his head most emphatically. The rest of the men joined his frantic nonverbal gesture of denial. They feared the extra-tall being with the overly large eyes easily espied even through his sunglasses. They feared he might somehow have stowed away that sword he referred to, somewhere in the folds of his bioluminescently bejeweled batwing cloak. "Not even a glimpse!" the man went on, head still shaking. "I was contemplating your robe. I was asking myself, most seriously, 'Might this be that most divine, hundred-headed snake god, Shesh Naag, who holds the celestial bodies in their place? Has Shesh Naag come down to Earth, in male form, to admonish us?' And admonish us quite rightfully, I might add?"

This question was intended of course to flatter the extraterrestrial out of entering a murderous rage. But by the time the terrified man finished asking it, the Fafamafalafama found himself caught up in the spirit of the dance, inspired by tinkly percussion nearby. He was circling Sasamara as she circled him, likewise caught up.

"Pah!" the silk-shirted pimp spit upon the ground in disgust. "We know we are dirt! We have never pretended to be anything more than dirt!"

Do you mean the dirt without which you would have no place to walk? telepathed Oodle-Noodle to all the armed men. *Don't demean yourselves, nor the dirt!*

"Ruff!" barked the dachshund therapy dog, positioning himself in between the girls and the men. Far more dramatic, though, was what the additional colorful water balloon color splatters against Effy revealed.

The ephemeral dragon had risen up on his hind legs to his full, impressive height. He spread his wings wide, dwarfing the display the Fafamafalafama put on with his cape.

The men who came to reclaim their prostitute slaves looked up in horror, then turned to flee. Some dropped their guns as Effy let loose with a blowtorch exhalation immense enough to lick at their rear ends. Although, like unto all other attempted violence in recent hours, Effy's righteous flames mutated into more harmless splashes of color, rather than actually scorching anyone.

"Ah," nodded Professor Aquinas, who couldn't be more delighted. "More data for Professor Skepticus to deal with, on his mission to prove the ephemeral dragon is some lifeless, conscious-less as well as conscienceless phenomenon! What we have here is that this supposed randomly thrown-together bag of chemicals not only is attracted, like metal filings to a magnet, to chocolate chip cookies, which it then proceeds to incinerate. It also makes itself appear attracted to butt-sniffing when someone of the canine persuasion is near. And, AND, there is something about persons of bad character. Is it some special, hitherto undiscovered pheromone perhaps? Whatever it is, the professor's impossibly extraordinary phenomenon reacts by attempting to torch their behinds! And that is the whole point! Such a phenomenon, presumed lifeless, is impossible!"

Aquinas's only regret was that Skepticus had stayed back aboard the Smoke and Mirrors. Thereby was Aquinas deprived of the opportunity to rant directly in his face.

Meanwhile, Captain Taylor was coming to realize something most sobering. True, her entourage succeeded in travelling very far forward on foot despite the craziness.

However, their efforts might have been for naught, save of course for their salvation of the abused girls and young women.

They had been after a decent view of whatever was going to happen next with the stadium-sized oval UFO hovering down close to the Ganges River. But it didn't look like that was going to happen for Helena and company. In fact, Captain Entroper and *her* company enjoyed the better seats back up in space, receiving video feeds from various drones. The same could be said for the Tictoctickians.

What moved Captain Taylor to such a bummed-out assessment was what she witnessed up ahead. Thousands of people were piled high...

"Wait a minute!" Helena did a double-take. "I don't see any bleachers!"

"Captain," broke in Yoon-hee. One of the emaciated girls with Down Syndrome was gathered up in her arms. "Are my eyes playing tricks, or again am I seeing something I would have bet Kevin's merciless tickles was impossible?"

"Don't let Kevin hear you say that," said Helena, "because I am seeing it too. All those people, they look like they're sitting comfortably up levels of stadium seating,-"

"On nothing," Chris completed her sentence. "Unless- Would the seats be transpar- Wo!"

Chris couldn't even finish saying "transparent" before the next incredible thing happened.

The crowd which had filled in again ahead of the motley starship crew procession was suddenly floating way up off the ground. They were gently deposited on invisible, totally intangible seating. This included a Maharaji atop his elephant, both of them together.

There was no time to turn and run, nor to ponder what would happen next. Prior to any of that, the Smoke and Mirrors entourage found itself most gently leaving the dignified soil behind.

Oodle-Noodle felt moved to telepath, *What we are experiencing might be proof that nothing, nothing is more powerful than a most wonderful dream!*

⚬ ⟊⟐ ⚬ ⟊⟐ ⚬ ⟊⟐ ⚬

"If yer tellin' me you see what I see, then we're both aff our heads!"

"I don't want to say that, Jim me boy, but the tele gives me no choice!"

Jim MacShank and Donnie Spriggs were seated behind the clubhouse counter for their minimally maintained golf course, the Tinkywink Links. They were commenting on what their fifty-inch flat-screen had just revealed. People, an elephant, and two tree beings were levitated by no visible agency. Then they were gently set down to float, essentially, in a semi-circle, sports stadium fashion. Every "seat" enjoyed an excellent view overlooking the Ganges River as well as the enormous oval UFO in hover mode.

Tinkle!

The door chimes caught both men by surprise, but not completely. A small incident had lodged to irritating effect in back of their minds. And it remained lodged, even while they marveled nearly a-gasp at what was transpiring some eleven thousand miles away, as revealed on their television.

There had been the sound of galloping not too far from the clubhouse, mere minutes after an unprecedented experience. Jim and Donnie saw two UFOs whiz by and appear to land on the back nine of their golf course. Neither man could work up the courage to go check, nor to warn the foursome they guesstimated had reached the fourteenth hole. Both pretended confidence nevertheless, discounting the galloping noise as having issued from a local herd of red deer. They wanted to believe those deer were spooked into a stampede by the landing flying saucers. However...

The scout saucers landed in a large patch of rough beside the fourteenth green. Pursuant to which, Captain Rek-mek-a-nek led his away team onto the two-lane road nearby. Shortly thereafter, they came upon a small sign for the Tinkywink Links. It featured one eye closed while the other eye sported a golf ball pupil. Golfing irons took the place of eyebrows. Also, an arrow indicated the direction towards the clubhouse.

Rek-mek-a-nek and company went down on all fours for a steady trot where the arrow pointed. That is when they heard a screech of burning rubber. They sidestepped with great haste over to the right side of the road, and just avoided being hit by a mini-van barreling up behind them at full speed.

A few steps further on, the deer creatures came across abandoned golf bags. They were left by the foursome of three sons with father, in fleeing panic from what they saw exit the landed flying saucers.

"I assume we can secure something to eat. If it is only plant food like the Akt visitors to Tictoctic fed former Commander Kwit-Nik, good enough. After that, these bags of clubs mean we will not need to share. Together with the clubs we've brought along, carved for us by the tree creatures from Koombk, there will be plenty for all of us," Captain Rek-mek-a-nek baaed reflectively. He marveled at how the one club he drew from its container appeared to consist of two different types of metal. One comprised the shaft, the other comprised the club-head.

This contrasted with the single piece of carved wood that comprised a typical tree-creature club.

Captain Rek-mek-a-nek's away team from the two scout saucers reared back up onto their hind legs to approach the Tinkywink clubhouse. But they had to duck their heads low to avoid bumping into the clubhouse ceiling with their antlers. They had to bow so low, they returned down on all fours for sidling up to the check-in counter.

Jim worked furiously to make of the Tictoctickians something at least remotely conventionally plausible. The best he could conjure led him to say, "If it's Halloween yer up to high don on celebratin', I'm afraid yer got the wrong time of th'- Wo!"

Captain Rek-mek-a-nek pulled his air igniter from his holster, and aimed it at the golf course co-owner.

"Let's calm doon, now! No need to skelp our wee behinds!" said Donnie.

Jim and Donnie both raised their hands in nervous surrender.

Captain Rek-mek-a-nek's ears twitched with perplexity. Tongue-click sounds did emit from his translator the Tictocticians adopted from the Earthlings. But half of them were emerging as pure gibberish. "We are not here to harm you! That is if you can provide us with food, and then allow us to play kooft with our kooft clubs and kooft balls!" This is how the captain's tongue-clicks translated, when he finally regrouped his thoughts enough to speak.

"Supper and a roon of whatever it is ye haver wi' the 'kooft,' is it?" said Donnie. Gradually, he was becoming more impressed with how ridiculous the group appeared. Where he was concerned, they were just five stags somehow dressed up in military-looking gear and dragging along bags of golf clubs. The sheer absurdity of how these creatures presented themselves temporarily overtook any worry Donnie might have felt. That is, worry over the space-age-looking rifle the lead stag was aiming at him and Jim both, swiveling it back and forth between them. "Well, I'll hae ye to know, all that what yer askin' of us cannae come cheap. Just how ye ae payin' fur it?"

"Ye glaekit scunner! (*You stupid nuisance!*)" Jim slapped Donnie upside the head. "Ye see tha' *Star-Trek*-type phaser he be totin'?! He could vaporize us like that!" Jim MacShank snapped his fingers in his business partner's face, intent on waking him up more fully to their peril. "It is goin' to be plenty enough if they nae be killin' us into th' bargain!"

The remarks by Jim and Donnie came out the translator another half-garbled mess of random tics and tocs.

Captain Rek-mek-a-nek reared himself up onto the counter with one articulated cloven hoof-hand. That way, with his other hoof-hand he got his air igniter in the club owners' faces. And yet he still kept his antlers from scratching against the varnished pinewood ceiling. He tersely brayed, "You are going to have to speak more clearly so our translator is not missing anything. Otherwise, I will assume you are plotting against us, and make you two the choices on our menu!"

"The- The proper English is it that you re- require? Okay, we can do that," nervously labored Jim to keep any more of his Scottish brogue out of his speaking. "And- And as an act of diplomacy, to better the relations ba- between your planet and ours, we want to offer you supper, plus a roon- no, I mean, a game of 'koofk,' the game and a supper, for free! That is what we will do, correct, Donnie?"

"I am wi'- I am with you, Jim!"

Rek-mek-a-nek backed down off the check-in counter, to the Earthlings' considerable relief. Sweat was streaming down the back of their necks despite the late winter chill.

A cold wind was blowing in from where the deer aliens left the clubhouse door propped open.

Jim shouted, "Noni Doogan?! Come out here! We have some special guests! They are guttin'- Sorry, I mean they are hungry for supper, and a game!"

Noni Doogan was a big-boned, bigger-muscled woman of enormous stature. Even without any antlers, she had to duck her head under the door frame to emerge from the back room.

Soon as Jim realized she was carrying the clubhouse menu, he swiped it from her before she could protest. In that same, swiping motion, he tossed it behind the counter. He didn't want weapon-toting, uniformed deer to catch any glimpse of what accompanied the venison sandwich on the menu. The words by themselves were not likely to mean anything to the antlered aliens, Jim figured. But that photo laminated beside it...Noni herself was proudly slapping a filet onto the grill. More importantly, that filet was sliced from what could clearly be seen were the insides of a split-open red stag carcass...

"Sae when did ye decide, Jim, ye wee scunner, ye need tae practice th' king's Sassenach some mair? Wo!" Noni's ample arms flew apart in surprise as she grew aware of the armed Tictoctickians.

"We need to be careful with choosing how we speak, dear," said Jim. By holding on tightly to the counter, he was trying not to let his arms tremble. "Their translator is not adjusted to our dialect," he went on. "They are visitors from another planet, as best we can tell, who came here in flying saucers. Maybe it has something to do with that spectacle down in India. Our television and, according to the reporters, all the other televisions are tuned in to it, whether people want to be tuned in or not."

"Enough about that!" Captain Rek-mek-a-nek harshly tongue-clicked. He reinserted his air igniter into the conversation.

"So Noni, you can serve them up a good fesh supper before we caddy- um, I mean, before we help them aroon- around the golf course?"

On Jim completing this question, the five extraterrestrial deer, their ears all a-flutter, looked up at Noni Doogan. They gave her what she found to be a most discomforting look, maddening as well. The tips of their tongues travelled a full circle around their thin-lipped mouths.

"A fesh supper," Noni answered. "And if you don't mind, I think I should be the one to show them across Tinkywink."

"Two, no, three questions." Rek-mek-a-nek directed his remark at Jim. "How is it," he indicated Noni with his air igniter, "going to show us around after our flesh supper? Will it be giving up only one of its upper limbs? Is that the part of its flesh you consider the most savory? And third, how are you able to keep your cattle that tame, just before its slaughter? Is there some tranquillizing property to the clothing you have it wearing?"

Jim strove to clear up the grisly confusion caused by Rek-mek-a-nek's translator. It mistook for the word, flesh, his dialect pronunciation of "fish" as "fesh."

But something, something pillowy-looking, diverted Donnie's attention away from his partner's panicky effort. It burst orange-yellowish from the underside of the immense oval object hovering over the Ganges River, as seen on live television. And it was accompanied by a poof! loud enough to be heard from the clubhouse flat-screen TV.

⚜ ⚜ ⚜

"Mr. President," said Captain Entroper. She could see President Carey's solemnly huddled visage on the left half of the panoramic view-screen aboard the Barack Obama. The right half of the screen was itself split into two. The upper right quadrant gave Entroper a drone feed of the incredible events transpiring down by the Ganges River. The lower part displayed the sunlit side of the Earth, which included India as it appeared from the Obama's high orbit. "Mr. President, we are now fully coordinated with the leader of the saucer forces from Tictoctic who calls himself Ak-keek-teek. They are prepared to target the objective with magnetic pulse-beams from two of their warships. They will do this, of course, in tandem with the fighter jet payload delivery plus laser cannon barrages from the Obama and Eisenhower. Do we have a go, Mr. President?"

"Mr. President." Chair of the Joint Chiefs of Military Staff General Sandy Warlor, also aboard the starship Obama, had finally worked up the courage to lodge her concern.

Louisa Entroper spasmed her double-take.

"Mr. President," repeated General Warlor, "regarding that payload delivery, we have to remember something. We- We shouldn't allow clinical language to insulate us from- from facing the full reality." Warlor was trembling visibly as she continued, "We are talking about dumping a fifty-megaton hydrogen bomb over a city of eight million people. Yes, we are h-hoping to destroy the alien spacecraft. And those other aliens, the Tic- Tictoctickians, they are as bothered as we are, even though this- this isn't their home planet. But the death and the radioactive pollution from that device alone...Even were we not to supplement it with our laser cannon fire and the other aliens' magnetic pulse-beams..."

"Wait, General Warlor." Dr. Magdalena Wang stepped into the discussion, also from aboard the Obama. "You are assuming the hydrogen nuclear explosive supplemented by the lasers and pulse-beams will be enough. That it will prove sufficient to finally overwhelm the means by which our rainbow invaders have managed to suspend several known laws of physics. This is why I say that if we do survive this crisis, if we do get past it, Mr. President, we must devote sufficient resources to developing bigger, better weapons. And then we must launch starship missions to track down any more of these extraterrestrial devils. We must destroy them before they can ever again come here, like the rainbow aliens have. Never again can we allow the rainbow aliens to control innumerable separate events all across our globe! Never again can we allow them to leave us defenseless against whatever they ultimately have in mind!" She stomped her magboot-wearing foot against the floor of the navigation bridge.

"Let's not get ahead of ourselves." President Carey raised a cautionary hand from his desk in the oval office of the White House in Washington, D.C.

"Let's not ignore, Dr. Wang, what the control from the rainbow has entailed. It has prevented anyone on Earth from doing violence to anyone else on Earth," said General Warlor. She was fiercely intent on making this point regardless of how the president or anyone else responded to the munitions expert. Her conscience was already feeling a tad bit better for her effort.

"I think some folks made a cogent point about that earlier," said Secretary Spinner. "There might be a lot to do with the rainbow invaders preferring their meat free from bruising, like we prefer our fruit."

"That speculation has absolutely nothing to b-back it up." Warlor got all trembling again as she made this particular observation.

"But we have to assume the worst in these situations, Madame Chair," argued Spinner. "Now, I'm certainly not accusing you of anything. However, it does seem to me there's a big problem here. None of us should be wasting any time reflecting on those lovely telepathed sweet nothings from the mind-reading tree creatures. I am concerned some people might be seduced into letting down their guard, where the cruel workings of the larger universe are concerned. And letting down their guard is exactly what our friends aboard the Smoke and Mirrors appear to have done. As a result, they have made themselves sitting ducks along the Ganges. They are about to become collateral, if our weaponry combined with Tictoctickian weaponry finally manages to overwhelm the suspension of normal physics. Either that, or they are about to be subjected to whatever is in store from whoever occupies that bright, shiny UFO!"

"Dr. Wang," said the president of the American Union, "your position is that the joint effort with those Tictoctickians has a good chance of working, no?"

"That is my position, Mr. President."

"Which means millions of people, the entire population of a five-thousand-year-old city in India, will be incinerated. They will be incinerated along with the crew of the Smoke and Mirrors plus their accumulated fellow travelers. Yes, Chief Warlor," President Carey nodded his concession. "The horror of that is unimaginable. But," he hunched his shoulders in a cringe, to Warlor's increasing irritation, "the alternative could be even more unimaginably terrible. Billions rather than just-no, we can't call it 'just.' It could be billions rather than millions. And if this is our only chance before whoever-they-are entrench themselves to such an extent that we can't stop them..."

And what if this is to be your civilization's only chance to acquire a path away from the self-destruction to where your logic is inevitably leading you? telepathed Oodle-Noodle for all parties to this conversation.

"You see, Oodle-Noodle," Captain Entroper reflexively reacted, in her own trembling rage. "Y-You have just insultingly imposed your rhetorical question upon us! You have bored it into our heads whether we wish to listen to you, or not! And to take it seriously, we would have to trust you and your companion, who I understand both *insisted* on joining the Smoke and Mirrors crew, insisted! We would have to trust you are not setting a trap on behalf of the rainbow invaders!!"

"Let us assume," President Carey once more held up a cautioning hand. "Let's assume the tree creature is correct. Let's assume our successful bombardment not only amounts to massacre on a scale not seen on Earth since World War 2." General Warlor's sudden severe stare prompted Carey to add, "Okay, far worse than anything *during* World War 2. All the same, it's a safe bet we will doom the aliens who rolled out the rainbow carpet for themselves. Whether their intent was evil or good, doesn't that at least allow us to imagine it was good? Build on the many ways they stopped us from doing violence to one another over the past day? Have a worldwide conversation about creating a more just planet? Wouldn't that be the best possible memorial for those who perish today? And meantime, of course, Dr. Wang, you do get provided the resources for bigger and better defenses, just in case.

"My other thoughts are these: Again suppose all the rainbow aliens really are that peace-loving. Their relatives who sent them here might be mad at us. But, and this might sound callous, they probably won't seek revenge for us blowing their diplomatic mission to Kingdom Come. They might even feel moved to make sure any future attempts to communicate with us won't come off so ambiguously. Besides which, the power of one of our fifty-megaton nuclear explosions should have the added benefit of teaching the extraterrestrial stags a lesson. It should convince them to stop messing with trying to add us to their food supply."

There is no room in any of your formulations, is there, Mr. President, for taking a chance on love?

⁕⁖⁘⁙⁕⁖⁘⁙⁕⁖⁘⁙⁕

A pillowy material glowing bright oranges and yellows finished ballooning out from underneath the stadium-sized oval UFO in a motionless hover just above the Ganges River. Its emergence was punctuated by a series of poofs. From the pillowy material's lower extent, a platform protruded that for many Earthlings could have been a tongue-shaped cloud protruding from a cloud monster's mouth. The platform nearly touched an upper step of the enormously wide and long ghat stairway descending into the murkily littered Ganges River.

Two lean, light-green humanoid figures popped upside down out of the circular aperture from where the brightly glowing pillowy material had issued. They wore silvery blue tunics, and their faces reminded Chris of a praying mantis's triangular bug-eyed visage, save for their earhole-to-earhole grins. One after the other, these beings somersaulted softly onto the pillowy material, landing there butt first. They proceeded to descend in spiral circles making clear they were on an immense slide, obfuscated by the fluffiness into which it was embedded. They gleefully cried, "Wheeeeee!" the entire way. Leaping off at the bottom, both landed solidly with their webbed feet onto the tongue-shaped, fluffily enshrouded platform. Thereafter, they looked out at their enormous audience, and they spread their very skinny arms wide open.

Chris was reminded, somehow, of Thing One and Thing Two running out from a box delivered by Dr. Seuss's *Cat In The Hat*.

The Maharaji's elephant uncoiled its trunk for a trumpeted blast.

"We would love, love, LOVE to levitate all who wish to experience our disembarkation slide," started to explain the slightly shorter thin, green, tunic-dressed humanoid. Her voice insinuated itself at just the right volume in everyone's ear, and in just the right language as well. This included for everyone around the world watching on televisions and other computer screens. "However," the slim green extraterrestrial went on, "our power to suspend your violence IS finite. It can only be sustained for so much longer. Therefore, we must strive to streamline our presentation."

This is as far as the shorter humanoid got before strange whining distressed the assembled multitude.

That whining issued from a huge hydrogen bomb falling towards the stadium-sized UFO. Accompanying it was the crackling, air-splitting thunder from house-sized red balls of laser cannon fire and targeted magnetic pulse-beams of neon blue.

Everyone covered their ears.

Time seemed to Helena Taylor to slow down as the discharged weaponry converged on the hovering oval UFO...

...until it metamorphosed into harmless splatters making the immense, mysterious alien spacecraft appear even more magnificently colorful than before.

"This," the taller thin green humanoid extended her skinny right limb heavenwards, "is the sort of behavior, the anticipated greeting which made our decision take so much longer than it might have. Although, imagine this were not the case. Imagine this were not the greeting we would have expected from your species. In that scenario, our decision would most likely not have been necessary in the first place."

"We do come in peace," went on the smaller green humanoid. "It would have been nice of your world leaders to have accepted this. They should have determined our motivation from our quantum filtration of any and all violence your species may have tried to inflict since our arrival.

"All the same, my name is Freamis-Framis. And here," she pointed at the taller one, "is Simarfagus, my eternal love."

Both females embraced. Pursuant to which they looked out upon their enraptured audience to say, in unison, "We are the Nuah-cherpels!"

"We have arrived here-"

"Again," inserted Freamis-Framis.

"-from a star located on the far opposite side of our common central singularity, the black hole core of our shared Milky Way Galaxy," went on Simarfagus. "We dreamed our way here, about which means of transportation we have too much else to relate for explaining any further than that."

"But it runs along the same lines of how we are able to dream everyone on this planet into seeing us clearly, as well as understanding us thoroughly," Freamis-Framis couldn't help adding.

"Many of you wonder, we well know," said Simarfagus. "Why have we picked Varanasi for our destination on Earth? Why not one of your centers of political and economic power, such as Washington, D.C. or Tokyo, Japan? Or some other such place? Why Varanasi, India which, as large as it is, is still a city separated from some more affluent parts of its country by the quarantine wall?"

"In the beginning," the shorter Freamis-Framis once again picked up the narrative thread, "we believe there was a non-material, non-anything sense of being. So infinitely profound was its loneliness, it split into two, to keep itself company..."

"And the creation was thus begun," the taller Simarfagus completed her lover's sentence. "But what forever after continued to be the case was that, in any direction you might go from your present location, infinity awaits you. This is true whether through three-dimensional space, or through four-dimensional time, or beyond."

"Which means," Freamis-Framis continued tag-teaming, "every last one of you, every last most minute speck of conscious awareness in the universe, dwells at its very center."

On this remark, Helena and Chris held hands ever tighter. They glanced from each other's eyes down to the pendant Helena wore as a bracelet. The Fafaman, Sasamara, had made it for Helena. But she had to leave it behind when she and the Fafamafalafama joined the Earthlings' escape from Fafama. Nevertheless, Chris's mother was waiting to hand it to Helena when they returned to Oomb. How exactly Samantha Olsen could have come into possession of the pendant wasn't at all clear. However, Helena suspected it had something to do with the space-time conundrum. The pendant must have taken a multi-trillion mile trip into the past, despite an alteration to a certain event that should have made such travel impossible. And Helena suspected she knew exactly what that certain event was. In an alternate universe, the planet Fafama was catastrophically wrecked by the water-shedding comet crashing into it. Creatures' resultant suffering gouged large wounds into the space-time continuum. Then the pendant must have been propelled through one of those wounds. It emerged out the other side falling from a thunderstorm onto a neighborhood in north Philadelphia, in the universe where Helena presently found herself. Helena recalled again the two missiles that were supposed to cause the comet to crash into Fafama. Their trajectories had suddenly, most enigmatically shifted towards deep space, where they both exploded harmlessly.

"The development of centers of power on your planet,-"

"-and on other planets as well,-"

"-can lead you away from this most basic truth. So we thought it vital we make our presentation amidst so many who have been treated as though they are not to be treasured as much as others."

"Besides," went on Freamis-Framis, "we discerned a synchronously poignant celebration happening in Varanasi, where our mission is concerned. It is the Holi celebration."

"What is Holi about? What does it mean for the rest of you Earthlings around the world who might not know? From what we have learned," said Simarfagus, "it boils down to this, as the saying from many a civilization throughout the galaxy goes, whether still extant or already self-destructed. King Hiranyakashipu's son, Prahlad, refused to respect his father as someone more special than all other creatures. For this, the king wanted his son dead."

"None of the king's attempts to inflict violence worked, though," went on Freamis-Framis. "Through prayer, Prahlad peacefully dreamed his safe escape from attempts on his life. Until at the last, the king had an enchantress named Holika try burning him to death with her special fire."

"But such violence only ended up destroying its perpetrator," continued Simarfagus. "Holika's flames were no more successful than the weapons were just a few moments ago, when they were inflicted upon our spacecraft." The lean green humanoid swept an arm back towards the colorfully stained, hovering, stadium-sized oval object.

"And so, on the day of Holi all across India and other parts of your world, pistols spray harmless water, most colorfully dyed and nicely scented. And people strive to mend broken relationships, if only for a few hours."

༄༠•ᨀ༠•ᨀ༠•ᨀ༠

"Okay, I am going to have to demand you put that thing away," Captain Rek-mek-a-nek tongue-clicked with terse impatience. He motioned his air igniter at Noni Doogan's computer phone, on which she was monitoring events way down the globe in Varanasi, India. "Yes, we found it a most satisfactory meal, the fried filets of sea creature together with fried filaments of plant root tubers. However, you need to understand something. Suppose we should have the slightest impression you were using your device to signal some of your fellow creatures to come imprison us. Such is the curiosity of our palates that we could easily succumb to it. We could easily make you our next meal aboard our scout saucer as we leave your planet's atmosphere behind. So once again I order you: Put that thing away! Return attention to our intended game of koofk!"

Noni Doogan fought down an impulse to push back and say, *Hand your wheesht! (Be quiet!)*, followed by an explanation of what she was doing. Plus, there would have been a question for these clothed, weapon-and-golf-bag-toting deer from outer space. That question would have been: Why were they not any more curious than they apparently were, about the epic goings-on with another extraterrestrial species into the mix, even?

What helped Noni suppress her otherwise inevitable reaction was the threat posed by futuristic-looking weapons the deer creatures were wielding. Although, what she had seen on her computer phone already transpire in Varanasi did set her to wondering...

"Okay, so this is the first tee box," Noni went on instead. She tucked away her phone in her rear pants pocket.

"'Tee,'" Rek-mek-a-nek's bleat came out, not requiring any translation. "That is this, correct?" The saucer captain pulled a three-foot-long stick from his oof bag woven from Oombian palm fronds. The stick had a concave platform at its broader end for placing the ball.

"Whoa!" exclaimed Noni. "I thought that was one of your clubs, specially prepared for swinging when you're down on all fours!"

"On another planet, we were shown it goes into the ground, like this." The captain of the Fifth Celestial Breath worked the stick's pointed end into the sandy soil until it stood straight without him holding on. "And then you place a koofk ball here for hitting either with a club, or with your execration end." Captain Rek-mek-a-nek made a butt wiggle towards where the ball was teed up over two and a half feet.

"Whoa! Not with your bahookie you don't! I mean, you can't expect your ball to go anywhere at all, strikin' it with your butt," Noni edited herself. She remembered "butt" was the English term for "bahookie."

"We saw a tree creature other-worlder hit the ball a long way towards the hole with its kakookie!" protested Rek-mek-a-nek. He had easily deciphered from the context what "bahookie" meant, even without Noni's redo.

"A tree with a 'kakookie,' as you called it? Well I was ready to bet most of me possessions that trees dornt have rear ends. But if they do, I suppose it is also just as likely they can use them to send a ball sailin' through the clouds, although..." She paused to wiggle her butt, trying to imagine. "For my own self, I suspect I would be pushin' my shot way out to the right, attempting such a stunt. Okay, so you have seen a mobile tree from another planet perform the miracle of launching a golf ball with its butt. Have you ever done that, yourself?"

The Tictoctickians exchanged looks all around. Only then did Captain Rek-mek-a-nek confess, "No. We have only made practice swings."

"Well, then." Noni Doogan took long, assertive strides up onto the tee box. She even shoved aside an officer along the way. "We will have none of this with the cricket-bat-length tee. I am making an executive decision as your new caddie. Especially since I now know that none of you have any business on a full-sized course. The lot of you ought to have found yourselves a driving range to practice before you entered the field of battle here. Oh, is that how it's going to be, is it?" When Noni looked up from pulling the three-foot-long tee out of the ground, she saw the five dressed deer creatures training their air igniters on her. "Let me tell you: I noticed something in the latest news coverage that has only now sunk in. I think you are goin' to see that if you actually fire yer ray guns at me, well you're liable to find yerselves sorely disappointed."

Still hoping to bluff the female Earthling back into feeling intimidated, Rek-mek-a-nek suddenly swung around his air igniter. He aimed it at the wood fence along the road to unleash a torching barrage. In seconds, the rails and posts crumbled apart, leaving a long but narrow mound of ash and cinders where fence once stood. The ash and cinders were already being blown away by a steady brisk breeze off the North Sea.

Puffy cumulus clouds scudded by overhead on an otherwise bright, sunny day.

"Somewhat impressive," nodded Noni. "But let's see what happens when you take a shot at that stand of poplars." She indicated a row of tall yet thin trees lining the far side of the road from where the fence had been.

After trotting up close to them, Rek-mek-a-nek lost no time unloading at the trees. To his consternation, though, the blowtorch stream from his air igniter turned to harmless, colorful splatters when it struck those evergreens.

"Ah," nodded Noni again, feeling more confident than ever about her bluff-calling. "So, ye cannae do violence to no living thing, can ye? Can ye?" She got up into Rek-mek-a-nek's twitching nostrils. "And now," she extracted her computer phone from her rear pants pocket, turned it back on, and put the video screen in the captain's eyes. "Would ye mind explainin' to me why you and your pint-sized herd are up here lookin' for supper and a free golf lesson? And that is golf, not 'koofk' or whatever ye were callin' it. Why are you wastin' my time? Why, instead, aren't you joining yer fellow travelers I saw darting about in their flying saucers on my phone?? And don't deny they are yer fellow travelers! They were using the same kind of saucers my partners spotted you landing near the fourteenth green!"

After he briefly contemplated what was unfolding on the smartphone screen, Captain Rek-mek-a-nek looked up plaintively into Noni's eyes. He had to overcome feeling intimidated by her severely arched eyebrow to even humbly baa, "We were sent on a mission to collect some of your fellow beings in one of our trawl nets. We were to add them to our food supply. It was supposed to turn out not unlike how you described netting those sea creatures we had for kupperk. However, we quickly realized a disturbing fact. We have no idea what the strange power is which emanates from the mysterious rainbow that arced here from deep space. Whatever it is, though, it won't let us catch any of your fellow beings. After I reported this to my superior, we were put on standby. Meanwhile, one of our scout saucers discovered your kolfk layout, and, well, we were intrigued by the game. And we happened to have along a bag of clubs given us by the tree creatures. I thought, maybe we can get a little something to eat here, and satisfy our curiosity about the game."

"But how do ye end up in one of the most remote regions of Scootlund? There are courses bunched together further south, around St. Andrews for instance!"

"This area reminded us the most of kolfk layouts we saw on the planet Koombk. Plus, we wanted to go where it looked like we would not have to deal with too many of your fellow Akt beings."

"So we have got ourselves an excellent selling point for outer space travelers, have we? Is it a little taste of 'Koombk' instead of a little taste of home? And you would rather be here swingin' clubs, your bahookies if I had allowed? You would rather be doin' that than findin' out what the extraterrestrials the appearance of wee leprechauns from Ireland are settin' to do?"

Noni sensed pleading in Captain Rek-mek-a-nek's voice as his baas faded ever meeker. "Sooner or later," said the captain, "we are going to be called, ordered back to our mission, reconfigured perhaps to abandon the original plan. When that happens, it is probable we will never have this chance, ever again. In addition, I am experiencing the strangest feeling. My fascination with your game might be fueled by something I will get out of it, something well beyond my meager imagination at this time."

To which admission, the other four Tictoctickians nodded agreement. They tossed their air igniters aside. Also nodding agreement were the several other deer extraterrestrials watching through their Captain's antler-cam from aboard the Fifth Celestial Breath. That immense flying saucer had long since been set into geosynchronous orbit some seven thousand miles straight up.

Big-boned Noni Doogan looked back and forth, between Rek-mek-a-nek and events unfolding in Varanasi, India as displayed on her phone. Finally she said, "Okay, I like it. Now let's go back up on the first tee box, with a reasonably sized tee. Good thing the first hole is a short par four. It's a wee bit over two hundred yards, although I suspect that unit of measurement means nothing to ye. But understand this: Any other group what comes along, we are goin' to allow them to play through. And I am only goin' to allow you to play for as many holes as I can put up with yer lack of experience. And put up also with a group numbering two more than common sense permits. Which includes me into the bargain, demonstratin' how it's done. AND, when I tell ye to pick up yer ball on a hole, ye do as I say, got it? Any time any of you wish to quit, maybe because you got out of it whatever it is yer spirit is tellin' you that you will get out of it, well that might be the better, okay? So here we go. I will hit first, give ye somethin' to model yerselves after, even though I am proportioned very differently from you. Also, I am not luggin' around a set of those antlers. I dornt know, it still remains to be seen how ye are goin' to look down at the ball with that stuff on yer head, without losin' yer balance and tippin' forward!"

Noni teed up her ball. She took a casual-looking swing at it with her five- wood, and sent it flying nearly the entire distance to the green. From where it landed, it rolled all the way on then all the way off the back, down the hill into a long-grassed collection area.

"That's what we call, 'too much of a good thing'!" Noni raised her clenched fists triumphantly high, holding her five-wood tightly by one of them.

Captain Rek-mek-a-nek and his crew drew back. They cowered intimidated by Noni's prideful display, especially since their air igniters were useless and their antlers unlikely to do any better.

"Nice and easy does it!" Ms. Doogan advised in her continuing exultation. "Swingin' too hard, that comes from a lack of faith in what ye can accomplish and, well, a lack of faith isn't going to get you very far. Now, why don't you go next, as you were fixin' to before with that

Loch Ness Monster's toothpick?" She directed her attention at Rek-mek-a-nek. "Only use this instead." She held out to him one of her two-inch-long tees.

The saucer captain wielded an especially large-headed club originally carved on Oomb.

Noni Doogan was surprised to find that actually, the uniformed deer creature having to balance his antlers helped his form; he stacked perfectly. "Aff you go; give it a good smack," she said, impatient for Rek-mek-a-nek to swing before he moved out of what looked to her like a decent setup.

The saucer captain topped his ball. He sent it scudding not more than twenty yards across the patchy-grassed ground just off the tee box. It moved not unlike the clouds scudding across the deep blue sky, Noni thought, at least until it came to a halt. "Ay," she groaned. "You didn't keep yer head doon, errr, down! Didn't keep yer head down! Now listen, all of ye, ye have to keep yer eyes on the ball until after ye hit the wee scunner, errr, the round little thing!

"Let me explain: My mother used to tell me that God, errr, I dornt know what you call it. If you want, I'll call it the creator of the universe. Okay, me mum, my mother, she used to say the creator of the universe made time so that everything wouldn't happen at once. Time gives yer spirit a chance to appreciate experience bit by bit, instead of having to swallow it all at once and thereby miss out on most of the flavor. So you're supposed to pick through step by step, with faith that the whole is a masterpiece. Looking to the next step before the one ye are on is done, though, that comes from a lack of faith in what lies ahead. Do that, and ye stumble. It's what I think, anyway. It's what happens when ye dornt keep yer head down on the ball. Ye got to have faith in how what is next is goin' to go! So, let's tee up yer ball where it landed, and try again! Remember, keep yer eye on it until after ye hit it!"

Rek-mek-a-nek's second contact with the ball wasn't quite perfect, but it was good enough. It sent that dimpled, spherical object on a low trajectory resulting in enough roll for reaching the front end of the green. The ball came to rest no more than fifteen feet from the pin.

Noni was about to enthuse over the saucer captain's success. However, that was when what she feared would happen, happened. It was the main motive for her insistence on accompanying these aliens, even had one of the co-owners fought her for the opportunity. She didn't expect this development so soon, but figured to herself, *Oh, well.*

Three female red deer, three young does, suddenly leapt out from behind gorse along the left side of the fairway. They came to a halt looking the golfers' way. Noni could smell they were in heat.

෴

The little green alien named Freamis-Framis, smartly attired in a silvery blue tunic, continued with her and her mate's presentation.

The green aliens' immediate audience was comprised of close to a million people, including two extraterrestrial trees from the planet Oomb. They all found themselves feeling unexpectedly comfortable in mid-air. They were suspended at varied heights so everyone could have the best seat in the house along a ghat on the Ganges River in Varanasi, India.

"We have borne sad witness," Freamis-Framis lamented, "to the self-destruction of numerous civilizations such as your own, and such as the civilizations on Tictoctic and Fafama. Incidentally, at this very same time both of those civilizations are receiving a comparable intervention from fellow Nuah-cherpels."

For her part, Captain Helena Taylor finally worked up the courage to sit back in her mid-air suspension. She found, not entirely unexpectedly, a gently firm if invisible back rest. Thereby was she reminded, once again, of Louisa Entroper's team-builder.

It seemed so very long ago when Helena closed her eyes and trusted others to catch her, prevent her from falling all the way.

"We have also extended our intervention to Tictoctic's binary sister planet, Chonora. Time travel has been required for that one, however. The faithless assault of Chonorans on Tictoctickians doomed them to extinction several solar orbits ago," added the taller Simarfagus.

"Yikes!" Purple inky fluid squirted from Chig-cher's neck. This happened over his distress hearing what happened to his fellow beings back home. Earthlings had essentially broken the news to him previously, but still...

"Ours is one of the few civilizations in our galaxy to have made it past your crisis point. It is as simple as this," said Freamis-Framis. "Most collectives of highly advanced creatures do not evolve their faith rapidly enough in the ultimate divine benevolence of the universe. And so their belief systems cannot keep pace with their technological progress. Their belief systems are too slow to catch up on the need for renouncing war. Sluggish thought hastens their self-destruction. Take for example your science fiction fantasies of insect giants advanced as us, able to maraud the stars on deadly conquest. This does not happen in reality, any more than the amount of anti-matter in the universe is ever able to approach the full amount of matter."

"The great debate among us," Simarfagus took it from there, "has been over how much intervention. To what extent should we inject ourselves into the grand historical narrative? Especially when we discover a civilization such as yours headed on an inevitable course for global suicide? Some of our fellow beings have argued that if we are not careful, we might enable an even bigger nightmare scenario to emerge. That is, a scenario even worse than one where the civilization of concern literally goes up in smoke. We might make it possible for a warfaring planet to advance that agenda to the stars, and indeed become the stuff of your futuristic adventures, after all."

"For some while now," continued Freamis-Framis on a wave her direction from her lover, "our compromise has been to unobtrusively provide little tweaks to your civilization. They were intended to lend you extra time. We were hoping you would thereby work out a better understanding of the benevolent ways of the universe, on its evolution towards a more perfect love. But those tweaks were not meant to save you, if that better understanding did not catch up soon enough with your technological advances."

"For example," said Simarfagus, "there was a day back in your year 1982. A nuclear missile launch was going to take place, accidentally. That would have precipitated a civilization-ending, all-out nuclear holocaust from which you never would have recovered. Until now, your political leaders and UFO investigators have only known one thing about what happened instead. The missile system of concern went off-line mysteriously during a nearby UFO sighting."

"That was the extent of our meddling," Freamis-Framis's turn again, "until we made breakthroughs in dream psychokinetic time travel propulsion. Plus, we enjoyed another major development, of quantum filter waves. For a finite period, those waves are capable of selecting out violence generated by intelligent species, and transmogrifying them into harmless events."

⟡ ⟡⟡⟡⟡⟡ ⟡⟡⟡⟡⟡ ⟡⟡⟡⟡

"I'm telling you," said Dr. Wang. She was watching the panoramic view-screen on the navigation bridge aboard the Obama. "A bigger, more prodigious application of weaponry, with that application we should be able to run out their 'finite period' earlier than they expect!"

"And then hope," added Captain Entroper with gritted teeth and clenched fist, "that someday, the world will appreciate what we have done, to save it from a far worse fate!"

General Warlor nodded. She wasn't nodding acceptance of her colleague's ranting, though. She well understood their mission was beyond futile. Creatures from an ultra-advanced civilization managed to fling themselves across untold light-years on what they said amounted to a dream. Besides which, they were able to gently whisper in people's heads an invite to attend their presentation ongoing. Surely, they were also well aware that Earthlings and deer aliens, alike, were plotting an additional military bombardment of their behemoth, oval spacecraft. And that this bombardment was to be even more fearsome than the first...and that they would weather it just as easily.

No.

What the Chair of the Military Joint Chiefs of Staff Sandy Warlor was nodding about accepting was that the whole enterprise of her life amounted to one gigantic waste of time and effort. Thank goodness these little green guys were going to save her and her fellow

Earthlings, hopefully. They were going to save them from the sick, twisted logic of war into which she had bought for so long...a logic making her colleagues, and the deer aliens also, apparently, blind to the likely failure of what they intended repeating on a far larger scale.

* * *

"With our newfound powers," was continuing Freamis-Framis, "our great debate became much more poignant. How should we use those powers? Should we make an all-out effort to not only save your civilization and others from self-destruction, but also to dramatically rewrite multiple planets' histories? It became clear to us such a dramatic rewrite was the only realistic chance we had for fulfilling our desire."

"Two situations in particular helped to tip the scales." Simarfagus suddenly appeared miraculously, impossibly to leap from her lover's mouth to proceed. "One involved a woman among you now, named Sasamara."

On this utterance of the original name of the former Varalawa, the Fafamafalafama's one-and-now-only found herself gently levitated. She was carried to where everyone could have a good look at her.

Pedro and Ludi, hands clenched tightly together, marveled at how easily they made out the nocturnal-eyed woman's features despite her distance from them. It was as though they were viewing her through some form of magnification. Similarly, the little green extraterrestrial women's shiny tunics had proven easy to discern in fine detail.

"Back on her planet Fafama, Sasamara was caught up in a system that regarded women as cattle. Fafaman women were treated only marginally better than how cattle are treated, since they were not ever fattened up for slaughter. Of course, we understand you still strain to honor and venerate your cows and bulls here in India, rather than prepare them for consumption."

On this observation, subtle hand motion by Simarfagus resulted in levitation of the same cow to whom a Tictoctickian soldier had tried to hand his air igniter. "Mooooooo!!" she mooed triumphantly. She was feeling the love, the thunderous applause before she was set down again, back behind the magically elevated seating for everyone else.

"Despite Sasamara's circumstance, or maybe because of it..." Freamis-Framis squeezed herself from the cow's udder on the cow's descent. She squirted back onto the brightly glowing platform, accompanied by much oo-ing and ah-ing. "...she labored in secret to engrave two golden pendants with:"

Before Freamis-Framis could go on, from Sasamara's bracelet pendant beamed golden rays. They resolved into a holographic image, emblazoned across the sky. Each of the image's multitudinous facets featured one of the remaining literate languages on Earth, Fafama, Tictoctic and Chonora. Each literate audience member found she or he could easily focus on that facet displaying the language best known.

"From every single awareness," Freamis-Framis continued, "the universe spreads out infinitely,

In all directions.

For this fact, every awareness dwells at the center,

Its import rippling out everywhere, forever,

As from a pebble dropped into a never-ending sea.

A couple honors that import with their devotion to one another.

I wish to honor that import with you!

"Various of your people have taken journeys of loving, peace-filled faith. Notable in that regard is a woman not present here, a woman who had no idea what was engraved on the pendant. Nevertheless, she completed a cycle of passing it along. Her faith in something good about the pendant triumphed over her fear of the void. Or worse yet was her fear the void is an intentional force named evil. Her journey argued powerfully, where many of us were concerned, for going ahead with an enormous intrusion on your history." Freamis-Framis pulled up on her tunic, thereby revealing her belly button. She proceeded to rub it as though, Chris fancied, she were Alladin rubbing his magic lamp. Sure enough, Simarfagus emerged from there like a genie.

Chris and Helena went arm and arm ever tighter. They both were fingering the pendant bracelet on Helena's wrist.

"But we weren't quite there yet," went on Simarfagus to more oos and ahs. "That final event which pushed us over the edge, as it were, happened on the planet Fafama. It happened there when the starship Smoke and Mirrors flew into the past to save Fafaman civilization from a comet's catastrophic collision. That collision was engineered for the sake of trying to destroy a rebellion. Two brave men struggled with trying to re-position the ballistic missiles that were going to change the comet's course onto a downward destructive path. Those men had concluded-"

"Yep, that's me!" Sergeant Frankly raised a forefinger. "What?! Don't I get my own honorary floating-light-as-a-feather?!"

"-one of them must die to accomplish the deed. And so, in their dedication to one another, they fought, they battled, over who would make the sacrifice. That is when Tanya stepped in."

On the pronouncement of Tanya's name, she and her husband Ali, both, found themselves elevated as had happened to Sasamara and the cow.

"Tanya and Ali!" Freamis-Framis made this introduction even before she finished spiraling out of Simarfagus's left ear. "In their synergistic joining to honor one another's ascendant centeredness, Tanya conceived, Tanya imagined a third option. She dreamed an accomplishment of the objective where no life sacrifice, no fighting, no violence, no fear of the void which by its very definition does not exist, especially as a conscious entity, was necessary. This tipped enough of us over the edge, immediately thereafter we were on our way." Freamis-Framis squatted and farted profusely. From what their epic audience could gather with laughter and gasps, Simarfagus pooped from her rear end to proceed, "But the attention we have given the few should not detract from the specialness of the all, for which the infinity is granted to fully elaborate upon. Just one example, before we must move events along, is this gentle spirit, Mukul..."

Mukul in his rumpled business suit, and unshaven for days, was levitated.

"Mukul has labored for years in obscurity, trying to make whatever progress he can to push for the cleaning up of the Ganges River. He has done this despite several decades of broken promises by politicians. In their own lack of faith, they have succumbed to the sick logic of the quarantine walls, plus the acceptance of bribes from arms manufacturers."

⋯⋯⋯

Ay, how me extraterrestrial golf apprentices and those does are lookin' one another's way, there may as well be lightnin' sparkin' between them! Noni Doogan was thinking to herself with disdainfully shaking head. *I'm also not likin' how me furry-tailed scunners from outer space are comin' down on all fours.* "Listen to me! All of ye!" she consequently burst out. She gave Captain Rek-mek-a-nek and his away team head-jerking startlement. "There will be none of yer goin' over for sniffin' snouts with them, 'cause I can tell that will lead to sniffin' other places what cannae be discussed in polite company! Plus, you need ta know there is a bull stag hidin' behind the gorse. He might want to say a thing or two on this matter with his own considerable set of antlers! Let's say he has a mind to use those antlers, run you through your chests uniforms and all! I am not so clear on how that would turn out, from what I have been hearin' those wee extraterrestrial leprechauns say down in the Middle East. What's protectin' us from killin' each other is not necessarily goin' to protect you!"

Rek-mek-a-nek and company immediately stood back up on their hind legs. They focused on the thick, thorny bushes blanketed in bright yellow flowers along the left side of the fairway. Sure enough, they spotted a stag rearing its head from there. And that head was surmounted by a set of antlers far more intimidating than their own.

"I want you to think about this most carefully," Noni continued. She was ever thankful for her expectation proving out of a stag bull red deer close by, monitoring the situation. "When you hit a 'koofk' ball, whatever you want to call it, you will often see hazards along the way. Some of them will make you a-feared. Others, like those naked girls, will be distractin' you in other ways. But for your ultimate fulfillment, ye have to keep yer focus on yer goal, neither fearing nor succumbing to temptation!"

"So what would you have us do?" the starship saucer captain brayed plaintively. "We have not been home on planet leave for the longest time! And sexual intercourse...it is like a bowel movement!"

"So makin' love is like a bowel movement, ye say? Well aren't ye the romantic?!" snapped Noni. "Here is what I want ye and those under yer command to do for me. I want ye to look from here for yer ball on the green. I want ye to see if ye can see it. If ye can, focus on it for a wee bit. And then, if ye still feel ye need to do what ye was set on doin', well I'll just turn and look t'other way! I won't be stoppin' ye, and I also won't be responsible for the consequences!"

The four other extraterrestrial deer creatures understood Captain Rek-mek-a-nek's subtle nod for exactly what it was: an order to follow through on the hefty human female's request. Not five seconds later, they were squinting towards the front edge of the green. It took not too many more seconds for every single one of the deer creatures to realize something exceedingly odd: The "koofk" ball the captain had succeeded in hitting so well on his second try appeared inordinately large. It appeared much too large for how far away they stood. They could even make out individual dimples.

If Noni fancied reminding her odd golf apprentices to take a while contemplating that ball, she wouldn't have needed bother. Not a one of them could pull themselves away from doing just that.

The longer Captain Rek-mek-a-nek pondered the ball, the more he found himself admitting that going through his head was a deep yearning. On ground leave from the saucer under his command, he mated with a variety of does. But it was always the same one when he was lucky enough to be with her, the one with whom he had to fight down a feeling of deep regret. He had to fight down associated guilt when he clung to the other does from behind. Now he could allow his guilt-entangled regret to surface, and finally come to terms with what it meant. What it meant was that he wanted to take that special doe away from the mating collective, with her permission. Her permission was as important as anything because that would mean the feeling was mutual. Again assuming she felt what he felt, they would set up to raise a family, just the two of them. And Captain Rek-mek-a-nek was determined he should be the one staying home to care for their children. That way he could make possible the great achievements of which he sensed she was capable. Other of his fellow creatures used to dwell on trivial matters in their spare time. However, she used to encourage speculation on exactly how underground water tables might be tapped. She wanted to transform Tictoctickian deserts into lush farmland.

If the saucer starship captain could have but known it, their own contemplations led two of his officers to give one another a telling look. Back inside the privacy of one of their stalls aboard ship, they had something most special to confess each other.

At last, the magnificent bull stag red deer leapt from behind the gorse. He stationed himself between his harem and the extraterrestrials with his chest swelled out proudly. He made a couple of sways of his most formidable antlers, and he stamped upon the ground with his right hoof.

The does ran off the other side of the fairway, in amidst a stand of poplars.

Captain Rek-mek-a-nek would never forget the look the stag gave him before he bounded away to join them.

Rek-mek-a-nek would have sworn it was filled by a certain wistful melancholy.

As for Noni Doogan, she knew right then and there that she had eaten her last venison sandwich, ever.

⚬⟊⟐⚬⟊⟐⚬⟊⟐⚬

Freamis-Framis pressed her forefinger against her left nostril, to inhale through her right nostril. Then she pressed her forefinger against her right nostril, to exhale a multi-colored streamer from her left nostril. It shot high into the air before bursting apart into a confetti-like substance, fluttering down all over. "We have invoked your Hindu religious tradition, and now we will lean on your planet's Judeo-Christian and Islamic faiths," she announced. "In your religious texts, the Bible and the Quran, Aaron was the older brother of a leader well known to many on your planet as Moses. Aaron worked on making peace between couples, between neighbors, and even, through amiable conversation, between enemies."

On Freamis-Framis's next nasal expulsion of an impossibly long and colorful streamer, Simarfagus emerged like he was riding that streamer on a surfboard.

So thought Guy Hanson with an arm draped securely around Yulala's shoulders. Goolafala was dozing off amazingly quietly, placidly in Yulala's arms, despite her pulsating purplish glow.

"We hope that our providing you with a sustained quantum violence filter has been having a pacifying benefit to honor the spirit of Aaron," said Simarfagus. He came floating back down to rest on the platform attached to the hovering oval spacecraft by the billowing spiral slide in between. "But we are intent on doing far more. After this presentation is concluded, we will finish preparation for a massive time travel experiment. Starting one hundred fifty years ago, we shall be endeavoring to confiscate weapons on all sides of many of your ancestors' most bloody conflicts. World War 1, for example."

Freamis-Framis suddenly poked her head out of Simarfagus's tunic. She turned and gave her lover a big, loud, sloppy kiss. Then she leapt out from that tunic, to land on the platform again as gently as a falling leaf. "The guns, the bombs, the destructive ordinances on all sides of the conflict, poof!" Freamis-Framis flew her hands apart. "We will make away with them. By the time the quantum wave retraces its steps to the particular interval we chose, your ancestors will find those weapons gone. Left in their place will be all that metal melted down into far better things. There will be windmills, solar panels, and many other useful products, well ahead of when your people would have naturally invented them. They will give the physicists of your past something to scratch their heads over.

"We won't try to control how people behave as a result. If they choose to knock out one another by hitting themselves over the head with a photovoltaic array, so be it."

"But we will be making these conversions for situations big and small, well known and obscure," went on Simarfagus ballooning out from under Freamis-Framis's tunic. "For example, there was a massacre in Ponce, Puerto Rico, on that island's south coast back in 1937. Violence became the response to peaceful dissent against a nearby super power. That super power, I think you know who they are. They were extracting far more value than they were putting in. Upon our arrival, the rifles and other guns used for their act of suppression, poof!"

Tears streamed down Pedro's cheeks. In his family, he had heard of a great great grandfather who lived on the south coast of Puerto Rico...

"We will also be presenting ourselves to world leaders, here and there." Freamis-Framis went sky-diving off the enormous oval spacecraft as she continued, "We will be telling them we intend to take violent solutions off the table, and keep on doing that until those options are given up voluntarily.

"No more Nazi holocaust. No more East Timor massacre. All of you know something, deep down inside if not close to the surface due to the recent loss of a loved one. You know you wish the awful parts of your history could be rewritten." Freamis-Framis's tunic billowed out, parachute-wide, to deposit her safely back onto the presentation platform.

But to where had her partner gone off, this time? Freamis-Framis closed her eyes. Then she opened them wide, sending out soft, golden rays that resolved themselves into Simarfagus, who thereafter proceeded with, "Tonight, one of two things will occur. Either you will manage to fall asleep easily despite what I am about to tell you, or exhaustion will finally overtake you. But know that when next you wake up, for the most part you will do so at varying times in your past, or the future even.

"The benefits we expect from our intervention will dramatically decelerate population growth, but not to worry. Our research has long since verified, confirmed the conservation of spirits. You will find your world much improved, and memories of how it used to be but a series of sporadic, curious nightmares having nothing to do with your present circumstances. Your families, your loved ones, all those relationships you will find still intact. And more.

"And what about us? Well. Again, scattered throughout your recent history, enigmatically marvelous inventions will suddenly appear. There will be strange rumors of other-world beings attending secretive meetings of world leaders. Beyond those impenetrable mysteries, however, it will be as though we never existed. Our intervening will have become unnecessary where believe us, if we hadn't intervened, you would have soon been doomed. A nihilistic act would have forced the moon into a collision with your planet.

"But imagine our intervention, our Great Healing, does not manage to take hold. Imagine your species cannot be brought over to faith in peaceful conflict resolution, by a century's worth of mysterious confiscation of weapons and killing chambers. In that situation, we are agreed we will have to leave your fate to the forces of a caring cosmos. And be forewarned: It is a caring cosmos that does not allow war to spread for more than a brief while, when at all, off any planet from where it might originate."

Captain Helena Taylor had become enraptured, captivated, by the little green extraterrestrials' explication. So enraptured, so captivated, she didn't notice initially the second wave of nuclear warheads and targeted magnetic pulse-beams. They were nearly upon the enormous oval hovering craft when Helena finally managed to fully key in on their whining and air-splitting thunderous crackling.

There was a blinding flash of light, everything blazing yellowish-white. Helena's last cogent whiff of a thought couldn't have been more horrific. Namely, it was that the destructive power of Earth-based combined with Tictoctickian-based assault must have finally triumphed. Those forces must have overwhelmed the physics-thwarting machinery of the little green aliens' so-called violence quantum filter. If there was personal existence beyond personal death, she was about to find out.

But no.

Next thing Helena and the multitudinous others there knew, a yin-yang-looking sphere spun in mid-air above the platform down near the Ganges River. That spinning sphere split back apart into Freamis-Framis and Simarfagus. They turned towards each other and gave themselves a hi-six (the number of digits on their hands). Then they turned their backs on one another, and gave themselves a grinding butt-bump. At the last, they turned towards their epic audience, extended their arms outward and shouted, "Ta-daaa!!"

The elephant in attendance trumpeted her approval as Buddy Leung wondered to himself, *Did that assault actually almost succeed?, but they somehow saved the day with a last-microsecond time travel trick?*

Helena thought to herself, *Heaven help us; were fellow humans really that dead set against revisiting our planet's history in a way that might defuse much of its horror? Were they so dead set, in fact, they were willing to commit a level of mass slaughter that for all they know could have also engulfed the entire Earth in nuclear winter?*

What Buddy and Helena, among many others, would never learn was that the little green extraterrestrials were not themselves sure exactly what just happened. Their butt-bumping celebration was a bluff. Yes, the quantum filter worked hard to thwart the attack. But Freamis-Framis and Simarfagus were both certain it had come close to giving out, even without an extra challenge added. They could only conclude there was something to do with the UFOs that haunted *their* civilization!

"We will be escorting the both of you back to where your vehicle has been stowed," assistant Fleek-tok baaed in garbled fashion to Michel and Priscilla DeFarge.

Behind them, Dek-Fook-Tek was no longer able to keep his head held high. For several solar orbits, it had been overloaded with a ridiculously overgrown set of antlers, thanks to his steroid-strewn diet. But now, fellow deer creatures were no longer willing to act as his antler handlers. So there was nothing else for him than to be carried away on a stretcher, utterly defenseless.

"You will be free," Fleek-tok continued garbling for the DeFarges, "to fly yourselves as far as your technology will take you from here. That is, before we are awoken to the new reality promised by the new other-world intruders. Burp! We would imprison you for the war crime you have committed, but that would appear ridiculous. If we understand correctly what those new other-worlders told us, you will no longer have committed it once they are done altering the past!"

"Well I'll be damnably damned if the translator you brought us can make out a tiny mouse's dick of what you have been baaing with your mouth full!" Michel DeFage spat out and blustered. "What the hell have you been eating?! Huh?!"

"Oh, sorry." Fleek-tok made a production out of swallowing the remainder in one big gulp. "It was a kokolate kip kookee from the recipe one of your fellow other-world beasts brought us. One of my biggest regrets is that when next we wake up, I will have never tasted it. It will be like it never happened. But I ruminate on delicious hopes for the historical rewrite we are on the meadow's edge of experiencing! Shall we meet again under peaceable circumstances, where I will get to eat more kookees than ever! Burp!"

Chapter 36

The ebb and flow of waves, hurled crashing against the shore...

Bright and sunny, temperatures in the mid-fifties, sea air carried on gentle breezes out of the southeast... However, not many people were roaming the boardwalk of Rehoboth Beach, Delaware, along the Atlantic coast of the United Americas. But most who were, that weekday in mid-March, 2064, crowded around a most curious gathering.

Husband Guy Hanson was finally showing wife Yulala his favorite beach resort, and had the rest of the gang from aboard the Smoke and Mirrors along for the fun. Beach resorts were unheard-of on Fafama, due mainly to the sunset storm line.

For the briefest while, Yulala used to be the twenty-third wife of the Fafamafalafama. Presently, she was bemusedly contemplating the antics of a small shore bird, how it played tag with the surf. That creature advanced and retreated on toothpick legs a blur of motion. Its stops lasted only long enough to poke the sand in search of some tender crustacean morsel.

Oodle-Noodle and Wafoodle-boodle, branch in branch, were reminded by the small shore bird of the Oonzy-Ootzies on their home planet Oomb. The Oonzy-Ootzies were constantly jiggle-waddling out of the sea, then back in again, regardless of how rough the Oombian surf got, though it never got very rough.

Fred and Ciela's two adoptees would most certainly have reprised their own Oonzy-Ootzy imitation to mock the shore birds. They would have acted heedless of ocean water chill, and the mess they would have made of their clothes. And they would have corrupted their three new friends, Manjeeta, Numila and Peenu, into joining them. This would have happened despite how emaciated those girls adopted by Tanya and Ali still were from their awful circumstances back in Varanasi, India. But all five adoptees had joined many other people from aboard the Smoke and Mirrors to feast on boardwalk fries, or waffle cones from a hundred-flavor ice cream shop. Almost more ice cream was on some faces than inside their mouths.

Yulala broke off from watching the shore bird's antics, to check her own waffle cone's condition. She wanted to make sure it wouldn't drip on anything when she took her next lick. "Guy dahling," she once more proudly strove to speak in English rather than leaning on the translator. "Whaht is thah flavah of thais ice crahm ahhgain?"

Guy Hanson looked up from gently rocking their wonder baby, Goolafala.

Goolafala was already lulled into deep, deep sleep by the sea air. It was an even deeper sleep than she had enjoyed only hours earlier in Varanasi, India, despite the extreme agitation and excitement there.

Anyway, Guy Hanson noticed three sea gulls soaring directly overhead, cawing as seagulls do. No available translator could let anyone know precisely what they were communicating. Hanson hoped one of them wasn't going to poop on Yulala or her waffle cone. Also, he marveled at how they were riding gentle updrafts, the same as the starship Smoke and Mirrors rode gentle light beams. "Actually, it's a special flavor inspired by the Smoke and Mirrors," he finally answered Yulala. After snatching a lick off his wife's cone, he continued, "It's named 'Light Speed Chocolate.' Those multi-colored sugar sprinkles that used to be called jimmies are now called photon bits. Plus, there are chocolate and peanut-covered malt 'asteroids' that 'crash through' the dark chocolate."

"Yes," nodded Tanya Petrovsky. "I think one of those asteroids must have crashed into my Ali's shirt, and left debris field there!"

"Hmm," hmmed Counselor Magabu. He looked down at his sky blue uniform with a fancifully smiling sun stitched onto it. That's when he realized the full extent of the mess he had made...and guessed that mess was stressing out his better half. The prospect of a lasting chocolate stain probably raised her blood pressure far more than saving lives by means of her shuttle pod piloting prowess. "I suppose I could open my shirt as a tourist attraction for ants," supposed Ali. "Shall I charge them admission for a truly most delicious inspection of the chocolate crater?"

Tanya would have pushed herself to embrace her husband's good-natured effort to defuse her from freaking out over his mess. She would have accomplished this feat by asking whether she should set up a forty-five-minute wait sign like they have for certain theme park rides. And then explaining that's how long the line of ants, wanting to have a go at his dripped ice cream, was liable to grow.

At the same time, tentacle-armed Chig-cher from the planet Chonora would have offered to relieve Magabu of the shirt. Chig-cher's shirt hadn't gotten nearly as stained by ice cream cone runoff.

Before either Tanya or Chig-cher could open their mouths, though, Yulala went translation-less with her communication again. She said, "How beautahhfahl thah beach ahnd thah oceahn ahre in thah full lahght of day; it is ahlmost enough to convert me frahm nocternahl into a blinding lahght dwellah! Ahnd it is true, mah Guy, there is nevah any sunset stormlahn?"

"No storm line on such a regular basis, Yulala." Guy shook his head while switching from rocking Goolafala in his arms to holding her, still fast asleep, against his shoulder. "Sometimes, there is a procession of thunderstorms along a cold front. That can seem like the sunset storm line. Less frequently, we have a monster heat transfer storm called a hurricane. It's far more destructive than the typical Fafaman storm line. Of course, we are also dealing with the rising sea level from our self-inflicted global warming; you noticed that row of breakers way off shore?"

Sergeant Hanson was going to explain about the artificially maintained sand bar buffer zones. But before he could, Helena found herself shouting for Ludi and Pedro's benefit, despite their standing so close by. "You see that little woman approaching us from the beach?! Ludi?! Pedro?! That can't be…"

It is, telepathically confirmed Oodle-Noodle.

Captain Taylor together with Chris, Chris's grand uncle Pedro and grand aunt Ludi were already sprinting off the boardwalk onto the warm sand, chuff!, chuff!, chuff! They were closing the gap with the person in question, as fast as possible.

"Ay Diomio is you, Doña Galleta!" Ludi Perez enthused. Ludi drew the diminutively short woman's mousey-gray-haired head to her chest.

Ludi's two-and-a-half-year-old daughter Alexita had been running alongside her. She gave the cookie lady a hug around one leg.

Pedro held back. He didn't want to overwhelm Doña Galleta, as delightedly amazed as he was to see her after so many years. He also forced himself to refrain from asking, *Where are the chocolate chip cookies?*

"Ahh, to find you here on this beautiful day full of hope and promise," Doña Galleta gushed in English on her forceful exhale of a most exuberant inhale of the sea air. But as impassioned as her utterance was, her audience still had to strain to hear her frail voice above the gentle surf. They had to listen extra closely to make it out as something distinct. "I wanted to share a last thought with you," she continued, "before you are on your way to assist further with the Great Healing. You see this split-open nautilus shell I have brought along with me?" She held it out for everyone's inspection. "The shell's spiral design, the chambering, those features are solutions for problems of water pressure adjustment and locomotion. They tell us that inevitably, there is loving beauty inherent to the universe's solutions to problems. The universe's faith in its capabilities steadily grows. Each being's faith in its capabilities steadily grows. As this happens, there are ever more beautiful, ever more loving solutions to be expected, whether they be solutions to pain, depravity, death, whatever."

"I am not so sure," intruded the Fafamafalafama with a grandiose swirl of his ever-bioluminescent cape. He also made a final swipe of ice cream from his chin with a tiny, ice-cream-shop napkin. His sword had long since been left behind, literally light-years away.

Otherwise, Chris mused to himself, surely he would have unsheathed it to scrape off the ice cream like he was shaving.

The former ruler of Fafama continued, abetted by the translator device given him way-back-when by Captain Taylor. "On Fafama," he fa-la-laed, "we have the giant ahtpah. Your comparable multi-legged, exoskeletoned creature is, I understand, named the spidah. What they share in common is the instinctive production of webs that might be beautiful to behold, but certainly are NOT loving. They trap various other creatures for very un-lovingly injecting them with chemical paralysis, then sucking out their insides. What happens with the universe's love in THEIR circumstances?"

Professor Skepticus listening in raised a forefinger as though, Chris mused further, to add, *I'll have what he's having.* Skepticus said, "An excellent point I would have wanted to have made myself!"

Doña Galleta nodded her resignedly tranquil understanding before she responded, "The universe is still developing. It is still growing faith in its ability to have its love permeate down through its teensiest nooks and crannies. On the planet from where you have come as well as on this one, it has taken tens of millions of solar orbits for creatures such as yourselves to evolve. It has taken that long for creatures to find themselves wanting to look beyond killing other creatures for their food. And even daring to imagine spiders and atpahs developing a peaceful co-existence with fellow creatures, well beyond the vague discomfort I believe they experience every time they claim another victim."

We concur, telepathed Oodle-Noodle and Wafoodle-boodle. *How all the centers of being can be brought into harmony is the great, central project of the universe.*

"Your thoughts are as beautiful as that shell." The Fafamafalafama nodded towards the split-open nautilus. It reminded him of the foofafa back on Fafama. "But despite what we have experienced today, I am not yet convinced. In so many ways, the universe is still a very perilous place where the wickedness always threatens to overwhelm the goodness."

Sasamara, arm in arm with her beloved, gave the former ruler of Fafama an extra tight squeeze.

It wasn't until then that something sank in for Helena. Ever since the Fafamafalafama and Sasamara landed in a shuttle pod at Rehoboth Beach, there had been a certain, wistful melancholy about this extraterrestrial couple. That melancholy persisted despite how clearly much they relished both the ice cream and the boardwalk fries, not to mention the general seaside ambience.

"Captain!" Chief Medical Officer Deborah Davis-Murphy ran up, her face white as a ghost. She and Geena had been browsing numerous small tourist shops along Rehoboth Avenue. They only just then caught up with the main group. "These malnourished children from India, consuming so much ice cream! Not to mention the adult extraterrestrials..."

"I don't think the children will have room for the adults after they finish their ice cream, even if the adults are prepared using a tempting Tictoctickian recipe!"

"Ho! Ho! Ho! Captain! You know what I'm talking about!"

"Yes I do, Deb, and you can cool it. Tanya and Ali handed out chewable lactose wafers all around."

"I'm with you on that, Mr. Fafamafalafama!" Fred Frankly shouted loudly enough for everyone to hear clearly within a hundred feet of him. "Believe me, I am all in on the alien leprechauns' scheme! I relish time-skipping here and there in the past to pull the weapons rug out from under battles big and small! That's going to save loads, just in killed and crippled war vets alone. But I'm still not sure what's going to happen when humanity is left to its own devices. I'm afraid they're just going to revert back to violent ways again, sooner or later! Although I suppose if I'm to consider this coming in from the opposite direction, Ms. Oodles of bleepin' Noodles... I'm callin' it bleepin' for all the little runts' sake here, bein' the fine gentleman I've f- Okay, what I was sayin' was that now I'm not sure you're not correct with your peace and love stuff. Confession time, maybe I've lost a little faith in my original lack of faith in those future potentialities! Ow! Yeah, Ciela, you've given me some pause as well! No need to go pinchin' me like that, risk triggering my cuss reflex! Why are you doing that? I was just about to call Guy's attention to my use of another six-million-dollar word, 'potentialities'!"

"Mom! Dad! You've kept moving so much, I've had a tough time catching up!"

"Shelly! You are going to join us?!?" No sooner did Captain Helena Taylor ask this question, though, than she noticed a telltale, if brief, digital blemish on her daughter's forearm...and that her sandaled feet were leaving no imprints in the sand.

Shelly bit at her lower lip and she shook her head. "Mom, there is a special man in my life, but he has done something awful. Suppose I enter the conundrum with you and Daddy. Even if I see him again afterwards, in the reawakened world when we return...the memory of what his circumstances moved him to do will still haunt me, I'm afraid. I need to stay here so I can reawaken as well, with his having not done what he did, even in my memory, and hope for our miraculous reconnection."

Helena and Chris's eyes watered when they gave the holographic projection of their daughter a hug that none of them could feel. "We will look forward to meeting him," Helena said. "And don't be jealous," added Chris, "but I will look forward to introducing him to a bag of golf clubs!"

"Daddy!" protested Shelly.

"Excuse me, sir."

It took the Fafamafalafama a full minute to realize a little boy was tugging on his long cape. He had become too utterly absorbed in the farewell playing out between Helena and Chris, and their daughter Shelly. "Yes?!" he boomed in his deepest voice when he turned to acknowledge, take full stock of the interruption to his focus. He strained not to raise his left eyebrow threateningly when he realized the situation. That would have remained hidden from the young child's view behind his anti-glare goggles, but still...

"Sir, are you the real Fala-lala-la? Are you the king of Fafama?"

One other little boy, plus two little girls, had gathered by then beside the little boy who worked up the courage to initiate conversation with the tall extraterrestrial. Deborah keeping an eye on the unfolding scene figured none of the children could have been more than six years old.

"I WAS the king of the planet Fafama," the Fafamafalafama nodded. "See this!" He abruptly spread out his arms to open his cloak to its full extent. He could have been some dragon about to fly off, Ali Magabu mused.

With her daughter Shelly's holographic image totally dissipated, Captain Taylor wondered anew. Why was there still the solemn undercurrent to the Fafamafalafama's voice, despite his dramatic flourish?

"This," went on the Fafamafalafama, "is my official king's cape!" That is how his fa-la-las translated.

"Wow!"

"Cool!"

"Awesome!"

"Zowee kapowee!"

"What are those green sparkles?" the young boy who initiated conversation with the Fafamafalafama fearlessly asked.

"Those green sparkles are the ever-glowing lights from a certain special moss. The moss was scraped off rock walls of an interior passageway of my planet's great pyramid, a pyramid that stretches up past the clouds, almost into outer space! The moss was woven into the fabric, where with a little wet spray every six days, it continues to glow, INDEFINITELY!!"

The two boys and two girls leapt backwards. One of the girls thereby tripped over a washed-ashore horseshoe crab exoskeleton. She fell sprawling uninjured on the sand.

"Ah!" the Fafamafalafama exclaimed as he stooped over to pick up the horseshoe crab's hollowed-out remains. He found its tail to have a sharp point, plus a serrated edge its full length. "This will be perfect, for turning you into contestants for who will become the next Fafamafalafama!" With that, the former ruler of a planet snapped off the horseshoe crab's tail from the rest of its exoskeleton. Then he wielded it to tear four, roughly equal-sized pieces of cloth from his cape. He handed one piece to each child.

"Gee, thanks, Mister!"

"Thank you! Wow!"

"I'll spray mine every night!"

"Zowee kapowee!"

When the Fafamafalafama looked up he saw one child's parent, the mother, waving. She silently mouthed what he had heard enough English to lip-read was a big *thank you.*

"I am the Fafamafamafalala!"

"No! I am the Falafalamamala!"

"That's me!"

"You're all wrong! That's me!"

"A very nice thing you have done, 'sir,'" said Helena Taylor. Arm in arm with Chris, she approached the Fafamafalafama and Sasamara. The children were charging at one another's cape fragments like they were bull and bullfighter, both, as Helena went on, "Umm, Freamis-Framis has telepathed we need to be headed up soon to join them for their mission."

With a broad, wistful grin, the Fafamafalafama shook his head. He said,

"Cahptahn, I cannot go with you."

"Neither can I," Sasamara's fa-la-las immediately thereafter translated.

Helena slowly, tentatively nodded acknowledgement of the Fafaman couple's response. "You know, of course, that entering into the conundrum with us guarantees you will not, uh, get lost to each other. We're talking about the reawakening after our rainbow alien friends have tampered with the histories of our planets."

"We fully understand the risk to our relationship, Cahptahn," the former Fafaman ruler somehow managed to boom quietly. "But here is the problem: To get to where we have gotten, there are things we have both done..." His lips actually quivered as he and Sasamara arm-in-arm hugged each other ever closer. Helena guessed if not for his anti-glare goggles, she would have seen his eyes watering, Sasamara's as well. "We have a chance to reawaken to a past on Fafama made more peaceful by the little green aliens' weapons removal. It is a past where those acts would no longer be weighing on us, because we would not have committed them. Knowing that..."

"We understand the memory of what we did might drop away regardless, were we to accompany you." Sasamara held out a protesting hand Helena's direction while she said this, as in, *No need to remind us of that.* "But we fear our lives would be forever haunted by nightmares of our horrendous deeds, even if faded into mystery as to their origin."

"Well," sighed Helena, "I guess I do understand. I can only hope most earnestly that you will both manage to reconnect with one another, whenever you end up reawakening."

"What she said," added Chris. "I will sincerely look forward to the next time we meet. I mean to say, when the first encounter between our two civilizations is rewritten. Maybe I can help you set up golf courses on Fafama despite the sunset storm line and occasional ahtpah!"

"And you two will learn how to sleep with regularity on a tralalafa!" boomed the Fafamafalafama. He stirred the air with his forefinger as though he were once more wielding his sword.

"Oh! Doña Galleta!" Helena suddenly looked around for her. Then she said to nobody in particular, maybe Chris, "Before we pick up some Grotto Pizza and Dolle's popcorn to carry back aboard the Smoke and Mirrors…" She trailed off, having spotted who she thought might be Cookie Lady, unaccountably standing up to her knees in the gentle surf. However, that image somehow resolved itself into a dolphin's dorsal fin. The dolphin was gently slowly arching her back out of the water on her way down the coast, looking for fish. Another dorsal fin soon broke the surface alongside her. No sea monsters were anywhere in evidence.

"Captain Helena Taylor!"

Helena recognized another deep, booming voice, this time from television news anchor Paul Berger. He was rushing up beside her with microphone in hand and body cam attached to a bandana around his forehead. She had been wondering how long it would take the news media to catch up to where the Smoke and Mirrors crew had gone from India. "Please make this brief," she said. "I've just received word we need to get ready to go."

"That's fine," Paul spoke into his mike. "I can keep to one question for now. Captain, how does it feel to be cooperating with an extraterrestrial intelligence clearly far superior to our own, which appears intent on rewriting our history? Some people believe this is the work of the devil, of an evil force."

"An evil force that wants us to abandon violence? I don't know whether you remember the press conference when I was privileged to introduce the Smoke and Mirrors. I quoted from the English novelist, Charles Dickens. For my quote this time, I'm going to travel even further back in time to the Bible, from First Corinthians." Helena found herself glancing away from the reporter as she proceeded. She noticed Ciela and Fred's two adopted sons joining the children who had received the Fafamafalafama's cape fragments. Imaginary sword play was transpiring. Shouts were continuing, of how one or the other was the real "Falalalamafamama." "'When I was a child, I spoke as a child, I understood as a child, I thought as a child, but when I became a man, I put away childish things.' I do believe those aliens with whom we will be cooperating have come in peace, to encourage us to put away our childish things."

"Do you think they will succeed?"

"I'm not sure," Helena answered without hesitation.

When Captain Taylor walked onto the navigation bridge of the starship Smoke and Mirrors, accompanied by Chris, Guy and Yulala, the first question she received came from Kevin Smith-Park. He was already strapped in at his engineering console. "Okay, Captain," he said, "so where's this Grotto Pizza that Sergeant Hanson has been raving about?"

"Stored in a mess hall refrigerator, Kevin. We're going to wait on the feast until we've hit light speed, so we don't have crust crumbs floating everywhere. Oh!" Captain Helena Taylor gasped.

On the panoramic view-screen, a reprise of the extraterrestrial-generated, impossible, impossibly wide rainbow unrolled like a runway carpet. It came from somewhere underneath where the starship was holding in geosynchronous orbit above the Earth. And it extended into deep space, where it narrowed to a needle-sharp point.

"That must be the path Freamis-Framis telepathed we would need to accelerate into, for our supplementing their mission," said Helena.

"We're following the rainbow instead of a yellow brick road, Captain," nodded Yoon-hee seated at her navigation console. "Shall I bloom the mirror arrays?"

"Fore and aft approaching full tilt as you charge the EM field to sixty percent. That should do it, Officer Park-Smith."

"And we are off!" happily declared Buddy Leung. He laughed anew as though he had just delivered the funniest punch-line. "First stop, Rwanda, 1994!"

"Ah, yes, a truly awful massacre," nodded Counselor Magabu. "My grandparents told me what they remembered about that from the news when they were growing up. Truly awful."

"So this is our trial run, yes?" said Guy Hanson. While he spoke, he couldn't help marveling at the fairy dust exhaust from the Smoke and Mirrors photon evacuation shaft, as revealed in the rearview half of the split-screen. How many times he had seen it before didn't matter, where his child-like wonder was concerned. "The aliens are going to round up the machetes, bombs, guns, and whatever was used to bring down the government plane?"

"Correct, Sergeant," confirmed Ali. "Apparently that plane crash was the trigger for the bloodbath. After we thereby remove the excuse for all-out civil war, we are going to leave the Rwandans with plans for agricultural and economic development."

"Together with what we reconstitute after we melt down the weaponry," added Buddy. "They are going to find themselves rolling in piles of solar panels, farming equipment, guitars, drums,-"

"And golf clubs. Don't forget the golf clubs," Chris finished off this recap. He made a hi-five, hand to branch, with Oodle-Noodle, who was standing well-rooted in a bowl of moist soil.

"Yes, all this and more, which won't be completed until well after the quantum wave has caught up to us. Then we're off to confiscating a-bombs, tanks, and grenades; leaving love notes on Hitler's desk while he is still a teenager...What could possibly go wrong?" Kevin's voice dripped with sarcasm.

Pedro joyfully continued to contemplate the personal telepath he received from Freamis-Framis some hours earlier. It contained the little green woman's reassurance she and her partner would definitely be defusing the massacre in Ponce, Puerto Rico. There, Pedro's great

great grandfather had suffered even worse than a broken back.

"Think I've finally got it!" Professor Skepticus rose from his chair and snapped his fingers during the intensifying gravitational pull from light-speed acceleration through the time rift. "This is all some wildly elaborate nightmare I have been having! There ARE no rational explanations for the innumerable impossible things I have been experiencing! None! Because it is a hopeless jumble of randomly firing neurons inside my head! I only await the painful enough pinch to bring me out of this somnolent delirium!"

Whoomf!

"Ouch!" Skepticus reflexively grabbed at his buttocks. Smoke was rising from there courtesy of another blowtorch exhalation by Effy, the ephemeral dragon.

"I say, Professor Skepticus," said Professor Aquinas, readjusting the bridge of his glasses on his nose in perpetual search for the sharper, more comfortable view. "Have you woken up yet? Or shall I endeavor to inflict on you an even more painful experience?"

"Officer Olsen-Taylor?"

"Yes, Captain?" Chris responded with a jump. He still couldn't help his surprise whenever his wife called on him in an official capacity.

"Can you share some music appropriate for the occasion?"

"Right away, Captain." Chris would have commanded his amplet to fill the navigation deck with "Supper's Ready," by an English symphonic rock group from the late twentieth century named Genesis. With the miraculous workings of the leprechaun-ish aliens, he had been finding himself haunted by that epic piece's conclusion. Vocalist Peter Gabriel sang, "Lord of lords, king of kings, has come to lead his children home, to take them to the new Jerusalem!" But Chris didn't want to press his luck having his wife and the rest of the crew sit through the piece's twenty-plus-minute length. They might even arrive at their first stop before it was over. So he went, instead, with the concluding, exuberantly ascendant instrumental conclusion of a piece by Yes, another late-twentieth-century symphonic rock group. It was entitled "Starship Trooper."

The sound of her husband's snoring had never before been as welcome as it was on that late March morning in 1998, when Doña Galleta awoke beside him. She was having a nightmare of epic proportion that seemed to go on for the longest time. She well knew most dreams actually lasted no more than seconds before someone emerged from the lighter phase of their slumber. But this one...!

In her nightmare, Doña Galleta lived with her husband, Silverio, in a poor, destitute area of some large east coast city of the United States. She couldn't be sure whether it was supposed to be Philadelphia or New York. But it was filthy and polluted, especially from the burning of so much fossil fuel, and from so many people having to make do bunched so close together. Galleta and her husband were just scraping by.

But then one night, Silverio was coming home from his late shift at a local fast-food restaurant. That's when someone shot and killed him for a few dollars plus his credit card. Then there was a cylindrical gold pendant glowing luminescent green in the shadows. Somehow, Doña Galleta needed to deliver that pendant to a location she never quite reached. She was climbing a tenement row-house building to enter through a window, despite its being shut. The climbing action was what seemed to have climbed Doña Galleta awake to where she realized, concerning her nightmare,

That was not how it happened.

Fossil fuel use was abandoned virtually planet-wide decades earlier. What little remained by way of fuel combustion engines and the like remained mostly as museum artifacts. Those east coast cities were fast transforming into sprawled-out town centers. Most people could go everywhere they needed to on foot or bicycle. And Galleta had not moved there. Above all else, her Silverio was not shot; he was sleeping comfortably beside her.

Doña Galleta snuggled up behind her husband. She spooned him whilst wrapping an arm round his waist. That's when the "co-qui, co-qui" of the teensy Puerto Rican tree frog prompted her to rise off the mattress.

She walked over to the bedroom window to peak through the blinds. In a nearby field, arrays of solar panels were imperceptibly moving in unison. They were following the sun from dawn onto its path across the sky. Two brightly colored Puerto Rican parrots were circling one another in a mating dance. They were flitting from one coconut palm to the next. And much higher up in the sky, a flying saucer was zipping by. It probably carried passengers on the twenty-minute flight from San Juan Airport to the landing pads at Disneyworld,

Which somehow reminded Galleta: President Coretta Scott King was going to address the nation on television later that morning. She was going to announce a bold new task for her vice president, Robert Byrd. Vice President Byrd came from the great, prosperous state of West Virginia also known as the heart of solar panel country. Its last case of black lung disease was diagnosed over a decade ago, a full thirty years since the shutdown of its last coal-mining operation. President King was putting Byrd in charge of a joint mission with the European Union, the East Asian Collective, Brazil, the Arab-Israeli-Palestinian Confederation of Diversity, and the United States of Africa. They were going to artificially boost the gravitational field of Mars, in advance of a terraforming project planned for there at the turn of the century...

...which also reminded Doña Galleta: A telepathed voice in her head had told her this was the day when crew members aboard a spaceship from the future were going to visit her. Their purpose was to personally thank her for what she made possible. Part of what the voice in Doña Galleta's head referred to was a settlement on another planet in another solar system, a mysterious settlement of Puerto Ricans and people from India. The voice claimed that Galleta's civilization was going to run across them some seventy years from then, during the first interstellar voyage.

Heaven only knew what recipes inside of recipes that resulted from, but, *Oh, well, I better get going. I need to prepare lots of chocolate chip cookies and flan to welcome them. I also better prepare some extras for mi coqui tan grande, my tree frog so big, my very own center of the universe, Silverio!*

Imagine...

A Tale of More Than Four Thank-yous

People too numerous to mention are responsible for this story turning out far better than it otherwise ever could have. Any of its remaining faults are my bad, and my bad alone.

Nevertheless, a few admittedly inadequate acknowledgements: Don Koher and Angel Romero Ruiz for their thorough reading followed by insightful comments; Rob Adkins and Paul Berger for especially detailed reactions that had to have taken lots of extra time; Amal Malfouz for her cheerleading; son Danny for his enthusiastic reading (I will never be able to adequately express to him how much this has met to me) and other son Eddie for encouraging me to shoot for the moon and beyond (there will be a screenplay, I promise!); Bobby Bernshausen at Virtual Bookworm for his patience and enthusiasm despite not-the-most-robust sales; and lastly, my center of the universe, Maria, who has been a good sport about enthusiastically reading through the trilogy despite science fiction not being her thing; I owe her a murder mystery!

Beltsville, Maryland, April 2019